COLLINS'
COLLECTORS' CHOICE

Collins' Collectors' Choice

Four Great Thrillers

DAY OF JUDGMENT
THE VIOLENT ENEMY
STORM WARNING
WRATH OF THE LION

by

Jack Higgins

Introduced by the author

COLLINS
St James's Place, London
1981

William Collins Sons and Co Ltd
London · Glasgow · Sydney · Auckland
Toronto · Johannesburg

First published 1981

Higgins, Jack
Four great thrillers. –
(Collins' Collectors' Choice)
I. Title
823'.914[F]   PR6066.A87

ISBN 0-00-243345-1

Photoset in Baskerville by Unwin Brothers Limited
Made and Printed in Great Britain by
Butler & Tanner Ltd.,
Frome, Somerset

CONTENTS

INTRODUCTION

Long before THE EAGLE HAS LANDED was published it became clear that we had a bestseller on our hands, although at that stage I don't think anyone realized just how successful the book would be around the world. The novel which followed would, in a sense, be even more important. The world of publishing is littered with examples of writers who have produced an outstandingly good book and have never been able to repeat that success again

I was determined that this should not happen and the gods certainly seemed to be on my side when, by sheer chance, I came across an article in an obscure magazine which gave a brief account of the epic voyage of a group of German expatriates who had managed to sail from South America to Germany in a square rigger during the First World War. In the same week I found the extraordinary story of a spectacular lifeboat rescue during the Second World War when the boat had had to be dragged several miles overland by women, children and old men.

So STORM WARNING was born and was in the hands of my publishers in the very week that EAGLE was published. As I recall they had only one complaint, which was that Gericke's exploit in penetrating the boom at the British Naval base at Falmouth in a U-boat, entering the harbour and torpedoing two corvettes, was stretching things a bit. I was able to tell them that the incident really had taken place earlier in the war and details had been suppressed for obvious reasons. STORM WARNING, I am happy to say, was a great success, selling in America even more copies than THE EAGLE HAS LANDED.

DAY OF JUDGMENT was written following a period of extremely bad health when, for a while, all the signs seemed to indicate that I was very possibly not long for this world. Perhaps because of this the book, although a fast and exciting thriller set in the Berlin of the Cold War during President

Kennedy's famous visit to that city, takes a very downbeat look at life in our times.

On re-reading the novel for the purposes of this present edition, I was filled with a most haunting sense of times past. Of all my books DAY OF JUDGMENT is the one most firmly based on my own direct experience as a serving soldier concerned with security duties in the area described. The entire second half of the book came to me in a dream one afternoon when catnapping in front of the study fire. On awakening I went straight into the kitchen and described it to my wife. I never felt the slightest need to make notes of what I had experienced and when I reached that section of the book, it seemed to write itself. On the one hand JUDGMENT is intended to be an exciting, rather violent thriller, concerned with the attempt to rescue a Jesuit priest from East Germany, a story full of twists and turns. The other side of the coin is rather different. The book contains many questions of morality. Are the rights of the individual more important than the needs of the State? Is Christianity preferable to Communism? As I said earlier, a long cold look at the times in which we live.

A great many people have written to me over the years, saying that they consider DAY OF JUDGMENT an important book because of the questions it poses and certainly the most impressive thing I have written. Perhaps that is why it did not enjoy the same level of success as THE EAGLE HAS LANDED and STORM WARNING.

To make up the omnibus we decided to include two much earlier books, each chosen for special reasons. THE VIOLENT ENEMY marked a considerable turning point in my life. It was written while I was still a college lecturer, starts with a very carefully researched prison escape from Dartmoor and proceeds to the Lake District, perhaps an unusual locale for a thriller, but not for one which was concerned with proving that it was still possible to rob a mail train in spite of the additional precautions taken after the Great Train Robbery. Alan Ayckbourn, then a drama producer for radio in Yorkshire, very much wanted to sign up VIOLENT ENEMY as a *Saturday Night Theatre* production. The BBC did not share his enthusiasm. The following week we sold the film rights

– so much for the front office pundits. When I telephoned Alan to tell him the news he was delighted. The film was made, with considerable changes, starring Susan Hampshire, that fine actor Tom Bell as Rogan and Ed Begley, a famous Hollywood character actor who had just received an Oscar for *Sweet Bird of Youth*. My entire life was changed, for the film money gave me two years' salary as a senior lecturer in a lump sum. I resigned my post and at the grand old age of forty turned to writing as a full-time career.

WRATH OF THE LION was written some eighteen years ago. It has long been out of print in hard cover and many readers have written to me asking if we could make it available again. I was pleasantly surprised to find how well the story stands up at such a distance in time. But what makes the book something of a literary curiosity is the fact that it marks the first appearance of a character with whom I am obsessed. Mallory, the ex-paratroop officer, ruined and disgraced because of the hard line he took with terrorists in Malaya, is firmly based on fact. He reappears as Major Vaughan in SAVAGE DAY and DAY OF JUDGMENT, with the location of his previous activities set in Borneo.

For thirty years Britain has been engaged in a series of dirty little wars where the rules have gone to the wall. Malaya, Kenya, Cyprus, Aden, Borneo, the Gulf States, Ireland. It's the soldiers who have to do the fighting, often with the gloves off, and it is the soldiers who have to pick up the bill when the politicians turn away. Men like my Mallory-Vaughan character I see as the true heroes of our times; they go in through the window, for rather low rates of pay, when the rest of us watch on television – witness the Iran Embassy siege.

So, four-in-hand and, in their separate ways leading up to the spectacular success of SOLO and LUCIANO'S LUCK; but that, of course, is another story.

JACK HIGGINS
1981

DAY OF JUDGMENT

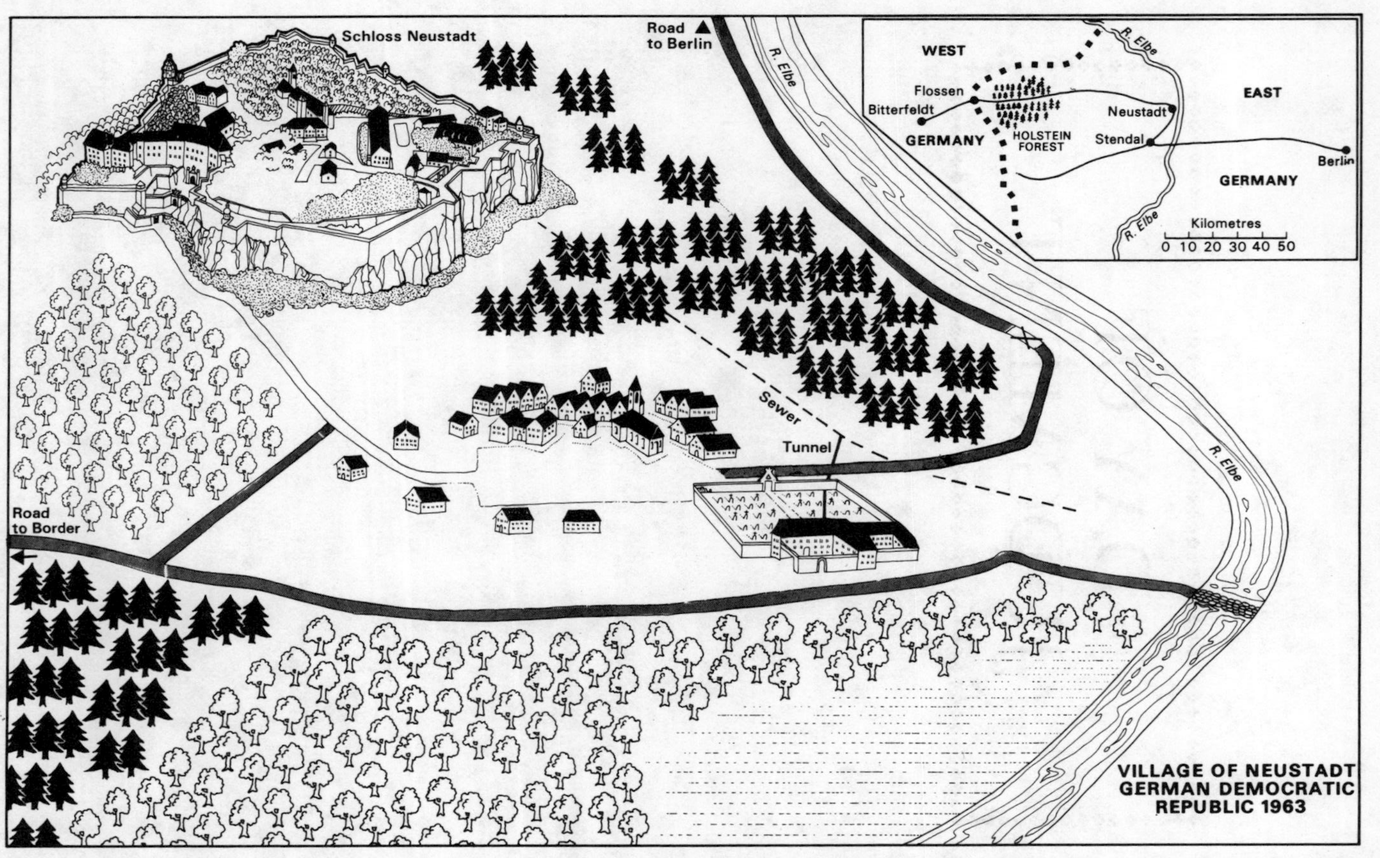
Schloss Neustadt
Road to Berlin
R. Elbe
WEST
Flossen
Bitterfeldt
GERMANY
HOLSTEIN FOREST
EAST
Neustadt
Stendal
Berlin
GERMANY
R. Elbe
Kilometres
0 10 20 30 40 50
Sewer
Tunnel
Road to Border
R. Elbe
VILLAGE OF NEUSTADT
GERMAN DEMOCRATIC
REPUBLIC 1963

— 1 —

AS MEYER turned the corner in the old hearse he reduced speed, his hands slippery with sweat as they gripped the wheel, his stomach tightening as he drove towards the checkpoint, clear in the night under the harsh white light of the arc lamps.

'I must be mad,' he said softly. 'Crazy. The last time, I swear it.'

There were two Vopos at the red and white barrier wearing old-fashioned Wehrmacht raincoats, rifles slung. An officer lounged in the doorway of the hut smoking a cigarette.

Meyer braked to a halt and got out as one of the sentries opened the door. The street ran to the wall itself through an area in which every house had been demolished. Beyond, in a patch of light, was the Western Zone checkpoint.

He fumbled for his papers and the officer came forward. 'You again, Herr Meyer. And what have we this time? More corpses?'

Meyer passed his documents across. 'Only one, Herr Leutnant.' He peered anxiously at the officer through steel-rimmed spectacles. With his shock of untidy grey hair, the fraying collar, the shabby overcoat, he looked more like an unsuccessful musician than anything else.

'Anna Schultz,' the lieutenant said. 'Age nineteen. A trifle young, even for these hard times.'

'Suicide,' Meyer explained. 'Her only relatives are an uncle and aunt in the Western Zone. They've claimed her body.'

One of the Vopos had the back of the hearse open and was starting on the brass screws of the ornate coffin lid. Meyer hastily grabbed his arm.

The lieutenant said, 'So, you don't want us to look into the coffin? Now why should that be, I wonder?'

Meyer, wiping sweat from his face with a handkerchief, seemed at a loss for words.

At that moment a small truck pulled in behind. The driver leaned out of the window holding his documents. The lieutenant glanced over his shoulder impatiently and said, 'Get rid of him.'

One of the Vopos ran to the truck and examined the driver's papers quickly. 'What's this?'

'Diesel engine for repair at the Greifswalder Works.'

The engine was plain to see, roped into position on the truck's flat back. The Vopo returned the documents. 'All right – on your way.'

He raised the red and white pole, the truck-driver pulled out from behind the hearse and started towards the gap in the wall.

The lieutenant nodded to his men. 'Open it.'

'You don't understand,' Meyer pleaded. 'She was in the Spree for a fortnight.'

'We shall see, shall we?'

The Vopos got the lid off. The stench was immediate and all-pervading so that one of them vomited at the side of the hearse. The other flashed his torch for the lieutenant to peer inside. He moved back hurriedly.

'Put the lid on, for God's sake.' He turned to Meyer. 'And you, get that thing out of here.'

II

The truck passed through the barriers on the other side and pulled in at the checkpoint hut. The driver got out, a tall man in a black leather jacket and flat cap. He produced a crumpled packet of cigarettes, stuck one in his mouth and leaned forward to accept a light from the West German police sergeant who had moved to join him. The match, flaring in the sergeant's hands, illuminated a strong face with high cheekbones, fair hair, grey eyes.

'Don't you English have a saying, Major Vaughan?' the sergeant said in German. 'Something about taking the pitcher to the well too often.'

'How do things look back there?' Vaughan asked.

The sergeant turned casually. 'There appears to be a little confusion. Ah yes, the hearse is coming now.'

Vaughan smiled. 'Tell Julius I'll see him at the shop.'

He climbed into the cab and drove away. After a while he kicked one heel against the front of the bench seat. 'Okay in there?' There was a muffled knock in reply and he grinned. 'That's all right then.'

III

The area of the city into which he drove was one of mean streets of old-fashioned warehouses and office blocks, alternating with acres of rubble, relic of the wartime bombing campaign. Some fifteen minutes after leaving the checkpoint, he turned into Rehdenstrasse, a dark street of decaying warehouses beside the River Spree.

Half-way along, a sign lit by a single bulb read Julius Meyer and Company, Undertakers. Vaughan got out, unlocked the large gates, opened them and switched on a light. Then he got into the truck and drove inside.

The place had once been used by a tea merchant. The walls were of whitewashed brick and rickety wooden steps led up to a glass-walled office. Empty coffins were stacked on end in one corner.

He paused to light a cigarette and the hearse drove in. Vaughan moved past it quickly and closed the doors. Meyer switched off the engine and got out. He was extremely agitated and ceaselessly mopped sweat from his face with the grimy handkerchief.

'Never again, Simon, I swear it. Not if Schmidt doubles the price. I thought the bastard was on to me tonight.'

Vaughan said cheerfully, 'You worry too much.' He leaned into the cab of the truck, fumbled for a hidden catch so that the front of the bench seat fell forward. 'All right, you can get out now,' he said in German.

'This is a life, this life we lead?' Meyer said. 'Why do we have to live this way? What are we doing this for?'

'Two thousand marks a head,' Vaughan said. 'Paid in advance by Heini Schmidt, who's got so many of the poor bastards lined up over there that we can do it every night if we want to.'

'There's got to be an easier way,' Meyer told him. 'I know one thing. I need a drink.' He started up the steps to the office.

The first passenger, a young man in a leather overcoat, crawled out of the hidden compartment and stood blinking in the light, clutching a bundle. He was followed by a middle-aged man in a shabby brown suit whose suitcase was held together by rope.

Last of all came a girl in her mid-twenties with a pale face and dark sunken eyes. She wore a man's trench-coat and a scarf tied peasant-fashion round the head. Vaughan had never seen any of them before. As usual, the truck had been loaded in advance for him.

He said, 'You're in West Berlin now and free to go anywhere you please. At the end of the street outside you'll find a bridge across the Spree. Follow your nose from there and you'll come to an underground station. Good night and good luck.'

He went upstairs to the office. Meyer was sitting at the desk, a bottle of Scotch in one hand, a glass in the other which he emptied in one quick swallow.

He refilled it and Vaughan took it from him. 'Why do you always look as if you expect the Gestapo to descend at any moment?'

'Because in my youth there were too many occasions when that was a distinct possibility.'

There was a tapping at the door. As they both turned the girl entered the office hesitantly. 'Major Vaughan, could I have a word with you?'

Her English was almost too perfect, no trace of any accent. Vaughan said, 'How did you know my name?'

'Herr Schmidt told me when I first met him to arrange the crossing.'

'And where was that?'

'In the restaurant of the old Hotel Adlon. Herr Schmidt's name was given to me by a friend as a reliable man to arrange these matters.'

'You see?' Meyer said. 'Every minute it gets worse. Now this idiot hands your name out to strangers.'

'I need help,' the girl said. 'Special help. He thought you might be able to advise me.'

'Your English is really very good,' Vaughan told her.

'It should be. I was born in Cheltenham. My name is Margaret Campbell. My father is Gregory Campbell, the physicist. You've heard of him?'

Vaughan nodded. 'Between them, he and Klaus Fuchs handed the Russians just about every atomic secret we had back in 1950. Fuchs ended up in the dock at the Old Bailey.'

'While my father and his twelve-year-old daughter found sanctuary in East Germany.'

'I thought you were supposed to live happily ever after,' Vaughan said. 'Socialist paradise and all that. Last I heard, your father was Professor of Nuclear Physics at Dresden University.'

'He has cancer of the lung,' she said simply. 'A terminal case. A year at the most, Major Vaughan. He wants out.'

'I see. And where would he be now?'

'They gave us a place in the country. A cottage at a village called Neustadt. It's near Stendhal. About fifty miles from the border.'

'Why not try British Intelligence? They might think it worth their while to get him back.'

'I have,' she said. 'Through another contact at the university. They're not interested – not any longer. In my father's field, you're very quickly yesterday's news and he's been a sick man for a long time now.'

'And Schmidt? Couldn't he help?'

'He said the risk involved was too great.'

'He's right. A little border-hopping here in Berlin is one thing, but your father – that's Indian territory out there.'

Whatever it was that had kept her going went out of her then. Her shoulders slumped, there was only despair in the dark eyes. She seemed very young and vulnerable in a way that was curiously touching.

'Thank you, gentlemen.' She turned wearily, then paused. 'Perhaps you can tell me how to get in touch with Father Sean Conlin.'

'Conlin?' Vaughan said.

'The League of the Resurrection. The Christian underground movement. I understood they specialized in helping people who can't help themselves.'

He sat staring at her. There was silence for a long moment.

Meyer said, 'So what's the harm in it?' Vaughan still didn't speak and it was Meyer who turned to her. 'Like Simon said earlier, cross the bridge at the end of the street and straight on, maybe a quarter of a mile, to the underground station. Just before it, there's a Catholic church – the Immaculate Heart. He'll be hearing confessions round about now.'

'At four o'clock in the morning?'

'Night workers, whores, people like that. It makes them feel better before going to bed,' Vaughan said. 'He's that kind of man, you see, Miss Campbell. What some people would term a holy fool.'

She stood there, hands in pockets, a slight frown on her face, then turned and went out without a word.

Meyer said, 'A nice girl like that. What she must have gone through. A miracle she got this far.'

'Exactly,' Vaughan said. 'And I gave up believing in those long ago.'

'My God,' Meyer said. 'Have you always got to look for something under every stone you see? Don't you trust anybody?'

'Not even me,' Vaughan said amiably.

The judas gate banged. Meyer said, 'So you're just going to stand there and let a young girl walk all that way on her own and in a district like this?'

Vaughan sighed, picked up his cap and went out. Meyer listened to the echo of his footsteps below. The door banged again.

'Holy fool.' He chuckled to himself and poured another glass of Scotch.

IV

Vaughan could see Margaret Campbell pass through the light of a street lamp thirty or forty yards in front of him. As she crossed the road to the bridge and started across, a man in slouch hat and dark overcoat moved out of the shadows on the far side and barred her way.

The girl paused uncertainly and he spoke to her and put a hand on her arm. Vaughan took a .38 Smith & Wesson from his inside pocket, cocked it and held it against his right thigh.

'No way to treat a lady,' he called in German as he mounted the half-dozen steps leading to the bridge.

The man was already turning very fast, his hand coming up holding a Walther. Vaughan shot him in the right forearm, driving him back against the rail, the Walther jumping into the dark waters below.

He made no sound, simply gripped his arm tightly, blood oozing between his fingers, lips compressed, a young man with a hard, tough face and high Slavic cheekbones. Vaughan turned him around, rammed him against the handrail and searched him quickly.

'What did he say to you?' he asked Margaret Campbell.

Her voice shook a little as she replied. 'He wanted to see my papers. He said he was a policeman.'

Vaughan had the man's wallet open now and produced a green identity card. 'Which, in a manner of speaking he is. SSD. East German state security service. Name of Röder, if you're interested.'

She seemed genuinely bewildered. 'But he couldn't have followed me. Nobody could. I don't understand.'

'Neither do I. Maybe our little friend here can help us.'

'Go to hell,' Röder said.

Vaughan hit him across the face with the barrel of the Smith & Wesson, splitting flesh, and Margaret Campbell cried out and grabbed him by the arm.

'Stop it!'

She was surprisingly strong and during the brief struggle, Röder ran to the end of the bridge and stumbled down the steps into the darkness. Vaughan finally managed to throw her off and turned in time to see Röder pass under a lamp at the end of the street, still running, and turn the corner.

'Congratulations,' he said. 'I mean, that really does help a lot, doesn't it?'

Her voice was the merest whisper. 'You'd have killed him, wouldn't you?'

'Probably.'

'I couldn't stand by and do nothing.'

'I know. Very humanitarian of you and a great help to your

father, I'm sure.' She flinched at that, her eyes wide, and he slipped the Smith & Wesson into his inside pocket. 'I'll take you to see Father Conlin now. Another one big on the noble gesture. You and he should do rather well together.'

He took her arm and together they started across the bridge.

V

Father Sean Conlin had, with Pastor Niemoller, survived the hell of both Sachsenhausen and Dachau. Afterwards, five years in Poland had made him realize that nothing had really changed. That he was still fighting the enemy under a different name.

But a tendency to do things in his own way and a total disregard for any kind of authority had made him a thorn in the side of the Vatican for years, on one famous occasion censured by the pope himself, which perhaps accounted for the fact that a man who was a legend in his own lifetime should still be a humble priest at the age of sixty-three.

He sat in the confessional box, a frail, white-haired man in steel-rimmed spectacles, dressed in alb, a violet stole about his neck, cold and tired for there had been more than usual that morning.

What he very much hoped was his last client, a local streetwalker, departed. He waited for a while, then started to get up.

There was a movement on the other side of the screen and a familiar voice said, 'You know, I've been thinking. Maybe people decide to give themselves to God when the Devil wants nothing more to do with them.'

'Simon, is that you?' the old man replied.

'Together with a true penitent. A young woman whose confession runs something like this: Forgive me, Father, for I have sinned. I am Gregory Campbell's daughter.'

Conlin said quietly, 'I think you'd better bring her into the sacristy and we'll have a cup of tea and see what she's got to say for herself.'

VI

The sacristy was almost as cold as the church itself. Conlin sat at the small deal table with a cup of tea, smoking a cigarette while the girl told him about herself. She was, it seemed, a doctor by profession; had only taken her finals at Dresden the previous year.

'And your father? Where is he now?'

'Near Stendhal, in the country. A village called Neustadt. A very small village.'

'I know it,' he told her. 'There's a Franciscan monastery there.'

'I wouldn't know about that, but then I don't know the place well at all. There is an old castle by the river.'

'That will be Schloss Neustadt. It was presented to the Franciscans by some baron or other at the beginning of the century. They're Lutherans, by the way, not Catholic.'

'I see.'

He said to Vaughan, 'And what do you have to say?'

'I'd give this one a miss.'

'Why?'

'The SSD man at the bridge. What was he doing there?'

'It could be that they are on to you and Julius. Bound to happen after a while.'

'Excuse me, but is Major Vaughan's opinion relevant?' Margaret Campbell asked.

The old man smiled. 'You could have a point there.'

Vaughan got up. 'I think I'll take a little walk, just to see how things stand.'

'You think there could be others?' she asked.

'It's been known.'

He went out. She said to Conlin, 'He scares me, that one.'

Conlin nodded. 'A very efficient and deadly weapon, our Simon. You see, Miss Campbell, in the kind of game he plays he has a very real advantage over his opponents.'

'What is that?'

'That it is a matter of supreme indifference to him whether he lives or dies.'

'But why?' she demanded. 'I don't understand.'

So he told her.

VII

When Vaughan went back into the sacristy they were talking quietly, heads together. The old priest glanced up and smiled. 'I'd like you to see Miss Campbell safely back into East Berlin later today. You'll do that for me, won't you, boy?'

Vaughan hesitated. 'All right,' he said, 'but that's as far as I go.'

'No need for more.' Conlin turned to Margaret Campbell. 'Once back on their side, return to Neustadt and wait for me. I'll be there the day after tomorrow.'

'Yourself?'

'But of course.' He smiled almost mischievously. 'Why should others have all the fun?' He stood up and put a hand on her shoulder. 'Never fear, my love. The League of the Resurrection has something of a reputation in this line of work. We won't let you down.'

She turned and went out. The old man sighed and shook his head. Vaughan said, 'What are you thinking about?'

'A child of twelve who, with only her father's hand to hold on to, was suddenly spirited away by night from everything warm and secure and recognizable, to a strange and rather frightening country with an alien people whose language she didn't even understand. I think now that in some ways she is still that lost and frightened little girl.'

'Very touching,' Vaughan said. 'But I still think you're wrong.'

'O, ye of little faith.'

'Exactly.'

VIII

Margaret Campbell was at the church gate when Vaughan caught up with her.

The street was deserted, grim and forbidding in the grey morning light. As they started along the pavement she said, 'Why do you live like this, a man like you? Is it because of what happened out there in Borneo?'

'Conlin and you *have* been improving the shining hour,' he said calmly.

'Do you mind?'

'I seldom mind anything.'

'Yes, that was the impression I got.'

He paused in a doorway to light a cigarette and she leaned against the wall and watched him.

Vaughan said, 'The old man was very taken.'

He very carefully tucked a wet strand of hair under her headscarf. She closed her eyes and took a hesitant step forward. His arm slipped around her waist and she rested her head against his shoulder.

'I'm so tired. I wish everything would stand up and walk away and leave me alone to sleep for a year and a day.'

'I know the feeling,' he said. 'But when you open those eyes of yours, you'll find nothing's changed. It never does.'

She looked up at him blankly. 'Not even for you, Vaughan? But I thought from what Father Conlin said you were the kind of man for whom the impossible only takes a little longer?'

'Even the Devil has his off-days, didn't he tell you that as well?'

He kissed her gently on the mouth. She was suddenly filled with a kind of panic and pulled away from him, turned and continued along the pavement. He fell in beside her, whistling cheerfully.

There was an all-night café by the bridge. As they neared it, it started to rain. He reached for her hand and they ran, arriving in the entrance slightly breathless and very wet.

The café was a small, sad place, half a dozen wooden tables and chairs, no more. A man in a dark blue overcoat was fast asleep in a corner. He was the only customer. The barman sat at the zinc-topped counter reading a newspaper.

She waited at a table by a window overlooking the river. Behind her, she could hear Vaughan ordering coffee and cognac.

As he sat down she said, 'You speak excellent German.'

'My grandmother came from Hamburg. She grew up by the Elbe, I was raised on the Thames. She lived with us when I was a boy. Raised me after my mother died. Made me speak German with her all the time. Said it made her feel at home.'

'And where was this?'

'Isle of Dogs near the West India Docks. My old man was captain of a sailing barge on the Thames for years. I used to go with him when I was a kid. Down to Gravesend and back. Even went as far as Yarmouth once.'

He lit a cigarette, the eyes dark, as if looking back across an unbridgeable gulf. She said, 'Where is he now?'

'Dead,' he said. 'A long time ago.'

'And your grandmother?'

'Flying bomb, November '44. There's irony for you.'

The barman appeared with a tray, placed a cup of coffee and a glass of cognac in front of each of them and withdrew. Vaughan took his cognac in one easy swallow.

'A little early in the day, I should have thought,' she commented.

'Or too late, depending on your point of view.'

He reached for her glass, she put a hand on his. 'Please?'

There was something close to surprise in his eyes and then he laughed softly. 'Definitely too late, Maggie. You don't mind if I call you that, do you? In fact, very definitely far too far gone. You know that poem of Eliot's where he says that the end of our exploring is to arrive where we started and recognize the place for the first time?'

'Yes.'

'He was wrong. The end of our exploring is to recognize the whole exercise for what it's been all along. One hell of a waste of time.'

He reached for the glass again and she knocked it over and sat staring at him, her face very white.

'And what's that supposed to prove?'

'Nothing,' she said. 'Just take it as sound medical advice.'

He sighed. 'All right. If you're ready, we'll move on. I'm sure you can't wait to get back on your side of the fence anyway.'

As they started towards the bridge she said, 'You still don't trust me, do you?'

'Not really.'

'Why?'

'No particular reason. Instinct, if you like. A lifetime of bad habits.'

'Yet you'll take me back across the wall because Father Conlin asked you to. I don't understand.'

'I know. Confusing, isn't it?'

He took her arm and they started across the bridge, footsteps hollow on the boards.

— 2 —

IT WAS TEN O'CLOCK on Tuesday evening when the old army truck loaded with turnips pulled up the hill out of the village of Neustadt. About a quarter of a mile further on it turned in to the side of the road under pine trees.

Father Conlin wore a corduroy jacket and peaked cap, a grimy blue scarf knotted around his neck. His companion, the driver of the truck, wore an old army tunic and badly needed a shave.

'This is it, Karl, you are certain?' Conlin asked in German.

'The cottage is a couple of hundred yards from here at the end of the farm track through the woods, Father. You can't miss it, it's the only one,' Karl told him.

Conlin said, 'I'll take a look. You wait here. If everything's all right I'll be back for you in a few minutes.'

He moved away. Karl took the stub of a cigar from behind his ear and lit it. He sat there smoking for a while, then opened the door, got down and stood at the side of the truck to relieve himself. There was no sound at all, so that the blow that was delivered to the back of his head came as a total surprise. He went down with a slight groan and lay still.

II

There was a light at one of the cottage windows for the curtains were partially drawn. When Father Conlin approached cautiously and peered inside he saw Margaret

Campbell, dressed in sweater and slacks, sitting in front of a blazing log fire reading a book.

He tapped on the pane. She glanced up, then crossed to the window and peered out at him. He smiled, but she did not smile in return. Simply went to the door and opened it.

Conlin moved into the warmth of the room, shaking rain from his cap. 'A good night for it.'

'You came,' she said in a choked voice.

'Didn't you think I would?' He was warming himself at the fire and smiled at her. 'Your father – how is he?'

'I wouldn't know,' she said tonelessly. 'I haven't seen him for weeks now. They wouldn't allow me.'

He saw it then of course, saw all of it, now that it was too late. 'Oh, my poor child,' he said and there was only concern for her in his voice, compassion in the faded blue eyes. 'What have they made you do?'

The kitchen door creaked open behind, a draught of air touched his neck coldly and he turned. A man was standing there, tall, rather distinguished-looking, dark hair turning to silver, a strong face – a soldier's face. He wore a heavy overcoat with a fur collar and smoked a thin cheroot.

'Good evening, Father Conlin,' he said in German. 'You know who I am?'

'Yes,' Conlin said. 'Helmut Klein. I believe you once enjoyed the dubious distinction of being the youngest full colonel in the Waffen SS.'

'Quite right,' Klein said.

Two men in raincoats emerged from the kitchen to stand beside him. At the same moment, the outside door opened and a couple of Vopos entered armed with machine-pistols, followed by a sergeant.

'We got the truck-driver, sir.'

'What, no comrade?' Father Conlin said. 'Not very socialistic of you, colonel.' He turned to Margaret Campbell. 'Colonel Klein and I are old adversaries, at a distance. He is Director of Section Five, Department Two of the State security service which is charged with the task of combating the work of refugee organizations in Western Europe by any means possible. But then, you'd know that.'

Her eyes were burning, her face very pale. She turned to Klein. 'I've done what you asked. Now can I see my father?'

'Not possible, I'm afraid,' Klein said calmly. 'He died last month.'

The room was very quiet now and when she spoke it was in a whisper. 'But that can't be. It was only three weeks ago that you first sent for me. First suggested that I . . .' She gazed at him, total horror on her face. 'Oh, my God. He was dead. He was already dead when you spoke to me.'

Father Conlin reached out for her, but she pulled away and launched herself on Klein. He struck her once, knocking her back into the corner by the door. She lay there dazed. As Conlin tried to move towards her, the two men in raincoats grabbed him and the Vopos advanced.

'Now what?' the old priest asked.

'What do you expect, whips and clubs, Father?' Klein asked. 'Nothing like that. We have accommodation reserved for you at Schloss Neustadt. Comfortable – or otherwise – the choice is yours. A change of heart is what I seek. As publicly as possible, naturally.'

'Then you're wasting your time entirely,' the old man said.

Behind them, the door banged as Margaret Campbell slipped out into the night.

III

She had no idea where she was going, her brain unable to focus properly after the stunning shock she had received. Klein had lied to her. Used her love for her father to betray a remarkable man.

Her mind rejected the idea totally so that she ran as if from the consequences of her action, blundering through the trees in the darkness, aware of the cries of her pursuers behind. And before her was only the river, its waters, swollen by heavy rain, flooding across the weir.

One of the Vopos loosed off a burst from his machine-pistol and she cried out in fear, running even faster, one arm raised against the flailing branches, tripped over a log and rolled down the steep bank into the river.

The Vopos arrived a moment later and the sergeant flashed

his torch in time to see her out there in the flood, an arm raised despairingly, and then she went under.

IV

It was just after eight o'clock on the following evening when the black Mercedes saloon drew up to the entrance of the Ministry of State Security at 22 Normannenstrasse in East Berlin. Helmut Klein got out of the rear and hurried up the steps to the main entrance for he had an appointment to keep – probably the most important appointment of his entire career – and he was already late.

Section Five was located on the third floor. When he went into the outer office, his secretary, Frau Apel, rose from her desk considerably agitated.

'He arrived ten minutes ago,' she whispered, glancing anxiously at the three men in dark overcoats who stood by the inner door. Hard, implacable faces, ready for anything and capable of most things, from the look of them.

There was a fourth man, lounging in the window-seat reading a magazine. Small, with good shoulders, dark hair and grey eyes that had a transparent look to them. The left-hand corner of the mouth was lifted into a slight ironic half-smile that contained no humour, only a kind of contempt directed at the world in general. He wore a dark trenchcoat.

Klein gave his coat to Frau Apel and moved towards him, hand outstretched. He spoke in English. 'Well, we got him, Harry. It worked, just like you said. The girl did exactly as she was told.'

'I thought she might.' The voice was soft and pleasant. Good Boston-American. 'Where is she now?'

'Dead.' Klein explained briefly what had happened.

'What a pity,' the small man said. 'She was rather pretty. You've got the man himself in there, by the way. I almost got to touch the hem of his garment as he swept by.'

Klein glanced quickly at the security men by the door and dropped his voice. 'Exactly the kind of remark we can do without. When I call you in, try and behave yourself.'

He opened the door to his office and entered. The man in the trenchcoat stuck a cigarette in the corner of his mouth, but didn't bother to light it. He smiled down at Frau Apel and for some reason she was aware of a slight flutter of excitement.

'Big night, eh?' he said in German.

'A great honour.' She hesitated. 'They may be a while. Perhaps I could get you a cup of coffee, Herr Professor?'

He smiled. 'No, thanks. I'll just go back to the window-seat and wait. I get an excellent view of your legs from there under the desk. You really are a very disturbing person, did anyone ever tell you that?'

He returned to the window. She sat there, her throat dry, unable to think of a thing to say and he stared at her with those grey, dead eyes that gave nothing away, the perpetual smile as if he was laughing at her. She reached for a sheet of typing paper quickly. As she put it into the machine, her hands were shaking.

V

When Klein entered his office, the man behind the desk glanced up sharply. His suit was neat, conservative, the beard carefully trimmed, the eyes behind the thick lenses of the glasses apparently benign. Yet this was the most powerful man in East Germany – Walter Ulbricht, chairman of the Council of State.

'You're late,' he said.

'A fact which I sincerely regret, Comrade Chairman,' Klein told him. 'Several main roads leading into the city from the west are flooded. We were obliged to make a detour.'

'Never mind the excuses,' Ulbricht said impatiently. 'You got him?'

'Yes, comrade.'

Ulbricht showed no particular emotion. 'I fly to Moscow in the morning and as I shall be away for a week at least I want to make sure this thing is fully under way. The man you have chosen to accomplish the task, the American, van Buren. He is here?'

'Waiting outside.'

'And you believe he can do it?'

Klein opened his briefcase, took out a folder which he placed on the desk before Ulbricht. 'His personal file. If you would be kind enough to have a look at it before seeing him, comrade. I think it speaks for itself.'

'Very well.' Ulbricht adjusted his glasses, opened the file and began to read.

VI

In the early months of 1950 Senator Joseph McCarthy charged that he had evidence that a number of employees of the American State Department were Communists. Arthur van Buren, a Professor in Moral Philosophy at Columbia University, was injudicious enough to write a series of letters to the *New York Times* in which he suggested that in this new development the seeds of a fascist state were being sown in America.

Like others, he was called to Washington to stand before a Senate sub-committee in the greatest witch-hunt the nation had ever seen. He emerged from it totally discredited, branded a Communist in the eyes of the world, his career in ruins. In March 1950 he shot himself.

Harry van Buren was his only son, at that time twenty-four years of age. He had majored in psychology at Columbia, researched in experimental psychiatry at Guy's Hospital in London, taking his doctorate at London University in February 1950.

He arrived home in time to stand beside his father's grave when they buried him. He didn't really know what to make of it all. His mother had died when he was five.

His father's brother was in the machine-tool business and almost a millionaire; his Aunt Mary was married to a man who owned forty-seven hotels. They seemed more concerned with the possibility that the senator from Wisconsin had been right. That his father was indeed a Red. It was up to Harry to restore the family honour, which he did by joining the Marine Corps the moment the Korean war started.

Nonsensical behaviour, of course. As a professional psychologist he could see that. Could even understand the reasons for it and yet he went ahead, lying on his enlistment papers about his education; a need, he told himself, to purge some kind of guilt.

He pulled mess duty, swabbed out the heads, endured the close proximity of companions he found both brutal and coarse and kept himself to himself. He took everything they handed out to him and developed a kind of contempt for his fellows that he would not have thought possible.

And then came Korea itself. A nightmare of stupidity. A winter so cold that if the M1 was oiled too much it froze. Where grenades did not explode, where the jackets of the water-cooled heavy machine-guns had to be filled with antifreeze.

In November of 1950 he found himself part of the First Marine Division facing northwards to Koto-Ri to end the war at one bold stroke as General Douglas MacArthur intended. Except that the Chinese Army had other ideas and the Marines walked into a trap that was sprung at the Choisin Reservoir and led to one of the greatest fighting retreats in the history of war.

For a while he played his part with the others who fought and died around him. He killed Chinese with bullet and bayonet, urinated on the bolt mechanism of his carbine when it froze, and staggered on with frostbite in his left foot and a bullet in the right shoulder. And when a boot in the side stirred him into waking one misty morning, it was something like a relief to look up into a Chinese face.

It was at the camp in Manchuria that he'd decided he'd had enough after the first month in the coal mine. The indoctrination sessions had given him his opportunity. The chief instructor was crude in the extreme. Easy enough not to contradict, but to reinforce the points he was making. A few days of that and van Buren was sent for special interrogation during which he made a full and frank confession of his background.

He was used at first to work as a missionary amongst his fellow prisoners until he came to the attention of the famous Chinese psychologist, Ping Chow, of Peking University, who at that time was making a special study of the behaviour patterns of American prisoners of war. Chow was a Pavlovian by training and his work on the conditioning of human behaviour was already world famous at an academic level.

In van Buren he found a mind totally in tune with his own.

The American moved to Peking to research in the psychology department of the university there. There was no question in his own mind now of any return to America.

Soon enough both the Pentagon and the State Department became uncomfortably aware of his existence, but kept quiet about it for obvious reasons so that he remained on that list of those missing, presumed dead, in Korea.

By 1959 he was an expert in thought reform and by special arrangement moved to Moscow to lecture at the university there. By 1960 his reputation in the field of what the press popularly termed 'brainwashing' was already legendary. There was not a security department in any Iron Curtain country which had not called upon his services.

And then, in April 1963, while lecturing at the University of Dresden in the German Democratic Republic, he had received a visit from Helmut Klein, Head of Section Five in the State security service.

VII

Walter Ulbricht closed the file and looked up. 'There is one flaw in all this.'

'Which is, Comrade Chairman?'

'Professor van Buren is not, and never has been, a Communist.'

'I agree entirely,' Klein said. 'But for our purposes he is, if I may say so, something far more important – a dedicated scientist. He is a man obsessed by his work to an astonishing degree. I have every faith in his ability to accomplish the task we set him.'

'Very well,' Ulbricht said. 'Show him in.'

Klein opened the door and called. 'Harry – in here.'

Van Buren entered, hands in the pockets of his coat. He stood in front of the desk, that slight, mocking smile set firmly in place.

'You find something amusing?' Ulbricht enquired.

'My deep regrets, Comrade Chairman,' van Buren said. 'But the smile is beyond my control. A Chinese bayonet in the face at Koto-Ri in Korea in the winter of 1950 when I was serving with the American Marines. Eight stitches, very badly administered by a medical orderly who didn't really know much better. He left me looking on the bright side permanently.'

'This Conlin affair,' Ulbricht said impatiently. 'You understand the implications?'

'They've been explained to me.'

'Then allow me to refresh your memory. Conlin, as you know, stood beside Niemoller in opposition to the Nazis. Went to Dachau for it.'

'And survived,' van Buren said. 'Which means he must be quite a man. I've been looking him up. At his trial in 1938 the Nazis were able to prove that his organization had helped more than six thousand Jews to escape from Germany over a two-year period. The Israelis gave him honorary citizenship two years ago.'

'None of which is material to the present issue,' Ulbricht said. 'We have a situation in which thousands of misguided comrades persist in attempting to cross over to West Germany. In the main, they have to rely on the help of organizations based on the other side who operate purely for financial gain.'

'Or try Conlin?'

'Exactly. This League of the Resurrection of his asks for nothing.'

'Very charitable of them.'

'Which unfortunately makes for excellent publicity,' Klein said. 'It has made Conlin a celebrity again. He was featured on the front of *Life* magazine in America only four months ago. Last year he was recommended for a Nobel peace prize and had to turn it down because the Church didn't approve.'

'I should imagine that must have been the first time in years he took any notice of the Vatican,' van Buren commented.

Ulbricht said, 'You know that President Kennedy visits Berlin next month?'

'I had heard.'

Ulbricht was angry now, removed his glasses and polished them vigorously. A dedicated Communist of the old school, he had managed to prevent, in East Germany at any rate, the de-Stalinization movement which had swept Eastern Europe after the death of the Russian dictator. There was no one he hated more than the present American president, especially since his triumph in the Cuban crisis.

'If it could be proved in a public trial that Father Conlin's actions were motivated not so much by Christian ideals as by political ones; if he could be made to admit to the world his involvement with the American CIA and their espionage activities directed against our Republic; this would have the most damaging effect on Kennedy's visit to Berlin. It would, in fact, make it totally worthless as a diplomatic gesture.'

'I understand.'

'For God's sake, man.' Ulbricht was almost angry now. 'Rats in cages, dogs oozing saliva at the sound of a bell. I know as much of this Pavlovian psychology as anyone, but can you really change a man? Make him act like a different person? Because that's what we need. Conlin to stand up in court before the cameras of the world and freely admit to having been a political agent acting for the Western powers.'

'Comrade,' Harry van Buren said crisply, 'I could make the Devil himself think he was Christ walking on the water, given enough time.'

'Which is exactly what we don't have,' Klein said. 'The problem of the Campbell girl and her knowledge of the affair has solved itself, but there will be others. Conlin's associates in this League of Resurrection will be aware, within a matter of days, that something has gone badly wrong.' He hesitated then said carefully to Ulbricht, 'And then, of course, comrade, there are certain traitors in our own ranks still . . .'

'I know that, man, I'm not a fool,' Ulbricht said impatiently. 'What you are saying is that there are those in the West who will discover what's happened and attempt to do something about it?' He shook his head. 'Not officially, believe me. The Americans are heavily concerned to improve relations with Russia at the moment and Pope John's attempts to come to terms with the Eastern bloc speak for themselves. And what can they say? Conlin has simply ceased to exist. After all, he shouldn't have been here in the first place, should he?'

He actually permitted himself a smile.

'Of course, comrade,' Klein said.

'I have every confidence in your ability to deal with any such attempts with your usual efficiency, colonel.'

There was a slight silence. Ulbricht adjusted his glasses and said to van Buren, 'You have a month. One month, that's all, before Kennedy's visit. You have those papers, Colonel Klein?' Klein produced a sheaf of documents instantly and laid them before Ulbricht, who took out his pen and signed them, one after the other.

'These give you full authority, civil and military, in the district of Neustadt where Conlin is being held at the Schloss. Power of life and death, total and complete, comrade. See that you use it wisely.'

Van Buren took them from him without a word and Klein came forward with the chairman's coat as Ulbricht stood up. He helped him into it, then escorted him to the door.

Ulbricht turned, looking from one to the other. 'When I was a boy, my mother was very fond of reading the Bible to me. "Well done, thou good and faithful servant." I remember that phrase particularly. The Council of State feels exactly like that, Comrades, towards those who succeed, but for the failures . . .'

He put on his hat and went out, closing the door behind him.

Klein turned to van Buren. 'So, my friend, it begins,' he said.

— 3 —

FOR MARGARET Campbell re-birth was a nightmare. Of suffocation, of freezing cold and then a long darkness from which she finally surfaced to find a middle-aged, grey-haired man at her side. He wore a brown habit, with a knotted cord at his waist from which a large crucifix was suspended.

Her mouth was dry so that she found it impossible to speak and he got an arm around her shoulders and put a glass to her lips.

'Easy now,' he said in German.

She coughed a little and said hoarsely, 'Who are you?'

'Brother Konrad, of the Franciscan order of Jesus and Mary. This is our house at Neustadt.'

'How did I come here?'

'One of my brothers found you this morning, caught on the weir, draped across the trunk of a tree. The Elbe is in flood because of the heavy rains.'

She tried to move and was aware of an excruciating pain in her left leg. Her hand, moving instinctively to the spot, encountered heavy bandages. 'Is it broken?'

'I think not. Very badly sprained. A torn thigh muscle.'

'You seem very sure.'

'I'm not without experience in these matters, fräulein. During the war I served as a volunteer with the medical corps, mainly on the Russian front. Unfortunately the nearest doctor is at Stendhal, but if you think it necessary . . .'

'No,' she said. 'The nearest doctor is here.'

'I see.' He nodded calmly. 'On the other hand, although our Lord said, "Physician, heal thyself", this is not the easiest of precepts to follow.'

'I am in your hands, it would seem.'

'Exactly.' He gave her two white tablets and a glass of water. 'Take these, they will help with the pain.' He arranged the pillow behind her head to make her more comfortable. 'Sleep now. We will talk again later, fräulein . . .?'

'Campbell,' she said. 'Margaret Campbell.'

'Is there someone I can notify of your safety?'

'No.' She leaned back, staring up at the ceiling. 'There is no one.'

II

It was towards evening and she was wide awake when he came in, her head turned to one side, trying to look over the sill out of the window.

He put a hand to her forehead. 'Better,' he said. 'The fever has gone down. A miracle when one thinks how long you were out there in the water.'

His face was full of strength, firm, ascetic and touched with a tranquility that she found completely reassuring.

'The Society of Jesus and Mary?' she said, and remembered her first meeting with Conlin. 'You're Lutherans, isn't that so?'

'That's right,' he told her. 'Our movement started in England in the closing years of the last century. There was a great interest in that time in the work of St Francis and a desire, by some people, to continue his mission within the framework of the Church of England.'

'And how did you end up in Neustadt?'

'A lady called Marchant married the Graf von Falkenberg, the greatest landowner in these parts. On the death of her husband, she offered Schloss Neustadt to the order. They came here in 1905, led by Brother Andrew, a Scot. There were twelve friars then, just like the disciples, and eight nuns.'

'Nuns,' she said blankly. 'There are nuns here?'

'Not any more.'

'But this is not Schloss Neustadt,' she said. 'It can't be.'

He smiled. 'We were moved out of the castle in 1938. The army used it as a local area headquarters for a time. Towards the end of the war it served to house prominent prisoners.'

'And since then?'

'The State has failed to find any particular use for it, but on the other hand has never shown any great desire to return it. This house, in which we have lived for some years now, is called Home Farm. If I raise you against the pillows you can see the river and the Schloss on the hill above.'

He sat beside her, an arm about her shoulders, and now she could see a pleasant garden surrounded by a high wall. On the other side there was a cemetery. To the right, the River Elbe raced between trees, a brown, swollen flood. Beyond, on the hill above the village, stood Schloss Neustadt behind its massive walls, pointed towers floating up there in the light mist, the approach road zig-zagging up the face of the hill towards the great gate of the entrance tunnel.

The door opened and another middle-aged man entered carrying a tray. 'And this,' Konrad said, 'is Brother Florian who fished you out of the river.'

Florian placed the tray across her knees. There was soup

in a wooden bowl, black bread, milk. She put a hand on his sleeve. 'What can I say?'

He smiled again and went out without a word. 'He cannot speak,' Konrad told her. 'He is under vow of silence for a month.'

She tried a little of the soup and found it excellent. 'The nuns,' she said. 'What happened to them?'

His face was grave now, something close to pain in his eyes. 'They left,' he said. 'The last of them about two years ago. There are only six of us here now, including myself. A year from now I should imagine we'll all be gone if the State has its way.'

'But I don't understand,' she said. 'It states quite clearly in the constitution that no individual shall be prevented from practising whatever religion he chooses.'

'True. The youngest among us, Franz, joined our order only six months ago in spite of every obstacle that officialdom tried to put in his way. Are you a Christian, Fräulein Campbell?'

'No,' she said. 'When it comes right down to it, I don't suppose I'm anything.'

'The State is rather more equivocal. The rights to religious free expression, as you have said, are enshrined in the constitution. At the same time Walter Ulbricht himself has told the country in more than one speech that Church membership is not compatible with being a good Party member.'

'But the constitution remains. What can they do?'

'Provide State services as substitutes for Christian ones. Marriage, baptism, funeral – all taken care of. To go to church is to deny the State, which explains why there hasn't been a Catholic priest here for five years and why, in what has always been a mainly Catholic area, the church door remains barred.'

Her mind was full of disturbing emotions. Religion had never interested her. There had been no place for it in her home background, for her father had been an atheist for most of his adult life. Her education had followed the path set for the children of all important officials in the Socialist Democratic Republic. Privileged schooling and an open door to university. A private, enclosed world in which all was perfection. What Brother Konrad was saying was new to her and difficult to take in.

'Why did the nuns go?' she said.

'There was an article in *Neues Deutschland* implying that orders such as ours were immoral. Old wives' tales, common for centuries. That in pools near convents, the bodies of newborn infants had been discovered. That sort of nonsense. Then the State medical authorities started monthly inspections for venereal disease.' He smiled sadly. 'It takes great strength of will to stand up to such ceaseless pressure. The nuns of our order, one by one, gave in and returned to life outside, as did most of our brothers.'

'But you hang on,' she said. 'A small handful, in spite of everything. Why?'

He sighed. 'So difficult to explain.' And then he smiled. 'But perhaps I could show you.'

III

He brought an old wheelchair, a robe to put about her shoulders, and took her out and along the stone-flagged corridor into the courtyard, pausing only to push open the gnarled oaken door on the far side.

It was like plunging into cool water, a tiny, simple chapel with no seating at all. Whitewashed walls, a wooden statue of St Francis, the plainest of altars with an iron crucifix, a small rose-coloured window through which the evening light sprayed colour into the room.

'For me,' Konrad said, 'there is joy in simply being here, for in this place I am aware of all my faults and weaknesses with utmost clarity. Here it is that I see myself as I truly am and here also that I am most aware of God's infinite compassion and love. And that, fräulein, gives me joy in life.'

She sat, staring up at that rosy window and made her decision. 'Have you ever heard of the League of the Resurrection?'

'Why do you ask?'

'Have you and your friends ever assisted with its work?'

'We are an enclosed order,' he said gravely. 'The contemplative life is what we seek.'

'But you know of the work of Father Sean Conlin?'

'I do.'

'And approve?'

'Yes.'

She swung to face him. 'He's up there now in Schloss Neustadt. Dachau all over again and it's all my fault.'

IV

It was cold with the bedroom window open, but her face was hot, burning as from a fever again, and the evening breeze eased it a little. She stirred restlessly in the chair and the door opened and Konrad entered with a glass.

'Cognac,' he said. 'Drink it down. It will make you feel better.' He pulled a chair forward. 'Now tell me more about this American professor, van Buren.'

'I first met him in Dresden about eighteen months ago. I was just finishing my medical studies and he was lecturing on para-psychology, a fringe interest of his. He made a point of visiting my father. Said he'd always admired his work. They became good friends. He even obtained a medical appointment for me in his own department at the Institute of Psychological Research. A wonderful opportunity – or so I thought at the time.'

'You didn't like working there?'

'Not really. Harry van Buren is a remarkable man – certainly the most brilliant intellect I've ever been exposed to. But it seems to me he has one fatal flaw. He's obsessed with his subject to such a degree that human beings become of secondary importance. At the Institute I saw him turn people around, change them completely. Oh yes, there were the psychotics where it was a good thing – a miracle, if you like. But the others . . .'

Konrad said gently, 'So – he betrayed you?'

'My father was ill – terminal cancer of the lung. They took him into hospital several weeks ago – I'm not certain of the exact date. They told me that the medical superintendent wanted to see me. When they took me to his office, I found Harry and a Colonel Klein from state security.'

'What happened then?'

'Colonel Klein told me that the radio-therapy treatment needed to keep my father alive was costly and the equipment needed elsewhere. It was usual medical policy to allow such cases to run their own course. If I did as I was told, they might be able to make an exception.'

'Which was to entice Conlin over the border for them?'

She nodded. 'Harry explained why it was necessary in the finest detail. It was as if he was trying to persuade me. How Father Conlin could be made to stand up before the world and say exactly what he had been told. Harry said it was necessary because Conlin was an enemy of the State. That he and his organization had been engaged in espionage.'

'And you believed him?'

'My only thought was for my father.'

'Honestly put.'

She carried on. 'Harry calls his technique thought reform. And it works. He'll have Father Conlin denying everything he's ever believed in before he's through.'

There was a long pause, then Konrad said, 'And what is it you would have me do, fräulein?'

'When they sent me across, they used a man called Schmidt in East Berlin who specializes in such matters. Klein said they allowed him to operate because it suited their purposes. Sometimes they put agents across to the other side in the guise of refugees. That sort of thing.'

'Which makes sense. And they had you followed?'

'Oh yes. An SSD operative, not that he lasted very long. The man who handled the actual crossing was an Englishman – a Major Vaughan. He and his partner have an undertaker's establishment in Rehdenstrasse in the West Zone. Julius Meyer & Co.'

'You think he can help?'

'Perhaps. He was the only one who could see I was lying. Isn't that a strange thing?'

She broke down then, harsh sobs racking her body. Konrad rested a hand on her shoulder briefly, turned and went out. He paused for a moment, a slight frown on his face, then went to the far end of the corridor and opened a door which gave access to the farmyard at the rear of the main building. There was a monotonous jangle of cowbells as the small dairy herd was shepherded in from the water-meadow by Brother Urban, a frail old man with white hair who wore a sack across his shoulders.

Brother Konrad opened the main door to the cow byres for him. 'Tell me,' he said, 'what time does Franz deliver the milk to the inn in the morning?'

'Seven-thirty is the usual time, I believe, brother,' the old man replied.

'And Berg, from the Schloss? What time does he collect his milk? Do you know?'

'He's usually waiting at the inn when Franz gets there.'

'Good.' Brother Konrad nodded. 'When you see Franz, tell him that in the morning I will take the milk.'

Strange how cheerful he felt. He slapped the rear cow on its bony rump and they all tried to squeeze through the entrance into the byre together, bells clanking.

V

In the bedroom, Margaret Campbell stood at the open window awkwardly, all her weight on one leg as she leaned across the sill to cool her burning face. It was almost dark and yet it was still possible to discern the darker mass of Schloss Neustadt against the evening sky.

There was a light up there, gleaming faintly from one window after another as if someone was moving along a corridor. It was suddenly extinguished. She thought of Conlin alone up there in the darkness and was afraid.

VI

The car which Klein had placed at van Buren's disposal was a Mercedes staff car of the war years. It was in excellent condition, a pleasure to handle, and he enjoyed the hour and a half's run from Berlin in spite of the poor visibility towards evening.

It gave him time to think about the task ahead, and in any case he liked being alone like this. But then, he always had. An onlooker instead of a participant. In that way one could see things more clearly. Sum up the strength of the opposition, which, in this case, meant Conlin.

It was almost completely dark when he reached Neustadt. There were lights at the windows in the village, but the Schloss was in complete darkness. He drove up the narrow approach road, negotiating the sharp bends with care as it climbed the hill. There was a sentry standing in the mouth of the entrance tunnel out of the rain.

Van Buren held his identity card out of the window. 'Captain Süssmann is expecting me.'

The Vopo examined the card by torchlight and nodded. 'Straight on to the main courtyard. I'll telephone through and tell them you're on your way.'

Van Buren drove on, along the dark tunnel. There was a barrier at the far end, another sentry who examined his identity card again before raising the pole and allowing him through. Security was thorough enough, or so it seemed.

He drove across the inner courtyard and braked to a halt at the foot of a row of wide stone steps rising to a massive wooden door which stood open. A small group of Vopos waited to greet him. Two privates holding lanterns, a sergeant and a young man whose uniform carried a captain's tabs.

The captain saluted as van Buren got out of the car. 'A pleasure to meet you, Herr Professor. Hans Süssmann.' He nodded to the sergeant, a large, brutal-looking man. 'Becker.'

Van Buren looked up at the dark bulk of the Schloss. 'What's going on here?'

'The place has its own power plant from the days when it was an army group headquarters. The dynamo is giving trouble. Nothing serious. There are a couple of electricians working on it now.'

Van Buren took out a leather case and selected a cigarette. Süssmann offered him a light. The American said, 'You've had your orders from Colonel Klein? You understand the situation here?'

'Perfectly.'

'How many men have you got?'

'Twenty. All hand picked.'

'Good. Let's go in.'

The entrance hall was impressive, a marble staircase lifting into the darkness above. A silver candelabrum stood on the table in the centre with half a dozen lighted candles in it. A short, stocky man stood there. His dark beard was flecked with grey, his hair tangled, and the elbows of his old tweed jacket were crudely patched.

'This is Berg,' Süssmann said. 'The caretaker. The place hasn't been occupied for any official purpose since the war.'

Van Buren said to Berg, 'We spoke on the telephone earlier. You've done as I said?'

'Yes, Herr Professor.'

'Good – I'll see Conlin now.'

Süssmann nodded to Berg, who picked up the candelabrum and led the way up the marble stairs. As they followed, van Buren said, 'What's the situation in the village?'

'Population, one hundred and fifty-three – agricultural workers in the main. The local innkeeper is the mayor – Georg Ehrlich. He's Berg's brother-in-law. There has never been any trouble here – not from anyone. Oh, there are a handful of monks in the old farm at the bottom of the hill by the river.'

'Good God!' van Buren said, genuinely astonished.

'Franciscans. Berg says they supply the village with milk.'

They were passing along an upper corridor now, the light from the candelabrum in Berg's hand throwing shadows on the walls.

At the far end, two guards stood outside a door. Süssmann unlocked it. Van Buren said, 'I'll see him alone first.'

'As you wish, Herr Professor.'

Süssmann opened the door for him. Van Buren took the candelabrum from Berg and moved inside.

VII

It was a fairly ornate bedroom with a painted ceiling. Conlin was crouched at the end of the bed, his wrists handcuffed to one of the legs. He glanced up, blinking in the sudden light. Van Buren stood there, the candelabrum held high, looking down at him. He placed it carefully on the floor and squatted, taking out a cigarette and lighting it.

'I understand you smoke rather heavily?'

'It's been said.'

Van Buren placed the cigarette between the old priest's lips. 'Enjoy it while you can. The last for a long time. My name is Harry van Buren. Does that mean anything to you?'

'Oh yes,' the old man said calmly. 'I think you could say that. Thought reform – an interesting concept.'

'You know what to expect, then.'

'You're wasting your time, boy.' Conlin smiled. 'I've been worked on by experts.'

'Not really,' van Buren said. 'You only think you have.' He took the cigarette from Conlin's mouth, turned to the door and opened it. He handed the candelabrum to Berg and said to Süssmann, 'We'll take him below now.'

VIII

At the rear of the main staircase in the great hall an oak door gave access to the lower reaches of the Schloss.

As he unlocked it Berg said, 'There are three levels, as I explained to you on the telephone, Herr Professor, dating back to the fourteenth century.'

They descended a long flight of stone steps and then a tunnel which sloped into darkness before them. Berg led the way, holding a lantern, and van Buren and Süssmann followed, Becker bringing up the rear with Conlin between two Vopos.

Berg had to unlock two gates to reach the lowest level. It was very cold now and damp. He paused finally at an iron-bound door and unlocked it. The passageway stretched onwards into darkness.

Van Buren said, 'Where does that go?'

'More tunnels, Herr Professor. Dungeons, storage cellars. The place is a rabbit-warren.'

Berg opened the door. Van Buren followed him in and the caretaker held up his lantern. The cell was very old, stone walls smoothed by time, shining with damp. There was no window. The floor was stone-flagged and the only furnishing was an enamel bucket in one corner and an iron cot with no mattress. The door had a small flap at the bottom for food to be passed through.

'Is this what the Herr Professor wanted?'

'Exactly.' Van Buren turned to Süssmann. 'Let's have him inside. No shoes – shirt and trousers only and leave the handcuffs on.'

He moved out, ignoring Conlin as Becker and the two guards hustled him in. 'Nothing to say, professor?' the old man called.

'Why yes, if you like.' Van Buren turned to face him through the open doorway. 'Frances Mary. Will that do?'

Conlin's face sagged, he turned white. Becker and the two guards came out, the sergeant closed the door and locked it.

'I'll take the key.' Van Buren held out his hand for it. 'And I want a sentry here at all times – understood?'

'Yes,' Süssmann said.

'He stays in here for a week. Total darkness and no communication in any way. One meal a day. Bread and cheese, cold water, passed through the flap at the bottom of the door. Above all, no noise. Better make your sentries wear socks over their boots or something like that.'

'I'll see what can be done.'

'Good. I'm returning to Berlin tonight. If anything comes up, contact Colonel Klein.'

'And we shall see you again?'

'Exactly seven days from now. Then we really start to get down to it.'

They moved away along the passage, leaving Becker with one of the guards. The sergeant gave him his instructions, then followed.

IX

Inside the cell, Conlin stood listening, aware only of the muffled sounds of their going. *Frances Mary*. So long since he had thought of her. And if van Buren knew about her, what else did he know? His heart raced and the anguish at that moment was physical in its intensity.

He took a deep breath and shuffled cautiously through the darkness until he found the cot, then lay down on it carefully, the springs digging into his back. It was very quiet, 'Phase One,' he thought. 'Sensory deprivation leading to complete alienation of the subject.'

The darkness seemed to move in and complete panic seized him as he remembered Dachau. To be alone, so alone, of course, was the worst thing of all – and then it occurred to him, as it had many times before, that he was not. He closed his eyes, folded his hands, awkwardly because of the handcuffs, and started to pray.

X

It was just before seven-thirty on the following morning when Brother Konrad and Franz pulled their hand-cart, loaded with milk churns, into the courtyard of the local inn. Berg's old truck stood beside the front door and the caretaker leaned against it, smoking a pipe and talking to his brother-in-law.

Georg Ehrlich was a small dark man with an expression of settled gravity on his face that never altered. A widower, he left the running of the inn mainly to his daughter, for not only was he mayor, but chairman of the farm co-operative and local Party secretary.

He managed a smile for the Franciscan. 'Konrad – we don't often see you.'

'I wanted a word,' Konrad said. 'Official business, and besides – I thought the boy here might like a little help for a change.'

Franz, who at nineteen was the youngest member of the order and built like a young bull, grinned and swung a full milk churn to the ground with ease.

Berg said, 'I'm going to need at least one of those a day from now on. Put it on the truck for me, Franz, there's a good lad.'

'A full churn?' Konrad said in surprise. 'What on earth for?'

'Vopos up at the Schloss. Twenty of the bastards.'

'Come on in,' Ehrlich said. 'Sigrid's just made fresh coffee.'

They moved along a whitewashed corridor and entered an oak-beamed kitchen. Ehrlich's daughter Sigrid, a pretty, fair-haired girl of seventeen in a blue dress and white apron, fed logs into the stove. She glanced up and Ehrlich said, 'Coffee and perhaps a brandy to go with it? A cold morning.'

'That's kind of you,' Konrad said, 'but a little early in the day for me.' He turned to Berg. 'What's all this about Vopos up at the Schloss? I don't understand. What are they doing?'

'Guarding a prisoner they brought in the night before last. Twenty of them plus a sergeant and captain for one man. I ask you.'

Konrad accepted the cup of coffee Sigrid passed him with a smile of thanks. 'Someone important, obviously.'

'That's not for me to say, is it?' Berg said. 'I only follow orders like we all have to these days.' He leaned forward, the hoarse whisper of his voice dropping even lower. 'I'll tell you one thing you'll never believe. You know where they're holding him? In a cell on the third level. Solitary confinement to start with. A full seven days before we even open the door on him again. That's what the man from Berlin said and off he went with the key in his pocket. Van Buren, his name is. Professor van Buren.'

Konrad frowned. 'Merciful heaven! I would have thought that even the rats might have difficulty surviving down there.'

'Exactly.' Berg emptied his glass. 'I'd better be getting back with that milk now. They'll be wanting their breakfasts up there.'

He went out. Ehrlich took down his pipe and started to fill it. Konrad said, 'Some political prisoner or other, I imagine.'

'I don't know and I don't care,' Ehrlich said. 'In times like these it pays to mind your own business. He talks too much, that one.'

'He always did.'

The innkeeper applied a match to his pipe. 'What was it you wanted to see me about?'

'Ah yes,' Konrad said. 'I'd like a travel permit, to go to Berlin to see my sister. I think I mentioned when we last spoke that she'd had a heart attack.'

'Yes, I was sorry to hear that,' Ehrlich said. 'When do you want to go?'

'This morning, if possible. I'd like to stay a week. I'll remember, of course—' here he smiled – 'to wear civilian clothes.'

Ehrlich said, 'I'll make you a permit out now.' He reached for the bottle. 'But first, that brandy I mentioned, just to start the day right.'

'If you insist,' Konrad relented. 'But just a small one.' When he raised the glass to his lips, he was smiling.

XI

Margaret Campbell had spent a restless night. Her leg ached and she had fallen into a sleep of total exhaustion just before dawn. She was awakened at eight-fifteen by a knock at her door and Konrad entered with a breakfast tray. She had a splitting headache and her mouth was dry.

He took her temperature and shook his head. 'Up again. How do you feel?'

'Terrible. It's the leg mainly. The pain makes it difficult to sleep. The pills you gave me last night didn't do much good.'

He nodded. 'I've something stronger in the dispensary, I think. I'll leave them out for Urban to give you while I'm away.'

He placed the tray across her knees. She looked up in surprise. 'You're going somewhere?'

'But of course,' he said. 'West Berlin, to see this Major Vaughan of yours. Isn't that what you wanted me to do?'

There was an expression of utter astonishment on her face. 'But that's impossible.'

'Not at all. The co-operative produce truck leaves the square at nine for Stendhal, from which there are regular buses to Berlin. I'll be there by noon.'

'But how will you get across?'

'The League will help me.'

'The League of the Resurrection? But when I asked if you and your friends had ever assisted with its work, you said . . .'

'That we are an enclosed order. That the contemplative life is our aim.'

She laughed suddenly for the first time since he had known her, so that for the moment it was as if she had become a different person.

'You are a devious man, Brother Konrad. I can see that now.'

'So I've been told,' he said, smiling, and poured her coffee.

XII

In West Berlin, Bruno Teusen stood at the open window leading to the terrace of his apartment in one of the new blocks overlooking the Tiergarten and sipped black coffee. He was at that time fifty, a tall, handsome man with a pleasant, rather diffident manner, that concealed an iron will and a razor-sharp mind.

A lieutenant-colonel of ski troops on the Russian Front at twenty-five, a serious leg wound had earned him a transfer to Abwehr headquarters at Tirpitz Ufer in Berlin, where he had worked for the great Canaris himself.

His wife and infant son had been killed in an air raid in 1944 and he had never remarried. In 1950 when the Office for the Protection of the Constitution, popularly known as the BfV, was formed, he was one of the first recruits.

The function of the BfV was primarily to deal with any attempted undermining of the constitutional order, which, in practice, came down to a constant and daily battle of wits with the thousands of Communist agents operating in West Germany. Teusen was Director of the Berlin office, a difficult task in a city whose inhabitants still tended to equate any kind of secret service with the Gestapo or SD.

It had been a hard day and he was considering the merits of dining on his own and having an early night or phoning a young lady of his acquaintance when his bell rang. He cursed softly, went to the door, and peered through the security bullseye.

Simon Vaughan was standing there, Brother Konrad behind him, wearing corduroy trousers, a reefer jacket and tweed cap.

Teusen opened the door.

'Hello, Bruno.'

'Simon.' Teusen looked Konrad over briefly. 'Business?'

'I'm afraid so.'

'You'd better come in, then.'

He closed the door and turned to face them. Konrad took off his cap. Vaughan said, 'This is Colonel Bruno Teusen. Bruno, Brother Konrad of the Franciscan Order of Jesus and Mary at Neustadt on the other side. I think you'll want to hear what he has to say.'

He walked across to the drinks cabinet, poured himself a Scotch and went out on the terrace. It was really very pretty, the lights of the city down there, but for some reason all he could think of was Margaret Campbell, trapped at Neustadt with her injured leg and probably frightened to death.

'Poor stupid little bitch,' he said softly. 'You shouldn't have joined, should you?'

XIII

It was perhaps fifteen minutes later that Teusen and Konrad came out on the terrace.

'Not so good,' the colonel said.

'Can you do anything?'

'For Conlin?' Teusen shrugged. 'I don't hold out much hope. I'll get in touch with the Federal Intelligence Service in Munich, but I don't see what they can do, other than inform interested parties.'

'And who might they be?'

'The Vatican, for one. He is a priest, after all. Where was he born – Ireland?'

'Yes, but he's an American citizen.'

'They might be interested then, but I wouldn't count on it. And we haven't any proof that Conlin's over there. If anyone approaches the East German government officially, they'll simply deny any knowledge of him. In any case, from the sound of it, getting him out of Schloss Neustadt would take a company of paratroopers dropping in at dawn, and Skorzenys are thin on the ground these days.'

Brother Konrad said, 'And the girl?'

'We might be able to do something for her.' Teusen turned to Vaughan. 'Would you be willing to help there?'

For a moment Vaughan saw again her pale face, the dark weary eyes in the early morning light on the bridge over the Spree. He smiled. 'Julius won't like it.'

'I know. Something for nothing again.' Teusen glanced at Konrad. 'When do you have to be back?'

'My permit allows me a seven-day stay in East Berlin.'

'And where are you staying now?'

Konrad turned uncertainly to Vaughan, who said, 'At our

place in Rehdenstrasse. You might have to sleep in a coffin, but it's home.'

Teusen said, 'I'll be in touch. Possibly tomorrow – certainly by the day after. We should have the responses of all the interested parties by then.'

He closed the door behind them and poured himself a cognac. Then he went to the telephone, dialled a Munich number and asked to speak to General Reinhardt Gehlen, Director of BND, the Federal Intelligence Service. Strange that he no longer felt tired.

— 4 —

IN ROME, on the following morning, in an upper room of the Vatican, His Holiness Pope John XXIII, close to death due to the effects of a stomach tumour from which he had been suffering for a year, held audience propped up by pillows in his bed.

A young monsignor sat by his side, reading from one letter after another in a low voice. His Holiness listened with closed eyes, opening them occasionally to sign a document when requested and again when his physician entered to administer a pain-killing injection.

The phone at the side of the bed buzzed and the monsignor answered it. He said, 'Father Pacelli is here.'

The pope nodded. 'Admit him.'

'This is not good,' the doctor said. 'Your Holiness knows . . .'

'That he has very little time, and a great deal to do.'

The doctor turned away, closing his bag, and the monsignor opened the door to admit a tall, gaunt old man with white hair and deepset eyes, a strangely medieval figure in the plainest of black habits.

'You look more like a bird of prey than usual this morning,' the pope said.

Father Pacelli smiled slightly, for this was an old game between them. He was almost seventy years of age, a Jesuit, second only in that illustrious order to the Father General himself, Director of Historical Research at the Collegio di San Roberto Bellarmino on the Via del Seminario, from where he had been responsible for more than twenty-five years for the organization of the closest thing the Vatican had to a secret service department.

The pope looked up from the document he was reading. 'You Jesuits, Pacelli. The plain black habit, the lack of pomp. A kind of humility in reverse, don't you think?'

'I remind myself of the fact in my prayers each day, Holiness.'

'Soldiers of Christ.' The pope waved the document at him. 'Like Father Conlin. He reminds me strongly of a certain colonel of infantry I knew when I served as a military chaplain during the First World War. Whenever he went over the top to lead an attack he never ordered his men to follow him. Simply took it for granted that they would.'

'And did they, Holiness?'

'Invariably. There's a moral arrogance to that sort of action that I've never been too sure about. Still . . .' He handed the document to the young monsignor. 'You're certain as to the accuracy of this information?'

'It comes from my valued contact in the West German Intelligence Service.'

'And the Americans – have they been informed?'

'Naturally, Holiness. Father Conlin is an American citizen.'

'For whom they can do nothing.'

Pacelli nodded. 'If the facts are as stated, the East Germans would certainly deny his presence.'

'Even to us,' the pope pointed out.

There was a moment's silence. Pacelli said, 'There would, of course, be the inevitable moment when they produce him for this show trial.'

'Like Cardinal Mindszenty, saying all the right things? That the Church with the aid of the CIA is engaged in some kind of underground struggle aimed at the destruction of the

German Democratic Republic and everything Ulbricht and his friends stand for?'

'A suggestion not entirely without merit,' Pacelli said. 'But in my opinion, Holiness, it seems to me that on this occasion it is not so much the Church that is the target as the Americans. It would certainly cause President Kennedy considerable embarrassment if they succeeded in stage-managing the affair to coincide with his trip to Germany.'

'Exactly; and the Berlin visit is of primary importance. When he stands at the Wall, Pacelli, he places himself in the forward trench. He shows the Communist bloc that America is firm with the other Western powers.'

The pope closed his eyes, one hand gripping the edge of the damask coverlet of his bed. There was sweat on his face and the doctor leaned over him and sponged it away.

Pacelli said, 'So, Holiness, we do nothing?'

'To do anything official is not possible,' Pope John said. 'On the other hand, Father Conlin is a member of the Society of Jesus, which has always, or so it seems to me, proved singularly apt at looking after its own.' He opened his eyes, a touch of the old humour there again in spite of the pain. 'You will, I trust, find time to keep me informed, Pacelli.'

'Holiness.' Pacelli leaned down to kiss the ring on the extended hand and went out quickly.

II

The black limousine bearing the licence plates of the pope which had brought Pacelli to his audience returned him to the Collegio di San Roberto Bellarmino within twenty minutes of leaving the Vatican City, in spite of the heavy traffic.

When he entered the small library which served as his office on the first floor overlooking the courtyard at the rear of the building, Father Macleod, the young Scot who had been his secretary for two years now, rose to greet him.

'Neustadt,' Pacelli said. 'Have you come up with anything of interest?'

'I'm afraid not,' Macleod told him. 'An agricultural village, typical of the region. These Franciscan Lutherans are the only remarkable thing about the place.'

'And we have no church there?'

'Yes, Father. Holy Name. Founded in 1203. It's been closed for five years.'

'Why?'

'Officially, because there's no congregation.'

'The old story. You can't be a good Party member and go to church as well.'

'I suppose so, Father. Is there anything further you would like me to do in this matter?'

'Contact Father Hartmann, at the Secretariat in East Berlin. Get a message to him by the usual means. I wish to see him in West Berlin at the Catholic Information Centre the day after tomorrow. Get me a seat for the morning flight on that day. Inform him of Father Conlin's predicament and tell him I will expect the fullest possible information.'

'Very well, Father. The file on the American, van Buren, is on your desk.'

'Good.' Pacelli picked it up. 'Get me the Apostolic Delegate in Washington on the telephone. I'll be with the Father General.'

The young Scot looked bewildered. 'But Father, it's three o'clock in the morning in Washington. Archbishop Vagnozzi will be in bed.'

'Then wake him,' Pacelli said simply, and walked out.

III

The Father General of the Jesuits, leader of the most influential order in the Catholic Church, wore a habit as plain as Pacelli's. He removed his glasses and closed the file on van Buren.

'The Devil and all his works.'

'A genius in his own way,' Pacelli said.

'And how will Father Conlin fare at his hands, would you say?'

'He survived Sachsenhausen and Dachau.'

'A remarkable man.' The Father General nodded. 'We all know that, but times have changed. New techniques of interrogation. The use of drugs, for example.'

'I have known Sean Conlin for forty years,' Pacelli said. 'His is a faith so complete that in his presence I feel humble.'

'And you think this will be enough to sustain his present situation?'

'With God's help.'

The phone rang. The Father General lifted the receiver, listened, then handed it to Pacelli with a slight, ironic smile. 'For you. Archbiship Vagnozzi – and he doesn't sound too pleased.'

IV

It was a surprisingly chilly evening in Washington for the last day in May, and in the White House the Secretary of State, Dean Rusk, stood at a window in the Oval Office. The room was dark, the only light the table lamp on the massive desk, the array of service flags behind it. The door clicked open and as he turned the president entered.

John Fitzgerald Kennedy had celebrated his forty-sixth birthday only three days before and looked ten years younger. He wore dinner jacket and black tie, white shirt-front gleaming.

He smiled as he moved behind the desk. 'We were just going in to dinner and I've got the Russian Ambassador down there. Is it important?'

'The Apostolic Delegate came to see me this evening, Mr President. It occurred to me that it might be advisable for you to have a word with him.'

'The Conlin affair?'

Rusk nodded. 'You've read the file I prepared for you?'

'I've got it right here.' The president sat down at his desk and opened a folder. 'Tell me – did this come in through the German desk of the State Department?'

'No. A coded message to me personally from Gehlen himself.' There was a pause while the president leafed through the file. Rusk said, 'So what do we do?'

The president glanced up. 'I'm not certain. It's one hell of a mess, that's for sure. Let's see what the Vatican has to say.'

V

The Apostolic Delegate, the Most Reverend Egidio Vagnozzi, wore a scarlet zapata on his head and the red cassock of an archbishop. He smiled warmly as he entered the room and the Secretary of State brought a chair forward for him.

'It's good of you to see me on such short notice, Mr President.'

'A bad business,' the president said.

'And one which could be a considerable personal embarrassment to you if Father Conlin is brought to trial, as is suggested. I refer, of course, to your Berlin visit.'

'Does the Vatican intend to make any kind of official representation to the East German government?' Dean Rusk asked.

'What would be the point? At this stage in the game they would certainly deny having him in their hands, and there are other considerations. The position of Roman Catholics, indeed of all declared Christians, is a difficult one in East Germany these days. We must tread very carefully.'

'In other words, you'll do nothing,' the president said.

'Nothing official,' Vagnozzi said. 'On the other hand, Father Pacelli of the Society of Jesus is going to Berlin as soon as possible to assess the situation.'

The president smiled. 'Pacelli himself, eh? So you're letting him off the leash? Now that is interesting.'

'His Holiness, in spite of his unfortunate illness, is taking a personal interest in this matter. He would like to know, in view of the fact that Father Conlin is an American citizen, what your own views are.'

The president stared down at the folder, a slight frown on his face, and it was the Secretary of State who answered. 'There are various aspects which are far from pleasant. This man, van Buren, for example, has been a considerable embarrassment to us for years. Naturally, we've kept a very low profile on him, and so far that's worked.'

'And then there's Conlin's own position,' the president said. 'They'll try to brainwash him into saying his Christian underground has been a tool of the CIA for years. The point of the exercise: a total smear to ruin every good thing I'm hoping to achieve by the German trip. The improvement in relations between ourselves and Moscow since Cuba has been considerable. Together with the British, we're to resume three-power talks in Moscow aimed at a nuclear test-ban treaty. In a few days' time I'm making a speech here in Washington at the American University in which I intend to make clear our recognition of the post-war status quo in Eastern Europe.'

'A move of profound significance,' Vagnozzi said.

The president continued. 'As far as East Germany is concerned, Ulbricht is a Stalinist. He hates Krushchev, so my visit to Berlin is of great importance in the general scheme of things because it shows Ulbricht that we mean business.'

'Which helps Krushchev to handle him.'

'But more than that – it shows the Russians where we stand also. That trying to be reasonable doesn't mean we've gone soft. We stand by West Berlin.'

Vagnozzi said, 'So there is nothing we can do about Conlin?'

The president shook his head and the steel that was always there just beneath the surface showed coldly in the eyes for a moment. 'I didn't say that. What I'd like you to do is give me a little more time, that's all.'

Vagnozzi stood up. 'Very well, Mr President. I will delay making my official reply until I hear from you.'

'Before morning,' the president assured him. 'I think I can promise you that.'

The archbishop went out. Dean Rusk said, 'With the greatest respect, Mr President, I must point out that to attempt an official move at this time – to involve the CIA, for example – would be madness. If anything went wrong, it could only add substance to the kind of charges they intend to bring against Conlin anyway.'

'Exactly,' the president said. 'Which is why anything that is done will have to be on a completely unofficial basis.' He reached for a copy of the *Washington Post*. 'Did you know Charles Pascoe was in town?'

'No.'

'There's an article here on page three. He's giving the Vanderbilt Memorial Lecture at the Smithsonian tonight.'

'I thought he'd given up the academic life,' the Secretary

of State said. 'I heard his brother died last year and left him a fortune.'

'No, he's still Professor of Modern English Literature at Balliol.' The president folded the newspaper, stood up and eased his back. 'I'd like to see him – when he's finished his lecture, of course.'

'As you say, Mr President.'

The Secretary of State started for the door and President Kennedy called softly, 'And – Dean?'

'Yes, Mr President?'

'Let's make it the west basement entrance when you bring him in. No press on this one – by request.'

VI

Professor Charles Pascoe was bored, for the subject of his lecture at the Smithsonian, Aspects of the Modern Novel, was one he found increasingly unrewarding, as he did the company of the academics who surrounded him at the reception afterwards. The arrival of the polite young man from the State Department with a request that he visit the White House that very night had come as a happy release.

Charles Browning Pascoe was at that time sixty-six. The second son of a Birmingham cutler, he had chosen to go to the University of Heidelberg in 1914, an error of judgment which had cost him three years of internment. He had finally escaped to England by way of Holland and spent the last year of the war in Military Intelligence.

Afterwards came a brilliant academic career which had included eight years as Professor of Modern Literature at Harvard before a return to Oxford to his old college, Balliol. And then came Hitler's war, during which he was called back to Intelligence, first working with Masterman at MI5, helping to smash the German spy network in England, then transferring to Special Operations Executive where, more than anyone else, he had been responsible for the successful organization of the British and American Intelligence network in occupied France.

His wife had died in 1943. There were no children. After the war he had returned to Oxford, to the academic life that was his first love. And then, in the summer of 1962, his elder brother Robert, who had created one of the major electronics firms in England, died, leaving him a fortune which even after heavy death duties was considerably in excess of one million pounds, a circumstance which had occasioned him little excitement. Certainly nothing like as much as he felt now, leaning back against the seat as the car moved along Constitution Avenue.

VII

The limousine delivered him to the west basement entrance at the White House. The polite young man in the blue raincoat who had escorted him from the Smithsonian led the way past the secret service agents in the corridor and straight through to the Oval Office where the Secretary of State was waiting.

He smiled and held out his hand. 'Professor Pascoe. We have met, I think? A reception at the ambassador's house in London three years ago.'

Pascoe was slightly built, with stooped shoulders, a shock of iron-grey hair falling across his forehead. He wore a dark evening coat over his dinner jacket, an old-fashioned wing collar and black tie.

'And just exactly what is all this about?'

The Secretary of State indicated the manilla folder on the desk. 'If you'd be kind enough to read that, I think it covers the situation more than adequately.'

'And then?'

'The president himself will explain what comes after. I'll leave you now.'

The door closed behind him. Pascoe sat down without removing his overcoat, took a pair of half-moon reading glasses from his breast pocket, put them on and opened the file.

VIII

Twenty minutes later the door opened and President Kennedy entered, followed by the Secretary of State. Pascoe glanced up.

'I couldn't resist trying the seat of power, if only for a time.'

Kennedy grinned and turned to the Secretary of State. 'You know, when *While England Slept* was published, this man wrote me a letter twenty-two pages long, taking it apart word by word.'

'A necessary stage in your education, Mr President.' Pascoe smiled mildly, and closed the file.

'Interesting?' Kennedy asked.

'Yes – I think you could say that. I've admired Conlin's work for many years. He's a remarkable man. I'm sorry to see him in such a plight.' Pascoe removed his glasses. 'A strange coincidence here, by the way. Colonel Teusen, the West German Intelligence Officer who passed on the news from Berlin, is an old adversary.'

The president frowned and the Secretary of State said, 'Teusen served under Canaris at Abwehr Headquarters in Berlin during the war.'

'Another remarkable man, the admiral.' Pascoe stood up. 'However . . .'

The president moved to the window, looked out and said, 'You spoke about the seat of power. You know what power is? Real power? It's not being able to do a damned thing because you're president and you've got to think of the country or the UN or what the Russians will do – or not do.'

Pascoe said, 'Yes, I can see how hard it must be to have to stand back and watch a good man go down the drain like this.'

'Oh no.' The President shook his head gently. 'I'm not prepared to do that, and in any event I can't afford to. The Berlin trip is too crucial.'

'The point is, we can't do anything official – not at this stage,' Rusk said.

'So where do I come in?' Pascoe asked.

'Donovan once expressed the opinion that you were the greatest mind at work in Intelligence operations on either side during the war,' the president told him.

'As Mark Twain said, I can live for two months on a good compliment.'

'One is all you've got. My European schedule has me visiting West Berlin on 26 June.'

Pascoe said, 'You're serious? You really want me to try and do something about Conlin?'

'How many times did you handle similar operations during the war?'

'True.' Pascoe nodded. 'But that was eighteen years ago.'

'No official help, of course. Not from anyone. The West German Government can't afford any kind of involvement at this stage.'

'And the Vatican?'

'Pacelli arrives in Berlin tomorrow,' the Secretary of State said. 'Again, entirely unofficially. Do you know him?'

'Worked with him at a distance during the war, but we never met.

There was a pause. The president said, 'There would be the question of the necessary funds.'

'Hardly a problem,' Pascoe told him. 'My situation in that respect has changed considerably of late. I'm more concerned with my tutorials. My students are expecting me back next week. But I suppose something could be arranged.'

The Secretary of State said, 'If I might suggest, Mr President. Archbishop Vagnozzi . . .'

'The Apostolic Delegate,' the president said to Pascoe. 'He's fully informed on the whole affair. It might be a good idea if you had words with him before leaving. He could arrange a meeting with Pacelli when you arrive in Berlin.'

'And when exactly did you plan that to be, Mr President?' Charles Pascoe enquired.

'I had a word with my appointments secretary while you were reading the file. There's a BOAC flight that leaves for London just before midnight, which would give you time to speak with Vagnozzi. You'd be in Berlin tomorrow afternoon.'

'Presumably they have space available?'

'Already booked,' the president said.

Pascoe nodded. 'Very well. I have only one stipulation.'

'Yes?'

'A meeting with Teusen and a request that he has ready, on my arrival, all possible information known to the West German Intelligence Service on the situation at Neustadt.'

The president glanced at the Secretary of State, who nodded. 'I don't think there will be any difficulty there.'

'Good.' Pascoe picked up the file. 'I'm in your hands, it would seem. We don't have too much time if I'm to catch that plane.'

They started towards the door. The president said, 'I'd like to thank you, professor.'

Pascoe smiled. 'Did I really have any choice? It is rather in the nature of a royal command, after all.' He turned and followed the Secretary of State out.

— 5 —

FATHER ERICH Hartmann SJ, of the Catholic Secretariat in East Berlin, was an extraordinarily handsome man, yet he seldom smiled and there was a faintly chilling quality in the blue eyes that made most people who dealt with him proceed with considerable caution.

This included the Vopos at Checkpoint Charlie who had grown used to the young priest in the battered little Volkswagen in which he regularly passed through to the West Zone on Vatican business. After six months he was a familiar sight, as was the man in the black leather raincoat who followed him at a discreet distance on a light motor-cycle.

Erich Hartmann was thirty-three, born in Dresden in 1930, the son of a butcher who was not only a Communist, but also local Party secretary. He had continued his activities after the rise to power of the National Socialists and on 3 February, 1934 his wife had found him, hanging from a meat hook in his cold store. The official verdict was suicide.

Frau Hartmann sold the business and sent her son to her brother in New York. She herself stayed on, working actively against the Nazis with the Communist underground until she was arrested in October of 1944 and sent to Dachau, where she was executed by firing squad just before Christmas of that year.

Her brother and his wife were devout Catholics, who raised the boy in the faith and spoke nothing but German in the home against the day when he could be re-united with his mother.

The news of her death, not confirmed until 1946, affected him deeply. He had always been something of an introvert. Now, he withdrew completely into himself, even during his period at Notre Dame where he was not only a brilliant scholar, but an All-American quarterback two years running.

No one had been particularly surprised when he declared his vocation for the priesthood. In the Society of Jesus he found an order of discipline and intellect that was perfectly in tune with his own rigid attitude to the world about him.

Except for a brief curacy in Naples he had been employed mainly in the administrative section of the order, where Pacelli had discovered him and the curious fact that he was still officially a citizen of the German Democratic Republic.

His transfer to the Catholic Secretariat in East Berlin had been immediate, to duties ostensibly of an administrative nature, but in reality to be his superior's eyes and ears in the capital.

II

It was just after two-thirty when Hartmann pulled in to the kerb in front of the Catholic Information Centre in Budapesterstrasse. As he got out of the Volkswagen, the man in the black leather coat parked his motor-cycle by a tree on the opposite side of the road and dismounted. He started to light a cigarette and Hartmann crossed over.

'If you get bored, there's the Zoological Gardens behind you, Horst. I might be quite some time.'

The man smiled genially. He had high cheekbones and a slightly flattened nose that gave him the look of an ex-prize-fighter.

'On the other hand, Father, you could be on your way again before I know where I am and that would never do.'

Hartmann shrugged, turned and hurried across the street. He ran up the steps of the old building and moved straight through the reception hall, nodding briefly to the young woman behind the desk as he went up the stairs. He passed along an uncarpeted corridor, opened a door marked 'Private' without knocking and went in.

It was a small untidy room, furnished as an office and cluttered with filing cabinets. Pacelli sat behind a desk by the window, reading a typed report. He glanced up and smiled.

'You're looking well, Erich.'

'I can't complain, Father.'

Hartmann moved to the window and looked out across the road at the man in the leather coat sheltering under a tree. Pacelli joined him.

'SSD?'

'His name is Horst Schaefer. A Section Six man. Surveillance of all important Church leaders is their speciality.'

'You should be flattered.' Pacelli sat down, watching as Hartmann took off his coat. The old man smiled. 'But then, you couldn't allow such an unworthy emotion.'

'If you say so.'

'You have the look, Erich, of some fanatical Roundhead in the England of Cromwell's time. The kind of man who could cry out on the Lord with fervour and in the same breath cheerfully burn young girls as witches.'

'You sent for me, Father.'

'Yes, you're quite right. I did.'

He explained the situation quickly. When he was finished, Hartmann said, 'I heard van Buren lecture at the University of Dresden only three months ago.'

Pacelli got up and walked to the window. 'How regularly have you been making the crossing?'

'Twice a week – sometimes three times. I've even stayed the night on occasion.'

'What about our friend with the motor-cycle when you stay over? Don't tell me he stands out there all night? Or does someone else take over?'

'No,' Hartmann said. 'One agent per priest. That's bureaucracy for you. I usually warn him. A ridiculous situation, but no more than the world we live in. There's a small hotel with a bar just along the street. The sort of place streetwalkers use. He stays there. I always give him the keys of the car. It reassures him. He's a simple man.'

'So?' Pacelli went back to the desk. He opened a black leather briefcase, took out a large envelope and pushed it across.

'As at the moment your movements are restricted to East and West Berlin only, here's a present from the Vatican, signed by the Cardinal Secretary of State himself in the name of the Holy Father. A formal request that you be allowed to visit Neustadt without delay to consider the possibility of re-opening the church there.'

Hartmann opened the envelope and took out the letter. It was an imposing-looking document, stamped with a red seal. 'This must be submitted to the Ministry of State Security, as you well know, Father, which means the information will automatically pass to Klein at Section Five.'

'Who will be expecting something – some move or other from someone – or I miss my guess. You are correct. Father Conlin's presence at Neustadt and our official request for your visit is beyond coincidence, but my own feeling is that they will grant you leave to go. Under surveillance, of course.'

'Why should they?'

'Why not? We have the right, under the constitution and under the Secret Treaty of Accord signed with the Vatican only last July.' He smiled slightly. 'And they can hardly use Conlin's presence as a reason for saying no, can they?'

'But what is the purpose of all this?' Hartmann demanded. 'What do we gain?'

'Submit your request to the Ministry of State Security immediately on your return this afternoon,' Pacelli told him. 'You should have a decision one way or the other, tomorrow. I'll expect to see you back here the day after – and be prepared to stay overnight. It may be necessary.'

Hartmann said, 'Do I understand you to mean by all this that you contemplate an attempt to . . .' he hesitated. 'To retrieve Father Conlin?'

'I'm not sure what I intend at this stage. I've a meeting with Colonel Teusen of West German Intelligence later today. He's expecting Charles Pascoe to arrive from America this afternoon, which could prove interesting.'

'Pascoe?'

'Before your time. One of the great minds behind the British Intelligence system during the Second World War.'

'So – you think something could be done?'

Pacelli said, 'I'd formed the opinion that you did not approve of Father Conlin?'

'Of his work – no. I've always doubted the usefulness of this League of the Resurrection of his.'

'A little too dramatic for your taste?'

'Something like that. But the man himself . . .'

'I know exactly what you mean. Infuriating, isn't it? The people's saint, *Life* magazine called him. Vulgar, but apt.' Pacelli got up and went to the window and peered down at Schaefer. 'He's still there, waiting for you. Better be off.'

Hartmann picked up his raincoat and moved to join him. 'He isn't such a bad sort.'

'As a Communist or as a man?'

'Three daughters and his wife is pregnant again.'

He buttoned his coat. Pacelli looked out of the window and sighed. 'You know, Erich, I was just thinking how nice it would be to be a child again when life is full of innocent surprise.'

'Interesting, Father, but hardly practical.'

Hartmann went out. Pacelli stayed at the window, saw him emerge on the pavement below and get into the Volkswagen. As it moved away, Schaefer mounted his motor-cycle and went after it.

III

It was evening again when Charles Pascoe moved on to the terrace of Teusen's apartment and looked out across the lights of the city. He should have been tired after his long journey, but instead felt a sense of exhilaration. There was a footstep behind him and the German emerged, a glass in each hand.

'You may find this difficult to believe,' Pascoe said, 'but this is my first visit and yet, twenty years ago, there wasn't a day in my life that wasn't focused completely on Berlin and Section Three of Abwehr Headquarters on the Tirpitz Ufer where a certain Oberstleutnant Bruno Teusen gave me considerable trouble.'

'Who, in his turn, concentrated his attentions on SOE Headquarters at St Michael's House, 82 Baker Street. It used to take you twenty minutes to walk there from your flat in Ardmore Court each morning – when you didn't stay overnight. Do you still like to ruin excellent Courvoisier with three large cubes of ice?'

Pascoe took the glass with a smile. 'Do you still prefer those appalling Russian cigarettes you picked up a taste for in the Winter War?'

'You know, Pascoe, I learned so much about you, the most intimate of details, that in the end I actually grew to like you. Isn't that strange?'

'We could have met in June of '45,' Pascoe told him. 'I was offered the chance to handle your interrogation. I refused.'

'May I ask why?'

'It would, I think, by then have been too personal. Like turning over one's own stone. Still . . . to business. You've had certain orders about this Conlin affair, I believe?'

'Not orders – just a phone call from General Gehlen.'

'You know who I'm acting for?'

'Yes.'

'Again, quite unofficially.'

'Just like Pacelli from the Vatican, who's also here unofficially. I'm expecting him within the hour. They're all rather fond of that word, aren't they – as if we really had choice? Afterwards, of course, win, lose or draw, they'll say it never happened.'

Pascoe said, 'Can I count on your full co-operation as regards use of resources?'

'That's what I take my instructions to mean. There could be limits, of course. We'll just have to take each item on its merits. There is another factor of some importance also – Conlin himself.'

'You know him?'

'A marvellous man.'

'Good.' Pascoe emptied his glass and placed it down carefully. 'I'd like to get started, then.'

IV

In the study there were several files on the desk, and on the wall a map of the general area from the border to Neustadt. There was also a large-scale plan of Schloss Neustadt, with several photographs pinned beside it.

'Thorough as ever, I see?' Pascoe put on his half-moon reading glasses and peered at the plan. 'Where did you get it?'

'In the files,' Teusen said. 'No difficulty at all. It was an army group headquarters for most of the war, then a prison for *prominenti*.'

Pascoe examined the photos. 'It certainly looks formidable.'

'During the First War it was used as a prison for French officers. There was not one single recorded instance of escape.'

Pascoe nodded. 'That I can believe.'

'You'll find other maps and various drawings on the desk. Army engineers' stuff. New roads at various times during the war – drains. That sort of thing.'

Pascoe turned to the desk. 'And the rest?'

'Information on the various people involved. The Franciscans, for example, although I'll take you to meet this Brother Konrad later. The caretaker at Schloss Neustadt, Heinrich Berg, who served in entirely the wrong branch of the SS. And there's as much information there as we have on van Buren, which is considerable.'

'The Secretary of State provided me with a very comprehensive file on that gentleman before I left, courtesy of the CIA. No – I think this man Vaughan you were telling me about is the man I'm interested in at this stage.'

'Then this is the one you need.' Teusen pushed a manilla folder across the desk. 'Something of a cosmopolitan, our Simon, German grandmother, Irish mother.'

'What was his father?'

'Captain of one of those sailing barges on the Thames for many years. He died just before the war.'

'And what happened to Vaughan?'

'It seems that in 1917, when serving on the Western Front, the father carried in his colonel under fire. He was severely wounded during this exploit and awarded the Distinguished

Conduct Medal. On hearing of his death, his old colonel insisted on making himself responsible for the boy's education. Sent him to Winchester, which I have always understood to be one of your most important public schools.'

'My God,' Pascoe said.

'Exactly.' Teusen tapped the manilla folder. 'I think you'll find it makes interesting reading.'

V

It was an hour later when Teusen came back to the study. Pascoe had turned the swivel chair behind the desk and sat, arms folded, looking up at the plan of Schloss Neustadt.

'You think there's a way?' Teusen said.

'Oh yes.' Pascoe removed his glasses and ran a hand over his face. 'There's always a way, if only one looks close enough. You were right about Vaughan. A fascinating story. I've had a look at the rest of the stuff, only briefly. I'll work through it more thoroughly later.'

'Father Pacelli is here.'

'Excellent.' Pascoe swung round in his chair. 'Let's have him in.'

VI

Pacelli was wearing a collar and tie, and a rather nondescript tweed suit under an old raincoat. Pascoe went round the desk to meet him.

'A real pleasure. How many years is it since we were last in touch?'

Pacelli took his hand. 'Almost twenty. 1943 when you warned us of the Führer's ridiculous scheme to kidnap the pope.'

'Don't look at me, either of you,' Teusen said. 'Even Skorzeny nearly had a heart attack over that one. Your coat, Father?'

'No need. I only have a few minutes, so I'd like to get down to business right away.'

'Certainly.' Pascoe waved him to a chair and sat down himself.

Pacelli said, 'I had a call from Archbishop Vagnozzi in Washington who explained to me that you would be acting in this affair, professor.'

'If I can see any way to act,' Pascoe said mildly. 'May I enquire your intentions?'

VII

When Pacelli was finished, Pascoe said, 'He sounds an interesting man, your Father Hartmann. How did you get the East German authorities to accept his appointment to your secretariat over there? I'm thinking particularly of his American background now.'

'He's a citizen of the German Democratic Republic by birth. Even more important, both his father and mother were Communists who died for the cause. We can staff the secretariat as we choose. In their eyes, he would perhaps seem a better choice than most.'

'If they have to have your people there at all?'

'Exactly. The position of the Church, of all Christians over there, is an ambiguous one. Guaranteed by the constitution. The existence of these Franciscans at Neustadt, for example, is proof of this.'

'But subject to continual harassment?'

'Exactly.'

Pascoe nodded. 'So what do you think you gain, by sending Hartmann to Neustadt?'

'I haven't the slightest idea. We have the right to ask that he be given permission to inspect the situation of the church there. A right which I happen to think, for rather delicate political reasons vis-à-vis the Vatican, they will not deny.'

'Under surveillance?'

'Naturally.'

'And you accept that the request will indicate to Klein that you know they have Conlin there?'

'Of course.'

Pascoe glanced up at Teusen. 'An interesting situation.'

'Which is putting it mildly,' the German commented.

Pacelli said carefully, 'Are your own plans in any way advanced in this matter?'

'Hardly,' Pascoe said. 'Why do you ask?'

'It occurs to me that Father Hartmann's presence in Neustadt could be useful.'

'True,' Pascoe said. 'But in a way that might not prove acceptable to you.'

'As a kind of tethered goat, you mean, to draw the tiger?'

'No, more of a Trojan horse.'

'You have something in mind?'

'The glimmering of an idea only. Not far enough advanced to discuss at this point. It would mean Father Hartmann becoming the focus of their attentions.'

'While something quite different was going on behind their backs?'

'That would be the point of the operation.'

There was a long pause. The old Jesuit nodded calmly. 'That would be perfectly acceptable.'

'And Father Hartmann?' Teusen asked.

'Will comply with whatever is required of him.' Pascoe started to speak and Pacelli raised a hand. 'Let me make something quite clear. I have known Sean Conlin for the best part of forty years. He is a stubborn and rebellious old Irishman, who loves his fellow creatures so much that he has proved totally incapable of following anything but the dictates of his own conscience all his life. He has been on many occasions a considerable source of embarrassment both to the Church and the order he serves. In so doing, he has become a living symbol of faith in action to thousands of people. We, of the Society of Jesus, are not prepared to see him go under. Do I make myself plain?'

'I think so,' Pascoe said.

'Good.' Pacelli got up and buttoned his raincoat. 'When may I hear from you?'

'You expect Father Hartmann to return the day after tomorrow?'

'Yes.'

Pascoe glanced up at Teusen. 'Perhaps you'll arrange a meeting then?'

Pacelli didn't offer to shake hands. 'Let's hope, in the mean time, that you come up with something substantial.'

He went out, followed by Teusen. When the German

returned Pascoe had swivelled in the chair again and was looking up at the plan of Schloss Neustadt. Teusen took out a cigarette and lit it.

Pascoe removed his glasses and ran a hand over his face as if weary. Teusen said, 'You could do with some sleep.'

Pascoe looked up at him. 'Good God, no! At my age, my dear Bruno, there's time enough for that when you're dead.' He got to his feet. 'No, I think, if you'd be so good enough to take me, it's time I made the acquaintance of Major Vaughan.'

VIII

The Mercedes turned into Rehdenstrasse and pulled up in front of the sign Julius Meyer and Company, Undertakers.

'Is this wholly a front or do they really offer a service?' Pascoe asked as they got out.

Teusen smiled. 'Oh yes. They're quite prepared to bury you, if that's what you want.'

He opened the judas gate and led the way through. The garage was in darkness, but there was a light in the glass-walled office.

The door opened and Meyer looked out. 'Who's there?'

There was a certain alarm in his voice. Teusen paused at the bottom of the rickety wooden steps. 'It's me – Bruno. I've got a friend with me. Is Brother Konrad there?'

'Yes – come on up.'

Pascoe followed Teusen up the stairs. There was a chess-board on the desk and Konrad, who was sitting on the other side, got to his feet.

Meyer switched off the cassette-player. 'Where's Simon?' Teusen asked.

'He went to the bar at the end of the street for cigarettes. Who's this?'

'My name is Pascoe,' the professor told him. 'Charles Pascoe.'

Meyer ignored him and addressed himself to Teusen again. 'What's he want?'

'To offer you a great deal of money,' Pascoe said. 'In return for your help in retrieving Father Sean Conlin from his present predicament.'

Meyer gazed at him in total astonishment. 'What is this? Some kind of joke?'

'Ten thousand pounds, Mr Meyer. Perhaps more,' Pascoe said calmly.

Brother Konrad said carefully in halting English, 'Is this true? You really intend to do something about Father Conlin?'

'That would depend,' Pascoe said. 'On many things. On you yourself, for example, and your friends at Neustadt.'

The judas gate banged and Vaughan appeared from the shadows below. He paused at the bottom of the steps and it was Pascoe who moved out on the small landing first and looked down at him.

'Good evening, Major Vaughan.'

Vaughan glanced up and went very still.

'You know who I am?' Pascoe asked.

'You're on the syllabus at Sandhurst, didn't they ever tell you that?'

Pascoe started down the steps and Vaughan sat on a coffin, unzipped his jacket and took out a cigarette. Teusen and Brother Konrad stayed on the landing.

Meyer came down the steps. 'Money can't buy a life, Simon. Tell him that.'

'Money,' said Pascoe, 'always helps. One of the sadder facts of this grey little world, or so I've always found.'

Vaughan lit his cigarette. 'You've come for Conlin?'

'That is correct. Naturally, I'd like your assistance.'

'Not interested.'

'Ten thousand pounds.' Pascoe glanced at Meyer. 'Each.'

'Money' – Vaughan shrugged – 'at the best of times is only a medium of exchange.'

Meyer turned and went up the steps. He said to Teusen, 'You want a drink, because I need one. Maybe even two. When he starts talking to himself, that Devil down there, I know I'm in trouble again.'

He vanished into the office. Pascoe said, 'Do it for Conlin, then. I understand you like him?'

'He's been walking bare-footed towards some kind of stake since the day he was born.'

'All right,' Pascoe said patiently. 'Do it for yourself. Because there isn't really anything else left for you to do.'

'Isn't there?'

'Let's look at the facts. Simon Vaughan, born 27 July 1926, not a stone's throw from the West India Docks.'

'I'm a Sun-Leo,' Vaughan said. 'Most fortunate week of the zodiac. Did you know that?'

'A hell of a leap from the Isle of Dogs to Winchester. Did you make it?'

'Not really.' Vaughan smiled without humour. 'It's in the voice mainly. They got to me too late to make me word perfect.'

'So you joined up in 1944, a year under age and served with the twenty-first Independent Parachute Squadron at Arnhem. Military Medal there. Afterwards, when someone discovered you spoke surprisingly good German, thanks to that grandmother of yours, they commissioned you into the Intelligence Corps. After the war, they kept you on. Even sent you to Sandhurst.'

'See what a Labour government can do for you,' Vaughan said.

'Captain with Field Intelligence in Korea, captured on the Hook, spent nearly two years in a Chinese prison camp. Afterwards, back to Military Intelligence where you specialized in handling subversives, revolutionary movements generally and so on. The Communists in Malaya, six months chasing Mau-Mau in Kenya, then Cyprus and EOKA. The DSO for that little lot and a bullet in the back that nearly put paid to things.'

'I wonder how I managed to fit it all in.'

'And then Borneo and the confrontation with the Indonesians. You commanded a company of native irregulars. The area around Kota Baru was rotten with terrorists. You were told to go in and clear them out.'

'No one can say I failed to do that.'

'You were certainly thorough. How many prisoners did you have shot? How many captives interrogated and tortured in custody? The newspapers made a lot of that at the time. What did they call you? The Beast of Selangar. I suppose it was your medals that saved you. And the time in prison camp must have been useful. At least you weren't cashiered.'

'Previous gallant conduct,' Vaughan said. 'Must do what we can. Pity the Military Academy couldn't make a gentleman out of him.'

'To sum up,' Pascoe said. 'You were told to clear the last terrorist out of Kota Baru and you did just that. A little ruthlessly, perhaps, but you did it. Your superiors heaved a sigh of relief and threw you to the wolves.'

'Leaving me with the satisfaction of having done my duty.' Vaughan stuck another cigarette in the corner of his mouth. 'Water under the bridge, Professor. Meyer knows Berlin. I speak fluent German. It isn't much but it's a living.'

There was a long pause. Pascoe said, 'Well?'

'All right,' Vaughan said. 'I'll call your bluff. Twenty thousand – each,' he added.

'You know, somehow, I thought you might prove reasonable – in the end.'

IX

Teusen woke just after three o'clock in the morning with a bad headache. He found an aspirin and went to the kitchen to get a glass of water. To his astonishment, there was a light under the study door. He opened it, to find Pascoe seated at the desk, working his way through the files.

'Good God,' Teusen said. 'Haven't you been to bed?'

'Couldn't sleep.' Pascoe removed his glasses. 'Actually, I'm glad you're here. You can fill in a blank for me.' He swivelled to the map. 'Here, along the border, there must be dozens of crossing points, especially on the country back roads. Are there any where your intelligence people have a special arrangement to come and go when it suits them?'

'If you mean, are there border guards on the other side who are bribable, yes,' Teusen said. 'But it's getting tighter all the time.'

'What about here, west of Neustadt? The direct route out?'

'Yes.' Teusen moved closer, then found what he was looking for. 'There's a crossing at Flossen. A hell of an area. Holstein

Heath. I used to go shooting there when I was a youth. Wild boar.'

'So – it could be arranged?'

'Yes, I think so. It would be difficult. Also expensive. If you want me to, I'll get in touch with my man in the area in the morning.'

'It's morning now,' Pascoe pointed out.

He put on his half-moon spectacles and returned to his files. Teusen stood looking down at him for a moment, feeling strangely helpless, then he turned and went out, closing the door behind him. He went back into his bedroom and sat on the edge of the bed.

'Now I know how we lost the war,' he said to himself wearily, and reached for the telephone.

— 6 —

PASCOE, AS A RULE, did not enjoy flying in small aircraft. They were noisy, uncomfortable and lacking in the more obvious amenities, but he could certainly find no fault with the plane Teusen had arranged to fly them from Tempelhof to East Germany at eleven o'clock that morning. It was a Hawker-Siddeley 125 and not long from the factory, a twin jet executive aircraft of some luxury in which it was actually possible to conduct a conversation without shouting.

'We land here,' Teusen ringed a spot on the map with pencil. 'Bitterfeld. A Luftwaffe night fighter base during the war. Not been used for years, but very convenient for the border. The field agent for the area will pick us up there.'

'And how far to this crossing you mentioned at Flossen?'

'Seven or eight miles.'

Pascoe examined the map in silence for a while, then opened his briefcase, took out a file and started to make notes.

Teusen said, 'When are you going to tell me what you have in mind?'

'When I know myself.'

The German produced a case and extracted one of his Russian cigarettes. 'But Vaughan provides an essential ingredient, I think?'

'Oh yes.' Pascoe closed the file and replaced it in his briefcase. 'Perfect for our purposes. A highly trained professional soldier. He speaks German as well as he does English – rather better, in fact. Also excellent Russian and passable Chinese. A legacy of nearly two years in that prison camp in Manchuria.'

'A killer by trade and by instinct.'

'But with brains. A combination not always to be found.'

Teusen shook his head. 'A great tragedy, what happened to Vaughan. A brilliant career in ruins – and for what?'

'He did his duty as he saw it.'

'You sympathize with him, I think?'

'Men like Vaughan are like the hangman,' Pascoe said. 'They carry the guilt for the rest of us. It takes a rather special brand of courage to do that.'

'You think he was right to do what he did?'

'Not necessarily, but he did and that's what's important.'

'So did the SS.'

Pascoe smiled slightly. 'Point taken, but in this present situation, it's a purely academic one. Whether he was right or wrong to do what he did out there doesn't concern me. I need him now. That's all that matters.'

II

They landed at Bitterfeld twenty minutes later. There were four hangars and the watchtower was still intact, but the grass between the runways was waist-high and there was an air of desolation to everything.

A black Mercedes was parked in front of the old operations building and a small, heavily-built man in a hunting jacket and forester's hat got out quickly as the Hawker-Siddeley taxied towards him.

Teusen was first out and shook hands. 'This is Werner Böhmler, the field agent for the area.'

'Herr Professor – a pleasure.'

Pascoe had turned and was looking out across the runway. 'This place is entirely unused, you say?'

'That's right.'

'Good.' Pascoe opened the rear door and got into the Mercedes. 'Can we get started, then?'

III

Father Conlin opened his eyes. Not that it mattered for it was still dark. For a little while he lay there, his body so numb that he couldn't even feel the springs of the iron cot digging into his back and then something clicked in his brain and he was filled with a sense of dreadful unease. Of some horror beyond understanding, crouched there on the far side of the cell.

He got to his feet, took a hesitant step forward and blundered into a stone wall. He took two paces back, hand outstretched and touched the other side. Three cautious paces brought him to the rear wall. From there to the door was four more. He was in a stone womb. Unbelievably cold. There was no beginning, no end. Only the fact of it.

I am a man. I exist, he thought. I will not give in. He lay down carefully on the bed and started to pray.

IV

When Klein went to van Buren's office at the University Medical Centre in East Berlin, there was only a young medical secretary available, a pretty, dark-haired girl in a white hospital coat.

'Colonel Klein,' he said.

She jumped at once. 'Oh yes, comrade. Professor van Buren is expecting you. If you'd follow me, please.'

She led the way along the corridor, knocked at a door at the far end, opened it and motioned him through into a small room, neatly carpeted and furnished only with several easy chairs. Van Buren was sitting in one of them by what appeared to be a window looking into the next room. It was in semi-darkness but as Klein approached, he saw that there was a man in there, strapped into what looked like a dentist's chair.

'What is this?' he demanded.

'General observation. I like to see how my patients are going on,' van Buren told him. 'He can't see us, by the way.'

In the other room, a picture appeared on a screen. A girl – very young and extremely pretty. Suddenly the shadowy figure in the chair bucked, straining against the straps, and from the sound-box above the window there issued a cry of agony. Van Buren reached up and turned it off and slid a panel across the window.

'What was that?' Klein demanded.

'One of the techniques we try here. The subject has a long history of rape and he prefers them young. We show him suitable pictures, which naturally arouse him, then administer severe electric shock. If he's a bad boy, he gets hurt you see. Childish, but extremely effective. The trouble is, it takes rather a long time.'

'My God,' Klein said.

'There are also several drugs which can be used in place of the electric shock to induce severe vomiting, but that becomes rather unpleasant for everyone. What did you want to see me about?'

'We're having trouble with the Vatican.'

'To do with Neustadt?'

'Yes. It's still in the hands of the Ministry for State Security so I can't give you full details yet. I'll see you this evening. Seven o'clock at my office.'

'All right.' Van Buren lit a cigarette. 'I'm glad you looked in. I wanted a word with you about Conlin.'

Klein sat down. 'Nothing wrong, is there?'

'No, but I think there's something we should get straight. There isn't enough time for a thought reform programme.'

Klein paused in the act of lighting one of his cheroots. 'But you told Ulbricht . . .'

'What he wanted to hear.'

There was something close to horror on Klein's face. 'Then what are you going to do?'

'To Conlin?' van Buren said calmly. 'Oh, break him, I

think. It's all there's time for. Reduce him to a state where he'll simply do as he's told.'

'You think you can do that?'

'I've done it before. In my early days in Peking I saw Ping Chow break a Catholic priest very effectively by putting him in a cell with ten other prisoners. Ordinary criminals. They had to take turns at keeping him awake, otherwise they didn't get fed. Within a couple of weeks, he was so disorientated that he was agreeing to anything his interrogators told him.'

'Then why aren't you down there at Neustadt now? Why are you here?'

'I've left Conlin to rot for a week in his own filth in total darkness,' van Buren said. 'He comes out on the seventh day, then we start.'

Klein stood up, walked nervously to the door, then turned. 'I hope you know what you're doing, Harry, because if you don't . . .'

'Then both our heads will roll. I'll see you later.'

Van Buren turned, slid back the screen and peered into the other room and Klein opened the door and left hurriedly.

V

Peter Bulow was a large, pleasant-looking man, in spite of the bad shrapnel wound on his right cheek. He was a sergeant in the people's police in command of the border post at Flossen, not because he was a good Communist, but because the small farm on which his parents had raised him had found itself a quarter of a mile on the wrong side of the line at the end of the war.

Flossen itself was half a mile into Western Germany. Bulow had attended the village school as a boy. Half his relatives still lived there, which explained his frequent visits. And there was the village store, of course, where he could obtain delicacies not so readily to hand on his own side.

But that morning he had a special mission for it was his daughter Lotte's birthday. He had ordered a dress for her a month previously. Something very special from Hamburg to surprise her with at her party that evening.

He hurried up the single street past the inn and crossed to the store. He went inside and unbuttoned his jacket.

Muller, the storekeeper, looked up and smiled. 'Ah, there you are, Peter. I was beginning to think you'd forgotten.'

They were second cousins and Bulow grinned as he shook hands across the counter. 'Has it come?'

'Of course – I'll get it for you.'

He went into the back. Bulow walked to the window and peered out into the street, taking out his pipe. He put a match to it and turning, found Böhmler and Bruno Teusen standing behind the counter.

'Hello, Peter,' Teusen said.

'Herr Oberst.' Bulow was no longer smiling.

'I'd like a word with you.'

'No.' Bulow put a hand out as if to ward him off. 'No more. You promised.'

'I know, Peter, but this is special,' Teusen said.

'How special?'

It was Pascoe who answered him, pushing back the curtain at the rear entrance to join them. 'Fifty thousand marks.'

Bulow gazed at him in astonishment, then turned back to Teusen, who said, 'Plus asylum for you and your family in West Germany, a good job and housing guaranteed.'

'Or the same in the USA if you prefer it,' Pascoe added.

There was a moment's silence. Böhmler said, 'You would do well to listen to the Herr Professor, Peter.'

'No, thanks. For that kind of offer this has to be big – too big for me.'

'Not at all,' Böhmler said. 'All you have to do is let a little traffic through on a few selected occasions during the next three or four weeks. For the next month you and young Hornstein will be on the night shift. I know that. Six p.m. till six in the morning. Is he still sneaking over twice a week to visit the mayor's daughter?'

'The same terms for him,' Pascoe said.

Bulow shook his head violently. 'I won't do it. We nearly got caught passing that agent of yours through in March and there's Sergeant Hofer to consider. He's got a mind like a steel trap. A solid Party member, too.'

'He'll be on the day shift,' Böhmler pointed out. 'What he doesn't know won't hurt him.'

'No,' Bulow said.

Teusen sighed. 'I could get very unpleasant, Peter. I could point out that a word in the ear of the right person in Berlin about your activities on our behalf in the past would have the SSD on your back before you knew it.'

'You wouldn't,' Bulow said.

'No – because there isn't any need. Tell him, Werner.'

Böhmler said, 'The good times are coming to an end, Peter. We know of a secret meeting at highest government level last week in which Ulbricht ordered a crash programme aimed at strengthening the border in rural areas, with the specific intention of keeping you lot firmly on your own side.'

'No more visits to the store,' Teusen said.

'It's also been decided as a matter of policy to transfer people like you, men with local connections, to duties in the east. By autumn, all men on frontier guard duty will be from other parts of the Republic.'

'You're lying,' Bulow said, but there was no conviction in his voice.

'Don't be stupid,' Böhmler told him. 'You've been expecting something like this for a year now.'

'And now it's come and here we are throwing you a lifeline,' Teusen told him. 'You should be grateful. Hornstein will be interested, would you say?'

Bulow sighed wearily and sat down in a chair by the counter, shoulders slumped. 'Yes – I've been expecting him to defect for months now. He's crazy about the Conrad girl. He'll jump at a chance like this.'

'Excellent.'

'My wife – my daughter?'

'It will all be taken care of. When you come over for the last time, so do they – and Hornstein, of course.'

'All right – what do you want me to do?'

'For the moment, nothing,' Teusen said. 'Werner will be in touch with you again during the next few days.'

'Very well.' Bulow got to his feet. He seemed to have aged ten years since entering the shop and looked very tired. 'Can I go now?'

Muller moved forward from the back of the store hesitatingly, holding a large package which he placed on the counter. His face was grave.

'The dress. And there's a ham and a bottle of wine with my compliments.'

Bulow gazed at him blankly and then something clicked. 'Of course – how stupid of me. Thank you.'

'I'm sorry, Peter,' Muller said.

'For what?' Bulow replied bitterly. 'Russia was worse, but only just.'

He went out. Teusen moved to the window and watched him go. 'We use people,' he said. 'Even when we think we're in the right, we use people as if they were paper coffee cups to serve our purpose and be tossed on one side.'

'Yes,' Pascoe said calmly. 'War *is* hell and make no mistake, my dear Bruno. That's exactly what we're engaged in.' He glanced at his watch. 'And now I think we'd better be getting back to Berlin. I've seen what I want to see here.'

VI

In East Berlin towards evening storm clouds moved in across the city, and in Klein's office, Harry van Buren, seated behind the massive desk, worked his way through Erich Hartmann's file. Klein was standing at the window, peering out morosely and drinking coffee.

'My God,' he said. 'What weather. I've never known such a June.' He turned. 'What do you think?'

Van Buren held Hartmann's photo under the light. 'Interesting face. He and Ulbricht would have a lot in common.'

Klein frowned. 'I don't understand?'

'Religious obsession on the one hand – political on the other. Two sides of the same coin.'

Klein, who had been raised a Catholic, was aware of a faint anger stirring somewhere deep inside. Strange how one could never quite erase the imprint of those early years.

'You would dismiss religion so lightly?'

'I don't see why not. Fear of the dark – a rage against dying. People have to have something and if there's nothing there, they invent it. When was this application made?'

'Late yesterday, to the appropriate department. They passed it straight to me.'

'I like the phraseology.' Van Buren picked up the typed letter. 'Father Erich Hartmann, appointed Vatican Inspector General to report on the state of the church at Neustadt to the Holy Father.' He helped himself to a cigarette from the box on the desk. 'Presumably you're going to tell them where to put their application?'

'No.' Klein shook his head. 'Not possible.'

Van Buren glanced up sharply, a look of genuine astonishment on his face. 'But this is nonsense. That church in Neustadt has been closed down tight for five years now and they haven't done a thing about it. This application isn't just coincidence. It means they know we've got Conlin.'

'Exactly.'

'And Hartmann. Good God, you know what he is? A Vatican spy. It's here in your own file.'

'Of course I know,' Klein said calmly. 'And Hartmann's superiors know that I do.'

'Oh, I see,' van Buren said. 'It has a certain ring to it, I must admit. A kind of lunatic logic.'

'Politics, Harry,' Klein said. 'Let me explain. Last year, we signed the Secret Treaty of Accord with the Vatican. A kind of blueprint for future relations.'

'Which doesn't mean a thing. You're still screwing the Catholic Church into the ground at every chance you get.'

'But we have to continue some sort of dialogue at governmental level. A political decision on the part of the Council of Ministers.'

'Under the inspired leadership of our esteemed Comrade Chairman.'

Klein ignored the remark. 'Relations with the Vatican have altered considerably. Unavoidable with a man like Pope John at the helm. His Peace on Earth encyclical in April was warmly received, I must remind you, not only in the West but as far east as Moscow.'

'Beautiful,' van Buren said. 'I hope you're all having a fine time. But underneath all that garbage, I presume what you're really trying to tell me is that Hartmann comes to Neustadt whether I like it or not. Do you actually expect some sort of rescue attempt?'

'Not really. I think he's going there to sniff out what he can, that's all. I'll hold him off for ten days.'

'That's very kind of you.'

'Naturally he'll have a Section Six operative tugging at the skirt of his cassock. A man called Schaefer. He'll have orders to report to you.'

'That's it then.' Van Buren got up, belting his coat and crossed to the door.

Klein sat down behind the desk. 'Cheer up, Harry. After all, what can Hartmann hope to accomplish? I would have thought you might find the situation quite amusing.'

'Just what I'm looking for, something to lighten the more depressive periods of my daily round.'

He opened the door. Klein said, 'I must say I'd like to be there at that first meeting. What will you say to him, Harry?'

'Oh, that's an easy one.' Van Buren smiled. 'Bless me, Father, for I have sinned.'

VII

When Vaughan opened the judas gate and went into the warehouse, everyone seemed to be there. Meyer, Teusen, Brother Konrad, and at the top of the steps in the glass-walled office he could see Charles Pascoe with Father Pacelli and a grey-haired man.

Meyer, who was pacing up and down, hurried forward. 'You got my message.'

'I'm here, aren't I?' Vaughan unzipped his jacket. 'What is this, a board meeting?'

'Something like that,' Teusen said, without getting up from the coffin on which he was sitting with Konrad.

Vaughan nodded to the Franciscan. 'Still here?'

Konrad smiled. 'So it would seem.'

'Who are the new arrivals?' Vaughan looked up to the office.

Teusen said, 'The grey-haired one is Kurt Norden, professor of forensic pathology at the university.'

'Forensic pathology?' Vaughan said in astonishment. 'Now what in the hell does he need him for?'

Teusen shrugged. 'I presume that in his own good time he'll tell us.'

Meyer smiled tightly. 'More corpses.'

'It comes to us all, Julius,' Vaughan told him cheerfully. 'And the other one?' he asked. 'Who's he?'

'Later, Simon,' Teusen said.

Vaughan shrugged, lit a cigarette and leaned against the side of the truck. There was silence and then the office door opened and Pascoe appeared with Norden.

'My thanks,' he said in English. 'I look forward to receiving your report, Herr Professor.'

Norden shook hands, then came down the steps, a tall, thin man with stooped shoulders in a tweed overcoat. He paused at the bottom, a slightly bemused look on his face, then pulled on a tweed hat that matched his overcoat, hurried to the gate, opened it and disappeared into the night.

Pascoe looked down at them calmly. 'Ah, there you are, major. Good. We can get started, then. If you'd kindly come up.' And he turned and went back into the office.

VIII

On the wall were pinned a map of that section of the border stretching from Flossen to Neustadt and one of the large-scale military plans of the Schloss and the village which Teusen had provided.

Pascoe said, 'I'll take things step by step, gentlemen, and if you bear with me, I think you will see how several apparently disparate items join together to make a whole in the end.'

No one said anything and he carried on. 'To start with, here just outside Flossen at Bitterfeld is a disused Luftwaffe fighter station which will serve as our base. The border post at Flossen itself is in our pocket. The Vopo sergeant and private who will form the night shift for the next twenty-eight days have agreed to come over. That gives us unrestricted access to the other side, within limits.'

'And when you get there what have you got?' Vaughan put in. 'Around fifty miles to Neustadt and most of that is Holstein

Heath, one of the most sparsely populated areas in the country. A few woodcutters, a handful of farmers and very little else.'

Pascoe nodded. 'I should imagine the traffic, such as there is, would tend to be Vopo military vehicles and prowler guards.'

'Prowler guards?' Meyer said.

'Vopo motor-cyclists with no set routine. Their brief is to roam the area at will, so that no one can ever be certain where they will be next.'

Vaughan said, 'In other words, anyone else passing through, even in an old potato truck, is going to stick out like a sore thumb.'

'Oh, I don't know.' It was Teusen who spoke. 'We have a saying in the Harz mountains. If you want to hide in a forest, you must pretend to be a tree.'

'Exactly,' Pascoe said. 'I presume you are capable of riding a motor-cycle, Major Vaughan?'

'I always did look better in uniform.' Vaughan turned to Pascoe. 'Nice one, professor. Yes, I think I could manage that. What kind of machine? Cossack?'

'Yes,' Teusen told him.

'Good.' Pascoe said. 'In principle, what I am saying is that any transport we use between Flossen and Neustadt will be of a military nature. Colonel Teusen assures me he can supply any kind of Vopo vehicle we need.'

'No problem,' Teusen said. 'And the real thing, too. So many of them have come over to our side during the last couple of years.'

'The map, of course, will have to be studied in detail and the roads committed to memory, so that the chosen route and at least two alternatives to allow for unforeseen contingencies can be tackled by night at reasonable speed. Under most conditions, I see no reason why the trip from Neustadt to the border should ever take longer than an hour and a half.'

There was another of those pauses while everyone seemed to wait and Vaughan said patiently, 'All right, so now we're at Neustadt, where Conlin is being held . . .'

'By only twenty men.'

'. . . in a fortress so impregnable that when it was used as a prison for officers, there wasn't a single recorded instance of escape, am I right, Bruno?' Teusen looked uncomfortable and Vaughan carried on, 'Look at it. That zig-zag approach road, walls like cliffs, tunnel entrance, one guarded gate, then another. A Panzer column would have difficulty getting in.'

'But not a plumber or an electrician if they were needed,' Pascoe said. 'It isn't getting in that's the problem. It's doing it in such a way that you can come out with Conlin.'

'All right, surprise me.'

Pascoe indicated the plan of Schloss Neustadt again. 'Three levels – and our information is that Conlin is kept on the lowest, which makes sense because conditions will be extremely bad down there. Now, look at this.' He unrolled another plan. 'During the war, when the Schloss was an army group headquarters, there were considerable improvements made to the sewage system. Here, in the third level, not far from the cells, an inspection chamber gives access to a sewer pipe, concrete lined and eight feet in diameter, dropping through several levels to the Elbe, which it never reached, by the way. According to the engineer's working report, work stopped a hundred and fifty yards from the river.'

'Why?'

Teusen shrugged. 'It was 1945 and the Russians were coming. No one needed army group headquarters any more.'

Vaughan looked down at the plan, a slight smile on his lips, for there was a certain black humour to the whole thing which rather appealed to him; the thought of those wretched army engineers labouring away down there in the darkness while their whole world collapsed above them.

'Which hardly helps Conlin.'

'It does if you notice the interesting fact that the tunnel passes close by the Home Farm, which is the headquarters of the Franciscan Order of Jesus and Mary at Neustadt,' Pascoe pointed out. 'There is a large barn, as you can see, directly on the boundary line. From there, sixty-five feet in a straight line to break into the main sewer.'

'Through a cemetery,' Vaughan said to Meyer. 'Now you see why the forensic pathologist was called in. I wonder just how many terminal diseases can be caught digging through that kind of compost heap?'

'Nothing that can't be handled with proper precautions and

the right drugs,' Pascoe said. 'And as Miss Campbell is at Neustadt it does give us the advantage of having a doctor on site.'

'And who does the digging?' Vaughan turned to Konrad. 'Your people, is that the idea? All six of you? And just how long do you expect it would take?'

'A week' Pascoe said. 'Ten feet down and easy soil, so Brother Konrad informs me.'

'Then what? So Conlin comes out through this – this rabbit hole. How long before the bloodhounds find their way to the farm?'

'By then the cupboard will be bare. Brother Konrad and his friends come over too.'

Konrad smiled almost apologetically. 'We were nearing the end of things in any event. I do not think we could survive another year with the kind of political pressure mounted against us.'

Vaughan nodded towards Pacelli. 'Who's this?'

'My name is Pacelli,' the old man said. 'I represent the Society of Jesus in this affair. Of which Father Conlin is a member.'

'What's he talking about?' Meyer looked bewildered.

'Jesuits, Julius,' Vaughan told him. 'Soldiers of Christ. They had such a fun time playing devious games with Elizabeth the First that they've never been able to stop since. And where does your little lot fit in, Father?'

'We will arrange for one of our representatives in East Berlin, Father Hartmann, to visit Neustadt to report on the state of the church there which has been closed for five years.'

'And what do you hope to gain from that?'

'Nothing,' Pacelli said serenely.

'East German Intelligence would be justified in expecting someone,' Pascoe said.

'So you give them Hartmann?'

'To keep them occupied.'

'And he's happy about that?'

'Perfectly,' Pacelli interjected.

'Good for him.' Vaughan shrugged. 'That's it then. What happens now?'

'Brother Konrad returns tomorrow, the same way he came.

You follow in two, perhaps three days, but we can discuss that later. There is one other point. It occurs to me that Conlin's state of health is likely to be such that, once out, it might be advisable to get him to the West as fast as possible. I see here on the map, a quarter of a mile south of the farm, a meadow beside the river.'

'Water Horse Meadow,' Konrad said. 'I don't know where it got the name. It is good firm ground. Three hundred yards of open space between trees.'

'I understand it's not unknown for light aircraft to fly in by night on occasion under their radar screen to bring people out,' Pascoe said. 'Would you know anyone that foolhardy, Bruno?'

Teusen shook his head. 'No, but they would.'

Pascoe waited and Vaughan sighed and looked at Meyer. 'Any idea what Max is doing these days?'

'Max,' Pascoe said, 'is good, I presume.'

'The Luftwaffe thought so.'

'A long time ago.'

'He did shoot down seventy-two Lancasters by night, and some things you never forget.'

'Can you find him for me?'

'I can try.'

'Good. As soon as possible, please.'

Pacelli stood up. 'If there is nothing else, I'd like to get back. I've work to do.'

'Of course,' Pascoe said. 'Major Vaughan, perhaps you could drive Father Pacelli back to the Catholic Information Centre?'

The old man shook his head. 'Not necessary. Just point me in the direction of the nearest underground station, major. I need the exercise.'

IX

'I wanted a chance to talk to you, Major Vaughan,' Pacelli said as they walked along the canal towards the bridge.

'So?' Vaughan said.

'You were a prisoner of war in Korea, I understand. The Chinese had you for two years so you're something of an expert on Pavlovian and similar techniques. What will happen to Conlin?'

'I can only guess,' Vaughan said. 'Because this isn't a normal case.'

'Explain.'

'Our friend van Buren doesn't have much time. And time is what you need for really good long-term results with thought reform. He's got to go for quick answers, possibly helping things along with drugs. But a lot can be done in two or three weeks if you can find the right soft spots.'

'And Father Conlin is an old man and in failing health.'

'That could be in his favour. They don't want him dead, remember. Another thing – they'll have to go easy on the physical side of things and not just because the bruises would show. I wouldn't have thought his heart would take too much at his age.'

'So – how will van Buren begin?'

'Sensory deprivation, I'd say. A week or so in a dark room cut off from human contact. Can lead to a feeling of alienation so terrible that some subjects will grab the first hand that reaches out.'

'This was done to you?'

'Several times.'

'And you survived?'

'Let's say the cracks don't show.' Vaughan smiled. 'I've a vivid imagination, Father. The Irish bit of me. I used to make up stories to pass the time.'

Pacelli smiled. 'Father Conlin will survive.'

'For a while. On the other hand, I don't know what his soft spots are. If van Buren finds them, then he could be in trouble.'

'And you think Father Conlin has these weaknesses? These soft spots you speak of?'

'He's a man, isn't he? What is it the Bible says? Conceived in wickedness? We're all touched by original sin, I thought that was what you lot preached.' They had reached the bridge and went up the steps. 'Follow your nose on the other side and you'll find an underground station about a quarter of a mile along the road.'

Pacelli turned to face him. 'So you will see this thing through, Major Vaughan, but not for the money, I think.'

Vaughan stopped smiling. 'What then?'

'Nor the young lady. Oh, in part perhaps, but that would be too easy an answer. No, major, you can be a hard man, your record proves it, but this is only surface stuff. The protecting shell. Underneath is the boy who crewed his father's barge that long, long summer on the Thames and never wanted it to end. The boy who found life more corrupt than he had hoped.'

'You go to hell,' Vaughan said harshly and he turned and went back down the steps.

— 7 —

IN ROME on the following day, His Holiness Pope John XXIII died at the age of eighty-one. In his bedchamber at the Vatican Palace the circle of kneeling cardinals chorused the *De profundis*, first of the millions who, throughout the world, would mourn the best-loved pope of modern times.

In his office at the Collegio di San Roberto Bellarmino, the Father General of the Jesuits was standing at the window when there was a light tap at the door and Father Macleod entered.

'You wanted me, Father?'

'Yes – Father Pacelli. Contact him in Berlin. He is to return with all possible speed.'

'And Father Hartmann?'

'Is Father Pacelli's concern,' the Father General replied, without looking round.

The door closed softly and he dropped to his knees and began to pray for the repose of the soul of the man who had started life as Angelo Giuseppe Roncalli.

II

Pacelli was standing impatiently at the window of his office at the Catholic Information Centre in West Berlin when the battered little Volkswagen turned into Budapesterstrasse and pulled in at the kerb below. The old priest gave an exclamation of relief and Vaughan, who had been sitting in a chair in the corner reading a newspaper, got to his feet and joined him at the window.

'So that's him,' he said as Hartmann got out and crossed the road to Schaefer, who was pulling his motor-cycle up on its stand.

'And that's Schaefer, his Section Six man.'

'They seem pretty chummy.'

'You're sure you can handle him?'

Vaughan nodded. 'I should think so.'

'Good. I would offer you my blessing, but somehow I do not think it would be well received.' The old priest smiled and held out his hand. 'I can only wish you luck, then, Major Vaughan.'

'Which always helps,' Vaughan said and went out.

After a while there was a tap, the door opened again and Hartmann entered.

'Ah, there you are, Erich.'

'Father.'

He was carrying a leather briefcase which he placed on the desk. Pacelli said, 'You've heard the news?'

Hartmann stared at him blankly. 'News, Father?'

'The chair of Peter is vacant, Erich. The pope is dead. I received word only an hour ago.'

Hartmann was visibly shocked and crossed himself automatically. Pacelli sat down behind the desk. 'You were successful?'

'Yes, Father.' Hartmann opened the briefcase, produced a large official-looking envelope and passed it across.

Pacelli opened it and unfolded the document it contained. 'Excellent,' he said. 'And countersigned by the minister himself.'

'You will notice that I am not permitted to proceed to Neustadt for several days.'

Pacelli shrugged. 'So they delay things as long as possible. It was to be expected.'

'And I am also to consider myself at the orders of the military governor for the district.'

'Who will probably be van Buren.' Pacelli nodded, folded the permit and handed it back. 'I had hoped to stay to see you through this thing, Erich, but now I must return to Rome. You understand?'

'Yes, Father.' Hartmann hesitated, then said carefully, 'The new situation in Rome. Does it change things?'

'Will the new pope approve, do you mean?' Pacelli smiled coldly. 'I think not, if the candidate who immediately springs to mind succeeds. He was once heard to say that he had little time for the Mafia, whether it was in or outside the Church.'

'And that is how he sees our order?'

'The Society of Jesus has always had its enemies, Erich, you know that. Those who object to our power, our influence.'

'So your orders in this matter could be countermanded?'

'Not if we move fast. There are eighty-two members of the Sacred College who should be present at the conclave in the Sistine Chapel when the new pope is elected. Cardinal Mindszenty can't come, he's still trapped in the US legation in Budapest and the Primate of Ecuador is too old to travel, but the rest will come, from every corner of the globe, and that will take time.'

'How long?'

'A fortnight at the earliest, probably closer to three weeks before we see a pope in Rome again.'

'And the general plan concerning Father Conlin is well advanced now?'

Pacelli nodded. 'At our last meeting I mentioned an Englishman to you – Professor Charles Pascoe.'

'I remember.'

'He is now in complete charge – of everything.' Pacelli emphasized the phrase. 'From now on you will take your orders from him. A meeting is arranged for you this afternoon when the entire operation will be explained in detail. I think you'll find that Pascoe has an aptitude for this sort of thing.'

'And Schaefer?' Hartmann walked to the window. 'What about him?'

Pacelli joined him. 'No problem. When you leave here, go down to the basement garage. You'll find an old truck there with Meyer & Company painted on the side. Just climb in the back and you'll be taken to meet Pascoe.' He smiled and placed a hand on the younger man's shoulder. 'Are you frightened, Erich, at the prospect of Neustadt?'

'No, Father.'

Pacelli sighed. 'No, I didn't really think you would be, and in some ways that's a pity.'

'Father!' Hartmann hesitated and Pacelli knew that he was debating whether to ask for a blessing.

Pacelli said gently, 'You'd better go now, Erich. Professor Pascoe will be waiting.'

Hartmann went out. Pacelli crossed to the window. Schaefer was pacing up and down under the trees, collar turned up, looking thoroughly miserable. Pacelli felt sorry for him, but that would never do. He went back to his desk and started to pack his small case.

III

The basement garage was surprisingly large. It contained half a dozen cars and the truck, as Pacelli had indicated. Hartmann approached the rear and started to climb over the tailboard as ordered. He hesitated, then walked round to the front and peered into the cab.

Vaughan leaned back in the driver's seat, cap over his eyes. He pushed it up and sighed. 'In the back, the man said. Rule number one in this game, always do as you're told.'

Without a word Hartmann turned, went round to the rear and climbed over the tailboard. He sat down on the floor, his back against the cab, well out of view, and a moment later the truck moved away.

IV

In Teusen's study, Hartmann sat at the desk and worked his way through the last of the files Pascoe had given him – the one concerning Simon Vaughan. He closed it and leaned back with a sigh, running his hands over his eyes.

The door opened and Pascoe entered. 'Finished? So – now you know as much as I do, Father. Our intentions in the matter. The background details of those you will be working with.'

'Yes – most interesting. This Major Vaughan, for instance.'

'You don't approve?'

'His motives worry me.'

'I'm not interested in whether a man is a thief, Father. Only in whether he's a reliable thief. Vaughan works for wages. That makes him very reliable indeed.'

There was a knock at the door and Teusen looked in. 'Konrad is here, Charles. He's ready to go.'

'Good. Show him in.'

Konrad entered. In his corduroy trousers, reefer coat and tweed cap, he looked more like a workman than ever.

'Father Hartmann, this is Brother Konrad of the Franciscan Order of Jesus and Mary at Neustadt.'

The two men shook hands. 'You return to Neustadt today?' Hartmann enquired.

'No, only to East Berlin. I shall spend the night at my sister's house. Go on to Neustadt tomorrow.'

'What situation will I find there?' Hartmann asked. 'There are still good Catholics in the village, I presume?'

'Plenty, but it's the old story. You can't be a good Party member and go to church at the same time. You know what happened at Holy Name, do you?'

'Yes – it was closed five years ago. Lack of support was the official excuse.'

'The last priest was Father Honecker. A marvellous man and much loved. He was eighty and very frail and the district commander was displeased because his congregation was so large. Honecker welcomed everyone, you see. It didn't matter to him if you were a Party member or not.'

'What happened?'

'There was a famous cross at Holy Name – medieval, I think – called the Cross of St Michael. It was oak with a marvellous carving of Our Saviour on it. It stood in a stone socket by the altar. One night the district commander had it removed and taken down to the bottom of the hill and planted in a grove of trees by the Elbe. Honecker went to see him. He was told that the church stayed shut until the Cross of St Michael was restored to its rightful place. The only stipulation was that Father Honecker had to carry it himself, which as the thing weighed around a couple of hundredweight was hardly likely.'

'He tried, of course.'

'And died of a heart attack.'

There was a silence and beyond Konrad, Hartmann was aware of Vaughan in the doorway.

Pascoe said, 'Yes, well, we mustn't detain you, Konrad.' He picked up an envelope from the desk and handed it to the Franciscan. 'That's for Doctor Campbell, Professor Norden's report.'

'Good.' Konrad slipped it into his breast pocket and turned to Vaughan. 'So – I will expect you when? The day after tomorrow?'

'I don't see why not,' Vaughan said.

Konrad turned to face them all and bowed in a strangely old-fashioned way. 'Gentlemen.'

He went out. Pascoe said to Hartmann, 'Right, Major Vaughan will take you back to the Catholic Information Centre now and this is what I want you to do.'

V

Schaefer was out of cigarettes, cold and thoroughly miserable when Hartmann came out of the Catholic Information Centre and crossed the road to join him.

Schaefer managed a smile. 'There you are, Father. Can we go home now?'

'Sorry, Horst,' Hartmann said. 'I'm afraid I'm going to have to stay the night. I hope it won't inconvenience you too much.'

'It won't have to, will it?'

Schaefer tried to sound injured, but women were his one great weakness and his pulse had already quickened at the prospect of the streetwalkers who patronized the Astoria Hotel. He could see the entrance now, a hundred yards down on the other side of the road.

'I'll have to have your car keys, Father.'

'Of course.' Hartmann gave them to him. 'There's one other thing I wanted to mention. Next Sunday . . .'

'You go down to Neustadt, some village or other that God forgot on the edge of Holstein Heath. Yes, I had heard, Father. The office does like to keep me informed about little things like that.'

'How very efficient of them. I could be there for a couple of weeks, I'm afraid.'

'The country air will be good for me. I smoke too much.'

'And your wife?'

'She'll be fine. The baby isn't due for another three months and besides, she has her mother living with us now. Another good reason to get away for a while. I'll see you in the morning, Father.'

He kicked his BMW down off the stand and pushed it along the pavement towards the Astoria and Hartmann hurried back across the road. When he went into the office on the first floor, Vaughan and Meyer were standing by the window.

'He took it quite well,' Hartmann told them.

'Is that a fact?' Vaughan said. 'Julius, take Father Hartmann to Bruno's place. Come back for me in an hour.'

Hartmann looked puzzled. 'You're staying here?'

'That's right.'

Vaughan ignored him, intent on Schaefer down there, almost at the hotel. Hartmann hesitated, then followed Meyer out. Schaefer was at the Astoria now. He parked the BMW outside, locked the rear wheel with a chain and padlock and went in. Vaughan brought a chair to the window, lit a cigarette and settled himself down to wait.

VI

When Schaefer went into the Astoria's tiny bar he saw, to his disappointment, that it was quite empty except for the hotel's proprietor, Willi Scheel, a grossly fat man who was never seen anywhere else except perched on a stool behind the zinc cash register reading the sports papers.

He looked up. 'Herr Schaefer. Nice to see you. You're staying, I hope?'

He reached for a bottle of cognac, opened it and poured some into a glass which he pushed across.

'Just for tonight, Willi.' Schaefer took the cognac down in one swallow. 'I'll have a packet of cigarettes. Trade a little slack?'

'Early yet,' Scheel told him. 'They'll be packed in here like sardines in another couple of hours with the weather like it is.' He touched the lapel of Schaefer's coat with one podgy hand and shuddered. 'You're wet through. What you need is a hot bath.'

'Sounds good,' Schaefer said.

Scheel raised his voice. 'Jutta? Where are you? Get in here.' He poured Schaefer another cognac.

'Jutta?' Schaefer asked. 'New, is she?'

Scheel nodded. 'God knows, it's difficult enough to get decent help these days, but this one is the limit. An absolute slut. Around anything in trousers she's like a bitch in heat.'

Schaefer drank a little of his cognac. 'Is that so?'

'You'll have to watch yourself with this one.' Scheel smiled amicably.

'Yes, what do you want?'

The voice was hoarse, petulant. Schaefer turned and found a young woman standing in the entrance to the bar. She was small with high cheekbones and almond-shaped eyes and had the face of a corrupt child. Her black dress was far too short, crumpled and soiled. The one incongruity was the shoes which were black patent leather with immensely high heels.

Schaefer almost choked on the rest of the cognac as Scheel said, 'Take Herr Schaefer up to number nine and run him a bath. You can take your break then.' He pushed the bottle of cognac across the bar to Schaefer. 'Better take this, do you good. Bring on a sweat when you're in the bath, eh?'

He started to laugh and Schaefer took the bottle, throat dry, and hurried after the girl. She was already half-way up the stairs, the skirt straining at the seams across her buttocks; there were ladders in her black stockings. He stood close behind her as she fumbled with the key in the door and she pushed back against him and he felt the same old excitement surging inside him that never failed.

She turned to look at him calmly. 'Better get that coat off quick. You'll catch your death. I'll turn the bed down for you.'

Schaefer put down the bottle and unbuttoned his coat and she leaned across the bed to turn back the coverlet, the skirt sliding back to expose bare flesh at the top of the dark stockings. It was more than he could stand and he seized her from behind, his hands sliding over her breasts.

'Naughty,' she said as he pushed against her. 'You'll catch your death, I warned you. What you need is a good stiff drink to warm you up.'

'And then?' he demanded.

'We'll see.'

She went into the bathroom and came back with a glass which she filled almost to the brim. He was already down to shirt and trousers.

She held out the glass. 'There we are, sweetheart. A nice big one, just to slow you up. I mean, you'd like that, wouldn't you?'

He almost choked getting it down, and then he dropped the glass and pulled her to the bed, sprawling across her thighs, his hands at the buttons of her dress. His fingers felt thick and clumsy and the buttons refused to obey. She was talking to him, but he couldn't hear what she was saying and then she just wasn't there at all.

VII

The girl adjusted her dress, then went to the window, opened it and leaned out. She came back to the bed, searched in the pocket of Schaefer's jacket, found his cigarettes and lit one. Then she lay on the bed beside him, propped against a pillow and waited.

After a while the door opened and Vaughan entered. 'Oh, very nice,' he said in German. 'The Blue Angel, slightly rundown version, if that's possible.'

The girl smiled and her voice when she spoke, was now crisp and very upper-class. 'I don't know what you put in the bottle, but it's certainly knocked him cold. Only just in time, too. The original randy bull, that one.'

Vaughan lifted one of Schaefer's eyelids. 'Good for ten or

twelve hours, I'd say. Good stuff, but you need a strong heart to stand it. Hope he qualifies.'

'You bastard,' she said.

He went through Schaefer's jacket and found the wallet. It contained a few hundred marks, a photo of Margarete and the children, army discharge papers in the rank of sergeant, Schaefer's SSD identity card and various social security papers.

He replaced them in the wallet. 'I'll have this back to you in two hours. Put it back in his jacket, then you can go.'

'Thanks very much.'

'Are you working at the moment?'

'I've got a television play next week and an audition in Munich the week after for a war picture.'

'All go, isn't it?'

Vaughan went out, closing the door gently behind him. She lit another cigarette and leaned back, staring at the ceiling. Beside her Schaefer started to snore gently.

VIII

Teusen examined the identity papers in the light of his desk lamp and nodded in satisfaction.

'I told Jutta she could have the wallet back within a couple of hours,' Vaughan said.

'No problem. I'll have one of my men deliver it.'

'Good – I think she'd like to get out of there. She's a good actress, but playing the whore on a television stage is one thing – the reality is something else again.'

'You haven't said anything to Hartmann about this?'

'Didn't think he'd like it.'

Teusen nodded. 'Yes, he could be a problem, that one.'

'Where's Pascoe?'

'At the American Embassy. They had a call booked for him on the scrambler to the Secretary of State. What are you going to do now?'

'Is Pascoe still keen on the idea of using a light plane to bring Conlin out?'

'Yes.'

'Then I'd better find Max Kubel and quick.'

'Do you anticipate any problems there?'

'Not really. You know how Max moves around, but Julius has put a few feelers out. Maybe he's come up with something.'

They went into the other room. Hartmann was standing on the terrace looking out across the city. Meyer was on the telephone. He replaced it and turned to Vaughan.

'That was Ziggy. He doesn't know where Max is playing this week, but it seems he's been using Madame Rosa as post-office.'

'Playing?' Teusen looked puzzled.

'Piano,' Meyer said. 'He makes his rent money playing jazz in some of the clubs.'

Vaughan said, 'We'll call on Rosa and drop you off on the way, Father.'

Hartmann said, 'Perhaps I could accompany you? It sounds as if it could be interesting.'

'Possibly even rough. Too rough for that collar.'

Teusen went into his bedroom and returned with a black silk evening scarf which he handed to Father Hartmann. 'Whose side are you on?' Vaughan demanded.

Hartmann adjusted the scarf to conceal his clerical collar. 'Satisfied, Major?'

'Why not?' Vaughan said. 'It could be an interesting evening,' and he led the way out.

IX

Vaughan drove, the three of them crammed into the cab of the truck. Over the Kurfürstendamm, West Berlin's smartest street, towered the floodlit Kaiser Wilhelm Memorial Church.

'Berlin,' Meyer said. 'What a place. Would you believe it, Father, but a third of it is green. There are more than a hundred working farms within the city limits, twenty theatres, the Berlin Philharmonic . . .'

'And a considerable variety of more fleshly levels of entertainment for those inclined,' Vaughan added drily.

'Still the finest city in the world to eat in.'

'You wouldn't think the Gestapo chased him out of the place in '39', Vaughan said.

But Meyer ignored him. 'It's a terrible thing for an old

Jew to confess, Father, but I adore Berlin food and it's anything but kosher, believe me.'

Vaughan turned into a street of old-fashioned apartment houses, pulled in at the kerb and got out. He went up the steps and checked the cards.

Hartmann said. 'You've been together some time?'

'Not really,' Meyer said. 'Simon was in the army, then he had a little trouble in the Far East.'

'Yes, I know about that.'

'He was chief of police in a little Arab state in the Gulf when I met him. He saved my skin.'

'You think a lot of him.'

'He's a good boy.'

Vaughan called, 'This is it.'

He pressed the bell-push, then spoke into the wall mike. As they arrived, the door clicked open and he led the way inside. It was decent enough, the walls painted in cream and carpet on the narrow stairs. The apartment was on the first floor and the brass plate on the door said: Rosa – Chinese Astrologer.

'My God,' Meyer said. 'The people we deal with.'

'You don't approve?' Hartmann asked.

'Astrology, Chinese or otherwise, is a nonsense.'

The door opened. The woman who stood there was very old. She wore a long black dress, gold ear-rings, and white hair was drawn back tightly from the parchment face. The eyes were darkly luminous.

'When were you born?' she said to Meyer in a voice that was little more than a whisper. 'December twenty-eight or nine?'

He was genuinely shocked. 'Twenty-seventh.'

'Typical Capricorn', she said. 'If he was dying and they brought him a doctor he'd ask to see his diploma.'

Vaughan grinned. 'I'd say that was pretty accurate reading, wouldn't you, Julius? I'm looking for Max, by the way. Max Kubel. Ziggy Schmidt thought you might be able to help.'

'Max?' she said. 'You're friends of his?'

'Definitely.'

'All right, come in.'

The sitting-room was warm, a good fire in the stove, two

white cats sleeping in front of it. Untidy but comfortable, and there were books everywhere.

She sat down at a circular mahogany table and motioned them to join her. 'I thought you might have come for a reading.'

It was Hartmann who answered. 'And why not? A little something for your time. How much?'

'Any gift is welcome.' She was looking at him intently and he took out his wallet and produced a hundred-mark note. 'Which year were you born? With the Chinese it is the year which is important.'

'1930.'

'Year of the Horse.' She nodded. 'Late April, I think.'

'That's right.'

'Horse Taurus, then. You serve a hard master. The hardest in the world to follow, I think.' She reached forward and pulled the scarf to one side. 'See, I am right.'

'So it would appear.'

'Driven by fire and by fire consumed. You must take care.'

'Thank you, I will,' he replied gravely.

She turned to Meyer who held his hands in front of his face. 'No – not a word. I don't want to listen to such nonsense.'

'Don't waste your time,' Vaughan said. 'Try me. 27 July 1926.'

'The Tiger and the Lion,' she said. 'Both beasts of prey and all men fear the tiger by night. You walk on corpses, major.' She stood up. 'I'm tired. You'll find Max at a club called Tabu in Josephstrasse.'

She walked out. Hartmann said softly, 'Madame Sosostris, the wisest woman in Europe. You are familiar with the quotation, major?'

'Particularly the line which comes later,' Vaughan replied. ' "I do not find the Hanged Man." I've a feeling she just did. Eliot knew what he was talking about.'

'Eliot?' Meyer demanded. 'Eliot who?'

'Never mind, Julius.'

'This club – the Tabu. You know it?' Hartmann asked.

'The Berliner, Father, likes to boast that he can offer you anything from the most elegant nightclubs in the world to seedy bars that can't supply much more than an odour of urine and petty crime.'

'And the Tabu?'

'It could be worse, but not much. Maybe we'd better drop you off on the way.'

'Nonsense,' Erich Hartmann said. 'A necessary stage in my education, wouldn't you say, major?'

— 8 —

DURING the Second World War there was an almost incredible superiority of German fighter pilots in terms of confirmed victories. The Luftwaffe's leading ace was credited with almost nine times as many victories as his British and American adversaries and no less than thirty-five Germans had scores in excess of one hundred and fifty, which charmed circle did not include Max Kubel, who had ended the war with a score of one hundred and forty-nine.

He was only twenty years old when he first saw combat flying with the Condor Legion in Spain. In Poland he was shot down and parachuted to safety, the first of eight such occasions.

The heady summer of the Battle of Britain when victory had seemed so near had been followed by the Eastern Front. Shot down near Kiev on 12 June 1943, and taken prisoner by the Russians, Kubel had escaped, seized a Yak fighter and flown back to German-held territory.

This exploit earned him the Oak Leaves to his Knight's Cross and made him something of a hero to the German people for some considerable time after. Forbidden to fly in combat, he had endured a desk job with the Luftwaffe inspectorate for almost a year before securing an active posting with a night fighter unit in the spring of 1944.

In September 1944 he had joined a test unit operating the

Messerschmitt 262, at that time the most advanced jet fighter plane in the world. On the morning of 2 October that year, he crashed in flames near Hamburg and on Goering's personal instructions, was flown to a hospital at Weissach in Bavaria, which had developed special techniques in the treatment of half-cooked human flesh. It was March of 1946 before he had been judged fit enough to emerge into the outside world again.

II

Seated at the piano in the Tabu, he seemed considerably younger than his forty-five years with his fair hair and the insolent blue eyes that women found so appealing.

He looked rather dashing in the old black leather Luftwaffe flying jacket and he was surrounded by girls on the stand above the small dance floor. As Vaughan, Hartmann and Meyer leaned over the balcony rail, he moved into a solid, driving arrangement of 'St Louis Blues.'

'He's good,' Hartmann said.

'He'd agree with you. Max is a great one for self-advertisement. He'd wear his Knight's Cross if he thought he could get away with it.'

Meyer sat down at the table, called over a waiter. 'You want something to eat, you two?'

Vaughan glanced at Hartmann and shook his head. 'Bottle of wine, maybe. Niersteiner. Something like that.'

Kubel glanced up and caught sight of them and waved. Hartmann said, 'Such a flight by night would require great courage.'

'At Innsbruck they have one of the oldest ski jumps in the world. When you take off you can see one of the city's cemeteries by the church at the bottom. If you're genius standard you may just land in one piece three hundred and sixteen metres below.' Vaughan lit a cigarette. 'Max still does that kind of thing for fun. He was wounded so many times during the war I think they must have taken his nerves out while they were at it.'

Max Kubel stopped playing and an accordionist took over. The club was crowded, mostly middle-aged men or older, and the girls were on the whole past their prime.

'Love for sale,' Vaughan said.

'A strange phenomenon,' Hartmann observed. 'We always assume we can give it, but we usually mean on our own terms. And why should you assume that sin should shock me, major? The average priest listens to more evil and wickedness in the confessional in a week than the average man experiences in a lifetime.'

Kubel appeared at the head of the stairs at that moment. He paused to light a cigarette, then pulled a chair forward and joined them at the table.

'Simon – Julius.' He examined Hartmann coolly and then his eyes widened. He reached out and pulled the scarf to one side. 'Good God.'

'Don't worry, he isn't after your soul.'

'Not this time, at any rate.' The priest smiled and held out his hand. 'Erich Hartmann.'

The waiter was unloading his tray and Kubel reached for the bottle of wine. Vaughan said casually, 'Are you still flying the Black Bitch?'

'Wouldn't part with her.'

'Where do you keep her?'

'Private club field near Celle.' Kubel's voice was lazy, but there was an alert wariness in the eyes.

'Black Bitch?' Hartmann asked.

'An old Fieseler Storch spotter plane that Max owns. Painted black for camouflage on certain night flights he's in the habit of making.'

'Not any more,' Kubel said. 'They're getting too good over there these days. One of their MiGs intercepted Heini Braun in his Henschel in April and blew him out of the skies.'

'A load of Russian rubbish,' Vaughan said. 'You could handle that, an old-timer like you.'

Kubel smiled beautifully. 'I've decided to settle for the simple things in my old age, Simon. A good piano, a glass of wine, an accommodating lady . . .'

'Nothing more?' Hartmann said. 'Is there nothing more than this that you would like in the whole world?'

Kubel turned to him. 'Not really, Father. All is vanity. Isn't that what the Bible says?'

Vaughan leaned forward. 'One flight, Max, some time

during the next two weeks. Neustadt on the Elbe, fifty miles inside the line. Twenty minutes in – twenty out. Two passengers.'

'I told you, you're wasting your time.'

'One hundred thousand marks, or any other currency you prefer.'

'My God, who do you want to bring out, Walter Ulbricht?'

'Not quite.'

Kubel's fingers tapped restlessly on the table as he thought about it. 'Who would I be working for?'

'I can take you to meet him now.'

A buxom woman of forty or so had been hovering anxiously for some time. Her make-up had been applied a little too carefully and the blonde hair was piled up in several layers in a style that would have suited a younger girl, but she did have a certain undeniable appeal.

Kubel smiled. 'Good. Then we go to see this friend of yours, but later, Simon.' He reached for the woman's hand. 'First I must dance with Frau Ziegler because she is the owner of this disgusting establishment and one must always keep the boss happy.'

Hartmann and Vaughan leaned on the rail and watched Kubel and the woman move on to the crowded dance floor.

'I thought he'd bite,' Vaughan said.

'You consider yourself a man of sound judgment, major?'

'I understand men like Max,' Vaughan said calmly. 'They're a breed on their own.'

'Why?'

'His is a world of the senses. You think about it – he just does it.'

'And what exactly do you mean by it?'

'Politics or conversation. Philosophy or sex.' Vaughan glanced down to the centre of the dance floor where Kubel was massaging Frau Ziegler's buttocks with some feeling. 'See what I mean?'

'And you, Major Vaughan?'

'When I was fifteen my old grandma told me there were three things to avoid like the plague. Drink, cards and loose women.'

'Have you followed her advice?'

'Well, I don't play poker, Father, because I've nothing to lose.'

'On the contrary,' Hartmann told him, 'I would have said everything.'

Vaughan laughed out loud and turned to Meyer who had just finished eating. 'Hear that, Julius? There's hope for me yet. For God's sake, let's pick up Max and get out before our friend here starts preaching from the balcony.'

III

Outside, rain poured down relentlessly. The street was badly congested because one side of it had been excavated so that the old sewer pipe could be renewed. There was some sort of commotion going on at the far end. A small crowd had gathered, made up of workmen and passers by. A police car drew up and then another.

'Where did you park?' Kubel asked, looking up at the rain with distaste.

'In the next street,' Vaughan said. 'I couldn't get any closer.'

As they neared the crowd, he caught at the arm of one of the workmen hurrying past. 'What's going on? Car accident?'

'One of the pipe-layers is trapped in the storm drain and the water level's rising by the minute with this rain.'

He pulled himself free and Hartmann strode forward. The ease with which he forced his way through the crowd was immediately apparent and for the first time Vaughan was aware of the size of the man, the breadth of his shoulders.

'What's he playing at?' Meyer demanded as Hartmann paused to speak to a police sergeant.

In the sewer excavation below, water swirled three feet deep in a chaos of mud and broken planking.

A figure emerged from the dark mouth of the pipe, followed by three others. They reached wearily and willing hands pulled them up.

'I've ordered everyone out,' the first man said. 'Had to. There's only a couple of feet of headroom left between the waterline and the roof and the level's rising all the time.'

Hartmann said, 'Is he still alive, the man in there?'

'Not for long. There was nothing we could do. A half-ton block on his legs.'

'What's his name?'

'Günther Braun.'

'Good.' Hartmann handed his raincoat to Vaughan. 'Hold this, please, major.'

He leapt down into the excavation, ducked inside the dark mouth of the tunnel and disappeared.

'Is he mad?' Meyer cried.

Vaughan didn't bother to answer, simply shoved the priest's coat into Meyer's hands, grabbed a handlamp from an astonished policeman, jumped into the pit and went after Hartmann.

IV

The pipe was perhaps five feet in diameter and the level of the water was now closer to four than three. He found Hartmann at once, the beam from the lamp picking him out of the darkness and the white desperate face of Günther Braun, the waters of the storm drain running with such force that they were already washing across his head.

As the light revealed Hartmann's clerical collar, Braun cried, 'That's all I need, a priest. Come to hear my confession, Father?'

'Not at all, my friend.' Hartmann leaned over him, feeling under the water.

Vaughan crouched beside them. 'You're wasting your time. That block weighs half a ton. You heard what the foreman said.'

'Just hold his head,' Hartmann said calmly. 'And pull him clear when he tells you to.'

'Mad!' Braun cried. 'Crazy!'

The Jesuit took a deep breath and plunged his head under the surface. The mighty shoulders heaved and then, incredibly, his face came up out of the water, carved in stone, every muscle taut.

Braun screamed and Vaughan lurched backwards, dropping the lamp, plunging them into darkness, aware of the man's body floating free. A moment later he emerged into the excavation crater to the astonishment of the crowd. There were excited cries and men dropped in to help.

Max Kubel reached down to pull him up. Vaughan said, 'Half a ton, Max. The bastard lifted half a ton with his hands under water.'

Hartmann had appeared beside them, soaked to the skin, his face streaked with mud. Meyer helped him into his raincoat, an expression of awe on his face.

For the moment, the attention of the crowd was concentrated on Braun as he was lifted into a waiting ambulance. Hartmann said, 'I think we'd better go now, gentlemen, while the going's good.'

'He's right,' Meyer said. 'The last thing he needs is his picture on the front page of the *Berliner Zeitung*.'

Hartmann moved away quickly and they followed. Kubel said, 'A remarkable man, this priest of yours.'

'I know,' Vaughan said. 'Just what I needed. Another holy fool.'

— 9 —

EMERGING FROM the Berlin air corridor into Western Germany, Max Kubel banked south and took the Storch down to a thousand feet.

Pascoe, sitting next to him, said, 'I don't fly myself, but it seems a beautiful plane to handle. Wasn't it one of these Skorzeny used to airlift Mussolini off Gran Sasso in '43?'

'That's right, and during the last week of the war Hannah Reitsch landed one under Russian artillery shells on the east-west axis in the heart of Berlin.'

Bitterfeld was below them now and as Kubel turned into the wind and dropped the Storch down in a landing that was pure perfection, the black Mercedes drove to meet them,

Werner Böhmler at the wheel. Kubel switched off the engine and they sat there in the silence.

'You've never used this place, not even in the war?' Pascoe asked.

Kubel shook his head. 'No. You say the landing lights still work?'

'So I'm informed. Also the radio communication system in the watchtower is regularly serviced by the Luftwaffe in case of need.'

'What for?' Kubel said. 'Do those bastards at HQ think we might get lucky third time around?' He looked angry. 'I always did hate their guts. Big men behind desks.'

'Like me?' Pascoe said.

'Exactly like you, professor. Different uniform.'

'Of course,' Pascoe said. 'But to the business in hand. Could you make the kind of flight I require to Neustadt under the conditions described?'

'No problem.'

'And those MiG interceptors the East Germans are flying in the area – they don't worry you?'

'Of course they do,' Kubel said. 'On the other hand, their radar can't reliably discriminate between low altitude targets and ground clutter, which means that if I take this old bitch in under six hundred feet all the way, they won't even know I'm there. And those kids they have flying those things – all they have is flight training. No combat experience at all.'

'So you'll do it?'

'I suppose so,' he said morosely. 'Deserted airfields always did bring out the worst in me. This is a bad place. Good men died here. Not that it matters. The same for all of us in the end.' He shivered and opened the door. 'Come on. You'd better introduce me to this man of yours.'

II

In Washington, it was still very early in the morning and President Kennedy, unable to sleep because of the pain in his back, sat at his desk in the Oval Office and worked on one of his speeches for the coming visit to Germany.

There was a light tap on the door and Dean Rusk looked in. 'I heard you were up.'

The president put down his pen. 'Anything important?'

'The Conlin affair. I've heard from Pascoe.'

'Fine. Help yourself to coffee and bring me up to date.'

Dean Rusk did so. When he was finished the president said, 'I suppose Pascoe knows what he's doing. God help them, that's all I can say.'

Rusk stood up. 'Oh, and General Gehlen has briefed Chancellor Adenauer on this one, as you requested. I think that just about covers everything for the moment.'

'Good,' the president said. 'Keep me informed.'

Rusk went out and the president moved to the window, pulled a curtain and peered outside. It was still dark – no sign of light at all and for some unaccountable reason, he felt depressed. But that, as always, was something to be fought against. He went back to his desk, picked up his pen and started to write again – 'for unless liberty flourishes in all lands, it cannot flourish in one.'

III

It was just before three o'clock in the afternoon when the co-operative produce truck pulled up in front of the inn at Neustadt and Konrad climbed down. Georg Ehrlich and Berg were standing in the porch talking and the mayor smiled and waved.

'So you're back, Konrad.'

A Mercedes staff car crossed the square and drove past. Harry van Buren was at the wheel and a young woman in Volkspolizei uniform sat beside him.

'My God,' Berg said. 'That's him – the new boss. Back a day early. I'd better get up there.' He jumped into his pick-up truck and drove away at once.

'Poor Heinrich,' the mayor said. 'For him, life is just one damn thing after another. How was Berlin?'

'As Berlin always is.'

'And your sister?'

'About the same, thank you. How about here? Have the changes up at the Schloss made any difference to things?'

'Not really. Some of the Vopos come in for a drink. The commander is a Captain Süssmann and there's a sergeant called Becker who's the original bastard. Still, it takes all sorts. Have you time for a coffee?'

'Not just now, thank you. Later perhaps. I'd like to see how things have been getting on at the farm.' Konrad told him, and went back down the steps.

IV

Margaret Campbell was sitting by the window in her wheelchair reading when he entered her room. She glanced up and her delight was immediate.

'Brother Konrad. How marvellous to see you.' She dropped her book to the floor and held out her hands.

Konrad said, 'You're looking well. Are you walking yet?'

'A little. But never mind that. What happened?'

He walked to the window and looked up at Schloss Neustadt. 'He's back.'

'Who is?'

'Van Buren. He just drove through the village in his car. He had a Vopo lieutenant with him. A woman.' He turned to face her. 'I saw him, this Major Vaughan of yours.'

'My Major Vaughan?' She was blushing now.

'Oh yes, I think so. A remarkable man.'

'But can he *do* anything?'

'You could ask him yourself. If everything goes according to plan, he should be here tomorrow night.'

She went very pale and held out her hands again. 'Tell me – tell me everything.'

V

The room which Berg had shown van Buren into was at the top of the main stairway leading up from the hall. It was comfortable enough, furnished as an office with a large, empty, stone fireplace.

'Yes, this should do very well,' van Buren said. 'Especially when you get a fire in here.'

'This was always the general officer commanding's office

both for our own people and the Russians when they were here.'

Van Buren had been going through the desk drawers and smiled, holding up a Russian pineapple grenade. 'Evidently. There's at least a dozen of these things in here. The last man in charge must have been the kind of paranoid who expected the paratroopers to drop in at dawn.'

'Another advantage . . .' The caretaker moved to a door in the corner and opened it.

Van Buren joined him and peered down a dark stone spiral stairway. 'Where does that go?'

'The rear courtyard. It makes a convenient private entrance in case of need.'

He glanced nervously at the lieutenant standing by the window, a military overcoat with fur collar slung from her shoulders.

'Lieutenant Leber will require a room,' van Buren said coldly.

'Certainly, Herr Professor.'

Süssmann hurried in, buttoning his tunic. 'My apologies, comrade. I was only just informed of your arrival.'

'Lieutenant Ruth Leber. She'll be with us for a while.'

'Comrade.'

Van Buren said, 'All right, Berg. See that she gets the best.'

Berg picked up her suitcase and she followed him and Süssmann watched her go, frank admiration in his eyes.

Van Buren said, 'Let me make one thing clear. She isn't here to supply comforts for the troops. She's important to my plans for Conlin.'

'As you say, comrade.'

'How is he?'

'I have no idea. As you ordered, he has been left in total isolation.'

'Take me to him now.'

On the third level it was cold and very damp and the sentry outside the cell wore a winter greatcoat and woollen scarf.

'Anything to report?' Süssmann demanded.

'No, comrade, Not a sound.'

'Open the trap,' van Buren ordered.

The sentry did so and the American crouched. The stench from inside the cell was immediately apparent.

'Perhaps he's dead,' Süssmann suggested.

'No, he's fine.' Van Buren kicked the trap shut. 'I have an instinct for these things. He's just as I want him and tomorrow, we get to work.'

VI

Margaret Campbell sat by the window in her wheelchair reading Professor Norden's report. It was succinct and to the point and quite fascinating.

She read it once, sat thinking about it for a while, then worked her way through it again.

> Working in a cemetery in the manner indicated should not pose too many difficulties. The area, being close to the river, must be fairly damp. Most of the occupants will be poor- to middle-class in simple wooden coffins rather than lead.
>
> If the working party were to come across a recent body, that is, one buried within say twelve months, things could be very nasty.
>
> The coffin will have dropped to pieces owing to gas pressure. The body will have distended, cavities will have ruptured and copious putrid gas and fluid will be permeating the soil.
>
> There will be streptococci present of a virulent kind. If any of the working party were to cut themselves, the result would be disastrous with the possibility of the infection leading to gas gangrene very quickly.
>
> Most of the bodies will have been there for some time. They will have become partly converted to adipocuere, a fatty substance with an all-pervading stench. This is not dangerous, but the stench is appalling. There is a remote chance of infection by anthrax and TB but so remote as to be hardly worth considering.
>
> Although the usually accepted depth for a grave is six feet, this is not always so. In this part of East Germany, nine feet is common and in any case, changes in subsoil and compacting means that human remains may be found up to twelve feet deep.
>
> The sewer could be the dangerous place, depending on how it has been used. There are often pockets of CO_2 and methane – choke damp and fire damp. The first will suffocate. The second will not only suffocate, but will explode from a spark if conditions are right. The immediate risk is to fall in the effluent. Nausea, vomiting and rapid death within hours can occur due to a gutful of human pathogenes.
>
> There is also the possibility of viral hepatitis. No obvious scratch

is needed for this. It may be transmitted orally and manually. There is a ten per cent morbidity rate.

It cannot be stressed too strongly that any kind of scratch or abrasion contracted during any phase of this operation MUST receive immediate drug therapy. If this procedure is not followed, septicaemia will be contracted within twelve hours, if not something worse.

So there it was. She sat there with the notes on her lap, thinking about it. After a while, the door opened and Konrad came in.

'Ready?' he asked.

'As I ever will be.'

He wheeled her out.

VII

They were all seated round the wooden dining table in the kitchen when Konrad wheeled her in.

God, but they are all so old, she thought as she looked from one serene face to another. It just isn't possible.

There was Franz, of course, who was only nineteen and built like a young bull, but Florian, Gregor and Augustin were all in late middle age and Brother Urban was just a frail old man with not long to go under any circumstances.

They were waiting. She said, 'Brother Konrad has told me of your decision and I think it's marvellous, but do you really think it's possible?'

'Oh yes,' Konrad said. 'Gregor was an officer of engineers during the war. He considers it entirely practical.'

'The soil in question is extremely light,' Gregor said. 'Easy enough to work. We have plenty of wood for props and a considerable amount of corrugated iron sheeting in the barn which we can utilize as lining.'

'Won't there be a problem with air supply?' Margaret asked.

'No – not at that depth. And the length of the tunnel will be quite short, remember. Naturally one will need to see how work progresses for the first day or two, but I think it could be managed in a fortnight at the outside, possibly sooner.'

'All right,' she said. 'Fine, but there is one unusual aspect here. The fact that we'll be digging through a cemetery. This will involve certain grave health risks. Brother Konrad has brought me a detailed report from a very eminent Berlin pathologist on what to expect. I'd like to go through it with you now.'

VIII

The trap at the bottom of Conlin's door was pushed open. Light gleamed as a plate was pushed through. The trap was closed again. He waited, listening, and heard the rustle in the darkness of the solitary rat which had taken to appearing each day exactly at mealtime.

The fear left him then, as quickly as it had come, and he chuckled and said softly, 'Conditioned reflex, my friend. Pavlov would have approved of you.'

Then he lay down on the cot again, folded his hands and started to say his office from memory.

IX

At Flossen, as darkness was descending, the heavy farm truck passed through the guard post on the West German side, through the neutral zone, and paused at the barrier pole where Private Gerald Hornstein stood waiting, rifle slung from his shoulder. The door of the guard hut opened, Peter Bulow emerged and approached the truck.

Werner Böhmler was at the wheel. He wore an old army fieldcap, filthy overalls and badly needed a shave. He held out his papers without a word. Bulow inspected them, then handed them back. He nodded to Hornstein, who raised the barrier and Böhmler drove through.

Ten minutes later he rolled to a halt at the side of the narrow road in thick forest, went round to the rear of the truck and unfastened the high tailgate, lowering it so that it formed a sloping ramp to the road.

There was the roar of an engine firing inside and Vaughan ran a Cossack motor-cycle and sidecar down the ramp and braked to a halt. He wore full Vopo uniform: heavy dispatch-rider's raincoat, ankle-length, helmet and heavy goggles which just now were pulled up. Across his chest was suspended on a sling a Russian AK assault rifle with folding stock, a thirty-round magazine in place, ready for instant action.

'Well, you look the part anyway,' Böhmler said.

Vaughan grinned. 'Let's hope the opposition thinks so. See you tomorrow night. Eleven-thirty as arranged. I'll try not to keep you hanging about.'

Böhmler listened until the sound of the Cossack had faded into the distance, then he got into the truck and drove back towards Flossen.

Vaughan rode on, the yellow beam of his headlight cutting through the darkness, pine trees crowding in on either side. He had burned the map into his brain, reducing the journey to a kind of formula beforehand. Right at the first crossing. Then left. Right at the crossroads. Then came the first village. Ploden. Half a dozen houses and an inn.

There was a Vopo field car parked outside, a uniformed driver lounging beside it as if waiting for somebody. He raised a hand in salute as the Cossack went by. Vaughan waved back. It was as easy as that.

Filled with a sudden fierce exhilaration, he opened the throttle wide and roared on into the night.

X

Margaret Campbell was sitting in her wheelchair in the chapel. Ever since that first occasion on which Konrad had taken her there, the place had held a peculiar fascination. It was not that in any sense she had experienced a religious conversion, she was honest enough to admit that, but there was peace here of a kind she had never known before, with the wooden statue of St Francis smiling down at her in the candlelight. She didn't know what it meant yet, but that didn't matter.

The door creaked open behind and Konrad peered in. 'Ah, there you are,' he said. 'I was looking for you. Someone to see you.'

He stood back and a Vopo in ankle-length raincoat, helmet and goggles, a submachine-gun across his chest, moved into the room. She felt a moment of complete panic and then he pushed up the goggles.

Brother Konrad left them. Vaughan put a canvas pack he was holding in her lap.

'Present for you from Professor Norden.'

She found difficulty in speaking, so great was her emotion. 'What is it?'

'Medical supplies. Various drugs he thought you might find useful.'

She gazed up at him, eyes burning. 'You were right, weren't you? You saw through me like clear glass. The only one.'

He took off his helmet and put it down. 'You've had a hard time. It shows.'

'I'm so glad to see you. So glad.'

He smiled lit a cigarette and sat down beside her. 'That's all right then.'

XI

It was just after ten when Heinrich Berg stumbled out of the inn and made his way to his truck. He wasn't exactly drunk, but he did have a weakness for apricot brandy and that last glass had definitely been one too many.

He clambered up behind the wheel and fumbled for the key and the barrel of a pistol nudged his right ear. A cold voice said softly,' 'Up the road towards the Schloss, there's a disused barn on the left hand side on the edge of the wood.'

'What is that?' Berg said. 'What do you want?'

'Do it!'

The pistol barrel screwed into his ear painfully and he hurriedly switched on the lights, aware that the other man was a Vopo, no more than that. The pistol nudged him again.

'Come on! Move it! I haven't got all night.'

In total panic now, Berg pressed the starter button and drove away rapidly.

XII

It was cold and damp in the barn, but quiet as Berg moved uncertainly round into the light of the headlamps where Vaughan stood.

'Look, what is this?' Berg tried to sound firm. 'What do you want?'

'It's really quite simple,' Vaughan said. 'You've got a man called Conlin up there in the Schloss in a cell on what you call the third level. Am I right?'

Berg moistened dry lips. 'But that is a state security matter. The SSD are in charge.'

'Exactly,' Vaughan said cheerfully. 'But some friends of mine would like to get him out and we thought you might give us a hand.'

Berg gazed at him in total horror. 'You must be insane. Why should I do such a thing?'

'Because you've been a naughty boy, old chum. Staff-Sergeant Heinrich Berg, or should I say Hauptscharführer. Isn't that what they called the rank in the SS?'

Berg tried hard. 'This is nonsense. I don't know what you're talking about. I was an army man. Infantry for the whole of my service.'

'SS,' Vaughan said softly and took a bundle of papers from his pocket and laid them on the bonnet of the truck. 'Not Waffen SS. At least they were fighting men. You were Einsatzgruppen. Extermination squads, recruited from the gaols of Germany. You never faced a soldier in battle in your life. All you did was execute people. Lots of people. Anyone they told you to.'

'It's a lie!'

'See for yourself. Those are photostats of your military career, although as an ex-professional soldier myself, I must say it sticks in my throat having to use a phrase like that in connection with you.'

'If I was SS I would have my blood group tattooed under my left armpit,' Berg whispered.

'Normally, but in your case, you didn't finish training at Dachau until the autumn of '44 and by then your superiors knew the game was up. The tattooing was stopped. I mean, they didn't want to make it too difficult for you after the war. It's all there, read it.'

With trembling hands, Berg opened the papers and Vaughan carried on relentlessly, 'Amazing how detailed these SS records are. They certainly had a mania for putting things on paper.'

'Go to hell!' Berg launched himself forward and Vaughan kicked him casually under the right kneecap, dodging out of the way as Berg fell to the ground.

'Which method did you favour? The gas chamber, a phenol injection or just a bullet in the back of the neck?'

On his knees now, Berg crumpled the papers in his hands. 'I'll tell. I'll confess. Why shouldn't I? There are SS at every level of government. The police, the SSD, are full of them.' He was momentarily beside himself, almost unaware of what he was saying. 'And when I tell them about you, they'll be grateful.'

'You'll still lose your head one way or the other,' Vaughan said. 'Here, let me show you. See here on the last sheet. Mauthausen, 8 April 1945. You executed a man called Willi Stein, a man who'd been operating with the Communist underground against the Nazis right through the war.'

'I don't recall.'

'You should do. It's right here in the records. You hung him on a meat hook.'

And Berg remembered. It showed in his face. 'So?'

'I don't know how hot you are on political history, but back in 1933 when the Nazis came to power, one of the first things they did was to crush the old KPD, the German Communist Party, of whom a prominent member was Walter Ulbricht. Present Chairman of the Council of State. You have heard of him?'

'Yes,' Berg whispered, waiting for the axe to fall.

'Ulbricht escaped arrest because one of his closest friends in the movement risked everything to get him out. And you know who that man was?'

'God, no!' Berg cried.

Vaughan said, 'I wonder what Walter Ulbricht would do to the man who butchered Willi Stein?'

Berg crouched beside the truck, head in hands. Vaughan went to the door and peered out. As he turned, Berg stood up.

'What alternative do you offer?'

'Much as we object to helping a pig like you, asylum in the West with a guarantee of no criminal proceedings. You'll be transported out of here with everyone else involved at the appropriate time. No problems.'

'All right. What do you want me to do?'

'Van Buren came back today, didn't he?'

'Yes.'

'What's he like?'

'What can I tell you?' Berg shrugged. 'He's a cold fish.'

'Why do you say that?'

'Well, he's taken over the suite of rooms that's always been used by the commandant. It has a private entrance. A spiral staircase going down to a door in the rear courtyard. I thought I was doing him a favour when I mentioned it to him, especially with this woman he's brought with him. The Vopo lieutenant.'

'But he didn't think you were?'

'No.'

'Maybe he just doesn't like women.' Berg stirred uncomfortably and Vaughan lit a cigarette. 'All right, now you tell me about the set-up at the Schloss – everything. And then I'll tell you what you're going to do.'

— 10 —

'I WILL BLESS the Lord who gives me counsel, who even at night directs my heart. I keep the Lord ever in my sight. Since he is at my right hand I shall stand firm.'

The words, whispered aloud, comforted Conlin and it was necessary to hear a voice occasionally, even if it was only his own. It was an old story, this. He had experienced solitary confinement before at both Sachsenhausen and Dachau concentration camps under the Nazis, in company with that great and good man, Pastor Niemoller.

Niemoller had taught him how to fight using every resource of brain and intellect. To be especially strong at those darkest moments that sometimes struck on waking when the fear was for some nameless horror that would end all things.

The technique was a simple one. There was the missal to remember page by page, the correct order of services and so on. Then poetry which could be recited out loud. It was amazing how much came back, particularly the Irish of his youth which he'd not used for so long. *The Midnight Court*, for instance. As a boy, he had been able to recite the whole of it. Had received his own leather-bound Bible from his grandfather for doing so.

> *Ba ghanth me ag siubhail le chiumhais na na habhann,*
> *Ar bhainseach ur's an drucht go trom . . .*
> I used to walk the morning stream,
> The meadows fresh with the dew's wet gleam.

And then there were the books. *David Copperfield* for one. He'd read that many times anyway. It had all the reassurance of an old friendship.

He was re-living again the death of Steerforth in that terrible storm off Yarmouth when the door opened with total unexpectedness and light poured in.

Harry van Buren was standing there, Süssmann and Becker behind him. The cell stank like a sewer and Süssmann stepped back hurriedly.

Van Buren held a handkerchief to his face. 'How are you, Father? Fighting fit?'

The rat streaked from under the bed and disappeared into the darkness of the far corner and van Buren's eyes followed it.

'You really are being rather stupid if you do intend me to make my appearance in court, whole and unblemished,' Conlin said. 'As an old concentration-camp hand, I can assure you that six to twelve days after a rat bite in conditions like these, with human excrement present, it's usual for the victim to develop Weil's disease.'

'Is that so?' van Buren said.

'Death follows due to liver failure in up to thirty per cent of cases.'

Van Buren turned to Süssmann. 'Bring him up, then have this place cleaned out.'

He turned and walked away along the passage and Süssmann and Becker followed, holding Conlin gingerly between them.

II

When Vaughan pushed Margaret Campbell into the old barn at the Home Farm, they found Konrad and Franz already waist-deep into a large hole over in the far corner. Brother Gregor pushed an empty wheelbarrow in through the open doorway to the next room. He started to fill it again from the growing pile of loose soil.

'How's it going?' Vaughan asked.

Konrad climbed up out of the excavation, wiping sweat from his brow with the back of one hand. 'So far so good.'

'How are you getting rid of your soil?'

'The least of our problems. Come, I'll show you.'

Brother Gregor had just filled his barrow again and Konrad took it into the next room and Vaughan followed, pushing the girl in front of him. The room had a stone floor and there was a jumble of rusting agricultural machinery. There was a well in the far corner, its wooden cover pulled back, into which Konrad tipped the contents of the barrow. It seemed a long time before they heard a splash.

'Seventeenth-century,' he explained. 'We haven't used it in years. I should think it will accommodate our tunnel refuse adequately.'

They moved back to the other room. Margaret said, 'Where are the rest?'

Konrad picked up his shovel. 'There is work to be done, Fräulein. The farm to run, milk and eggs for the villagers. We must keep up appearances. Brother Urban is too old for such work as this. He sees to the cows and chickens. Florian handles our milking and deliveries in place of Franz, and Augustin sees to the cooking and other household chores.'

'I could do that,' she said. 'It's time I got up on this leg more and I can operate from the wheelchair when I feel tired.' He looked uncertain and she pulled at Vaughan's arm. 'Tell him, Simon! Make him see! The courtyard gate is always barred. To gain admittance outsiders have to ring the bell. That means I can't be caught out.'

'She's right,' Vaughan said. 'Which would free Augustin to do what he can here. And while we're at it, if you can give me something to wear instead of the pretty uniform, I've got the rest of the day to kill.'

III

The bath was very old with brass taps and the water, when it came, spouted from the mouth of a cherub. None of which mattered, for the only important thing was that when Süssmann and Becker lowered him into it, it was blissfully warm. Conlin sighed and closed his eyes.

Van Buren nodded to the two Vopos who went out. Lieutenant Leber came in. She wore a white overall and carried towels over her arm.

'Wash him thoroughly and disinfect the water.'

'Have I got you worried then?' The old priest smiled and opened his eyes. And then he saw the woman. His smile faded, his hands moved down to cover himself defensively.

'You're ashamed to be seen naked by a trained nurse?' van Buren said. 'Now there's an unhealthy attitude. There's nothing obscene in the human form, or did they teach you differently at the seminary when you were a boy? I've often wondered about those places. Celibate priests and adolescent boys.'

'I find it even stranger that a man of your training should find the notion of celibacy so difficult to take.' She was soaping his body now and Conlin winced. 'What is this supposed to be? A study in conscious humiliation?'

'You know, I really do find it interesting,' van Buren said, 'that you should find the situation so disturbing. So shameful?'

For the first time, the old man lost his temper. 'God forgive me for saying it, but why don't you go to hell?'

'Ah, but I see now,' van Buren said, as if suddenly gaining

insight. 'Not shameful, but frightening. You're afraid in such a situation. That is interesting.' He turned to the woman and said in German, 'Have him out now and dress him. I'll see him when he's eaten.'

He left and Ruth Leber helped Conlin out of the bath and towelled his body without a word, handling him gently as if he were a child. Then she brought clean underwear, corduroy pants, a shirt and warm sweater, socks, slippers and waited for him to dress, still without speaking.

When he was ready, she opened the door and led the way into the next room. Van Buren was not at his desk, but a great fire of logs blazed on the stone hearth and a meal was waiting on a small card table in front of it.

She held the chair for him to sit, then walked to the door. As she opened it, he said in German, 'Thank you, my child.'

She didn't even pause, but kept right on going, closing the door softly behind her. Conlin sighed, reached for his fork and raised a piece of beef to his mouth. It was really excellent and the wine was Chablis, his favourite, and beautifully chilled. He was under no illusions as to the purpose of all this, none at all, but his body needed all the strength it could get to sustain it in the days to come.

IV

When Berg went down to the third level, he found the Vopo sentry swilling out Conlin's cell with buckets of water carried from a tap in the passageway.

'He's still up above then?' Berg asked.

'That's right. What have you got there?'

Berg carried a spotlamp in one hand, a bucket in the other, and he lifted it up. 'Rat poison. Like some?'

The boy shuddered. 'No, thanks. Will you lay it in here?'

'No. Lower down. That's where the bastards breed,' Berg said. 'I'll see you later.'

He moved along the passageway and turned the corner, his spotlamp cutting into the total darkness ahead. A hundred yards, descending all the way and he entered a vaulted chamber. What he was seeking was in the centre, a heavy metal plate, bolted and padlocked. He knelt down, took a bunch of keys from his pocket and got to work.

He had never had occasion to open the plate before and had to try six keys before he found the right one. The plate was heavy and took both hands and all his strength to lift.

He probed the darkness below. There was an iron ladder perhaps ten feet deep and he descended it quickly. The tunnel stretched before him, ten feet in diameter, sloping downwards and perfectly dry.

It was twenty minutes later when he emerged. He snapped the padlock back into place, then reached for the bucket and laid down some of the rat poison, thinking of Vaughan as he did so. He'd like to have had him back at Mauthausen in the old days. By God, he'd have made him dance. But the bastard did have the whiphand. The prospect of what would happen to him if Ulbricht ever got a sight of his SS service record was too terrible to contemplate.

On the other hand, there were certain advantages to this situation. It meant he could go to the West and in safety, relieved at last of the nagging fear which had plagued him for years that his past would catch up with him. As he retraced his steps along the passageway, he began to whistle softly.

V

Conlin rationed himself to one glass of wine and was just finishing the last of the food when van Buren came in.

'You look like a different article.' He settled himself into the wing-back chair on the other side of the fire and lit a cigarette.

'What now?' Conlin asked.

'What do you think?'

'First you were nasty, then you offer me comfort. Nothing very extraordinary in that. The Gestapo were just the same when I first found myself in the cellars at Prinz Albrecht-strasse. There was the brute who beat me half to death with a whip, then the clean-cut boy who begged me to confess to save myself.'

'And in the end he turned out to be worse than the other guy. Right?'

'What is it you want of me?'

'Not me,' van Buren said. 'I only work here. Klein wants the Christian underground. Names, places. The works. Plus details of your connection with the CIA. That's the general idea.'

'But there isn't one.'

'Does it matter? What's truth? What's reality? It's all a question of perspective. It's a chain reaction in a way. Klein wants to please Ulbricht by giving him what *he* wants and I want to please Klein.' He smiled beautifully. 'And that means, old buddy, that you've got to please me.'

'I'm afraid I'd find that very difficult.'

'I thought you might.'

'So what happens now?'

'You tell me.'

'Phase two, the object of which will be to drive me to the edge of insanity. To take me to pieces, then put me together again in your image. Good Marxian psychology which believes that each man has his thesis, his positive side, and his antithesis, the dark side of his being. If you can find out what that is and encourage its growth, then the guilt will be too much for me to bear. Isn't that what you would tell your students?'

'Very good,' van Buren said. 'And where would you say I should probe for your antithesis? In the sexual area? You certainly did seem a little disturbed over that slight incident in the bathroom with Lieutenant Leber.'

'Why is it you people find the notion of celibacy so bewildering?' Conlin asked. 'You really should pull yourself together, boy. Read a different class of book.'

Van Buren wasn't in the slightest put out. He pressed a button on the desk and Süssmann came in. 'Take him back now.'

Conlin stood up. 'Is that all?'

'Should there be any more?' Van Buren selected another cigarette. 'Good night, Father. Sleep well.'

Süssmann didn't say a word on the way back to the third level until they reached the cell where the sentry stood guard.

Conlin paused at the door and Süssmann said, 'No, the next one, if you please.'

The cell was exactly the same as the other except that it

was clean and fresh. There was a chemical toilet, a mattress on the bed, blankets.

'You will be more comfortable here, I think, Father. Good night to you.' The door closed, the key turned in the lock.

A moment later, the light was switched off. Conlin unfolded the blankets. At least he had a breathing space. Why, he didn't know, but he at once relaxed, tension draining out of him and knelt down beside the bed to say his prayers.

The cell was filled with a hideous, frightening clamour. He scrambled to his feet and saw that a large bell was fixed just above the door that rang continually while a red light flickered on and off rapidly.

What a fool he'd been. The key rattled in the lock, the door was flung open and Süssmann and Becker appeared to drag him away along the passageway between them.

VI

Vaughan climbed up out of the excavation wearily and young Franz dropped in beside Gregor to take his place. They were about seven feet down and the going was harder now.

Florian came in from the other room pushing the empty barrow. 'Had enough?'

'Just about. Not used to hard labour.' Vaughan glanced at his watch. 'In any case, I'm going to have to get moving.'

Margaret Campbell swung in through the door on a pair of old wooden crutches, followed by Konrad carrying a jug of coffee and several mugs on a tray.

'What's all this?' Vaughan demanded.

'Konrad found them for me,' she laughed. 'It makes me feel half-way like a human being again.'

The gate bell rang. In the pit Franz paused, his pick raised above his head to swing. Everyone waited. Konrad said, 'I'll get it,' and went out.

Vaughan peered through the crack of the half-open door out through the rain. Margaret Campbell moved beside him and whispered, 'What do you think?'

Konrad had the gatelight on and was unbarring the postern. He opened it and Heinrich Berg stepped through. He muttered something to Konrad and peered around the courtyard nervously. Konrad shut the gate and came back to the barn.

'He wants you, major.'

Berg paused inside the door, cap in hand, his dark, watchful eyes taking in everything. The excavation in the corner – the girl. Everyone waited. He managed an ingratiating smile. 'Major? I didn't realize.'

'Did you find it?' Vaughan asked impatiently.

'Oh yes, Herr Major, just like you said. A heavy manhole cover in the lower chamber. Padlocked and bolted.'

'And you went in?'

'Yes.'

'Tell me.'

'There was a ladder – a steel ladder, maybe twelve or fifteen feet down. The tunnel was around ten feet in diameter and sloped down all the way. At other stages there were two further ladders to descend. Ten foot each – no more.'

'You went all the way?'

'Yes. It's all concreted except for the last thirty or forty feet. That's still rough. You can see where they were digging when they finished and there's a certain amount of rubble.'

'And you were able to breathe – no foul air?'

'Fresh and clean. There was some water – perhaps a foot deep in places. Not sewage – spring water, I think.'

Konrad said, 'If the air is fresh, it means the tunnel must be vented to ground level and in more than one place.'

'Exactly.' Vaughan said to Berg, 'You've done well. I won't be seeing you for a while. A week at least.'

'Is there anything else you want me to do in the meantime?'

'Find out as much as you can about the day-to-day treatment of Father Conlin. Keep Brother Konrad informed – say every two days.'

'As you say.'

'All right, you can go now.'

Konrad saw him out and bolted the postern again. When he came back he said, 'You think we can trust him?'

'He doesn't have any other choice. He'd sell us out if he could, but he can't. For people like Berg life is just a series of accommodations.' He glanced at his watch. 'I'd better get changed. I don't want to keep my friend hanging around at the border.'

VII

When he stepped out into the porch, he was once more in the heavy dispatch-rider's coat and helmet, the AK assault rifle across his chest.

Margaret Campbell said, 'I don't like you in that.'

'You're not meant to.' Behind her, Konrad pushed the Cossack and sidecar out of a shed into the courtyard, then went to open the gate.

Vaughan touched her cheek briefly with the back of a gloved hand. 'You look too good to leave standing there in the lamplight, Maggie my love, and nicely helpless on those crutches.'

'And what would you do with me?'

'I'll think of something.' He mounted the Cossack. 'See you at the week-end.'

He drove out through the gate. Konrad closed it. The girl stood there, listening to the sound of the engine fade into the night, then she turned and went back inside.

VIII

In the old operations room at Bitterfeld, Pascoe sat at the controllers' desk, examining the plan of Schloss Neustadt in the light of a reading lamp. Bruno Teusen was asleep in a chair in the far corner. It was very quiet – almost midnight – and Pascoe wondered what had happened. What had gone wrong. And then there was a knock on the door and Vaughan stepped into the room, followed by Böhmler.

Pascoe leaned back in his chair and smiled. 'You know, for a while there I was beginning to worry. I must be getting old. Everything went all right at the border?'

Vaughan removed his helmet. 'Like a charm. I didn't see a soul between Neustadt and Flossen, until I made contact with Böhmler here.'

'That was just after eleven,' Böhmler said. 'We put the bike in the back of the truck and proceeded to Flossen where Bulow passed us straight through – no fuss.'

'Excellent,' Pascoe said. 'Now, tell me what happened out there. Everything.'

IX

Böhmler and Vaughan crossed the airstrip at Bitterfeld to what had been the officers' mess in the old days.

'It's not bad,' Böhmler said. 'Army cots, I'm afraid, but there are plenty of blankets and the caretaker got the boiler working again today. There should be plenty of hot water by tomorrow.'

One of the hangar doors stood partially open, light seeped through and there was the sound of an electric drill. 'What's going on?' Vaughan asked.

'That crazy friend of yours, Kubel. He seems to work on that plane of his every hour of the day or night.'

'I'll catch up with you,' Vaughan told him.

When he went into the hangar, he found the Storch standing all alone in the immensity of it. Max Kubel was working on one of the wings with an electric drill, whistling cheerfully. He wore a pair of black mechanics' overalls that had certainly seen better days.

He switched off the drill and grinned. 'So, return of the hero. What was it like?'

'Interesting. I see you still love planes more than women.'

'Much more reliable. Tell me, my friend, the girl you mentioned. You found her well?'

'About the only thing I'm sure of any more is that I did find her.' Vaughan paced restlessly to the partly opened door.

'And how do you feel?'

'Uneasy.'

'For whom? Yourself or this young woman of yours?' He laughed out loud. 'My poor Simon.'

'You go to hell,' Vaughan said and made for the door.

'Undoubtedly,' Max Kubel shouted cheerfully, and he picked up his electric drill and switched it on again.

X

Father Conlin crouched in the corner of a cell on the first level. It was painted white, contained no furniture at all and seemed filled with a hard, white light that hurt his eyes.

He was aware of a dull, solid, slapping sound, a continuous rhythm that never ceased. It seemed to be very near and yet far away. It made no sense.

The door opened and van Buren appeared with a young Vopo guard. 'Bring him,' the American ordered.

When the Vopo got Conlin into the corridor, the old priest found van Buren standing at the next cell, peering in through a barred window. The slapping sounds continued and when the guard hustled Conlin close enough, he saw, inside the cell, a man in tattered shirt and trousers spreadeagled across a bench. Süssmann and Becker, stripped to the waist, were systematically beating him with rubber hoses.

The man on the bench moaned, turning his head, and Conlin saw to his horror that it was Karl, the driver who had delivered him by truck to Margaret Campbell's cottage that first night.

'What does this prove?' he asked van Buren. 'He knows nothing about the underground. He can't tell you a thing – that's the way I organized the system.'

'Oh, I believe you,' van Buren said. 'But without a penitent, reform is not possible, isn't that what your church teaches? Shouldn't we take an interest in his soul? And pain is a purgative. I mean, take the Cross. What a way to go. Squalid, filthy and degrading, and yet three days later . . .'

— 11 —

IT WAS JUST after eight o'clock on Saturday when Bulow waved the truck through at Flossen. About a mile up the road Böhmler forked left into a forest track, and a couple of hundred yards later emerged into a clearing in which stood the ruins of an old saw-mill beside a fast-flowing stream. The wheel which had once provided its source of power had not turned in years and the doors at the front of the building sagged on their hinges.

He drove inside, took a handlamp, went round to the rear and dropped the tailboard. The Cossack and sidecar were inside, together with various other items and Vaughan, once more a Vopo. He passed down a foot pump with a long hose attached and a couple of plastic buckets. Böhmler took them without a word and went and filled them at a tap in the corner.

Rain started to drum against the roof and he grinned. 'Twenty minutes earlier and it would have saved us some work.'

'And exposed us to the chance that some nosey-parker might have seen a piece of Volkspolizei hardware entering East Germany from the West and wondered what was going on?' Vaughan pointed out.

He put the end of the foot pump in one of the buckets and started to operate it vigorously as Böhmler sprayed the truck. Very quickly, the dirty-grey water paint with which it had been painted dissolved away and the truck now stood revealed for what it was, a Volkspolizei field truck painted in the dark green and brown camouflage colours of the forest sector and bearing divisional and group signs.

Ten minutes was all it took and Böhmler went and threw the pump and buckets into the mill race. He came back, wiping his hands on a rag. 'All yours, major.'

Vaughan clambered up behind the wheel. 'One hour after midnight. Okay?'

The engine roared into life and he drove out across the clearing. Böhmler went after him and by the time he reached the main road, the sound of the field truck had faded into the night. He turned and started to jog back towards the border post.

II

Vaughan should have known that it was too good to last. No matter how good your organization, it was always the unexpected that fouled things up. The stupid little things you hadn't planned for.

The first ten or fifteen miles passed uneventfully enough. Nothing but trees and darkness and then, as he passed through Ploden, he noticed a Cossack and sidecar that was twin to his own parked outside the inn. Obviously a regular stopping-off point for Vopo patrols. On the other hand, it was probably the only pub for miles.

The truck slewed violently as one of the rear tyres burst. He fought to control the wheel, stamping hard on the brake and managed to come to a halt in one piece in the grass verge.

Cursing softly, he got out, took the jack from the tool box and unbolted one of the two spare wheels. It was dark – too dark to see what he was doing so he got the handlamp from the cab, placed it on the ground and started to unfasten the wheel bolts. They were apparently immovable and it struck him suddenly that they had probably been tightened automatically in the garage. It took all his strength, concentrating fiercely. It was perhaps because of that that he was unaware of the sound of the approaching engine until it was too late to do anything about it.

The Cossack pulled on to the verge and the Vopo came forward and stood over him. In other circumstances it might have been funny, for he could have been Vaughan's twin; helmet, goggles, coat, even the AK across the chest.

'Trouble, comrade?'

'What do you think?' Vaughan demanded sourly. His hand slid into his right pocket, found the butt of the Walther he carried there and he slipped off the safety-catch.

'I'll give you a hand.'

The Vopo started to pump up the jack vigorously. 'Where are you heading?'

'Stendhal,' Vaughan told him. 'Divisional machine stores.'

An establishment which existed, he knew that. His new-found friend wrestled the old wheel off. 'What, on a Saturday night?'

Vaughan rolled the spare forward. 'An emergency. One of our recovery trucks ran off the road near Flossen and broke an axle. It's needed for Monday, so that means getting the part tonight and working through tomorrow.' He started to tighten the wheel bolts. 'There goes my week-end.'

He released the jack and air hissed. The Vopo chuckled. 'Had something good lined up, did you? Not Dirty Gerty at the inn at Ploden. Is that who you mean? I heard she was a certain turn.'

Vaughan slung the jack into the tool locker. 'Beggars can't be choosers, not in a dump like this.' He scrambled up behind the wheel. 'Anyway, thanks, comrade. Got to get moving.'

The Vopo said, 'Hang on, you've forgotten the wheel you took off. I'll sling it in the back for you.'

Vaughan heard the footsteps go round to the rear and didn't wait for the reaction, simply stamped on the accelerator, and drove away.

III

He didn't stand a chance, not in any kind of a race with a machine as powerful as the Cossack. In his mirror he was aware of its headlight coming up fast and he swerved across the road as it tried to overtake him.

This manoeuvre served him well for a while, but then he ran out of forest and emerged on to the dyke road above the Holstein Marshes, a causeway three miles long that ran across the wilderness of mudflats and great pale barriers of reeds higher than a man's head. An alien world inhabited only by birds.

And here it was no longer possible to weave because the slightest miscalculation would have the field truck over the causeway and into the marsh. Very sad for Sean Conlin and Margaret Campbell, not to mention Simon Vaughan.

Perhaps if he kept in close, inviting the Vopo to overtake, there would be a chance to crowd the Cossack over the edge into the marsh. Vaughan tried it, but the Vopo showed no intention of accepting the invitation, staying right on his tail.

There was a shot, then another as he fired his AK one-handed and Vaughan, doing the only possible thing, braked hard, skidding to a halt. He left his engine ticking over, slid across the passenger seat, went under the far door and crouched beneath the field truck.

The Cossack had stopped and footsteps approached. The boots, the tail of the coat, passed close to his face. The driving door was wrenched open.

There was silence and Vaughan came up from beneath the field truck behind the Vopo. His knee went into the small of the back, the left arm around the throat, bending the body back in an agonizing bow. The right hand jerked the helmet back hard against the nape of the neck. It broke cleanly as the Vopo gave one frantic choked cry and died.

Vaughan held him in his arms for a few moments, breathing heavily, then dragged him back to the motor-cycle and eased him into the sidecar, which wasn't easy because he was a large man. Then he mounted the machine. When the engine was ticking over nicely, he jumped off and twisted the accelerator. The Cossack surged forward under its own power, over the edge of the causeway, into the marsh.

He got the handlamp from the field truck. The Vopo had been pitched forward, the machine falling on top of him. It didn't take long to disappear, but Vaughan waited anyway, not satisfied until the surface mud was calm again.

So – one Vopo missing from patrol plus his machine, which with luck would indicate to security that he had defected to the West. And even if the marsh did decide to reveal its secret, there was nothing to indicate anything more than an unfortunate accident.

He got behind the wheel and lit a cigarette. It tasted foul.

He threw it out of the window and drove away, gripping the wheel too tightly.

IV

Vaughan walked down the sloping ramp of planks into the excavation with Brother Gregor and peered along the length of the tunnel.

'How far?' he asked.

'About twenty feet. It's really gone very well.'

It was well lit with electric light bulbs strung from a long flex at regular intervals. The roof and sides were lined with rusting corrugated iron sheets and propped up with baulks of timber.

'You can't exactly swing a pick in there,' Vaughan observed.

'No – admittedly only one man can actually work at the face itself with a labourer at his shoulder to help fill the cart. Four feet wide, three foot six high.'

'Couldn't you advance faster if two men could actually work on the face at the same time?'

'By widening the tunnel? Not really because the volume of soil to be brought out would increase dramatically. I spent some considerable time on the mathematics of it.' Gregor smiled apologetically. 'The engineer in me still comes out occasionally.'

'You're in charge,' Vaughan said. 'After all, as long as that tunnel is wide enough for a man to get through, that's all that's needed.'

'Exactly. I had the same problem during the final days in Stalingrad with trench communication.'

'I can imagine.'

There were three sharp raps from up ahead and Gregor looked up at Konrad and the others standing above. 'Haul away.'

Someone pulled on a rope and as Vaughan watched, a wooden cart mounted on a set of old pram wheels appeared, loaded with earth. It came straight out on crude rails and continued on up the ramp, where Konrad started to shovel the earth into a wheelbarrow.

Vaughan ducked into the tunnel and crawled along the

centrepiece of wooden planks until he came to Franz, crouched at the soil face, hacking away with an old trenching shovel, Florian crouched at his shoulder. They were both stripped to the waist, their bodies streaked with sweat and dirt.

Franz grinned. 'Back again, major. Do you want a shovel?'

'No, thanks,' Vaughan said. 'You seem to be enjoying yourself.'

'A nice, safe, enclosed feeling. Like being back in the womb. And interesting souvenirs.' He searched in the loose soil with his hand and came up with a finger bone. 'There you are. A present from Neustadt.'

Vaughan crawled back, out into the pit and went up the ramp. 'Nothing unpleasant so far?'

Gregor shook his head. 'Only old bones. I've inspected the cemetery and this side is mainly seventeenth-and eighteenth-century.'

'And what comes after?'

Konrad paused, leaning on his shovel. 'Considerably later, I'm afraid. Some graves as recent as last year.'

There was a nasty silence. No one seemed to know what to say and then the barn door opened and Margaret Campbell limped in, no crutches now. Just a heavy walking stick to lean on.

'Supper everyone,' she said, and when she smiled at Vaughan, it was as if a lamp turned on inside.

V

It was towards the end of the meal that the gate bell sounded.

'That should be Berg,' Konrad said. 'I was expecting him tonight.'

He went out and came back presently with the caretaker. Berg was obviously surprised to see Vaughan and stood just inside the room, nervously twisting his cap in his hands.

'You're back, major.'

'So it would appear. What's happening up there?'

'They don't exactly take me into their confidence. I only get to see some things.'

'Get on with it, man,' Vaughan told him.

'Well, Conlin is in good condition. I mean he can walk

under his own power. I saw him leaving van Buren's office this afternoon under guard.'

'Is he still on the third level?'

'Yes.' Berg hesitated. 'They've been concentrating on another man.'

'Who?'

'I overheard Captain Süssmann talking to Becker. It seems this man drove the truck Father Conlin was in when he first came here.'

'And what have they done to him?'

'Everything,' Berg said simply. 'They had him in the yard for hours tied to a pole. I'd say he hasn't got long myself.'

Margaret Campbell's distress was apparent to everyone. Vaughan took her hand under the table and held it tight.

'The Vopo officer – the woman he brought with him? What's her story?'

'Lieutenant Leber. A nurse from the medical corps.' He shrugged. 'Frankly, I hardly ever see her. She's up there with van Buren most of the time.'

There was a pause while Vaughan thought about it, then he nodded. 'All right, you'd better stay and hear what I have to say as you'll be a part of it.' He stood up. 'Tonight I drove here in a Vopo field truck, a troop carrier. It's in one of the sheds in the courtyard.'

'And that's our way out when the time comes?' Konrad asked.

'Exactly. There are Vopo uniforms and rifles in the back for everyone including you. Berg. Even if the whole countryside is roused, in such a vehicle, you'd never be questioned.'

Berg cleared his throat. 'But surely all border posts would be notified by phone to allow no traffic through.'

'Exactly,' Vaughan said. 'By happy chance, the one we shall use is in the hands of friends.'

'And what about a timetable?' Margaret Campbell asked. 'How can you possibly arrange that?'

'No need for one.' He went to the sideboard and picked up a leather army knapsack. He brought it back to the table, opened it and took out a small black wireless transmitter.

'You intend radio communications?' Konrad said. 'But such a thing is madness. The security forces have dozens of units whose sole task is to monitor all radio frequencies. They would track you down in a matter of hours.'

'Exactly,' Vaughan said. 'But bear with me and you'll understand. At Bitterfeld, from next Wednesday on, my friends will be on constant standby. A Storch spotter plane is waiting with a pilot who has made this sort of flight many times. The day I decide to go in for Conlin, this transmitter is switched on. It sends out an ultra-high-frequency signal, specially coded, and switches itself off automatically after two minutes. That alerts them at Bitterfeld. That procedure will be repeated the moment I bring Conlin out, and when that signal is received at Bitterfeld, the Storch will take off.'

'And how long will the flight take?' Margaret asked.

'Twenty minutes at the outside. The pilot will land at a spot called Water Horse Meadow by the Elbe about half a mile from here.'

'But can he land in such a place at night?'

'This pilot can and I have all the help he needs right here in this knapsack, Konrad will deliver me to the landing site with Conlin. The old man and I will return to Bitterfeld in the Storch.'

'And the rest of us?' Berg demanded.

'Konrad drives back here to pick you all up, in uniform, of course.' He smiled at the girl. 'There's even one for you.'

'I didn't know they made them that small.'

'Neither did I. You'll have to pull your cap down over your eyes. There's a map in the truck with the fastest route to Flossen clearly marked. You'd better find time to memorize that, Konrad.'

'Of course.'

'And one more thing and burn this into your brains. On the night in question, whenever it is, it's absolutely essential that everyone does what they have to exactly on time. If anyone is missing at the final stage, then they're on their own.' He turned to Konrad. 'You don't hang about for anyone.'

Berg shook his head. 'Crazy,' he said. 'Absolutely crazy.'

'No, it isn't,' Konrad told him. 'It's really very simple, if you think about it. One part fitting neatly into another like a good Swiss watch.'

'And you know what happens to those when something goes

wrong with one of the parts,' Berg said morosely. He pulled on his cap. 'Anyway, I'd better be off. I'll see you again the day after tomorrow.'

Konrad took him out and the others got up. 'Back to the salt mines,' Franz said cheerfully and they all went out.

The girl turned to Vaughan and there was concern in her eyes. 'You look tired.'

For a moment he almost told her of the incident on the causeway. That he had recently killed a man. But it was better left unsaid. She was not someone who would ever be able to accept such things lightly, however good the cause.

'I must be getting old,' he said, and smiled.

Konrad came back in. 'What time do you leave?'

Vaughan glanced at his watch. 'In about an hour. My contact man expects me at one o'clock on the dot.'

The girl put a hand on his arm. 'You're going back tonight?'

'Yes, it's necessary. I've got things to do. But I'll be back next Wednesday. You know about that.'

Konrad said, 'You think it will work, this scheme of yours?'

'I don't see why not.'

'And Father Hartmann? You haven't told him?'

'I'd rather present him with the situation as a fact. He might argue about it.'

'You know best.' Konrad hesitated, glancing from one to the other. 'I'll leave you for a while, if I may, and see how things are progressing in the barn.'

He went out. Vaughan lit a cigarette. Margaret Campbell folded her arms and leaned back in her chair, watching him.

'How long have I known you? A year? A hundred?'

'It never pays to be specific.'

'Have you any idea how I felt on the bridge that morning? How much I wanted to tell you everything?'

He leaned across and touched her face. 'More water under the bridge.'

'And you believe in all this?' she said. 'Believe in what you're doing? You must do. You couldn't go to such lengths otherwise.'

'If you mean do I dislike what goes on over here, then you'd be right,' he said. 'There are thirty thousand troops guarding the wall, did you know that? Any soldier who prevents the escape of a fellow guard gets promotion two ranks, the Merit Badge of the National People's Army, five hundred marks and a vacation in Moscow for two. I don't suppose they told you that at university.'

'No, they didn't.'

'Not that it's doing the bastards much good. More than two thousand guards have defected already. You see, they'd rather experience the fleshpots of Western capitalism than the purity of Marxist ideology.'

'You're angry,' she said.

'Am I?'

'Tell me about Borneo.'

'Why?'

'I'd like to know, from your point of view. Please.'

She laid a hand on his arm very lightly.

VI

'Last year, in Borneo, there was an area around Kota Baru that was absolutely controlled by terrorists and most of them weren't Indonesians. They were Chinese Communist infiltrators. They burned villages wholesale, coerced the Dyaks into helping them by butchering every second man or woman in some of the villages they took, just to encourage the others.'

'And they put you in to do something about it?'

'I was supposed to be an expert in that sort of thing so they gave me command of a company of irregulars, Dyak scouts, and told me to clean things up. I didn't have much luck until they burned the mission at Kota Baru, raped and murdered four nuns and eighteen girls. That was it as far as I was concerned.'

'What did you do?'

'An informer tipped me off that a Chinese merchant in Selangar named Hui Lui was a Communist·agent. I arrested him and when he refused to talk, handed him over to the Dyaks.'

'To torture him?'

'He only lasted a couple of hours, then he told me where the group I'd been chasing were holed up.'

'And did you get them?'

'Eventually. They split into two groups which didn't help, but we managed it.'

'They said you shot your prisoners.'

'Only during the final pursuit when I was hard on the heels of the second group. Prisoners would have delayed me.'

'I see. And Mr Hui Lui?'

'Shot trying to escape. Absolutely true and that's the most ironic part of it. I was quite prepared to take him down to the coast and let him stand trial, but he tried to make a break for it the night before we left.'

'And do you regret any of this now?'

'What I did to him he'd have done to me. The purpose of terrorism is to terrorize. Lenin said it first and it's on page one of every Communist handbook on revolutionary warfare. You can only fight that kind of fire with fire. I did what had to be done. Malaya, Kenya, Cyprus, Aden. I'd seen it all and I was tired of people justifying the murder of the innocent by pleading it was all in the name of the cause. When I finished, there was no more terror by night in Kota Baru. No more butchering of little girls. That should count for something, God knows.'

Her face was very calm, the eyes hooded, brooding, arms folded beneath her breasts as she leaned on the table. 'So you ruined yourself. Career, reputation – everything.'

'I'd better go now.'

He got up, took his long dispatch-rider's raincoat from behind the door and buttoned it up. He slung the AK assault rifle across his chest and put on his helmet, adjusting the strap. 'Will I do?'

'I should think so.'

He had the door open when she said softly, 'I see now what it was I saw in you from that first moment – sensed and never understood. There is always in your heart, I think, a sense of justice outraged.'

There was silence between them. The door closed softly and he was gone.

VII

It was just after 2 a.m. and Meyer was lying in one of the narrow military cots of Bitterfeld, blankets piled thickly about him, for he felt the cold easily. He was reading one of Vaughan's books, a critical appreciation of the philosophy of Heidegger.

The door opened and Vaughan came in. 'Simon, you're back!' Meyer said.

'You sound surprised.' Vaughan stripped off his helmet and raincoat, sat wearily on the edge of the bed and lit a cigarette.

'Everything go all right?'

'I had to kill a Vopo prowler guard who tried to stop me on the road.'

'My God!'

'Don't worry. I dumped him and his motor-cyle in a place called the Holstein Marsh. With any luck, his superiors will think he's defected.'

'There are times when all you can do is close the windows and wait for darkness to pass,' Meyer said gravely.

'A century or so ago when I was seventeen, I used to go dancing, Julius, at the old Trocadero. Your kind of music. You'd have loved it.

'So what's the point?'

'That seventeen is an age of infinite promise. Seventeen is walking girls home five miles from a dance in the rain for not much more than a kiss. Seventeen is being filled with a restless excitement, the knowledge that something is waiting just around the next corner. Seventeen is standing under a street lamp with a girl in your arms and rain drifting down like silver spray.'

Meyer said, 'That was then, this is now, Simon. You're thirty-seven years of age and you've been a professional soldier for twenty of them. Let's face it, business is business and killing is your trade. You can't stop. Malaya, Kenya, Cyprus – all those little wars you served in. Now this. For you, there'll always be another little war because you can't stop it, this game you play. In the end it has you by the balls, my friend, and one day, no matter how good you are, how smart, a sniper is waiting on a rooftop somewhere to put a bullet in your back. No honour there.'

'I spent two years in a Chinese prison camp,' Vaughan said wearily. 'That's honour enough for one lifetime.'

'You're damaged goods, Simon. Let her go, there's a good boy. Get her out safe for a mitzvah, a good deed, then let her go. She's entitled to a life.'

Vaughan got undressed and climbed into the other bed. Meyer said, 'Do you mind if I keep on reading? Does the light bother you?'

'No.'

'Interesting fellow, this Heidegger. He says that for authentic living what is necessary is the resolute confrontation of death. Do you agree?'

Vaughan's voice was muffled when he replied, 'A good man in his day, Heidegger. Just like me.'

VIII

Walter Ulbricht's office was furnished with spartan simplicity. A framed photograph of Stalin with a dedication occupied a prominent position on one wall and the generally chilly atmosphere was not solely the product of the Comrade Chairman's well-known dislike of central heating.

Early morning sunlight streamed into the room through one of the narrow windows, but did little to lighten the sombre atmosphere as he sat there at the desk, methodically working his way through a pile of papers presented to him by a male secretary, signing the occasional letter where requested.

There was a tap at the door and Helmut Klein entered. He made a distinguished enough looking figure in the heavy overcoat with the fur collar, and yet in the presence of the older man he seemed to shrink. Ulbricht ignored him for a while, continuing to sign letters. Finally he paused, removed his glasses and ran a hand over his eyes.

'Leave us,' he said softly, and the secretary went to the door at once, opened it and left without a word.

Ulbricht looked up at the other man for a full minute before speaking. 'Well, Klein, I'm waiting. I've been back from Moscow two days and no word from you.'

'Comrade Chairman,' Klein began, 'these things take time.'

'You told me that this American, van Buren, was the best. I wasn't happy about his lack of political commitment, but you assured me that didn't matter. You promised me results. In fact, it wouldn't be exaggerating the position to say that you actually guaranteed me results.'

Klein's mouth was bone dry. He moistened his lips and managed to whisper, 'Yes, Comrade Chairman.'

'Good. Failure in this affair will not be tolerated. I hold you personally responsible. I look forward to hearing from you soon with favourable news.'

He picked up his pen and returned to his documents and Klein got out as fast as he could

IX

He had his driver take him to the Ministry of State Security at Normannenstrasse at once. When he entered the outer office of Section Five, Frau Apel rose to greet him. 'Good morning, colonel. The Leipzig office has been on the line.'

'Never mind that now,' Klein told her. 'Get me Captain Süssmann at Schloss Neustadt.'

He went into his office and sat behind his desk without taking off his coat. He saw now that he stood on the brink of a precipice. He had placed his life, his career, entirely in Harry van Buren's hands.

The phone rang, and when he picked it up the voice said, 'Süssmann here.'

'What's happening there, Süssmann? Is he getting anywhere? The truth, now.'

'Not in my opinion. Too much conversation. Now if Sergeant Becker and I could have a free hand . . .'

'No,' Klein said. 'Another week and then we review the situation. Naturally, I expect you to report to me on van Buren's activities in minutest detail.'

'Of course, comrade.'

'This affair could mean considerable advancement for you, Süssmann, if we can reach a successful conclusion.'

'I'll do my best.'

'Another thing. This priest, Hartmann, will be turning up the day after tomorrow. I want to know what he gets up to as well. Telephone me at any hour. You have the private number where you can reach me at night if I'm not at the office. Now transfer me to van Buren.'

X

Van Buren was alone in his office with Ruth Leber, going over his notes on the last session with Conlin when the phone rang.

He picked it up and Klein said Cheerfully, 'Hello Harry, I haven't heard from you for a few days so I thought I'd see how things were going.'

'Fine,' van Buren said. 'I'm making real progress.'

'Good. It's just that I had to see Chairman Ulbricht on other matters this morning and he did mention the Conlin affair. He told me he expects to see some really positive result quite soon now. If Conlin's trial is to coincide with Kennedy's visit, then preparations must be put in hand as soon as possible.'

'I see.'

'Would it help if I came down?'

'No, that wouldn't do at all,' van Buren said hastily. 'The whole technique of this thing depends on the closeness of my personal contact with him. The fact that no one else is allowed to enter the private area of our relationship.'

'A week, Harry, that's all I can give you.'

'But that's ridiculous.'

'No, it isn't. It's Ulbricht.'

The line went dead. Van Buren replaced his receiver and sat there frowning.

'Trouble?' Ruth Leber asked.

'No, I don't think so. We're just going to have to move a little faster, that's all.' He stood up. 'I think I'll have another word with Conlin.'

XI

When he opened the cell door, Conlin was sitting on the bed staring at the wall. He looked very frail, the flesh on his face reduced so that every bone showed clearly.

'You don't look too good,' van Buren said.

'I'm getting old, that's all.'

Van Buren lit a cigarette and the smoke was pungent on the cold air. Conlin smiled drily. 'A waste of time. I've gone through my nicotine withdrawal symptoms. I haven't breathed so well in years. You've done me a favour there, Harry.'

It was totally unexpected, the use of his name and van Buren was aware of a spurt of anger – or was he trying to rationalize a fear syndrome? Perhaps deep inside he felt the old man's familiarity as a personal threat.

He said to Becker, 'Bring him along,' went out and along the passage and unbolted the door to another cell.

The truck-driver, Karl, lay in the corner. Blood oozed from his nostrils, the corner of his mouth, his eyes were fixed as if on some spot in the middle distance.

'We pride ourselves on a sense of logic and order,' van Buren said, 'but inside, we are savages. A predisposition to violence is man's most enduring attribute.'

Conlin got down on his knees painfully and leaned over the broken body. There was a flicker of recognition, the lips moved. Karl said, 'Save me, Father. Help me.'

He tried to clutch at the old man's shirt front, but he hadn't the strength, and slumped back again. 'For pity's sake, Harry,' Conlin said, 'get him a doctor.'

'Too late,' van Buren told him. 'But I've done the next best thing. I've brought him a priest.'

He went out, the door closed, the bolts rammed home. Conlin put an arm around Karl and leaned the broken head against his shoulder.

'Karl,' he whispered, 'I want you to make an act of contrition. Say after me, O my God, who art infinitely good in thyself . . .'

12

L'OSSERVATORE Romano is one of the world's oldest newspapers, but its distribution is not confined to the Vatican alone and there are special weekly versions in English, French, Spanish and Portuguese.

Although the editorial staff pride themselves on their coverage of general world news, there is little doubt that anything of significance to the position of the Roman Catholic Church has special importance for them. The report from one of their German correspondents was received on Wednesday morning and a reporter took it straight into Manzini, the managing editor.

'Where did this come from?' he asked.

'West Berlin. You think there could be any truth in it?'

'I don't know. If there is, it could be a hot one. Leave it with me and I don't want it discussed. Not with anyone.'

The reporter went out. Manzini sat there thinking about it for a while, then reached for his phone and told his secretary to get him the Father General of the Jesuits at the Collegio di San Roberto Bellarmino.

II

Over six hundred thousand people, the greatest number ever assembled to honour a Roman pontiff, had filed past the embalmed body of Pope John as it lay in state for three days in St Peter's Basilica. In addition to the Italian president and his entire cabinet, diplomatic representatives of fifty-five countries had been among the mourners. And finally, he was buried in the Crypt of St Peter in private, in accordance with his dying wish.

For Pacelli, it had been a busy time. So many Church dignitaries arriving in Rome from all over the world; conferences to attend with various departments of the Italian security services; new policies to be hammered out.

When he knocked on the door and went in, the Father General was standing by the window. He turned. 'Ah, there you are. I've just had Manzini on the phone, from *L'Osservatore Romano*. They've got wind of the Conlin affair.'

'To what extent?'

'A minor report from one of their Berlin correspondents, totally unconfirmed, that Conlin has disappeared and that the East Germans have him.'

'What did you tell Manzini?'

'I asked him not to use the story, naturally. I told him that matters of the gravest security were concerned. He agreed at once. He is a man of the utmost dependability. He did point out that if the rumour exists, then sooner or later it must come to the attention of other news agencies, and there is nothing we can do about that.'

'An unfortunate situation,' Pacelli said. 'It's amazing how minor leaks of this nature can take place, no matter how strict one's security system. I'll see about the other news agencies. We do have a certain influence in these areas.'

'Do what you can.'

'May I remind you that it is today that Father Hartmann proceeds to Neustadt?'

The Father General, who had sat down behind his desk, looked up. 'Then we must pray for him.'

'Indeed we must,' Pacelli said, 'for he will need all our prayers, I think.'

III

In the basement garage of the Catholic Secretariat in East Berlin, Erich Hartmann was loading his suitcase into the back of the Volkswagen. The garage was dimly lit. There were only two other cars to be seen and a State Medical Service ambulance. He wondered what it was doing there and then there was the rattle of a motor-cycle engine and Schaefer came down the ramp on his BMW.

He wore his trenchcoat, a cap and goggles, and there was

a canvas suitcase strapped to the luggage carrier of the BMW. He pulled the machine up on its stand and walked across, pushing up his goggles.

'Why couldn't we have gone down this afternoon, Father, in daylight? I hate biking after dark.'

'I had a considerable amount of paperwork to clear up this afternoon,' Hartmann said, which was not strictly true. He had left his departure until eight o'clock at night because Pascoe had asked him to, although there had been no explanation why.

'All right, Father, we might as well get started.'

'This is nonsense,' Hartmann said. 'Why can't you drive down with me in comfort?'

'Regulations,' Schaefer replied. 'Where you go, I follow.'

'Which seems to me to be stretching bureaucracy to the limits.'

'That's democratic socialism for you, Father.'

Hartmann smiled. 'How's your wife?'

'Glad to get rid of me for a week,' Schaefer grinned. 'I'll tell you what, Father. Half-way there on the far side of Rathenow there's a roadside café called the Astor. Pull up there and I'll let you buy me a coffee.'

'Done,' Hartmann said, and he got into the Volkswagen and drove out of the garage.

Schaefer paused to pull on his gloves and a voice called softly from behind, 'Excuse me.'

He turned and found a tall man advancing towards him, hands in pockets. There was something strange about him, something Schaefer couldn't put his finger on, and then he realized what it was. The other man was wearing a trenchcoat that was twin to his own, tweed cap, navy blue polo-neck sweater, grey tweed trousers. All the same.

'Horst Schaefer?'

Schaefer, sensing that something was very badly wrong here, reached for the holstered Walther under his left armpit. Too late; for already he found himself staring down the muzzle of its twin.

'So am I,' Vaughan smiled.

The ambulance rolled forward and braked to a halt and two men in white uniforms got out. One of them jerked

Schaefer's arms behind and handcuffed him and Vaughan removed his wallet. He took out the identity papers only and slipped them into one of Schaefer's pockets. He kept the more personal items, a letter from Schaefer's father, a couple of snaps of his wife and children.

He produced identical identity papers which he slipped into the wallet, then put it in his own inside breast pocket. He removed Schaefer's goggles and put them on.

'What is this?' Schaefer was frightened now. 'Who are you?'

'I'm Horst Schaefer,' Vaughan told him amicably. 'These two gentlemen are members of what you could call an illegal organization – the Christian Underground. I wouldn't advise you to give them any trouble. They're not too good at turning the other cheek.'

One of them led Schaefer to the rear of the ambulance, the other opened the door and they pushed him inside and down on one of the bunks. Before he knew what was happening, a hypodermic appeared and the needle was jammed into his arm, right through the leather sleeve.

On the opposite bunk there was a body totally covered by a red blanket. Vaughan pulled it back to disclose the waxen features of a young girl, eyes closed in death.

'We always try to make it a young girl. It makes the Vopos feel bad at the checkpoint.'

'I don't understand.' Schaefer could hardly keep his eyes open now and his limbs felt as heavy as lead.

'Into the Western Zone. All quite legitimate. These gentlemen have got the papers.'

A concealed trap was lifted in the floor, a space revealed about the size of a coffin. Schaefer was lowered into it, his senses already slipping away from him as the lid was lowered.

IV

It was a quiet night at the Astor café. There were only four people in the place, the girl behind the counter, two truck-drivers having their evening meal and Erich Hartmann who sat with a cup of coffee in front of him at a corner table.

He made a conspicuous enough figure in his broad-brimmed

shovel hat and black cassock and the others watched him curiously. He wondered what could be keeping Schaefer, for traffic on the road had been light. He became aware of the sound of a motor-cycle engine outside and looked out and saw the BMW turn into the car park and pull up beside the Volkswagen.

'Fräulein?' he called to the girl. 'Another coffee, if you please.'

A moment later, the door opened. He turned with a smile and then the smile faded as, to his total astonishment, Simon Vaughan entered the café.

V

Vaughan spooned sugar into his coffee. Hartmann waited for the girl to go back behind the counter before whispering, 'What on earth is going on here?'

Vaughan took out his wallet, extracted his card and passed it over. 'Horst Schaefer, your friendly local SSD man.'

The card was a perfect facsimile of Schaefer's own, except that the thumbprint, the physical characteristics, where appropriate, and the photo, were Vaughan's.

Hartmann passed the card back. 'Where's Schaefer? What have you done with him?'

'Should be in West Berlin right about now,' Vaughan told him. 'Sleeping soundly and when he wakes up, he'll find Bruno Teusen at his bedside.'

Hartmann's face was calm, but there was anger in the eyes and his right fist had clenched. 'Why wasn't this discussed with me?'

'Because it was felt you might argue about it. Now you can't.'

'Damn you, Vaughan.'

'Strong words for a man of the cloth, Father,' Vaughan said. 'And while we're on the subject, why the fancy dress? Conspicuous consumption by any standards, I should have thought.'

'I want them to know who I am when I get to Neustadt. I thought that was the idea. To pull all attention on to me.'

'Something like that,' Vaughan said. 'Well, is it war or peace between us?'

Hartmann smiled ruefully. 'Do I have a choice?'

He got up and moved out and Vaughan followed him.

VI

It was shortly after ten when Hartmann pulled up in front of an inn at Neustadt. A Vopo field car was parked a few yards away. Hartman sat there for a while, then reached for his suitcase and got out. He went up the steps to the entrance, paused, then opened the door.

Georg Ehrlich was behind the bar with Sigrid. Heinrich Berg and half a dozen of the village men sat in a circle together drinking beer, Süssmann and Becker were at a table by the fire, plates of stew before them.

It was Sigrid who saw Hartmann first and sucked in her breath sharply. And then the whole room went silent. Hartmann put down his suitcase and moved to the bar.

'Are you Herr Ehrlich, the mayor here?'

'That's right.'

'My name is Hartmann. I believe you've been warned to expect me. I'm here to consider the question of the church.'

Ehrlich's eyes flickered nervously to the two Vopos by the fire. 'Yes,' he said slowly. 'I received word from the Ministry of State Security some days ago. 'You're wasting your time here, Father, you must know that.'

The door opened and Vaughan entered carrying his canvas holdall. 'So you made it, Father?' Heinrich Berg stared at him, his mouth gaping in astonishment, a kind of horror in his eyes, and Vaughan nodded, cheerfully.

Süssmann got up, wiping his mouth on a napkin and walked across the room. He stood for a moment, looking them both over. 'Papers,' he said curtly.

Hartmann handed him his Ministry of State Security permit. Süssmann examined it, handed it back to him without a word, then turned to Vaughan.

'And you?'

'Schaefer – Section Six.'

Vaughan proffered his SSD card and Süssmann checked it. 'So where he goes, you follow?'

'Something like that.'

He returned Vaughan's card and Hartmann said, 'Would you be the military commander of this area?'

'No,' Süssmann said. 'Why do you ask?'

'I was told to report my presence to him on arrival.'

Süssmann hesitated. 'The person you seek is busy tonight. You must try tomorrow. In the morning at Schloss Neustadt.'

He walked back to the table and sat down, saying something to Becker who laughed coarsely. Hartmann said, 'Have you room for us to stay, Herr Ehrlich?'

Ehrlich shook his head. 'That is not possible.'

'I see,' Hartmann said calmly. 'Is there a priest's house still?'

'Yes,' Ehrlich said reluctantly. 'But it has not been used for some time. I have the key.'

'Perhaps if you could spare a few blankets,' Hartmann said, 'I'm sure Herr Schaefer and I could manage, unless, of course, you can find him room here.'

Ehrlich looked hunted and Vaughan said cheerfully, 'Can't let you out of my sight, now can I, Father? I think we'd better stick together.'

'All right,' Ehrlich said. 'I'll find you some blankets and get the key.'

'And the church?' Hartmann said. 'Have you the key to the church?'

'The church stays locked.' It was Süssmann who had spoken.

Hartmann turned to look at him and Ehrlich said hurriedly, 'I'll get the blankets,' and fled.

The villagers were discussing the situation among themselves in low tones and Hartmann and Vaughan sat down at a table to wait. Sigrid brought two beers without a word. She was a pretty girl in traditional costume, her flaxen hair plaited about her head. She gazed at Hartmann in fascination, unable to take her eyes off him.

He toasted her, 'Thank you, that's very kind.'

Becker got up and swaggered forward, a stein of beer in his left hand. He emptied it, put it down on the table and stood over Hartmann, looking down at him contemptuously.

'Skirts on men. What next?' He made a kissing sound with his lips and patted Hartmann's cheek.

Hartmann's hand fastened around his wrist and the smile was wiped from Becker's face. He staggered, then fell to one knee, forced down by the relentless pressure of all that enormous strength. Hartmann released him suddenly so that Becker lost his balance and fell back. His rage was terrible to see and he pulled at the flap of his pistol-holster.

'Becker!' Süssmann called. 'Enough!'

The sergeant got to his feet, his hand on the butt of his Walther now. This time, when Süssmann spoke there was iron in his voice. 'Becker! For the last time!'

The sergeant went back to the table and Ehrlich returned with the blankets and an oil lamp. 'All right, gentlemen, if you'll follow me.'

VII

The house was next to the church, a small, two-storeyed building with wooden shutters which were closed.

'I'm surprised you haven't let someone move in,' Hartmann said.

'There is no shortage of housing in this village, Father. Agriculture is declining in these parts and most young people move to Berlin if they can to get work in the factories there. I'm afraid the electricity is not connected, which is why I've brought the oil lamp, but there's water on tap and a lavatory. You should be all right.'

The front door opened on to a stone-flagged passage. There was a wooden staircase going to the upper floor and he led the way along to the kitchen. There was a wooden table, chairs and an old iron stove.

'Plenty of wood out at the back if you want to light a fire. Two bedrooms upstairs. I don't know what condition the mattresses will be in.'

'We'll manage,' Hartmann said. 'You've been very kind.'

'That's all right, Father,' Ehrlich told him gruffly. For a moment it seemed as if he might say something more; then he thought better of it and went out.

'Now what?' Hartmann said.

'Make a fire. Fill in a little time. Then I'd like to see how the Franciscans have been getting on.'

'May I come with you?'

'If you like. One thing is definite. We stay as far away from that place as possible during the day. Not even a hint of a connection.'

'As you say.'

Vaughan lit a cigarette. 'I like what you did to that big ox back at the inn. I didn't know your lot went in for things like that.'

'Soldiers of Christ, Major Vaughan. Didn't you know?' Hartmann picked up the lamp. 'And now, I'll see if I can find some wood in the yard.'

VIII

The gate bell made a lonely sound, rather eerie, and there was no response for some considerable time, then footsteps. The shutter was opened and frail old Brother Urban peered out. The bolt was withdrawn, he opened the gate.

'Major,' he said in his dry old voice. 'They're in the barn.'

'How are things?'

'Not good.'

It was the smell which was most noticeable the moment Vaughan opened the door. Konrad and Florian were loading on the edge of the excavation and both of them were wearing bandages wrapped about their faces to cover mouth and nose. The half-light of the barn enhanced the effect, strange and disturbing.

When Konrad paused to speak, leaning wearily on his shovel, his voice was thick, muffled. 'Good, you made it. Did everything go all right?'

'Perfectly. This is Father Hartmann.'

'I won't shake hands,' Konrad said. 'For obvious reasons.'

Hartmann moved to the edge of the excavation, his face pale. 'Is it bad in there?'

'I'm afraid so. We've made excellent progress, but we've started to hit more recent graves and it isn't nice.'

'That smell is terrible.'

There was a movement down below and someone emerged

on hands and knees. When he stood, Vaughan saw that it was Gregor, in spite of the fact that the head was swathed in bandages as well as the mouth and nose. He carried a piece of sacking in both hands, holding it out in front of him, and from the bulge it was obvious that it contained something.

'An arm, or what's left of one,' he said to Konrad. 'It's not going to be pleasant getting the rest out.'

He went through to the other room. 'The well?' Vaughan asked.

Konrad nodded. 'Then lime and more soil. Nothing else we can do.'

'Where's Doctor Campbell?'

'In the house attending to Franz. He cut himself and she's most insistent that every injury, even the slightest scratch, is treated at once.'

'We'll have a word with her.'

They found her in the kitchen with Franz who was stripped to the waist. There was a large zinc bath of heavily disinfected water on the table and an assortment of drugs. She was giving him an injection as they went in and Vaughan saw the dressing at once on the boy's left arm, fastened into place by surgical tape.

'Simon.' She smiled, but her cheeks were sunken.

'How goes it?'

'Fine. Have you seen Konrad?'

'Yes, we took a look. Nasty.'

Franz said, 'I'll get back now.'

'And don't forget,' she told him. 'The slightest thing – any kind of ache or pain or headache – come and see me at once.'

'Fräulein.' He grinned. 'I ache all over already.'

He went out and she said, 'So this is Father Hartmann.'

Hartmann took her hand and smiled warmly. 'A pleasure Fräulein. I've heard a great deal about you.'

'Can I get you coffee?'

He hesitated, glancing at Vaughan. 'No, thanks. I think I'd like to go back to the barn. There may be something I could do.'

'Tea and sympathy,' Vaughan said with brutal directness. 'No more than that. They've got their job to do – you have yours. I don't want you getting your cassock dirty. Spend too much time in there and the villagers will smell you coming as you cross the square.'

'All right,' Hartmann said angrily, 'I take your point.'

When he'd gone, Vaughan turned to the girl. She was putting the kettle on the stove and turned to face him, looking tired and somehow past everything that ever was and totally vulnerable.

'You've no idea how glad I am to see you,' she said and came into his arms.

Every resolve he had made faded away. He held her close. 'Bad, is it?'

When she looked up at him, her eyes were filled with a deep disgust. 'Horrible, Simon. Like something out of a nightmare and the trouble is, I think it's going to get worse.'

IV

It was cold in the early dawn and still dark when the two Vopos dragged Conlin into the courtyard. He stood between them, shivering, wondering what was to come. The headlamps of a field car parked close by were switched on and their twin shafts picked Karl out of the darkness, strapped to a post in the centre of the courtyard.

Süssmann and Becker appeared and the captain said, 'Bring him,' and went forward with the sergeant, the two Vopos dragging Conlin behind.

Karl hung in the straps, his head lolling to one side. Becker peered closely at him. 'I think he's dead,' he announced.

'Make sure,' Süssmann said coldly.

Becker took out his Walther, cocked it and fired into the skull at point blank range. Pieces of bone and blood sprayed, the body sagged. Conlin cried out sharply. Süssmann and Becker walked away, the two Vopos released their grip and Conlin sank to the ground at Karl's feet, all strength going out of him.

Footsteps approached, the damp air was scented with cigarette smoke. Harry van Buren squatted beside him.

'You could have prevented this if you'd been sensible. He'd have still been alive if it hadn't been for that incredible self-righteousness of yours. The insistence that you must be right in all things, even when it kills people.'

'Go away,' Father Conlin said in a low voice.

'Like poor Karl here,' van Buren told him. 'Or your sister.'

He stood up and walked away quite quickly, his footsteps echoing on the cobbles. Conlin crouched there, his head against Karl's knee.

'Oh dear God, Frances Mary,' he said. 'I never wanted it, you know that.'

For the first time in years he started to cry.

X

Vaughan and Hartmann sat on two chairs on the landing outside van Buren's office and waited. After a while, Vaughan got up, went to the balustrade and looked down at the imposing sweep of the great staircase, the hall below.

'Perfect for a remake of *The Prisoner of Zenda*, but not exactly comfortable,' Hartmann remarked.

The door opened and Süssmann looked out. 'He'll see you now – together.'

Hartmann led the way into the room, Vaughan at his heels and Süssmann closed the door behind them and stood against it. Van Buren waited, seated at his desk. Hartmann produced his permit.

Van Buren ignored it and looked him over, an amused, slightly contemptuous smile on his face. 'Are you going to a costume ball?'

'I think you know why I am here,' Hartmann said carefully. 'I was ordered to report to the area commander on arrival and I have now done so. Am I permitted to leave?'

'Very good,' van Buren clapped his hands solemnly. 'Nothing like a religious education for teaching a man how to behave.'

'I heard you lecture at Dresden three months ago. The Psychological Basis of Religious Persuasion. You were very eloquent.'

'But failed to make my case?'

Hartmann said, 'I happen to believe that in every human

being there is something profound and mysterious that can never answer to your more rational explanation.'

Van Buren held up a hand to cut him off. 'No, thanks, I'm not interested in philosophical argument, not at this time of day. Let's stick to the facts. Just what do you intend to to while you're here?'

'Examine the state of the church. Meet the people. Discuss their religious needs.'

'With a view to re-opening the church itself?'

'If that is what people want. The right of cach and every citizen to follow the religion of his choice is part of the constitution.'

'So is censorship of the papers. And the fact that trade unions are forbidden the right to strike. Which is right, which is wrong!'

'I thought you said you'd no time for philosophical discussion at the moment?'

Van Buren smiled. 'Your point, Father.' He lit a cigarette and leaned back. 'All right. Play your little games if you must, but don't get underfoot. Any incident of the most minor nature and I'll have you back to Berlin within the hour.'

'As you say. There is one thing. I understand you have the key of the church?'

Van Buren sat staring up at him for a while, then opened a drawer, took out three large keys on a ring and threw them across the desk. 'There you are, but no public services.'

'Which means you think I'll actually get a congregation. Thank you. That's most encouraging. And thank you for your time.'

Hartmann moved to the door. As Süssmann opened it for him, van Buren said in English, 'They tell me you were at Notre Dame. All-American quarterback two years running.'

'That's right.'

Van Buren laughed. 'A jock,' he said. 'In a black frock. That I should live to see the day.'

Hartmann refused to be drawn and went out without a word. Van Buren laughed, got up and moved to the fire, not a bit put out. He threw on another log and turned to Vaughan. 'So you're Schaefer?' he said in German.

'That's right, comrade.'

'I hear you've moved into the priest's house with him.'

'There was little choice. The mayor said he couldn't accommodate us at the inn and besides, I like to stick close to him. That's my job.'

'And that's exactly what you will do,' van Buren said. 'Stick like glue. Anything he does that's the slightest bit out of the ordinary, I want to know about it.'

'You're in charge, comrade.'

Van Buren nodded. 'All right. On your way and stay in touch.'

Vaughan went out and Süssmann closed the door.

'Are you going to let him get away with it, this priest?'

'His permit is signed by the Minister for State Security himself. All a question of politics, Süssmann. Tell Lieutenant Leber I want her, will you?'

The captain went out and van Buren sat down at his desk and, opening a drawer in search of blank paper, discovered the Russian grenades again. He took one out and saw that it was very similar in design to the American version. A ring pin to pull with finger or teeth, the safety-lever to hold until the final second before throwing.

He was handling one when Süssmann came back. 'Nasty little item,' van Buren said.

'A fragmentation grenade.'

'Yes, we used babies like this in Korea and they suffer from the defects of their kind. If you ever want to throw one, make sure you're under cover. They can scatter fragments for a two hundred metre radius.'

Süssmann, who had never seen action and secretly envied van Buren his war experience, nodded. 'I'll remember that, comrade. Lieutenant Leber will be along in a moment.'

'Good.'

'Is there anything else, comrade?'

'Yes, you'd better bring Conlin up here again and we'll see how he's getting on.'

— 13 —

THE CHURCH WAS cold and smelt of damp, which was only to be expected. It was rather dark, the glass of its narrow windows stained in sombre hues that were not particularly pleasing.

'Nineteenth-century,' Hartmann said. 'But these pillars are medieval.'

It took Vaughan straight back to his boyhood and the forced attendance at church each Sunday evening with his grandmother. There had been a church smell then, there was a church smell now. Nothing changed.

There was a row of oak pews on either side of the aisle, a small dark chapel to the left with an image of the Virgin floating there in the half-light. Hartmann walked along the aisle and genuflected in front of the altar.

Vaughan followed him and Hartmann said, 'See, here beside the altar rail.'

There was a square hole set into the floor and lined with brass.

'What is it?' Vaughan asked.

'The socket for St Michael's Cross, I should imagine.' He stared across the church, a slight frown on his face. 'There's something unusual here. Have you noticed how clean everything is?' He ran a finger along the altar rail. 'Not only is there no dust, but it smells of polish.'

He crossed to the sacristy and opened the door. There wasn't much in there. A table, chairs, a cupboard which, when he opened it, contained the church registers and also a plentiful supply of candles.

It was Vaughan who made the most interesting discovery of all, for when he tried the side door, it proved to be unlocked and opened to his touch.

'Now, what do you make of that?' he asked. 'At least we

now know how the cleaning staff get in.'

'I wonder if our friend the mayor knows about this?' Hartmann tried the light switch which proved to work. 'See,' he said. 'Even the electricity is still connected, which is more than you can say for the house. I wonder why?'

Vaughan lit a cigarette. 'Probably there are hordes of lovable peasants out there just aching to come back to the arms of Mother Church.'

'Perhaps,' Hartmann said. 'Tell me, do you think it at all possible that Brother Konrad and his friends might manage what he was talking about last night?'

'What, break through within the next three days? I don't see why not. Is it important?' And then Vaughan saw the way things were going. 'You'd like more time here, is that it? You'd like to really get your teeth into the situation. Well, forget it, Father. We're not here to save souls. We're here to save Conlin.'

Hartmann didn't reply, but got up and went back into the church. Vaughan sat there finishing his cigarette, and suddenly, to his complete astonishment, heard organ music.

When he went in, he couldn't see Hartmann at first, then discovered him seated at the organ masked by a curtain above the choir stalls. As Vaughan went up the steps to join him, Hartmann was experimenting, pulling out one stop after another, his hands running over the keys.

'Something else you managed to pick up in the football squad at Notre Dame?'

'Not good,' Hartmann said. 'But not bad. One could hardly expect an outstanding instrument in a village like this and the reed stops have suffered in all this damp.'

He moved into the opening of the Bach Prelude and Fugue in D Major and he was good. Vaughan sat down in one of the choir stalls, hands in pockets, head back, and simply listened, and one didn't have to be a music lover to enjoy it. The music filled the church, echoing into the rafters as Hartmann played on, lost in some private world of his own.

Finally he stopped. Vaughan said quietly, 'You should have made All-American for that, too.'

Hartmann turned on the seat, smiling hugely for the first

time since Vaughan had known him, obviously genuinely pleased, and then he paused, looking out over Vaughan's shoulder.

When Vaughan turned, he found Sigrid Ehrlich sitting in the front pew.

II

A scarf was bound round her head and her tweed coat was simply slung from her shoulders as if put on in a hurry. She sat there, clutching it about her, her eyes never leaving Hartmann, a kind of awe in them.

He came down the steps from the choir stalls, smiling. 'Fräulein Ehrlich, isn't it? It's good to see you here.'

'Father.' Her voice was almost a whisper.

'And what brings you?' He sat down in the pew beside her.

'I could hear the organ.'

'In the inn?'

'Yes.'

'You must forgive me. I was obviously forgetting myself.'

She leaned forward eagerly. 'No – not at all. It was wonderful, It's a long time since I heard anything like it. Father Honecker used to play, but I was only a child then and didn't really appreciate such things.'

'You knew Father Honecker?'

'Oh yes.'

'I see,' Hartmann said carefully. 'Tell me, are you a Catholic, fräulein?'

She flushed. 'I – I am baptized, Father, but there has been no priest here since Father Honecker's death.'

'Yes, I know that.' There was a slight pause. She stared down at her hands, folded now in her lap. Hartmann said gently, 'The church is obviously well looked after. Clean, sweet. Do you do that?' She glanced at Vaughan, her face troubled. 'Come on, you can speak freely. Herr Schaefer won't tell.'

'All right. Several of the older women come in regularly each week.'

'I see.' He was not smiling, but there was a light in his eyes that somehow illuminated his entire face. 'I will pray for you, my child. All of you.'

He started to get up and she caught hold of his sleeve, her face strained and anxious. 'Father, hear my confession.' He seemed transfixed, staring down at her, his face pale.

And suddenly she was on her knees, clutching at his hand, tears running uncontrollably down her cheeks. 'Oh, Father, it's been so long.'

'Of course, my child.' He raised her up and sat her down. 'Stay there.'

He went out into the sacristy and Vaughan followed, but when he got there, there was no sign of Hartmann. He opened the side door and saw the priest going into the house.

Vaughan sat on the table and lit a cigarette. 'Oh my God,' he whispered, 'that's all I need. A truly good man.'

A few moments later, the door opened and Hartmann entered holding a black velvet bag. 'Don't tell me,' Vaughan said. 'Let me guess. Your vestments and other assorted goodies.'

Hartmann opened the bag and started to take things out. 'You surely didn't think I came unprepared, major.' He put on his alb and threw a violet stole over his shoulder.

'Would it be too much to ask you to remember why we're here?'

Hartmann paused, a hand on the door. 'Major Vaughan, there is one thing I have that I share with the pope himself. Whatever else I am, whatever my background, however high I rise, I am still priest, first and foremost. That is something I can never escape. It is my reason for being.'

'So we're back in the drainpipe again?'

'If you like.'

Hartmann went into the church and Vaughan followed him to the door, watched him speak to Sigrid Ehrlich. She stood up and they walked together to the confessional box and entered their separate compartments.

There was a murmur of voices and then the sound of passionate weeping from the girl. Vaughan shivered as if suddenly aware that he had no right to be there. He closed the door softly, let himself out into the garden and walked up and down aimlessly under the plane trees, smoking.

III

It was a good half-hour before Hartmann and the girl appeared. He had taken off his alb and stole and was once more attired in black cassock and dark hat. The girl gazed up at him intently as he talked to her.

As they approached, Hartmann said cheerfully, 'Ah, there you are, Horst. Kind of you to wait.' He smiled down at Sigrid. 'Herr Schaefer is in some respects my keeper.' She glanced up at Vaughan, a certain alarm in her eyes and Hartmann laughed. 'Don't worry. He won't bite. We have what you might call a working relationship.'

He was in excellent spirits, more animated than at any time since Vaughan had known him. 'You've finished in there, I presume?'

'For the moment, yes. Sigrid's going to show us the Cross of St Michael, down by the river.'

'That should be nice,' Vaughan said.

The irony in his voice seemed totally lost on Hartmann. 'How far did you say it was, Sigrid? A mile? Then we'll walk, I think.'

It was a nonsense, of course, the whole affair, but in a sense Vaughan was trapped, a fact of which, he decided, Hartmann was only too well aware. He trailed along behind the priest and the girl, across the square and along the main street, attracting curious glances from the few villagers that they passed. Beyond the last house, the road sloped down to the Elbe between a double row of pine trees and the view was rather beautiful.

At one point, the girl laughed and he heard Hartmann say, 'But there is no law forbidding priests to visit you. Surely one or two must have come here during the past five years, from neighbouring villages perhaps?'

'With Party cards in their pockets,' she said contemptuously. 'They only seem like priests.'

The road turned to the right to follow the course of the river. To the left, a rough track led to a grove of trees and the cross stood there, plain to see, black heavy oak as was the figure of Christ nailed to it. It was obviously the work of a peasant hand and had no great artistic merit, but it possessed a certain dignity for all that. It had been set into the earth and grass grew thickly about the base.

Hartmann stood looking up at the figure of Christ intently. 'And Father Honecker tried to lift this on his own?'

'He must have been mad,' Vaughan said.

'No. Desperate, I think.'

'He died here,' Sigrid said. 'Died trying, here on this very spot.'

Hartmann bowed his head in prayer.

Vaughan took the girl by the elbow and led her some little distance away.

The Elbe rushed by, brown and swollen, and he took out his cigarettes. 'Do you use these things?'

'No,' she said.

'Good for you.' He put one in his mouth and lit it.

'My father says you're a policeman.'

'You could put it that way.'

'Why are you always with Father Hartmann?'

'Oh, he needs looking after, wouldn't you say?'

'He's a good man,' she said. 'A wonderful man.' And turned to where Hartmann stood at the foot of the cross.

His voice was blown to them by the wind, strong and firm. '*Requiem oeternam dona eis, Domine, et lux perpetua luceat eis.*'

He was saying the Mass for the Dead.

IV

On the way back, Vaughan expressed interest in the Catholic cemetery and the girl took them in. It was surprisingly well looked after, the grass cut, some of the newer graves decorated with flowers. The tunnel line stretched from the wall of the barn to the north-east corner of the cemetery, Vaughan knew that, but above ground things looked perfectly normal. A fall down there, of course, and that would be something else again. The consequences would be disastrous.

He turned away and followed Hartmann and the girl out of the entrance and across the street to the church. The mayor was standing in the porch of the inn and came down the steps and moved a few paces towards them.

'Sigrid, go in at once, you're needed.'

She glanced uncertainly at Hartmann. He nodded gently and she hurried past her father and went inside.

'Don't be angry with your daughter, Herr Ehrlich,' Hartmann said. 'She was kind enough to show me one or two places I wanted to see.'

Ehrlich moved close and his voice was low and full of passion. 'She was in the church. Do you think I don't know this? I don't want her in there again. I don't want her mixed up in this sort of thing, you understand? In the world we live in today, Father, it's too dangerous.'

'It's always been dangerous, my friend,' Hartmann said. 'But surely as mayor and local Party secretary, you'd be the last person to deny the constitution under which each individual has the right to exercise free will in the matter of religion?'

'Oh, go to the Devil!' Ehrlich turned and hurried back towards the inn.

'What are you after?' Vaughan demanded as they went up the steps to the entrance of the church. 'What are you trying to prove?'

'I'm supposed to provide a diversion, am I not? I should have thought I was succeeding admirably.' Hartmann opened the door and moved inside, and then he stopped with an intake of breath.

There were flowers everywhere or so it seemed. In the Lady Chapel and on the altar. And more. There was a ruby glow to the sanctuary lamp. Hartmann walked slowly down the aisle and stood at the bottom of the steps. There were even fresh candles, neatly stacked beside the offertory box.

'So, Sigrid is not alone, it would seem.' He picked up a candle and placed it in one of the holders and said to Vaughan, 'Light it, please.'

Vaughan struck a match and touched it to the wick. As the candle flared Hartmann turned to him and smiled. 'To St Jude, patron saint of the impossible.'

V

Conlin was tired and listless, eyes sore from lack of sleep. When he closed them, all he could see was the back of Karl's skull dissolving as the bullet fragmented bone endlessly and, occasionally, he seemed to hear the voice in his ear, begging him to confess.

Which was all perfectly understandable, of course. Such hallucinations were common under conditions of extreme stress and his physical state was not good now. Experience and logic told him as much, but it didn't help him sleep. It didn't enable him to close his burning eyes.

He vomited into the bucket and the guard looked in to see what was happening. Conlin sat on the bed feeling very ill indeed. Finally he heard steps approaching, the door was opened and van Buren appeared. Lieutenant Leber was with him in her white coat, carrying her medical bag. It occurred to Conlin, and for no particular reason, that he had never heard her talk.

Van Buren said, 'Are you ill?'

'It's nothing,' Conlin told him wearily. 'I was sick a couple of times, that's all, and I can't sleep.'

'We can do something about that at any rate,' van Buren said solicitously and turned to the woman. 'Give him a shot.'

Conlin didn't argue. There would have been no point. She produced a hypodermic and gave him an injection in his right arm. It hurt rather a lot because there wasn't too much flesh on his bones now, but he was really past caring. When she rubbed it afterwards, her fingers were particularly light and soothing.

Van Buren said, 'We'll leave you. Try and get a good night's sleep. I need you fresh for the morning.'

'What was it she gave me?' Conlin asked, already aware of the languour that seeped through his veins.

'Something good, I promise you.' The door clanged shut. The echo seemed to go on for a very long time and then there was silence.

VI

He was lying on a bed and it was not dark and there was a pale, diffused light to things which he found rather pleasant. It was warm, which was an improvement for he seemed to have been cold for so long now.

He was aware of a slight movement and turned his head and saw Lieutenant Leber standing on the other side of the room. She was wearing her Vopo uniform – tunic, skirt and leather boots. Her face was very calm as she started to unbutton the tunic.

Underneath, she wore a white cotton blouse and when she moulded her hands to her waist the blouse tightened, a nipple blossoming at the tip of each breast.

She came across to the bed, leaned down and put a hand on him. He tried to push her away, but there was no strength in him at all, his arms moving in a kind of slow motion.

She spoke in a distorted and remote voice, 'There's nothing to fear. Nothing to be ashamed of.'

She unfastened the zip at the side of her skirt and slipped out of it. And then she sat on the edge of the bed and unfastened the blouse. Her breasts were round and full and very beautiful and then, as she leaned over and put a hand on him, he started to laugh uncontrollably, his entire body shaking with helpless mirth, eyes tightly shut.

And after a while, when he opened them again, she had gone.

VII

Van Buren was standing staring down into the heart of the fire, a glass of cognac in one hand, when there was a knock on the door and Ruth Leber entered. She was in full uniform, including her greatcoat which was unbuttoned at the front. The one incongruous feature was the small vanity case she carried in one hand.

'I left one or two things in the bathroom,' she said. 'Can I get them?'

'Help yourself.'

He lit a cigarette and she returned and stood looking at

him, as if waiting for something. 'Are you sure you want me to go?'

'Nothing for you to stay for, is there?'

'I don't suppose there is.'

'You can take the Mercedes.'

She paused, a hand on the door. 'Is there any way you can get out of this thing, Harry?'

He turned to look at her, surprise on his face. 'Why should I want to?'

'How many times have I worked with you? How many cases? Fifteen – twenty?'

'So?'

'He's different, this old man. He isn't like the others.'

'Why? Because he's got God on his side?'

'Perhaps.'

He smiled coldly. 'Careful, angel. If Klein heard you talking like that . . .'

'Goodbye, Harry.'

The door closed softly behind her.

VIII

He sat, slightly dazed, in front of van Buren's desk, a blanket around his shoulders. His mouth was dry, obviously the after-effect of the drug, and he sipped eagerly at the coffee provided. After a while the door opened and van Buren came in. He sat down on the other side of the desk.

'How do you feel?'

'Terrible. Sorry about that drug of yours, whatever it was.'

'We'll have to go back to the lab and try again.'

'That poor girl.' Conlin shook his head. 'What was she supposed to do? Prove I'm a sinner like anyone else? I already know that. Arouse my dormant sexuality? Induce an erection?' He shook his head. 'There are times, Harry, when I despair of you. Didn't it ever occur to you that the Almighty might consider that a perfectly reasonable chemical reaction?'

Van Buren smiled in spite of himself. 'You could have a point there.'

'I could indeed. Man is a creature of instinct as well as

reason. Even that old fraud Sigmund Freud admitted that sometimes a cigar is only a cigar.'

'You'll have to be careful,' van Buren said. 'Much more of this and you'll leave me only one choice.'

'The same as you gave Karl? But I'm not afraid to die, Harry. Maybe that's the difference between you and me. One loses consciousness – sleeps. The corruption of the body afterwards is something else. One isn't involved. We die from the day we're born.'

'Only some of us go rather sooner than others,' van Buren said. 'Frances Mary, for instance.'

IX

It was just after eight when Vaughan went across the square to the inn. When he went in, van Buren was sitting at the best table, the one beside the fire, with Süssmann. They were deep in conversation. Becker sat at a smaller table on his own, obviously excluded and not liking it. He scowled at Vaughan, who ignored him and went to the bar.

Ehrlich nodded formally. 'What can I get you?'

'A bottle of hock would be fine and what about something to eat?'

'Potato soup, cold sausage, sauerkraut. I can do nothing more.'

'That would be fine.'

Ehrlich withdrew, and van Buren called, 'And where's the Holy Father tonight?'

If he'd expected to draw a laugh from the locals, it failed miserably and the silence which followed was one of disapproval.

Vaughan moved across. 'Seeking out the faithful. He's like a travelling salesman, going round knocking on doors, hoping someone will buy.'

Süssmann said, 'Shouldn't you be with him?'

Schaefer's position in the SSD gave him the equivalent rank of a lieutenant in the Volkspolizei, so Vaughan didn't see any pressing need to be polite to Süssmann, He said, 'My official brief is to keep him under observation and know where he is at all times. As far as I'm concerned, I do.'

He nodded to van Buren, walked across to another table and sat down. Becker was scowling at him harder than ever. Sigrid came in from the kitchen with a tray. There was soup and black bread, a bottle of Hock with the cork already drawn.

'Where's your father?' Vaughan asked.

'In the kitchen. He thinks he's a better cook than I am.'

She was really very pretty in her peasant skirt.

As she went back to the bar, Becker grabbed her hand and pulled her on to his knee. He acted as if two-thirds drunk, but Vaughan suspected otherwise. There was too much of the brute to Becker for his liking. A suggestion of the animal.

As the girl struggled, Becker laughed, one hand fondling her left breast, the other sliding up under the skirt. She writhed, tears of humiliation in her eyes, and he laughed again coarsely.

'You like that, eh?'

Vaughan glanced across at the villagers. No one made a move. *They're frightened to death*, he thought and turned to van Buren and Süssmann. The Vopo captain seemed totally unconcerned and van Buren poured a glass of wine and threw another log on the fire. But now it was beyond enduring. There was only lust on Becker's face and the girl moaned in pain. Vaughan said, 'Let her go!'

Becker turned his head sharply. 'What was that?'

'I said, let her go. I mean, she doesn't know where you've been, does she?'

Van Buren was interested now, his eyes watchful over the rim of his glass as Becker pushed Sigrid to one side and got up. He crossed the room with exaggerated slowness and leaned on the table with both hands.

'You know what I'm going to do with you?'

Vaughan was in the act of pouring a glass of Hock. In an almost casual gesture, he reversed his grip and smashed the bottle across the side of the Vopo's head. As Sigrid cried out, Becker staggered and fell to one knee.

Vaughan picked up a chair and brought it down across the great shoulders. Becker grunted and started to heel over and Vaughan smashed the broken chair down again. He threw the pieces to one side and backed away.

Slowly, painfully, Becker reached for the edge of the table

and pulled himself up. He hung there for a moment, then turned to Vaughan, wiping blood from his face casually.

And then, incredibly, he charged, head down, hands reaching out to destroy. Vaughan judged his moment exactly, swerved to one side and punched him in the kidneys. Becker cried out and fell to the floor. He tried to get up again, but there was nothing left and he rolled on to his back, moaning.

Sigrid's face was very white and she was trembling. Her father, who had appeared from the kitchen, drew her behind the bar. Süssmann came forward, his face angry and knelt down beside Becker.

He looked up at Vaughan. 'This is a serious matter.'

Van Buren pulled on his coat, smiling cheerfully. 'Nonsense. He asked for it – he got it. You'd better see if you can wire him together again while I have words with our good comrade here.'

Vaughan followed him outside. Van Buren paused at the top of the steps to light a cigarette. 'Very good for a Section Six man. I didn't think your training took you quite that far.'

'We do our best,' Vaughan said warily.

'And Father Hartmann? Has he been behaving himself? He's not trying to pack them in there or anything, is he?'

'Not as far as I know.'

Van Buren was already on his way across the square and Vaughan followed. The American pushed open the main door and they went in. Candles flickered in many places now and half a dozen women and three men sat in a row beside the confessional box, waiting their turn.

'Now what do you make of that?' van Buren said. 'Very naughty indeed, I'd call it.'

'I know,' Vaughan said. 'Karl Marx was right. Opiate of the people. Just like cigarettes. One taste and you're hooked again.'

'That's good. I'll remember that one.' Van Buren pulled up his collar. 'So far and no farther. Tell him that from me.' He turned and went out.

Vaughan waited for a while, but it was obvious that Hartmann was going to be some little while yet and it was time he checked on how things were going at the farm. He went out, hurried across the square and disappeared into the darkness of the side street opposite.

X

His pull on the gate bell was answered by old Brother Urban, and as he crossed the yard Konrad opened the barn door and peered out.

'Oh, it's you. What about Hartmann?'

'About God's holy work,' Vaughan said. 'I think he's decided Neustadt needs him.'

'He could be right, major. Stranger things have happened.'

There was mild reproof in Konrad's voice, no more than that and they went into the barn. Gregor was doing some measurements on a plan opened out on a small table. Margaret Campbell stood beside him pouring coffee into several mugs, and Berg was there also, peering over Gregor's shoulder, a cigarette in his mouth.

Augustin, stripped to the waist, came in from the other room pushing a barrow. He wore no bandaging about his face and Vaughan suddenly realized that the dreadful all-pervading smell had gone.

'Considerably fresher than when I was last in here.'

Konrad nodded. 'In that respect, things have improved tremendously. We have made real progress. Far, far better than any of us could have hoped.'

'Where are the others?'

'Franz and Florian are working at the coal face, which is what we call it now.'

As he talked, Vaughan was watching the girl. She had not looked at him directly. She had a scarf tied around her hair and seemed absurdly young, with great sunken eyes.

He pulled himself together and turned to Berg. 'Well, how are things up at the Schloss?'

'Not so good. The truck-driver, Karl. You remember?'

'What about him?'

'They executed him. Tied him to a pole in the courtyard and shot him. I saw it all from an upstairs window.'

'When was this?'

'Very early this morning – dawn. It was still pretty dark, you understand, but I managed to see enough.'

'And Father Conlin?'

'He was there too. They made him watch. When I left earlier this evening, he was back on the third level.'

'Anything else to report?'

'I don't think so. Oh, yes. The woman – the Vopo lieutenant.'

'What about her?'

'She's gone – drove back to Berlin this evening.'

Gregor said, 'Fifty feet by my reckoning. We're almost at the cemetery boundary and the sewer pipe is approximately six feet on the other side.'

'We could reach it by tomorrow afternoon,' Konrad said.

'Easily. Perhaps sooner.'

'You're sure of this?' Vaughan demanded.

'I don't see why not. There's the question of breaking into the sewer pipe but that shouldn't present any kind of difficulties,' Gregor told him.

'Which means we could try to bring him out tomorrow night,' Konrad said. 'Unless you think that too soon for any reason.'

'Good God, no.' Vaughan shook his head. 'The sooner the better. We can't be sure from one day to the next what van Buren might try with Conlin. The wrong kind of drugs, for instance.' He turned to Berg. 'You go down there again tomorrow with your rat poison and get the padlock off that manhole cover.'

'I understand,' Berg said. 'But at what time will things really start to happen? When do we leave?'

'It must be after dark for obvious reasons. I'd say nine o'clock would be as good a time to strike as any.'

'Call in with some milk churns at six,' Konrad said. 'I'll give you the final details then.'

Berg nodded. 'Fine. I'll go now.'

He went out. Konrad turned to examine the plan again with Gregor and Margaret Campbell handed Vaughan a mug of coffee without a word. They walked to the door, which was partly open. Rain drifted through the courtyard light outside. It was as if they were alone.

'You look tired,' he said.

'Everyone is tired. So much must be done at night and there's the appearance of things. The milk and eggs to be delivered round the village each day. The cows to be taken to pasture and so on. There things must be seen to be done, otherwise someone might wonder what's happening.'

'How's your leg?'

'I manage very well.' Her shoulder touched his, she leaned against him wearily. 'Not long now, Simon.'

'Not long.'

'And then what?'

'You'll be able to go home.'

'And where would that be?' There was a bitterness, an anger in her voice that he had never heard before. 'If you find out, let me know, major. I've never been too sure myself.'

And suddenly, he was desperately anxious to say the right thing, for her, not himself. 'You've got to start fresh, Maggie. Unstamped metal. All right, you've had one hell of a life so far, but the kind of knowledge you get from bitter experience has a limited value. It sets your thinking in a pattern built on that experience and that's no good.'

'So what do I do?'

'Practise your trade, I suppose. You're a doctor, aren't you? Pascoe should be able to get you a choice of England or America if you want. Or you could stay in West Germany.'

'And you?' Thc eyes were darkly watchful as if someone was inside looking out at him.

He remembered what Meyer had said about the sniper on the roof and tried hard. 'God knows. Something will turn up. It always does for people like me.'

'And what kind of person are you? How do you see yourself?'

'Old Chinese saying,' he said. 'There's always an official executioner. If you try to take his place, it's like trying to be a master carpenter and cutting wood. You'll only hurt your hand.'

'And what is that supposed to mean?'

'It means, give it up, Maggie. Let me go.'

'No,' she said simply. 'Which doesn't mean that I approve

of you or how you live, or what you've done in the past. It simply means I love you.'

Her hand was on his arm, her eyes serene, calm. He gazed down at her, suddenly desperate. From behind them in the tunnel came the most dreadful cry he had ever heard.

XI

Franz had turned to take the sheet of corrugated iron from Florian when it happened. There was a trickle of soil on his head. He glanced up.

Florian scrambled back. 'Careful, I think the roof goes.'

The soil bulged, a rotting coffin appeared. The end broke away and two decaying feet poked through, minus the toes. The stench was immediate and appalling. Franz cried out in horror and tried to scramble back. As he moved the entire coffin descended, the rotting wood breaking to reveal what was left of the corpse inside.

XII

Vaughan and Gregor slipped through the darkness of the cemetery and crouched by the wall.

'This should be the place,' Gregor whispered.

Vaughan switched on his torch. There was a grave – a comparatively recent one. An old man who had died ten months previously. It was more ornate than some, a marble slab on the ground surrounded by railings.

'Is this the one?'

Gregor nodded. 'It has to be. Thank God for that slab. Without it there might have been one hell of a hole to explain.'

They returned to the farm quickly. There was that smell in the barn again only worse now, and Konrad and Augustin had the bandaging wrapped around their faces. Margaret Campbell had the medical chest open on the table and was filling a hypodermic.

'I'm going to give everyone a shot. Just as a precaution and that includes you, major. The possibilities of infection are appalling.'

'Where are Franz and Florian?' Vaughan asked. 'Not still in there surely?'

'But of course,' Konrad said. 'It must be brought out, that thing, before we can break through the final few feet.'

There was a movement below and Florian appeared, pulling a long, sacking-enshrouded bundle. Franz appeared at the other end. Konrad jumped down to help them and they struggled up the ramp.

In spite of the sacking, the smell was terrible and he said, 'Keep back, the rest of you.'

They went into the other room and Vaughan followed in time to see them drop the body into the well. Konrad poured a sack of lime after it, Florian followed this with a barrowful of soil.

When they returned, Margaret Campbell was waiting to give them their injections. Franz was breathing hard, his eyes wild, and the stench on him was terrible.

Konrad said, 'Better go and have a bath, Franz. We'll carry on here.'

'A bath?' Franz glared at him. 'You think I can wash that thing in there off me with soap and water? It will be with me till the day I die.'

He rushed out. In the silence, Konrad picked up a shovel and said calmly, 'Last lap, my friends, so let's get to it,' and he went down the ramp and crawled into the tunnel.

XIII

Hartmann was sitting in the sacristy at the table reading *The City of God* by St Augustine. It was very quiet. There was the lightest of taps at the outside door. It opened and Sigrid looked in.

'May we come in, Father?'

To his astonishment, he saw that her father was with her. Georg Ehrlich looked embarrassed and thoroughly uncomfortable.

'What is it?' Hartmann asked. 'What can I do for you?'

'Go on, Father,' the girl urged.

'It's my aunt,' the mayor said. 'She's an old woman. Eighty-two.'

'Well?'

'She's dying, Father,' Sigrid told him simply. 'And she hasn't seen a priest in a long time.'

'I'll come at once,' Hartmann said. 'Is it far?'

'The edge of the village.'

He opened his vestment bag and rummaged in it quickly. There was a ciborium from which he took a Host and hung it in a silver pyx around his neck, a small silver jar containing holy oil to anoint the dying woman's ears, nose, mouth, hands and feet.

He threw a stole over his shoulder and picked up his missal. 'I'm ready.'

The door opened and Vaughan entered. The mayor was obviously considerably put out. Vaughan said, 'What's going on?'

'Herr Ehrlich's aunt is dying, Horst. She needs me. You can come if you want, but we haven't got time to argue.'

He took Sigrid's arm and went out like a strong wind. Vaughan said to Ehrlich, 'I'm supposed to follow him everywhere, did you know that? Not only the day but half the bloody night as well. I'll be glad when they transfer me to another assignment.'

He went out, the mayor hurrying at his side. 'She's an old woman, my aunt, and old people, you have to humour them. On the other hand, it could be very embarrassing for me in the Party if this got out, comrade. You know what I mean.'

Vaughan turned up his collar against the rain, 'Yes,' he said sourly, 'I know exactly what you mean.'

XIV

The bedroom was on the ground floor, the door half-open. Vaughan could see the old woman clearly, propped up against pillows. Hartmann was celebrating Mass and she followed every move, hands clasped together. After he gave her communion she started to cry and he held her hands at the end.

'*Ite, missa est.*'

'*Deo gratias*,' she said through her tears.

And Sigrid, too, was crying, as she hurried from the room.

XV

As they walked back towards the church, Vaughan explained in detail what had taken place at the Home Farm.

Curiously enough, Hartmann didn't refer to the incident of the body in the tunnel, but simply said, 'So you could be ready for Father Conlin tomorrow night? That's much sooner than I'd imagined.'

'Or any of us did,' Vaughan said. 'You almost sound sorry.'

'There's work to be done here. A real need to be filled.' Hartmann smiled. 'Remember what I told you? One is always a priest before everything else. Still . . .'

They went up the steps of the church and he opened the door. A man and a woman were sitting in one of the rear pews with three young children. They stood up at once and the woman pushed the children forward. The eldest looked no more than seven.

'Please, Father,' she said. 'I'd like them baptized.'

Her husband stood at her side, cap in hand, his face anxious. Beyond them Vaughan saw another half-dozen people at the confessional box.

'But it's two o'clock in the morning.'

Erich Hartmann smiled. 'You see, my friend?' he said. 'You see now what I mean?'

— 14 —

THE FRANCISCANS worked on relentlessly through the night and it was just before five o'clock in the morning when Franz's shovel sliced through soft earth and rattled against something harder.

'I think we're there,' he said to Gregor who was acting as labourer. He renewed his attack with vigour, pulled the soil away and the curved side of the great concrete pipe started to take shape.

'I'll be back,' Gregor said excitedly and crawled away.

Franz kept on working, shovelling the soil back into the cart, until the pipe wall was completely clear. Gregor returned with Konrad. They carried a sledgehammer and a couple of steel crowbars.

'Give it to me and keep back,' Franz said.

He took the sledge and when they had pulled the cart out of range swung it with all his strength against the pipe. There was a hollow booming sound, but he had made no visible impression on the concrete. He tried again slightly awkwardly, for because of the confined space it was only possible to swing sideways.

Gregor crawled forward. 'Try it this way,' he said.

There was a join where one length of pipe had been cemented to another. He got the sharp end of the crowbar into it and lay flat, keeping his head down.

Franz swung again, connecting squarely with the head of the crowbar which sank in immediately. He grunted with effort, swinging again with all his strength and a crack appeared in the concrete and then another.

'I hoped that might happen,' Gregor said. 'It's pre-stressed.'

Franz swung against the concrete this time and a large piece fell inwards. There was an immediate blast of cold air, a draught sweeping the length of the tunnel. He swung the hammer again and again, Gregor working beneath him with the crowbar, and within a few minutes had made an entrance large enough to pass through.

II

From the kitchen window of the priest's house, Vaughan could see Berg standing beside his truck outside the inn talking to Ehrlich. The milk cart appeared from the direction of the Home Farm. To his surprise, he saw that Brother Konrad was pushing it.

Hartmann was at the stove frying eggs. Vaughan said, 'That's interesting. Konrad's doing the milk round himself this morning. I think I'll see what's going on.'

He found a jug and went out. As he approached the inn, Konrad was helping Berg lift a couple of churns on to the back of the truck. Ehrlich was standing watching.

Vaughan said, 'Good morning, comrade.'

The mayor mumbled a reply and went inside. Vaughan held out his jug for Konrad to fill. 'We broke through at five o'clock,' he said.

'And how are things?'

'Fine. Gregor, Franz and I went the whole length of the sewer as far as the exit. The manhole cover is, of course, closed.'

'You get down there as soon as you can and get that padlock off,' Vaughan said to Berg. 'I want you at the farm tonight as late as possible with any news at all on the state of the game up there. Say seven o'clock.'

'All right.' Berg climbed into his truck and drove away.

'Anything else you want me to do?' Konrad asked as he picked up the shafts of the cart.

'Activate the transmitter as soon as you get back,' Vaughan said. 'That will alert them at Bitterfeld to expect something tonight.'

The Franciscan moved away and Vaughan went back into the house. 'Anything I should know?' Hartmann asked, passing him a plate with two fried eggs and a slice of black bread on it.

'They'vc broken through.'

'So – tonight it is.'

Vaughan found that the eggs were really quite reasonable. 'You should be at the farm no later than nine, by the way.'

'Why?'

'To get yourself ready to move out with the others.'

'We made no such arrangement.'

'Good God, you can't stay here, man. You can't stay anywhere in East Germany. Within five minutes of finding Conlin gone, they'll put two and two together and make it five where you're concerned. You've no choice. You've got to leave with the others while you can.'

'Yes, I suppose you're right,' Hartmann said. 'It hadn't really occurred to me before.'

Strange how he had suddenly lost his appetite. He pushed the plate away from him.

III

Berg removed the padlock from the manhole cover, slipped it into his pocket, then picked up his lamp and went to check his poison bait. There were several dead rats and he collected half a dozen and went back up the passage, holding them in one hand by their tails.

As he came to the Vopo outside Conlin's cell he held them up. 'Six at one blow, just like the tailor in the fairy tale.'

The young Vopo shuddered. 'Stinking things. I can't stand them.'

Berg laughed and moved on up the passage to where the next guard stood at the door to the steps leading to the second level.

IV

In his cell, Conlin slept fitfully. He couldn't get the fact of Karl's death out of his mind and the knowledge, as van Buren had said, that he could have saved him, just as he could have saved Frances Mary. At the thought of her, all the pain, all the distress welled up in him again as it had not done for years.

She was his only sister, nine years his junior and they had always been close, especially since the death of their parents. She had lived with an old aunt during the years of his training, was so delighted when a parish appointment took him back to Dublin.

And then she'd fallen in love with Michael, a young assistant lecturer in History at Trinity College, a Protestant, but a lovely boy for all that. And then there was the child coming.

He could hardly breathe, remembering, his hands clutching at the blanket. That December night, just before Christmas. The car skidded, overturned, killing Michael instantly. And Frances Mary, seriously injured, had gone into labour.

It was two o'clock in the morning when he'd got there and the doctor in charge of the case had faced him with a terrible decision. She needed immediate surgery; under the circumstances, there was no question that she could be allowed to continue in labour and in the condition she was in, a Caesarian was impossible.

What they wanted was simple: Conlin's permission for them to destroy the child; and that was something he could not give for such a thing ran contrary to everything he had believed all his life.

'All right,' the doctor had said. 'If we wait until after the birth, there's a strong possibility your sister will die. The choice is yours.'

But as a good Catholic, he had no choice. And he sat and waited until four in the morning when the doctor had returned to tell him they were both dead, Frances Mary and the daughter who had barely lived.

It was snowing when he left the hospital and bitterly cold – almost as cold as it was now. What was it Donne said?

Under the rod of God's Wrath having been.
He hath broke my bones, worn out by flesh and skin.

Oh God, help me, he thought. I killed Karl, just as I killed my own sister out of my own selfish stubborn pride. The iron conviction that I alone know what is right and true.

In that moment he was in total despair, at the bottom of a pit so dark there seemed no way out. He had never felt so totally alone in his life.

'God forgive me,' he said. And wept.

A hand reached out to take his and a fierce aching excitement filled his heart. It was as if it was the third day and he was waiting for the stone to roll aside.

V

At Bitterfeld, Pascoe went into the hangar and found Kubel working on the Storch, Meyer sitting on a box watching him. The plane had had a fresh coat of dull black paint and looked remarkably sinister.

'How goes it?' Pascoe asked.

Meyer chuckled. 'If he touches that engine once more it'll complain to the union.'

'Half the airmen who bought it during the war weren't shot down by the enemy. They died through engine failure of one sort or another,' Kubel said. 'That's why I made sure I knew more about them than the mechanics.'

There was the sound of running steps and Teusen appeared in the hangar entrance, so much out of breath that he could hardly speak.

'What is it?' Pascoe demanded.

'It's come – the preliminary signal. We've just picked it up.'

There was silence. Max Kubel walked across to the hangar door and looked out. Grey clouds hung heavily over the airfield and a curtain of rain swept towards the hangar.

'Ah well,' he said softly to himself. 'At least it should prove interesting.'

VI

Süssmann and Becker took Conlin into the room between them and sat him down in the chair opposite van Buren.

'Wait outside,' he said.

They withdrew. Conlin straightened himself wearily. 'Well?'

'You look tired.'

'Yes, I'll admit to that.'

'Which isn't surprising. The unfortunate business with Karl. My reminding you of Frances Mary.' Van Buren shrugged. 'There's a limit to how many stones we can turn over.'

'It's no good, Harry.' Conlin smiled gently. 'You're wasting your time. I didn't kill Karl – you did. And I didn't kill Frances Mary either. It was the circumstance of life that killed her – something I was unable to prevent because of my religious belief. I have no right to judge myself. God will do that for me.'

'You still find time for belief?'

'Oh yes, I think you could say that. In the depths of total despair, I reached out and he was there like a cold wind on the face in the morning. Excitement, Harry – the indescribable hollow, frightening excitement of knowing totally. I discovered then that nothing could ever touch me again.'

'And that's your final word?'

The old man smiled gently. 'Harry, your father was a fine man. What happened to him was a terrible thing, but that doesn't excuse you making war on the whole world. Rats aren't people, Harry. A rat in a cage does what you teach him to do, but a man in a cage always has free choice.'

Van Buren had gone very pale, his fingers interlocked tightly together. He said slowly, 'I have a new drug with me which is used as a muscle relaxant in certain surgical operations, but the crucial point about it is that the patient has to be unconscious. You see, the effect on a conscious person is so horrifying that where accidents have occurred, the standard procedure is to inject scopolamine to erase the incident from the patient's memory.'

'You learn something new every day,' Father Conlin said.

Van Buren opened a drawer, took out a bottle and a hypodermic syringe and started to fill it. 'Succinyl choline causes convulsive muscular spasms, then leaves the subject totally paralysed, unable to breathe, in agonizing pain – but conscious. You'll feel yourself dying of lack of oxygen. The effect only lasts for two minutes, but the experience is so terrible that few people can stand the threat of a repeat performance.'

And Conlin knew fear then as he had never known it in his life before. His mouth went dry and his hands started to shake so much that he could only still them by clasping them tightly behind him.

And in the end, can the human spirit be broken so easily? Did you really intend such a thing, Lord? No, I can't believe it. I stand by my faith, now and always.

He took a deep breath and managed the bravest smile of his life. 'Come on, boy. Surely you can do better than that? If the measure of a man is to be decided by which drug you pump into him, then where does that leave you, Harry?'

Van Buren stared at him fixedly, then pressed the buzzer on his desk, the door opened and Süssmann and Becker entered.

'Hold him,' he said.

VII

It was just before seven when Vaughan went up the steel ladder and gently raised the manhole cover. The chamber above was in total darkness. He listened for a few moments, then lowered the cover again and went back down the ladder. Ten minutes later he was crawling along the cemetery tunnel back into the barn.

They were all waiting and Berg had arrived while he'd been exploring the tunnel.

'Satisfied?' Konrad asked.

Vaughan nodded. 'Ten minutes at the outside to get there, five to get Conlin, ten – maybe fifteen – to get back.'

'You'll have to carry him,' Berg said. 'I saw him leaving van Buren's office an hour ago over Becker's shoulder, and he didn't look good.'

'Had he been beaten?'

'Not that I could see.'

Vaughan reached for his leather trenchcoat and pulled it on. 'Probably drugs. There are some pretty nasty ones in use for van Buren's kind of purpose these days. You get back up to the Schloss. Stay there till about eight-forty-five and keep your eyes open. Anything happens before then, get down here with the news as fast as you can.'

Berg nodded and went out. Konrad said, 'What now?'

'We wait. I'll go and see Hartmann. Fill him in on what's happening, if I can tear him away long enough from his endless confessions and baptisms. The only thing he hasn't done is hold a public service.'

As he moved to the door, Margaret Campbell joined him. They crossed the courtyard together, his arm about her shoulder.

He said, 'Once things start hotting up I may be too busy to notice what you're doing, so promise me to do as Konrad tells you and get into that truck at the right time like a good girl.'

'We could have breakfast together at Bitterfeld,' she said.

'I don't see why not.'

'And that café on the end of the bridge in Berlin. You'll take me there again if I ask you?'

'We'll see.' He touched her cheek lightly with the back of his hand. 'Look after yourself.' He stepped out through the gate and hurried away.

VIII

It was just after eight o'clock when Hartmann opened the side door and went into the sacristy and found Vaughan waiting for him.

'Where in the hell have you been?' Vaughan demanded.

'Visiting the sick. House calls,' Hartmann said. 'I told you there was a need here. Why?'

'Because at approximately nine I go in,' Vaughan said. 'At nine-twenty I come out again with Conlin, at nine-forty Kubel will pick us up at Water Horse Meadow, and shortly after that you'll all be on your way to the border in the field truck. So – get together what you want of your things and you can come back to the farm with me now.'

'No,' Hartmann said. 'I've been thinking about that and I think I have a rather better idea. My only real purpose in this whole affair was to act as a decoy to a certain degree. It seems to me I'd be most useful doing that right now.'

'What in hell are you talking about?' Vaughan demanded.

So Hartmann told him.

IX

Van Buren was going over his notes when there was a knock on the door and Süssmann entered with Becker.

'Trouble?' Van Buren said.

'In a manner of speaking. I've just had a phone call from the village. An anonymous well-wisher who was in the inn a short while ago when the priest came in and spoke to the mayor.'

'And?'

'It seems he told him he intended to bring the Cross of St Michael back to the church.'

'I don't understand.'

Süssmann explained briefly. When he had finished, he

added, 'An act of direct defiance, or so it seems to me. You did warn him.'

Van Buren said. 'Where is this cross?'

'I know,' Becker said. 'By the Elbe about half a mile outside the village. I've seen it. I was told the story by Berg, the caretaker, when I first got here.' He laughed contemptuously. 'Hartmann must be crazy. There's no way he could carry that thing over such a distance.'

'If he did, of course, and claimed the right to open the church again for public worship . . .' Süssmann said.

Van Buren nodded. 'No, we can't have that.' He smiled. 'An interesting situation, though. Let's go and see how he's getting on.'

X

At that precise moment, Erich Hartmann was attacking the ground at the base of the cross vigorously with a spade. Twenty or so villagers, women as well as men, some with lanterns stood in a half circle some little distance away and watched.

Sigrid and her father were closest. The mayor said, 'Father, this is madness. When the news reaches the castle, the military will come.'

Hartmann said, 'You see, Sigrid, we make progress. He worries for me.'

'They'll arrest you, Father,' Ehrlich said.

Hartmann kept on digging. 'Did you phone them up there to tell them what I intended to do? After all, you are the local Party secretary.'

'No,' Ehrlich said. 'I did not.'

'Then they will arrest you too, my friend. That's the kind of people they are. The kind of society you have.' He turned to address the crowd now. 'And you use the word democratic to describe it.'

The cross swayed and started to fall. He threw the spade aside and caught it, easing it down. The evidencc of his enormous strength drew an audible gasp from the crowd.

Sigrid ran forward and put a hand on his arm. 'Please,

Father, don't do it.' Her face was strained, pleading. 'You'll kill yourself.'

'But I must, my child,' he said gently. 'You see, it occurs to me now that this is very likely what it's all about, my life up to now, I mean. What I do now is what gives it purpose.'

He looked at the hill, black in the rain, rising up towards the village. 'Dear God, give me strength,' he murmured.

He hoisted the cross on his left shoulder, braced himself to the weight and started forward.

XI

Brother Konrad, in the uniform of a Vopo lieutenant, was standing at the table in the barn with Margaret Campbell, examining the sewer plans, when Vaughan came in. He wore dark pants and sweater, and a black balaclava helmet covered most of his face, giving him a sinister and deadly appearance.

Margaret Campbell's eyes widened. 'You look . . .' She hesitated.

He scooped up dirt from the floor with his hands and rubbed it over the exposed part of his face. 'Look like what?' he demanded.

'Different – another person.'

He was filled with a fierce energy that seemed to crackle around him like static electricity.

'The real me,' he said. 'The man I've always been. Rising to the occasion because this is what I'm good at.'

There was something close to hurt in her eyes. He turned from it and said to Konrad, 'Is Franz in the tunnel?'

'Yes.'

Vaughan took a Mauser from his belt, the pre-war model with the bulbous silencer, specially manufactured for the Gestapo and still the best silenced handgun in his experience. He checked the clip, then pushed the Mauser back into his waistband.

'I wonder which Station of the Cross Hartmann's reached now?'

There was anger in Margaret Campbell's voice when she said, 'He's doing what he thinks is right. It's not proper for you to make fun of him.'

'A holy fool,' Vaughan said. 'Just like Sean Conlin, which is why we're all here if you think about it. God, the trouble the good of this world cause the rest of us.' He glanced at his watch and saw that it was a quarter to nine. 'To hell with it,' he said. 'I'm not going to wait any longer.'

'And this?' Konrad touched the transmitter which stood on the table. 'What about this?'

'Press that button at ten past nine,' Vaughan said. 'That should be about right.'

'But what if something should go wrong?' Margaret Campbell said in a sudden panic. 'The timing is the critical point, you said so yourself.'

'Not any more,' he said. 'From now on, things just happen. You see, we don't control the game any longer – it controls us.'

He ducked into the tunnel and was gone.

XII

At Bitterfeld, Teusen had switched on the outside lights. Heavy mist blanketed the airfield. The Storch was ready on the apron and Max Kubel, Pascoe and Meyer stood in the shelter of the hangar.

Meyer said, 'Look at the weather. It's times like these I wonder if there's a God. What a thing to happen.'

Kubel wore his old flying jacket, a white scarf wrapped around his neck. He was smoking a cigar and looked enormously cheerful. 'Taking off in filth like this is nothing, Julius. It's landing that's the difficulty.'

'And if it's like this at Neustadt?' Pascoe asked him.

'Then we have a problem,' Kubel said simply.

XIII

Never had Hartmann carried such a weight on his shoulders and as he came up to the crest of the hill, he paused. His entire body was one great ache, his left shoulder was rubbed raw and the right, to which he had shifted position, was no better.

The crowd had swelled considerably and people were still

arriving. The strange thing was their silence. Only the occasional murmur of a voice, here and there.

He started forward again, giving an involuntary groan of pain as the weight settled on his shoulder. He lost his balance almost at once and went down heavily and lay there, under the cross.

There was a rush of feet as people surged forward to help. 'No!' he shouted. 'No!'

They paused. He stayed there, on his hands and knees for a while. And then Sigrid started to recite the creed in a firm, clear voice. 'I believe in one God, the father, the almighty, maker of heaven and earth, and of all things, seen and unseen.'

Another voice joined in, hesitantly at first and then another and another.

Hartmann had never known such joy. 'I am not worthy of this burden,' he murmured. 'I accept it as a cross.'

And then he was on his feet again and going forward over the brow of the hill.

XIV

Franz waited at the bottom of the steel ladder with the lamp while Vaughan went up and cautiously raised the manhole cover. It was dark in the chamber, but a certain amount of diffused light indicated the entrance to the passageway. He lifted the manhole cover back carefully, then climbed out, taking the Mauser from his belt and cocking it.

When he peered round the corner, he saw the Vopo guard at once, leaning against the wall negligently, an AK slung from one shoulder. Fifty or sixty feet away and the corridor was well lit, but there was no choice. Vaughan started forward, keeping to the wall, holding the Mauser against his right thigh. It was all a question of how close he could get before his presence was noted.

At that moment, another Vopo emerged from the gloom at the far end of the passage, rifle slung and carrying a jug in one hand. He saw Vaughan at once and cried out in alarm. He dropped the jug and started to unsling his rifle. Vaughan fired twice, both bullets ripping into the heart, killing the man instantly.

Even as the Vopo went down, the Mauser was already arcing towards the other guard, whose AK was just coming up. Vaughan shot him in the right shoulder, the heavy bullet turning him around in a circle. The next shattered his spine, slamming him against the cell door. His greatcoat started to smoulder at the point of entry and there was a tiny flicker of flame as he slid to the floor.

The silenced pistol had made virtually no sound at all, but there was the question of the first Vopo's cry. Vaughan ran along the passage lightly and paused at the door at the bottom of the steps, listening. There was no sound and, satisfied, he came back.

He pulled back the bolts on the cell door and went in. Father Conlin lay on the bed, fully clothed, breathing heavily, apparently sleeping, but when Vaughan shook him, there was no response.

Vaughan pushed the Mauser back into his belt, lifted the priest into a sitting position, leaned down and took him across his shoulder. He went out and hurried back to the chamber.

Franz was peering over the edge of the manhole as he arrived. 'Trouble, major?'

'Nothing I couldn't handle,' Vaughan said. 'He's unconscious. Drugged, I think. I'll pass him down to you.'

Franz stood at the bottom of the ladder and gently took the old man's weight, cradling him in his arms like a child. Vaughan followed, pulling the manhole cover back into place.

He glanced at his watch. It was just coming up to ten past nine. 'Okay, let's get moving.'

They started forward and a moment later Brother Konrad in the barn pressed the button on the transmitter that sent that final, vital signal to the West.

XV

At Bitterfeld, Max Kubel boosted power and let the Storch go, the Argus engine responding magnificently. The landing lights had been switched on, but he could only see the first few – not that it mattered.

As the fog swallowed him up, Meyer, standing by the

hangar entrance with Pascoe and Teusen, said, 'Right, so he made it. What happens now?'

'The worst part, as it always is,' Pascoe said. 'The waiting.'

XVI

Even before they got to the square, van Buren could hear the singing. Becker was driving the field car, Süssmann beside him in the front seat, and when they turned into the square most of the village seemed to be there. Heinrich Berg, standing at the back of the crowd, saw them at once, and he moved back into the shadows.

'We would appear to have a religious revival on our hands,' van Buren observed.

Süssmann stood up, holding on to the top of the windshield. 'I can see him now.'

Hartmann entered the square on the far side, moving steadily, the crowd surging around him. He kept on coming doggedly and people started to clap and cheer. As he neared the bottom of the broad steps leading up to the church door, van Buren got out of the field car and moved to cut him off.

'Father Hartmann!' he called.

Hartmann paused. The singing died away, there was silence. It started to rain, heavily in a great rush as they confronted each other.

'I told you that if you gave me any trouble, I'd pack you back to Berlin.'

Süssmann stood up in the field car to address the crowd. 'Go home – all of you. That's an order.'

No one moved. Hartmann said, 'I'm taking the cross into the church. It is my right.'

He started up the steps. Van Buren said to Becker, 'I've had enough of this charade. Stop him.'

Becker went up the steps quickly and grabbed at one end of the cross, pulling Hartmann off balance, putting him down on one knee. Becker kicked out, sending him toppling.

'You're under arrest,' he said.

Hartmann ignored him completely, got on one knee again and picked up the cross. Becker took out his Walther and cocked it.

'No!' he said as Hartmann rose to his full height.

The priest stood there swaying, obviously tired, and when he moved, he almost lost his balance, one arm of the cross catching Becker a painful blow, sending him back against the church doors. Becker, in a kind of reflex action, fired twice. Hartmann fell back across the steps, the cross on top of him.

XVII

There was an immediate uproar. The crowd surged forward and Sigrid was the first to reach Hartmann, falling on her knees beside him. Süssman drew his own pistol and fired it into the air.

'Go home!' he shouted. 'I order you to disperse – all of you.'

Van Buren leaned over Hartmann. The Jesuit's eyes were open, there was a touch of blood at one corner of his mouth. Becker came down the steps.

'You fool,' van Buren told him. 'There was no need for this.'

'Murderer!' Sigrid cried.

'Oh no,' van Buren said. 'He's still with us, but not if you leave him lying out here.'

Behind him another field car appeared in a hurry, scattering the crowd. The Vopo driver jumped out and hurried forward. It was bad news, van Buren could tell by his face, before he even got close enough to start pouring out his story.

XVIII

When Berg pulled on the bell at Home Farm, it was Brother Florian who let him in.

'Where's the major?' Berg demanded.

'Left five minutes ago in the field truck,' Florian said. 'It all worked perfectly. He and Franz brought Conlin out between them and now Konrad's taken them to meet the plane.'

Margaret Campbell appeared in the entrance to the barn. 'There seems to be quite a disturbance in the village. What's been going on? Where's Father Hartmann?'

'Dead or dying from what I saw,' Berg said, and explained what had happened.

She went into the barn without a word and returned with her medical bag.

'Take me to him.'

'Don't be crazy,' he said. 'Konrad will be back here very soon now and we've all got to be ready to leave with him.' He added desperately, 'Look, he was shot twice at close quarters. He must be dead by now.'

'Take me to him,' she said.

Brother Florian opened the gate. 'Hurry. I'll tell Konrad when he returns. We'll wait for you.'

XIX

Van Buren came out of Conlin's cell and stood looking down at the dead guard by the door.

'Impossible,' Süssmann said. 'It doesn't make sense.'

'Of course it does,' Van Buren told him. 'There must be another way out of this rat trap somewhere down there in the darkness. If you search, you'll probably find it.'

He started to walk away and Süssmann called, 'And you, professor? Where are you going?'

'To visit the priest. It seems to me a remarkable coincidence that he should be putting on such a conspicuous display at the same time this little lot was going on.'

He stepped over the other body and hurried away along the passage.

XX

The field truck was parked at the northern edge of Water Horse Meadow. Brother Konrad was looking after Conlin while Vaughan, after checking the wind direction, took half a dozen cheap cycle lamps from his knapsack, switched them on and laid them out in a row. Then he ran to the other end of the meadow, following the direction of the wind, and laid two more. Simple but effective, and Kubel, coming in fast at six hundred feet a few minutes later, saw the pattern at once. He'd had an excellent flight on the whole, except for that earlier part where things had been so dirty he had been compelled to go up rather higher than he would have liked. Still . . .

As the Storch dropped in for a perfect landing, Vaughan put Conlin across his shoulder and said to Konrad, 'Off you go, then. See you at Bitterfeld at about eleven o'clock.'

Konrad got in the truck and drove away as Vaughan ran across to the Storch where Kubel waited for him, the door open. He leaned out to catch Conlin under the armpits to pull him in and Vaughan scrambled up to join them, slamming the door.

The Storch was already turning into the wind for take-off. Max grinned. 'See, my friend, nothing to it.'

He boosted the engine, the Storch surged forward and lifted into the night.

XXI

Hartmann was quite dead, Margaret Campbell knew that from the moment she entered the crowded bedroom at the priest's house, but she went through the motions of searching for a pulse and listening for a heartbeat. He looked very calm, very peaceful, and she started to put her stethoscope away.

Georg Ehrlich said, 'He is dead, then?'

'I'm afraid so.'

Sigrid, on her knees at the bedside, started to weep and there was a general murmuring among those who crowded into the room.

Ehrlich said, 'We haven't met. Are you new to the district, doctor?'

'Passing through.'

She closed her bag, stood up and found Harry van Buren standing in the doorway.

'Hello, Margaret,' he said. 'This *is* a surprise.'

— 15 —

MAX KUBEL, pushing the Storch towards the border at one hundred and sixty miles an hour, had been in trouble for some considerable time. On his run in, he had climbed to a height of just over one thousand feet because of bad visibility. He had been able to go down again within minutes, but during the intervening period, his presence had been noted on the radar screens at Allersberg.

Such a brief appearance could indicate a ghost image or ground clutter due to wave reflection. On the other hand, it could be an intruder and the chief controller at Allersberg was not one to take chances.

The rain had reduced visibility considerably and Kubel decided to go up. It was only six or seven minutes to the border now anyway. He pulled back the control column and the Storch started to climb, emerging into clear air at just over a thousand feet.

There was a quarter moon, pale, rainwashed, but it touched the low clouds with a kind of luminosity. He turned and shouted to Vaughan across the head of the unconscious Conlin. 'Not long now.'

There was a roaring that filled the night, the Storch bucked like a wild horse in the turbulence so that it took everything Kubel had to hold her as a dark shadow banked overhead and took up station to starboard.

'What is it?' Vaughan demanded.

'MiG fighter. We've got trouble, my friend.'

The MiG waggled its wings. 'He's signalling,' Vaughan said.

'I know that.' Kubel switched on the radio. Reception was very clear. The voice said, 'Adopt course three-four-zero for Allersberg airbase. I will follow you down.'

Kubel switched off the radio. 'This doesn't look too good. Those cannon of his could blow us to pieces.'

'Is there anything you can do?'

'In this kind of contest a jet's speed can be a disadvantage. I'm really too slow for him to handle. I'll go down low and see if I can make him do something stupid.'

He banked to port and went down fast and the MiG banked too in a sweeping curve that would bring him in on the Storch's tail. He started to fire his cannon, too soon, his speed so excessive that he had to bank to starboard to avoid collision.

Kubel was at six hundred when the MiG came in again, and this time the Storch staggered under the impact as cannon shells punched holes in the wings.

The MiG turned away in a great curve, then came in again, and once more the Storch shuddered under the impact of cannon shell. The windscreen disintegrated and Kubel cried out sharply.

Vaughan said, 'Are you all right?'

Kubel's flying jacket was ripped just under the left shoulder. When Vaughan reached over to touch it, he found blood.

'Never mind that, I'll live,' Kubel said. 'Just hang on tight because this time I'll show the bastard how to fly.'

They were now down to five hundred feet, the countryside clear below them, the border very close. The MiG came in for the kill, sliding in on their tail perfectly. Pieces flew off the wings as the cannon shells struck home and Kubel dropped his flaps.

The Storch seemed to stand still in mid-air and the pilot of the MiG, totally unprepared, banked steeply to starboard to avoid collision. Too steeply and the MiG, with no space to work in, ploughed straight into the forest below.

There was a mushroom of flame, spectacular in the night, and then it was behind them, already fading as they pushed on to the border.

The engine seemed to miss a beat and Kubel worked at the controls frantically. 'Come on, you bitch. Don't let me down now.'

Vaughan checked Conlin. The old man was still unconscious, but his breathing seemed regular enough.

'Is he okay?' Kubel shouted.

Vaughan nodded. 'Are you?'

'So I've taken a little steel in the back. I've had worse and this time it was worth it.' He laughed out loud. 'Don't you see, Simon? I've got my one hundred and fiftieth.'

A moment later, they coasted across the border and he banked to starboard and commenced his descent for Bitterfeld.

II

Franz closed the barn doors and barred them with a baulk of timber. Like the others, he was dressed in the uniform of the Volkspolizei. They stood by the field truck in the rain, each man with an AK rifle slung across his chest in approved fashion.

Konrad peered out through the side gate anxiously. 'Come on,' he whispered. 'Where are you, Margaret?'

Gregor moved to join him. 'It's no good, we must go. It is only a matter of time before our tunnel is discovered. We can't afford to stay here any longer.'

There was the sound of running footsteps and Berg appeared from the darkness, face distraught, totally panic-stricken. Konrad brought him to a halt and held him at arm's length.

'What is it? Where's the girl!'

Berg, struggling to catch his breath, had difficulty in speaking. 'He's got her. Van Buren's got her.'

Konrad shook him. 'What are you talking about?'

'She went to see the priest to see if there was anything she could do, but he was dead. Then van Buren turned up.'

'And?'

'They took her away in a Vopo field car. To Schloss Neustadt.'

Konrad gazed at him in horror, still holding on to the front of Berg's coat. Berg said urgently, 'We must go, don't you see? It's only a matter of time and they'll be here.'

'He's right,' Gregor said gently to Konrad. 'Remember Major Vaughan's orders? We were to wait for no one.'

'But we can't leave her,' Konrad said. 'We must do something.'

'She's at Schloss Neustadt by now,' Gregor said. 'We can do nothing.' He prised Konrad's fingers away from Berg's jacket. 'You get in the back of the truck.' He turned to the others. 'All of you – mount up.'

Konrad said in a dead voice, 'What a thing to happen after all this. As if she hasn't suffered enough.' He turned and his voice was savage now. 'You know something, Gregor. This God I've been serving all these years – I'm beginning to wonder whether he's at home any more.'

He climbed up behind the wheel and Gregor got in beside him. Konrad pressed the starter and drove out through the gates.

The sound of the engine faded into the night, the courtyard lay silent and deserted. It was a good twenty minutes before there were the first sounds of movement inside the barn and someone started banging on the door.

III

'The Resurrection was astonishing,' van Buren said. 'If true, that is, which I've always doubted, but your case, Margaret – that's what I call a miracle. Old mother Elbe was supposed to take you to her bosom weeks ago.'

She sat there beside the desk, hands folded in her lap, very calm. 'I've nothing to say.'

'Nothing new in that,' he said. 'You always were an introverted little thing. Understandable, of course, after the kind of conditioning you went through.'

The door opened and Süssmann hurried in. 'A manhole cover on the lower level gives access to a sewer pipe from the war days that's never been used. We found a tunnel from it leading under the cemetery, emerging in the barn at the Home Farm.'

'The Home Farm?'

'The Franciscans.'

Van Buren laughed out loud, head thrown back. 'Oh, but that's beautiful. That really is a pearl. They're not there now, of course?'

'No. The place is deserted.'

Van Buren turned again to Margaret Campbell. 'So that's where you've been hiding out for the past few weeks?'

She made no reply. Süssmann said, 'Berg, the caretaker, appears to be missing, also Schaefer.'

'Schaefer?' van Buren said sharply. 'But of course, that would fit very nicely. Schaefer and the priest. I always did wonder about him.'

'Another thing. There's been a report of a light aircraft landing and taking off again in the vicinity of the river some time during the past hour.'

'Is that so?' Van Buren appeared curiously indifferent.

'For God's sake,' Süssmann said. 'What are we going to do?'

'I don't know,' van Buren told him amiably. 'Call out the guard. Alert the border. After all, you're the military genius around here.'

'But we must get Conlin back again,' Süssmann shouted, 'or we're all finished, and this bitch can tell us where he is.'

'You obviously weren't very good at mathematics when you were at school,' van Buren said patiently. 'If a plane landed and took off again within the past hour, who the hell do you think was on it?'

Süssmann turned and strode angrily from the room, slamming the door behind him. He went down the staircase quickly and entered his office where he found Becker waiting.

'What happens now?' the sergeant asked.

'God knows, Rudi,' Süssmann said. 'We could all find our heads on the block for this one. Get on the phone to HQ. Send out a red alert to all Volkspolizei units between here and the border to pick up anyone they find on the roads who is in the slightest way suspicious.'

Becker went out. Süssmann lit a cigarette and paced up and down nervously.

IV

'Schaefer,' van Buren said. 'He has to be the key figure. I should have known after he knocked hell out of Becker so superbly. He won't get far.'

'The plane,' she said serenely.

'He was also on board, was he? So he's safe and that pleases you.' He leaned back, watching her closely. 'Are you in love with him?'

'Too late for games,' she said. 'You've lost. If I were you, I'd be packing my bags right now.'

'But where would I go?' He smiled gently. 'I've been everywhere, that's the problem. But to get back to Schaefer. If he was on the plane, that means he left you and that doesn't fit. He isn't the type.'

She was silent and he continued. 'You were supposed to leave with the others, weren't you? And then you heard about Hartmann and just had to play doctors. He isn't going to like that, Schaefer, or whatever his name is.'

'Vaughan.' There was pride in her voice. 'Major Simon Vaughan.'

'English? Now, there's a thing.' He nodded slowly. 'He'll come back for you.'

'Don't be absurd.' She was genuinely alarmed now.

'He'll come back for you, Margaret. That kind of man always comes back. It's my business to know these things,' he said cheerfully. 'I am, after all, one of the world's better psychologists.'

'No,' she said. 'No!' as if by repetition she could make it so.

He poured himself an enormous brandy. 'You've got a problem, I can help you.' His grimace was painful. 'The only trouble is, and this will make you fall about laughing, I could never understand my own. Problems, I mean.'

There was silence while he brooded. For no accountable reason she said, 'I'm sorry.'

'Well, that's handsome of you. Excuse me for a moment, will you?'

Instead of going out, he simply picked up the phone and dialled Klein's office number. Frau Apel answered at once.

'Working late, aren't you?' he said. 'Is he in?'

'I think so, professor.'

A moment later Klein came on. 'Hello, Harry, I was just leaving. What's the news at your end?'

'All black,' van Buren said. 'Conlin escaped.'

'What?' Klein said. 'That isn't possible.'

'My dear Helmut, anything is possible in this wicked old

world of ours,' van Buren told him. 'I'd have thought a man of your varied experience would have realized that by now. The details aren't important at the moment. The fact is that an assorted group, which included that damn priest of yours, got Conlin out of Schloss Neustadt earlier this evening and flew him out by light plane. For some obscure reason, I wanted the pleasure of telling you all this myself.'

'You're sure of your facts?' Klein said. 'You're certain he's got clean away?'

'Goodbye, Helmut.' Van Buren put down the phone and poured another brandy.

'What happens now?' she asked.

'We wait,' he said. 'We wait to see if I'm right about this Major Vaughan of yours.'

V

Süssmann was just about to leave his office when the phone rang. When he picked it up, Klein was on the other end.

'I've just heard from van Buren. I want your version of what's happened there tonight. Quickly now.'

Süssmann told him, leaving nothing out. When he was finished, there was silence. He said tentatively, 'Colonel, are you there?'

'Yes,' Klein said. 'I was thinking.'

'What do you want me to do, colonel?'

'You're a promising officer, Süssmann. A pity to see you pulled down by your association with a man who is most certainly a traitor to the State. The only conceivable explanation for this whole sorry affair. I should be there in about a couple of hours to interrogate van Buren personally. Naturally, if he attempts to leave before I arrive, you would be within your rights to prevent him by any means possible. Such action would redound to your credit. You understand me?'

'Good, I'll see you later.'

Süssmann put down the phone, then he took out his Walther and checked the clip.

VI

After speaking to Süssmann, Klein turned to the rows of books which lined the wall behind him. He removed several to reveal a small wall-safe which he opened quickly. He took out a very ordinary-looking office file and a set of false identity papers which he had long had ready for such a day. The file contained a list of the identities of all agents of his department at that time operating in West Germany.

He slipped it into his briefcase and checked the false identity papers. A good thing that as a security chief, his face was not generally known to the military. He slipped the papers into his breast pocket, pulled on his coat and picked up his briefcase.

Frau Apel was still at her desk. She glanced up. 'You're going now, colonel?'

'Yes. Good of you to stay so late, Clara. Get yourself home now and I'll see you in the morning.'

He went out, whistling cheerfully. Twenty minutes later he passed through a little used checkpoint near Koenigstrasse and presented himself to the policeman on duty on the other side with the astonishing request that he be put in touch at once with General Reinhardt Gehlen, Director of the Federal Intelligence Service.

VII

It was still raining at Flossen where Bulow paced up and down outside the guard hut impatiently. At nine-thirty he had received the red alert signal from the HQ which meant no traffic of any description to be allowed through. His wife was already safe on the other side with their child and all he wanted now was to join them.

Hornstein, who had moved a little way up the road, turned excitedly. 'There's a vehicle coming.'

He moved to the sergeant's side. They waited anxiously and then a Volkspolizei field truck moved out of the night and braked to a halt.

Konrad leaned out of the window. 'I believe you've been waiting for us.'

Bulow didn't even bother to reply. Hornstein was already

raising the barrier. They both scrambled over the tailgate, helped by willing hands as the field truck started to roll again, moving across to the West.

VIII

Pascoe was in the control room at Bitterfeld on his own when Böhmler came in to tell him that the truck had arrived safely. They went across to the hangars together and found a state of some confusion. The Franciscans were standing by the truck talking to Teusen and Meyer.

As Pascoe entered, Meyer said passionately, 'Madness, that's the only word for it. He goes to his death.'

'What's going on?' Pascoe demanded.

'I'm afraid we lost Doctor Campbell, professor,' Konrad told him. 'She is now in van Buren's hands at Schloss Neustadt.'

'Simon says he's going back for her,' Teusen said.

There was the sound of footsteps. They all turned and Vaughan entered the hangar once again in his Vopo uniform and dispatch-rider's raincoat. The AK was slung across his chest and he was fastening his helmet strap.

Pascoe said, 'There's no point to this.'

Vaughan ignored him and said to Konrad, 'Is there much activity over there?'

'Oh yes,' Konrad said. 'We passed several patrols, but no one bothered us. They assumed we were after the same game.'

'So why should they treat me any differently?' Vaughan mounted the Cossack and kicked the engine into life.

Teusen said, 'Don't be a fool, Simon.'

'You want to do something for me, keep that crossing point open for as long as you can.' Vaughan opened the throttle and roared away.

There was silence. Pascoe sighed and turned to Sergeant Bulow and young Hornstein. 'It would seem you gentlemen are going to have to return to duty for a while.'

'Oh no,' Bulow said. 'That wasn't in the contract.'

'But my dear man, you must see the necessity. If your HQ phones through and you're not there to answer, they'll come looking.'

'That may have happened already,' Bulow said.

'We'll just have to take our chances on that one.'

'No!'

There was an AK rifle on the driver's seat of the truck. Pascoe picked it up and cocked it. 'I'm not disposed to argue. You go back over there and I'll go with you.'

'Let me,' Teusen said.

Pascoe smiled wearily. 'No, Bruno, for once, this is my show. I was always good at sending other men out into the field, but not this time.' He turned back to Bulow. 'After you, sergeant, if you please.'

IX

Vaughan drove up the narrow approach road to Schloss Neustadt with care and when he went over the crest of the hill, he found a sentry standing in a box at the tunnel entrance out of the rain.

Vaughan brought the Cossack to a halt. 'Dispatch for Professor van Buren from Berlin.'

The sentry waved him on without hesitation and Vaughan drove in through the dark tunnel. This time there was no sentry at the other end and he moved on across the cobbled square past the main entrance, following the narrow passage between high walls that brought him finally into the rear courtyard.

He switched off the engine and dismounted, remembering Berg's description of the private entrance to the commandant's quarters. It had to be here somewhere. He unslung his AK and moved forward.

X

Margaret Campbell lay on the bed in van Buren's bedroom in the dark, her eyes open. She was thinking about Vaughan, wondering what had happened to him. But most of all, she was praying that he wouldn't act in the way van Buren had predicted.

At that moment the door opened and the light was switched

on. Van Buren stood looking at her, a glass in his hand. 'Come in here,' he said, and went back into the other room.

When she joined him, he was standing by the fire pouring another brandy. He seemed more than a little drunk. 'He disappoints me, this boy-friend of yours. Where is he?'

There was a slight creak, a sudden cold draught. They both turned as the narrow door in the far corner swung open and Vaughan stepped into the room, holding the AK at the ready.

Margaret Campbell ran to his side. 'Oh, you fool – you marvellous bloody fool. Wasn't once enough for you? Haven't I been enough trouble?'

He smiled. 'I decided to forgive you all that.' He put an arm around her.

Van Buren laughed delightedly. 'You see, I'm never wrong. The mind of man is an open book to the great van Buren.'

Vaughan said, 'If you make a sound, I'll cut you in half with this thing.'

'And bring every man in the castle on the run? Don't be stupid, Schaefer or Vaughan or whatever your name is.'

'I'm taking her out of here.'

'Who's stopping you?'

Van Buren poured another brandy and turned away. Vaughan lowered the gun. 'What's going on here?'

Margaret Campbell put a hand on his arm. 'Don't argue, Simon. Just go.' She turned to van Buren. 'I'm sorry, Harry. In spite of everything you did concerning my father, I'm still sorry for you.'

'So am I.' Van Buren raised his glass. 'L'Chayim. Now get out of here.'

Vaughan led the way quickly down the spiral stone staircase. At the bottom, he opened the door and peered out, but there was no one in evidence. He took her arm and hurried her across to the Cossack.

'You'll have to crouch down in the sidecar cockpit and I'll cover you with the rain tarpaulin.'

She climbed in and as she settled herself, said, 'What was it he said up there just before we left?'

'L'Chayim,' Vaughan told her. 'It's a Hebrew word. It means "to life".'

She didn't say anything to that, simply crouched down as

he had instructed her. He stretched the rain cover across the cockpit, snapping the studs into place, then he swung a leg over the Cossack and started the engine. A few moments later, the sentry was waving them through the main entrance.

XI

Van Buren stood in front of the fire, staring back into the past. 'Well, at least I was a pretty good corporal of Marines,' he said softly. 'Maybe that counts for something.'

He emptied his glass, put it down, then crossed to the door and opened it, intending to look for Süssmann. There was a murmur of voices from the hall below and when he peered over the balustrade he saw Süssmann and Becker standing down there.

'The sooner it's done, the better,' Süssmann was saying. 'When Klein gets here, he wants to find him dead. It's important for all of us, Rudi. He takes all the guilt.'

Becker took out his Walther and checked it and van Buren stepped back into his office. A few moments later, he came out again and stood at the head of stairs as they started up.

'Ah, there you are, Süssmann. I wanted a word with you.'

The two men paused on the landing half way up the stairs and took out their Walthers. 'You're under arrest,' Süssmann said. 'For treason against the State. You will deliver the woman Campbell into my charge.'

'Not possible, I'm afraid,' van Buren told him. 'I let her go ages ago.'

'You're lying.'

'No, my friend, with all my faults that's something I never did do. When does the shooting start?' Becker glanced uncertainly at Süssmann and van Buren said, 'Shot while trying to escape. Isn't that how it goes?'

'If you say so.'

Süssmann fired three times. As van Buren cried out he opened both hands, dropping the two Russian pineapple grenades he was holding. They bounced down the stairs, one after the other. Becker uttered a cry of fear and, turning to run, collided with Süssmann. The grenades exploded a second later.

XII

It was half past two when the Cossack emerged from the darkness and braked to a halt where Bulow and Hornstein stood waiting outside the guard hut at Flossen. Pascoe appeared in the doorway, the AK in his hands. Vaughan pushed up his goggles wearily.

'Were you successful, major?'

Vaughan pulled back the canvas rain cover and Margaret Campbell sat up. 'Are we here?' she asked. 'Are we in the West?'

'No,' Vaughan said. 'But we soon will be.'

He drove on and Charles Pascoe, Bulow and Hornstein followed on foot. Behind them, the telephone started to ring in the guard hut. It rang for quite some time before it stopped. It was quiet then, only the door creaking a little as it swung to and fro in the slight wind.

— 16 —

ON 21 JUNE in Rome, Cardinal Giovanni Battista Montini was elected to the papal throne by the Sacred College, taking the name of Paul VI. In a room at the Collegio di San Roberto Bellarmino, Father Sean Conlin was in bed, propped up against pillows and reading a book when Pacelli entered to give him the news.

Conlin said, 'So – life goes on?'

'So it would appear.'

'But not for Erich Hartmann. Tell me, Father, what was he like? What was he really like?'

'Who knows? A mystery – like all men – known only to his maker.'

'A bit of a saint, would you say?'

'Certainly not. Erich was entirely lacking in the kind of

humility needed for that office. What he did at Neustadt was magnificent nonsense – but thank God for it.'

'Ah, well,' Sean Conlin sighed. 'I'll remember him in my prayers for the rest of my life.'

'I, too.' Pacelli smiled. 'And now you must excuse me. I have a great deal to do. The work goes on.'

He went out. It was very quiet in the room as Father Conlin closed his eyes, folded his hands and prayed for the repose of the soul of Erich Hartmann.

II

On 26 June President Kennedy paid an eight-hour visit to West Berlin. Landing at Tegel airfield in the French sector, he made a thirty-mile drive through the city, accompanied by Dr Adenauer and Willi Brandt, amid the frenzied cheering of one million, two hundred and fifty thousand people.

The party finally reached the West Berlin town hall in Schöneberg where the president was expected to make the most important speech of his tour.

The room on the first floor to which he was taken was crowded, and among those waiting there were Charles Pascoe and Simon Vaughan. The president moved through the crowd, stopping here and there.

When he got to Pascoe and Vaughan he shook hands, the smile easy and relaxed, no different from what it had been for the others. Only his words carried their own meaning.

'Gentlemen, we are glad, believe me, to see you here today.'

He moved out on the balcony to an enormous cheer from the crowd. He started to speak. Pascoe said, 'I know I'm getting old, but it's still better to travel hopefully. He could be what we all need, that man. At least he says the right things. The things that should be said.'

Kennedy's voice drifted in. 'Today in the world of freedom, the proudest boast is *Ich bin ein Berliner*.'

He was leaning over the balcony, touched by light, and then it was as if a shadow passed over the face of the sun, and the light on him died, but only for a moment.

For some unaccountable reason, Vaughan went cold. He

said to Pascoe, 'Let's get out of here. You can read all about it in the papers.'

He turned and worked his way through the crowd, Pascoe following him. Margaret Campbell was standing against the wall at the head of the stairs with Meyer.

She reached for his hand. 'What's wrong, Simon? What is it?'

'Nothing,' he said. 'Someone just walked over my grave, that's all.'

As they went down the stairs, the president's voice rang out across the crowd like a trumpet blast. 'Freedom has many difficulties and democracy is not perfect, but we never had to put up a wall to keep our people in.'

THE VIOLENT ENEMY

— 1 —

ON THE CREST of a tor where the moor lifted to meet the blue sky in a sharply defined edge, Vanbrugh paused to catch his breath, sat on a stone and took out an old briar pipe and a tobacco pouch.

He was a tall, heavily built man in his middle forties, hair greying a little at the temples, shoulders solid with muscle under the old tweed jacket, and carried about him that indefinable quality that only twenty-five years as a policeman gives, a mixture of strength and authority and a shrewdness that was apparent in the light blue eyes.

A few moments later, Sergeant Dwyer joined him and slumped to the ground, chest heaving.

'You should do this more often,' Vanbrugh observed.

'Give me some leave and I will,' Dwyer said. 'I'd like to point out that I've been working a seventy-hour week since February and my last day off was so long ago it's become a fond memory.'

Vanbrugh grinned and put a match to his pipe. 'You shouldn't have joined.'

Somewhere in the distance an explosion echoed flatly on the calm air, and Dwyer sat up quickly. 'What was that?'

'They'll be blasting up at the quarry.'

'Prison working party?'

'That's right.'

Dwyer looked out across the moor, narrowing his eyes into the distance, relaxed and at ease with himself for the first time in months, the sharp, clear air driving the taste of London from his mouth. It was a happy chance that the old man should have chosen to make this mysterious personal visit to the most notorious of Her Majesty's prisons on such a glorious day, but one couldn't help feeling curious.

On the other hand, one thing he had learned in his two years with the Special Branch was that Chief Superintendent

Dick Vanbrugh was very much a law unto himself, as many on both sides in the great game had discovered to their cost over the years.

'We'd better be moving,' Vanbrugh said.

Dwyer scrambled to his feet and caught sight of the skeleton of a sheep impaled on a gorse bush in a hollow to the left.

'Death in life, even here on a day like this.'

'No escaping it wherever you go.' Vanbrugh turned and looked across the moor again. 'Whenever the mist creeps in, this place becomes a waking nightmare. A man can walk all day and end where he began.'

'No one ever gets off the moor,' Dwyer said softly. 'Isn't that what they say?'

'Something like that. In the whole history of the place, there's only one recorded instance of a man getting clean away and he's probably lying at the bottom of a bog. Some of them could swallow a three-ton truck.'

'The right sort of place for a prison.'

'That's what they thought when they built it.'

Vanbrugh set off down the slope towards the car parked at the side of the narrow road below and Dwyer followed, stumbling over the tussocks of rough grass and patches of marshy ground, water seeping in through the laceholes of his smart town brogues.

When he reached the car, Vanbrugh was already sitting in the passenger seat and Dwyer climbed behind the wheel, pressed the starter and drove away.

He was hot and tired, his feet were wet and his sweat-soaked shirt clung to his back. A small spark of temper flared inside him, but he pushed it away with a determined effort.

'A one-hundred-and-seventy-mile drive, wet feet and the makings of a good sprain in my ankle. I hope he's worth it, sir.'

Vanbrugh turned sharply and the blue eyes were very cold. '*I* think so, sergeant.'

Dwyer took a deep breath, aware that one of those violent storms for which Dick Vanbrugh was so notorious was about to break over his head, but the moment passed. Vanbrugh applied another match to the bowl of his pipe and Dwyer concentrated on his driving and on the sheep and wild ponies which frequently wandered across the unfenced road. Ten minutes later they came over a slight rise and saw the prison in the hollow below.

II

The moors lifted in a purple swell fading almost imperceptibly into the horizon, and at the head of the quarry a red flag danced in the slight breeze.

The explosion, when it came, echoed into the distance, the sound of it beating against the hills like thunder. As a great shoulder of rock cracked into a thousand pieces, smoke drifted in a white pall that curled over the edge of the rock and across the moor like some living thing.

A whistle sounded, and as the convicts emerged from shelter a Land-Rover came over the edge of the escarpment, rolled down the dirt road and stopped.

The youth at the wheel had very fair hair and blue eyes that somehow made him look even younger than he was. His uniform was brand new and he was painfully conscious of that fact as he got out of the Land-Rover and moved past a group of convicts loading a truck.

Mulvaney, the duty officer, moved to meet him, a black and tan Alsatian at his heels. He grinned. 'Hello, Drake. Putting you to work already, are they?'

Drake nodded. 'I've got a chit here for a man called Rogan. The governor wants to see him.'

He produced a slip of paper from his breast pocket. Mulvaney initialled it and waved towards a small hollow at the bottom of the slope.

'That's Rogan down there. You're welcome to him.'

The man indicated worked stripped to the waist and was at least six foot three, the muscles in his broad back rippling as he swung a sledgehammer above his head and brought it down.

'God in heaven, the man's a giant,' Drake said.

Mulvaney nodded. 'They don't come much bigger. Brains and brawn, that's Sean Rogan. Pound for pound, about the most dangerous man we've ever had in here.'

'They didn't send anyone with me.'

'No need. He's expecting his discharge any day now. That'll be what the governor wants to see him about. He's hardly likely to make a run for it at this stage.'

Drake moved down the slope. Bronzed and fit, his body toughened by hard labour, Sean Rogan looked a thoroughly dangerous man and the ugly puckered scars of the old bullet wounds in the left breast seemed strangely in keeping.

Drake paused a yard or two away and Rogan glanced up. The skin was stretched tightly over high Celtic cheek-bones, a stubble of beard covering the hollow cheeks and strong pointed chin. The eyes were grey like water over a stone or smoke through trees on an autumn day, calm and expressionless, holding their own secrets. It was the face of a soldier, a scholar perhaps. Certainly this was no criminal.

'Sean Rogan?' Drake said.

The big man nodded. 'That's me. What do you want?'

There was no hint of subservience in the soft Irish voice and Drake, for some unaccountable reason, felt like a young recruit being interviewed by a senior officer.

'The governor wants a word with you.'

Rogan picked up his shirt from a nearby boulder, pulled it over his head and followed Drake up the slope, the sledge-hammer swinging easily in one hand. He dropped it beside the duty officer. 'A present for you.'

Mulvaney grinned, took a battered silver case from his breast pocket and offered him a cigarette. 'Is it likely at all, Sean Rogan, that I might be seeing the back of you?'

Rogan's face was illuminated briefly by a smile of great natural charm. 'All things are possible, even in this worst of all possible worlds. You should know that, Patrick.'

Mulvaney touched him briefly on the shoulder. 'Go with God, Sean,' he said softly in Irish.

Rogan turned and walked quickly towards the Land-Rover and Drake found himself trailing a step or two behind. As they passed the group of convicts loading the truck, someone shouted, 'Good luck, Irish!' Rogan raised a hand in reply and climbed into the passenger seat.

Drake got behind the wheel and drove away rapidly, feeling uncertain and ill-at-ease. It was as if Rogan had taken charge, as if at any moment he might order him to take the next turning on the right instead of keeping straight on to the prison.

The Irishman smoked his cigarette slowly from long habit, gazing out over the moor. Drake glanced sideways at him a couple of times and tried to make conversation.

'They tell me you're hoping to get out soon?'

'One can always hope.'

'How long have you been here?'

'Seven years.'

The shock of it was like a blow in the face and Drake winced, thinking of the long years, the wind across the moor blowing rain, grey mornings, a brief summer passing quickly into autumn and the iron hand of winter.

He forced a smile. 'I've only been here a couple of days myself.'

'Your first posting?'

'No, I was at Wakefield for a while. Came out of the Guards last year. Didn't fancy another hitch and then I saw this advert for prison officers. It looked a good number so I thought I'd try it.'

'Is that a fact now?'

For some unaccountable reason Drake felt himself flushing. 'Somebody has to do it,' he said defensively. 'The pay could be worse and quarters and a pension at the end of it. You can't grumble at that, can you?'

'I'd rather be the devil,' Sean Rogan said with deep conviction. He half-turned, folding his arms deliberately, and stared out across the moor, cutting off all further attempts at conversation.

III

'It's certainly one hell of a record,' the governor said, looking down at the file on his desk, 'but then I don't need to tell you that, superintendent. I was hoping we'd see the back of him this time.'

'So was I, sir,' Vanbrugh said.

'There are days when I distinctly welcome the fact that I retire in another ten months.' The governor pushed back his chair and stood up. 'He'll be here in about fifteen minutes. In the meantime, I've one or two things to do. You make yourselves comfortable in here and I'll have them send you in some tea.'

The door closed behind him and Dwyer moved from the window to the desk. 'I don't know a great deal about Rogan, sir. A bit before my time. Wasn't he a big man in the IRA?'

'That's right. Sentenced to twelve years in '56 for organizing escapes from several prisons in England and Ulster. Remember the famous invasion of Peterhead in '55? They went over the wall under cover of darkness like blasted commandos and brought out three men. Got clean away.'

'He was behind that?'

'He led them in.' Vanbrugh opened the file. 'It's all here. He spent most of his early life in France and Germany. His father was in the Irish political service. He was a student at Trinity College, Dublin, when he was wounded and caught during a weekend raid over the Ulster border. That would be just before the war.'

'What did he get?'

'Seven years. He was released in 1941 at the request of the Special Operations Executive because of his fluency in French and German. That's when I first came across him. I was working for them myself at the time. He was given the usual training and dropped into France to organize the Maquis in the Vosges Mountains. He did damned well, saw the war out, told them what to do with their medals and demobbed himself the moment it was over.'

'What did he do then?'

'Got up to his old tricks. Five years at Belfast in 1947. They let him off lightly because of his war record. Not that it made any difference. He escaped within a year.' Vanbrugh grinned wryly. 'He made a habit of that. Parkhurst in '56, but never got off the island. Peterhead the following year. Three days on foot across the moor, then the dogs ran him down.'

'Which explains why he was finally sent here?'

'That's it. Maximum security. No possibility of escape.' Vanbrugh started to fill his pipe again. 'If you examine the file you'll find a confidential entry at the back. It refers to an incident the commissioners prefer to keep quiet about. In July

1960 Sean Rogan was picked up in the early hours of the morning crossing the field at the rear of the officers' quarters.'

Dwyer frowned. 'Isn't that outside the wall?'

Vanbrugh nodded. 'The principal officer had been playing cards late at another house. He had his Alsatian with him and on the way home, it picked up Rogan's scent.'

'But how did he get out?'

'He wouldn't say. The commissioners wanted it kept out of the press so the enquiry was very hush-hush. It was finally decided that he must have hidden himself in a car or truck on its way out.'

'At that time in the morning?'

'Don't worry. No one really accepted that one. They had him on maximum security for a couple of years after that. When the governor finally made things a little easier for him, Rogan told him that it didn't matter because he wasn't going to try again. He said that getting out was easy. It was getting anywhere without help once you were out that was difficult. I think he decided to sweat out his sentence and hope for remission.'

'Which is what he's just applied for?'

Vanbrugh nodded, 'When the IRA called off its border campaign in Ulster recently it just about went into liquidation. Most of its members serving sentences in English gaols have since been released. In fact the Home Office has been under considerable pressure to release them all.'

'And what's the answer on Rogan?'

'They're still frightened to death of him. Now I've got to tell him he's still got five years to serve.'

'Why you, sir?'

Vanbrugh shrugged. 'We worked together during the war. Since then, I've arrested him on three separate occasions. You might say I'm the Yard's Rogan expert.'

He walked to the window and stood looking out into the courtyard. 'England's the only country in the civilized world that doesn't make special provision for political offenders, did you know that, sergeant?'

'I hadn't really given it much thought, sir.'

'You should do, sergeant. You should do.'

The door opened and the governor came in quickly. 'They're

bringing him up now.' He sat down behind his desk and grinned tightly. 'I really don't have much stomach for this one, superintendent. I'm glad you're here.'

The door opened again and the principal officer came in. 'He's here, sir.'

The governor nodded. 'Let's get it over with, then.'

Outside, Drake stood beside the door waiting, and Rogan leaned against the wall, arms folded as he stared through the window at the end of the corridor.

Life was, on the whole, an act of faith. He'd read that somewhere once, but twenty years of hard living, of violence and the dark places had taught him to look only for the unexpected on the other side of each new hill.

Everyone in the place, including the screws, expected his pardon to go through. To Rogan, that was sufficient reason in itself for something to go wrong. When the door opened and the principal officer called him in, he was prepared for the worst.

The presence of Vanbrugh confirmed what was already apparent from the atmosphere in the office, and he stood in front of the desk, hands behind his back and looked out of the window over the governor's head. He noticed that the trees on the hill beyond the wall were stripped quite bare of leaves now and the untidy nests of the rookery were clearly exposed to view. He watched a rook flap lazily through the air from one tree to another and became aware that the governor was speaking to him.

'We've had a communication from the Home Office, Rogan. Chief Superintendent Vanbrugh brought it down with him specially.'

Rogan turned slightly to face Vanbrugh, and the big policeman got to his feet, suddenly awkward. 'I'm sorry, Sean. Damned sorry.'

'Then there's nothing to be said, is there?'

The hard shell with which he had surrounded himself was something they could not penetrate. In the heavy silence, the governor glanced helplessly at Vanbrugh, then sighed.

'I think you'd better come in from the quarry for a while, Rogan.'

'Permanently, sir?' Rogan said calmly.

The governor swallowed hard. 'We'll see how you go on.'

'Very well, sir.'

Rogan turned and walked to the door without waiting for the principal officer's order. He stood in the corridor, face expressionless, aware of the murmur of voices as the door closed behind him.

'You can go now, Drake,' the principal officer said, then turned to Rogan and said briskly, 'All right, Rogan.'

They went downstairs and crossed the courtyard to one of the blocks. Rogan stood waiting for the door to be unlocked, aware from the expression on the duty officer's face that he knew, which wasn't particularly surprising. Within another half hour every con, every screw in the place would know.

The prison had been constructed in the reform era of the nineteenth century on a system commonly found in Her Majesty's prisons. Half a dozen three-tiered cell blocks radiated like the spokes of a wheel from a central hall which lifted a hundred feet into the gloom to an iron framed dome.

For reasons of safety each cell block was separated from the central hall by a curtain of steel mesh. The principal officer unlocked the gate into D block and motioned Rogan through.

They mounted an iron staircase to the top landing, boxed in with more steel mesh to prevent anyone who felt like it from taking a dive over the rail. His cell was at the far end of the landing and he paused, waiting for the principal officer to unlock the door.

As it opened, Rogan took a step forward and the principal officer said, 'Don't try anything silly. You've everything to lose now.'

Rogan swung round, his iron control snapping for a brief moment so that the man recoiled from the savage anger that blazed in the grey eyes. He slammed the door shut quickly, turning the key in the lock.

Rogan turned slowly. The cell was only six by ten with a small barred window, and a washbasin and fixed toilet had been added in an attempt at modernization. A single bed ran along each wall.

A man was lying on one of them reading a magazine. He

looked about sixty-five, with very white hair, and eyes a vivid blue in a wrinkled humorous face.

'Hello, Jigger,' Rogan said.

In that single moment, the smile died on Jigger Martin's face and he swung his legs to the floor. 'The bastards,' he said. 'The lousy rotten bastards.'

Rogan stood looking out through the small barred window and Martin produced a packet of cigarettes from beneath his mattress and offered him one. 'What are you going to do now, Irish?'

Rogan blew out a cloud of smoke and laughed harshly. 'What do you think, boyo? What do you think?'

IV

As the gates closed behind them, Dwyer was conscious of a very real relief. It was as if a great weight had been lifted from him, and he took out his cigarettes.

He offered one to Vanbrugh who was driving, his face dark and sombre, but the big man shook his head. When they reached the crest of the hill, he braked, turned and looked down at the prison.

Dwyer said softly, 'What do you think he'll do, sir?'

Vanbrugh swung round, all his pent-up frustration and anger boiling out of him. 'For God's sake, use your intelligence. You saw him, didn't you? There's only one thing a man like that can do.'

He moved into gear and drove away rapidly in a cloud of dust.

— 2 —

DURING MOST of September it had been warm and clear, but on the last day the weather broke. Clouds hung threateningly over the moor, rain dripped from the gutters and when Rogan went to the window, brown leaves drifted across the courtyard from the trees in the governor's garden.

Behind him Martin shuffled the cards on a small stool. 'Another hand, Irish?'

'Not worth it,' Rogan said. 'They'll be feeding us soon.' He stood at the window, a slight frown on his face, his eyes following the roof line of the next block of the hospital beyond, and Martin joined him.

'Can it be done, Irish?'

Rogan nodded. 'It can be done all right. It took me just over two hours last time.' He turned and looked down at Martin. 'You'll never make it, Jigger. You'd break your bloody neck half-way.'

Martin grinned. 'What would I be wanting to crash out for? Nine months and I can spit in their eyes once and for all. My old woman's got a nice little boarding house going in Eastbourne. They won't see me back here again.'

'I seem to have heard that one before,' Rogan said. 'Can you still work that trick of yours on the door?'

'Always happy to oblige.'

Martin took an ordinary spoon from his bedside locker and went to the door. He listened for a moment, then dropped to one knee.

The lock was covered by a steel plate perhaps six inches square, and he quickly forced the handle of the spoon between the edge of the plate and the jamb. He worked it around for several minutes and there was a slight click. He pulled and the door opened slightly.

'Now that's one thing that always impresses me,' Rogan said.

'There's thirty years' hard graft there, Irish. The best screwsman in the business.' Martin sighed. 'The trouble is I got so good they could always tell when it was me.'

He pushed the door gently into place and worked the spoon round again. There was another slight click and he stood up.

'There have been times in my life when I could have used you,' Rogan said.

'You don't want to start consorting with criminals at your age, Irish.' Martin grinned. 'An old lag's trick. Plenty of cons in this place could do as much. These old mortice deadlocks are a snip. One of these days they'll get wise and change them.'

He went back to his bed, produced a packet of cigarettes and tossed one across to Rogan. 'There's at least six other gates to pass through between here and the yard and most of them are guarded, remember. It'll take more than a spoon to get you out of this place.'

'Anything can be done if you put your mind to it,' Rogan said. 'Come to the window and I'll show you.'

Martin held up a hand quickly and shook his head. 'Nothing doing. What I don't know can't hurt you.'

Rogan frowned. 'You're no grass, Jigger.'

The old man shrugged. 'We can all be pushed just so far in a place like this.'

There was a rattle at the door and, turning quickly, Rogan was aware of an eye at the spyhole. The key turned in the lock and the principal officer came in.

'Outside, Rogan. Someone wants to see you.'

Rogan frowned. 'Who is it?'

'A bloke called Soames. Lawyer from London. Something to do with an appeal. Seems you've got friends working for you.'

As he waited in the queue outside the visiting room, Rogan wondered about Soames, trying to decide what could be behind his visit. As far as he was aware, there was no chance of an appeal against the Home Secretary's decision for at least another year, and to his certain knowledge there was no one working for him on the outside. Since the organization had gone into voluntary liquidation the previous year, he'd become a dead letter to most people.

When his turn came, the duty officer took him in and sat him in a cubicle. Rogan waited impatiently, the conversation on either side a meaningless blur, and then the door opened and Soames came in.

He was small and dark with a neatly trimmed moustache and soft pink hands. He carried a bowler hat and briefcase and wore a neat pin-striped suit.

He sat down and smiled through the wire mesh. 'You won't know me, Mr Rogan. My name's Soames – Henry Soames.'

'So I've been told,' Rogan said. 'Who sent you?'

Soames glanced each way to make sure that no individual conversation could be overheard in the general hubbub, then leaned close.

'Colum O'More.'

A vivid picture jumped into Rogan's mind at once, one of those queer tricks that memory plays. He had just volunteered to 'go active' as they'd called it in the organization in those days, a callow, seventeen-year-old student. They'd taken him to a house outside Dublin for the final important interview and had left him alone in a small room to wait. And then the door had opened and a giant of a man had entered, the mouth split in a wide grin as he laughed back over his shoulder at someone outside, wearing his strength and courage for all to see like a suit of armour. Colum O'More – the Big Man.

'Are you sure, *avic*?' he'd said to Rogan. 'You know what you're getting into?'

Mother of God, who wouldn't be sure and face to face with such a man?

'So Colum sent you?' Rogan said.

'Not directly.' Soames smiled faintly. 'I believe there's something like half of a ten-year sentence still hanging over his head in this country. He *is* in England at the moment, but we've only met personally once. Since then I've been working through an accommodation address.'

'If you're thinking of raising my case again with the Home Secretary, you're wasting your time.'

'I couldn't agree more.' Soames smiled slightly. 'To be

perfectly frank, Colum O'More was thinking of adopting more unorthodox means.'

'Such as?' Rogan said calmly.

'Assisting you to leave without the Home Secretary's permission.'

'And what makes you think I could?'

'A man called Pope,' Soames said. 'I believe he shared a cell with you for a year? He was released six months ago.'

'I still have the stink of him in my nostrils,' Rogan said contemptuously. 'A cheap, two-a-penny tearaway. The worst kind. Was a peeler with the Metropolitan and got done for corruption. He'd sell his own sister on the streets if you made it worth his while.'

'He tells an interesting story, Mr Rogan. He insists that in 1960 you were caught in the early hours of the morning outside the walls of this prison. That to this day the authorities have never been able to find out how you got out.'

'He has a big mouth,' Rogan said. 'One day someone will be closing his eyes with pennies.'

'Is it true?' Soames said, and for the first time there was an urgency in his voice. 'Have you a way out?'

'And if I had?'

'Then Colum O'More would be glad to see you.'

'And how could that be managed?'

Soames leaned even closer. 'You know the quarry and the hamlet between it and the river – Hexton?'

'I've been working there for the past year.'

'Below the quarry there's an iron footbridge. On the other side of the river you'll find a cottage. You can't miss it. It's completely isolated.'

'Will Colum be there?'

'No, Pope.'

'Why him?'

'He's proved very useful. He'll have clothes, a car, even an identity for you. You could be clear of the moor within half an hour.'

'And where do I go?'

'Pope will have full instructions. They'll take you to Colum O'More. That's as much as I can tell you.'

Rogan sat there, a slight frown knitting his forehead,

considering the situation. He wasn't happy about Pope, and Soames was a hollow man if ever he'd seen one, but was there really any choice? And if Colum O'More was behind the organization . . .

'Well?' Soames said.

Rogan nodded. 'How soon can Pope be ready?'

'He's ready now. I'd heard you were a man who doesn't like to let grass grow under your feet.'

'It's Thursday today,' Rogan said. 'Better make it Sunday.'

'Any particular reason?'

'It's dark by six and we're locked up for the night at half past in my wing. From then on there's only one duty screw who works from the central hall checking blocks. If I'm not missed, and there's no reason why I should be, they won't find I'm gone till they turn out the cells at seven on Monday morning.'

'Which sounds sensible.' Soames hesitated and then said carefully, 'You're certain you can get out?'

'Nothing's certain in this life, Mr Soames, I'd have thought you'd have found that out for yourself by now.'

'How right you are, Mr Rogan.' Soames picked up his bowler hat and briefcase and pushed back his chair. 'I don't think there's anything more to discuss. I'll look forward to Monday's newspaper with interest.'

'So will I,' Rogan said.

He stood there watching as Soames walked to the door and waited. A few moments later, the principal officer came for him and they went back into the corridor.

As they went back across the courtyard, he said, 'Any joy?'

Rogan shrugged. 'You know what these lawyers are like. Big with their promises and fees, but short on hope. I gave up counting my chickens a long time ago.'

'The best way of looking at things and the most sensible.'

When they reached the top landing, the bell was sounding for the midday meal and when Rogan went back into his cell, Martin already had the plates ready on the small table. When the door closed, he waited for a moment, then looked at Rogan questioningly.

'And what was all that about?'

For a moment, Rogan was going to tell him and then he

remembered the old man's words earlier. That in a place like this a man could only be pushed so far. He was right, of course. If Sean Rogan had learned one thing from the thirteen years of his life spent between four walls, it was that no one was ever completely dependable.

He shrugged. 'Some friends of mine on the outside have clubbed together and dug up a lawyer. He wanted to meet me personally before trying the Home Secretary again.'

Martin's face creased into the perpetual smile of hope of the long serving convict. 'Hell, Irish, maybe things are looking up.'

'You can always hope,' Sean Rogan said and moved to the window.

It was still raining and a slight mist curled across the top of the hill beyond the walls where the quarry lay. If you listened carefully you could almost hear the river; dark, peat-stained, splashing over great boulders on its long run down to the sea.

— 3 —

RAIN DASHED against the window as Rogan peered into the darkness. After a while, he went to the door and stood listening, and from below the steel gate clanged hollowly as the duty officer closed it after him.

He turned and grinned tightly, his face shadowed in the dim light. 'A hell of a night for it.'

Martin was lying on his bed reading a book, and he pushed himself up on one elbow. 'For what?'

Rogan crouched beside him and said calmly, 'I'm crashing out, Jigger. Whose side are you on?'

'Why, yours, Irish, you don't need to ask.' The old man's face was grey with excitement and he swung his legs to the floor. 'What do you want me to do?'

'Open the door,' Rogan said. 'Just that. When I've gone, you leave it unlocked, get back on your bed and stay there till they turn out the cells at seven.'

Martin licked his lips nervously. 'What happens when they bring me up in front of the governor?'

'Tell him you got the shock of your life when I opened the door, that you lay there and minded your own business.' Rogan grinned coldly. 'After all, that's just what he'd expect you to do. Any con who did anything else under similar circumstances wouldn't last twenty-four hours before the boys got him. The governor knows that as well as you do.'

The threat was implicit and Martin got to his feet hastily. 'Hell, Irish, I wouldn't do anything to ball things up, you know that.'

Rogan turned over his mattress, slid his hand through the seam at one side and pulled out a coil of nylon rope and a sling with snap links at the end, of the type used by climbers.

'Where in the hell did you get those?' Martin asked.

'They use them up at the quarry when they're placing charges in the cliff face.' Rogan took out a narrow-handled screwdriver and a pair of ninc-inch wire cutters which he tucked into his belt.

'These came by way of the machine shop.' He nodded towards the door. 'Okay, Jigger, let's get moving. I'm on a tight schedule.'

Martin took out the spoon and knelt in front of the door, his hands shaking a little. For a moment he seemed to be having some difficulty and then there was a slight click. He turned, his face very pale in the dim light, and nodded.

Rogan quickly arranged his pillow and some spare clothing from his locker into some semblance of a human form under the blankets on his bed. He moved to the door.

'I just thought of something,' Martin said. 'You know how the duty screw pussyfoots in carpet slippers?'

'He'll have a look through the spyhole, that's all,' Rogan said, 'and if he can tell that it isn't me in that bed in this light, he's got better eyes than I have.'

Suddenly, Martin seemed to undergo a change. It was as if ten years had slipped from his worn shoulders and he laughed softly. 'I can't wait to see the expression on that screw's face in the morning.' He clapped Rogan on the shoulder. 'Go on, son, get to hell out of it and keep on running.'

The landing was dimly lit and the wing was wrapped in quiet. Rogan stood in the shadow of the wall for a moment, then moved quickly to the stairs at the far end.

The great central hall was illuminated by a single light, and above him its roof and the dome were shrouded in darkness. He climbed on to the rail and scrambled up the steel mesh curtain to the roof of the cell block. He hooked the snap links of his sling into the wire, securing himself in place and took out the wire cutters.

It didn't take him long, cutting in a straight line against the wall, to make an aperture perhaps three feet long through which he pulled himself. Once on the other side, he again hooked himself into place and carefully closed up the links one by one so that only a close inspection could reveal his passage. His previous escape had been made from B Block on the opposite side of the hall and in three years no one had discovered his route out from there.

Steel supporting beams lifted into the darkness, each one supported on a block of masonry which jutted from the main fabric of the wall. He reached the first one with ease and wedged himself against the wall, judging the five-foot gap to the next carefully. A quick breath, a leap into darkness and he was across. He repeated the performance three times until he had completed the necessary half-circle which brought him to the beam close to B Block.

A door clanged and he glanced down and saw the duty officer and the chief walk through the pool of light below to the desk. They were talking together in low tones, the voices drifting up as the duty officer made an entry in the night book. There was a burst of laughter and they crossed the hall, unlocked the door leading to the guardroom and disappeared.

Rogan slipped the sling around the beam and his waist, snapped the links together and started to climb, leaning well out.

The difficulty lay in the fact that the beam itself started to curve, following the line of the wall, leaving only an inch or two for the sling. It was now that his perfect physical condition and massive strength stood him in good stead. He gritted his teeth and heaved his way up into the darkness almost inch by inch and the pool of light receded beneath him. A few moments later, he reached his objective, a large steel ventilation grille, perhaps two and a half feet square.

It was held in place by two large screws on either side and he braced himself against the wall, leaning back in the sling, took out the screwdriver and set to work.

The screws were brass and came out easily, but he left one partly in position so that the grille swung down, no longer obscuring the entrance, but still securely held.

He had now reached the most difficult moment. He carefully unhooked the spring links securing the sling and pushed it into the shaft quickly, then forcing his fingers behind the beam he walked up the wall and pushed himself feet first into the zinc-lined ventilating shaft. Clouds of dry dust arose, filling his nostrils. He choked back a cough and reached out and swung the grille back into place. Very carefully he pushed his fingers through and replaced the screw he had removed, covering his tracks completely.

On his previous attempt he'd had an electric torch, something he hadn't managed to get hold of this time, and from now on he had to work in darkness, relying completely on memory.

He had worked out the route after a fast ten minutes with a map of the prison's ventilation system carelessly left on a bench in the machine shop by a heating engineer, but that had been three years ago and there had been structural alterations since then. He could only pray that the section he was using had been left alone.

He moved backwards into darkness, the dust filling his eyes and throat, sweat trickling down his face, and after a while, came to another opening. He went into it head first and slid gently down a shallow slope, slowing his descent by bracing his hands against the sides.

At the bottom, he paused. It was completely dark, no chink of light anywhere. He was boxed in as securely as if he had been in his own coffin. He pushed the idea away from him and inched forward again.

He came to a side shaft and then another and paused. Six or was it seven? No, six before he roped down to the first level. He pushed forward again, counting until he reached the shaft on his left. He ran his hand along the right side and found at once the supporting bracket he had forced from the wall as a support on that other occasion. He pushed forward, then eased himself backwards into the hole. He supported himself with his arms, uncoiled the nylon rope, looped it into a running line around the bracket he had forced out from the wall, then lowered himself carefully down the shaft. Thirty feet below, it curved into a straight line and he moved into it backwards on his belly, pulling the rope down after him. He coiled it carefully and inched backwards.

Light showed through in several places and he paused at a grille and peered down into the main kitchens. There was a light on, but they were quite deserted and he moved on, emerging into a slightly larger shaft. He twisted round and went forward on his hands and knees.

He was now at the far end of the central block and perhaps forty minutes had elapsed since he left his cell. He moved on quickly and came out into the bottom of a wide shaft that lifted vertically above his head, bands of yellow light cutting into it from grilles set at several levels.

The zinc lining of the shaft was held in place by a network of steel stays which provided excellent footholds and he started to climb quickly. His objective was a side shaft at the very top which ran through the roof and out across the courtyard to the hospital on the other side.

He became conscious of a strong current of air and a low, humming sound, and frowned. This was something new and the heart moved inside him. A few moments later he reached the top of the shaft and his worst fears were confirmed. Where there had previously been only the entrance to the link with the hospital, there was now a metal grille protecting an electric extractor fan. He stayed there for a moment, tracing the edge of the grille with his free hand, knowing it was hopeless, then started down.

The first grille he came to was only a foot square and he moved on down to the next. This was perhaps two feet square, a tight squeeze certainly, but possible. He could see into a quiet corridor, dimly lit and remembered that these would be the bachelor quarters for unmarried officers.

He hesitated for only a moment, wedged there in the narrow shaft, then took out the screwdriver and pushed his hand as far between the bars of the grille as it would go, holding the screwdriver by the shaft. He felt for the head of the left hand screw and to his relief it started to move at once. A moment later, the screw fell to the floor and he forced the grille down with all his strength.

He went back up the shaft a little way so that he was able to lower himself through the grille feet first. There wasn't much room, and for a moment he seemed to stick and then went through in a rush, shirt tearing, landing six feet below in the corridor.

He picked himself up quickly, turned and forced the grille back into position, then moved along the corridor. He could hear a radio playing and there was a quick burst of laughter, strangely muted and far away. At the end of the corridor, he came to the stairhead and looked over the banisters. Three floors below he could see the entrance hall quiet and still in the light from a single yellow bulb. He went down quickly, keeping to the wall.

At the bottom he paused in the shadows then crossed quickly to the door, then opened it and hesitated in the porch. A lamp jutted from the wall, casting a pool of light to the path below, and he went down the steps quickly and moved into the darkness at the front of the walls.

The rain was falling heavily now, bouncing from the cobbled courtyard like steel rods and he glanced up at the ventilating shaft high above his head stretching across to the hospital. It had originally given him access to the hospital roof, now he had to find another route.

He kept to the shadows of the wall, working his way round the courtyard until he reached the hospital and moved round to one side. It was then that he remembered the fire escape. He found it a moment later and started quickly, head lowered against the driving rain.

The final landing was outside a door directly under the eaves of the roof and he climbed on to the rail, reached up to the gutter and tested it quickly. It seemed reasonably secure and he took a quick breath and heaved himself up and over.

He scrambled up on to the ridge of the building and moved

along it, a foot on either side, hands braced against the tiles. It took him a good five minutes of careful work to reach the end of the building and the chimney stack of the incinerator.

No more than fifty feet away from him through the darkness was the spiked edge of the outer wall of the prison, and beneath him an iron drainage pipe cut through space to meet it. Rogan uncoiled his nylon rope, flung one end round the chimney stack and went straight over the edge gripping the double strand tightly.

His feet slipped on wet brickwork and he swung wildly, skinning his knuckles and bruising his shoulder painfully and then his legs banged against the pipe.

He sat on it, legs astride, and pulled the rope down, coiling it again, then he started across. The narrow pipe cut into his crotch and he moved painfully on, pushing away the thought of the cobbles forty feet below, concentrating on the task in hand. Was it now, or was it three years previously? There was no way of telling and life seemed a circle turning upon itself endlessly. His fingers touched stone and he looked up to see the darker line of the wall against the sky.

He carefully stood up, reached for the rusty spikes and pulled himself on top. With hardly a pause, he uncoiled the rope, looped it around a couple of spikes and went over the edge, using the same double strand technique as in descending from the hospital roof. A few moments later he dropped ten feet into wet grass at the foot of the wall, pulling the rope down after him.

He was soaked to the skin and for a moment he lay there, his face in the coolness of the wet grass and then he scrambled to his feet. He coiled the nylon rope quickly, hooked it over his head, turned and moved quickly away through the darkness.

Remembering his previous experience, he gave the married quarters a wide berth, striking up the hillside to the open moor and the quarry.

Darkness was his friend and five minutes later he reached the crest of the valley and paused to look back. Below in the hollow the prison lay like some primeval monster crouching in the darkness, shapeless, without form, a yellow light gleaming here and there and at its feet the houses crouched.

Rogan was suddenly filled with a fierce exhilaration. He laughed out loud, turned and started to run across the moor. It took him fifteen minutes to reach the quarry and beyond it, the river, swollen by rain, tumbled over boulders in the darkness.

Half-way across the iron footbridge, he paused and tossed the rope, screwdriver and wirecutters into the foam. Somehow there was a finality about the act. This time there would be no going back. He ran across the bridge and moved along the bank, and a few moments later the lights of the cottage gleamed through the dark trees of the wood.

— 4 —

IT WAS COLD in the stone-flagged kitchen and Jack Pope shivered involuntarily as he piled logs into the crook of one arm. He moved back along the passage and went into the living room of the small cottage.

Flames flickered across the oak-beamed ceiling, casting fantastic shadows that writhed and twisted convulsively and he piled more logs on to the already large fire..

He went to the dresser, took down a bottle of whisky and half filled a glass.

Outside the wind moaned, driving the rain against the window with the force of lead shot and he shivered, remembering the place on the other side of the hill beyond the river where he had spent five years of his life. He emptied the glass quickly, coughing as the raw spirit burned its way down his throat, and reached for the bottle again.

There was no sound, and yet a small cold wind touched him gently on the right cheek. He turned slowly, the hair rising on the nape of his neck.

Rogan stood in the doorway, shirt and trousers plastered to his body, moulding his superb physique, rain mingling with the dust from the ventilating shafts, washing over him in a patina of filth.

And Jack Pope knew fear, real primeval fear that loosened the very bowels in him so that in the presence of this strange, dark man he was like a frightened child, completely dominated by some elemental force he couldn't even comprehend.

He moistened his lips and forced a ghastly smile. 'You made it, Irish. Good for you.'

Rogan crossed the room, soundlessly, took the glass from Pope's hand and poured the whisky down in one quick swallow. He closed his eyes, took a long breath and opened them again.

'What time is it?'

Pope glanced at his watch. 'Just after half past eight.'

'Good,' Rogan said. 'I want to be out of here by nine. Is there a bath?'

Pope nodded eagerly. 'I've had the water heating all afternoon.'

'Clothes?'

'Laid out in the bedroom. What about something to eat?'

Rogan shook his head. 'No time. If you've got a vacuum flask fill it with coffee and make a few sandwiches. I can eat them on the way.'

'Okay, Irish, anything you say. The bath's at the end of the passage.'

Rogan turned abruptly and went out, and immediately the forced smile was wiped from Pope's face. 'Who the hell does he think he is, the big stinking Mick. God, how I wish I could turn him in.'

He went into the kitchen, put the kettle on the stove, then he rummaged in a drawer till he found a breadknife, took down a loaf and started viciously to cut it into slices.

The bathroom was a recent extension to the rear of the cottage and the bath itself was small. Not that it mattered. Rogan filled it with hot water, stripped off his wet clothes and climbed in. For a brief moment only he sat there enjoying the warmth, then he started to wash the filth from his body. Five minutes later, he stepped out, dried himself quickly, then went along the passage to the bedroom, a towel about his waist.

He found everything he needed laid out neatly across the

bed. Underclothing, shirts, even the shoes were the right size and the two-piece suit in Glencarrick thornproof looked as if it had been made to measure. There was also a battered rain hat and an old trenchcoat. A nice touch that, he had to admit, however grudgingly. He took them with him when he returned to the living-room.

Pope followed him in from the kitchen carrying a large vacuum flask and a tin biscuit box. 'Sandwiches are inside; it'll save you having to stop.'

'And just where am I supposed to be going?'

'O'More wants to see you.'

'Where do I find him?'

Pope shrugged. 'God knows. I've been working through an accommodation address in Kendal. Do you know where that is?'

'The Lake District, isn't it? Westmorland?'

'That's right. You're in for a long drive. It's all of three hundred and fifty miles from here and you've got to be there by seven in the morning.'

Which was the precise moment at which they would be turning out the cells at the prison and Rogan smiled slightly. They were hardly likely to be looking for him in a place like Kendal. It would take them at least three days to realize that he'd got off the moor and even then they wouldn't be sure.

'Why seven?'

'Because that's the time you're being picked up. You drive into the car park of the Woolpack Inn – that's in Stricklandgate – and wait.'

'Who for?'

'I honestly don't know. As I said, I've been writing to an accommodation address in Kendal. Maybe it's just a jumping off place to somewhere else.'

Rogan shook his head. 'Not good enough, Pope. You wouldn't go into anything blindfold.'

'It's the truth, Irish, as God's my judge. I'll admit I opened my mouth about that escape of yours when I got out and the word must have got around among the boys. You know how these things are.'

'What about Soames, the lawyer.'

'Been disbarred for the past five years. A villain down to

the soles of his feet. He came to see me a couple of weeks ago. Said a client of his had heard this rumour about you having a way out and they'd traced it to me. It didn't take him long to get down to brass tacks. He's a downy bird.'

'And what's your cut?'

'For setting this little lot up? A couple of centuries and my expenses.'

Rogan helped himself to a cigarette from a packet on the table and lit it, an abstracted frown on his face. On the fact of it, it didn't make sense – not any of it. And yet Colum was as cunning as a fox. It would be like him to cover his tracks again, making any direct route to him difficult to find.

'All right, for the moment, I'll buy it,' he said. 'How do I get to Kendal?'

Pope produced a small white folder and grinned. 'Nothing like being efficient, so I went to the top. Got you an AA route guide. It starts at Exeter and takes you straight through to Kendal.'

He went over it quickly, indicating the route on the excellent sketch maps provided. At Exeter Rogan would pick up the A38 and follow it through Bristol and Gloucester. From there, the new M5 motorway would take him north past Worcester and Birmingham, joining the M6 for the long run up through Lancashire to the Lake District.

'You'll find some sections of the motorways are still under construction,' Pope said, 'but on the whole, you should have a pretty clear run.'

'What kind of car have you got for me?'

'Nothing special. A Ford brake, two years old but the engine's perfect. I've had it checked. You'll find a few samples of animal feed in the back. You're supposed to be a salesman for an agricultural firm.' He picked up a briefcase and produced various documents. 'Here's a couple of printed business cards in the name of Jack Mann and a driving licence. Hope you can still remember how.'

Rogan shrugged. 'I'll get by.'

There were insurance papers and log book, all in the same name. Even an AA membership card. Rogan tucked them all into his inside breast pocket.

'You seem to have thought of everything.'

'We aim to please.' Pope took out a worn leather wallet and passed it across. 'You'll find forty quid in there. No sense in carrying more. If you were stopped and searched it would only excite suspicion.'

'The police mind,' Rogan said. 'You can never get away from it, can you?'

Pope flushed, but managed to force a smile. 'That's about it.' He glanced at his watch. 'Almost nine. You'd better be on your way.'

Rogan pulled on the trenchoat, belted it around his waist and picked up his hat. They went out through the kitchen and Pope flicked on an outside light, opened the door and led the way across the small courtyard to an old barn. He opened a large door, and two cars were revealed.

One of them was a large dark shooting brake, the other a green saloon. Rogan paused in the entrance, looking at them.

'Two?' he said.

'Well how in the hell do you think I'm going to get out of here at this time of night?' Pope said. 'It was bad enough having to walk five miles to the nearest bus stop yesterday after driving out here in the Ford. I picked up the saloon in Plymouth this morning.'

Which was a good story had it not been for the fact that the wheels of both vehicles were still damp and muddy from the day's rain.

Rogan let it pass. 'I'd better be on my way.'

Popc nodded. 'Make sure it's the right one. No detours to Holyhead for the Irish boat.'

Rogan turned very slowly, his face quite expressionless. 'And what would you be meaning by that?'

Pope forced a smile. 'Nothing, Irish, nothing. It's just that the Big Man's invested a lot of money in you. He's entitled to see some return.'

The next moment, a hand had him by the throat, pulling him close and the rush of blood seemed to be forcing out his eyeballs.

'When I do a thing, it's because I want to,' Rogan said softly. 'Always remember that, Pope. Nobody crowds Sean Rogan.'

Pope went staggering back against the whitewashed wall

and slumped to the ground. He crouched there, sobbing for breath, aware of the Ford starting up and moving out across the yard, the engine fading into the distance.

A footstep scraped on stone and a voice said calmly, 'Friend Rogan plays rough. A dangerous man to cross.'

Pope looked up at Henry Soames and cursed savagely. 'I hope you know what you're doing.' He groaned, swaying a little as he got to his feet. 'If I'd any sense I'd pull out of this now.'

'And lose out on all that lovely money?' Soames patted him on the shoulder. 'Let's go back inside and I'll go over it again. I think you'll see things my way.'

Round the bend of the road, Rogan parked the car by a five-barred gate and walked back the way he had come. There were several reasons for such a course. In the first place he didn't like Pope; in the second, he didn't trust him. And there was the intriguing fact that the tyres of both cars had been wet although the brake had supposedly been under cover since the previous day.

Nearing the cottage, he left the road, pushed his way through a plantation of damp fir trees and crossed the yard at the rear. A curtain was drawn across the window, but when he bent down he could see most of the living room through a narrow crack.

Henry Soames and Pope were sitting at the table engaged in earnest conversation, the whisky bottle between them. Rogan stayed there for only a moment, then turned and retraced his steps.

So – the plot thickened. Most puzzling thing of all, how did Colum O'More come to be mixed up with such people? There was no answer, could be none till he reached Kendal. He leaned back in his seat and concentrated on the road ahead.

— 5 —

AFTER MIDNIGHT Rogan had the road pretty much to himself, although from Bristol to Birmingham and north into Lancashire he came across plenty of heavy transport working the all-night routes.

Just after 2 a.m. he stopped at a small garage near Stoke to fill up, staying in the shadows of the car so that the attendant didn't get a clear look at his face.

He made good time, always keeping within any indicated speed limits, and dawn found him moving north along the M6 motorway east of Lancaster.

The morning was grey and sombre with heavy rain clouds drifting across his path, and to the west the dark waters of Morecambe Bay were being whipped into whitecaps. He opened the side window and the wind carried the taste of good salt air and he inhaled deeply, feeling suddenly alive for the first time in years.

He stopped the car, took out the vacuum flask and stood at the side of the road looking out at the distant sea while he finished the coffee. It was difficult to believe, but he was out. For a brief moment, the strange, illogical thought crossed his mind that perhaps this was only some dark, hopeless dream from which the rattle of the key in the lock of his cell door would awaken him at any moment, and then a gull cried harshly in the sky and rain started to fall in a sudden heavy rush. He stood there for a moment longer, his face turned up to it, and then got back into the car and drove away.

He arrived in Kendal just after seven and found the place, like most country market towns at that time in the morning, already stirring. He located the Woolpack Inn in Strickland-gate without any trouble, pulled in the car park and switched off the engine.

It was a strange feeling waiting there in the car, like the old days working with the Maquis in France, and he remembered that morning in Amiens with the rain bouncing from the cobbles and the contact man who turned out to be an Abwehr agent. But then you never could be certain of anything in this life, from the womb to the grave.

He opened the packet of cigarettes Pope had given him, found it empty and crushed it in his hand. A quiet voice said, 'A fine morning, Mr Rogan.'

She was perhaps twenty years old, certainly no more. She wore an old trenchcoat belted around her waist and, in spite of her headscarf, rain beaded the fringe of dark hair which had escaped at the front and drifted across her brow.

She walked round to the other side, opened the door and sat on the bench seat beside him. Her face was smoothly rounded with a flawless cream complexion, the eyebrows and hair coal black and her red lips and an extra fullness that suggested sensuality. It was the sort of face he had seen often on the west coast of Ireland, particularly around Galway where there had been a plentiful infusion of Spanish blood over the centuries.

'How could you be sure?' he said.

She shrugged. 'I had the number of the car and Colum showed me a photograph. You've changed.'

'Haven't we all?' he said. 'Where do you fit in?'

'You'll find out. If you'll let me get at the wheel, we'll move out.'

He eased himself across the seat. She slid past him. For a moment he was acutely conscious of her as a woman, a hint of perfume in the cold morning air, the edge of the coat riding above her knees. She pulled it down with a complete lack of self-consciousness and started the engine.

'I'd like to stop for some cigarettes,' Rogan said.

She took a packet from her left pocket and tossed them across. 'No need. I've got plenty.'

'Have we far to go?'

'About forty miles.'

She was perfectly calm, her hands steady on the wheel as she took the brake with real skill through the narrow streets and the early morning traffic, and he watched her for a while, leaning back in the corner.

A fine, lovely girl this one, but one who had been used by life and not kindly. The story was there in the shadow that lurked behind the grey-green eyes. Hurt, but not broken – the courage showed in the tilt of the chin, the sureness of those competent hands. The pity of it was that she would never let anyone get close to her again and that was the real tragedy.

Her voice cut sharply into his musing. 'You'll know me next time?'

'And would that be a bad thing?' he grinned lightly. 'Liverpool-Irish?'

'Is it that obvious?'

'No accent like it in this world or out of it.'

She smiled in spite of herself. 'You needn't think you sound like any English gentleman yourself.'

'And why would I be wanting to?'

'You were a major in their army, weren't you?'

'You seem to know.'

'I should do. At one time, I used to get the great Sean Rogan for breakfast, dinner and supper and precious little else.'

They were now on thc outskirts of the town and she pulled in beside a low stone wall topped by iron railings. A little farther along there was an open iron gate and a sign which read *Church of the Immaculate Heart* with the times of mass and confession in faded gold letters beneath.

'Do you mind?' she said. 'I don't get in very often.'

'Suit yourself.'

He watched her pass through the gate, a small girl with a ripe peasant figure and hips that were too large by English standards. So, she still kept to the faith? Now that was interesting, and proved she wasn't an active member of the IRA, which carried automatic excommunication.

On impulse he opened the door and followed her along the flagged path. It was warm inside and very quiet. For a little while he stood there listening intently and then he sat down in a pew at the back of the church.

She was on her knees by the altar. As he looked down towards the winking candles it seemed to grow darker. He leaned forward and rested his head on a stone pillar. All the strain and excitement of the past twelve hours catching up on him. In some strange way it was as if he were listening for something.

He pushed the thought away from him and sat back and watched as she got to her feet and walked back along the aisle. She became aware of him there in the half darkness and paused abruptly.

'That was foolish of you. You could have been seen.'

He shrugged, stood up and took her arm as they went to the door. 'If you think like that you act suspiciously; if you act suspiciously, you get caught. I'm an old hand at being on the run.'

They stood on the step and the wind blew a fine drizzle of rain into the porch as she looked up at him searchingly. She smiled and it was as if a lamp had been turned on inside.

'Hannah Costello, Mr Rogan,' she said and held out her hand.

He took it and grinned. 'A fresh start makes old friends of bad ones,' he said. 'A proverb my grandmother was fond of. Would it be too much to ask where you're taking me?'

'The other side of the lakes. On the coast, near a place called Whitbeck.'

'Is Colum O'More there?'

'Waiting for you.'

'In the name of God, let us go then. There's a farm in Kerry my father's growing too old to cope with. It's time I was home again.'

The smile vanished from her face and she gazed up at him searchingly. She seemed about to speak, but obviously thought better of it and turned and led the way back to the car.

II

Dick Vanbrugh was tired, damned tired, and the heavy rain driving against the bathroom window wasn't calculated to improve the way he felt. He finished shaving and was towelling his face tenderly when the door opened and his wife looked in. 'Phone, darling. The assistant commissioner.'

Vanbrugh stared at her, a deep frown creasing his forehead. 'You're joking, of course.'

'I'm afraid not. I'll get your breakfast on the stove now. From the sound of him, you'll be moving off in a hurry.'

Vanbrugh pulled a shirt over his head, tucking it into his trousers as he went downstairs. His tiredness had vanished completely. Whatever this was, it was something big. You didn't get the assistant commissioner on the phone at seven-thirty in the morning just because somebody's warehouse had been turned over.

He picked up the phone from the hall stand and leaned against the wall. 'Vanbrugh here, sir.'

'Morning, Dick. I'm afraid I'm going to put you off your breakfast.'

'Not the first time,' Vanbrugh said.

'Rogan's out.'

Vanbrugh suddenly felt a little light-headed. He took a deep breath, closing his eyes, and then opened them again.

'When?'

'Some time during the night. They found him missing at seven o'clock turn-out. The governor's just been on the line to the old man.'

'How did he get out?'

'Nobody seems to know. They may come up with something later, but the first quick check disclosed nothing.'

Vanbrugh laughed gently. 'In the Maquis, they called him The Ghost, did you know that, sir?'

The assistant commissioner ignored the remark. 'You're in charge, Dick.'

Vanbrugh took a deep breath and stood up straight. 'I'd rather not—not this time.'

'He won't take no for an answer, Dick. After all, you know Rogan better than anyone else.'

'That's the trouble, sir.'

'There's a fast train for the West Country at nine from Paddington. Take Dwyer with you. I'll see that the local constabulary give you every co-operation. The longer he's out, the worse it will be. The newsboys will start digging up his war record and so on and before you know where you are, we'll be in it right up to our necks.'

'Would that be such a bad thing, sir?' Vanbrugh said. 'It might make the Home Secretary think again if nothing else.'

'Respond to this kind of emotional blackmail? You must be mad.' The assistant commissioner snorted. 'For God's sake try to remember you're a copper and get moving.'

Vanbrugh replaced the receiver, stood there thinking for a moment, then put through a quick call to Detective Sergeant Dwyer at his home. When he was finished he went into the kitchen. His wife turned from the stove, a frying pan in her hand, and he shook his head.

'Just coffee, love. I've got to get moving.'

She filled his cup, placed it on the table before him, then ran her fingers through his greying hair. 'Twenty-five years, Dick. I should know you by now. What's gone wrong?'

'It's Sean,' he said. 'Sean Rogan. He's on the loose. The old man wants me to go down to the West Country to take charge of the hunt personally.'

'Oh, no, Dick.' A spasm of pain crossed her face and she sank into the opposite chair. 'Haven't you done enough?'

'I'm a policeman, Nell,' he said. 'You knew it when you married me. Sean knew.'

'But, Dick, he saved your life.'

'God in Heaven, do you think I don't know that?' he demanded.

When she put out her hand and gently touched his face there were tears in her eyes. He turned the hand and brushed his lips against the palm.

'I'd better get moving, love. I haven't got much time.'

He got to his feet, turned and went out slowly.

III

It was still raining when Rogan and the girl reached Bowness and took the ferry across Lake Windermere. The boat was deserted and they stood at the stern rail taking in the beauty.

'What do you think of it?' she said.

'It's certainly spectacular.'

'The most beautiful place in England. In the summer these roads are crowded with holidaymakers. At this time of the year, you won't see a soul. That's when I like it best.'

There was a glow to her cheeks and she wiped moisture

away from her brow carelessly and looked across at Belle Isle. Rogan watched her, aware of beauty and gladdened by it.

On the other side, they took the road to Hawkshead, then turned down the far side of Coniston Water to Broughton-in-Furness and Whicham. From there, they turned north along the coast road and a mile beyond Whitbeck Station they came to a signpost carrying the legend, Marsh-End. She turned off the road and bumped over a rutted track towards the sea.

They followed the course of a winding creek that twisted like a snake, losing itself in a country of rough grass marshes and mud flats where wild ducks nested in the reeds and fog drifted in from the sea, dulling the edges of things so that they lacked definition, formless as in a dream.

The brake turned into another track which led through a clump of fir trees, and on the other side a lonely farmhouse stood at the head of a creek.

It stood in a clump of beech trees at the water's edge, an ancient grey-stone building with a good barn and a walled yard. It was only as they approached that Rogan became aware of the decay that hung over everything, of the broken fences, peeling paintwork.

Grass grew between the cobbles, and as the car rolled to a halt Hannah Costello switched off the engine and grimaced.

'Not much of a place. Over the years, the tides have eroded all the pasture. No one could make a living here except by wildfowling and fishing. The agents were glad to lease it for a year.'

He frowned. 'A long time.'

'Anything less would have looked suspicious.'

She hesitated and then went on, 'How long is it since you last saw Colum O'More?'

'Ten years.'

'You'll find him changed. Try not to show it. I think his pride means a lot to him.'

Before Rogan could reply, the door behind him opened and he turned quickly. The man who stood there leaned heavily on a stick, head slightly forward from the great hunched shoulders.

'Sean,' he said in a hoarse whisper. 'Sean Rogan, by all that's holy.'

The shock was like a physical blow and Rogan swallowed hard and moved to meet him, hand outstretched. 'Colum, you old devil. A long time.'

For a moment in their handclasp there was a touch of the old strength he remembered, but only for a moment and Colum O'More laughed harshly. 'They say time changes all things, Sean. Me, he decided to kick straight in the teeth. I'm glad he's dealt better by you.'

He turned and limped along the whitewashed corridor and Rogan followed him, aware of the clothes hanging in folds upon the skeleton of the man he had once known.

The living room was simply furnished with a table, a couple of easy chairs by the fire on the open hearth and rush matting on the floor. Colum O'More sank into one of the chairs and looked at Hannah.

'There's a bottle on the sideboard, girl, and glasses, and don't be telling me I shouldn't. I'm past caring.'

Rogan unbelted his coat, took it off and sat in the other chair. 'What happened, Colum?'

The old man shrugged. 'The hard life I've led, past sins catching up on me. Does it matter?' He shook his head. 'I've never seen a man look better from seven years in an English gaol.'

Rogan shrugged. 'Remember what Tom Clarke wrote? Never give in. Keep fighting and hang on to your self-respect?'

O'More nodded. 'And didn't he do just that for fifteen years?'

Hannah poured whisky into two glasses and brought them across and the old man slipped an arm around her waist. 'Lucky for her I'm not thirty years younger, Sean. A hundred per cent, this one.' He smiled up at her. 'Make him some breakfast, girl, while we talk.'

She looked once at Rogan, an unspoken message in her eyes, and went out. O'More drank some of his whisky and sighed with pleasure. He took out a pipe and started to fill it from a worn leather pouch. 'You've just been on the news. By now they'll be running round in circles blocking every road off that damned moor and here you are, three hundred and fifty miles away where they'd least expect to find you. There must be a small laugh in that, surely.'

Rogan toasted him briefly. 'Thanks to the Big Man.'

'The organization looks after its own,' Colum O'More said. 'The time we've taken, I'll admit, but that was no fault of mine.'

There was a small silence and Rogan said carefully, 'And what would be the quickest way to Kerry from here, Colum?'

'Well, now, Sean, wasn't it that I wanted to discuss with you?'

There was something deep here, something he as yet didn't understand, that had been under the surface of things since Soames had made his visit to the prison a hundred years ago. Rogan took out a cigarette and lit it with a burning splinter from the fire.

'It's been a long time, Colum, too long for awkwardness between us. Say what you have to say.'

The old man shrugged. 'It's simply told. We have a job for you.'

'We?'

'The organization.'

'I understood it had folded when they called off the border war.'

Colum O'More chuckled. 'A tale for fools and old women, but times have been difficult, Sean. We're reorganizing on a big scale, we need money.'

'And where would we be finding that?'

The old man turned to the table, opened the drawer and took out a map which he unfolded on the floor. It showed the Lake District in detail and he used his stick as a pointer.

'The Glasgow to London mail train comes down through Carlisle and Penrith. Notice that it doesn't touch Kendal. That's served by a local line. It joins the main line at Rigg Station eight miles south of Kendal.'

'So?'

'Every Friday, the Central Banks Association sends an armoured van from Penrith. It does a sort of circle through the Lakes and down the coast, calling at Keswick, Whitehaven, Seascale and so on. From Broughton, which you'll have passed through on your way here, it goes up to Ambleside, then down through Windermere to Kendal. It arrives at Rigg Station at three in the afternoon where it meets up with the London Express.'

'What kind of stuff do they carry?'

'The usual weekend cash surplus, mainly old notes for re-pulping. You know what the banks are like. They don't like it lying around these country branches. Usually around a quarter of a million.'

'A useful sum.'

'It would be to the organization.'

Rogan laughed harshly. 'God save us all, but here's madness for you!' He paced across to the window, then swung round angrily. 'Was it for this you helped me out after seven years, Colum O'More?'

'You're the best brain we ever had,' O'More said calmly, 'the best organizer. We needed you.'

'And if you hadn't, where would I be now, Colum O'More?'

'It took a lot to get you out, lad, and not only in hard cash. I'm depending on you.'

'Then you'll be disappointed.' Rogan shook his head and moved back to the fireside. 'I've had it up to here, Colum, can't you see that? Forty years old and I've spent twelve of them in gaol. As far as I'm concerned, the game's played out. The organization must find another way to get what it wants. I've had my bellyful.'

The old man nodded. 'And what will you be doing?'

'There's a farm in Kerry waiting for me now, you know that as well as I do. My father's been running it since he retired from the political service ten years ago. He's getting old, Colum, and so am I.'

'Aren't we all?' The old man sighed. 'So be it. North of here there's a place on the coast called Ravenglass. I'll give you the name of a man I know. He'll see you across the water for a hundred pounds.' He opened the drawer again, took out a packet of banknotes and tossed them on the table. 'Good luck to ye, Sean Rogan.'

Rogan picked up the notes, weighing them in his hand, a frown on his face. 'And you?'

'God save us, lad, I've a job to do and men waiting ready for it back there in those mountains. I'll see this thing through on my own.'

Rogan stood staring at him for a moment, then he turned without a word, flung open the door and moved outside.

— 6 —

THE TIDE WAS drifting in, gurgling in crab holes, stippled water covering the mud-flats with an expanse of shining silver that moved among sea asters, and somewhere a curlew cried, lonely in a sombre world.

Rogan crossed a narrow stone causeway and followed a path through rough marsh grass and reeds that were head high. On impulse he took an even narrower path to the right and, pushing his way through the undergrowth, emerged at the side of a narrow creek and found a motor launch moored to the bank.

There was no sign of life and he jumped down on to the deck and moved into the wheelhouse. Although the boat was obviously old, it was in good condition and the interior had recently been swept. The brass compass mounting and engine controls were brightly polished. There was a movement out on thc deck behind him and he turned to see Hannah Costello standing watching him.

He moved out to join her and she tossed his trenchcoat across. 'I thought you might need this.'

He pulled it on, turning up the collar against the rain, and lit another cigarette. 'Is this Colum's?'

She nodded. 'He sailed it down from Ravenglass himself.'

'His quick exit when the job's done?' She nodded and he shook his head. 'Well not me, I'm moving out now.'

'No one's stopping you.'

With a sudden rush of rain increased into a solid downpour and he stared out across the marsh. 'A strange place this, like nowhere I've ever been. You'd swear there were eyes watching you from every thicket.'

'Spirits of the dead,' she said. 'This is an ancient place. Ravenglass was a port even in Roman times. They called it Glannaventa. Not much more than a hundred years ago they found a longboat aground on the mud-flats at dawn half-filled with blood and a dozen revenuers with their throats cut. The free-traders used the farmhouse as their headquarters.'

'Nothing changes,' he said.

She nodded. 'The hardest lesson to learn. All my life I've been trying to change things, change me even. I always end up back at base.'

'How do you fit into all this?'

'That's an easy one. I live with my uncle, Paddy Costello, at a place called Scardale, in the fells north of Ambleside. He has an excuse for a sheep farm up there that's just about on its last legs. He and my father were members of the Big Man's organization in the North of England during the war. He found out about this bank van six months ago and got in touch with Colum.'

'Why should he do that?'

'Because drunk or sober – which isn't often – he lives in a dream world of action and passion and God Save Ireland, cried the heroes. He sees himself still one of them carrying on the gallant struggle.'

'And is that such a bad thing?'

'It's a foolish dream,' she said, 'which is worse. An echo of something that's gone for ever. The world's changed and it doesn't need men like my uncle any longer.'

'Or me?'

'If the cap fits. Are you going to take that boat out of Ravenglass?'

'I'd be a fool if I didn't.'

She leaned against the rail and stared back into the past. 'When I was a kid in Liverpool, all I ever got was Sean Rogan – the great Sean Rogan. My old man was by way of being a fan of yours. At least that's what he said loudly across every bar counter on the waterfront. But that's as far as it ever went. After my mother died, the drinking really got a hold on him.'

'I've seen it happen,' Rogan said. 'A bad thing.'

'Funny how someone can destroy themselves in front of you,' she said. 'Even your love for them. I didn't end up hating him, I just didn't care. When he started mistaking my bedroom for his when he staggered in, I thought it was time to move on. He died the following year.'

'What did you do?'

'What every girl in my position does – went to London.'

'How old were you?'

'Sixteen, but that turned out to be a distinct advantage. Girls of that age have a strong appeal for some men.'

'So I've heard,' he said gravely.

'I got a job as a waitress, but that wouldn't keep me in room and board. Then one of the customers offered me a job in his club. I was always a good dancer.' She smiled calmly. 'They're right when they go on about the importance of the little sins – the Church, I mean. It's amazing how quickly you can become what you never thought you would.'

'It sounds like a bad plot.'

'It gets even better. The police moved in and it turned out the boss had been squeezing some of the more respectable customers dry on the side. He dragged three of us down with him.'

'What did you get?'

'Six months. When I got out, I wrote to Uncle Paddy. His wife had died and he needed a woman round the place. He's got a son, Brendan, aged seventeen. Had meningitis when he was a kid.' She touched her head. 'Needs looking after.'

'And now you're up to your ears in this lot? Why don't you just pack your bags and get out?'

She shrugged, and watched the mist creeping in from the sea. 'Why does anybody do anything? You become involved, I suppose, just like a fish in a net. Choose which way you twist, there's no way out.' She looked up at him, her face quite calm. 'That's how I've been all my life, Mr Rogan, trapped in an invisible net with no way out.'

There was a stillness about her, a strange, brooding calm, and the green eyes held his steadily. It was as if she wanted him to say something, perhaps offer some solution, but there was nothing of value he could say.

'I've been trying to crash out of something all my life and I'm forty years old.'

She nodded slowly. 'I think you are a man held too easily by old loyalties.'

Which was a remarkably shrewd observation and Rogan lit another cigarette and changed the subject. 'What kind of a set-up has Colum got back there in the mountains?'

'At Scardale? Nothing very complicated. He's recruited a couple of tearaways from Manchester. Professional crooks; they've been there a week now.'

'What are they like?'

'Smash their way in, smash their way out and God help anyone who gets in the way. You know the type. Only one of them is really dangerous. That's Morgan – Harry Morgan. He's got brains of a sort. Fletcher's just a blunt instrument.'

'Nice people Colum O'More's got himself mixed up with.'

She shrugged. 'For this kind of job, you need experts and Morgan and Fletcher are that all right.'

'How did he get in touch with them?'

'I think Soames found them for him.'

'Have you ever met him?'

She shook her head. 'Colum has, but only once. That was in Liverpool. Since then, we've used an accommodation address – a back-street newsagent's in Kendal. I've usually collected the letters by hand.'

'So Soames doesn't know about this place?'

'Marsh-End?' She shook her head. 'Even my uncle hasn't been here. Morgan's tried following me a few times, but I've always given him the slip.'

'There was a man called Pope – Jack Pope. He was waiting for me when I got out. Where does he fit in?'

'As far as I know, he was paid to do a particular job and that was the end to it. Soames handled all the negotiations at that end.'

'How much was Soames paid?'

'Five hundred and his expenses.'

Rogan shook his head. 'Not enough. His kind live under stones. He'll want more.'

She frowned. 'How could he get it?'

'I don't know, but he and Pope are up to something and whatever it is, it isn't going to do Colum any good.' He flipped his cigarette down into the water. 'Come on, let's get back.'

She caught his sleeve and held him a moment. 'What are you going to do?'

'God knows, but he's an old man. I can't let him put his head on the block without doing something about it, now can I?'

He turned, scrambled over the rail and pushed his way through the wet undergrowth back towards the farmhouse.

II

Colum O'More sat at the table, a large scale map of the Lake District in front of him. When the door clicked open behind him, he didn't bother to move and Rogan sat on the edge of the table.

He looked down at the map, a slight frown on his face. 'One thing I don't understand, Colum? Why you? Where are the young and active ones? Safe in their beds?'

The old man shrugged. 'I first heard about this bank van through an old comrade, Paddy Costello. Hannah's uncle.'

'She told me about him.'

'I put the idea before the headquarters staff in Waterford. They said it couldn't be done. That it was too risky.' He chuckled harshly. 'I thought I'd show them there was life in the old dog yet.'

'The money that got me out,' Rogan said. 'Where did that come from?'

'Does it matter?'

'It might.'

Colum O'More shrugged. 'I had some savings. That and a mortgage on my house in Lismore.'

Rogan shook his head. 'No fool like an old one.'

'Oh, don't be worrying about me. I'll get my expenses paid out of the proceeds of this one.'

Rogan shook his head. 'It won't work, Colum. You're too old.'

The old man went very white, eyes like hot coals. The stick swung up as if he would strike Rogan across the face with it and then a spasm of pain racked his face. He clapped a hand to his mouth too late and a quantity of brown vomit erupted, spilling across the stone floor.

There was a quick exclamation from the doorway and when Rogan turned Hannah was standing there. 'A cloth,' he said, 'and some water. Quickly now.'

He held the old man's head up until the girl came back. She gently swabbed away the vomit with a damp cloth and Rogan took his arm and pulled him up.

'He'll be better lying down.'

The bedroom was on the ground floor at the rear, and he sat the old man on the edge of the bed, took off his jacket and loosened his collar. Colum O'More lay back with a sigh and Rogan raised his feet and threw a coverlet over him.

He walked with the girl to the door. 'Have you seen him like this before?'

She nodded. 'Once. It was exactly the same. He was all right again within half an hour.'

There was a ghostly chuckle from the bed and when Rogan turned, O'More was looking at him through half open eyes. 'I received my sentence from the finest physician in Dublin three months ago, lad. A couple of years, maybe three and there's an end of it.'

Rogan stood at the side of the bed looking down at him. 'Will you be all right?'

'Fine. Right as a trivet in half an hour. I've had these attacks before.'

'Good,' Rogan said. 'Just take it easy then and don't worry about a thing.'

When he closed the door, the girl was standing in the passage, a puzzled frown on her face. 'Why – I don't understand?'

He could have talked to her of old loyalties, of what he owed to a man whose proud boast had been that he had never let a friend down in his life come hell or high water. But the thing went deeper than that.

From the moment he had dropped over the wall back there on the moor, he had been caught in a current from which there was no escaping until he reached the pre-ordained end. That was the Celt in him speaking and still a poor reason.

'Make him a cup of tea and lace it with whisky. I'll sit with him for a while.'

He pushed her along the passage, opened the bedroom door

and went back inside. He sat on the edge of the bed, took out his cigarettes and lit one slowly.

'All right,' he said to O'More. 'I want the lot. Places, names, who does what and when.'

'You'll do it, Sean?' the old man said eagerly. 'You'll handle it for me?'

'I'll look into it,' Rogan said. 'I'll go to Costello's place and I'll take a look at the set-up. More than that I won't promise.'

Colum O'More's breath was exhaled in a long sigh. 'And that's good enough for me.'

— 7 —

HARRY MORGAN came awake and stared up at the stained and peeling ceiling. Looked at long enough, it became a pretty fair map of London, and he recalled with nostalgia a little bar off Dean Street in Soho that had been a favourite haunt of his in the old days, and the Greek girl who ran it. Now there was a woman . . .

His throat was dry and his mouth tasted bad. He pushed himself up on one elbow and groped under the bed until he located a bottle. It was empty and he dropped it to the floor and stood up, a lean dark man with red hair, black eyes and a mouth that curled sardonically at the corners.

He pulled an old sweater over his head and moved to the door outside; then there was a howl of rage. As Morgan opened the door and moved into the white-washed passage, Costello's half-witted son, his mouth gaping in fear, stumbled into him, Fletcher hard on his heels.

Fletcher, a great ox of a man, grabbed for the boy and Morgan barred his way with an outstretched arm. 'Now what?'

'The bloody little swine's pinched all my fags. There were three packets under my pillow. They've all gone.'

'You lost them to me at brag last night,' Morgan said. 'You were too damned drunk to remember.'

'You can stick that for a tale.'

Fletcher pushed him roughly to one side and grabbed at the boy, who ran to the end of the passage and pulled open the door. What happened next was so quick and confusing, that afterwards Fletcher had difficulty in recalling the incident clearly.

One moment he was reaching for the scruff of the boy's neck, the next he was stumbling headlong to the cobbles of the yard. He started to turn and a foot pushed down hard across his throat. Fletcher began to choke and then the pressure was relieved. When he managed to control his breathing again, he found himself looking up into a hard, implacable face.

Jesse Fletcher had never been afraid of anything or anybody in his entire life and he felt no fear now, only the natural wariness of a born fighting man who senses the same qualities in another.

'Get up!' Sean Rogan said.

Behind him, Hannah Costello stood by the brake, an arm around the boy's shoulders and Morgan laughed gently from the doorway. 'A touching scene.' He came forward as Fletcher scrambled to his feet. 'I'm Harry Morgan, Mr Rogan, and this relic of a more primeval time is Jesse Fletcher. You'll have to excuse his lack of manners. They weren't handing out brains the day he was born.'

'One of these days I'll fill that big mouth of yours full of dirt,' Fletcher said viciously and turned and went inside.

'Where's my uncle?' Hannah demanded.

'He went into Ambleside in the truck for supplies. I'll be surprised if we see him back before the pubs close.'

He stood to one side with a slight, mocking grin and Rogan moved past him into the house. When he went into the large, stone flagged living-room, Fletcher was sitting in a chair by the window, a bottle in one hand, a glass in the other.

Rogan ignored him and turned as Hannah and Morgan followed him in. 'Where's the boy?'

'Taken himself off into the hills,' she said. 'He won't be back till dark. He often does that.'

'What about beds?'

'There are two rooms upstairs. I've got one, my uncle and Brendan share another.'

'Jesse and I are across the passage,' Morgan said.

Fletcher snorted. 'Maybe he'd like us to move out?'

Rogan looked at him calmly. 'When I do, I'll let you know.'

He brushed past Morgan and followed Hannah along to the kitchen. Fletcher swallowed his whisky with a curse. 'The great Sean Rogan – what a laugh. Just a big Irish bogtrotter. One belt in the right place and he'd split clear down the middle.'

'Why don't you tell him that, Jesse?'

'Maybe I'll do just that.'

Morgan chuckled. 'Let me know when, I'd like to be there.'

In the kitchen, Rogan sat on the edge of the table and lit a cigarette, and Hannah took off her coat and hung it behind the door. 'Ham and eggs all right?'

'Fine,' he said and walked to the window.

The wind rushed through the old beech trees which encircled the place, plucking most of the remaining leaves from the branches and lifting them high over the roof top, and his eyes lifted to the heather-covered hill-side and the mountains beyond.

'Quite a place. Anyone ever come here?'

'Only a few fell walkers or climbers and we see them mostly during spring and summer. The road peters out a quarter of a mile from here. A hundred and fifty years ago they mined for lead up there till the vein ran out. You can still see the old workings. Brendan can tell you all about that.'

'He seemed a nice enough kid.'

She nodded. 'A bit slower than other people, that's all. Uncle Paddy treats him like a dog, that's a lot of the trouble.'

'A sweet bunch Colum's surrounded himself with.'

'What did you think of the two in there?'

'Fletcher's just a second-rate tearaway. A good man in a clinch with an iron bar or at putting in the boot. Morgan's a different proposition. For one thing he's got brains.'

'Don't let that fool you,' she said. 'Fletcher I can understand. He's too ignorant to be anything else, but Morgan's bad because he wants to be. You'll have to watch him. His favourite occupation seems to be stirring up trouble, then standing back to watch the fun.'

'The best way I know to burn your fingers,' Rogan said. 'Someone should tell him.'

She placed ham and eggs before him and a plate piled high with fresh bread and butter and sat on the other side of the table, a cup of tea in her hands, and watched him eat.

'You needed that,' she observed when he finally pushed the empty plate away with a sigh.

He smiled slightly. 'And not because I was hungry. I'm the great one for symbolic actions. Not that they fed us too badly in there. It's just that it tastes different on the outside.'

They lit cigarettes and sat there smoking in a companionable silence, rain tapping lightly against the window, and after a while Morgan came in and found them there. He took a cup, helped himself to tea from the pot and sat on the edge of the dresser.

'How was O'More?'

'In good shape,' Rogan said.

Morgan laughed harshly. 'No need to keep that up with me, big man. When Jesse and I met him in Manchester a couple of weeks back it was taking him all his time to stay on his feet.'

'So?'

'The way I see it he's on the way out. It takes a good man to run a thing like this, a strong man.'

'I know,' Rogan said softly. 'That's why I'm here.'

'Who the hell says so?' Jesse Fletcher filled the doorway, the ugly scarred face flushed in anger. 'Who says we even need you? Maybe Morgan and me got our own plans.'

'O'More told me you were working for wages,' Rogan said. 'Five grand apiece. Right?'

'That's what the contract says.'

'Then tell the hired help here to shut his big mouth.'

Fletcher took a convulsive step forward and Morgan said sharply, 'Hold your fire, Jesse, fighting among ourselves won't get us anywhere.' He turned to Rogan and shrugged. 'Jesse gets annoyed easily. It's understandable. Since that one meeting in Manchester we haven't clapped eyes on O'More. Hannah is the only link we've got with him. Even her uncle doesn't know where he's staying.'

'Caution's his second name,' Rogan said, 'No harm in that. You'll see him at the right time.' He stood up. 'What about this plan of yours?'

'I've got a map in the living-room,' Morgan said. 'Let's go through.'

Outside the rain had stopped and the sky had cleared a little over the mountains as evening fell. It was dark in the living room, shadows gathering in the corners, and Hannah lit an oil lamp and placed it in the centre of the old mahogany table. Morgan took a large scale map of the area from a drawer and unfolded it.

'Here's Scardale,' he said. 'Five miles north of Ambleside below Scardale Fell. Ambleside to Windermere, five miles, then straight into Kendal. Rigg Station's five miles south.'

'About twenty-five miles in all.'

'That's it. Rigg's only a way station. The sort of place that has a stationmaster-cum-porter. Busy during the season when all the holiday trains pass through to the Lake District. Like a grave at this time of the year.'

'What about this Friday afternoon mail train? Can a passenger board it at Rigg?'

Morgan shook his head. 'It isn't a scheduled stop any more. The railways have been doing a lot of reorganization during the past couple of years and Rigg Station's just the sort of place where the axe has fallen. In fact the stationmaster, if you can call him that, is more of a caretaker than anything else. He doesn't even live on the premises any more. Comes out from Kendal each day.'

'What about the armoured van? From what Colum said, it sounds like a tough nut to crack.'

'Just a bloody great steel box on wheels, the sort of thing the Central Banks are using all the time these days, and they've got a radio telephone hook-up to county police headquarters. They call in every half-hour.'

'Where's the weak link, Rigg Station?'

Morgan shook his head. 'The van never arrives more than five minutes before the train. There's an unloading ramp at the side of the station and they back up to it and sit tight till the train comes.'

'You're sure about that?'

'Ask Hannah. She sat outside in the car the other Friday and the week before that, Fletcher and I saw everything through glasses from a wood on the hillside. If you're thinking about taking them there, forget it. There wouldn't be time and the train's got a radio telephone as well. They all have since someone took them for a couple of million the other year.'

'A tough one.'

Morgan nodded. 'The old man seemed to think we could simply ambush the van on a quiet stretch of the road between Rigg and Kendal which shows you how much he's behind the times.'

'And you have a better idea?'

Fletcher laughed harshly. 'The best thing you ever heard of, Jack. Go on, tell him, Harry.'

'We've got an old Morris van out in the barn,' Morgan said. 'Now the way I see it, only one thing would tempt those two guards to break the rules and get out of their van – a bad road accident.'

'And you intend to provide one?'

'That's it. There's a good place about two miles out of Rigg Station. We've checked it half a dozen times. Only the occasional farm truck uses the road. At the right moment, we heave the old van over on its side, spill a little petrol and set it on fire. Even better, one of us lies in the road with blood on his face. They're bound to stop for that. No man on earth would go driving by.'

'Which is when the rest move in?'

Morgan nodded. 'Simple, isn't it?'

'Too simple.'

Rogan glanced across at Hannah, who returned his gaze calmly, no expression on her face and Fletcher said, 'You've got something better, I suppose?'

'Not yet,' Rogan said, 'but one thing's certain. It couldn't be any worse.' Morgan's lips tightened in anger, but Rogan carried on, 'There are two king-size flaws. In the first place the moment they come across the crash, the van guards will contact county police headquarters. They're bound to do that every time something out of the ordinary happens. You'd have a car on its way from Kendal within five minutes, and they'd expect another message from the armoured van, the moment the crash had been investigated. If they didn't get one, they'd turn the county out.'

What he had said was so obviously true that Fletcher and Morgan were reduced to silence, but Rogan carried relentlessly on. 'Even if we assume that I'm completely wrong, that the van guards are so upset at the sight of the crash, that they don't bother contacting police headquarters, you still have the situation at Rigg Station to consider. What happens when the van fails to show? You said yourself that all mail trains carry radio telephones now. The first thing the guard will do will be to contact the proper authorities to notify them that the van hasn't shown up. Within minutes, the whole county would be buzzing like a hive of bees. They'll have a master plan ready for this sort of thing – they always do.'

Hannah laughed somewhere deep down in her throat and Fletcher turned angrily. 'You keep your mouth shut.'

Morgan put a hand on his arm and shook his head. 'No, he's right, Jesse. Every damned thing he says makes sense.' He looked across at Rogan, his eyes dark shadows in the lamplight. 'You've got something better?'

'There's always something better if only you can find it,' Rogan said. 'I'll look the situation over in the morning.'

At that moment, an old, high-sided cattle truck turned in through the gate, one battered wing scraping the stone post, and bumped across the cobblestones. It halted a foot from the wall of the house, the door swung open and an old man almost fell out.

He walked past the window, swaying from side to side and Morgan shook his head in disgust. 'In and out of every boozer in Ambleside shooting off his big mouth and spending money like water.'

'And no affair of yours if he does,' Hannah said, an angry red spot in each cheek.

The outer door opened and a rich, fruity voice broke into song:

God save Ireland, cried the heroes,
God save Ireland, cry we all,
Whether on the scaffold high or the battlefield we die,
Sure no matter when for Ireland dear we fall.

He paused in the doorway, a stupid grin on his blotched whisky face. 'God save all here.'

There was a slight pregnant silence and then Rogan said calmly, 'God save you kindly.'

The mouth gaped in the old man's face and he stared fixedly at Rogan. 'Holy Mother of God,' he said in a whisper. He staggered across the room and seized Rogan's hand. 'The great day this is for me, Mr Rogan. The great day.'

He blinked his rheumy eyes several times and Rogan wrinkled his nose in disgust at the stale, beery smell that surrounded him.

'You've been into Ambleside?' he said.

'I have indeed, Mr Rogan. A little matter of business connected with the farm.'

'Did you hear anything about me?'

The old man took a folded evening newspaper from his pocket and passed it across. 'There's an item at the bottom of the second page.'

It was no more than half a dozen lines. A brief mention of his escape and the fact that every exit from the moor had been blocked. There was no photo.

Rogan tossed the paper on to the table and turned back to Costello. 'You don't go into Ambleside again, or anywhere else for that matter unless I give you permission. Understand?'

'Oh, I do, Mr Rogan. I do indeed.'

'And that goes for the rest of you.'

He left the room, went along the passage and stood by the cattle truck looking across the yard and down the valley towards Ambleside. Lake Windermere was a distant flash of silver in the dusk, and on either hand the mountains lifted steeply. There was the scrape of a shoe behind and he turned to see Fletcher and Morgan in the doorway.

'The girl tells me the road peters out a quarter of a mile up the valley?'

Morgan nodded. 'There's a few broken-down cottages up

there and an old lead mine. The sort of place that gives you the creeps. I've only been up there once.'

Rogan looked down the valley again at the dirt road white in the gloaming. 'One way in and one way out. That doesn't sound too healthy.'

'You're telling us,' Fletcher said. 'Half a dozen scuffers down there with a couple of cars across the road and we've had it. Christ knows why O'More had to pick a place like this.'

'Because anywhere else, you two would have stuck out like a couple of sore thumbs,' Rogan said and walked away across the yard to the gate.

The two men watched him turn into the road and climb the slope towards the head of the valley and Fletcher spat viciously. 'God, how I'd like to cut that bastard down to size.'

'Never mind that,' Morgan said. 'We've got more important things to think of.'

They went back into the living room and found Costello in a chair by the fire, a glass of whisky in his hand. 'Where's the girl?' Morgan demanded.

'Making me a sandwich in the kitchen.'

'Did you see Pope?'

The old man nodded. 'He's staying at a small hotel just outside Ambleside – The White Grange. I told him you'd ring him some time tomorrow.'

'And how in the hell do I do that?'

'There's a public call-box at the bottom of the valley where the track joins the main road.'

Morgan sat on the edge of the table, a frown on his face, then turned and looked down at the map. 'I'd like to know what Rogan intends to do.'

'He won't know that himself till he's looked things over,' Fletcher said.

Morgan shook his head. 'I wouldn't be too sure. He's got it up here, that one.' He tapped his forehead. 'He's thought of something already, I could tell.'

'Then sooner or later, he's got to tell us what it is,' Costello said. 'He can't pull the job on his own.'

He laughed foolishly, whisky dribbling from the corner of his mouth and Morgan grabbed him by the tie, pulling him up from his chair. 'You'd better lay off that stuff, Dad. You're beginning to make me nervous. Just remember you're in this with the rest of us right up to your chin, and Rogan's no fool. The slightest slip from any of us and he'll smell a king-sized rat and a minimum of fifty thousand quid each is too much to lose because an old soak like you can't keep off the booze.'

A draught touched him lightly on the face and he turned and saw Hannah standing in the doorway, a tray in her hands. She moved in, her face expressionless and placed the tray on the table.

'You keep on sneaking around as quietly as that and we'll have to put a bell on you,' Morgan said.

She ignored him and spoke to her uncle. 'Coffee and sandwiches. If you want any more you'll have to get them yourself.'

She left the room, and a moment later they saw her pass the window and cross the yard to the gate. 'Do you think she heard anything?' Fletcher said.

Morgan frowned. 'One thing's for sure. We'll have to keep an eye on her. I don't like the way she looks at that big Mick.'

'Do me a favour,' Fletcher said. 'He's twice her age.'

Morgan shook his head pityingly. 'You know, there are times when you amaze me, Jesse, you really do.'

He turned, slapped the old man's hand as he reached for a sandwich and started to eat them himself.

On the slope above the farm, Rogan sat on a stone and lit a cigarette. In the far distance, Lake Windermere cut into the heart of the hills, black with depth near the centre, purple and grey at the edges. In the desolate light of gloaming, the tops of the mountains were streaked with orange.

The beauty of it was too much for a man and he breathed deeply on the sweetness of the heather, damp from the day's rain, filled with pleasant nostalgia.

'It's quite a view, isn't it?' Hannah Costello said.

He turned and found her standing a few yards away, watching him. 'I didn't hear a thing,' he said. 'I must be getting old.'

He took out his cigarettes and offered her one, and when she bent her face to the match which flared in his cupped hands her eyes were fathomless, so deep a man might drown in them.

She sat on the tilted slab of stone beside him and blew out a plume of smoke. 'There's something going on down there.'

'Between Morgan and Fletcher?'

'My uncle too. They were arguing together. I heard them from the passage. Something about this man Pope, the one who was waiting for you when you got out. He's in Ambleside now.' Rogan nodded and she frowned. 'You don't seem surprised?'

'I'm not.' He told her about Jack Pope and Soames and of how he had seen them together on his return to the cottage on the moor. 'What else did they say?'

'Morgan's phoning him tomorrow from the call-box on the main road. I suppose he'll wait to hear your verdict on the job.'

'That's about the size of it.'

'Another thing. He was talking about fifty thousand pound shares. I thought they were supposed to be getting five thousand each?'

'It looks as though Morgan intends to cut the cake differently.'

'You still don't look worried.'

'It'll work out, you'll see.' He smiled warmly. 'It's nice to know someone's on my side, anyway.'

She flushed perceptibly and he looked over the valley into the dark arch of the sky where a single star shone. For several minutes they sat there in silence and then she said softly, 'What are you thinking about?'

'Kerry,' he said. 'I've a farm there, or rather my father has.'

'And you'd like to go back?'

'It's quite a place. Sea and mountains, green grass, soft rain, fuchsia growing on the dusty hedges, glowing in the evening. *Deorini Dei* – the Tears of God, they call it.' He laughed softly. 'And the prettiest girls in the world. I was almost forgetting.'

He turned and found her looking at him, something that was very close to pain upon her face. Instinctively, he reached out and took her hand. 'You'd fit into the scenery admirably.'

She gazed at him searchingly, the strange, orange light

playing upon her face and then her smile seemed to deepen, to become luminous, and he pulled her to her feet and kissed her gently on the parted mouth.

Her lips were soft and fresh and quite suddenly, he was trembling slightly, his stomach hollow with excitement. It was as if she were the first, as if this had never happened before. She turned her face into his coat, holding him tightly and above them, a single cloud of red fire burned itself out, leaving them wordless in the night.

— 8 —

THE MORNING was cold with no rain, and a trace of mist hung over the fields behind the house as Rogan leaned against the fence, smoking a cigarette, and looked up at Scardale Fell, shrouded by low cloud.

He had spent the night on a camp bed in the old harness room above the barn and had eaten breakfast with Hannah and young Brendan, the others being still abed. Now, feeling relaxed and strangely content, he waited for the girl to bring the car from the barn.

Behind him, the house door opened and Paddy Costello shouted angrily, 'Get out of it, you useless lump. Up on the fellside with you and don't come back without those sheep.'

Young Brendan dodged a kick and ran across the yard, his patched jacket flying behind him. As he passed Rogan, he looked at him quickly, the dark eyes in the thin face like those of some hunted animal and Rogan was aware of an instant sympathy.

The boy ran away along the road and Costello came towards Rogan. His eyes were tinged with yellow, the veins swollen with blood and the pouched and folded skin of his face looked somehow unclean.

'He'll be the death of me, that lad, Mr Rogan. The death

of me.' He pushed the tail of his shirt into his waistband. 'The early start you're getting.'

'I've plenty to do,' Rogan said. 'Are Morgan and Fletcher still in bed?'

The old man nodded. 'What else would you expect from a couple of low-lifes like them two, Mr Rogan?'

In the barn, an engine coughed into life and the shooting brake emerged, Hannah at the wheel. She stopped and Rogan opened the door and got into the passenger seat beside her. He wound down the window and looked out at her uncle.

'If you're thinking of taking a trip in the cattle truck or the Morris, forget it. I've taken the keys. Tell Morgan I'll be back some time this afternoon.'

As the old man's face slipped, Rogan wound up the window and nodded to Hannah who released the handbrake and took the brake out through the gateway and down the dirt road into the mist.

She was wearing slim-fitting navy-blue ski pants, a heavy sheepskin jacket and a silk scarf was bound around her head, and again, he was conscious of that same restless excitement he had known on the hillside the previous evening.

As if aware that he was watching her she coloured slightly, her eyes never leaving the road as she negotiated a dangerous bend around a shoulder of the mountain.

'Your uncle chased the boy off up the fellside,' he said. 'Something about some sheep.'

She nodded. 'He's been selling them off in half dozen lots lately. He has a powerful thirst. They spend most of their time up there on the slopes. Finding them can be difficult.'

'Shouldn't the boy have a sheepdog?'

'He did. A collie named Thrasher, the joy of his life. He fell into one of the old mine shafts last month and broke his back. Some of them are a couple of hundred feet deep.'

Rogan sat there thinking about it. At breakfast, the boy hadn't had a great deal to say for himself, and when he did speak it was obvious that he stammered badly. Probably only psychological and not surprising with a father like Paddy Costello.

'You don't like my uncle, do you?' she said.

He laughed shortly. 'The understatement of the age. I've

met too many of his breed. A big man with the drink taken and words pouring out of him by the hundred. I can see him now in front of a police inspector with a face like whey, the cap twisting in his hands while he spills out his unclean guts. God knows how Colum O'More could have been taken in by him.'

'But he wasn't. My uncle contacted him through an old comrade in Liverpool and Colum simply turned up at the farm a month later. He didn't like what he found. He squeezed my uncle dry with the help of a bottle of pot-distilled whiskey that put him on his back in two hours, then turned his attention to me.'

'Had you ever met before?'

'Never, but he seemed to take to me. He said that he always liked to work from a distance through a go-between. He offered me the job.'

'And you accepted.'

'Remember what you said yesterday about wanting to crash out of something? Well, Colum O'More offered me the chance to do just that. Two thousand pounds and a passage to Ireland with him at the end and he promised to take Brendan with us.'

'And that was important to you?'

She shrugged. 'I couldn't walk out and leave him. Uncle Paddy won't last much longer, not at the rate he's drinking and what would happen to Brendan then? An institution?'

'So you're the only one who knows where Colum's staying? Your uncle wouldn't like that.'

She chuckled. 'He's tried following me a time or two and so has Morgan, but it didn't get them anywhere.'

'You sound as if you've been enjoying yourself?'

'I suppose I have.' She frowned as if trying to explain it to herself and concentrated on the road. 'In a strange way, I've been in a sort of limbo, drifting aimlessly ever since I was released from prison and came to Scardale to live. A year of days passing, the rain falling, snow on the mountains, and somewhere else a world that I had cut myself out of.'

'Surgery is always painful,' he said. 'Some people never get over it.'

She smiled tightly. 'Anyway, like I said yesterday, what

else could I have done? There was nowhere else to go. I was in this thing up to my neck whether I liked it or not.'

From Ambleside, they followed the lake to Windermere, then took the road through Staveley to Kendal. There was very little traffic about and the mist, if anything, was a little heavier. In Kendal itself, it was raining heavily and they passed through a thin scattering of traffic and drove out of the town again.

She pointed out the site of the Roman fort of Alavna as solemnly as if he had been any ordinary tourist. 'The Romans never landed in Ireland, did they?'

'They knew better,' Rogan said and a wide grin split across his face.

She glanced at him briefly, a sudden light in her eyes. 'That's the first time you've laughed properly since I've met you. I was beginning to think you didn't know how.'

He smiled again. 'Give me time, Hannah. That's all I need.'

For a brief moment, the intimacy between them was almost physical and they were both aware of the fact. He groped for the right words, but before he could find them, they topped a small rise of the narrow country road and he saw Rigg Station in the hollow below.

She stopped the shooting brake on the edge of a small parking space covered with gravel and Rogan lit a cigarette and wound down the window. The small, single-storeyed building had a roof of red tiles and was constructed of large square blocks of granite. There was an arched entrance, a large clock above it and a scale map of the district was displayed in a glass case pinned to the wall. At the other end was the loading bay, double-doors giving access to the station.

'Let's take a closer look,' Rogan said.

They got out of the brake and crossed the patch of gravel to the entrance. Inside, there was a narrow hall, a barrier and a ticket window which was closed by a wooden shutter. The door to the platform stood open and they could hear cheerful whistling. When Rogan peered cautiously round, he could see an oldish white-haired man sweeping the platform at the far end.

'Keep him talking,' Rogan said to Hannah. 'Ask him if you

can still catch the London train from here, anything you like, but keep him on the platform. I'll take a look round.'

She nodded briefly and moved out through the door. The old man didn't see her until she was almost upon him and he leaned on the broom and smiled. As the murmur of their voices started to echo through the quiet station, Rogan moved quickly to the door marked Stationmaster and opened it.

Inside he found the usual cluttered office. There was a desk, a couple of wooden filing cabinets and two or three yellowing calendars on the walls. There were two other doors. One gave access to a small washroom, the other to a narrow arched baggage hall which cut through the building from front to rear linking the platform with the loading bay. He moved out on to the concrete bay, jumped to the ground and went back to the car.

When Hannah returned five minutes later, he was smoking a cigarette, hands thrust deep into his pockets, a curiously withdrawn look on his face. She slid behind the wheel and closed the door.

'I thought I was never going to get away. Did you see everything you wanted?'

He nodded. 'What did the old man have to say?'

She smiled. 'His name's Briggs, and he retires next month. He's got two daughters and six grandchildren and his wife died two years ago. He also told me I couldn't get the London train from here, but that was only incidental.'

'He didn't leave much out.'

'I could have been talking to him yet. I don't suppose he has much to do in a place like this. It must get pretty boring. Apparently he isn't here all the time. They just send anyone who's available from Kendal.'

Rogan looked out at the station building again, a slight frown on his face. 'Where were you last Friday when the van arrived?'

'On the other side of the road under that tree,' she said. 'I brought Brendan with me. We had a picnic.'

'Did you get a close look at the driver and the guard when they got out of the van?'

'Close enough.'

'What kind of uniform do they wear?'

'That's easy. I sat next to one of them in a transport café in Kendal last month. A double-breasted blue serge suit with black plastic buttons – the sort of thing naval petty officers wear. The cap was the only elaborate thing about him. Shiny black peak edged with gold and a fancy badge.'

'And the bags the money was in – you saw them, too?'

'As they pulled them out on to the ramp. They were just the usual GPO mailbags. Is it important?'

'It could be.'

He took a large-scale map of the area from the glove compartment and unfolded it across his knees. After a while, he nodded. 'Let's get moving. Take the road back to Kendal then out towards Staveley. About forty miles an hour. No faster. I'll tell you when to stop.'

She drove back into Kendal and took the Windermere road to Staveley. Just before the junction with the Bowness road and perhaps ten minutes after leaving Rigg Station, Rogan nodded and she slowed to a halt. A few yards away, a five-barred gate gave access to a track which disappeared into a plantation of fir trees. Rogan got out of the brake, walked across to the gate and fumbled with the rusty chain that fastened it to an old stone post. The gate swung open and he returned to the car and got in.

'Follow the track and take it easy. According to the map there should be some flooded gravel pits a couple of hundred yards in.'

The track was soggy with rain and overgrown with grass from long disuse. Hannah stayed in a low gear and took the brake forward cautiously. The fir trees closed in on either side, dark and sombre, and then they went over a small rise and dropped down into a clearing.

There was an old barn constructed of heavy grey stone, its roof gaping to the sky and, beyond it, water gleamed through the undergrowth.

Hannah cut the engine and Rogan got out and walked across. He looked up at the crumbling walls for a moment, then continued across the clearing and paused at the far edge. A mass of undergrowth sprawled in a confusion of twisted branches to spill over the lip of a fifty-foot cliff that lifted from the dark waters of the gravel pit below.

Rogan stood there looking down, the slight frown still on his face. After a while he nodded his head as if in confirmation of some secret, hidden decision, turned and found Hannah standing a couple of yards away watching him.

'Can it be done, Sean Rogan?'

He flicked his cigarette down into the water and smiled calmly. 'I think it's time I had another word with Colum O'More.'

He took her arm, and together they walked back to the brake.

— 9 —

VANBRUGH CURSED as he sank into a patch of bog, cold water slopping over the tops of his rubber boots. The sergeant and constable of the county constabulary who accompanied him pulled him back on to firm ground with impassive faces and they continued up the slope.

On the crest of the tor, cloud dashed cold rain in the face and mist hung in a damp grey curtain that reduced visibility to no more than fifty yards.

Vanbrugh turned to the sergeant. 'How long can a man last in conditions like this?'

'You'd be surprised sir. We've had them on the run for a week many a time. The classic case was the bloke who got out during the winter about five years back. He was on the loose for a fortnight.'

'How did he manage that?'

'Holed up in a holiday cottage no more than three miles from the prison. That's one of the difficulties. There are lots of places like that all over the moor. They're always empty at this time of the year and we can't keep them all under constant surveillance. We haven't got enough men.'

'I know, sergeant. I know.'

Vanbrugh turned and went back down the hill towards his car and police Land-Rover parked beside it. He was cold and tired and thinking about Sean Rogan somewhere out there in the mist, running like a hunted animal, didn't make him feel any better.

As he neared the two vehicles, another Land-Rover appeared from the mist and pulled in at the side of the road. Sergeant Dwyer got out and moved to meet him.

Dwyer shook his head. 'Not a smell of him so far. The chief constable seems to think a house-to-house search should be the next step in case he's holed up somewhere. Apparently there are lots of holiday bungalows and cottages scattered across the moor that are mostly empty out of season.'

'No guarantee he wouldn't pick on one that's already been searched,' Vanbrugh said. 'Did you get that list from the prison?'

Dwyer took a typewritten sheet from his pocket and unfolded it. 'Here you are, sir. They couldn't list his close friends over the past few years because he hasn't had any, but there are at least half a dozen men here who've shared cells with him since he came out of solitary confinement.'

Vanbrugh examined the list quickly. 'Some real villains here. At least one of 'em's back inside to my knowledge.' He frowned and an expression of distaste appeared on his face. 'So he shared a cell with Jack Pope?'

'You know him, sir?'

'I should do. He was a sergeant in the uniformed branch at West End Central. Got sent down for corruption ten or twelve years ago and he's been back inside since for fraud.' Vanbrugh shook his head and said grimly, 'I can't stand a crooked copper.' He handed the list back to Dwyer. 'Anything else?'

'There was a message from the Yard about that lawyer you wanted them to contact, the one who visited Rogan. He doesn't seem to exist.'

Vanbrugh swore softly. 'Then Rogan didn't just take off into the blue. The whole thing was arranged. Why else would a phoney lawyer visit him only a couple of weeks before the event?'

'Which means that Soames must have known that Rogan

had a way out, sir, and not many people did. It was kept pretty dark and Rogan doesn't sound the sort of man who'd open his mouth if it didn't suit him.'

'It's amazing what men find out about each other when they share a cell, sergeant. As far as I'm concerned, any one of those men on that list of yours could have taken the information out with them when they were released.'

The rain suddenly increased in force and they climbed into the rear of the Land-Rover. Vanbrugh took a large vacuum flask from a basket under the seat and poured coffee into two plastic cups.

As he handed one to Dwyer, the sergeant said, 'If what you surmise is true, sir, Rogan could be almost anywhere by now, perhaps even across to Ireland.'

Vanbrugh shook his head. 'We'd have been the first to know, believe me. He's something of a legend in his own time, remember. His homecoming would hardly pass unnoticed.'

He started to fill his pipe. Dwyer hesitated and then said, 'Do you think we'll get him, sir?'

'I hope not, sergeant. I hope not.' Vanbrugh looked up with a slight smile, the pipe jutting from the corner of his mouth. 'That surprises you?'

'It mightn't if you explained why, sir.'

'It's really quite simple.' Vanbrugh put a match to his pipe and puffed out blue smoke. 'Sean Rogan's no criminal. He's a political offender. That doesn't mean I think he's right, but it doesn't mean that I have to agree with a system which condemns him to the same treatment as a criminal. In any case, as the IRA has now officially called off its underground campaign, I don't see how any useful purpose can be served by compelling Rogan and men like him to work out their sentences to the bitter end.'

'I must admit it doesn't make sense to me, sir.'

Vanbrugh nodded. 'Which doesn't mean that I'm not going to do my damnedest to run him down and find the men who helped him out.'

'He must be quite a man.'

'And then some.' Vanbrugh flicked the match into the rain and stared into the past. 'I was working on special assignment in France back in '43 and Rogan was running the local underground. Someone opened their mouth and I was picked up by German Military Intelligence.'

'Things must have looked pretty grim.'

'There was a troop train passing through on its way to the Ruhr and they arranged for it to stop at a tiny local station called Blois to pick me up. I was escorted there by two tanks and a company of infantry. They weren't taking any chances on the Maquis interfering.'

'What happened?'

'When we reached Blois, the main escort stayed outside and I was marched into a small waiting room between two Intelligence officers who'd even taken the precaution of handcuffing themselves to me. Inside, we found Rogan in the uniform of a colonel of infantry and half a dozen of his men. They knocked my escort senseless and released me.'

'Then what?'

'They had an unconscious man on a stretcher, some local collaborator. Rogan took him out on the platform when the train arrived and handed him over in my place and I scrambled into a spare uniform they'd brought me. We then walked out of the waiting room past my escort, climbed into a couple of official cars and drove away. The whole thing couldn't have lasted more than five minutes.'

'By God, it must have taken nerve.'

'And brains. The kind of intelligence that can always find a solution to even the most hopeless situation.' He looked out into the driving rain. 'That's Sean Rogan for you.'

There was a long silence before Dwyer said, 'So you think we might be wasting our time here, sir?'

'We could be,' Vanbrugh said. 'Tell you what you do. Go back to London and see what you can find out about Soames. Try the Law Society for a start. Men who pose as solicitors have usually practised at some time in the past. Have a look through their list of members who've been disbarred during the past few years.'

'And what about the other list, sir?'

'Rogan's old cell-mates?' Vanbrugh nodded. 'Have each one run down and checked. Probably nothing there, but you never can tell at this game.'

'Very well, sir.'

As Dwyer got out of the Land-Rover and walked to his car through the rain, Vanbrugh leaned out and shouted, 'And Dwyer!'

The sergeant turned. 'Yes, sir?'

'Top priority. We haven't got much time.'

For a moment Dwyer hesitated. It was quite obvious that he intended to say something, but thought better of it and he turned and walked to his car. As he drove away, Vanbrugh leaned back in his seat and took out his matches again, a slight frown on his face.

Now what on earth had made him say that? Time for what? But there was no answer, just that strange sixth sense, product of twenty-five years as a policeman, that told him that there was more to all this than any of them realized. Much more.

— 10 —

RAIN HAMMERED lightly against the window and Colum O'More turned to look outside. 'More rain. It never seems to do anything else.'

He was sitting in his armchair by the fire, his stick beside him and Rogan sat in the opposite chair drinking coffee. He was shocked at the obvious deterioration in the old man's condition. The face was grey, the skin hanging from the great jaw in loose, yellow folds and a two-day growth of beard didn't improve matters.

'When did you last see a doctor?'

O'More shifted uncomfortably in his chair and made an impatient gesture. 'Don't start worrying about me. I look a damned sight worse than I am. We've got something more important to discuss.'

'Suit yourself.' Rogan took out a cigarette and lit it with a splinter of wood from the fire. 'What do you think?'

'Of the plan?' O'More chuckled. 'It has just about the right mixture of simplicity and cold nerve I might have expected from you.'

'You think it could work?'

'I can't see how it could fail, not if you get your timing right.'

'What about flaws?'

The old man stuffed tobacco into his pipe, a slight frown on his face. 'There's a goods train due in at Rigg half an hour after the mail train. Unloads things like cattle fodder and heavy machinery for local farmers.'

Rogan shrugged. 'That would still give us a margin of twenty-five minutes to get away.'

'But you couldn't get across here in that time and once the news is out, the whole area will be buzzing with peelers. There aren't many roads through these mountains, remember. They'll have no trouble in closing them.'

'As long as we can make it back to Costello's farm at Scardale I'll be satisfied. We'll come here on Saturday.'

O'More frowned. 'They'll be stopping everything in sight.'

'I've got an idea that should take care of that.' Hannah came in from the kitchen with fresh coffee and he held out his cup. 'The worst thing you can do in that sort of situation is to get hold of a fast car. I proved that time and time again in the old days with the Resistance in France. A battered old van or truck that had all on to do twenty miles an hour with a load of hay or turnips or a couple of pigs in the back was the best bet. The important thing is to look as if you belong, as if you're just going about your normal business.'

'Which is logical enough. What have you in mind?'

Rogan turned to Hannah. 'You said your uncle had been selling off his sheep lately? Where exactly?'

'Sometimes to some wholesale butchers in Kendal, sometimes at cattle auctions on market days.'

'Is there a market anywhere on this side on a Saturday?'

She nodded. 'Millom. That's about five or six miles south of here.'

'Good enough,' Rogan said. 'We'll drive over in Paddy Costello's old cattle truck with a dozen or fifteen sheep in the back. I don't think the police will give us much trouble.'

'There'll be plenty of other farmers on the same road,' Hannah said.

'That's settled then.'

Colum O'More nodded, a slight frown on his face. 'There's just one thing I'm not happy about. From what I know of the way this security van firm works generally, the driver will contact county police headquarters on the radio telephone twice. Once to signal his arrival at Rigg, and then again to let them know that the job's complete. How are you going to get over that second call? If the police don't get it, they'll send out a local car to check straight away, just as a matter of routine.'

'I thought of that one, too,' Rogan said. 'There's only one way out. We'll have to get them to phone in for us from the mail train. Tell them the set's gone dead in the van or there's been an accident or something. It's reasonable enough. That sort of thing must happen occasionally.'

They sat there in silence for several moments and then the old man slapped his knee. 'By God, I think it'll go, Sean.' He turned to the girl. 'What do you say, Hannah?'

'You're the experts.' She picked up the tray. 'I'll make something to eat.'

She returned to the kitchen and O'More laughed.

'You've taken ten years off me already.'

'Don't speak too soon.' Rogan walked to the window and looked out at the rain. 'Soames and Jack Pope, how much are they mixed up in this thing?'

'They aren't,' Colum said. 'They were paid in advance for their part. As far as I'm concerned, they don't even know where we are or what we're doing. I've seen Soames in person once. Pope I only know from a photograph. Since then I've used the Kendal accommodation address in the name of Charles Grant. I've covered my tracks every step of the way. That's why I decided to use Hannah as a go-between. Even her uncle doesn't know about this place.'

'I didn't like the way Pope was playing things. The night I crashed out, after I left, I parked the car down the road and went back on foot. He and Soames had their heads together in the living room of the cottage.'

The old man frowned. 'So what?'

'Jack Pope's in Ambleside now. He's already been in contact with Morgan. Hannah overheard him and Fletcher talking about it. From what she said, her uncle's in it up to the tide mark on his dirty neck.'

'The lousy bastards,' the old man said. 'They've sold me out.'

'You let Soames recruit them for you. The link was there from the start. How much have Morgan and Fletcher had already?'

'Five hundred each. The rest to be paid out two weeks after the job's finished, through a man I know in Liverpool.'

Rogan shook his head. 'Not enough, Colum. These men are professionals. When they work for wages they expect half in advance, half after the job's finished. You should have smelt a rat the minute they said they were willing to accept such a small advance.'

'And how would I be knowing that?' Colum O'More demanded angrily. 'When have I needed to work with riff-raff like this before?'

'No cause for alarm.' Rogan held up a hand and smiled coldly. 'This thing is beginning to interest me.'

'And me, too, by God.'

The old man leaned across to the table, opened a drawer and produced a heavy Colt automatic of the type used by American officers during the war. He tossed it across.

Rogan caught it deftly, extracted the magazine, checked it, then rammed it back into the butt. 'A long time since I handled one of these.'

'I'm not suggesting you leave any corpses around when you've finished, but it might come in handy,' the old man said. 'When do you think they'll make their move?'

'At the farm after the job's finished. If they tried anything earlier, they might really mess things up. I don't think Morgan's that stupid.'

Colum cursed and slammed his hand hard against his bad leg. 'I have to sit here, crippled and useless and you alone.'

'There's always Hannah. At least I can rely on her.' Rogan got to his feet. 'Don't worry, Colum, there's always a certain strength in knowing the opposition for what it is.'

Hannah came in from the kitchen, belting her raincoat. 'Are you ready?'

'As ever was.' Rogan punched the old man heavily on the shoulder. 'Every tinker to his own trade, Colum, and this is mine. The one thing I had a talent for.'

He went outside. It was raining heavily and he ran across the yard, scrambled into the shooting brake and switched on the radio. It was almost half past the hour and a few moments later, the news headlines came on. As he was listening, Hannah opened the other door and got behind the wheel.

There was a political crisis in the Far East, car workers were on strike again and the opposition seriously disagreed with the government's policy towards immigration. The final item was a brief mention of the fact that Rogan was still at large, that the moor was being combed thoroughly and that the chief constable confidently expected his early recapture.

Rogan switched off and turned with a slight smile. 'So far, so good. Let's get back to the farm.'

She moved into gear and took the brake back along the rutted track towards the main road.

— 11 —

'I'LL GO OVER it again,' Rogan said.

He leaned across the table, the map spread before him and they crowded around, Fletcher almost knocking over the oil lamp in his eagerness.

'Paddy leaves here first in the cattle truck and parks it at the gravel pits this side of Kendal. We follow five minutes later in the Morris van, Hannah at the wheel, the rest of us in the back with the dummy sacks. We pick Paddy up on the way.' He glanced at Morgan. 'You and Fletcher will be in uniform as I've described.'

'The post of honour,' Morgan said mockingly.

'There isn't one. We get to Rigg no more than five minutes before the armoured van. I go in with Paddy, handle the stationmaster. Hannah backs up to the loading bay and you two get those sacks inside on the double. Then Hannah takes off and waits at the gravel pits.'

Hannah nodded calmly and Rogan went on, 'Paddy gets into the stationmaster's uniform and starts to sweep the platform. We wait for the armoured van.'

'They don't get out till he tells them the train's coming,' Morgan said. 'That doesn't leave much time.'

'We'll have to work fast, that's all. The moment they drag the first couple of sacks off the loading bay into the baggage hall, you smack them down good and hard. We aren't playing patty fingers.'

'Then what?'

'You and Fletcher put on their caps. That's the one part of the uniform we can't duplicate.'

'What if they don't fit?'

'Make them fit. Wear them at an angle – anything. Then open the door and out with the dummy sacks.'

'How many?'

'God knows. We'll take six. If there's more, they'll have to have some money back. That kind of a sack stuffed with notes can weigh as much as a hundredweight. We don't have time to mess about.'

'What happens on the platform?'

'You play it by ear. According to Colum, the duty men on the train change as often as the van crews so nobody should question you. There'll be a clearance chit. Get it signed, crack a joke and that's it.'

'What about the stationmaster? How do we know they'll accept Paddy in his place?'

'No trouble there. They don't have a regular stationmaster at Rigg. They send out anyone available from Kendal.'

There was a small silence and Fletcher glanced at Morgan. 'What do you think?'

'Looks good to me.' He turned to Rogan. 'What about mailbags? They're not easy to come by, not in a place like this.'

'I was hoping you might be able to suggest something.'

'I know a bloke in Manchester who's good at that sort of thing.'

'Fine,' Rogan said. 'You and Fletcher can take a run down in the brake in the morning. You could pick yourself up a couple of uniforms at one of those war surplus places.'

'Suits me,' Morgan said. 'I could do with a look at the big city again.'

'No hanging around,' Rogan said. 'I want you back here by dark, and lay off that stuff,' he told Fletcher, who was pouring whisky into a tumbler at the sideboard. 'You'll need all your wits about you on Friday.'

'You mind your business, Jack, I'll mind mine,' Fletcher said and moved out into the passage.

Morgan lit a cigarette and flicked the match into the fire. 'Just one thing bothers me – what happens when we get back here?'

'We sit tight till Saturday, then go our separate ways.'

'When do we slice up the cake?'

'We don't. You get what's coming to you from O'More's agent in Liverpool a fortnight later as agreed.'

'Why not here on the great day?'

'You disappoint me, Morgan. I thought you had brains.' Rogan shook his head. 'We'll stick to the contract.'

'All right for you,' Morgan said. 'You've got your line of retreat worked out, but what about Fletcher and me? There'll be more scuffers than hikers on these roads before you know where you are.'

'Then lie up here for a week or two. Move out when the fuss dies down.'

Morgan nodded. 'Maybe you've got something there.' He yawned. 'Think I'll take a walk before turning in.'

'You do that.'

When he had gone, Paddy Costello laughed nervously and clapped his hands together. 'God save us, but it's the great day, Mr Rogan, and me feeling like a young 'un again. I'll just take a wee walk along to the kitchen and see what damage Fletcher's done to that bottle of mine.'

He went out and Hannah got up from the chair where she had sat in silence throughout the whole proceedings. 'What about Morgan? Do you think he's gone to phone Pope?'

'That's what I intend to find out. You hold the fort here. I won't be long.'

He hurried along the passage, took down a three-quarter length oilskin coat from a peg and opened the door. Rain drummed down against the roof, bouncing from the cobbles, silver in the broad band of yellow light that streamed from the window of the living-room. She stood in the window watching him, curiously still, her face grave and, for some unaccountable reason, a great tenderness moved inside him so that he wanted to reach out, to touch her face gently, tell her that he cared. But there was no time, probably never would be.

He hurried along the track in the darkness, keeping to the grass shoulder, for half a mile until he reached the main road. He saw Morgan at once, standing in the lighted telephone-box a hundred yards down the road. Rogan moved towards the box, keeping in the shadows, and paused in the shelter of the bush no more than ten yards away.

Morgan was speaking into the receiver and, after a while, he put it down. He opened the door, looked out at the heavy rain and lit a cigarette.

Rogan waited, rain soaking his head, streaming across his face. Once a truck passed going down towards Ambleside, but otherwise, Morgan in the lighted telephone-box might have been the only inhabitant of a dark world.

It was perhaps twenty minutes after Morgan had made his telephone call that Rogan heard the sound of an engine faintly through the rain from the direction of Ambleside. A moment later, a mini-cab braked to a halt and Jack Pope leaned out of the window.

Morgan got in beside him and they started to talk. It was impossible for Rogan to hear anything of their conversation at all. He watched for a moment or two more, then withdrew into the darkness and started back along the road to the farm.

Whatever it was they intended, they meant business, so much was certain. But where was Soames and what was he doing? That was the important thing. Or perhaps he was simply the man behind the scenes? God knows, he'd hardly looked like the active type.

The rain seemed to increase in force and Rogan bent his

head and pushed on. As he rounded the shoulder of the hill, the valley falling away steeply on his right, he could see the farm nestling in a hollow of darkness, the yellow light reaching out into the night, and Hannah screamed his name aloud.

He was running, splashing in puddles of water and not caring, a strange sense of unreality to everything and saw her, silhouetted in the doorway, her hands clawing at Fletcher's face as he towered above her.

Brendan was on his knees in a pool of water, dazed and shaken, blood on his face, and Rogan ran forward lightly, a terrible, cold anger surging through him. The girl's dress was torn to the waist and as Fletcher laughed drunkenly and bent to kiss her, she jerked her head away so that Rogan got a clear picture of her face. There was nothing of fear there, only rage and humiliation and disgust. He grabbed Fletcher by the collar and pulled him away in one easy movement.

Fletcher staggered backwards, lost his balance and fell to one knee. He stayed there for a moment, looking up at Rogan, an expression of bewilderment on his brutal face, then gave a cry of anger and flung himself forward, hands reaching out to rend flesh and muscle.

Rogan swayed to one side and slashed him across the kidneys with the edge of his hand as the big man ran headlong past. Fletcher screamed and hit the wall. As he turned, Rogan punched him with tremendous force beneath the breastbone, the sound of the blow like a mallet striking wood. Fletcher slid down on his knees, the breath coming out of him in a long sigh.

Rogan moved in close and incredibly, one gnarled hand grabbed for his ankle and pulled hard, jerking him off balance so that he fell heavily to the cobbles. Fletcher's great hand clawed across his body, reaching for the throat. Rogan grabbed at his wrists and they rolled over in the rain.

They cannoned into the wall beside the horse trough and Rogan, with a supreme effort, threw him to one side and got to his feet. Fletcher reached for the edge of the trough and pulled himself up. As he reached his full height, Rogan moved in fast and kicked him in the stomach. Fletcher doubled over and a knee like iron lifted into his face sending him back over the edge of the water trough.

He sprawled there, head under the surface and Rogan leaned on the edge to get his breath. After a while, he grabbed the big man by the shirt front and hauled him out. He dropped him on the cobbles and turned to find Hannah and Morgan watching him.

When he spoke, his voice seemed to be the voice of a stranger and the blood pounded in his ears. 'You tell him next time I see him with a bottle, I'll break it over his skull.' He pushed Morgan violently out of the way and lurched across the yard towards the house.

He was sitting in the chair beside the kitchen table, he was aware of that, and Hannah was wiping the blood from his face with a towel and warm water, tears pouring down her cheeks, and then she was in his arms and his lips were against the cool flesh and it was as if this had always been.

Outside in the rain, Morgan crouched beside Fletcher who was moaning in pain, eyes half open. 'What was it you called him, Jesse? Just a big Irish bogtrotter? Hit him in the right place and he'd split clean down the middle.'

He started to laugh, turned and walked to the house and left Fletcher lying there alone in the heavy rain.

— 12 —

MORGAN AND FLETCHER left for Manchester straight after breakfast the following morning, Fletcher sullen and angry, his eyes smouldering with hate whenever he looked at Rogan.

Rogan stood at the gate and watched the brake move away down the dirt road. He turned and looked up at the mountains, feeling relaxed and at peace. The morning was bright and clean, the moor purple with heather and the haze of autumn was on the land.

He turned and found Hannah watching him, a slight smile on her face. 'A fine morning.'

'With those two gone it's like being rid of a bad taste in your mouth.' He took a deep breath as a small wind lifted from the stream in the valley bringing with it the dank, wet smell of rotting leaves.

'My favourite season, autumn,' Hannah said. 'Always something a little sad about it. Old dreams like smoke in the air, lingering on for a moment before fading for ever.'

There was a poignancy in her voice that touched something deep inside him and he reached out and caressed her face gently with the back of his hand. She turned and kissed his palm, her face flushed and beautiful.

'What would you like to do?' he said. 'The way I see it, we've got the day to ourselves.'

She turned, shading her eyes, and looked up at the fells. 'I'd like to go up there, I think. It would be nice to be above the world for an hour or two. I could make some sandwiches.'

'Sounds fine to me,' Rogan said. 'What about your uncle?'

'Still sleeping it off. Brendan went up the valley half an hour ago. We'll probably see him up there.'

They returned to the house. Hannah went into the kitchen and Rogan had a shave. When he had finished, he helped himself to the oilskin jacket he had used the night before and an old tweed cap from a peg behind the door, and waited outside.

Hannah joined him a few minutes later. She was wearing leather knee-length boots and jeans and her sheep-skin jacket. A scarf was knotted around her head and she carried an old army knapsack.

'I'll take that,' Rogan said and he slipped his arms through the straps.

Over the mountains, the sky was grey and threatening and the sun had almost disappeared, but the prospect of more rain didn't seem to matter. They turned out through the gate and started up the valley.

The surface of the old road had almost disappeared under a creeping carpet of moss and rank grass that grew profusely from every crack and it followed the side of the hill, rising steeply. Beyond a shoulder they paused and saw in a hollow beneath them the ruins of the old mining village.

As they moved down, rain descended in a great rush,

splashing into the interiors of the roofless cottages, giving the place a setting that was somehow strangely appropriate.

'It must have been quite a place,' Rogan said.

Hannah nodded. 'I looked it up in the library in Ambleside once. There were two or three hundred people living here at one time. They mined for lead during the Napoleonic Wars.'

'What happened?'

'The vein ran out during the 1820s.' She sighed. 'It's rather sad when you come to think of it. This place was once alive and throbbing with love and laughter and children and chapel on Sundays and then the vein ran out.'

'That's life,' Rogan said gently. 'The vein always seems to run out when you least expect it.'

She turned, a shadow in her eyes. 'It isn't really fair, is it? It doesn't seem to give people much. You work and hope and then get kicked in the teeth.'

'God lets no man suffer too long.' Rogan smiled. 'A saying my grandmother was fond of.'

'Do you believe that?'

He shrugged. 'I believe in hope, Hannah. Hope above all things. Without it, life would be pretty pointless.'

They paused outside the little church and Rogan examined the slab above the door with the faded letters, moss-grown: Scardale Primitive Methodist Chapel 1805.

'The year of Trafalgar,' he said. 'A long time ago.'

'Another British victory?'

He grinned. 'There were more than fifty American citizens in the crew of Nelson's *Victory* and twice as many Irishmen. A way the British had with them.'

'We learn something new every day.'

They moved on, following the slope of the main street and came to a sizeable dam constructed of large blocks of granite stone, slippery and green with the years where moisture leaked through, the stream issuing from a stone sluice at the bottom.

On the far side of the dam higher up the valley were the actual mine workings. A dozen or fifteen sheep were penned together in an old stone enclosure. A few yards away, Brendan Costello sat on a large boulder throwing pebbles into the water. Hannah called to him and he turned quickly, eyes very dark in the white face.

He came towards them and nodded to Rogan, smiling shyly. Hannah ruffled his hair with obvious affection. 'What have you been doing?'

He spoke in short, rather clipped sentences, an obvious attempt to defeat his stammer by missing out those words which gave him most difficulty.

'He w-wants m-more sheep bringing down.'

Hannah nodded. 'We're having our dinner up here today. Would you like to come with us?'

He looked swiftly at Rogan and his face crimsoned with pleasure. 'C-can I?'

'If you like.'

'I c-could show you the Long C-cut, Mr Rogan. Y-you'd like that.'

Rogan turned to Hannah. 'The Long Cut?'

She pointed to the western end of the dam where it ran into a tangled mass of bushes at the face of a steep cliff. 'We'll take a look if you like. You can't see the entrance from here, but they ran a tunnel under the shoulder of the mountain into the next valley. It carries a canal. They used to take the ore out that way.'

They moved round the edge of the dam into a clump of trees, and beyond them a crumbling landing stage jutted into the water and the mouth of the tunnel gaped darkly. There was very little headroom and when Rogan squatted down and looked inside, he could see a tiny circle of light at the other end.

'How long is it?'

'Six or seven hundred yards.'

He whistled softly. 'It must have taken some doing.'

'There was a natural cave system. I think they just linked it up. Of course there wouldn't be any water in it until they built the dam.'

'Quite an achievement all the same.'

'We can go through if you like.'

She pointed, and when Rogan turned he saw the boy moving out of the undergrowth at the side of the dam hauling on a length of rope, to which was attached a heavy, high-sided punt of the type used by wildfowlers. There was a couple of inches of water in the bottom.

Rogan grinned. 'Are you sure it's safe?'

Hannah dropped into it and sat on one of the narrow wooden seats. 'You couldn't get any wetter than you are.'

Rogan joined her in a world of cold, clammy darkness, of walls that oozed moisture where water constantly dripped so low that Rogan actually had to bend his head, and when he looked over his shoulder he saw that the boy was lying on his back and propelling the punt along by walking his feet along the roof.

They passed into a large echoing cavern with a vaulted roof, crossed it and entered the tunnel again. They passed through two similar caves and then moved into the final stretch, and the opening at the other end seemed to increase in size quite suddenly.

They drifted out into another similar dam and bumped against the side of a stone landing stage. Brendan scrambled up and fastened the line to a rusting iron ring. Rogan followed him and turned to give Hannah a hand up.

They walked through a grove of trees past several ruined buildings. One of them, a stable, had a corrugated iron roof, and stout wooden doors of recent origin were secured with a padlock and chain.

'What's in here?' Rogan asked.

Brendan ran forward, slipped his hand under a flat stone beside the door and produced a key. He quickly unlocked the padlock, pulled away the chain and swung back the door.

An old jeep was parked inside. It had been fitted with a battered aluminium body in place of the old canvas tilt and the original olive green paintwork was chipped and scraped.

Rogan took off his knapsack and got behind the wheel. 'A long time since I drove one of these. It must be all of twenty years old.' He pulled out the choke and pressed the starter and the engine turned over at once. 'Who owns it?'

'Most of this valley is one big sheep ranch run by a syndicate', Hannah said. 'That's the way farming seems to be going these days. They always keep a jeep or a Land Rover up here fuelled and ready for action. They're particularly good in bad weather on the fellside. The shepherds use them as they used to use a horse or a pony in the old days.'

Rogan got out of the jeep and they moved back outside.

Brendan locked the door and replaced the key under the stone. Below them in the rain, the valley dropped down towards a shining expanse of water.

'What's that?' Rogan said.

'Rydal Water. If you move down the slope a little further you'll see the beginning of Grasmere to the west of it.'

He took an Ordnance Survey Map of the area from the pocket of his jacket and opened it, dropping to one knee. 'Let's suppose something had gone wrong with my original plan and I wanted to get from here to Marsh-End, how would I set about it?'

She examined the map with a slight frown. 'There *is* a back road. I found it by accident one day when Uncle Paddy tried to follow me. I think I can show you if we move further down the slope.'

They went down the track for perhaps a hundred yards. From that point, it was possible to see not only Rydal Water, but most of Grasmere as well.

'Can you see the stream linking the two lakes?' Hannah asked. 'There's a gate and a small bridge and beyond it a track goes as far as Elterwater. From there, there's a road, mainly unfenced, that takes you through Wrynose Pass between the mountains. About six miles from there, the road branches. If you take the one which follows the valley of the Duddon River through Seathwaite and Ulpha, you come to the Whicham road about ten miles further on.'

'And how far is Whicham from there?'

'Nine or ten miles.'

'And Marsh-End is only a couple of miles from there up the coast.' He nodded and folded the map. 'A lonely sort of road, would you say?'

'You probably wouldn't see a soul during the entire run. Not at this time of the year. Mind you, it could be hard going in bad weather over Wrynose. You'd need a good vehicle, especially if you had a load on. Uncle Paddy's old cattle truck would never take it.'

'I wouldn't be using it, not in the sort of situation I've been going over in my mind.' He lit a cigarette and put one foot on a boulder, resting an elbow on his knee. 'Scardale would be one hell of a place to be caught in with that one road out.

It seems to me that in an emergency Brendan's Long Cut would provide a very adequate back door and that jeep would be more than handy.'

'Are you thinking of dropping the idea of using the cattle truck?'

He shook his head. 'Not unless I have to. Does your uncle know about the Long Cut?'

She nodded. 'He's never been through, though. As far as I know, he doesn't think it's possible.'

'So Morgan and Fletcher don't know about it either?' Rogan nodded, a slight smile on his face. 'We'll keep it that way. What happens now?'

Hannah looked up through the rain at the top of Scardale Fell, low cloud and mist draped across it. 'We could climb up to the top. There's a climbers' hut we could eat in. Brendan could take the boat back through the tunnel and climb up the other side to meet us.'

The boy nodded eagerly, turned and ran back through the trees towards the old landing stage, and Rogan and the girl took a winding track that slanted up the side of the fell between rain-soaked, decaying bracken.

After a while, the track narrowed and Hannah went in front to lead the way. Rogan watched her as she bent to the slope of the hill, and when she paused and smiled back at him over her shoulder realized with a sense of wonder that she was beautiful.

'How are you doing?'

'Never mind about me,' he said. 'We've a thousand feet or more to go yet.'

He plodded on through the heavy rain and as the mountain lifted before him he was filled with a strange feeling that all this had happened before. What was it the psychologists called it – *déjà vu*? Previously seen? And then in one quick moment of complete recall he remembered.

September 1943. Out of France through the Pyrenees into Spain with papers that had to be in Gibraltar within a week. It had rained like hell and to make matters worse, a company of German mountain troops had got their scent.

He remembered how it had been on just such a hillside as this, his guide, a brown-skinned Basque mountaineer, a couple of yards in front. And then the rifle shot, flat, curiously muffled by the rain. The man had spun round, a dark hole between his eyes, surprise on his face and Rogan had jumped into the bracken and run for his life.

He came back to the present with a start, realizing that Hannah was calling to him. When he looked up, she was standing beside a low hut constructed of great slabs of stone and concrete about fifty feet above him on the edge of a small plateau.

'Any sign of Brendan?' he said as he joined her.

She shook her head. 'It'll take him another twenty minutes at least. Harder going on that side of the mountain.'

Inside the hut there were wooden benches, a table and kindling for a fire. They sat at the table and Rogan took off the knapsack. Hannah produced several packets of sandwiches, some fruit and a large vacuum flask. 'Shall we start or do you want to wait for Brendan?'

'We'll have a coffee and wait.'

He lit a cigarette and they sat there in companionable silence. After a while, she said hesitatingly, 'Is it going to work, Sean?'

He nodded and there was a calm certainty in his voice. 'It'll work all right.'

'And then what?'

'I'll go home,' he said. 'Back to Kerry and that farm I was telling you about.'

'And a good woman?'

He touched her gently on the face. 'I'm twenty years too old for you, have you considered that?'

'You've been in prison a long time,' she said, and a small devil looked out of her eye at him. 'Working that off should keep me going for quite a while.'

Laughter erupted from his throat and he reached across, tugging at her hair. 'The most dangerous remark you ever made in your life, my girl.'

She held on to his hand, her laughter matching his, and then it faded and she turned her face and kissed his palm. He went round the table in two quick steps, the bench going over with a clatter and pulled her into his arms. There were tears on her face and her whole body was trembling. He held her at arm's length and raised her chin with one hand.

'This is one hell of a place to be putting a question like this to you, but did anyone ever ask you to marry him before?'

He could not have stilled her more completely with a slap across the face. She stared at him in incredulous wonder, eyes wide and staring and then she stumbled into his arms, her head against his chest.

When she looked up, her eyes were shining. 'Nothing matters now. Nothing.'

'I know, Hannah. I know.'

There was the rattle of stones on the hillside above the little plateau, she pulled away from him quickly and wiped her eyes. She turned to the table and started to unpack the sandwiches as Brendan appeared in the doorway.

He came forward shyly and Rogan patted him on the shoulder. 'Sit down, son, we've been waiting for you.'

Brendan took the sandwich Hannah offered him, bit into it and sighed with pleasure. The strange thing was that when he spoke there was no trace of a stammer at all. 'I wish this day could go on for ever, Mr Rogan. Do you ever feel like that?'

Rogan looked across at Hannah, knowing what she must be thinking and shook his head. 'Nothing lasts for ever, son, that's one of the things we all have to learn.'

Hannah's eyes clouded for a moment, her face became a blank mask again. Rogan sighed, got to his feet and moved to the door. The rain was falling harder than ever and he looked out at it morosely. Whichever way you looked at it, life was neither a beginning nor an ending, but a constant state that covered every action a man had taken, good or bad, during his entire existence.

He was involved with this girl just as he was involved with Colum O'More and Harry Morgan, because every single thing he had done in his life had led him to this point. There was no point in regretting anything. Subtract any part of the whole and it no longer existed, which was an interesting thought. He sighed heavily and went back inside.

II

In the late afternoon as the shadows drifted in across the mountains they moved down the track towards the farm. As they rounded the shoulder of the hill, the shooting brake was turning through the gate into the yard. The two men got out, Fletcher went straight inside, but Morgan stood waiting for them.

'A hell of a day for a walk on the mountain,' he said, the characteristic sardonic smile tugging at the corner of his mouth.

'Any trouble?' Rogan said.

Morgan shook his head. He moved to the rear of the brake, opened the door and lifted a rug to disclose four mailbags neatly folded and a couple of brown paper parcels containing the uniforms.

'Four was all you could get?'

Morgan nodded. 'He had these in stock, so to speak. He could have got us more this evening, but I decided you wouldn't want us to hang around.'

Hannah and Brendan had gone into the house and the two men stood there alone in the heavy rain. 'That's it then,' Rogan said. 'All we can do now is wait.'

'That's all,' Morgan said and there was a slight, mocking edge to his voice.

Rogan looked at him steadily for a long moment. Only when Morgan flushed and looked away did he turn and walk to the house.

— 13 —

IT WAS JUST before noon on Thursday when Vanbrugh arrived at Paddington. Dwyer was waiting for him at the ticket barrier. They went into the station restaurant, ordered coffee and sat in a corner.

Vanbrugh looked tired and lit a cigarette, an unusual thing for him. 'Any sign of Pope yet?'

'I've managed to trace him to another address, since I wired you the photos of him and those other two prospects yesterday. Not far from here as a matter of fact. His landlady says he moved out a week ago with no forwarding address. I've got some men on it, but it's pretty difficult. You know what the manpower position is in the CID at the moment.'

'You don't need to tell me.' Vanbrugh ran a hand over his face. 'As it happens, you can stop looking. Pope's been out of town.'

'You've found him, sir?'

Vanbrugh shook his head. 'All I can tell you is that he hired a car in Taunton last weekend. The manager of the place recognized him at once from the photo you sent.'

'Hiring a car's hardly a criminal offence, sir.'

'Perhaps, but being in the area of the prison when his old cell-mate breaks out very probably is.'

'So you think Rogan's no longer in the vicinity of the prison?'

Vanbrugh chuckled. 'What is it they say? No one ever gets off the moor? Well, Rogan did and very probably within an hour of getting over the wall, from the way things are beginning to shape up.'

'Then he *must* be in Ireland by now, sir. This is the fourth day, remember.'

Vanbrugh shook his head. 'If he'd landed in Ireland, we'd have known about it, take my word for that. No, he's still in England, I'm certain of that. But why, that's the question.'

He stared down into his cup, a slight frown on his face. 'What about Soames?'

'I've got Scott on the final trace now. I think it's the right man. Real name Bertram Greaves. He was disbarred by the Law Society for malpractice ten years ago. Since then he's been mixed up in all sorts of things under various aliases. Soames must only be the latest of a dozen or more.'

'Any form?'

'Six months for false pretences in 1958. That was unusual. He's the sort who usually manage to skate on pretty thin ice without falling in.'

'Let's hope Scott comes up with something then. In the meantime, I'd like to see Pope's landlady. We're probably wasting our time, but you never can tell.'

Dwyer had a squad car waiting and they pulled up outside a narrow brownstone house in a mean street within ten minutes of leaving the station. The woman who opened the door to them was cold and hard, a cigarette dangling from one corner of her narrow mouth. Beneath the cheap silk scarf, her head was a mass of tightly rolled curlers.

'For Christ's sake, you again?' she said pleasantly when she saw Dwyer.

'Less of that,' he told her. 'Chief Superintendent Vanbrugh would like a word with you.'

Something close to respect appeared on her face and she opened the door wide. 'You'd better come inside.'

There was a stale smell compounded of urine and cooking odours, and an unwashed child, naked from the waist down, stood by the kitchen door and looked at them with wide eyes, a grimy finger in its mouth.

The woman took them up the stairs and opened a door at one side. 'He lived here for a week. I've got a Jamaican moving in Monday. A bloody sight cleaner than some of the bastards we get,' she added defensively.

The room was quite bare except for an old-fashioned wardrobe, a brass bedstead and a strip of linoleum. They went back downstairs and she led the way into the cluttered kitchen.

She stood with her back to the fire, one hand on the

mantelpiece. 'I told your man here all I knew, Mr Vanbrugh. I wish I knew where he was, honest I do. He owed me for his week's rent.'

'There's nothing you can remember? Nothing at all?' Vanbrugh said. 'A word, a name, anything?'

She shook her head stubbornly. 'Nothing.'

'No visitors, even?'

'If you mean birds, I don't run that sort of place.'

Vanbrugh sighed. 'What you're saying is that during the time he lived here, Jack Pope didn't have any kind of contact with anyone. Not even a letter.'

'That's right.' She nodded vigorously and Vanbrugh turned towards the door. 'Of course he did get a postcard one day. Last week I think it was.'

Vanbrugh's tiredness vanished at once. 'A postcard? Where from?'

'For Christ's sake, Mr Vanbrugh, how would I know?'

'Was it from a seaside place?' Dwyer suggested.

She shook her head. 'No, nowhere like that. I remember being a bit surprised.' Her face brightened. 'Windermere – that was it. Lake Windermere.'

Dwyer looked blankly at Vanbrugh. 'She must be joking, sir. Who in creation would Pope know in the Lake District?'

Vanbrugh turned to the landlady. 'You've been very helpful. Perhaps more than you realize.'

She shrugged. 'I know which side my bread's buttered on, Mr Vanbrugh. If you do see that sod, you tell him I want my rent.'

The child started to cry and as she moved towards it with a curse, Vanbrugh and Dwyer left hurriedly. As they went down the steps towards the car, the driver leaned out of the window. 'HQ on the radio, sir. They've got a message for you. Top priority.'

Vanbrugh nodded to Dwyer. 'You take it. Let's hope it's something good.'

Dwyer leaned in the window and Vanbrugh lit another cigarette, a slight frown knitting his brow. The Lake District. Now that *was* a turn-up for the book. Hardly the sort of place one would expect to hear about from a man like Pope or the sort of people he associated with.

Dwyer turned, excitement on his face. 'That was Scott, sir. He's traced Soames to an address in Hendon. He told the landlady he was going away for a week on business. That was last Saturday. She hasn't seen him since.'

'Let's get moving,' Vanbrugh said. 'This is beginning to get interesting.'

They moved into a calmer, more ordered, world of respectable semi-detached houses with neat hedges and, in spite of the season, well-kept gardens. There was little doubt that whatever else Soames and Pope had in common, it certainly wasn't a similar standard of living.

They found Scott waiting in his car outside a small detached house at one end of a quiet cul-de-sac. He was a tall, quiet young man with a clipped moustache that gave him rather a military air.

'Anything doing?' Vanbrugh demanded.

Scott shook his head. 'He moved out last Saturday. Told her he'd be away for a week on business. She hasn't heard of him since.'

Vanbrugh nodded. 'You stay here. We'll go in. What's her name?'

'Mrs Jones, sir. A widow lady and very upset about this, I might add.'

She had opened the door as soon as they had ascended the steps, a sure sign that she had been watching from behind the curtains. She was a rather fussy, pouchy-faced woman, with pale blue eyes and wearing a green dress.

'Mrs Jones? I'm Chief Superintendent Vanbrugh and this is Detective Sergeant Dwyer. I'd like to ask you a few questions about a man called Soames. I believe he's been staying here.'

'Really, superintendent, I told the young man who called here earlier everything I know.'

'There may have been a point or two he missed,' Vanbrugh said patiently. 'Perhaps we could see Mr Soames' room?'

She led the way upstairs, talking incessantly. 'What my other guests are going to think of all this I really don't know and Mr Soames seemed a most respectable gentleman. A solicitor, he told me. Somewhere in the City.'

'How long has he been staying here?'

'Since early May of this year. Just six months.'

She opened the door at the end of a lengthy passage and led the way in. The room was neat and comfortable. There was a modern washbasin in one corner, two fitted wardrobes and a neat single bed. At the other end, beyond a room divider crammed with books, was a fireplace, a desk, a couple of easy chairs and a french window leading on to a small balcony which overlooked the garden.

'Scott told me he'd been through everything, sir,' Dwyer said. 'Couldn't find anything in writing at all.'

Vanbrugh moved to the desk and opened the drawers one after another in quick succession. They were all quite empty. 'A cautious bird, our Mr Soames,' he commented.

Dwyer went through the two wardrobes quickly and draped various items across the bed. There was a dressing-gown, two suits and several shirts on hangers. Vanbrugh joined him and they went through the pockets.

There were one or two old bus tickets and the odd coin, but nothing else of value, and the drawers of the dressing table contained only underwear, socks and towels.

Mrs Jones had been watching them with a mixture of uncertainty and horror on her face. At any moment, Vanbrugh expected her to ask to see the search warrant he didn't have and he moved in to the attack without any further waste of time.

'You told Constable Scott that Soames left on Saturday, Mrs Jones?'

'That's right, superintendent. It was just before lunch. I remember it particularly because he asked if he could have something to eat a little earlier than usual. He said he had a train to catch.'

'Did he take a taxi?' Dwyer said hopefully.

'There's an underground station at the end of the road. It's quicker than a taxi these days, traffic being what it is.'

'And Soames gave you no hint at all as to his destination?'

She shook her head. 'Just said he was taking a little business trip. That he'd probably be away for a week or ten days.'

'Has he done this sort of thing before?'

'Oh, yes, often.'

'And he never leaves you a forwarding address for urgent mail and so on?'

'I asked him about that once, but he said there was no point, that he would be on the move the whole time.'

'What about his social life? Did he have many callers?'

'None at all. He once told me that he preferred to keep his business and private life completely separate. He was a quiet, well-mannered person who kept himself to himself. Most evenings, he took a walk down to The George on the corner for a drink, but he never stayed for more than half an hour. He was fond of television and he looked after the garden for me. He was very good with flowers.'

'What about mail? Did he get much?'

She shrugged. 'Two or three letters a day, mostly circulars and so on.'

'Anything particularly interesting?'

She bridled at once. 'I've better things to do, superintendent, than to go through my guests' mail.'

'I wasn't suggesting that you had been snooping, Mrs Jones,' Vanbrugh said patiently. 'But quite obviously, you must sort the mail every morning after it's been delivered. It would be only natural for an intelligent person to notice anything unusual, any change in the pattern.'

She responded immediately, almost as a reflex action. 'It's funny you should say that. Nearly all Mr Soames' letters used to come from the London area, but during the past few weeks they've been coming from all over the place.'

'Can you remember where?'

'He had a couple from Manchester and several from the Lake District. The day he left, he had one from Taunton. That's in the West Country,' she added. 'I spent my holidays near there last year.'

Dwyer had taken a sudden, involuntary step forward, but Vanbrugh stilled him with a quick gesture from one hand. 'These letters from the Lake District, Mrs Jones, can you remember where they were from?'

'Oh, yes,' she said. 'because he always replied within a day or two. Sometimes I posted the letters for him. Kendal, that was the place. He used to write to a Mr Grant at Kendal.'

'And you can't remember the address?'

She shook her head. 'I'm afraid not. It was addressed care of somebody else, I do know that. I always assumed it was a boarding house or something similar.' She patted her hair impatiently. 'You know there's really nothing more I can tell you, superintendent.'

Vanbrugh gave her his most charming smile. 'My dear Mrs Jones, you've helped us more than you'll ever know. I don't think we'll need to trouble you again.'

He went down the stairs quickly, Dwyer at his heels, opened the front door and went down the path. Scott was waiting for them. 'Any luck, sir?'

'You could say that.' Vanbrugh turned to Dwyer. 'An interesting coincidence, isn't it, Soames and Pope being in touch with someone in the Lake District.'

'But what on earth would they be doing there, sir?' Dwyer said. 'It doesn't make sense.'

'Oh, I don't know,' Vanbrugh said. 'It's remote, secluded and they'll pretty well have the place to themselves at this time of the year.'

'If they *are* there, sir,' Dwyer reminded him.

Vanbrugh grinned. 'When you've been at this game as long as I have, sergeant, you'll learn an interesting fact. That police work is mainly a matter of rather tedious routine, of question and answer, of sitting back, assessing the facts and looking for a pattern.'

'I know that much already, sir.'

'But that's not all,' Vanbrugh went on. 'As the years pass you'll find you develop a sort of extra faculty, an instinct that tells you a thing's so, even when you can't actually prove it. It's a good copper's most valuable asset.' He took out his pipe and gripped it firmly between his teeth. 'Soames and Pope are either in Kendal or somewhere near,' he said. 'I've never been so sure of anything in my life.'

'And Rogan, sir?'

Vanbrugh shook his head and some of the excitement died in him. 'Now there you have me. The trouble is, it doesn't make any kind of sense. Neither does the fact that he's mixed up with a couple of villains like Soames and Pope. They're just not his style.'

'What's the next move, sir?'

'Straight to the Yard. I'll see the assistant commissioner and make arrangements for us to leave for the Lake District at once. I'll get him to fix up full co-operation for us with the county constabulary.'

'We won't reach Kendal before nine or ten tonight, sir,' Dwyer pointed out. 'We wouldn't do much till tomorrow.'

'You said Soames was nicked in 1958, didn't you?' Vanbrugh demanded. 'The least you can do is get his picture from records and wire it to Kendal together with that one of Pope. The sooner we get the local men looking out for them, the better. And we'll need the county constabulary in on this, too.'

As the car moved away, he sank back against the padded seat, no longer tired, a hollow ache of excitement in the pit of his stomach. He was as certain as he had ever been about anything, that the answer to this whole affair lay in the last place in the country he would ever have thought of looking.

II

At that precise moment, Soames was crouched in a clump of bushes at the side of the coast road a few yards away from the signpost indicating the way to Marsh-End.

The small green saloon he had hired from a garage in Broughton-in-Furness was parked in a clearing to the rear. The fact that he was here at all was purely accidental. He had been waiting at the side of the Ambleside road for Pope who had gone up the valley on foot to keep a prearranged appointment with Morgan, when the shooting brake containing Rogan and Hannah Costello had come down from Scardale. Soames, his cunning mind working overtime, had simply seized the opportunity.

Rogan was not expecting to be followed. His decision to make a last visit to Colum O'More had been taken at a moment's notice, mainly because he had wanted to be alone with Hannah and in any case, he carried the keys of the cattle truck and the Morris van in his pocket.

They chose the long way round through Hawkshead, Coniston and Broughton and there was a fair amount of traffic on the road, which was greatly to Soames' advantage.

Cautious by nature, he was anything but a violent man and he knew just when it paid to take a chance and when it did not. When the shooting brake took the turning for Marsh-

End he drove by, then turned and quickly found somewhere to park. Then he moved cautiously through the trees until he came upon the farm and the brake parked in the yard. He returned to the main road at once and took up his position in the shelter of some bushes.

The rain continued to fall steadily during the hours that he waited, but finally the brake reappeared and he drew back into the bushes until the sound of its engine faded into the distance.

He left his car where it was and moved back through the trees towards the farm. There was no sign of life anywhere and he stood at the edge of the yard examining the windows for a moment, then crossed to the door.

It opened to his touch and he walked softly along the whitewashed passage. The living room door was slightly ajar and someone coughed. He pushed the door open and stepped in.

Colum O'More was sitting by the fire in the act of applying a match to the bowl of his pipe. He stared at Soames as if he had seen a ghost and a quick anger kindled in his eyes.

'What the devil are you doing here?'

'I thought it was time we had a little chat, Mr O'More.'

Soames moved forward, shook the rain from his hat and placed it carefully on the table.

'I've nothing to say to you,' O'More said. 'You've been paid for what you've done, well paid and there's an end to it.'

'I have a friend in Dublin, Mr O'Morc, did you know that?' Soames held his hands out to the fire. 'He's been making a few enquiries for me. Among the right people, you understand.' He smiled gently. 'The headquarters of your movement in Dublin, or what's left of it, don't seem to have heard from you in five years or more.' He shook his head reprovingly. 'You've not been telling the truth, Mr O'More. I wonder what Sean Rogan would say to that?'

— 14 —

A COLD WIND slanting across the square drove rain against the window with the force of lead shot as Vanbrugh stared morosely into the street. Already half-convinced that he was wrong, an abortive morning spent visiting every hotel in Kendal without finding a trace of either Soames or Pope, hadn't improved his temper. He wondered impatiently what was keeping Dwyer.

There was a knock on the door and a young constable entered with a cup of tea. As he turned to leave, Dwyer came in.

'You can make that two.' He shook rain from his hat and unbuttoned his coat. 'What a climate.'

'Any luck?' Vanbrugh demanded.

Dwyer shook his head. 'We've visited every guest-house and boarding house in Kendal without a trace. I've told the men to get some lunch and report back in an hour.'

'I didn't do any better at the hotels.'

The young constable brought in another cup of tea and Dwyer sipped it gratefully. 'Of course, there must be a lot of people in a place like this who take in paying guests, especially in the season.'

'Too many,' Vanbrugh said. 'It would take a house-to-house search to find them all. We simply haven't the men or the time.'

'It would explain the bit about this bloke Grant's address being care-of-someone else.'

'I've been in touch with the local postmaster about that,' Vanbrugh said. 'I know it's a long shot that a postman might remember something like that. I know from past experience that most of these fellows get to know their round well.'

'Any joy?'

'Not yet. Most of the men are still due in from the lunchtime delivery. He's going to see them all before they go off duty and give me a ring.' He glanced at his watch. 'Two o'clock. That gives us half an hour.'

'There's a pub just round the corner,' Dwyer said. 'We could probably get some sandwiches or a pork pie or something.'

'Something like a pint, you mean?'

'It's been a hard morning, sir.'

Vanbrugh grinned and took down his coat from behind the door. 'Well, if you're paying, sergeant. . .'

II

Looking over Hannah's shoulders through the flooded windscreen, Rogan could see Paddy Costello several hundred yards ahead, standing at the side of the road. The small man clambered into the passenger seat and closed the door with a curse.

'Christ Jesus, but I'm soaked to the bloody skin. It cuts into you like razor blades, that stuff.'

'Everything go off all right?' Rogan said.

'I parked it at the back of that ruined barn. Sure and there won't be a soul about on a day like this.'

Rogan eased back against the side of the van and lit a cigarette. He tossed the packet across to Fletcher who sat opposite, strangely formal in his navy blue uniform. The big man extracted a cigarette with hands that shook slightly.

'What's wrong with you?' Morgan demanded. 'Wetting yourself?'

'Why don't you get stuffed?' Fletcher leaned back and blew out a cloud of smoke with evident satisfaction. 'It's going to be all right, I can tell.'

'What did you do, write to Gypsy Rose?' Morgan asked sarcastically.

Fletcher turned, one gnarled fist balling and Rogan cut in sharply, 'Knock it off. You can cut pieces out of each other from tomorrow on as far as I'm concerned. Until then, I'm in charge.'

A few minutes later, they started to move through Kendal and he glanced at his watch. 'A quarter of an hour.'

He could see beads of sweat lining the folds of skin that draped over the back of Costello's collar and the old man pulled down his cap with a hand that shook slightly. Fletcher showed no apparent emotion and Morgan grinned.

'Nothing quite like it, is there?'

Rogan didn't reply, but he knew exactly what the man was getting at. The hollowness in the stomach, the tightness in the chest, the difficulty in breathing properly. It wasn't fear exactly, but something rather more subtle. A strange mixture of excitement and apprehension. A feeling he had known many times before that lasted until the exact moment that you made your first decisive move. After that, there was never time to think of anything but the job in hand.

The van moved along the narrow lane between high hedges and then, quite suddenly, they were turning into the parking space outside Rigg Station. Hannah braked to a halt, and reversed in one smooth motion until the back of the van was no more than a foot from the loading bay. Rogan opened the door, stepped out and moved into the booking hall.

A silk scarf was already knotted at the back of his neck and he pulled it over the lower half of his face and jerked down the peak of his old tweed cap. He opened the door of the stationmaster's office and stepped inside.

Briggs stood at the fireplace, one hand reaching for the kettle, a pint pot in the other. He started to turn and Rogan took the Colt automatic from his pocket.

The old man's face was a study in bewilderment. He opened his mouth as if to speak and his jaw went slack as the shock of what was happening hit him with the force of a physical blow.

Paddy Costello moved inside quickly, opened the other door and passed into the baggage hall. As Rogan heard the outer doors open, he said to Briggs, 'Do as you're told and you won't get hurt. Take off your cap, jacket and waistcoat and put them on the desk.'

The old man stood there staring at him, frozen by fear, his mouth open. Rogan stepped forward in one quick movement and touched him between the eyes with the cold barrel of the automatic.

'Now, not tomorrow.'

His action had exactly the psychological effect that he had hoped. Briggs put his pint pot on the mantelpiece and hurriedly took off his jacket. When Costello came back into the office, Briggs was standing by the fireplace, his shirt sleeves rolled above the elbow, one arm only half the thickness of the other, badly disfigured by the jagged distinctive scars of old shrapnel wounds.

'Where did you pick that lot up?' Rogan asked.

Briggs seemed to come to life a little and his head went back. 'The Somme, 1916.'

'If you got through that bloody lot, you'll survive anything. Lie on the floor and close your eyes.'

He nodded to Costello who moved forward quickly, a coil of rope in his hands. Rogan went into the baggage hall. Outside, the wheels of the old Morris van skidded on the loose gravel as Hannah drove away. Fletcher dragged in the fourth mailbag and Morgan closed the door.

He turned to Rogan, the skin drawn tightly across his cheekbones, eyes very bright. 'Everything okay?'

Rogan nodded and glanced at his watch. 'Five minutes, maybe sooner.'

Costello had knotted a scarf around the old man's eyes and gagged him with a piece of sticking plaster. He was tying his wrists behind him as Rogan went back into the office and the Irishman nudged him with the toe of his shoe.

'I'll finish that, you get changed.'

As Costello hurriedly took off his raincoat and pulled on the uniform waistcoat, Rogan dropped to one knee and lashed the old man's wrists together, securely, but not too tightly.

He patted Briggs on the shoulder. 'I'm putting you out of harm's way for a little while. Don't try anything silly and you'll be all right. Understand?'

The old man nodded and Rogan opened the door to the washroom, picked him up and carried him inside. He laid him on the floor, went back into the office and closed the door.

Costello buttoned his jacket and put on the cap. He

examined himself in the cracked mirror over the fire, turned and laughed nervously. 'Will I do?'

'Perfect!' Rogan said. 'Now get out on that platform and look busy.'

He stood at the narrow window watching Costello go to work with his broom, then went back into the baggage hall. Morgan had one of the double doors open slightly and was looking outside. He made a sudden, cutting gesture with one hand as Fletcher started to speak and, through the heavy rain, they heard the sound of an engine approaching.

Rogan moved beside him. As he peered through the narrow crack, the van turned off the road on to the parking space. It seemed strangely ordinary, its coachwork painted dark blue with no distinguishing characteristics except for the circular aerial on the roof.

It rolled to a halt a few yards away, giving him a clear view of the two occupants. The driver looked like an ex-Guards NCO, dark moustache bristling beneath the gold-rimmed peak cap. The guard was a younger man with a hard, bony face and a scar bisecting one cheek.

Rogan saw him yawn and pick up the radio telephone receiver. A moment later he started to speak. He replaced the receiver, put a cigarette in his mouth and reached across to the watch held out to him by the driver.

The door leading to the platform opened and Costello hurried in.

'It's coming.'

'All right. Get outside and give them a nod,' Rogan said.

Costello hesitated and Morgan kicked him viciously on the leg. 'Get moving, damn you!'

Costello opened the door, leaned out and raised a hand. The driver of the van nodded, turned in a half-circle and started to reverse.

Rogan could hear the train beginning to slow on the run in to the station and he gave Costello a shove across the baggage hall. 'On the platform and stay by the door.'

Rogan stepped back into the office leaving the other two waiting in the baggage hall. Morgan stood in one corner by the double doors, Fletcher in the other, each of them with a rubber truncheon ready in his right hand.

Then everything seemed to be happening at once. As the noise of the train filled the building, the double doors were pushed open, hiding Fletcher and Morgan from view. The driver came in first, a receipt book in one hand, dragging a mailbag behind him. The guard followed with another, cigarette still dangling from one corner of his mouth.

The doors swung back and Morgan and Fletcher moved in together, truncheons flailing down expertly. The driver dropped like a sack, unconscious from the first devastating blow. The younger man managed to turn, dropping his mailbag and reached for his own truncheon. His mouth opened in a soundless cry, drowned by the noise of the engine and Fletcher slashed him across the edge of the neck.

Rogan moved in fast, grabbed the driver's feet and dragged him into the office. As he dropped him behind the desk out of sight from the window, Fletcher followed with the other guard.

Rogan moved back into the baggage hall and Morgan came in from the ramp, the driver's gold peaked cap slanting across his eyes. 'The bloody van's empty. Only the two bags.'

So Colum O'More had been wrong for once, but there was no time to worry about that now. Rogan was already on one knee beside the two mailbags, a pair of pliers in his hand. Each bag was fastened by heavy wire, an official lead seal inscribed with several code words and a number. He snipped the wire and quickly laced it through the metal eyelet holes of one of the dummy bags which Fletcher dragged forward. He joined the broken ends of the wire as neatly as possible, twisting them together, then pushed the join out of sight through one of the eyelet holes in the mouth of the bag.

As he repeated the operation on the other, Morgan dropped to one knee beside him. 'Let's hope they don't check those too carefully.'

'Why should they?' Rogan said calmly and got to his feet. 'Out you go.'

The young guard's cap was a size too small for Fletcher, but he tilted it forward over his eyes and lifted up a mailbag. Morgan picked up the receipt book and the other bag and moved to the end of the baggage hall. He hesitated, opened the door and moved out. Rogan held his breath and waited.

It was strangely quiet on the platform, the muffled rumble of the diesel engines the only sound. Paddy Costello leaned on his broom by the door, making a great show of examining his watch, and the sliding door of the mail van stood open.

Morgan moved forward and an attendant leaned out and grinned. 'Aren't you beggars ever late?'

'Don't ask me,' Morgan said. 'First time we've done this run.'

He heaved his mailbag into the van and Fletcher followed suit. The attendant produced a pen and held out his hand. 'Let's have it.'

Morgan opened the receipt book and handed it to him. The attendant signed the top copy, tore it off and handed the book back. 'That's it then.'

He started to draw back and Morgan said, 'Christ, I was forgetting. Do me a favour, mate. I gave the radio a bit of a bash getting out of the cab and it's on the blink. Give 'em a ring at headquarters, will you, and tell 'em we're on our way in?'

'Anything to oblige.'

It was as simple as that. The sliding door closed and Costello raised a hand to the guard who leaned out of his window at the rear of the train. A whistle sounded faintly and, in a moment, the great diesel engines picked up and the train slid away.

As the rear of the train disappeared into the heavy rain, the three men crowded into the baggage hall excitedly. 'We made it, by Christ! We made it!' Fletcher said.

'A long way to go yet,' Rogan told him. 'Get those two mailbags into the van and don't forget the dummies. Don't leave them anything they might be able to trace.' He turned to Morgan. 'You help me in here.'

The van driver and his guard still lay unconscious by the desk and Rogan examined them. There was a trickle of blood at the back of the driver's ear and he looked up at Morgan grimly.

'You don't pull your punches.'

Morgan shrugged. 'I could never see the point.'

Rogan produced a couple of lengths of thin cord from his

pocket and they quickly tied the wrists of the two unconscious men behind them.

'Right, into the van and get that engine started,' Rogan said. 'I'll be out in a minute.'

He opened the washroom door and dropped to one knee beside Briggs. The old man was breathing heavily through the nose and Rogan pulled the sticking plaster away from his mouth. Briggs sucked in a lungful of air gratefully and Rogan patted him on the shoulder.

'You'll be all right, Dad. That goods train should arrive in exactly twenty-five minutes.'

The old man turned his head blindly towards him. 'God help you, lad, because you'll never get away with this.'

'You take a chance every day of your life.' Rogan hurried out through the baggage hall. The rear door of the van stood open, Costello peering out. Rogan stepped inside and closed the door and Morgan turned from the small armoured glass window and gunned the motor.

As the van moved at high speed along the narrow lane between the hedges, Rogan flicked the switch of the intercommunication system.

'Take it easy, especially on the way through Kendal. We've all the time in the world.'

'What kind of a steamer do you think I am?' Morgan said angrily, all the tension of the past ten minutes bursting out of him.

Rogan flicked the switch and sat down. Paddy Costello was slumped on the bench seat opposite, his facing shining with sweat, hands grasped tightly together.

'It's going to be fine,' Rogan said. 'Everything's going to be all right.'

The old man nodded, lips compressed together as if he couldn't trust himself to speak. In Kendal, traffic was light and Morgan had to stop only twice at traffic lights. Once through the town and on to the Windermere road, he increased speed and turned into the plantation of fir exactly eight minutes after leaving Rigg Station.

As the van braked to a halt, Rogan opened the door and jumped out. Hannah was standing beside the cattle truck and she came forward anxiously.

'Everything all right?'

Rogan nodded. 'Couldn't have gone better. What about the Morris?'

'Parked at the back of the barn.'

Costello and Fletcher were already transferring the mail-bags from the armoured van to the cattle truck and Morgan leaned out of the driver's window and watched. Fletcher gave him a shout and Morgan released the handbrake and took the van towards the rim of the flooded gravel pits, where he jumped clear. A second later, the van plunged over the edge. By the time Rogan and Hannah had joined him, it had already disappeared.

'Now the Morris,' Rogan said. 'We'd better shove her over a little further up.'

They ran the little van along the track which followed the edge of the pits and, as it dipped over the crown of a small rise, Rogan gave the wheel a twist and jumped back. The van, running on down the slope, veered sharply to the left and vanished over the edge.

Costello was already behind the wheel of the cattle truck, Hannah beside him in the cab. As the engine roared into life, Rogan and Morgan joined Fletcher in the back. The truck dipped over the rutted surface of the track, paused for a moment outside the gate while Hannah closed it, then turned into the main road and moved rapidly towards Windermere.

'How are we off for time?' Morgan demanded.

Rogan checked his watch. 'That goods train is due in at Rigg in exactly twelve minutes if it's on time.'

'Which they never are.'

'It'll take the crew at least five minutes to sort out what's happened and get in touch with the authorities, another ten for the police to get any kind of an alert out. That gives us at least twenty-seven minutes.'

'And Ambleside's only ten miles away.' Morgan laughed harshly. 'We're home and dry.'

Fletcher, sitting against one side of the truck, nudged a mailbag with the toe of his shoe. 'My God, but I'd like to know what's inside those two babies.'

'I should be able to tell you,' Morgan said. 'I haven't had time to look before.'

He took the receipt book from the pocket of his uniform and opened it quickly. 'It's headed "Consignment for pulping".'

'That means it's all old stuff,' Fletcher said. 'Just the job.'

'Bag Rs3, forty-five thousand in one pound notes, twenty-five thousand in fivers. Bag Rs4, fifty thousand in one pound notes, twenty in fivers.'

'Christ Jesus,' Fletcher whispered. 'That's a hundred and forty thousand quid in old notes.'

'Not bad,' Morgan said. 'Split three ways, that's better than forty grand apiece.' He grinned. 'An interesting thought.'

'Come on, let's have a look,' Fletcher said excitedly and reached for one of the bags. Rogan slammed the heel of his shoe across the back of the outstretched hand.

Fletcher scambled to one knee, snarling like an animal and found himself looking into the barrel of the Colt automatic. 'Colum O'More opens those bags, no one else.' Rogan reached forward and touched Fletcher between the eyes with the barrel. 'Another play like that and I'll kill you. That's a promise.'

— 15 —

THE PARKING space outside Rigg Station was more crowded than it had probably ever been in its previous existence, and as Vanbrugh moved to the edge of the ramp another patrol car rolled to a halt.

A couple of ambulance attendants came out of the baggage hall carrying the driver of the armoured van on a stretcher and two more followed with the guard. Vanbrugh opened his tobacco pouch and filled his pipe as he watched them place the injured men in the ambulance and drive away.

By sheer chance, he and Dwyer had been in conference with a Superintendent Gregory of the county constabulary at

Kendal police headquarters, discussing their abortive visit to the GPO, when the alarm had come through from Rigg. Vanbrugh, drawn by a more than professional interest, had accompanied Gregory at once.

As he applied a match to his pipe, Dwyer moved out of the baggage hall. 'It took nerve. You've got to give them that. Of all the bloody cheek. Imagine getting the train to phone in for them.'

'A touch of genius,' Vanbrugh said.

Dwyer appeared to hesitate and then continued, 'It's a familiar pattern, somehow, don't you think so, sir?'

Vanbrugh sighed heavily. 'Strange that I should have told you about that business in France during the war only the other day. This affair's been almost a carbon copy.'

Gregory joined them, a tall, spare man in a beautifully tailored uniform. 'I've been thinking, sir,' he said to Vanbrugh. 'This has been a big city job, no doubt about that. Any chance of your man Rogan being involved?'

'Every chance, I'm afraid,' Vanbrugh said. 'Mind if I have a word with the stationmaster?'

'Help yourself.'

They went into the office where old Briggs sat at his desk, a cup of tea held in both hands. A constable stood at the door and a sergeant sat on the edge of the desk, taking Briggs' statement. He stood to one side and Gregory smiled down at the old man.

'Feeling a little better, Mr Briggs?'

'Nothing wrong with me that a couple of rums won't cure,' the old man said.

'This is Chief Superintendent Vanbrugh of Scotland Yard. He'd like to ask you a few questions.'

Vanbrugh was reading quickly through the sergeant's notebook and he nodded and looked up. 'You say here that you never got a look at the face of the man with the gun?'

'Couldn't do. He was wearing a scarf.'

'He was a big man?'

'A giant, leastways, that's the way he looked to me.'

Vanbrugh nodded. 'What about his voice?'

'Well-spoken, an educated bloke.'

'Could he have been Irish?'

'It's possible. Irish or Scots, I wouldn't like to say which. To tell you the truth, he wasn't such a bad bloke.'

'What makes you say that?'

The old man held up his crippled arm. 'He asked me how I got that. When I told him the Somme, he laughed and said if I could get through that lot, I could survive anything. Another thing, he took the time to come back to the washroom afterwards to pull off my gag. I was near choking.'

Vanbrugh turned and nodded to Gregory. 'Rogan, without a doubt.' They moved out through the baggage hall to the ramp and he slammed a fist into the palm of his other hand. 'But why? It just isn't in character. I've known Sean Rogan for years. He isn't the type.'

'He's been inside a long time, sir,' Dwyer said gently. 'People change.'

Before Vanbrugh could reply, a police constable leaned out of the window of a patrol car and called, 'Superintendent Gregory. Message from Kendal.'

Gregory jumped to the ground and walked briskly to the car. He leaned in the window and Vanbrugh watched him take the receiver the constable offered him. A moment later, he straightened excitedly.

'That accommodation address you wanted,' he called to Vanbrugh. 'They've traced a postman who thinks he knows it. He's been off duty for a couple of days with a sprained ankle. That's why they didn't come up with him earlier.'

Vanbrugh jumped to the ground and moved forward quickly. 'You know what this could mean?'

'Don't I just.' Gregory smiled coolly. 'I'm afraid someone may be in for a rather nasty surprise.'

The address was that of a small back-street newsagent in Kendal and a patrol car was waiting when Gregory and the two Scotland Yard men arrived. The postman, a man named Harvey, was sitting in the back, a walking stick between his knees, chatting to the patrol car crew.

When Gregory leaned in the window, the two constables got out of the car at once. 'Mr Harvey – I'm Superintendent Gregory, county constabulary. You're sure about this?'

'About the letters addressed to Charles Grant, care of Tomlinson's? Oh, yes, sir. I remember kidding him about it and him saying how trade was bad and who was he to turn down ten bob a week just to accept delivery of a few letters.'

Gregory straightened and turned to the two constables. 'Have you been in?'

'Not yet, sir.'

He nodded to Vanbrugh. 'After you.'

Tomlinson was a middle-aged man with greying hair and horn-rimmed spectacles that had been badly repaired with electrician's tape. When they went in he was standing behind the counter, leaning forward to see what all the fuss was about.

'Mr Tomlinson?' Gregory said. 'I'm Superintendent Gregory, county constabulary. This is Chief Superintendent Vanbrugh and Sergeant Dwyer of Scotland Yard. We understand you might be able to help us in an investigation we're conducting.'

Tomlinson looked completely bewildered. 'I don't even know what you're talking about.'

'You've been allowing this address to be used by a Mr Charles Grant, isn't that so?'

Tomlinson nodded, a slight frown knitting his brow. 'Nothing wrong in that, is there?'

'We think Mr Grant may be a man we're looking for. Have you any idea as to his present whereabouts?'

'Not a clue,' Tomlinson said. 'I've only ever seen him once, that was the first time he came in. He was pretty old, walked with a stick. Irish, I think, which surprised me, him having a Scots name.'

'Have many letters come for him?'

Tomlinson nodded. 'Three or four a week, I'd say. They've been picked up by a young woman as a rule. She's usually looked in most afternoons.'

'Do you know her name?'

Tomlinson shook his head. 'No, but I've seen her at Ambleside Market a couple of times. She was with an old fella called Costello – Paddy Costello. Runs an excuse for a sheep farm up Scardale way. Big boozer and gambler. He's known in every pub in the district.'

Gregory was already moving outside. He leaned in the window of his car and said to the driver, 'Get through to HQ at once. Tell them to phone the station sergeant at Ambleside. Ask him what he knows about a man called Paddy Costello who keeps a farm somewhere Scardale way. And tell them this is top priority.'

He turned and took out a silver case as Vanbrugh and Dwyer joined him. 'From the sound of things, this could be it.'

He offered Vanbrugh a cigarette and they stood there smoking nervously, neither man speaking. Within an incredibly short space of time, Gregory's driver leaned out of the window.

'On Costello, sir. Station sergeant at Ambleside knows him well. A list of drunk and disorderly charges as long as your arm. Keeps a farm at the top end of Scardale below the old mine workings.'

'Does he live alone?'

'He has a son and his niece has been living with him for the past ten months. Hannah Maria Costello. She has a record, sir. Six months at Holloway on a vice charge last year.'

Gregory turned to Vanbrugh. 'Rather more than promising, I'd say.'

The driver interrupted. 'One more thing, sir. This man Soames that Chief Superintendent Vanbrugh wanted to see, they've picked him up in Broughton. They want to know what to do with him.'

'We've more important business in hand,' Vanbrugh said. 'Tell them to run him up to Kendal. I'll see him later.' He turned to Gregory, his face expressionless. 'I'd say we could do with a couple of dozen good men.'

'Don't worry, sir.' Gregory smiled gently. 'We breed them on the large side up here. Your pal Rogan may be in for something of a shock.'

— 16 —

WHEN THEY reached Scardale, Costello drove the truck straight into the barn and parked it behind the shooting brake. When he cut the engine, Rogan jumped to the ground and nodded to Morgan and Fletcher.

'Inside, you two, and stay there.'

As Hannah and Costello came round from the cab, Fletcher said, 'What the hell do you mean, inside? I've just about had enough of you and your bleeding orders.'

He came forward with a rush. Rogan waited till he was close, then pulled out his automatic and struck him heavily across the face.

As the steel sight on the end of the barrel sliced across his cheek, Fletcher gave a cry of agony, hands going to his face as blood spurted.

'You wait, you bastard,' he said through clenched teeth. 'I'll fix you. I'll fix you good.'

Rogan looked at Morgan coldly. 'Any questions?'

Morgan shrugged. 'You're the boss.'

Fletcher stumbled out of the barn and Morgan followed him. Rogan held out his hand to Costello.

'I'll take the truck keys.'

Costello handed them over hastily. 'Do you want me inside with the others?'

'For the time being.'

The old man went across the yard and Hannah pulled off her scarf and shook her hair free. 'You're harder than I ever thought you could be.'

'With scum like that, it pays.' He took her hand and pulled her close for a moment. 'How do you feel?'

'How am I supposed to feel?' She shrugged. 'Tired, washed out. I could sleep for a week.'

'What you need is a cup of tea with a drop of the right stuff in it and something to eat.'

She smiled wanly. 'Maybe you're right. What about you?'

'I'll be in later. Something I want to do here first.'

He pulled her into his arms and kissed her briefly and fine straw dust drifted down through the cracks in the loft above. When they looked up, they saw Brendan peering over the edge.

He dropped to the ground and scrambled to his feet, white with excitement. He tried to speak, his mouth opening and closing, but nothing emerged and Hannah put her hands on his shoulders.

'Take your time. Just take your time.'

The boy breathed in deeply and the words came out of him in a great rush. 'There's a man at the house. He came up the valley road just after you'd gone.'

'A big man with black hair?'

'That's right.'

'Jack Pope,' Rogan told Hannah.

'I think he was trying to find me,' the boy said. 'He looked everywhere, but I hid under the hay in the loft.'

Hannah looked at Rogan anxiously. 'What do you think they're up to?'

'I should have thought that was obvious.' He stood thinking, a slight frown on his face, then nodded. 'You go in and prepare a meal.' She opened her mouth to protest and he gave her a small push. 'Don't worry. I know what I'm doing.'

Fletcher sat on the edge of the kitchen table, cursing as Morgan fixed another large strip of sticking plaster across his cheek.

'Anybody'd think he had it in for you, Jesse,' Morgan said with a grin.

Fletcher cursed and snatched the tumbler into which Costello had just poured a generous measure of whisky. 'I'll fix that swine yet.'

'That'll be the day,' Morgan jeered.

He left them there and went along the passage to his bedroom. Rogan was tough all right and he'd be a hard nut to crack. But whatever happened, Morgan hadn't the slightest intention of allowing a hundred and forty thousand pounds to slip through his fingers without trying to do something about it.

He opened the bedroom door, turned to close it and found Jack Pope standing in the corner, a revolver in his right hand. The tension oozed out of Pope in a long sigh and he wiped sweat from his forehead.

'I thought it might be Rogan.'

'He's still in the barn,' Morgan said. 'Did you have any trouble getting in?'

'No, but I couldn't find the lad anywhere.'

'Not to worry. That kid wanders around all over the place.' Morgan pulled the revolver from Pope's grasp. 'Where did you get the shooter?'

'Soames picked it up in the Smoke. Thought it might come in useful.'

'Any spare slugs?'

'Half a dozen, that's all.' Pope handed them over. 'What was the take?'

'A hundred and forty thousand. Not as good as expected. There were only two mailbags.'

'And Rogan's got them?'

'That's it. Says he intends to hand them over to O'More intact.'

'I had a phone call from Soames last night,' Pope said. 'He's managed to trace O'More to a farm called Marsh-End. It's just off the coast road near Whitbeck.'

'Which means the old devil's probably got a boat all ready and waiting for a quick exit across the Irish Sea.'

'That's right. What's our next move?'

Morgan went to the door, opened it and called to Fletcher and Costello. They came in a moment later, Fletcher carrying the bottle of whisky in one hand and a tumbler in the other.

'So you got here?' he growled at Pope. 'A fat lot of bloody good it'll do you, the way things look at the moment.'

'I wouldn't be too sure.' Morgan held out the revolver in the palm of his hand. 'This might just even things up a little.'

'Saints preserve us,' Paddy Costello said.

'Have you still got the spare ignition key for the cattle truck?' Morgan demanded.

The old man produced it from one of his waistcoat pockets

and handed it over. Morgan moved to the window, staying behind the curtains as Hannah came out of the barn and crossed to the front door. They heard it open and she passed along the passage to the kitchen. He moved to the door, listened for a second, then returned to the window. Brendan emerged from the barn pushing a hand cart loaded with several bulging sacks.

'What's the kid up to?' he demanded. 'I didn't even see him go in there.'

Paddy Costello joined him at the window. 'Never mind him. He creeps around like a flaming ghost.'

Brendan pushed the cart out through the main gate and turned up the track towards the mine workings. 'Where's he taking that little lot?' Fletcher said.

'We've got some sheep penned in the enclosure up at the village. The ones I'm supposed to drive in to Millom market tomorrow. He'll be taking them some feed.'

Rogan came out of the barn, a mailbag over each shoulder. He stood looking after the boy for a moment, then walked across to the house.

'Let's take him now on his way in,' Pope said.

Morgan shook his head, weighing the revolver in one hand. 'He's had a lot of shooting experience. I wouldn't like to be the one to try anything from the front. We'll bide our time.' He turned to Pope. 'You stay here. You two come with me.'

When Rogan came in they were in the living-room, Morgan and Fletcher sitting on either side of the fire, Costello at the table.

The Irishman stood in the doorway, a mailbag in each hand, and looked at them calmly. Morgan could feel the revolver in his pocket and fought against the suicidal impulse to pull it out. There was a strange magnetism about Rogan, a sort of invulnerability that seemed to say that no one could ever touch him.

His ascendancy over the three of them was almost tangible as he tossed the two mailbags into a corner by the door and unbuttoned his raincoat.

'That kid of yours is beginning to give me the creeps,' he said to Costello. 'He was playing around in the hayloft back there in the barn. He'll never know how close he came to getting a bullet in him.'

'It's sorry I am to hear it, Mr Rogan,' Costello said hastily. 'I'll boot the behind off him when he gets in.'

Hannah called from the kitchen and Rogan sniffed. 'Bacon frying or I miss my guess. Nothing like a job of work well done to give you an appetite. We'd better go in.'

'Not me,' Fletcher said and reached for the whisky bottle.

Rogan took a single pace forward and pulled the bottle from his hand. He put it down on the sideboard and turned, his face quite calm.

'I said we eat.'

Fletcher sat there glaring and Morgan slapped him on the shoulder. 'Come on, Jesse.'

Paddy Costello was already on his way and Fletcher followed. In the doorway, Morgan paused and turned. 'Sometimes you can push people just a little too hard. Ever thought of that?'

'You're a good talker,' Rogan said. 'Keep it up long enough and you might convince yourself you could do something about me.'

Morgan's face turned very pale and all light died in his eyes. 'I did two years in a Chinese prison camp in Korea, Rogan, did you know that? When they released me, I had a double hernia from the number of times the guards had booted me in the crotch and TB in one lung.'

'So?' Rogan said.

'When I got home, I found that nobody gave a damn. They didn't seem to know a war had been going on.'

'What's that supposed to prove – that you had an excuse?'

Morgan laughed harshly. 'I haven't needed one since the day I was old enough to work out the odds in this lousy world for myself. I'll tell you one thing, friend. If I could survive those Chinese bastards, I can survive you. Just think about that.'

He went along the passage and Rogan smiled softly. Nothing like an open declaration of war to let you know where you stood. He hung his raincoat behind the door, took the Colt automatic from his pocket and pushed it down into his waistband at the rear so that it was covered by the tail of his jacket, the butt hard against the small of his back. He buttoned his jacket at the front and went along to the kitchen.

It was an uncomfortable meal and eaten in complete silence. Hannah moved from one to the other, refilling cups with fresh tea and bringing more bread from the dresser. On the occasions that she managed to catch Rogan's eye, her face was strained and anxious.

Finally, he pushed back his chair and said calmly, 'That'll do me for now. Let's go back to the living-room.'

Fletcher looked angrily at Morgan who made a slight gesture with his head and stood up. Fletcher followed him out of the door, Costello trailing after them.

Hannah moved acrosss to Rogan quickly. 'There's going to be trouble, Sean. I feel it.'

'Don't worry.' He smiled. 'I know what I'm doing. You stay here.'

When he went into the living-room, no one said a word. He picked up the bottle of whisky and a tumbler from the sideboard and sat on the edge of the table.

'Funny how you remember things. The last time I robbed a train was in France in '44. We had it all laid on to knock off one that was carrying a month's pay for a German Panzer Division. It would have been quite a haul.'

'What went wrong?' Morgan said.

'We never really found out. The important thing was that instead of the payroll, the train carried a company of German paratroops armed to the teeth and spoiling for action and let nobody kid you, those boys were good.'

'Somebody grassed?' Fletcher said, interested in spite of himself.

'One of three possibilities,' Rogan said. 'The first was a local farmer whose place we'd been using as headquarters for a while. He wet himself every time an ivy leaf tapped on the window.'

Costello flushed and looked away hurriedly and Rogan went on. 'Then there was a lovely specimen who'd been inside for just about every crime in the book. A big man at beating hell out of the prostitutes on the Marseilles waterfront when they objected to handing over half their takings.'

Fletcher's hand shook with rage as he raised his glass of

whisky to his mouth and drained it and Morgan said calmly, 'What about the third?'

'He was the most dangerous of the lot. He'd even done three years in a Jesuit seminary training for the priesthood.' Rogan tapped his forehead. 'A hoodlum with brains. The worst kind there is. Pure evil.'

'Lucifer, Prince of Darkness. The fallen angel,' Morgan said. 'Now that, I find interesting. What happened?'

'We took them out into the forest, what was left of us, and shot them.'

'All three?'

'Nothing else to do in the circumstances.'

'Holy Mother,' Paddy Costello whispered in horror.

Rogan stuck a cigarette in the corner of his mouth and leaned down to light it with a splinter from the fire. In the brief moment that his back was turned, Morgan seized his chance, pulled out the revolver and extended his arm.

'I could blow your head off right now. Make a wrong move and I will.'

Rogan turned slowly, hands held well away from his body and Morgan called,'Pope, get out here fast!'

There was a quick movement in the passage and Pope appeared in the doorway. 'What's going on?'

'Hello, Jack,' Rogan said. 'Fancy meeting you here?'

'Get a grip on those two mailbags,' Morgan said, 'and don't let them out of your sight. Jesse, get his gun.'

Fletcher came forward slowly, his ugly face splitting into a delighted grin. He stood looking at Rogan for a long moment and then quickly searched him. He frowned and turned.

'He hasn't got it on him.'

'That doesn't make sense,' Morgan said, suddenly wary. 'Look again, but watch him. He's a foxy bastard.'

'We can soon take care of that,' Fletcher said.

He turned back to Rogan and his fist swung in a short arc, catching the Irishman on the right cheek. Rogan rode the punch, allowing himself to stagger back. He went over the armchair, landing on his shoulders and pulled the automatic free at the same moment. He loosed off one quick shot that chipped splinters from the table and Morgan gave a cry of alarm.

'Get out of it, quick!'

He fired hastily and Rogan rolled for the shelter of the old horsehair sofa that stood against the wall. As he reached it, Morgan pushed Fletcher and Pope into the passage.

Rogan fired through the door, the bullet tearing its way through the flimsy woodwork and ricocheting between the stone walls of the passage.

Costello gave a cry of alarm, ran to the front door and wrenched it open and Pope went after him, the mailbags banging against his knees.

Morgan gave Fletcher a shove. 'Get after them, Jesse. We'll have to make a run for it in the truck.'

He fired through the door into the living-room, keeping his back flat against the wall, then turned and ran after Fletcher. The big man was half-way across the yard and Pope and Costello were already vanishing through the open double doors into the half darkness.

As Morgan started to run a chair came through the window behind him. He turned and fired a wild shot that chipped stone from the wall ten feet off target, then ran, zig-zagging from side to side. A single shot chased him into the barn, ploughing into a bale of hay at the rear.

Fletcher and Pope had already got the mailbags into the back of the cattle truck and Morgan shoved Costello up behind the wheel. He followed him into the cab, pushed in the ignition key and switched on.

'Get this bloody thing moving.'

The old man's face was grey with fear and spittle dribbled from the corner of his mouth. Morgan slapped him heavily across the face. 'Get moving,' he cried.

Rogan was half-way across the yard and he dropped to one knee behind the water trough, aimed carefully and fired. As Morgan and Costello ducked, the bullet drilled a neat hole through the windscreen. Costello gave a cry of fear. He pressed the starter and slammed the stick into first gear.

The old cattle truck roared through the entrance, knocking one of the half-open doors off its hinges and they bounced over the potholes towards the gateway. Morgan fired in the general direction of the water trough to keep Rogan's head down and then they were through with a crunch of metal as the right wing crumpled against one of the stone gateposts.

Costello changed into top gear and rammed his foot hard against the boards, his hands tight on the wheel and Morgan looked back and laughed harshly as Rogan came through the gateway and started to run down the road after them.

'A fat lot of bloody good that'll do you.'

As he turned, putting the revolver into his pocket, the truck swung round the shoulder of the mountain and his throat went dry. A police car was moving towards them, at least half a dozen other vehicles strung out behind it.

Costello gave a hoarse cry and the police car slowed to a halt, turning broadside to block the narrow road. 'Brake, you stupid sod! Brake!' Morgan cried.

Costello seemed to lose all control. When he rammed down his foot, it caught the accelerator instead of the brake pedal and the truck shot forward. Its offside wheels ploughed into the rain-soaked grass shoulder and the wheel spun in his hands. Morgan had one quick glimpse of the steep slope dropping a hundred and fifty feet to the boulders in the stream below and his hand grabbed for the door handle. He jumped as the truck started to go over and the door swung back behind him, smashing Costello in the face as the old man tried to follow.

Morgan somersaulted twenty feet down the slope, coming to rest against a gorse bush. As he picked himself up the cattle truck bounced against a rock shelf fifty feet below. It soared into space, turning over almost in slow motion and Fletcher was tossed out, arms and legs flailing wildly.

The truck landed upside down in the stream bed with a terrible, grating crunch, and Fletcher landed on top of it. The petrol tank exploded immediately like a bomb, and orange and yellow flames lifted into the rain.

Morgan scrambled up the slope. He was badly shaken and blood poured down his face from a gash above his right eye, but the instinct for survival was strong. As he crossed the road he heard voices and turned to see several uniformed policemen running towards him. He fired and one of them seemed to trip and fall headlong. The others immediately scattered and

Morgan ran for the shelter of a shallow ravine and followed its course up the side of the mountain.

II

Rogan had stopped running and was on his way back to the farm when he heard the first terrible crunch of metal as the truck went over the edge. He started to run back as the petrol tank exploded, and reached the point where the road curved round the shoulder of the mountain as Morgan fired at the police and staggered across.

A police car roared along the road and slewed broadside to protect the constable who had been shot. A large, heavily built man in a fawn trenchcoat jumped out and ran, crouching, to drop to one knee beside him.

Rogan recognized Dick Vanbrugh at once. The strange thing was his own lack of surprise, but he didn't stop to analyse that. He turned and ran back towards the farm. Hannah was standing in the gateway as he entered the yard.

'What is it? What's happened?'

'No time for questions. Grab your coat and get back out of here fast. We're leaving. I've still got a key for the shooting brake, remember?'

When he drove out of the barn, she was pulling on her sheepskin coat by the water trough. He opened the door and she scrambled in and slammed it as they drove away.

When they moved through the gate and turned left towards the head of the valley, she touched his arm. 'Where are we going?'

'Through the Long Cut, Brendan's waiting up there now with the mailbags. The two I brought into the house were the dummies.'

'What about the others? What happened back there?'

'The whole place is crawling with peelers. The truck went over the edge of the road.'

Her face was very white. 'And my uncle?'

'It went up like a torch.'

She turned away, crossing herself automatically. He reached out and took her hand and she held it tightly as they went over the brow of the hill and down into the village.

— 17 —

THROWN CLEAR by the force of the explosion, Jesse Fletcher floated face down in a pool of water three feet deep. Most of his clothing had been burned away and several ribs showed through the charred flesh of his back.

Gregory and Vanbrugh waded forward and turned him over. The strange thing was that his face was unmarked except for the bruises left by his clash with Rogan and his eyes stared vacantly into eternity, fixed for all time.

'Do you know him?' Gregory asked.

Vanbrugh shook his head. 'He's a new one on me.'

The truck was still burning furiously and as they approached, they became aware at once of the sickly sweet stench of burning flesh.

A constable turned, his face wrinkling in disgust. 'One of them's still in the cab, sir. You can just see him if you bend down.'

In the intense heat, things seemed to shimmer, to lose definition and the figure which lay doubled up, one arm reaching out through the crumpled window, no longer seemed human.

'A nasty way to go,' Gregory said.

Vanbrugh nodded and they stumbled across the stream, knee-deep in ice-cold water to where another constable knelt beside a body in the wet grass.

As they approached, he stood up and turned. 'Nothing doing here, sir. His neck's broke. Must have been thrown out of the back when the truck first landed.'

Jack Pope lay on his back, one arm bent, fingers curling slightly. His eyes had retracted slightly and his head lolled unnaturally to one side.

'What about this one?' Gregory said.

'Jack Pope. He's the one who shared a cell with Rogan.'

'The ex-policeman?'

'That's him.'

They turned and Vanbrugh shielded his eyes from the rain with one hand and watched half a dozen men move up the mountainside above the road in a thin line. Gregory gave a sudden grunt and pointed.

'There he is, just below the ridge.'

Vanbrugh caught a brief glimpse of Morgan moving fast, several hundred feet above his pursuers. A moment later he went over the ridge and disappeared.

'Red hair,' Gregory said. 'At least we know that much about the bastard.'

'So it wasn't Sean Rogan' Vanbrugh moved back across the stream and picked up a piece of red mailbag canvas that shredded in his hands, still smouldering.

'Just about settles it,' Gregory said.

'Looks like it.'

They climbed the steep slope and arrived back on the road in time to see the wounded constable being lifted into the rear of the Land-Rover. His face was twisted with pain, but he managed to grin when Gregory lit a cigarette for him and stuck it in his mouth.

'How is it?'

The constable gingerly touched the blood-soaked bandage that encircled his right thigh above the knee. 'Bloody awful, but I'll survive, sir.'

'Good man,' Gregory said. 'Don't worry. We'll lay him by the heels.'

As the Land-Rover moved away, a police car came down the road from the direction of the farm and braked to a halt. Sergeant Dwyer jumped out.

'Any luck?' Vanbrugh said.

'Not a soul to be seen, sir, but they've certainly been having themselves a high old time. Someone's been shooting the place up.'

'Now what in the hell is that supposed to mean?' Vanbrugh said, frowning.

'A hundred and forty thousand is a hell of a lot of money,' Gregory said. 'Maybe somebody wanted a bigger slice of the cake.' He turned to Dwyer. 'What about the car we heard driving away?'

'We found it a mile or so further on where the road peters out in the ruins of an old mining village. A green Morris Oxford shooting brake.'

'No sign of the occupants?'

'Not a smell. There's a sergeant and two men up there now, but they're going to need help.'

Vanbrugh turned to Gregory. 'Didn't you say there was no other way out of the valley?'

Gregory nodded. 'Not by road, but any reasonably active person could cross the mountain on foot.' He took a map from his pocket and opened it. 'You can see the village here and the old workings on the other side.'

Vanbrugh studied the map for a moment and pointed to the two dotted lines that marked the course of the Long Cut under the mountain. 'What's this? A canal?'

'It certainly looks like it. Probably used to ship ore through to the next valley in the old days.'

'If it were still navigable, it would make a convenient back door. The sooner it's plugged the better.'

Gregory moved to the nearest car and contacted headquarters on the radio. Vanbrugh looked up at the mountainside. The half dozen policemen were just below the ridge and they went over one by one as he watched.

'And a fat lot of good it'll do them,' he told himself. 'He'll be half a mile down the other side of the mountain by now and still running.'

Dwyer moved to join him. 'Anyone we know down there, sir?'

'Jack Pope,' Vanbrugh said. 'I couldn't identify the other two. One of them was burned to a crisp anyway.'

'It couldn't have been Rogan, then?'

'I don't think so. Too small.'

Gregory came back from the patrol car. 'They're giving us every spare car and man they've got to cover the immediate area.'

'What about the other valley?'

'There are two cars on the way there now.' Gregory wiped rain from his face and smiled confidently. 'We're bound to get them, you know. This isn't the big city with a maze of back streets to hide in. There are damned few roads round here. We can seal them all with no trouble at all.'

'Then we've nothing to worry about,' Vanbrugh said. 'I'd like to take a quick look over the farm now if that's all right with you.'

'What about this fellow Soames? Should I have him brought up here? Perhaps we could squeeze something useful out of him.'

'A damned good idea,' Vanbrugh said. 'At least we might get a few answers to some rather puzzling questions,' and he turned and followed Dwyer through the heavy rain towards the patrol car.

II

Soames' agile brain was working overtime, seeking a way out of the predicament in which he found himself as the patrol car turned off the Ambleside road and moved up the track towards Scardale.

His wrists were handcuffed together and a constable sat on either side of him. As they came to the place where the accident had occurred, the driver slowed to ease past the parked vehicles and several men staggered over the edge of the road carrying a stretcher.

Soames stared out at the shapeless form beneath the blanket. An arm hung down to the ground, flesh peeling from the fingers and he shuddered as the wind carried the sickly sweet smell through the open window.

The young constable on his right turned and looked at him coldly. 'You'll be lucky to get away with fifteen years for this little lot.'

Soames felt suddenly sick. Only once in his career had he been stupid enough to step just too far over the shadow line between what was legal and what wasn't. The subsequent experience had not been pleasant.

It came to him, with a thrill of horror, that this time he had gone in over his head and his mouth went dry. The car turned in through the gate and braked beside another which stood outside the farmhouse door.

The two policemen pulled him out and he followed them inside and along the narrow whitewashed passage. It was like something out of a bad dream and the look on the faces of the three men who waited for him in the sitting room didn't make him feel any better.

Vanbrugh examined him briefly. 'Henry Soames?'

Soames moistened dry lips. 'That's right. I'd like to know why I've been brought here.' He added feebly, 'I have my rights. I demand to see a solicitor.'

'A short while ago, a young policeman was shot by one of your pals,' Vanbrugh cut in coldly. 'A man with red hair. If that boy dies, I'll see you in the dock as an accessory to murder.'

Soames struggled for breath as fear turned his bowels to water. Finally he managed to speak. 'Morgan, that's the man you want. Harry Morgan. He's the one with red hair.'

'Who else was in on this?'

Soames stumbled over his words in his eagerness to get them out. 'Jesse Fletcher. He and Morgan came up together from Manchester. And there was the man who owns this farm, Costello.'

'And his niece?'

'That's right.'

'What about Jack Pope?' Dwyer put in.

Soames turned to him eagerly. 'Oh, yes, he was in on it, too.'

'When you visited Sean Rogan in prison, it was to arrange details of his escape?' Vanbrugh demanded.

'That's right. On the night he got out, Pope was waiting with a car and a change of clothes.'

'Who laid everything on?'

'A man called Colum O'More.'

Gregory frowned and looked at Vanbrugh. 'That's a familiar name.'

'It should be,' Vanbrugh said. 'He was a big man in the IRA in the thirties and during the early part of the war.' He turned back to Soames. 'So the IRA are in this after all? Funds for the organization, I suppose?'

'That's what Rogan believed.'

'Let me get this straight,' Vanbrugh said. 'Morgan and Fletcher were working for wages, right?'

'Five thousand apiece. Rogan was just working off a debt. O'More persuaded him that he owed the organization one last favour for breaking him out.'

'So the rest of the haul goes to IRA funds?'

'That's what O'More told Rogan.'

'But you know different?'

'You're telling me. The old spider wants the bloody lot for himself.'

Vanbrugh shook his head. 'It won't wash, Soames. I know Colum O'More, everything about him. He isn't the type to pull a stroke like that.'

Soames shrugged. 'He's a sick man, cancer of something. That kind of thing changes people.'

Gregory looked at Vanbrugh quickly. 'I'll buy that.'

Vanbrugh nodded. 'Where's O'More now?'

Soames moistened his lips. 'Can we make a deal?'

'I wouldn't cut you down if you were hanging,' Vanbrugh said calmly. 'Now tell me where O'More is or I'll kick you from here to the door and back again.'

'He's at an old farm just off the coast road near Whitbeck,' Soames said sullenly. 'Marsh-End, it's called.'

'Anyone with him?'

Soames shook his head. 'He's on his own. Rogan was supposed to drive over tomorrow with the money.'

'But you and your friends had ideas of your own about that?' Vanbrugh turned to Gregory. 'At least that gives us some sort of explanation for the shooting that's been going on here. They probably tried to get their hands on the loot and Rogan objected. Do you know this place, Marsh-End?'

'No, but I know Whitbeck. It'll take us about forty-five minutes to get there in weather like this.'

'Then let's get moving.'

Vanbrugh walked out quickly and Gregory and Dwyer went after him. Soames looked around him hurriedly for a possible exit and a middle-aged police sergeant came through the door, a broad grin on his face.

'Didn't think we'd forget you, did you?'

In the moment the full realization of what had happened

to him hit Soames with sickening force. Outside the patrol car moved away carrying Vanbrugh, Gregory and Dwyer. As he stood there listening to the sound of the engine fade into the distance, he felt more lonely than he had ever felt in his life before.

III

The ditch was half-full of water and Morgan waded along it for some fifty yards, then darted across to the shelter of the fir trees on the other side. A few moments later, a police car swept by, followed by another.

By now, they would have sealed every main road through the mountains, that much was obvious. It would take a miracle to get through and yet he had to reach the coast. His one chance of escape lay at Marsh-End with Colum O'More.

As he started to work his way through the plantation of firs, a motorcyclist passed along the main road and slowed to a halt thirty or forty yards further on. Morgan went forward cautiously and paused behind a bush.

A police motorcyclist stood beside an AA box, his machine parked a few feet away. He was examining a map. As Morgan watched, he slipped a cigarette into his mouth and flicked a lighter.

Morgan didn't even think about it. He gripped his revolver by the barrel, jumped forward and struck hard at the nape of the neck. The policeman gave a stifled cry and slumped to his knees. Morgan grabbed him by the shoulders and pulled him back into the bushes. Then he ran out into the road, kicked the stand from under the motorcycle and pushed it under cover in the plantation.

It took him five minutes to strip the policeman and dress in his uniform. When he was ready, he fastened the man's wrists behind him with his belt and moved towards the motorcycle.

At that moment, another patrol car swept by. He waited until the sound of its engine had faded into the distance, then ran the machine out into the road, mounted it and kicked the starter. As the engine roared into life, he pulled down the goggles and rode away.

Half a mile further on he came to a bridge. On the other side a police car was parked half across the road leaving room for single line traffic only and two constables blocked the way. Morgan changed down and started to slow, at the same time getting ready to accelerate.

There was no need. As he went over the bridge, the two constables moved out of the way and one of them waved a hand casually. It was as easy as that. Morgan changed into top gear and sped away into the rain.

— 18 —

WHEN ROGAN cut the engine and jumped out of the shooting brake, there was no sign of Brendan and the rain hissing down into the water of the dam was the only sound.

Hannah moved around the brake to join him. 'I wonder where he is?'

'God knows, but we've got to get moving. If we don't get through the tunnel and down to Ambleside Road within fifteen minutes, we've had it.'

There was a sudden restless baaing and several sheep ran between the ruined houses, scattering to avoid Brendan who raced after them brandishing a stick. They plunged up the mountainside and he paused, slightly out of breath, and grinned.

'I thought I'd better set them free.'

'Never mind about them now, we've got to get going. Where are the mailbags?'

'I put them in the punt, Mr Rogan.'

They hurried round the side of the dam and through the clump of trees that masked the old landing stage. Brendan had moored the punt to a rusty iron ring and several inches of water slopped in the bottom. The mailbags were in the prow where it was dry, and Hannah sat down on them. Rogan crouched in the centre and Brendan shoved off from the rear.

The sound of the rain faded as they moved into the cold darkness and he looked at his watch. It was almost five o'clock and it wasn't dark till seven-thirty, which didn't help. It wouldn't take the police long to work out what had happened when they found the shooting brake. One fast patrol car to block the end of the other valley was all that it would take. Certainly, if Dick Vanbrugh was in on things, the hunt was up with a vengeance.

And what happened if the jeep wasn't there? But he pushed that thought away from him. If they could get down to the Ambleside road and reach the track that led between Rydal Water and Grasmere to Elterwater they might stand a chance. Beyond was the lonely road over Wrynose and old packhorse tracks that crossed over the fells to the coast, places where only a jeep or a similar vehicle could go.

They drifted out into the heavy rain and bumped against the side of the stone landing stage. Brendan scrambled up and fastened the line, then gave Hannah a hand and Rogan passed up the two mailbags.

Brendan ran on ahead through the trees and Rogan and the girl followed. When they reached the old stable, the boy had already got the doors open, revealing the jeep.

He opened the rear door and Rogan heaved the two mailbags inside. 'All right, let's get moving.'

Brendan scrambled into the rear, Hannah got into the passenger seat and Rogan slid behind the wheel. He pulled out the choke and pressed the starter and the engine turned over at once. In one smooth movement he reversed out the stable, swung the wheel, moved into first gear and roared down the track towards the mouth of the valley.

'We'll try that route you told me about on Wednesday,' he said to Hannah.

'Do we stand a chance?'

'All depends on how quickly they get a car round to this side. If we can reach that track you told me about leading across to Elterwater and get off the main road, we might surprise them yet.'

He drove very fast, his foot hard against the boards and the jeep responded magnificently. Five minutes later, they turned up through a clump of fir trees and reached the main road.

Rogan barely paused, swung the wheel to the right and drove along the road towards Rydal. 'How far?' he shouted above the roaring of the engine.

'Half a mile, no more.'

Rain hammered against the windscreen so hard that the wipers had difficulty in coping. He leaned forward anxiously as a truck passed them going the opposite way and then Hannah was tugging at his arm.

He saw the gate in a clump of fir trees in the same moment and braked, skidding a little. As he swung the wheel and stopped, the girl jumped down and opened the gate. Rogan drove through and waited for her to close it again. A moment later, they were moving on through the trees and when he looked in the mirror, he could no longer see the road.

His throat was dry and there was sweat on his forehead. His head trembled slightly when he raised it to brush away the sweat.

'Would you look at that, now? I've got the shakes.' He gave her a quick grin. 'Maybe I'm getting too old for this sort of caper.'

'That'll be the day.'

She produced matches and cigarettes from one of her pockets, lit one and put it in his mouth. Rogan inhaled deeply and sighed. 'I needed that.'

'First hurdle over safely,' she said.

He nodded. 'That's about the size of it. How do you feel?'

'As if I'm really crashing out of something for the first time in my life.'

'Keep on believing that and it'll come true.'

They crossed the bridge and he changed down and drove along the narrow track between the trees. It took them no more than three or four minutes to reach the Elterwater road, another five to reach the village itself. The streets were deserted in the heavy rain and he drove quietly through, following Hannah's directions until, at Eltermere, he turned into a side road that skirted Little Langdale village. A quarter of an hour after leaving the Ambleside road, they were moving alongside

Little Langdale Tarn and starting the long climb up to Wrynose.

The road lifted steeply before them, mist crowding in across the mountains, and the jeep climbed steadily, its engine deepening to a full-throated roar as he changed down through the gears.

Gradually, the mist enfolded them, and when they reached the top of the pass visibility was down to twenty or thirty yards. Rogan stayed in a low gear on the way down the steep hill to Wrynose Bottom and they followed the course of the Duddon River. Ten minutes later, they came to the place where the road forked, one arm climbing to Hard Knott, the other following the valley to Seathwaite and Ulpha.

'Give me another cigarette,' he said.

The girl lit one and put it in his mouth and Brendan leaned over the back of the bench seat. 'H-how are we doing, Mr Rogan?'

'So far, so good, son.' Rogan pulled in at the side of the road. 'Let's have another look at that map.'

He examined it quickly, a slight frown on his face. 'No way round Seathwaite and Ulpha from the looks of things.'

'Are you expecting trouble?' Hannah said.

'It's possible. They've had plenty of time to pass the word around by now.'

She had another look at the map and traced a line across the fells. 'There's an unfenced road here. It won't be very good but it runs across Thwaites Fell to the coast. We'd still have to go through Ulpha, but it would cut out the other places.'

'Where does it start?'

'Beckfoot, a couple of miles on the far side of Ulpha.'

'Good enough.'

He drove away quickly, and as they passed through the little village of Seathwaite the mist seemed to be thinning a little, but the rain continued to fall relentlessly as they dropped down through the pleasant wooded valley.

The main street was deserted, but as they approached the village inn, Hannah clutched Rogan's arm tightly. A police sergeant in peaked cap and heavy blue raincoat stood on the steps talking to a middle-aged woman.

Rogan drove steadily past, but when he glanced in the mirror, they were both watching the jeep as it moved away along the main street. The sergeant turned and said something to the woman and they went into the inn quickly.

'Did you see that?' Hannah said.

Rogan nodded grimly. 'We'll have to take that unfenced road over the top now. No choice.'

He pushed his foot down hard until the needle flickered on sixty and the old jeep roared along the road, spurning the gravel. It took them no more than two or three minutes to reach Beckfoot and he braked, and flung the jeep into the side turning.

They climbed into another world, grey and sombre, dark crags, dripping with moisture, looming out of the mist on either hand. The road stretched before them, unfenced, but surprisingly well surfaced and the jeep slowed as the slope lifted before them.

The roaring of the engine in low gear was almost unbearable and the old aluminium body rattled alarmingly. Rogan checked the petrol gauge and saw they were down to the last gallon.

'How far have we got to go?' he shouted.

Hannah had another look at the map. 'About six miles to Bootle, but we don't need to go right in. There's a track branching down to the coast road. A mile, maybe two, to Marsh-End. Have we enough petrol?'

He nodded and changed into top gear as they breasted the slope and moved past Mere Crags across a jagged plateau, shrouded in fog.

It came to him, with something like surprise, that they had nearly made it, that with any kind of luck at all another ten minutes, fifteen at the most, should see them at Marsh-End. The road started to drop steeply into a grey void and he took it on the run, braking on the corners instead of changing to a low gear.

About a quarter of a mile outside Bootle they came to a finger-post sign carrying the legend Whicham, and turned into a narrow, rutted track that brought them on to the coast road three or four minutes later.

Mist drifted in across the marsh carrying the good salt smell of the sea, and Rogan's spirits lifted. The signpost for Marsh-

End loomed out of the gloom. He turned into the track and they lurched over the rutted surface through the trees beside the creek and rolled to a halt in the yard.

When he switched off the engine and turned to Hannah her eyes were shining. 'So we made it after all?'

He grinned and squeezed her hands. 'I hope you're a good sailor. It's a rough crossing in a small boat.'

Fog rolled in across the marsh, pushed by the wind, and he opened the door and got out. Brendan pulled the mailbags to the ground and dragged them round to him. The house was strangely quiet and the windows stared blindly down at them like dark eyes. Rogan frowned, picked up the mailbags and crossed to the door. Hannah opened it for him and led the way along the narrow passage.

Colum O'More was in the easy chair by the fire, his head lolling to one side. As Rogan dropped the mailbags, Hannah moved forward and examined the old man quickly.

'Is he dead?' Rogan said.

She shook her head. 'He's very cold, though.'

There was no fire in the grate and Rogan went to the sideboard, opened it and found a bottle of Irish whisky. He half filled a glass, went back to the chair and forced a little of it between the old man's lips.

Colum O'More coughed, his head shaking from side to side and then his eyes opened suddenly. He looked at Rogan blankly for a moment and recognition dawned.

'Sean boy,' he said in Irish. 'Is it yourself?'

'And none other, Colum Oge,' Rogan answered in the same language.

The old man's eyes moved to Hannah and he smiled. 'You too, girl, dear.'

She looked desperately at Rogan. 'I don't understand?'

'Give him a moment to pull himself together.'

O'More ran a hand over his face, shook himself and reached for the glass of whisky. He took it down with a single swallow and shuddered. 'God save us all, but that's better,' he said in English.

When he looked up there was a different expression in his eyes and he seemed more alert. 'But what are you doing here? What's gone wrong?'

'We're a day early, that's all,' Rogan said, 'and every peeler in the country on the prowl for us. We'll have to be moving, Colum.'

'You've pulled it off?'

Rogan dumped the two mailbags on the table. 'That we have.'

The old man stared at him incredulously. 'What time is it?'

'A little after seven.'

'But that can't be.' Colum O'More shook his head vigorously. 'I had a bad attack just after I got up this morning so I took some of my pills. Maybe more than I should have done.'

'Now that, I can believe. Are your things packed?'

'There's a suitcase in the bedroom, it's got everything I need.'

Rogan turned to Hannah. 'Make him a hot drink. I'll send Brendan on ahead to the boat with the suitcase. There are one or two things he can be doing to help us make a quick exit.'

Hannah nodded and went out and Rogan got the suitcase from the bedroom and took Brendan across the courtyard at the rear of the farm to where the track through the marsh began.

'You'll come to a stone causeway a couple of hundred yards from here,' he said. 'Just beyond it, there's a narrower path to the right. Follow that and you'll come to a motor launch. She's tied fore and aft. Cast off and hold her ready on a single line. We'll be along in ten minutes.'

The boy nodded eagerly and moved away, the case bumping against his right leg. Rogan went back into the house. O'More still sat in his chair by the fire and as Rogan entered the room, Hannah came in from the kitchen with a coffee pot and cups on a tray.

'What happens when we get to Ireland?' she said as she started to pour. 'Do we just sail boldly in?'

Colum O'More chuckled. 'Hardly that, girl. There's a quiet place I know and good friends not far away. That's where I'll be leaving you and Sean.'

She looked up at Rogan. 'Then what?'

'We'll go to my father's place in Kerry. I never made things easy for a peeler in my life, not even an Irish one. They can come for me, there.'

Her face clouded over at once. 'Prison again?'

O'More laughed harshly. 'But not for long, girl, make no mistake about that. What you might call a necessary formality. You'll be back in his arms inside a month.'

She looked up at Rogan anxiously. 'Is that the truth?'

'Since when have I lied to you?' Rogan kissed her gently on the forehead. 'Get your coat on, we'd better be making a move.'

He felt her stiffen in his arms as she looked behind him and a cold wind gently touched him on the back of the neck. In the mirror above the mantelpiece, he saw the door swing open, framing a police motorcyclist, strangely anonymous, broad goggles masking his eyes beneath the peak of the white uniform crash helmet.

He unfastened his chin strap, pulled off his helmet and goggles and Harry Morgan smiled out at them.

— 19 —

MORGAN'S FACE was lined with fatigue and the revolver he was holding trembled slightly. 'Make any kind of a wrong move and I'll kill you, I swear it,' he said harshly. 'Clasp your hands behind your neck.'

He moved to the table and patted the mailbags with his free hand. 'So the two we grabbed back there at the farm were dummies? I've got to hand it to you for nerve, Rogan. Turn round.'

Rogan did as he was told. When he raised his arms, his jacket gaped, revealing the Colt automatic in his waistband.

Morgan nodded to Hannah. 'Take out his shooter with your left hand and toss it across.' She hesitated and he raised the revolver quickly. 'I shot a copper back there at Scardale. I've nothing to lose now.'

'Do as he says,' Rogan told her.

She reached for the automatic with her left hand and threw it across awkwardly. Morgan grabbed for it, missed, and the gun skidded across the floor and came to rest under the table.

She took an involuntary step forward and he shook his head. 'Leave it.'

Rogan lowered his hands. 'What happens now?'

'I'm going to take a little boat trip, just me and the old man here like he arranged with Soames.'

Hannah sucked in her breath sharply.

Rogan turned and looked down at Colum O'More, a frown on his face. 'What's he talking about?'

The skin of the old man's face tightened across the cheekbones and his eyes were dark holes as he glared at Morgan. 'He's trying to make trouble, can't you see that?'

'You must be losing your touch, Rogan,' Morgan jeered. 'The old bastard's been stringing you along from the beginning. He didn't want funds for his blasted organization. He wanted a stake for his old age. He used you, Rogan, and Soames found out about it.'

'Is it true?' Rogan said calmly.

O'More looked down at the floor and Morgan laughed again. 'Is it true, the man says. That's why we were supposed to cut you out back at the farm. We were all going to meet here tomorrow and divvy up if things hadn't gone sour.'

O'More looked up sharply. 'I knew nothing of that, Sean, nothing about any plans concerning you. Soames found out, it's true, and threatened to tell you unless I cut him in. But that's as far as it went.'

'Funds for the organization, you said.'

'I'd have seen you all right, lad.'

'A high price to pay for my good name.' Rogan tapped his chest. 'I am Sean Rogan, a soldier of the Irish Republican Army and no thief.'

'To hell with the Irish Republican Army.' The old man slammed his stick hard against the floor. 'Forty years, Sean Rogan. Forty years I've given to the organization. Twenty of those I've served in gaol on both sides of the water and what have I got to show for it?' He coughed harshly, struggling for breath, and pulled at his collar. 'Old and broken, my lungs rotting. By God, I'll pass the time left to me in comfort or know the reason why.'

Rogan shook his head and there was something close to compassion on his face. 'It won't work, Colum. That kind of thing never does.'

'Don't let him kid you, old man,' Morgan said.

He took a clasp knife from his pocket, opened the blade with his teeth and slashed through the cord binding the neck of one of the bags. He dropped the knife on the table, put a hand inside and pulled out a packet of notes.

He threw it at Rogan who grabbed it instinctively. 'How much is that, Rogan? Five hundred, a thousand?' He patted the bag. 'Lots more in here, big man, and you're going to carry them down to the boat for me.'

Rogan examined the bundle of notes in his hand and a slow smile spread across his face. 'If the rest are like these there wouldn't be much point.' He dropped the bundle into O'More's lap. 'What do you think, Colum?'

Colum O'More pulled out several pound notes and held them up to the light. His eyes widened. 'Holy Mother of God, they're perforated, every last one of them.'

He passed one to Hannah who held it to the light, then looked at Rogan, surprise on her face. 'What does it mean?'

'They were talking about it in the prison a month or two back,' he said. 'A trick some of the banks are using now if they're shipping old notes in quantity for repulping. They run them through an electronic machine that perforates each one with a code number in large letters as you can see.'

'Making them useless?'

'As legal tender. That's the general idea.'

'What the hell are you talking about?'

Morgan upended the mailbag on the table, scattering packets to the floor. He examined one feverishly and then another and another. When he turned, his face was very white. 'They're all the same, every damned one.'

'This just isn't your day, Morgan,' Rogan said.

Colum O'More let out a great gust of laughter. 'If you

could see your face, you scut. Somehow, it makes the whole damned thing worth while.'

'This is your fault, you bastard,' Morgan spat at him. 'The whole bloody thing was a waste of time from the start. We'd have known that if your information had been right.'

'We all make mistakes, lad,' Colum O'More said, and pushed himself up.

Morgan shot him twice in the body, the force of the bullets knocking him back into the chair. As Hannah screamed, Rogan flung himself headlong under the table, his hand reaching for the butt of the automatic.

Morgan jumped back to get a clear view of him, but he was too late. Rogan's first shot caught him in the chest, the second in the stomach, knocking him back against the wall. He dropped his revolver and crumpled to his knees, his face wiped clean of expression, then fell forward.

Colum O'More was doubled over in pain. Hannah, on her knees beside him, tried to lift his head. Rogan dropped the automatic on the table and pushed the old man back into his chair. His eyes were tightly closed, teeth clenched against the pain and his forehead was beaded with swcat.

Rogan shook him gently. 'Colum, listen to me. How bad is it?'

The old man opened his eyes and death stared out at them. 'As bad as it's ever likely to get, lad.' He looked beyond them into space. 'The long road I've walked, a road I was proud to be on, and now this.' Hc coughed and a trickle of blood oozed from the corner of his mouth. 'It wasn't me, Sean, it wasn't the Big Man. It was the sickness inside me. I think a little of it must have touched my brain as well.'

Rogan stood up and turned to Hannah. 'Hang on here. I'm going for a doctor.'

'You're wasting your time,' Colum O'More called and Rogan stepped over Harry Morgan, and moved along the passage.

He heard the cars up on the main road as he opened the outside door and the furious jangle of the bell through the trees, muffled by the fog, as the first one braked hard and swung into the track. He slammed the door shut, bolted it and ran back into the living room.

'The peelers are here.' He grabbed Hannah by the arm, ran her into the kitchen and wrenched open the back door. 'You know the way to the boat. Get down there fast and wait for me.'

She tried to protest and he shook her brutally. 'Do as you're told. Haven't I enough to worry about?'

He pushed her into the fog, slammed the door and ran back into the living room. 'They'll be here soon, Colum. They'll be able to do more for you than I can.'

'There's no help for me on top of earth,' the old man said through clenched teeth, 'but there is for you. Now pass me that gun and get to hell out of here. Harry Morgan's death can be on my conscience, not yours.'

'For God's sake, Colum . . .'

'That's an order, damn you,' the old man spat at him. As Rogan passed him the gun a car braked outside and footsteps pounded across the cobbles. 'Get out of it!' Colum O'More shouted and Rogan ran through the kitchen and wrenched open the back door.

He was half-way across the yard when a young constable came round the corner on a dead run. Rogan swerved, his fist glanced off a cheekbone and the man grunted and went down. As cries broke out behind, he reached the shelter of the trees and was swallowed up by the fog.

II

Morgan pushed himself up slowly and fell back against the wall. His entire body seemed to be one great pain and there was blood in his mouth. He focused on Colum O'More and gave him a ghastly grin.

'I'll hang on, you old bastard. Long enough to make sure Rogan swings for me.'

'Is that a fact now?' Colum O'More said and shot him through the head. As the outside door gave, the automatic slipped from his grasp and he fell forward.

Vanbrugh was first through the door, Gregory close behind. He dropped to one knee beside the old man, raising his head gently, but Colum O'More stared blindly into eternity.

'This one's had it,' Gregory said, getting to his feet beside Morgan. 'What about him?'

Vanbrugh shook his head and picked up one of the packets of banknotes. 'Didn't do anybody much good, this little lot, did it?'

Dwyer came in from the kitchen in a hurry. 'Someone made a run for it through the back door and clouted a constable. Sounds like Rogan.'

'Better get after him then,' Gregory said.

Vanbrugh led the way through the kitchen and across the yard. It was almost nightfall, and the fog drifting through the trees turned the marsh into a place of shadows.

'You round up every man you can,' he told Gregory. 'Dwyer and I'll go straight in after him. He can't have gone very far.'

Gregory turned, blowing his whistle sharply and Vanbrugh ran forward into the trees, Dwyer at his heels. Branches lashed against his face and he held up an arm to ward them off and stumbled on. Within a few moments they came to a narrow track that led across a stone causeway. On the other side, there was a turning to the left through tangled undergrowth and Vanbrugh paused, struggling for breath.

'I'll try this one, you go on ahead. Whatever happens, don't try to take him on your own. You aren't that good. If you catch sight of him, blow your whistle and I'll come running.'

Dwyer nodded and moved into the fog and Vanbrugh turned into the track through the undergrowth and started to run.

Rogan could hear the police whistle muffled by the fog, but distinctive enough for all that, and he put down his head and ran, crashing through a plantation of young firs, the branches whipping his sides. He tripped and fell, rolling down a small incline and again heard the police whistle.

He got to his feet, staggered forward and blundered through a fringe of bushes into the side turning that led down to the creek. He started to run, his chest heaving painfully, and burst through the trees on to the bank of the creek beside the launch a few moments later.

Hannah ran to meet him, her face a pale blur in the evening light. 'Are you all right?'

'Never mind me,' he said. 'There are peelers all over the place. Get on board.'

Brendan stood in the stern with a ten foot pole, hopping with excitement. 'Are we ready to go, Mr Rogan? Shall I give the engine a turn?'

'And attract everyone for miles around?' Rogan shook his head. 'We'll let the tide take us out through the estuary.'

He ran to the single line that still held the launch to land and cast off. The vessel swung out from the bank at once, caught by the tide, and Hannah called anxiously, 'Quickly, Sean.'

As Rogan took a step forward, Vanbrugh ran out of the undergrowth and cannoned into him. They rolled over and over on the ground, fetching up against a line of old rotting palings. Rogan on top. His great hands fastened around the policeman's throat and then he recognized him. He released his grip and got to his feet.

'Get up.'

They stood facing each other in the half-light, police whistles sounding monotonously from every part of the marsh, and Hannah gave a stifled cry.

Vanbrugh looked at her, shadowy and insubstantial in the fog as the launch drifted away, then he turned back to Rogan. 'Well, get moving, for Christ's sake!'

Rogan plunged into the water. He waded out to the launch, pulled himself up over the rail and took the pole from the boy. He turned and looked back at Vanbrugh for a long moment, then raised his hand in a half salute and poled the launch into the fog.

Vanbrugh stood there staring into the grey void and, after a while, Dwyer arrived. 'Any sign of him, sir?'

Vanbrugh shook his head. 'Got a cigarette?'

Dwyer took out his case. As he was giving him a light, there was the faint, distant rumble of an engine breaking into life.

He frowned. 'Did you hear that, sir?'

Vanbrugh stood listening, head on one side. He shook his head. 'I didn't hear a damned thing, sergeant. Come on, we're wasting our time here.'

He turned and led the way back along the path through the undergrowth.

As the launch had drifted out of the estuary, waves started to slap against her hull and Rogan pressed the starter. The powerful diesel engines rumbled into life and he took the launch in a long sweeping curve out past the last point of land into the open sea.

He turned and smiled at Hannah standing there in the cockpit beside him, and slipped an arm around her waist, pulling her close. For the first time in his life he felt as if he were really crashing out of something.

STORM WARNING

From the Journal of Rear Admiral Carey Reeve, USN

. . . and this I find the greatest mystery of all – the instinct in man to sacrifice himself that others might live. But then, courage never goes out of fashion, and at no other time in my life have I seen it better displayed than in the affair of the *Deutschland.* In the midst of the greatest war history has known, people on opposite sides in that conflict were able to come together for a time, take every risk, lay themselves on the line, in an attempt to save a handful of human beings from man's oldest and most implacable foe – the sea. I have never seen the tragic futility of war better demonstrated nor felt prouder of my fellow men that at that time . . .

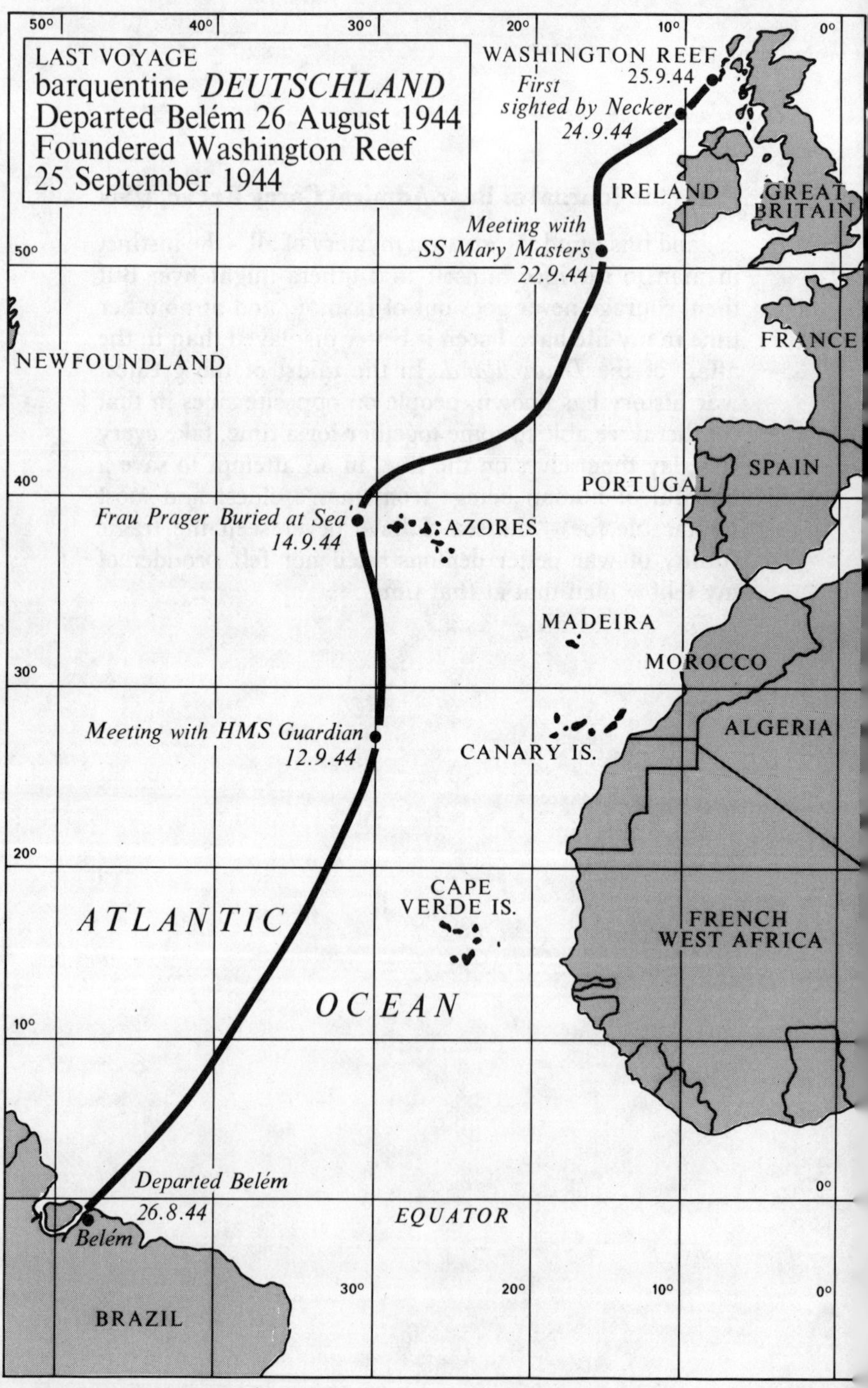
LAST VOYAGE
barquentine DEUTSCHLAND
Departed Belém 26 August 1944
Foundered Washington Reef
25 September 1944
50°
40°
30°
20°
10°
0°
WASHINGTON REEF
25.9.44
First
sighted by Necker
24.9.44
IRELAND
GREAT
BRITAIN
Meeting with
SS Mary Masters
22.9.44
FRANCE
NEWFOUNDLAND
SPAIN
PORTUGAL
Frau Prager Buried at Sea
14.9.44
AZORES
MADEIRA
MOROCCO
ALGERIA
Meeting with HMS Guardian
12.9.44
CANARY IS.
CAPE
VERDE IS.
ATLANTIC
OCEAN
FRENCH
WEST AFRICA
Departed Belém
26.8.44
Belém
EQUATOR
BRAZIL

— 1 —

Barquentine *Deutschland* 26 August 1944. Eleven days out of Rio de Janeiro. At anchorage in Belém. Begins hot. Moderate trades. Last of the coal unloaded. No cargo available. In ballast with sand for run to Rio. Hatches battened down and ready to sail. Rain towards evening.

AS PRAGER turned the corner, thunder rumbled far out to sea and lightning flashed across the sky, giving for one brief moment a clear view of the harbour. The usual assortment of small craft and three or four coastal steamers were moored at the main jetty. The *Deutschland* was anchored in mid-stream, distinctive if only for the fact that she was the one sailing ship in the harbour.

Rain came suddenly, warm and heavy, redolent with rotting vegetation from the jungle across the river. Prager turned up the collar of his jacket and, holding his old leather briefcase under one arm, hurried along the waterfront towards the Lights of Lisbon, the bar at the end of the fish pier.

There was the sound of music, muted yet plain enough, a slow, sad samba with something of the night in it. As he went up the steps to the verandah he took off his spectacles and wiped rain from them with his handkerchief. He replaced them carefully and peered inside.

The place was empty, except for the bartender and Helmut Richter, the *Deutschland*'s bosun, who sat at the end of the bar with a bottle and a glass in front of him. He was a large, heavily-built man in reefer jacket and denim cap, with long, blond hair and a beard that made him look older than his twenty-eight years.

Prager stepped inside. The bartender, who was polishing a glass, looked up. Prager ignored him and moved along the bar, shaking the rain from his panama. He dropped the briefcase on the floor at his feet.

'A good night for it, Helmut.'

Richter nodded gravely and picked up the bottle. 'A drink, Herr Prager?'

'I think not.'

'A wise choice.' Richter refilled his glass. 'Cachaca. They say it rots the brain as well as the liver. A poor substitute for good Schnapps, but they haven't seen any of that since '39.'

'Is Captain Berger here?'

'Waiting for you on board.'

Prager picked up his briefcase again. 'Then I suggest we get moving. There isn't much time. Has anyone been asking for me?'

Before Richter could reply a voice said in Portuguese, 'Ah, Senhor Prager, a pleasant surprise.'

Prager turned quickly as the curtain of one of the small booths behind him was pulled back. The man who sat there, a bottle of wine in front of him, was immensely fat, his crumpled khaki uniform stained with sweat and bursting at the seams.

Prager managed a smile. 'Captain Mendoza. Don't you ever sleep?'

'Not very often. What is it this time, business or pleasure?'

'A little of both. As you know, the position of German nationals is a difficult one these days. Your government is more than ever insistent on a regular report.'

'So, it is necessary that Berger and his men are seen by you personally?'

'On the first day of the last week in each month. Your people in Rio are most strict in this respect.'

'And the good Senhora Prager? I am given to understand she was on the plane with you.'

'I have a few days' leave due and she has never seen this part of the country. It seemed the ideal opportunity.'

Richter slipped out without a word. Mendoza watched him go. 'A nice lad,' he said. 'What was it he used to be? Chief helmsman on a U-boat. Obersteuermann, isn't that the word?'

'I believe so.'

'You'll have a drink with me?'

Prager hesitated. 'Just a quick one, if you don't mind. I

have an appointment.'

'With Berger?' Mendoza nodded to the barman who poured brandy into two glasses without a word. 'When does he leave to go back to Rio? In the morning?'

'I believe so.' Prager sipped the brandy, on dangerous ground now. He was sixty-five, an assistant consul at the German embassy in Rio until August 1942, when the Brazilians, enraged by the torpedoing of several of their merchant ships by U-boats, had declared war. Little more than a gesture, but it had presented the problem of what to do about German nationals – in particular the increasing number of sailors of the Kriegsmarine who found themselves washed up on her shores.

Prager, having spent twenty years in the country, and being acceptable in high places, had been left behind to cope with that. There were, after all, five thousand miles of ocean between Brazil and Germany so no need to set up expensive internment camps. The Brazilian government was content with the monthly reports he presented on his fellow citizens. As long as they were gainfully employed and not a charge on the State, everyone was happy.

Mendoza said, 'I've been harbourmaster here for two years now and for most of that time the *Deutschland* has been coming in regularly. Say every couple of months.'

'So?'

'A boat of that size usually manages with a master, mate, bosun, probably six foremast hands and a cook.'

'That is correct.'

Mendoza sipped a little of his brandy thoughtfully. 'According to my information, Berger has a crew of something like twenty this trip.'

He smiled genially, but the eyes in the fat face were sharp. Prager said carefully, 'There are many German seamen in Rio.'

'And more each day. The war, my friend, does not go well for you.'

'Berger is probably trying to employ as many as possible.'

Mendoza smiled beautifully. 'But of course. That explanation had not occurred to me. But I mustn't keep you.

Perhaps we'll have time for another drink tomorrow?'

'I hope so.'

Prager went out quickly. Richter was waiting on the verandah by the steps. Beyond, the rain hammered relentlessly into the ground. 'Everything all right?' he asked.

'Not really,' Prager told him. 'He knows something's going on. But how could be possibly suspect the truth? No one in his right mind would believe it.' He clapped Richter on the shoulder. 'Now let's get moving.'

The bosun said, 'I didn't get a chance to tell you inside, but there was someone asking for you.'

There was a movement behind and, as Prager turned, a nun in tropical-white habit stepped into the light. She was a small woman, not much over five feet tall, with clear, untroubled eyes and a calm, unlined face.

'Sister Angela,' Richter said.

'. . . of the Sisters of Mercy from the mission station on the Rio Negro. Introductions are not necessary, Helmut, Sister Angela and I are old acquaintances.'

He took off his panama and held out his hand which she clasped briefly in a grasp of surprising strength.

'It's good to see you again, sister.'

'And you, Herr Prager. I think you know why I'm here.'

'Why, yes, sister.' Otto Prager smiled warmly. 'I believe I do.'

II

An anchor light hung from the *Deutschland*'s forestay, as required by marine regulations, and this they saw first as Richter worked the dinghy across the harbour. Then suddenly she was very close, her masts and spars dark against the sky.

Prager looked up with conscious pleasure as he climbed the Jacob's ladder. She was a three-masted barquentine built by Hamish Campbell on the Clyde in 1881 and built with love and understanding and grace, with an elegant clipper bow to her and an extended jib-boom.

She had spent a lifetime in trade: Newcastle-on-Tyne with steam coal for Valparaiso; Chilean nitrates for America's west coast; lumber for Australia; wool for Britain . . . an endless circle, as sail died in a doomed attempt to combat steam, one owner after another through three changes of name until, finally, she had been bought by the Brazilian firm of Mayer Brothers, a family of German extraction, who had rechristened her *Deutschland* and put her to the coastal trade. Rio to Belém and the mouth of the Amazon – just the craft for such waters, having a draught of only eight feet fully loaded.

Prager went over the bulwark and extended his hand to Sister Angela. Richter was close behind on the ladder. Three seamen by the main mast gazed in astonishment as the little nun came over the side, and one of them hurried forward to take her other hand.

She thanked him, and Prager said to her, 'I think it would be better if I spoke to Captain Berger alone to start with.'

'Whatever you think best, Herr Prager,' she said tranquilly.

He turned to Richter. 'Take the good sister down to the saloon, then wait for me outside the captain's cabin.'

Richter and Sister Angela descended the companionway and Prager went aft towards the quarterdeck. Berger's cabin was underneath. He hesitated, then braced himself, knocked on the door and went in.

The cabin was small, spartan in its furnishings – narrow bunk and three cupboards and not much else except for the desk behind which Berger sat, making a measurement with parallel rulers on the chart spread before him.

He glanced up, and there was relief in his eyes. 'I was beginning to get worried.'

He was at that time forty-eight years old, of medium height with good shoulders, his wiry, dark hair and beard flecked with grey, and his face weathered by sea and sun.

'I'm sorry,' Prager said. 'We ran into a bad electric storm on the flight from Rio. The pilot insisted on touching down at Carolina until the weather cleared. We were there for four hours.'

Berger opened a sandalwood box and offered him a cheroot. 'What's the latest war news?'

'All bad.' Prager sat in the chair opposite and accepted a light. 'On the fifteenth of this month American and French forces landed on the Mediterranean coast. Two days ago French tanks entered Paris.'

Berger whistled softly. 'Next stop the Rhine.'

'I should imagine so.'

'And then Germany.' He stood up, crossed to one of the cupboards, opened it and took out a bottle of rum and two glasses. 'What about the Russians?'

'The Red Army is on the borders of East Prussia.'

Berger poured rum into the glasses and pushed one across. 'You know, Otto, we Germans haven't had to defend the soil of the Fatherland since Napoleon. It should prove an interesting experience.'

'Brazil might be the best place to be for the next year or two,' Prager said. 'A hell of a time to go home.'

'Or the only time,' Berger said. 'It depends on your point of view. Have you got the papers?'

Prager put his briefcase on the desk. 'Everything needed and I've checked again on the barquentine you mentioned when you first spoke of this crazy affair, the *Gudrid Andersen*. She's still in Gothenburg harbour. Hasn't been to sea since the first year of the war.'

'Excellent,' Berger said. 'Plain sailing from here on, then.'

'You are fully prepared?'

Berger opened a cupboard and took out a lifejacket which he dropped on the desk. The legend *Gudrid Andersen – Gothenburg* was stencilled on the back.

'And this, of course.' He produced next a Swedish ensign. 'A most important item as I'm sure you'll agree.' He smiled. 'Everything is ready, believe me. The official change of name we'll make once clear of the coastal shipping lanes.'

'And the log?'

'I've already prepared a false one in the name of the *Gudrid Andersen* for use with our friends from the other side if we should be so unlucky as to run into them. The true log of the *Deutschland* I shall continue to keep privately. It would not be correct to do otherwise.' He put the lifejacket and ensign back in the cupboard. 'As for you, old friend, what can I say? Without your hard work during these past few months, the information you have obtained, the forged papers, we could not have ever begun to contemplate such an enterprise.'

Prager said carefully, 'There is just one more thing to discuss, Erich.'

'What's that?'

Prager hesitated, then said, 'Seven passengers.'

Berger laughed harshly. 'You must be joking.'

'No, I'm perfectly serious. You've carried them before, haven't you?'

'You know damned well I have.' There was something close to anger in Berger's voice. 'I have accommodation for eight passengers. Two cabins on either side of the saloon, two bunks to each. I should also point out that this ship is amply crewed by ten men including myself. At the moment, we are twenty-two, as you very well know. Seven passengers would mean that the additional crew would have to bunk elsewhere. An impossible situation.'

'But you'll be in ballast.' Prager said. 'No cargo, and surely genuine passengers would only strengthen your cover story?'

'Who are these passengers?'

'Germans, like you and your men, who want to go home.' Prager took a deep breath and carried on. 'All right, you might as well know the worst. They're nuns. Sisters of Mercy from a mission station on the Negro. I've been visiting them regularly for the past two years, just like all the other Germans on my list. Every three months; a special dispensation from the authorities as the place is so difficult to get to.'

Berger stared at him in astonishment. 'For God's sake, Otto, am I going out of my mind or are you?'

Prager got up without a word and opened the cabin door. Richter was standing outside smoking a cigarillo. Prager nodded and the bosun hurried away.

'Now what?' Berger demanded.

'I brought one of them on board with me. The others are waiting on shore. At least hear what she has to say.'

'You must be out of your head. It's the only conceivable explanation.'

There was a knock at the door. Prager opened it and Sister Angela stepped inside. He said, 'Sister, I'd like you to meet Fregattenkapitän Erich Berger. Erich, this is Sister Angela of the Little Sisters of Mercy.'

'Good evening, captain,' she said.

Berger looked down at the tiny nun for a moment, an expression of astonishment on his face, then he grabbed Prager by the arm and pushed him outside into the rain, pulling the cabin door behind him.

'What in the hell am I going to do? What am I supposed to say?'

'You're the captain,' Prager told him. 'You make the decisions and no one else, or so I've always been given to understand. I'll wait for you here.'

He walked to the mizzen shrouds on the port side. Berger cursed softly, hesitated, then went back in.

She was standing behind the desk, leaning over the chronometer in its box under a glass plate. She glanced up. 'Beautiful, captain. Quite beautiful. What is it?'

'The seaman's measure of the heavens, sister, along with a sextant. If I can check the position of the sun, moon and stars then I can discover my own exact position on the earth's surface – with the help of tables as well of course.'

She turned to the desk. 'A British Admiralty chart. Why is that?'

'Because they're the best,' Berger told her, feeling for some reason incredibly helpless.

'I see.' She carried on in the same calm voice. 'Are you going to take us with you?'

'Look, sister,' he said. 'Sit down and let me explain.' He pulled another chart forward. 'Here we are at the mouth of the Amazon and this is the route home.' He traced a finger up past the Azores and west of Ireland. 'And if we get that far, there could be even greater hazards to face.' He tapped at the chart. 'We must pass close to the Outer Hebrides in Scotland, a graveyard for sailing ships, especially in bad weather – which is usually six days out of seven up there. And if we survive that, we only have the Orkneys passage, the run to Norway, then down through the Kattegat to Kiel,' he added with heavy irony. 'Five thousand miles, that's all.'

'And how long will it take us?'

He actually found himself answering, 'Impossible to say. Forty, maybe fifty days. So much depends on the weather.'

'That seems very reasonable, in the circumstances.'

Berger said, 'Tell me something. When you first came out here, how did you make the trip?'

'A passenger liner. The *Bremen*. That was just before the war, of course.'

'A fine ship. Comfortable cabins, hot and cold running water. Food that wouldn't disgrace a first-class hotel. Stewards to fetch and carry.'

'What exactly are you trying to say, captain?'

'That on this ship, life would be very difficult. Bad food, cramped quarters. A lavatory bucket to empty daily. Salt water only to wash in. And a blow – a real blow under sail – can be a frightening experience. In bad weather we can spend a fortnight at a time without a dry spot in her from stem to stern. Have you ever strapped yourself into a bunk in wet blankets with a full gale trying to tear the sticks out of the deck above your head?' He rolled up the chart and said firmly, 'I'm sorry. I can't see any point in prolonging this discussion.'

She nodded thoughtfully. 'Tell me something. How does a German naval officer come to command a Brazilian trading vessel?'

'I was captain of a submarine supply ship, the *Essen*, camouflaged as the US fuel ship *George Grant*. We were torpedoed in the South Atlantic on our third trip by a British submarine, which wasn't taken in by the disguise. You may consider that ironic in view of the fact that I intend to try and pass the *Deutschland* off as a similar ship of Swedish registration.'

'And how did you manage to reach Brazil?'

'Picked up by a Portuguese cargo boat and handed over to the Brazilian authorities when we reached Rio. The Brazilians have been operating a kind of parole system for any of us who can find work. The Mayer Brothers, who own the *Deutschland*, are coastal traders, Brazilian citizens but German by origin. They've helped a great many of us. We make the run from Rio to Belém and back once a month with general cargo.'

'And you repay them now by stealing their boat?'

'A point of view; for which I can only hope they'll forgive me when they know the facts. But we don't really have any choice.'

'Why not?'

'The Brazilians are starting to play a more active part in the war. Last month they sent troops to Italy. I think things could get much more difficult for us here.'

'And the other reason.'

'You think I have one?'

She waited, hands folded, saying nothing. Berger shrugged, opened the drawer of his desk and took out a wallet. He extracted a snapshot and passed it across. It was badly creased and discoloured by salt water, but the smiles on the faces of the three small girls were still clear enough.

'Your children?'

'Taken in '41. Heidi, on the left, will be ten now. Eva is eight and Else will be six in October.'

'And their mother?'

'Killed in a bombing raid on Hamburg three months ago.'

She crossed herself automatically. 'What happened to the children?'

'Herr Prager got word about them for me through our embassy in the Argentine. My mother has them in Bavaria.'

'Thank God in his infinite mercy.'

'Should I?' Berger's face was pale, jaw set. 'Germany is going under, sister, a matter of months only. Can you imagine how bad it's going to be? And my mother's an old woman. If anything happens to her . . .' A kind of shudder seemed to pass through his body and he leaned heavily on the desk. 'I want to be with them because that's where I'm needed, not here on the edge of the world, so far off that the war has ceased to exist.'

'And for that you'll dare anything?'

'Including five thousand miles of ocean dominated completely by the British and American navies, in a patched-up sailing ship that hasn't been out of sight of land in twenty years or more. An old tub, that hasn't had a refit for longer than I care to remember. An impossible voyage.'

'Which Herr Richter, your bosun, is apparently willing to make.'

'Helmut is a special case. The finest sailor I've ever known. He has invaluable experience under sail. Served his time as a boy on Finnish windjammers on the Chilean nitrate run.

That may not mean a lot to you, but to seamen anywhere . . .'

'But according to Herr Prager there are another twenty men in your crew who are also willing to make this so-called impossible voyage.'

'Most of them with a reason roughly similar to mine. I can think of at least seventy men in Rio who would gladly stand in their shoes. They held a lottery for the last ten places in a German bar on the Rio waterfront two weeks ago.' He shook his head. 'They want to go home, sister, don't you see? And for that, to use your own words, they'll dare anything.'

'And my friends and I are different, is that it? We too, have families, captain, as dear to us as yours. More than that, because of what lies ahead, home is where we are needed now.'

Berger stood staring at her for a moment, then shook his head. 'No. In any case, it's too late. You'd need Swedish papers, that's an essential part of the plan. Prager's arranged them for all of us.'

She got to her feet, opened the cabin door and called, 'Herr Prager!'

He moved in out of the rain. 'What is it?'

'My papers, please. May I have them now?'

Prager opened his briefcase. He searched inside, then took out a passport which he dropped on the desk in front of Berger.

Berger frowned. 'But this is Swedish.' He opened it and Sister Angela stared out at him from the photo. He looked up. 'I wonder if you'd be so kind as to step outside for a moment, sister. I'd like a few words with my good friend here.'

She hesitated, glanced briefly at Prager, then went out.

Prager said, 'Look, Erich, let me explain.'

Berger held up the passport. 'Not something you can pick up at twenty-four hours' notice, so you must have known about this for quite some time. Why in the hell didn't you tell me?'

'Because I knew you'd react exactly as you are doing.'

'So you thought you'd leave it until it was too late for me to say no? Well, you made a mistake. I won't play. And what about this mission station they've been operating? Is it suddenly so unimportant?'

'The Brazilian Department of the Interior has changed its policy on the Indians in that area; moving them out and white settlers in. The mission was due to close anyway.'

'They're a nursing order, aren't they? Surely there must be some other outlet for their talents up there.'

'They are also Germans, Erich. What do you think it's going to be like when those first Brazilian casualty figures start filtering through from Italy?'

There was a long pause. Berger picked up the Swedish passport, opened it and examined the photo again. 'She looks like trouble to me. She's been used to getting her own way for too long.'

'Nonsense,' Prager said. 'I knew her family from the old days. Good Prussian stock. Her father was an infantry general. She was a nurse on the Western Front in 1918.'

Berger's astonishment showed. 'A hell of a background for a Little Sister of Mercy. What went wrong? Was there some sort of scandal?'

'Not at all. There *was* a young man, I believe. A flier.'

'. . . who didn't come back one fine morning so she sought refuge in a life of good works.' Berger shook his head. 'It's beginning to sound like a very bad play.'

'But you've got it all wrong, Erich. The way I heard it, he simply let her think he was dead. She had a breakdown that almost cost her life and was just coming out of it nicely when she met him walking along the Unter den Linden one day with another girl on his arm.'

Berger held up both hands. 'No more. I know when I'm beaten. Bring her back in.'

Prager went to the door quickly and opened it. She was standing outside talking to the bosun.

Berger said, 'You win, sister. Tell Richter to have you taken ashore to collect the rest of your friends. Be back here by 2 a.m. because that's when we leave, and if you aren't here, we go without you.'

'God bless you, captain.'

'I think he's got enough on his plate at the moment without

me.' As she moved to the door, he added, 'Just one thing. Try not to let the crew know before they have to.'

'Are they likely to be disturbed by our presence?'

'Very much so. Sailors are superstitious by nature. Amongst other things, sailing on a Friday is asking for trouble. Taking any kind of a minister along as a passenger, the same. We should certainly pick up all the bad luck in the world with seven nuns sailing with us.'

'Five, captain. Only five,' she said and went out.

Berger frowned and turned to Prager. 'You said seven passengers.'

'So I did.' Prager rummaged in the briefcase and produced two more Swedish passports which he pushed across the desk. 'One for Gertrude and one for me. She, too, is waiting on shore with our baggage which includes, I might add, that wireless transmitter you asked me to try and get you.'

Berger gazed at him in stupefaction. 'You and your wife?' he said hoarsely. 'Good God, Otto, you're sixty-five if you're a day. And what will your masters in Berlin say?'

'From what I hear, the Russians are far more likely to get there before I do, so it doesn't really matter.' Prager smiled gently. 'You see, Erich, we want to go home, too.'

III

When Berger went up to the quarterdeck just before two it was raining harder than ever. The entire crew was assembled on the deck below, faces pale, oilskins glistening in the dim glow of the deck lights.

He gripped the rail, leaned forward and spoke in a low voice. 'I won't say much. You all know the score. It's one hell of a trip, I'm not going to pretend any different, but if you do as I tell you, we'll make it, you and I and the old *Deutschland* together.'

There was a stirring amongst them, no more than that, and he carried on, a touch of iron in his voice now. 'One more thing. As most of you will have observed, we're carrying passengers. Herr Prager, once assistant consul at our embassy in Rio and his wife, and five nuns from a mission station on the Negro.'

He paused. There was only the hissing of the rain as they all waited. 'Nuns,' he said, 'but still women and it's a long journey home, so let me make myself plain. I'll personally shoot the first man to step over the line, and so enter it in the log.' He straightened. 'Now everyone to his station.'

As he turned from the rail his second-in-command moved out of the darkness to join him. Leutnant zur See Johann Sturm, a tall, fair youth from Minden in Westphalia, had celebrated his twentieth birthday only three days earlier. Like Richter, he was a submariner and had served in a U-boat as second watch officer.

'Everything under control, Herr Sturm?' Berger enquired in a low voice.

'I think so, captain.' Sturm's voice was surprisingly calm. 'I've stowed the wireless transmitter Herr Prager brought with him from Rio in my cabin, as you ordered. It's not much, I'm afraid, sir. A limited range at the best.'

'Better than nothing,' Berger told him. 'And the passengers? Are they safely stowed away also?'

'Oh yes, sir.' There was a hint of laughter in the boy's voice. 'I think you could say that.'

A white figure appeared out of the darkness and materialized as Sister Angela. Berger swallowed hard and said in a low, dangerous voice, 'Could you now, Herr Sturm?'

Sister Angela said brightly, 'Are we leaving, captain? Is it all right if I watch?'

Berger glared at her helplessly, rain dripping from the peak of his cap, then turned to Sturm and said, 'Haul up the spanker and outer jib only, Herr Sturm, and let the anchor chain go.'

Sturm repeated the order and there was a sudden flurry of activity. One seaman dropped down the forepeak hatch. Four others hauled briskly on the halliard and the spanker rose slowly. A moment later there was a rattle as the anchor chain slithered across the deck, then a heavy splash.

Richter was at the wheel but, for the moment, nothing seemed to happen. Then Sister Angela, glancing up, saw through a gap in the curtain of rain, stars pass across the jib.

'We're moving, captain! We're moving!' she cried, as excitedly as any child.

'So I've observed,' Berger told her. 'Now will you kindly oblige me by going below.'

She went reluctantly and he sighed and turned to the bosun. 'Steady as she goes, Richter. She's all yours.'

And Richter took her out through the harbour entrance, drifting along like some pale ghost, barely moving, leaving a slight swirl of phosphorescence in her wake.

IV

Fifteen minutes later, as Captain Mendoza sat playing whist in his booth at the Lights of Lisbon with a young lady from the establishment next door, the man he had assigned to keep watch on the fish pier burst in on him.

'What is it?' Mendoza demanded mildly.

'The *Deutschland*, Senhor Capitan,' the watchman whispered. 'She is gone.'

'Indeed.' Mendoza laid his cards face down on the table and stood up. 'Watch her, José,' he called to the barman. He picked up his cap and oilskin coat and went out.

When he reached the end of the fish pier, the rain was falling harder than ever in a dark impenetrable curtain. He lit a cigar in cupped hands and stared into the night.

'Will you notify the authorities, senhor?' the watchman enquired.

Mendoza shrugged. 'What is there to notify? Undoubtedly Captain Berger wished an early start for the return trip to Rio, where he is due in eight days from now, although it would not be uncommon for him to be perhaps one week overdue, the weather at this time of the year being so unpredictable. Time enough for any official enquiry needed to be made then.'

The watchman glanced at him uncertainly, then bobbed his head. 'As you say, Senhor Capitan.'

He moved away and Mendoza looked out over the river towards the mouth of the Amazon and the sea. How far to Germany? Nearly five thousand miles, across an ocean that was now hopelessly in the grip of the American and British navies. And in what? A three-masted barquentine long past her prime.

'Fools,' he said softly. 'Poor, stupid, magnificent fools.' And he turned and went back along the fish pier through the rain.

— 2 —

> Barquentine *Deutschland*. 9 September 1944. Lat. 25°.01N., long. 30°.46W. Fourteen days out of Belém. Wind NW 6–8. Hove the log and found we were going twelve knots. In the past twenty-four hours we have run two hundred and twenty-eight miles. Frau Prager still confined to her bunk with the sea-sickness which has plagued her since leaving Belém. Her increasing weakness gives us all cause for conern. Heavy rain towards evening.

THE MORNING weather forecast for sea area Hebrides had been far from promising, winds 5 to 6 with rain squalls. Off the north-west coast of Skye, things were about as dirty as they could be – heavy, dark clouds swollen with rain, merging with the horizon.

Except for the occasional seabird, the only living thing in that desolation was the motor gunboat making south-west for Barra, her Stars and Stripes ensign the one splash of colour in the grey morning.

Dawn was at six-fifteen, but at nine-thirty visibility was still bad enough to keep the RAF grounded. No one on board the gunboat could have been blamed for failing to spot the lone Junkers 88S coming in low off the sea astern. The first burst of cannon shell kicked fountains of water high into the air ten or fifteen yards to port. As the plane banked for a second run, the 13mm machine-gun firing from the rear of the cockpit canopy loosed off a long burst that ripped into the deck aft of the wheelhouse.

Harry Jago, in his bunk below trying to snatch an hour's

sleep, was awake in an instant, and making for the companionway. As he reached the deck, the gun-crew were already running for the twin 20mm anti-aircraft cannon. Jago beat them into the bucket seat, hands clamping around the trigger handles.

Suddenly, as the Junkers came in off the water for the second time, heavy, black smoke swirled across the deck. Jago started to fire as its cannon punched holes in the deck beside him.

The Junkers was making its pass at close to four hundred miles an hour. He swung to follow it, aware of Jansen on the bridge above him working the Browning. But it was all to no purpose, and the Junkers curved away to port through puff-balls of black smoke and fled into the morning.

Jago stayed where he was for a moment, hands still gripping the handles. Then he got out of the seat and turned to Leading Seaman Harvey Gould, who was in charge of the anti-aircraft cannon.

'You were five seconds too late, you and your boys.'

The men of the gun crew shuffled uneasily. 'It won't happen again, lieutenant,' Gould said.

'See that it doesn't.' Jago produced a crumpled pack of cigarettes from his shirt pocket and stuck one in his mouth. 'Having survived the Solomons, D-Day and the worst those E-boat flotillas in the English Channel could offer, it would look kind of silly to die in the Hebrides.'

II

The pilot of the Junkers, Captain Horst Necker, logged his attack as having taken place at 09.35 hours precisely. A hit-and-run affair of no particular importance which had served to enliven an otherwise boring routine patrol, especially for a pilot who in the spring of that year, during the renewed night attacks on London, had been employed by the elite pathfinder *Gruppe* 1/KG 66 with the kind of success that had earned him the Knight's Cross only two months previously.

It had been something of a come-down to be transferred to KG 40 based at Trondheim, a unit specializing in shipping and weather reconnaissance, although the JU 88S they had given him to fly was certainly a superb plane – an all-weather machine capable of a top speed of around four hundred miles per hour.

His mission that morning had one purpose. To look for signs of a convoy expected to leave Liverpool for Russia that week, although the exact day of departure was unknown. He had crossed Scotland at thirty thousand feet to spend a totally abortive couple of hours west of the Outer Hebrides.

The sighting of the gunboat had been purest chance, following an impulse to go down to see just how low the cloud base was. The target, once seen, was too tempting to pass up.

As he climbed steeply after the second attack Rudi Hubner, the navigator, laughed excitedly. 'I think we got her, Herr Hauptmann. Lots of smoke back there.'

'What do you think, Kranz?' Necker called to the rear gunner.

'Looks like they made it themselves to me, Herr Hauptmann,' Kranz replied. 'Somebody down there knows his business and they weren't *Tommis* either. I saw the Stars and Stripes as we crossed over the second time. Probably my brother Ernst,' he added gloomily. 'He's in the American navy. Did I ever tell you that?'

Schmidt, the wireless operator, laughed. 'The first time over London with the port engines on fire, and you've mentioned it on at least fifty-seven different occasions since. I suppose it shows that at least one person in your family has brains.'

Hubner ignored him. 'A probable then, Herr Hauptmann?' he suggested.

Necker was going to say no, then saw the hope in the boy's eyes and changed his mind. 'I don't see why not. Now let's get out of here.'

III

When Jago went up to the bridge there was no sign of Jansen. He leaned against the Browning and looked down. The smoke had almost cleared and Gould was kicking the burned-out flare under the rail into the sea. The deck was a mess by the port rail beside the anti-aircraft gun, but otherwise things didn't look too bad.

Jansen came up the ladder behind him. He was a tall, heavily-built man and in spite of the tangled black beard, the knitted cap and faded reefer coat with no rank badges, was a chief petty officer. A lecturer in Moral Philosophy at Harvard before the war and a fanatical weekend yachtsman, he had resolutely defeated every attempt to elevate him to commissioned rank.

'A lone wolf, lieutenant.'

'You can say that again,' Jago told him. 'A JU 88 in the Hebrides.'

'And one of the Reichsmarschall's later models, to judge by his turn of speed.'

'But what in the hell was he doing here?'

'I know, lieutenant,' Jansen said soothingly. 'It's getting so you can't depend on anyone these days. I've already checked below, by the way. Superficial damage. No casualties.'

'Thanks,' Jago said. 'And that smoke flare was quick thinking.'

He found that his right hand was trembling slightly and held it out. 'Would you look at that. Wasn't it yesterday I was complaining that the only thing we got to fight up here was the weather?'

'Well, you know what Heidegger had to say on that subject, lieutenant.'

'No, I don't Jansen, but I'm sure you're going to tell me.'

'He argued that for authentic living what is necessary is the resolute confrontation of death.'

Jago said patiently, 'Which is exactly what I've been doing for two years now and you've usually been about a yard behind me. In the circumstances, I'll tell you what you can do with Heidegger, Jansen. You can put him where grandma had the pain. And try to rustle up some coffee while I check over the course again.'

'As the lieutenant pleases.'

Jago went into the wheelhouse and slumped into the chart-table chair. Petersen had the wheel – a seaman with ten years in the merchant service before the war, including two voyages to Antarctica in whalers.

'You okay?' Jago demanded.

'Fine, lieutenant.'

Jago pulled out British Admiralty chart 1796, *Barra Head to Skye*. South Uist, Barra and a scattering of islands below it, with Fhada, their destination, at the southern end of the chain. The door was kicked open and Jansen came in with a mug of coffee which he put on the table.

'What a bloody place,' Jago said, tapping the chart. 'Magnetic anomalies reported throughout the entire area.'

'Well, that's helpful,' Jansen said. 'Just the thing when you're working out a course in dirty weather.'

'Those islands south of Uist are a graveyard,' Jago went on. 'Everywhere you look on the damned chart it says "Heavy Breakers or Dangerous Seas." One hazard after another.'

Jansen unfolded a yellow oilskin tobacco pouch, produced a pipe and started to fill it, leaning against the door. 'I was talking to some fishermen in Mallaig before we left. They were telling me that sometimes the weather out there is so bad, Fhada's cut off for weeks at a time.'

'The worst weather in the world when those Atlantic storms start moving in,' Jago said. 'God knows what it must be like in winter.'

'Then what in the hell is Admiral Reeve doing in a place like that?'

'Search me. I didn't even know he was up here till I was told to pick up that despatch for him in Mallaig and deliver it. Last I heard of him was D-Day. He was deputy director of operations for Naval Intelligence and got himself a free trip on the Norwegian destroyer *Svenner* that was sunk by three Möwe-class torpedo boats. He lost his right eye and they tell me his left arm's only good for show.'

'A hell of a man,' Jansen said. 'He got out of Corregidor after MacArthur left. Sailed a lugger nearly six hundred miles to Cagayan and came out on one of the last planes. As I remember, he went down in a destroyer at Midway, was taken aboard the *Yorktown* and ended up in the water again.'

'Careful, Jansen. Your enthusiasm is showing and I didn't think that was possible where top brass was concerned.'

'But this isn't just another admiral we're talking about, lieutenant. He's responsible for an excellent history of naval warfare and probably the best biography of John Paul Jones in print. Good God, sir, the man can actually read and write,' Jansen put a match to the bowl of his pipe and added out of the side of his mouth, 'Quite an accomplishment for any naval officer, as the lieutenant will be the first to agree?'

'Jansen', Jago said. 'Get the hell out of here.'

Jansen withdrew and Jago swung round to find Petersen grinning hugely. 'Go on, you too! I'll take over.'

'Sure thing, lieutenant.'

Petersen went out and Jago reached for another cigarette. His fingers had stopped trembling. Rain spattered against the window as the MGB lifted over another wave and it came to him, with a kind of wonder, that he was actually enjoying himself, in spite of the aching back, the constant fatigue that must be taking years off his life.

Harry Jago was twenty-two and looked ten years older, even on a good day, which was hardly surprising when one considered his war record.

He'd dropped out of Yale in March 1941 to join the navy and was assigned to PT boats, joining Squadron Two in time for the Solomons' campaign. The battle for Guadalcanal lasted six months. Jago went in at one end a crisp, clean nineteen-year-old ensign and emerged a lieutenant, junior grade, with a Navy Cross and two boats shot from under him.

Afterwards Squadron Two was recommissioned and sent to England at the urgent request of the Office of Strategic Services to land and pick up American agents on the French coast. Again Jago survived, this time the Channel, the constant head-on clashes with German E-boats out of Cherbourg. He even survived the hell of Omaha beach on D-Day.

His luck finally ran out on 28 June, when E-boats attacked a convoy of American landing craft waiting in Lyme Bay to cross the Channel. Jago arrived with despatches from Portsmouth to find himself facing six of the best that the Kriegsmarine could supply. In a memorable ten-minute engagement, he sank one, damaged another, lost five of his crew and ended up in the water with shrapnel in his left thigh, the right cheek laid open to the bone.

When he finally came out of hospital in August they gave him what was left of his old crew, nine of them, and a new job: the rest that he so badly needed, playing postman in the Hebrides to the various American and British weather stations and similar establishments in the islands in a pre-war MGB, courtesy of the Royal Navy, that started to shake herself to pieces if he attempted to take her above twenty knots. Some previous owner had painted the legend *Dead End* underneath the bridge rail, a sentiment capable of several interpretations.

'Just for a month or two,' the squadron commander had told Jago. 'Look on it as a kind of holiday. I mean to say, nothing ever happens up there, Harry.'

Jago grinned in spite of himself and, as a rain squall hurled itself against the window, increased speed, the wheel kicking in his hands. The sea was his life now. Meat and drink to him, more important than any woman. It was the circumstance of war which had given him this, but the war wouldn't last forever.

He said softly, 'What in the hell am I going to do when it's all over?'

IV

There were times when Rear Admiral Carey Reeve definitely wondered what life was all about. Times when the vacuum of his days seemed unbearable and the island that he loved with such a deep and unswerving passion, a prison.

On such occasions he usually made for the same spot, a hill called in the Gaelic Dun Bhuide, the Yellow Fort, above Telegraph Bay on the south-west tip of Fhada, and so named because of an abortive attempt to set up a Marconi station at the turn of the century. The bay lay at the bottom of four-hundred-foot cliffs, a strip of white sand slipping into grey water with Labrador almost three thousand miles away to the west and nothing in between.

The path below was no place for the fainthearted, zig-zagging across the face of the granite cliffs, splashed with lime, seabirds crying, wheeling in great clouds, razorbills, shags, gulls, shearwaters and gannets – gannets everywhere. He considered it all morosely for a while through his one good eye, then turned to survey the rest of the island.

The ground sloped steeply to the south-west. On the other

side of the point from Telegraph were South Inlet and the lifeboat station, the boathouse, its slipway and Murdoch Macleod's cottage, nothing more. On his left was the rest of the island. A scattering of crofts, mostly ruined, peat bog, sheep grazing the sparse turf, the whole crossed by the twin lines of the narrow-gauge railway track running north-west to Mary's Town.

Reeve took an old brass telescope from his pocket and focused it on the lifeboat station. No sign of life. Murdoch would probably be working on that damned boat of his, but the kettle would be gently steaming on the hob above the peat fire and a mug of hot tea generously laced with illegal whisky of Murdoch's own distilling would not come amiss on such a morning.

The admiral replaced the telescope in his pocket and started down the slope as rain drove across the island in a grey curtain.

V

There was no sign of Murdoch when he went into the boathouse by the small rear door. The forty-one-foot Watson-type motor lifeboat, *Morag Sinclair*, waited in her carriage at the head of the slipway. She was trim and beautiful in her blue and white paint, showing every sign of the care Murdoch lavished on her. Reeve ran a hand along her counter with a conscious pleasure.

Behind him the door swung open in a flurry of rain and a soft Highland voice said, 'I was in the outhouse, stacking peat.'

Reeve turned to find Murdoch standing in the doorway and in the same moment an enormous Irish wolfhound squeezed past him and bore down on the admiral.

His hand fastened on the beast's ginger ruff. 'Rory, you old devil. I might have known.' He glanced up at Murdoch. 'Mrs Sinclair's been looking for him this morning. Went missing last night.'

'I intended bringing him in myself later,' Murdoch said. 'Are you in health, admiral?'

He was himself seventy years old, of immense stature,

dressed in thigh boots and guernsey sweater, his eyes grey water over stone, his face seamed and shaped by a lifetime of the sea.

'Murdoch,' Admiral Reeve said. 'Has it ever occurred to you that life is a tale told by an idiot, full of sound and fury and signifying precisely nothing?'

'So it's that kind of a morning?' Murdoch wiped peat from his hands on to his thighs and produced his tobacco pouch. 'Will you take tea with me, admiral?' he enquired with grave Highland courtesy.

'And a little something extra?' Reeve suggested hopefully.

'*Uisgebeatha?*' Murdoch said in Gaelic. 'The water of life. Why not indeed, for it is life you need this morning, I am thinking.' He smiled gravely. 'I'll be ten minutes. Time for you to take a turn along the shore with the hound to blow the cobwebs away.'

VI

The mouth of the inlet was a maelstrom of white water, waves smashing in across the reef beyond with a thunderous roaring, hurling spray a hundred feet into the air.

Reeve trudged along in the wolfhound's wake at the water's edge, thinking about Murdoch Macleod. Thirty-two years coxswain of the Fhada lifeboat, legend in his own time – during which he had been awarded the BEM by old King George and five silver and two gold medals for gallantry in sea rescue by the Lifeboat Institution. He had retired in 1938, when his son Donald had taken over as coxswain in his place, and had returned a year later when Donald was called to active service with the Royal Naval Reserve. A remarkable man by any standards.

The wolfhound was barking furiously. Reeve looked up across the great bank of sand that was known as Traig Mhoire – Mary's Strand. A man in a yellow lifejacket lay face-down on the shore twenty yards away, water slopping over him as one wave crashed in after another.

The admiral ran forward, dropped to one knee and turned him over, with some difficulty for his left arm was virtually useless now. He was quite dead, a boy of eighteen or nineteen, in denim overalls, eyes closed as if in sleep, fair hair plastered to his skull, not a mark on him.

Reeve started to search the body. There was a leather wallet in the left breast pocket. As he opened it, Murdoch arrived on the run, dropping on his knees beside him.

'Came to see what was keeping you.' He touched the pale face with the back of his hand.

'How long?' Reeve asked.

'Ten or twelve hours, no more. Who was he?'

'Off a German U-boat from the look of those overalls.' Reeve opened the wallet and examined the contents. There was a photo of a young girl, a couple of letters and a leave pass so soaked in sea water that it started to fall to pieces as he opened it gingerly.

'A wee lad, that's all,' Murdoch said. 'Couldn't they do better than schoolboys?'

'Probably as short of men by now as the rest of us,' Reeve told him. 'His name was Hans Bleichrodt and he celebrated his eighteenth birthday while on leave in Brunswick three weeks ago. He was Funkgefreiter, telegraphist to you, on U-743.' He replaced the papers in the wallet. 'If she bought it this morning, we might get more like this coming in for the rest of the week.'

'You could be right,' Murdoch crouched down and, with an easy strength that never ceased to amaze Reeve, hoisted the body over one shoulder. 'Better get him into Mary's Town then, admiral.'

Reeve nodded. 'Yes, my house will do. Mrs Sinclair can see him this afternoon and sign the death certificate. We'll bury him tomorrow.'

'I am thinking that the kirk might be more fitting.'

'I'm not certain that's such a good idea,' Reeve said. 'There are eleven men from this island dead at sea owing to enemy action during this war. I would have thought their families might not be too happy to see a German lying in state in their own place of worship.'

The old man's eyes were fierce. 'And you would agree with them?'

'Oh no,' Reeve said hurriedly. 'Don't draw me into this.

You put the boy where you like. I don't think it will bother him too much.'

'But it might well bother God,' Murdoch said gently. There was no reproof in his voice, in spite of the fact that, as a certificated lay preacher of the Church of Scotland, he was the nearest thing to a minister on the island.

There was no road from that end of Fhada, had never been any need for one, but during the two abortive years that the Marconi station had existed, the telegraph company had laid the narrow-gauge railway line. The lifeboat crew, mostly fishermen from Mary's Town, travelled on it by trolley when called out in an emergency, pumping it by hand or hoisting a sail when the wind was favourable.

Which it was that morning, and Murdoch and the admiral coasted along at a brisk five knots, the triangular strip of canvas billowing out to one side. The dead boy lay in the centre of the trolley and Rory squatted beside him.

Two miles, then three, and the track started to slope down and the wind tore a hole in the curtain of rain, revealing Mary's Town, a couple of miles further on in the north-west corner of the island, a scattering of granite houses, four or five streets sloping to the harbour. There were half-a-dozen fishing boats anchored in the lee of the breakwater.

Murdoch was standing, one hand on the mast, staring out to sea. 'Would you look at that now, admiral? There's some sort of craft coming in towards the harbour out there and I could have sworn that was the Stars and Stripes she's flying. I must be getting old.'

Reeve had the telescope out of his pocket and focused in an instant. 'You're damned right it is,' he said as the *Dead End* jumped into view, Harry Jago on the bridge.

His hand was shaking with excitement as he pushed the telescope back into his pocket. 'You know something, Murdoch? This might just turn out to be my day after all.'

VII

When the MGB eased into the landing-stage a woman was sitting on the upper jetty under an umbrella, painting at an easel. She was in her early forties, with calm blue eyes in a strong and pleasant face. She wore a headscarf, an old naval officer's coat, which carried the bars of a full captain on the epaulettes, and slacks.

She stood up, moved to the edge of the jetty, holding the umbrella, and smiled down. 'Hello there, America. That makes a change.'

Jago went over the rail and up the steps to the jetty quickly. 'Harry Jago, ma'am.'

'Jean Sinclair.' She held out her hand. 'I'm bailie here, lieutenant, so if there's anything I can do . . .'

'Bailie?' Jago said blankly.

'What you'd call a magistrate.'

Jago grinned. 'I see. You mean you're the law around here.'

'And coroner and harbourmaster. This is a small island. We have to do the best we can.'

'I'm here with despatches for Rear Admiral Reeve, ma'am. Have you any idea where I might locate him?'

She smiled. 'We have a saying in these islands, lieutenant. Speak of the devil and you'll find he's right behind you.'

Jago turned quickly and got a shock. When he'd received his Navy Cross from Nimitz at Pearl, Admiral Reeve had been one of those on the platform, resplendent in full uniform with three rows of medal ribbons. There was no echo of him at all in the small, dark man with the black eye patch who hurried towards him now wearing an old reefer coat and sea boots. It was only when he spoke that Jago knew beyond a doubt who he was.

'You looking for me, lieutenant?'

'Admiral Reeve?' Jago got his heels together and saluted. 'I've got a despatch for you, sir. Handed to me by the Royal Naval officer in command at Mallaig. If you'd care to come aboard.'

'Lead me to it, lieutenant,' the admiral said eagerly, then paused and turned to Jean Sinclair. 'I found Rory. He was with Murdoch at the lifeboat station.'

Her eyes were lively now and there was a slight amused smile on her mouth. 'Why, Carey, I thought you were going to ignore me altogether.'

He said gravely, 'I found something else down there on

Traig Mhoire. A body on the beach. A German boy off a U-boat.'

Her smile died. 'Where is he now?'

'I left him at the church with Murdoch.'

'I'd better get up there then. I'll pick up a couple of women on the way. See the lad's decently laid out.'

'I'll be along myself later.'

She walked away quickly, her umbrella tilted to take the force of the rain. 'Quite a lady,' Jago remarked.

The admiral nodded. 'And then some. As a matter of interest, she owns the whole damned island. Left it by her father. He was a kind of feudal laird round here.'

'What about that naval greatcoat, sir?' Jago asked, as they descended the ladder.

'Her husband's. Went down in the *Prince of Wales* back in '41. He was a Sinclair, too, like her. A second cousin, I believe.' He laughed. 'It's an old island custom to keep the name in the family.'

The crew were assembled on deck and as the admiral went over the rail, Jansen piped him on board. Reeve looked them over in amazement and said to Jago, 'Where did this lot spring from? A banana boat?'

'Chief Petty Officer Jansen, sir,' Jago said weakly.

Reeve examined Jansen, taking in the reefer, the tangled beard and knitted cap. He turned away with a shudder. 'I've seen enough. Just take me to my despatch, will you?'

'If you follow me, admiral.'

Jago led the way down the companionway to his cabin. He took a briefcase from under the mattress on his bunk, unlocked it and produced a buff envelope, seals still intact, which he passed across. As Reeve took it from him, there was a knock at the door and Jansen entered with a tray.

'Coffee, gentlemen?'

Reeve curbed the impulse to tear the envelope open and said to Jago as he accepted a cup, 'How's the war going, then?'

It was Jansen who answered. 'The undertakers are doing well, admiral.'

Reeve turned to stare at him in a kind of fascination. 'You did say Chief Petty Officer?'

'The best, sir,' Jago said gamely.

'And where, may I ask, did you find him?'

'Harvard, sir,' Jansen said politely, and withdrew.

Reeve said in wonderment, 'He's joking, isn't he?'

'I'm afraid not, admiral.'

'No wonder the war wasn't over by Christmas.'

Reeve sat on the edge of the bunk, tore open the package and took out two envelopes. He opened the smaller first. There was a photo inside and a letter which he read quickly, a smile on his face. He passed the photo to Jago.

'My niece, Janet. She's a doctor at Guy's Hospital in London. Been there since 1940. Worked right through the blitz.'

She had grave, steady eyes, high cheekbones, a mouth that was too wide. There was something in her expression that got through to Jago.

He handed the photo back reluctantly. 'Very nice, sir.'

'You could say that and it would be the understatement of the year.'

Reeve opened the second envelope and started to read the letter it contained eagerly. Gradually thc smile died on his face, his eyes grew dark, his mouth tightened. He folded the letter and slipped it into his pocket.

'Bad news, sir?'

'Now that, son, depends entirely on your point of view. The powers-that-be are of the opinion that the war can get on without me. That, to use a favourite phrase of our British allies, I've done my bit.'

Jago opened a cupboard behind him and took out a bottle of Scotch and a glass which he held out to the admiral. 'Most people I know wouldn't find much to quarrel with in that sentiment, sir.'

He poured a generous measure of whisky into the glass. Reeve said, 'Something else that's strictly against regulations, lieutenant.' He frowned. 'What is your name, anyway?'

'Jago, sir. Harry Jago.'

Reeve swallowed some of the whisky. 'What kind of deal are you on here? This old tub looks as if it might be left over from the Crimea.'

'Not quite, sir. Courtesy of the Royal Navy. We're only

playing postman, you see. I suppose they didn't think the job was worth much more.'

'What were you doing before?'

'PT boats, sir. Squadron Two, working the Channel.'

'Jago?' Reeve said and his face brightened. 'You lost an Elco in Lyme Bay.'

'I suppose you could put it that way, sir.'

Reeve smiled and held out his hand. 'Nice to meet you, son. And those boys up top? They're your original crew?'

'What's left of them.'

'Well, now I'm here, you might as well show me over this pig boat.'

Which Jago did from stem to stern. They ended up in the wheelhouse, where they found Jansen at the chart table.

'And what might you be about?' Reeve demanded.

'Our next stop is a weather station on the south-west corner of Harris, admiral. I was just plotting our course.'

'Show me.' Jansen ran a finger out through the Sound into the Atlantic and Reeve said, 'Watch it out there, especially if visibility is reduced in the slightest. Here, three miles to the north-west.' He tapped the chart. 'Washington Reef. Doesn't it make you feel at home, the sound of that name?'

'And presumably it shouldn't?' Jago asked.

'A death trap. The greatest single hazard to shipping on the entire west coast of Scotland. Two galleons from the Spanish Armada went to hell together on those rocks four hundred years ago and they've been tearing ships apart ever since. One of the main reasons there's a lifeboat here on Fhada.'

'Maybe we'd be better taking the other route north through the Little Minch, sir.'

Reeve smiled. 'I know – it's a hell of a war, lieutenant, but it's the only one we've got.'

Jansen said solemnly, 'As long as war is regarded as wicked it will always have its fascination. When looked upon as vulgar, it will cease to be popular. Oscar Wilde said that, sir,' he said helpfully.

'Dear God, restore me to sanity.' Reeve shook his head and turned to Jago. 'Let me get off this hooker before I go over the edge entirely.'

'Just one thing, sir. Do you know a Mr Murdoch Macleod?'

'He's coxswain of the lifeboat here and a good friend of mine. Why do you ask?'

Jago unbuttoned his shirt pocket and took out an orange envelope. 'The Royal Naval officer in command at Mallaig asked me to deliver this telegram to him, sir, there being no telephone or telegraph service to the island at the moment, I understand.'

'That's right,' Reeve said. 'The cable parted in a storm last month and they haven't got around to doing anything about it yet In fact at the moment, the island's only link with the outside world is my personal radio.'

He held out his hand for the envelope which he saw was open. 'It's from the Admiralty, sir.'

'Bad news?'

'He has a son, sir. Lieutenant Donald Macleod.'

'That's right. Commanding an armed trawler doing escort duty on east-coast convoys in the North Sea. Newcastle to London.'

'Torpedoed off the Humber yesterday, with all hands.'

Reeve's voice dropped to a whisper. 'No one was saved at all? You're certain of that?'

'I'm afraid not, admiral.'

Reeve seemed to age before his eyes. 'One thing they obviously didn't tell you, lieutenant, was that, although Donald Macleod was master of that trawler, there were four other men from Fhada in the crew.' He passed the envelope back to Jago. 'I think the sooner we get this over with, the better.'

VIII

The church of St Mungo was a tiny, weatherbeaten building with a squat tower, constructed of blocks of heavy granite on a hillside above the town.

Reeve, Jago and Frank Jansen went in through the lychgate and followed a path through a churchyard scattered with gravestones to the porch at the west end. Reeve opened the massive oaken door and led the way in.

The dead boy lay on a trestle table in a tiny side chapel to one side of the altar. Two middle-aged women were arranging the body while Murdoch and Jean Sinclair stood close by, talking in subdued tones. They turned and looked down the aisle as the door opened. The three men moved towards them, caps in hand. They paused, then Reeve held the orange envelope out to Jean Sinclair.

'I think you'd better read this.'

She took it from him, extracted the telegram. Her face turned ashen, she was wordless. In a moment of insight, Reeve realized that she was re-living her own tragedy. She turned to Murdoch, but the admiral stepped in quickly, holding her back.

Murdoch said calmly, 'It is bad news you have for me there, I am thinking, Carey Reeve.'

'Donald's ship was torpedoed off the Humber yesterday,' Reeve said. 'Went down with all hands.'

A tremor seemed to pass through the old man's entire frame. He staggered momentarily, then took a deep breath and straightened. 'The Lord disposes.'

The two women working on the body stopped to stare at him, faces frozen in horror. Between them, as Reeve well knew, they had just lost a husband and brother. Murdoch moved past and stood looking down at the German boy, pale in death, the face somehow very peaceful now.

He reached down and took one of the cold hands in his. 'Poor lad,' he said. 'Poor wee lad!' His shoulders shook and he started to weep softly.

— 3 —

Barquentine *Deutschland,* 12 September 1944. Lat. 26°.11N., long. 30°.26W. Wind NW 2–3. Overcast. Poor visibility. A bad squall last night during the middle watch and the flying-jib split.

SOME FIVE hundred miles south of the Azores, Erich Berger sat at the desk in his cabin entering his personal journal.

. . . Our general progress has, of course, been far better than I could ever have hoped and yet our passengers find the experience tedious in the extreme. For most of the time, bad weather keeps them below; the skylight leaks and the saloon is constantly damp.

The loss of the chickens and two goats kept for milk, all swept overboard in a bad squall three days out of Belém, has had an unfortunate effect on our diet, although here again, it has been most noticeable in the nuns. Frau Prager is still my main worry and her condition, as far as I may judge, continues to deteriorate.

As for the prospect of a meeting with an enemy ship, we are as ready in that respect as can reasonably be expected. The *Deutschland* is now the *Gudrid Andersen* to the last detail, including the library of Swedish books in my cabin. The plan of campaign, if boarded at any time, is simple. The additional men carried beyond normal crew requirements will secrete themselves in the bilges. A simple device admittedly, and one easily discovered by any kind of a thorough search, but we have little choice in the matter.

The *Deutschland* stands up well so far to all the Atlantic can offer, although there is not a day passes that shrouds do not part or sails split and, this morning, Herr

> Herr Sturm reported twelve inches of water in the bilges. But, as yet, there is no cause for alarm. We all get old and the *Deutschland* is older than most . . .

The whole ship lurched drunkenly and Berger was thrown from his chair as the cabin tilted. He scrambled to his feet, got the door open and ran out on deck.

The *Deutschland* was plunging forward through heavy seas, the deck awash with spray. Leutnant Sturm and Leading Seaman Kluth had the wheel between them and it was taking all their strength to hold it.

High above the deck, the main gaff topsail fluttered free in the wind. The noise was tremendous and could be heard even above the roaring of the wind, and the topmast was whipping backwards and forwards. A matter of moments only before it snapped. But already Richter was at the rail, the sea washing over him as he pulled on the downhaul to collapse the sail.

Berger ran to join him, losing his footing and rolling into the scuppers as another great sea floated in across the deck, but somehow he was on his feet and lending his weight to the downhaul with Richter.

The sail came down, the *Deutschland* righted herself perceptibly, the continual drumming ceased. Richter shouted, 'I'd better get up there and see to a new outhaul.'

Berger cried above the wind, 'You wouldn't last five minutes out there on that gaff in this weather. It'll have to wait till the wind eases.'

'But that sail will tear herself to pieces, sir.'

'A gasket should hold her for the time being. I'll see to it.'

Berger sprang into the ratlines and started to climb, aware of the wind tearing at his body like some living thing. When he paused, fifty feet up and glanced down, Richter was right behind him

II

There was a foot of water in the saloon, a sea having smashed the skylight and flooded in. Sister Angela went from cabin to cabin, doing her best to calm her alarmed companions.

When she went into the Pragers', she found the old man

on his knees at his wife's bunk. Frau Prager was deathly pale, eyes closed, little sign of life there at all.

'What is it?' Otto Prager demanded in alarm.

She ignored him for the moment and took his wife's pulse. It was still there, however irregular.

Prager tugged at her sleeve. 'What happened?'

'I'll find out,' she said calmly. 'You stay with your wife.'

She went out on deck to find the *Deutschland* racing north, every fore and aft sail drawing well, yards braced as she plunged into the waves. Sturm and Kluth were still at the wheel. The young lieutenant called to her, but his words were snatched away by the wind.

She made it to the mizzen shrouds on the port side, the wind tearing at her black habit, and looked up at the ballooning sails. The sky was a uniform grey, the whole world alive with the sound of the ship, a thousand creaks and groans. And then, a hundred feet up, she saw Berger and Richter swaying backwards and forwards on the end of the gaff as they secured the sail.

It was perhaps the most incredible thing she had ever seen in her life and she was seized by a tremendous feeling of exhilaration. A sea slopped in over the rail in a green curtain that bowled her over, sending her skidding across the deck on her hands and knees.

She crouched against the bulwark and, as she tried to get up, Berger dropped out of the shrouds beside her and got a hand under her arm.

'Bloody fool!' he shouted. 'Why can't you stay below?'

He ran her across the deck and into his cabin before she had a chance to reply. Sister Angela collapsed into the chair behind the desk and Berger got the door shut and leaned against it. 'What in the hell am I going to do with you?'

'I'm sorry,' she said. 'There was panic down below. I simply wanted to know what had happened.'

He picked up a towel from his bunk and tossed it across to her. 'A line parted, a sail broke free. It could have snapped the topmast like a matchstick, only Richter was too quick for it.' He opened a cupboard and reached for the bottle. 'A drink, sister? Purely medicinal, of course. Rum is all I can offer, I'm afraid.'

'I don't think so.' Berger poured himself a large one and she wiped her face and regarded him curiously. 'It was incredible what you were doing out there. You and Herr Richter, so high up and in such weather.'

'Not really,' he said indifferently. 'Not to anyone who's reefed main t'gallants on a fully-rigged clipper in a Cape Horn storm.'

She nodded slowly. 'Tell me, do you still think we're bad luck? A positive guarantee of contrary winds, wasn't that what you said at our first meeting? And yet we've made good progress, wouldn't you agree?'

'Oh, we're making time all right,' Berger admitted. 'Although she shakes herself to pieces around us just a little bit more each day.'

'You speak of her, the *Deutschland*, as if she is a living thing. As if she has an existence of her own.'

'I wouldn't quarrel with that. Although I suppose your Church would. A ship doesn't have one voice, she has many. You can hear them calling to each other out there, especially at night.'

'The wind in the rigging?' There was something close to mockery in her voice.

'There are other possibilities. Old timers will tell you that the ghost of anyone killed falling from the rigging remains with the ship.'

'And you believe that?'

'Obligatory in the Kriegsmarine.' There was an ironic smile on his face now. 'Imagine the shades who infest this old girl. Next time something brushes past you in the dark on the companionway, you'll know what it is. One Our Father and two Hail Marys should keep you safe.'

Her cheeks flushed but before she could reply, the door was flung open and Sister Else appeared, 'Please, sister, come quickly. Frau Prager seems to be worse.'

Sister Angela jumped to her feet and moved out. Berger closed the door behind her, then picked up the towel she dropped and wiped his face. Strange how she seemed to bring out the worst in him. A constant source of irritation, but then perhaps it was simply that they'd all been together for too long in such a confined space. And yet . . .

III

For most of the afternoon, HMS *Guardian*, a T-class submarine of the British Home Fleet, en route to Trinidad for special orders, had proceeded submerged, but at 1600 hours she surfaced.

It was the throb of the diesels that brought her captain, Lieutenant-Commander George Harvey, awake. He lay there for a moment on the bunk, staring up at the steel bulkhead, aware of the taste in his mouth, the smell of submarine, and then the green curtain was pulled aside and Petty Officer Swallow came in with tea in a chipped enamel mug.

'Just surfaced, sir.'

The tea was foul, but at least there was real sugar in it, which was something.

'What's it like up there?'

'Overcast. Wind north-west. Two to three. Visibility poor, sir. Slight sea mist and drizzling.'

'Succinct as always, coxswain,' Harvey told him.

'Beg pardon, sir?'

'Never mind. Just tell Mr Edge I'll join him on the bridge in five minutes.'

'Sir.'

Swallow withdrew and Harvey swung his legs to the floor and sat there, yawning. Then he moved to the small desk bolted to the bulkhead, opened the *Guardian*'s war diary and in cold, precise naval language, started to insert the daily entry.

IV

There were three men on the bridge. Sub-Lieutenant Edge, officer of the watch, a signalman and an able seaman for lookout. The sea was surprisingly calm and there was none of the usual cork-screwing or pitching that a submarine frequently experiences when travelling on the surface in any kind of rough weather.

Edge was thoroughly enjoying himself. The rain in his face

was quite refreshing and the salt air felt sweet and clean in his lungs after the hours spent below.

Swallow came up the ladder, a mug of tea in one hand. 'Thought you might like a wet, sir. Captain's compliments and he'll join you on the bridge in five minutes.'

'Good show,' Edge said cheerfully. 'Not that there's anything to report.'

Swallow started to reply and then his eyes widened and an expression of incredulity appeared on his face. 'Good God Almighty!' he said. 'I don't believe it.'

In the same instant, the lookout cried out, pointing, and Edge turned to see a three-masted barquentine, all sails set, emerge from a fog bank a quarter of a mile to port.

V

On board the *Deutschland* there was no panic, for the plan to be followed in such an eventuality had been gone over so many times that everyone knew exactly what to do.

Berger was on the quarterdeck, Sturm and Richter beside him at the rail. The bosun was holding a signalling lamp. The captain spoke without lowering his glasses. 'A British submarine. T-class.'

'Is this it, sir?' Sturm asked. 'Are we finished?'

'Perhaps.'

The *Guardian*'s crew poured out of her conning-tower and manned their positions. For a moment there was considerable activity, then a signal lamp flashed.

'Heave to or I fire,' Richter said.

'Plain enough. Reply: As a neutral ship I comply under protest.'

The shutter on the signal lamp in the bosun's hands clattered. A moment later, the reply came. 'I intend to board you. Stand by.'

Berger lowered his glasses. 'Very well, gentlemen. Action stations, if you please. Take in all sail, Herr Sturm. You, Richter, will see the rest of the crew into the bilges and I will attend to the passengers.'

There was a flurry of activity as Sturm turned to bark

orders to the watch on deck. Richter went down the quarter-deck ladder quickly. Berger followed him, descending the companionway.

When he entered the saloon, four of the nuns were seated round the table listening to a bible-reading from Sister Lotte.

'Where is Sister Angela?' Berger demanded.

Sister Lotte paused. 'With Frau Prager.'

The door of the consul's cabin opened and Prager emerged. He seemed haggard and drawn and had lost weight since that first night in Belém so that his tropical linen suit seemed a size too large.

'How are things?' Berger asked.

'Bad,' Prager said. 'She gets weaker by the hour.'

'I'm sorry.' Berger addressed his next remark to all of them. 'There's a British submarine on the surface about a quarter of a mile off our port beam and moving in. They intend to board.'

Sister Käthe crossed herself quickly and Sister Angela came out of the Pragers' cabin clutching an enamel bucket, her white apron soiled.

When Berger next spoke, it was to no one but her. 'You heard?'

'Yes.'

'We had a bad night of it, sister – a hell of a night. You understand me?'

'Perfectly, captain.' Her face was pale, but the eyes sparkled. 'We won't let you down.'

Berger picked up a broom that leaned against the bulkhead, reached up and jabbed at the skylight again and again, glass showering across the table so that the nuns scattered with cries of alarm.

He tossed the broom into a corner. 'See that you don't,' he said and went back up the companionway.

There was total silence, the nuns staring at Sister Angela expectantly. With a violent gesture she raised the bucket in her hands and emptied the contents across the floor. There was the immediate all-pervading stench of vomit and Sister Brigitte turned away, stomach heaving.

'Excellent,' Sister Angela said. 'Now you, Lotte, go to the lavatory and fetch a bucket of slops. I want conditions down here to be so revolting those *Tommis* will be back up that companionway in two minutes flat.'

She had changed completely, the voice clipped, incisive, totally in command. 'As for the rest of you, complete disorder in the cabins. Soak your bedding in seawater.'

Prager tugged at her sleeve. 'What about me, sister? What shall I do?'

'Kneel, Herr Prager,' she said. 'At your wife's bedside – and pray.'

VI

As the *Guardian* moved in, Harvey observed the activity on the deck of the *Deutschland* closely through his glasses.

Edge came up the ladder behind him. 'I've checked Lloyd's Register, sir. It seems to be her all right. *Gudrid Andersen*, three-masted barquentine, registered Gothenburg.'

'But what in the hell is she doing here?'

Harvey frowned, trying to work out the best way of handling the situation. His first officer, Gregson, lay in his bunk with a fractured left ankle. In such circumstances to leave the *Guardian* himself, however temporarily, was unthinkable. Which left Edge, a nineteen-year-old boy on his first operational patrol – hardly an ideal choice.

On the other hand, there was Swallow. His eyes met the chief petty officer's briefly. Not a word spoken and yet he knew that the coxswain read his thoughts perfectly.

'Tell me, coxswain, does anyone on board speak Swedish?'

'Not to my knowledge, sir.'

'We must hope they run to enough English over there to get us by, then. Lieutenant Edge will lead the boarding party. Pick him two good men – side arms only. And I think you might as well go along for the ride.'

'Sir.'

Swallow turned and at his shouted command, the forward hatch was opened and a rubber dinghy broken out. Edge went below and reappeared a few moments later buckling a webbing belt around his waist from which hung a holstered Webley revolver. He was excited and showed it.

'Think you can handle it?' Harvey asked.

'I believe so, sir.'

'Good. A thorough inspection of ship's papers and identity documents of everyone on board.'

'Am I looking for anything special sir?'

'Hardly,' Harvey said drily. 'The Germans last used a sailing ship as a surface raider in 1917, if I remember my naval history correctly, and times have changed. No, we're entitled to check her credentials and I'm consumed with curiosity as to the nature of her business, so off you go.'

VII

Sturm waited at the rail as the dinghy coasted in. Edge went up the Jacob's ladder first, followed by one of the ratings and Swallow, who carried a Thompson gun. The other rating stayed with the dinghy. Of Berger, there was no sign.

Sturm, who spoke excellent English, pointed to the ensign which fluttered at the masthead. 'I must protest, sir. As you can see, this is a Swedish vessel.'

'Ah, good, you speak English,' Edge said with a certain relief. 'Lieutenant Philip Edge of His Britannic Majesty's submarine *Guardian*. Are you the master of this vessel?'

'No, my name is Larsen. First mate. Captain Nielsen is in his cabin getting out the ship's papers for you. I'm afraid things are in a bit of a mess. We had a bad night of it. Almost turned turtle when a squall hit us during the middle watch. It caused considerable damage.'

Edge said to Swallow, 'You handle things here, coxswain, while I have a word with the captain.'

'Shall we take a look below, sir?' Swallow suggested.

Edge turned, taking in the watchful gun crew on the *Guardian*, the Browning machine-gun which had been mounted on the rail beside Harvey.

'Yes, why not?' he said and followed Sturm towards the quarter-deck.

The young German opened the door to the captain's cabin and stood politely to one side. Edge paused on the threshold, taking in the shambles before him. A porthole was smashed, the carpet soaked, the whole place littered with books and personal belongings.

Berger stood behind the desk, face stern, the ship's log and other papers ready on the desk before him.

'I'm afraid Captain Nielsen doesn't speak English so I'll have to interpret for you.' Which was far from the truth for Berger's English, though modest, was adequate. 'The captain,' Sturm added, 'is not pleased at this forcible boarding of a neutral vessel about her lawful business.'

'I'm sorry,' Edge said, considerably intimidated by the stern expression on Berger's face, 'but I'm afraid I must insist on seeing your ship's papers and log, also your cargo manifest.'

Berger turned away as if angry. Sturm said, 'But we carry no cargo, lieutenant, only passengers.' He picked up the ship's log, soaked in sea water, its pages sticking together. 'Perhaps you would care to examine the log? You will find all other relevant papers here also.'

Edge took it from him, sat down in Berger's chair and tried to separate the first two water-soaked pages which promptly tore away in his hand. And at that precise moment, Richter and the eleven other members of the crew secreted in the bilges with him, were lying in several inches of stinking water, aware of Swallow's heavy footsteps in the hold above their heads.

VIII

Edge left the cabin fifteen minutes later, having examined as thoroughly as he could an assortment of papers and clutching the Swedish passports offered for his inspection.

Swallow emerged from the companionway, looking ill. Edge said, 'Are the passengers down there, coxswain?'

'Yes, sir.' Swallow was taking in deep breaths of salt air rapidly. 'Five nuns, sir, and an old gentleman and his wife – and she doesn't look too healthy.'

Edge advanced to the top of the companionway and Swallow said hastily, 'I wouldn't bother, sir. Not unless you feel you have to. They've obviously had a rotten time of it in last night's storm. Still cleaning up.'

Edge hesitated, turned to glance at Sturm, Berger glowering behind, then started down.

The stink was appalling, the stench of human excrement

and vomit turning his stomach. The first thing he saw in the shambles of the saloon below were four nuns on their knees amongst the filth with buckets and brushes, scrubbing the floor. Edge got a handkerchief to his mouth as Sister Angela appeared in the doorway of the Pragers' cabin.

'Can I help you?' she asked in good English.

'Sorry to trouble you, ma'am. My duty – you understand?' He held out the passports. 'International law in time of war. I'm entitled to inspect the passenger list.'

He glanced past her at Prager who knelt beside his wife. Her face was deathly pale, shining with sweat, and she was breathing incredibly slowly.

'And this lady and gentleman?' He started to sort through the passports.

'Mr Ternström and his wife. As you can see, she is very ill.'

Prager turned to look at him, the agony on his face totally genuine, and Edge took an involuntary step back. Lotte chose that exact moment to be sick, crouching there on the floor like some animal. It was enough.

Edge turned hastily, brushed past Sturm and went back up the companionway. He leaned on the starboard rail, breathing deeply, and Swallow moved beside him.

'You all right, sir?'

'God, what a pest-hole. Those women – they've been through hell.' He pulled himself together. 'You've checked the holds thoroughly, coxswain?'

'Clean as a whistle, sir. She's in ballast with sand.'

Edge turned to Sturm who stood waiting, Berger a pace or two behind. 'I don't understand.'

'For many months we work the coastal trade in Brazil,' Sturm told him. 'Then we decide to come home. As you may imagine, no one seemed anxious to risk a cargo with us.'

'And the passengers?'

'The good sisters have been stranded in Brazil for more than a year now. We are the first Swedish ship to leave Brazil during that time. They were grateful for the opportunity for any kind of passage.'

'But the old lady,' Edge said. 'Mrs Ternström. She looks in a bad way.'

'And anxious to see her family again while there is still time.' Sturm smiled bitterly. 'War makes things difficult for us neutrals when we want to travel from one place to another.'

Edge made his decision and handed the passports back. 'You'll want these. My apologies to your captain. I'll have to confirm it with my commanding officer, but I see no reason why you shouldn't be allowed to proceed.' He moved to the head of the Jacob's ladder and paused. 'Those ladies down there . . .'

'Will be fine, lieutenant. We'll soon have things shipshape again.'

'Anything else we can do for you?'

Sturm smiled. 'Bring us up to date on the war, if you would. How are things going?'

'All *our* way now, no doubt about that,' Edge said. 'Though they do seem to be slowing down rather in Europe. I don't think we're going to see Berlin by Christmas after all. The Germans are making one hell of a fight of it in the Low Countries.'

He went down the ladder quickly, followed by Swallow and the other rating, and they cast off. 'Well, coxswain?' he asked as they pulled away.

'I know one thing, sir. I'll never complain about serving in submarines again.'

IX

On the quarterdeck Berger smoked a cigar and waited, Sturm at his side.

'What do you think, Herr Kapitän?' Sturm asked. 'Has it worked?'

In the same moment, the signal lamp on the bridge of the *Guardian* started to flash.

'You may proceed.' Berger spelled out. 'Happy voyage and good luck.' He turned to Sturm, his face calm. 'My maternal grandmother was English, did I ever tell you that?'

'No, sir.'

Berger tossed his cigar over the side. 'She's all yours, Herr Sturm. Let's get under way again as soon as may be.'

'Aye, aye, sir.'

Sturm turned, raising his voice to call to the men below, and Berger descended to the deck. He stood in the entrance to the companionway, aware of the stench, of Sister Angela's pale face peering up at him.

'Did it work?' she called softly.

'Remind me, when I have the time, to tell you what a very remarkable woman you are, sister.'

'At the appropriate moment, I shall, captain. You may be certain of that,' she said serenely.

Berger turned away. The *Guardian* was already departing towards the south-west. He watched her go, and behind him Helmut Richter emerged from the forrard hatch and came aft. His body was streaked with filth, but he was smiling.

'Can the lads come on deck and wash off under the pump? They smell pretty high after those bilges.'

'So I observe.' Berger wrinkled his nose. 'Give it another twenty minutes until our British friends are really on their way, Helmut, then turn them loose.'

He went into his cabin and Richter stripped his shirt from his body, worked the deck pump with one hand and turned the hose on himself. As he did so, Sister Lotte came out on deck clutching a full pail of slops in both hands. She got as far as the starboard rail and was about to empty it when Richter reached her.

'Never into the wind,' he said. 'That way you get the contents back in your face.' He peered down in disgust. 'And that, you can definitely do without.'

He carried the pail to the port rail, emptied it over the side, then flushed it out under the pump. She stood watching him calmly.

She was small and very slightly built, a lawyer's daughter from Munich who looked younger than her twenty-three years. Unlike the other nuns, she was still a novice and had been transferred to Brazil, by way of Portugal, the previous year, only because she was a trained nurse and there was a shortage of people with her qualifications.

She picked up his shirt. 'I'll wash this for you.'

'No need.'

'And the seam is splitting on one shoulder, I'll mend it.'

When she looked up, he saw that her eyes were a startling cornflower blue. 'It must have been horrible down there.'

'For you also.'

He handed her the pail, she took it and for a brief moment, they held it together. Sister Angela said quietly, 'Lotte, I need you.'

She was standing in the entrance to the companionway, her face calm as always, but there was a new wariness in her eyes when she looked at Richter. The girl smiled briefly and joined her and they went below. Richter started to pump water over his head vigorously.

IX

Berger sat behind the desk, surveying the wreckage of his cabin – not that it mattered. It could soon be put straight again. He was filled with a tremendous sense of elation and opened his personal journal. He picked up his pen, thought for a moment, then wrote: 'I am now more than ever convinced that we shall reach Kiel in safety . . .'

— 4 —

> Barquentine *Deutschland*, 14 September 1944. Lat. 28°.16N., long. 30°.50W. Frau Prager died at three bells of the mid watch. We delivered her body to the sea shortly after dawn, Sister Angela taking the service. Ship's company much affected by this calamitous event. A light breeze sprang up during the afternoon watch, increasing to fresh in squalls. I estimate that we are 1170 miles from Cobh in Ireland this day.

NIGHT WAS falling fast as Jago and Petty Officer Jansen went up the hill to St Mungo's. They found the burial party in the cemetery at the back of the church. There were twenty or so islanders there, men and women, Jean Sinclair and Reeve standing together, the admiral in full uniform. Murdoch Macleod in his best blue serge suit, stood at the head of the open grave, a prayer book in his hands.

The two Americans paused some little distance away and removed their caps. It was very quiet except for the incessant calling of the birds, and Jago looked down across Mary's Town to the horseshoe of the harbour where the MGB was tied up at the jetty.

The sun was setting in the sky the colour of brass, splashed with scarlet, thin mackerel clouds high above. Beyond Barra Head, the islands marched north to Bara, Mingulay, Pabbay, Sandray, rearing out of a perfectly calm sea, black against flame.

Reeve glanced over his shoulder, murmured something to Jean Sinclair, then moved towards them through the gravestones. 'Thanks for coming so promptly, lieutenant.'

'No trouble, sir. We were on our way to Mallaig from Stornoway when they relayed your message.' Jago nodded towards the grave into which half-a-dozen fisherman were lowering the coffin. 'Another one from U-743?'

Reeve nodded. 'That makes eight in the past three days.' He hesitated. 'When you were last here you said you were going to London on leave this week.'

'That's right, admiral. If I can get to Mallaig on time I intend to catch the night train for Glasgow. Is there something I can do for you, sir?'

'There certainly is.' Reeve took a couple of envelopes from his pocket. 'This first one is for my niece. Her apartment's in Westminster, not far from the Houses of Parliament.'

'And the other, sir?'

Reeve handed it over. 'If you would see that gets to SHAEF Headquarters personally. It would save time.'

Jago looked at the address on the envelope and swallowed hard. 'My God!'

Reeve smiled. 'See that it's handed to one of his aides personally. No one else.'

'Yes, sir.'

'You'd better move out, then. I'll expect to hear from you as soon as you get back. As I told you, I have a radio at the cottage, one of the few courtesies the Navy still extends me. They'll brief you at Mallaig on the times during the day I sit at the damned thing hoping someone will take notice.'

Jago saluted, nodded to Jansen and then moved away. As the admiral rejoined the funeral party, Murdoch Macleod started to read aloud in a firm, clear voice: 'Man that is born of woman hath but a short time to live, and is full of misery. He cometh up and is cut down like a flower . . .'

Suddenly it was very dark, with only the burned-out fire of day on the horizon as they went out through the lych-gate.

Jansen said, 'Who's the letter for, lieutenant?'

'General Eisenhower,' Jago said simply.

II

In Brest, they were shooting again across the river as Paul Gericke turned the corner, the rattle of small-arms fire drifting across the water. Somewhere on the far horizon rockets arched through the night and, in spite of the heavy rain, considerable portions of the city appeared to be on fire. Most of the warehouses which had once lined the street had been demolished by bombing, the pavement was littered with rubble and broken glass, but the small hotel on the corner, which served as Naval Headquarters, still seemed to be intact. Gericke ran up the steps quickly, showed his pass to the sentry on the door and went inside.

He was a small man, no more than five feet five or six, with fair hair and a pale face that seemed untouched by wind and weather. His eyes were very dark, with no light in them at all, contrasting strangely with the good-humoured, rather lazy smile that seemed permanently to touch his mouth.

His white-topped naval cap had seen much service and he was hardly a prepossessing figure in his old leather jerkin, leather trousers and sea boots. But the young lieutenant sitting at his desk in the foyer saw only the Knight's Cross with Oak Leaves at the throat and was on his feet in an instant.

'I was asked to report to the commodore of submarines as soon as I arrived,' Gericke told him. 'Korvettenkapitän Gericke, U-235.'

'He's expecting you, sir,' the lieutenant said. 'If you'd follow me.'

They went up the curving staircase. A petty officer, a pistol at his belt, stood guard outside one of the hotel bedrooms. The handwritten notice on the door said *Kapitän zur See Otto Friemel, Führer der Unterseeboote West.*

The lieutenant knocked and went in. 'Lieutenant-Commander Gericke, sir.'

The room was in half darkness, the only light the reading lamp on Friemel's desk. He was in shirt-sleeves, working his way through a pile of correspondence, steel-rimmed reading glasses perched on the end of his nose, and an ivory cigarette-holder jutting from the left corner of his mouth.

He came round the desk smiling, hand outstretched. 'My dear Paul. Good to see you. How was the West Indies?'

'A long haul,' Gericke said. 'Especially when it was time to come home.'

Friemel produced a bottle of Schnapps and two glasses. 'We're out of champagne. Not like the old days.'

'What, no flowers on the dock?' Gericke said. 'Don't tell me we're losing the war?'

'My dear Paul, in Brest we don't even have a dock any longer. If you'd arrived in daylight you'd have noticed the rather unhappy state of those impregnable U-boat pens of ours. Five metres of reinforced concrete pulverised by a little item the RAF call the earthquake bomb.' He raised his glass. 'To you, Paul. A successful trip, I hear?'

'Not bad.'

'Come now. A Canadian corvette, a tanker and three merchant ships? Thirty-one thousand tons, and you call that not bad? I'd term it a rather large miracle. These days two out of three U-boats that go out never return.' He shook his head. 'It isn't 1940 any longer. No more Happy Time. These days they send out half-trained boys. You're one of the few oldtimers left.'

Gericke helped himself to a cigarette from a box on the table. It was French and of the cheapest variety, for when he lit it and inhaled, the smoke bit at the back of his throat, sending him into a paroxysm of coughing.

'My God! Now I know things are bad.'

'You've no idea how bad,' Friemel told him. 'Brest has been besieged by the American Eighth Army Corps since the ninth of August. The only reason we're still here is because of the quite incredible defence put up by General Ramcke and the Second Airborne Division. Those paratroopers of his are without a doubt the finest fighting men I've ever seen in action, and that includes the Waffen SS.' He reached for the Schnapps bottle again. 'Of course they were pulled out of the Ukraine to come here. It could be they are still euphoric at such good fortune. An American prison camp, after all, is infinitely to be preferred to the Russian variety.'

'And what's the U-boat position?'

'There isn't one. The Ninth Flotilla is no more. U-256 was the last to leave. That was eleven days ago. Orders are to regroup in Bergen.'

'Then what about me?' Gericke asked. 'I could have made for Norway by way of the Irish Sea and the North Channel.'

'Your orders, Paul, are quite explicit. You will make for Bergen via the English Channel, as the rest of the flotilla has done, only in your case, someone at High Command has provided you with what one might term a slight detour.'

Gericke, who had long since passed being surprised at anything, smiled. 'Where to, exactly?'

'It's really quite simple.' Friemel turned to the table behind, rummaged amongst a pile of charts, found the one he was looking for and opened it across the desk.

Gericke leaned over. 'Falmouth?'

'That's right. The Royal Navy's Fifteenth MGB Flotilla operating out of Falmouth has been causing havoc on this entire coast recently. To be perfectly honest, it's made any kind of naval activity impossible.'

'And what am I supposed to do about it?'

'According to your orders, go into Falmouth and lay mines.'

'They're joking, of course.'

Friemel held up a typed order. 'Dönitz himself.'

Gericke laughed out loud. 'But this is really beautiful, Otto. Quite superb in its idiocy, even for those chairbound bastards in Kiel. What on earth am I supposed to do, win the war in a single bold stroke?' He shook his head. 'They must believe in fairy stories. Someone should tell them that when the tailor boasted he could kill seven at one blow he meant flies on a slice of bread and jam.'

'I don't know,' Friemel said. 'It could be worse. There's a protecting curtain of mines plus a blockship here between Pendennis Point and Black Rock and a temporary net boom from Black Rock to St Anthony's Head. That's supposed to be highly secret, by the way, but it seems the Abwehr still have an agent operational in the Falmouth area.'

'He must feel lonely.'

'Ships in and out all the time. Go in with a few when the net opens. Drop your eggs, up here in Carrick Roads and across the inner harbour and out again.'

Gericke shook his head. 'I'm afraid not.'

'Why?'

'We may get in, but we certainly won't get out.'

Friemel sighed. 'A pity, as I'll be going with you. Not out of any sense of adventure, I assure you. I have orders to report to Kiel and as the land routes to Germany are cut, my only way would seem to be with you to Bergen.'

Gericke shrugged. 'So, in the end, all roads lead to hell.'

Friemel helped himself to one of the French cigarettes and inserted it in his holder. 'What shape are you in?'

'We were strafed by a Liberator in Biscay. Superficial damage only, but my engines need a complete overhaul. New bearings for a start.'

'Not possible. I can give you four or five days. We must leave on the nineteenth. Ramcke tells me he can hold out for another week at the most. No more.'

The door opened and the young lieutenant entered. 'Signal from Kiel, sir. Marked most urgent.'

Friemel took the flimsy from him and adjusted his spectacles. A slight, ironic smile touched his mouth. 'Would you believe it, Paul, but this confirms my promotion as rear admiral in command of all naval forces in the Brest area. One can only imagine it has been delayed in channels.'

The lieutenant passed across another flimsy. Friemel read it, his face grave, then handed it to Gericke. It said: CONGRATULATIONS ON YOUR PROMOTION IN THE FULL AND CERTAIN KNOWLEDGE THAT YOU AND YOUR MEN WILL DIE

RATHER THAN YIELD ONE INCH OF SOIL TO THE ENEMY. ADOLF HITLER.

Gericke passed it back. 'Congratulations, Herr Konteradmiral,' he said formally.

Without a flicker of emotion, Friemel said to the lieutenant, 'Send this message to Berlin. Will fight to the last. Long live the Führer. That's all. Dismiss!'

The young lieutenant withdrew. Friemel said, 'You approve?'

'Wasn't that Lütjen's last message before the *Bismarck* went down?'

'Exactly,' Rear Admiral Otto Friemel said. 'Another drink, my friend?' He reached for the bottle, then sighed. 'What a pity. We appear to have finished the last of the Schnapps.'

III

It was still raining heavily in London at eight-thirty on the following evening when JU 88 pathfinders of *Gruppe* 1/KG 66, operating out of Chartres and Rennes in France, made their first strike. By nine-fifteen the casualty department of Guy's Hospital was working at full stretch.

Janet Munro, in the end cubicle, curtain drawn, carefully inserted twenty-seven stitches into the right thigh of a young auxiliary fireman. He seemed dazed and lay there, staring blankly at the ceiling, an unlit cigarette hanging from the corner of his mouth.

Janet was being assisted by a male nurse named Callaghan, a white-haired man in his late fifties who had served on the Western Front as a Medical Corps sergeant in the First World War. He strongly approved of the young American doctor in every possible way and made it his business to look out for her welfare, something she seemed quite incapable of doing for herself. Just now he was particularly concerned about the fact that she had been on duty for twelve hours, and it was beginning to show.

'You going off after this one, miss?'

'How can I, Joey?' she said. 'They'll be coming in all night.'

Bombs had been falling for some time on the other side of

the Thames but now there was an explosion close at hand. The whole building shook and there was a crash of breaking glass. The lights dimmed for a moment and somewhere a child started to wail.

'My God, Jerry certainly picks his time,' Callaghan remarked.

'What do you mean?' she said, still concentrating on the task in hand.

He seemed surprised. 'Don't you know who's here tonight, miss? Eisenhower himself. Turned up an hour ago just before the bombing started.'

She paused and looked at him blankly. 'General Eisenhower? Here?'

'Visiting those Yank paratroopers in ward seventy-three. The lads they brought over from Paris last week. Decorating some of them, that's what I heard.'

She was unable to take it in, suddenly very tired. She turned back to her patient and inserted the last couple of stitches.

'I'll dress it for you,' Callaghan said. 'You get yourself a cup of tea.'

As she stripped the rubber gloves from her fingers, the young fireman turned his head and looked at her. 'You a Yank then, doctor?'

'That's right.'

'Got any gum, chum?'

She smiled and took a cigarette-lighter from her pocket. 'No, but I can manage a light.'

She took the cigarette from his mouth, lit it and gave it back to him. 'You'll be fine now.'

He grinned. 'Can you cook as well, doc?'

'When I get the time.'

Suddenly, the effort of keeping her smile in place was too much and she turned and went into the corridor quickly. Callaghan was right. She needed that cup of tea very badly indeed. And about fifteen hours' sleep to follow – but that, of course, was quite impossible.

As she started along the corridor, the curtain of a cubicle was snatched back and a young nurse emerged. She was obviously panic-stricken, blood on her hands. Turning wildly, she saw Janet and called out – soundlessly, because at that moment another heavy bomb fell close enough to shake the walls and bring plaster from the ceiling.

Janet caught her by the shoulders. 'What is it?'

The girl tried to speak, pointing wildly at the cubicle as another bomb fell, and Janet pushed her to one side and entered. The woman who lay on the padded operating table, covered with a sheet, was obviously very much in labour. The young man who leaned over her was a corporal in the Commandos, his uniform torn and streaked with dust.

'Who are you?' The tiredness had left her now, as if it had never been.

'Her husband, miss. She's having a baby.' He plucked at her sleeve. 'For God's sake do something.'

Janet pulled back the sheet. 'When did she start?'

'Half an hour, maybe longer. We was in the High Street when the siren went, so I took her into the underground. Borough Station. When she started feeling bad I thought I'd better get her to hospital, but it was hell out there. Bombs falling all over the place.'

Another landed very close to the hospital now, followed by a second. For a moment, the light went out. The woman on the table cried out in fear and pain. Her eyes started from her head as the lights came on again and she tried to sit up.

Janet pushed her down and turned to the young nurse. 'You know what's wrong here?'

'I'm not sure,' the girl said. 'I'm only a probationer.' She looked at her hands. 'There was a lot of blood.'

The young Commando pulled at Janet's sleeve. 'What's going on? What's up?'

'A baby is usually delivered head first,' Janet said calmly. 'This is what's known as a breech. That means it's presenting its backside.'

'Can you handle it?'

'I should imagine so, but we haven't got much time. I want you to stand over your wife, hold her hand and talk to her. Anything you like, only don't stop.'

'Shall I get Sister Johnson?' the young nurse asked.

'No time,' Janet said. 'I need you here.'

Bombs were falling steadily now and from the sound of it, panic had broken out amongst the crowd that waited in general casualty for treatment. She took a deep breath, tried to ignore that nightmare world outside and concentrated on the task in hand.

The first problem was to deliver the legs. She probed gently inside until she managed to get a finger up against the back of one of the child's knees. The leg flexed instantly and so did the other when she repeated the performance.

The woman cried out and Janet said to the husband, 'Tell her to push. Push hard.'

A moment later, the legs delivered themselves. She held out her hands for the young nurse to wipe away the blood, then grasped the legs, fingers beneath the thighs and pulled down firmly until the shoulders were in sight.

Now the arms were extended. She twisted the child to the left until the shoulder flexed, hooked a finger under the elbow and delivered the left arm. Bombs were still falling but further away now as she repeated the performance with the right.

There was a tremendous hubbub outside, people running up and down the corridor and a smell of burning. She whispered to the young nurse, 'So far so good. Now for the head.'

She put her right arm beneath the child and got her forefinger into its mouth, then probed with her left hand for a grip on the shoulders and started to pull. Slowly, very slowly, it moved and yet the strength required was so considerable that sweat sprang to her forehead.

And then it was clear and safe in her hands. But it was obvious at once that it wasn't breathing and the whole body was deep purple.

'Cotton-wool, quickly!' The young nurse passed some across and Janet cleared the mouth and nostrils. 'Now you can get Sister Johnson, if she's available, or Callaghan. Anybody, only hurry.'

The girl went out on the run and Janet blew into the tiny mouth. Quite suddenly the child shuddered, gave an audible gasp and started to cry.

Janet looked up and found the young Commando staring at her wildly. 'A daughter,' she said. 'If you're interested.'

His wife gave a stifled moan and fainted. At the same moment the curtain was jerked back and Sister Johnson rushed in. Janet handed her the baby. 'This one's yours, sister,' she said. 'I'll see to the mother,' and she elbowed the young Commando out of the way and leaned over his wife.

IV

It was later, when the bombing had stopped and she had moved out on the porch to smoke a cigarette, that the tiredness hit her again.

'Oh God,' she said softly. 'Isn't it ever going to end, this war?'

There were fires on the other side of the Thames towards Westminster and the acrid smell of smoke filled the air. Behind her the blackout curtain opened briefly and Callaghan appeared, an American officer in raincoat and peaked cap with him.

'Oh, there you are, doctor,' Callaghan said. 'Been looking all over for you. This gentleman would like a word with you.'

'Colonel Brisingham, ma'am.' He saluted punctiliously.

Callaghan withdrew, leaving them alone in the dimly-lit porch. 'What can I do for you, colonel?' Janet asked.

'General Eisenhower would appreciate a word, ma'am, if you could spare him a few minutes of your time.'

He delivered the words gravely and courteously and yet, for Janet, the walls of the porch seemed to move in and out again, very slowly. She fell against the colonel, who caught hold of her arms.

'Are you all right?'

'It's been a long day.' She took a deep breath. 'Where is the general?'

'Just across the yard, ma'am, in his staff car. If you'd follow me. We haven't much time, I'm afraid. He has to be back in Paris by tomorrow morning.'

The car was parked in a corner by the main gate. She was aware of the jeeps surrounding it, the helmets of the military police, then Brisingham had the rear door open.

'Doctor Munro, general.'

Janet hesitated, then climbed inside and Brisingham closed the door. In the faint light from the dashboard she could only get the briefest impression. He was wearing a trenchcoat, a forage cap, she could see that, but not much of his face except for the brief gleam of teeth that went with the inimitable smile.

'Would it surprise you if I said I felt as if I already knew you?' Eisenhower said.

She frowned and then saw the solution. 'Uncle Carey?'

He chuckled. 'You were all he used to talk about over the coffee at SHAEF when we were putting Overlord together. But I knew him from long before then. Panama – 1922, 23. I was a major and he, as I recall, was a lieutenant-commander with a reputation for being difficult to handle.'

'He hasn't changed.'

'Not in the slightest.' He hesitated. 'When he went down in that Norwegian destroyer on D-Day, for example. He should never have been there. A direct contravention of his orders.'

'Which cost him an eye and most of one arm.'

'I know. Tell me. This place Fhada? This Scottish island he's staying on at the moment? What's he doing there?'

'His mother's family came from there originally. He was left a cottage by a cousin just before the war. He wanted somewhere to hide for a while and I suppose it seemed as good as any. It's a strange place.'

'You think he was looking for something?'

'Perhaps.'

The general nodded. 'Did you know he's been trying to get back into action?'

'No, but it doesn't surprise me.'

'Me neither. He couldn't change his nature this late in the day, but it just isn't possible, you must see that. One eye, an apology for an arm. He's given as much as any man could . . .'

'Except his life.'

'Dammit!' Eisenhower said. 'The Navy Department won't budge. They want him on the retired list now.'

'And you?'

He sighed heavily. 'He sent me a letter by hand, delivered by some young naval officer on leave. Lucky I happened to be in London today.'

'He asked for your help? Carey Reeve?' She smiled. 'Now that, general, is really something.'

'The same thought *had* occurred to me.' Eisenhower said. 'And can you help?'

'I've a job in Paris for him, starting the first of October. Supply and Personnel Co-ordination, Deputy Director.'

'A desk job?' Janet shook her head. 'It's action he's after.'

'Those days are over. If he wants a job, there's one for him. Otherwise it's the boneyard. He must understand that.'

'But will he?' she said softly and almost to herself.

Eisenhower said, 'Look, is there any chance you could get a few days off and go and see him?'

She hesitated. 'I suppose so. I haven't had more than a weekend in the past six months.'

'Wonderful,' he said. 'Naturally I'll have someone on my staff make all the necessary travel arrangements for you. I'll give you a letter, making clear the terms of my offer. But the real pressure must come from you.'

There was a tap on the window. Eisenhower lowered it and Brisingham leaned in. 'We'll have to get moving if we're to make that plane, general.'

Eisenhower nodded impatiently and wound up the window again. 'They won't leave me alone for a minute. A hell of a war, even for generals, believe me.'

V

Far out in the Atlantic, the horizon crackled with sheet lightning and rain started to fall heavily. The wind was Force 8 on the Beaufort scale, a mountainous sea running and the *Deutschland* fled under stay-sails only, Richter and Sturm at the wheel.

At four bells of the first watch a sudden vicious squall struck from the south-east with incredible force, driving hail before it like bullets. The *Deutschland* lurched to one side, swinging nearly five points off course, Sturm lost his balance and was swept into the scuppers by a cascade of water, leaving Richter to struggle desperately with the spinning wheel. The *Deutschland* staggered as the wind dealt her another savage blow and started to heel over.

Berger, unable to sleep, had been lying in his bunk for the best part of an hour, smoking a cigar and listening to the music of the gale. Every part of the ship creaked and groaned, and the wind whistled through the rigging with a hundred separate voices. He was wearing foul-weather gear, seaboots and oilskin coat, ready for any emergency.

The crisis, when it came, was so unexpected that he was thrown from his bunk before he knew what was happening and rolled across the cabin, fetching up against the desk.

The floor continued to incline as he tried to get up, 'Oh, dear God, she's going!' he said aloud. Then the tilting ceased. He scrambled across to the door, got it open and went outside.

The lightning that flickered constantly in the sky above illuminated an extraordinary scene. The *Deutschland* was lying over, almost on her beam ends, with her lee rail under and lower yardarm dipping into broken water.

Richter and Sturm were wrestling with the wheel and several members of the crew lurched and slithered across the sloping deck in complete panic.

'She's going! She's going!' one man screamed. Berger punched him in the jaw, sending him flat on his back.

He cried, 'Bring her round, for God's sake! Bring her round!'

Gradually and with considerable difficulty, the *Deutschland* started to turn into the wind, as Richter and Sturm got the helm up, but the deck remained at such a slope that no one could stand without hanging on to something.

Berger yelled at the two nearest men, 'Take the wheel and tell Richter and Herr Sturm to come to me.'

He managed to make it to the aft cargo hatch on his hands and knees and was wrestling with the ropes of the canvas cover when Sturm and Richter arrived. 'What do you think?' Sturm cried above the roaring of the sea.

'The ballast's moved, that's obvious,' Berger replied. 'But how much is the important thing. Let's have this hatch cover open and see the state of the game.'

VI

Below, for the passengers, there was total confusion. When the squall struck, Sister Angela and Sister Else had been sitting together on the bottom bunk in their cabin, discussing a passage of the scriptures, the usual evening task before bed. They were both thrown to the floor and the oil lamp fell from its hook in the ceiling to smash beside them. The spreading pool of oil flared but was almost immediately extinguished as the cabin tilted, the door burst open and water poured in.

Sister Angela started to make a final act of contrition. 'Oh my God, who art infinitely good in thyself . . .' But she choked on the words, every instinct rebelling against such a calm acceptance of death. She crawled to the door, calling to Sister Else to follow her.

The saloon was in total darkness, water pouring in through the shattered skylight. It was a nightmare world. Voices called hysterically. Someone lurched into her, she reached out and touched a face as an arm fastened about her in panic. And then a cabin door opened and light flooded out as Otto Prager appeared with a lantern in one hand.

The floor of the saloon was tilted at an angle of forty-five degrees, the dining table and chairs, all bolted to the floor, still in place, but on the port side at the bottom of the slope, water had gathered to a depth of three feet. Each time the *Deutschland* rolled, more came in through the broken skylight, newly repaired only the previous day after the *Guardian* episode.

Sister Angela found herself held by Sister Lotte, the youngest of the nuns. The girl was out of her mind with fear, and Sister Angela had to struggle to tear herself free.

She shook the younger woman vigorously and slapped her face. 'Pull yourself together, sister. Remember what you are.'

Sister Else managed to get to her feet beside her, waist deep in water, the skirt of her black robe floating around her and at that moment, the cabin door next to Prager's opened and Sisters Käthe and Brigitte peered through.

Prager, who seemed remarkably calm, said, 'Everything will be fine, sisters, no need to panic. Make for the companionway.'

Sister Angela got there first, an arm around Sister Lotte. Prager handed her the lantern and assisted the others, one by one, until they were all on the tilting companionway.

As he moved up to join Sister Angela the door at the head

of the companionway opened and Berger peered in, a storm lantern in one hand. 'Everyone all right?'

'I think so,' Sister Angela said.

He crouched down to speak to her. 'No point in putting you into one of the boats. It wouldn't last five minutes in this sea. You understand me, sister?'

'What must we do then, captain?'

'Stay here for the moment.'

'What's gone wrong, Erich?' Prager demanded.

'The ballast has shifted into the lee bow. Most of the crew are down there now trying to do something about it. We need you, too, Otto. If another squall hits while we're in this state she'll turn turtle.'

Prager moved out into the night without a word. Sister Angela said, 'Is there anything we can do, captain?'

'Pray,' Eric Berger told her. 'Very hard,' and he slammed the door shut and disappeared.

VII

When Otto Prager went down the ladder into the cargo hold it was like a descent into hell. The crew worked in the light of a couple of storm lanterns, furiously shovelling sand to windward. Each time the ship rolled men stumbled into each other and went down.

Prager stepped off the ladder and fell to one knee. Someone cried out in fear, but otherwise everyone shovelled away with a grim frenzy, the only sound the creaking of the ship's timbers and the gale outside.

A strong arm hoisted Prager to his feet and Helmut Richter grinned down at him. 'Just think, Herr Prager, you could have been safe in Rio at this very moment enjoying a drink before a late dinner, looking out from the terrace of the Copacabana at the lights in the bay . . .'

'Well, I'm not,' Prager told him, 'so just give me a bloody shovel and let's get to it.'

VIII

For some time now it had been obvious that the *Deutschland* was tilting to windward, but on the companionway in the half darkness it seemed an eternity before the door opened again and Berger peered in. He managed a smile, but only just.

'Did you pray, sister?'

'We did.'

'Well, for what it's worth, your prayers were answered. Somebody on this tub must live right. It isn't me, so it must be you.'

'I'm willing to admit that possibility, captain.'

'Excellent. We'll have the pump working as soon as we can, but it may not be possible to light a fire in the galley again before morning. I'm afraid you're going to find it rather uncomfortable down there for the rest of the night.'

'We'll manage.'

In a sudden outburst, he added roughly, 'Dammit, sister, it was you who insisted on coming. I warned you.'

'Yes, captain, I believe you did,' she said. 'And for that I thank you, amongst other things.' She looked down at the faces of the others, upturned in the dim light of the lamp. 'Shall we pray, my beloved sisters?'

She began to recite aloud the prayers for thanksgiving after a storm. 'So they cried unto the Lord in their trouble; and he delivered them from their distress.'

Berger shut the companionway door and turned towards Prager who leaned wearily on the hatch beside him. 'What a woman,' he said. 'What a bloody infuriating . . .'

'Wonderful woman,' Prager finished.

Berger laughed, then turned to look up at the quarterdeck where Richter had the wheel on his own now, for the wind had dropped a little although there was still a heavy sea running.

Sturm came down the ladder to join him. 'I've got a party on the pump, sir. Any further orders?'

'Yes,' Berger said. 'Wood, Herr Sturm. Every plank you can find. Gut the ship if needs be. Every cabin and locker, but I want that sand decked-off within twenty-four hours so it can't damn well move again, whatever happens.'

'Aye, aye, sir.' Sturm hesitated. 'A close one, captain.'

'Too close,' Erich Berger said. 'Let's try not to make a habit of it,' and he turned and walked towards his cabin.

— 5 —

Barquentine *Deutschland*, 17 September 1944. Lat. 38°.56N., long. 30°.50W. Wind hauled into the west during the middle watch and we braced the yards forward. Hove the log and found we were going 10 knots. Overcast cleared just before noon and allowed the sun to come through, the wind dropping to a flat calm.

THE *DEUTSCHLAND* seemed to float in space, completely still, every sail set, yards braced, perfectly reflected in a sea of green glass.

It was hot and airless. Conditions below were unbearable and, on the captain's orders, a canvas awning had been rigged aft of the main mast so that the sisters might be protected to some degree from the fierceness of the sun.

Most of the crew and passengers were suffering from sea boils now, a product not only of the unsatisfactory diet, but of the constant action of salt water on the skin. One of the men, a brawny Hamburger named Schirmer, was virtually crippled by a whole crop of them on his left leg. He leaned back groaning in a canvas chair while Sister Angela went to work with a lancet.

Forward from the mainmast, under the supervision of Sturm, four of the crew worked the heavy metal bar of the ship's two suction pumps and water gushed across the deck in a brown stream.

Richter, who had just finished a thirty-minute stint himself, dipped a pannier into the water bucket, wrinkling his nose in disgust. 'Have you seen this, Herr Leutnant?' he asked Sturm, and poured the contents of the pannier back into the bucket. The water was dark red.

'Rust from the tanks, I expect.' Sturm grinned. 'On this ship we think of everything, Helmut. You don't just get a drink of water. We throw in an iron tonic as well. Good for the constitution.'

'My belly doesn't agree.' Richter ran a hand across his stomach. 'Sometimes the cramps are terrible. Most of the lads will tell you the same.'

Sister Lotte was standing by the mizzen shrouds on the port side. Like the other nuns, she had put on her white tropical habit again, because of the heat. And, as always, Richter wondered how on earth she managed to keep it so clean. She made a rather appealing figure as she stood there, one hand on a rope, gazing out to sea.

Walz, the cook, came out of the galley and emptied a pail of garbage over the rail beside her. She moved back hastily.

'Sorry, sister,' he said, with total insincerity.

'That's all right, Herr Walz,' she answered in a low, sweet voice.

He looked her over boldly and grinned, showing bad teeth. The lust in his eyes was plain: her smile faded and she reached for the shrouds as if to support herself.

Walz turned back to the galley and found Richter leaning against the entrance. He was stripped to the waist, his muscular body burned brown by the sun, the long, blond hair and beard bleached white, a black Brazilian cigarillo between his teeth. A match flared in the bosun's cupped hands. As he leaned down to it, he said softly, 'Manners, you bastard. That isn't some San Pauli whore you're talking to.'

'So, you fancy her, too?' Walz grinned again. 'I don't blame you. It's a long trip home and women are women, as the captain said, whatever they choose to wear. It's what's between the legs that counts.'

He was hurled into the shadows of the galley, found himself back across the table, a hand of iron at his throat. There was a sharp click as the blade of the Finnish gutting knife in the bosun's right hand sprang into view.

'One wrong word, you lump of dung,' Richter said calmly, 'try even looking at her again as you did now and you go over the side – and I wouldn't like to guarantee it'll be in one piece.'

Walz almost fainted with terror, felt his bowels move. The bosun patted his face. 'That's it, Ernst. That's exactly the way

I like you. Frightened to death.'

He snapped the blade of the gutting knife back into place and went outside.

Sister Lotte was still standing by the mizzen shrouds and, at that moment, an albatross swooped down to where the garbage floated, motionless as the ship itself.

She turned, as if by instinct, and became aware that Richter was watching her. She smiled and he crossed the deck to join her.

'Herr Richter.' There was no attempt to conceal the pleasure in her eyes. 'That bird – what was it?'

'An albatross, sister. King of the scavengers. There'll be more around soon, when they get wind of our garbage.'

'So beautiful.' She shaded her eyes against the sun and watched it go.

'And so are you, by God,' Richter thought. 'They say an albatross is probably the ghost of a dead sailor.'

'And you believe that?'

Her eyes were very blue, her face a perfect oval framed by the white coif. Richter's throat was suddenly dry. He said. 'Of course not, sister. Superstitious nonsense.' He took a deep breath. 'Now, if you'll excuse me, I must see the captain.'

He had a rope burn on his right wrist. She reached for his hand and frowned. 'That's nasty. It could get worse. You must let me see to it for you.'

Her fingers were cool. There was sweat on his brow and then, across her shoulder, he saw that Sister Angela, seated under the awning, her medical case open beside her as she treated one of the seamen, was watching him gravely.

Richter pulled his hand away. 'No need, sister. It's nothing, believe me.'

II

Berger, seated at the desk in his cabin was entering the log.

> . . . 18 September 1944. A bad night. Rain and heavy seas. Lower t'gallant split during a sudden squall at six bells in the mid-watch. Weather changes again to flat

calm in the forenoon. Herr Sturm reports sixteen inches of water in the bilges.

He put down his pen and sat back, aware of the dull monotonous thumping of the pump. Not good. Not good at all for her to be taking so much water. Although he had said nothing to Sturm and Richter about it, he knew that the seriousness of the situation must be as apparent to them as it was to him.

There was a knock on the door and Richter entered. 'Herr Sturm's compliments, sir. From the sound of things, she's just about dry again.'

Berger nodded. 'What do you think, Helmut?'

Richter shrugged. 'She's old, sir. Too old, and I shouldn't think the copper's been off her in years. God knows what state her timbers are in.' He hesitated. 'And when that squall struck the other night, when she nearly turned turtle . . .'

'You think she took some damage that we weren't aware of?'

Before Richter could reply, there was a confused shouting on the deck, mixed with cheering. And a strange drumming. Berger was on his feet in an instant, got the door open and rushed outside with Richter at his heels.

It was raining, a freak tropical downpour. Most of the crew were running about the deck like madmen, those who had been able to find buckets holding them up to catch the sweet water. The nuns, sheltering under the awning, were laughing like children as water poured from it in a torrent. Sturm stood underneath the impromptu shower, water cascading over his head. He turned and, seeing Berger, moved aside hurriedly.

'Sorry, captain. Collective madness.'

He stood mopping his face with his neckerchief, like a schoolboy caught out. The rain ceased as suddenly as it had started, and steam began to rise from the decks.

Berger said, 'How's the pumping?'

'Sucked dry, sir.' Sturm hesitated. 'For the moment.'

Berger nodded, aware that most of the crew were hanging around, intent on picking up any information that was going. He made his judgement and acted on it. There was, after all, little point in pretending the situation didn't exist.

'Not good, Herr Sturm. Sixteen inches today. The same yesterday. Fourteen the day before. There has to be a reason.'

There was a heavy silence, broken only by the creaking of the rigging and the slapping of the empty sails.

Richter spoke first. 'Maybe I should go down and take a look, captain.'

He was an excellent swimmer, and self-evidently strong as a bull. With the ship totally becalmed, there was little danger. Berger nodded. 'All right.' He took a key from his pocket and handed it to Sturm. 'Get a rifle from the gun locker, just in case.'

As Richter pulled off his canvas rope-soled shoes, Sister Angela moved to Berger's side. 'Why the rifle, captain?'

Berger shrugged. 'Sharks. No sign now, but amazing how they appear with a man in the water, and all that garbage doesn't help.'

Sister Lotte turned pale. She moved to Richter's side where he stood at the rail, tightening his belt. 'It's – it's very deep, isn't it, Herr Richter?'

Richter laughed out loud, 'A thousand fathoms, at least. But don't worry, I'm not going all the way down.'

Berger, listening to this exchange, frowned, but the time was hardly appropriate to make any comment. Instead he said, 'You want a line, Helmut?'

Richter shook his head. 'Why bother? There isn't an inch of movement in her.' He put one foot on the rail, sprang up and dived cleanly into the water.

A shoal of small fish scattered before him, disintegrating in a silver cloud. He went down fast, through water that was like green glass, pale with sunlight. The planks of the hull of the *Deutschland* were coated with barnacles, and the seagrass sprouted everywhere in a gaudy carpet.

Years since her bottom's been scraped, he thought, and swam down to the keel, hanging on to it for a moment, then started to work his way along towards the prow.

On deck, they waited in silence. Richter surfaced once, for air, waved and went under again. Sister Lotte gripped the rail tightly, her knuckles white as she stared down into the water. Berger, watching her closely, glanced up and found

Sister Angela looking at him. Her face was calm but there was something close to pain in her eyes. He took out his pipe and started to fill it from the worn oilskin pouch. More problems. As if he didn't have enough on his plate. And why did it have to be Richter, the finest seaman in the crew?

At that moment the bosun surfaced and floated at the port rail, coughing, his hair plastered to his skull. Someone tossed him a line and he was hauled over the rail.

He squatted on the deck for a moment, shivering. Berger said, 'How was it? You can speak out. Let everyone hear.'

'Nothing marked, captain,' Richter said. 'No sign of any real damage. It's as we thought, she's a very old lady. In places there are gaps between her planks where you can stick two fingers. I'd say she needed recaulking ten years ago.'

Berger turned to address the men. 'You heard him. Nothing we can't handle. And with double the normal crew there won't be any difficulties in manning the pump.'

The faces around him were still filled with uncertainty, but at that moment the mainsail flapped, as a tiny wind rippled the water from the south-east.

Berger looked up as the sails started to fill and laughed. 'There you are, a good omen. We're on the move again. Back to work, Herr Sturm, if you please.'

Sturm barked orders and the crew broke away. Sister Angela said, 'If you have a moment, captain, I'd like a word with you.'

Berger glanced from her to Lotte who, with the other nuns, was clearing away her belongings from under the awning. 'All right, sister.'

In his cabin, she faced him across the desk, perfectly composed, hands folded. 'Lotte is the most vulnerable of those amongst my charges, captain. It is my sworn duty to see that nothing interferes with the path she has chosen.'

'What you're trying to say is that she isn't a proper nun yet,' Berger said. 'Not like the rest of you?' He shook his head. 'It doesn't make any kind of difference to me, I assure you. My orders to the crew are plain where you and your friends are concerned.'

'And Herr Richter?'

He leaned back and looked up at her. 'All right, so you've

caught him looking at the girl a few times. What do you expect me to do about that?'

'She was afraid for him when he went over the side and she allowed it to show.'

'He's a good-looking boy.'

'Which is exactly what's worrying me.'

Berger said, 'Helmut Richter was Obersteuermann on a U-boat before he fetched up in Brazil like the rest of us. Chief Quartermaster, to you. Iron Cross, Second and First Class. The finest seaman I've ever known and a remarkable young man in every way. You've nothing to worry about, believe me.'

'I have your assurance in this matter, then?'

'Yes, dammit.' He was unable to contain his exasperation, went to the door, opened it and called to Sturm, 'Send Richter in here.'

As he went back to his desk, Sister Angela made a move towards the door. Berger said, 'No, don't go. You might as well hear this.'

She hesitated and at that moment there was a knock on the door and Richter entered. He had put on a heavy sweater and reefer, but still looked pale.

'You wanted me, Herr Kapitän?'

Berger produced a bottle and a glass from his desk cupboard. 'Scotch whisky, Haig and Haig. The very best. You've earned it.'

'It was colder than I thought down there.'

Richter drank some of the whisky and Berger sat down. 'How long have we known each other, Helmut?'

'A year, captain. Fourteen months to be precise. Why do you ask?'

'The young nun,' Berger told him. 'Sister Lotte.' He hesitated, choosing his words. 'She was worried about you.'

Richter glanced at Sister Angela, his face paler than ever now, then placed his glass on the desk carefully. 'My affair, Herr Kapitän.'

'Don't play the fool with me, Helmut,' Berger snapped. 'The girl is still a novice. Do you know what that means to these people?'

'That she hasn't made up her mind yet,' Richter said evenly.

'And you'd like to make it up for her, is that it?'

Richter glanced at Sister Angela, then turned back to Berger. 'You don't understand, either of you, so let me make it plain.' He held up his left hand. 'Before I would see harm come to her from any man, I would cut this off. You understand me?'

'I believe you, boy. And what happens when we reach Kiel and dry land again will be none of my concern, but for the present, you'll stay away from her. I could make it an order, but I won't. I'll simply ask for your word instead.'

For a moment he thought that Richter was going to argue but the bosun's hesitation was only fractional. He braced himself, heels together. 'You have it, sir.'

'That's all right, then.'

Richter went out quickly and Berger said to Sister Angela, 'Was there anything else?'

'No, I don't think so. I appear to anger you at times, captain. I wonder why?'

'God knows, sister. I wish *I* did. I've experienced a few hard cases in my time: you get them in every crew. They can be handled well enough. With boot and fist if necessary, but you . . .'

She said gently, 'Poor Captain Berger. If only everything in life were capable of such a simple solution.'

She went out. Berger sat there, thinking about it, realizing suddenly that it was the first time he'd seen her smile.

III

Like many a distinguished sailor before him, sea-sickness was an old story to Rear Admiral Otto Friemel, and the foul weather which had allowed U-235 to make such an excellent surface run from Brest had had an unfortunate effect on his stomach. On arrival off the mouth of the Fal, he had accepted the offer of the bunk in Gericke's cabin on which to recover.

He slept surprisingly well and drifted up from darkness into a world of total silence. For a moment, he could not remember where he was and lay there frowning in the dim light. Then the curtain was pulled back and Gericke entered with a pot of coffee and two cups on a tray.

Friemel swung his legs to the floor. 'Things were a total blank. Does that ever happen to you?'

'Frequently.'

'A nasty feeling. Perhaps I'm getting too old. For this sort of thing certainly.'

Gericke said, 'It's the war, that's all. It's gone on too long.'

He took a chart from the shelf above the bunk and opened it out across the small table. Friemel said, 'It's damned quiet.'

'And so it should be. Most of the crew are lying down. Those who have to move are walking with rags round their boots.'

'How are they taking it?'

'The prospect of imminent death, you mean?' Gericke shrugged. 'They're good lads, and we've been together a long time. But they've been to Japan and back, remember, so there's a distinct feeling that we could be taking our pitcher to the well once too often.' He lit a cigarette and picked up a slide rule. 'Of course, it hasn't helped that I've taken the coding machine to pieces and distributed them around the crew in case the worst comes to the worst.'

'And you share their pessimism?'

'Not entirely.' Gericke traced a pencil across the mouth of the Fal from Black Rock Beacon to St Anthony's Head. 'According to the Abwehr's friendly local agent, the boom is positioned here. Getting in is no problem. There have been several ships in and out since we arrived, but so far they've always been singles. I'd rather follow a small convoy, if possible. It would give us better cover.'

Friemel inserted a cigarette in his holder. 'Another point in your favour, as I see it, is that at this stage in the war, the *Tommis* are hardly likely to expect a German U-boat to attempt to penetrate a major naval installation.'

'A comforting thought. But I'd rather not rely on it. Once in, we drop the mines through the stern tubes. Here in Carrick Roads; across the mouth of the Inner Harbour, what's left across the entrance to St Mawes . . .'

'And out again.'

'You forget the boom. We'll need a ship coming in or out for it to open again. We'll have to wait. And if anyone's unfortunate enough to touch off one of those mines in the meantime, the door, I assure you, will remain very tightly shut.'

'And what do we do then – scuttle?'

'There is another possibility. Not much of a one, but it's there.' Gericke ran his pencil across to Pendennis Point. 'Here, between the Point and Black Rock Beacon.'

'The minefield?' Friemel said. 'A death trap, surely.'

'Not the inshore run. South Passage, they call it. According to the Abwehr report, they haven't bothered to mine it. Simply stopped the hole by sinking an old merchant ship.'

Fiemel looked at the map. 'In six metres. It would surprise me if a mackerel could find room to squeeze past.'

'Six metres now,' Gericke said. 'But at high tide, which tonight is at twenty-three hundred hours, nine metres at least in that slot.'

Friemel examined the map again. 'Sorry, Paul, but I just don't see it. Barely room to submerge, even at high water. And the navigation would be impossible.'

'But I wasn't thinking of submerging,' Gericke said. 'Not completely. I'd stay on the bridge and give steering directions. I've memorized the chart.'

'God in Heaven!' Friemel whispered.

The green curtain was pulled aside and Oberleutnant zur See Karl Engel, the first watch officer appeared. 'Contact sir. Ships moving in from the east, line astern. Three, possibly four.'

Gericke glanced at his watch. It was a few minutes past nine. 'Sounds exactly what we've been waiting for. You know what to do. Ready to move out in five minutes from now. We follow them in blind. I'll take the helm myself.'

'No periscope?' Friemel said.

'Not until we're well into Carrick Roads.'

Engel disappeared and the curtain dropped back into place.

Gericke opened a cupboard under the bunk and took out a bottle and a couple of tin mugs.

'Schnapps?' Friemel asked.

'The best.' Gericke poured a generous tot into each mug. 'It's been to Japan and back, this bottle. The one I keep only for the most special occasions.'

'And to what shall we drink, my dear Paul?' asked Konteradmiral Otto Friemel.

'Why, to the game,' Gericke said. 'That would seem appropriate. To the bloody stupid and imbecile game we've all been playing for five years now, which would once more appear, as they say, to be afoot.'

IV

Janet Munro came awake reluctantly to the persistent buzzing of the front doorbell. She had a splitting headache, her mouth was dry. She lay staring up at the ceiling through the darkness, trying to pull herself together, hoping that damn noise would cease. But it didn't. Suddenly angry, she flung the bedclothes aside and reached for her bathrobe.

When she opened the front door, a tall, slightly-built young naval officer in reefer coat and peaked cap was reaching for the bell push again. He had stooped shoulders and seemed tired, particularly around the eyes, and a bad scar ran down the right side of the face.

She glanced at her watch. It was just after ten. She'd had three hours' sleep. Under the circumstances she found considerable difficulty in keeping her temper.

'Yes, what is it?'

'Dr Munro? My name's Jago. Harry Jago.'

'I'm afraid you've chosen the wrong night. I don't know who sent you, but I have to sleep. Maybe some other time.'

Jago's smile faded. He suddenly looked very young. 'You don't understand.' He produced a letter from his pocket and held it out to her. 'Your uncle asked me to deliver this.'

She frowned. 'Uncle Carey? I thought he was still in the Hebrides?'

'That's right. I spoke with him on Fhada the day before yesterday.'

She took the letter from him and nodded slowly as if still having difficulty in taking it all in. 'And what are you doing up there, lieutenant?'

'Oh, I run a kind of postal service round the islands,' Jago said cheerfully.

'Hardly the dead centre of the only war we've got.'

'While good men and true are fighting and dying elsewhere? It's a point of view.' He was no longer smiling. 'Anyway, you've got your letter, doctor, and if you're interested, the Admiral was in good health when I last saw him.'

She regretted the sarcasm instantly. She had become increasingly prone to such cruel remarks of late.

'Just a minute,' she said. Jago turned. She smiled. 'You'd better come in and have a drink while I read this.'

The living-room was small and untidy. She switched on the electric fire and sat down. 'Take off your coat and help yourself to a drink. You'll find some Scotch in the corner cupboard. No ice, I'm afraid. Something you learn to live without over here.'

'What about you?'

'A small one would be fine. Nice and straight.'

He took off his coat and cap and moved to the cupboard, and while he busied himself getting the drinks she read the letter. It told her nothing she had not already learned from General Eisenhower, and was mainly concerned with her uncle's desperate need to get back into the war again. Talking it out, she thought, just as if I was sitting in front of him, that's all he's doing.

She looked up as Jago came back with a couple of glasses and the first thing she noticed was the Navy Cross ribbon. She took the drink automatically, without even saying thank you.

'Sorry about the delay,' Jago said. 'The letter, I mean. I tried here yesterday evening but you were out, and when I called at the hospital today, they said you were too busy to see anyone.'

'You could have left it.'

'The admiral asked me to see that you got it personally.'

'You're a rotten liar, you know that?'

'I'm afraid so.'

'Why was it so important?'

'He showed me a photo of you.'

She laughed again. 'And what is that supposed to do – sweep me off my feet?'

'No, ma'am,' Jago said. 'You asked me, I told you, that's

all.' He stood up and reached for his reefer. 'I'd better be moving.'

'Oh, be your age, for God's sake.' She was suddenly angry again. 'Let me tell you something, lieutenant. Tonight I feel not only totally exhausted but old enough to be your mother.'

'You're twenty-seven,' he said. 'Birthday, November ninth. That's Scorpio and I can certainly see why.'

'Did you get that out of Uncle Carey, too? All right, I surrender. What is it you do in the Navy in those circumstances?'

'Strike your flag.'

'I've had a rather heavy afternoon,' she said. 'Fourteen flying bombs hit London today. Maybe you heard the bangs but I saw the results. I fell into bed exactly three hours ago. Then you arrived.'

He was on his feet again in a moment. 'I'm sorry. I just didn't realize.'

'You brought a letter for Ike as well, didn't you?' He hesitated and she carried on. 'Don't worry, you aren't giving away State secrets. He spoke to me about it last night. My uncle's trying to get back into the glorious fight.'

Jago didn't know what to say. He was fascinated by this strange, abrasive girl, by her wide, almost ugly mouth and her harsh, distinctive voice.

She said, 'When are you going back? The week-end?'

'That's right.'

'Me too. I mean, I'm going to see my uncle, courtesy of the Supreme Commander, but they haven't given me a date yet.'

'Maybe we'll be on the same train.'

She took an English cigarette from a packet on the mantelpiece and he lit it for her. 'And the rest of your leave? What do you plan to do with that?'

'I don't really know.' Jago shrugged. 'There doesn't seem to be too much fun in this town these days.'

'Oh, I don't know,' she said. 'You Yanks seem to do all right, with your cigarettes and whisky. Why, you can even get a cab when you need one, which is more than the locals can, believe me.'

'Is that how you see yourself? A kind of American Cockney?'

'I came out of Paris in 1940. I've been here ever since.'

There was a hiatus and Jago couldn't think of anything to say. Janet said, 'Where are you going now? Out on the town?'

'I don't think so. I've got a bed in one of the officers' clubs.'

'And just think – you could be walking along the Embankment with me.'

He stared at her. 'The Embankment?'

'Sure, why not? I could do with the air. Give me three minutes to throw something on.' She crossed to the bedroom door and paused to look back at him. 'You don't mind, do you?'

V

In Falmouth, coasting along at periscope depth, U-235 discharged the last of her mines across the entrance to St Mawes harbour and started to turn away. Gericke was at the periscope, Admiral Friemel and Engel beside him, and the Obersteuermann, Willi Carlsen, at the helm. The tension had been incredible, the crew padding about like ghosts, no one speaking above a whisper.

There was sweat on Engel's face. He said eagerly, 'And now we go home?'

'Bergen is home?' Gericke said as he started his sweep, checking the situation in the harbour.

But at that moment a tug, emerging from Carrick Roads, struck one of the mines. There was an instant searing explosion, a tongue of flame that illuminated the entire harbour area. The concussion drummed on the hull of the submarine.

'Oh my God,' Engel moaned.

Friemel, face ashen, plucked at Gericke's shoulder. 'A mine?'

'I'm afraid so. Strike one.' And then he seemed to go rigid, his shoulders hunched. He turned to look at them. 'There are two River-class frigates moored almost side by side just north of the inner harbour.'

'Not even you could be crazy enough for such a thing,' Engel said desperately. 'We wouldn't stand a chance.'

'And what chance do we stand now?' Gericke demanded. 'Frigates, Karl. Two of them.'

He seemed to crackle with electricity, his face very white,

his mad, dark eyes blazing. It was as if he had been sleeping and was now awake.

He turned on Friemel. 'Admiral?'

Friemel found himself shaking, not with fear, but with a kind of fierce joy. 'Why not, by God? A hell of a way to go, Paul.'

And Engel, touched now by the same madness, all fear leaving him, saluted, heels together. 'At your orders, Herr Kapitän.'

'Good man.' Gericke clapped him on the shoulder. 'Take her up. We'll have to do this the hard way. Prepare tubes one to four for surface firing.' He turned to Carlsen. 'You take the helm, Willi, and make it good.'

There was a sudden bustle of activity, the klaxon sounding battle stations. As Gericke moved towards the ladder, he added almost casually, over his shoulder, 'Perhaps you'd care to join me on the bridge, Herr Konteradmiral?'

VI

At the top of the ladder he waited. There was a hiss of compressed air, a rushing of water and then Engel called, 'The hatch is above water.'

Gericke unclipped it and scrambled out on to the bridge of the conning-tower. Heavy rain smacked solidly into his face and the waters of the harbour heaved in turmoil. The tug was almost under now, but the oil around it was on fire and when he focused his night glasses, men jumped into view, hurling themselves into the icy water.

In the forward torpedo compartment the crew worked frantically to make ready. Engel was already aligning the attack periscope as Gericke swung his glasses to focus on the two frigates.

Beside him, Friemel said, 'A lot of activity on deck. I'd say you've got three minutes before they chop those anchors and get out of there.'

Alarm klaxons echoed stridently across the water. There was considerable movement now on the harbour wall. Suddenly, there was a hollow staccato booming and brilliant balls of fire seemed to cascade towards them in a great curve, falling into the water to port.

'That's it,' Friemel said grimly. 'They know we're here.'

U-235 surged forward. Gericke said calmly, 'Tubes one to four prepare for surface firing.'

Engel called into the voice pipe. There was the briefest of pauses before he looked up. 'One to four ready, sir.'

'Six metres,' Gericke said. 'Line of sight. One and two on the starboard frigate, three and four take care of the gentleman to port. Distance one thousand metres, speed thirty-five. Director angle blue four.'

Engel relayed the orders through the voice pipe to Leading Seaman Pich, who manned the TDC, the complicated electrical device linking gyro compass, attack periscope and torpedo circuits, which from now on would, in effect, be responsible for the success or failure of the operation.

He made the final connection. Engel guided the aiming cross of the attack periscope on to the starboard frigate which, relieved of its anchor, was starting to swerve to port.

'Blue four, ready to fire, sir!'

'Fire,' Gericke called.

'Tube one fire. Tube two fire!'

The U-boat staggered as the torpedoes broke free and raced towards the target at thirty-five knots. The port frigate was moving now, surging forward as her captain gave her everything she had, the bow wave rising.

'She'll make it, Paul. She'll make it!' Friemel cried, his binoculars glued to his eyes.

'Oh no she won't,' Gericke said calmly. 'This is my night. Hard a-starboard,' he called. 'It's all yours, Karl. Fire at will.'

Machine-gun bullets rattled against the conning-tower, several shells landed close enough on the port side to cause the U-boat to roll violently. But it was Karl Engel's night, too – calm, detached, cooler than he had ever been, as the captain of the frigate made his one mistake, turning to starboard to bring all guns to bear, momentarily exposing his entire port side, a perfect target.

As the torpedoes were released, the U-boat corkscrewed in the heavy seas. 'Hard a-port,' Gericke called. 'And tell Dietz to give them everything he's got.'

There was a muffled explosion, followed by another as the first two torpedoes struck home. A cheer drifted up from the control room. Across the water, orange fire erupted from the first frigate and black smoke billowed into the night. The second was turning frantically now, as if her captain already sensed that the axe was about to fall, her guns still firing.

A moment later, number three torpedo hit, closely followed by the fourth. The frigate staggered drunkenly, her prow seemed to lift high into the air, then plunged. There was a further great explosion and flames towered into the night.

'That's it,' Gericke said. 'The magazine. It has to be.' He called to Engel. 'I said speed, damn you! Speed! Let's get out of here.'

All hell had broken loose now, guns firing across the harbour from the shore installations. Friemel, ducking between the steel canopy as a bullet ricocheted close to his head, said, 'Gun crew, Paul?'

'No,' Gericke said. 'We'd only give them a better target. We'll be out of it soon, believe me. They won't be expecting us to try the South Passage run. It isn't supposed to exist, remember.'

The wind rolled thick, oily smoke in a black pall across the harbour, blanketing the entire scene, and U-235, hidden from view, made towards Pendennis Point at full speed.

VII

The tide was running fast under the Point as they turned into the channel. In the control room, Engel had the helm, Friemel at his shoulder. Everyone seemed to have crowded in – Dietz, the chief engineering officer, young Heini Roth, the second watch officer.

The diesels had stopped and the propellers were being driven by the electric motors. It seemed very still and when Gericke's voice crackled over the Tannoy, Roth gave a startled gasp.

'We haven't got too much time to spare. The tide's beginning to ebb and there's a five or six knot current running, so let's get it right first time.'

His voice, clearly audible to every man on board, was

properly calm. Engel, speaking into the microphone box above his head, barely managed to keep his voice steady as he replied, 'Aye, aye, sir. Ready when you are.'

Gericke, on the bridge, was colder than he'd ever been in his life before. Reaction, he told himself, to all that action and passion. He managed a smile. He wore a lifejacket, headphones and a throat microphone, and was up to his chest in water.

It was not totally dark for an eerie phosphorescence, and considerable broken water, gave him a far better view of the general situation than he had expected. The hubbub on the far side of the harbour seemed muffled and far away, without reality.

'Course one-eight-two,' he said.

Engel's voice crackled in his ears. 'Seven metres under the keel . . . six metres under the keel.'

They surged on, caught by the current, white water all around and somewhere high above in the night, the turret on Pendennis Point lifted into the darkness. Gericke could hear traffic and wondered briefly whether there might be searchlights mounted.

There was sudden panic in Engel's voice, 'Two metres, sir. Only two metres under the keel . . . one metre.'

Gericke said calmly, 'Steady as she goes, Karl. Nice and easy. Half-ahead.'

'We would appear to have run out of water, my dear Paul,' Friemel's voice sounded equally calm.

U-235 seemed to shudder, there was a crunch, a long-drawn-out grating that set on edge the teeth of every man on board.

'Oh God, that's it,' Heini Roth said aloud in the control room.

And yet they were still moving, a long, continuous grating, that suddenly ceased as Gericke's voice called, 'Full ahead.'

There was a ragged cheer through the entire boat. 'He's done it!' Dietz said excitedly. 'As usual,' he added.

Gericke's voice sounded again, 'If you think we're out of the wood yet, forget it. We haven't passed the blockship. A hundred metres to go. I can see her plain. Half-engines and make ready to give me everything you've got when I give the word.'

On the bridge he faced the last obstacle. U-235 drifted forward in the grip of the current that coursed through South Passage as the tide started to ebb. The blockship was an old coaster, her single stack clear against the night sky, deck awash.

'Hard a-starboard,' Gericke said.

The slot between the rocks and the blockship seemed inconceivably narrow, but it was too late to turn back now. Again there was a grating under the keel.

Engel's voice was frantic. 'There should be six metres, sir. Six metres.'

The grating stopped as the U-boat slid on. 'Probably a chain.' Gericke said. 'Keep going, Karl. Not long now.'

Somewhere behind him, beyond the smoke on the other side of the harbour, there was a muffled explosion. He paid no heed, and gave all his concentration to the task in hand, gripping the rail with numbed fingers.

And then the boat seemed to be caught in a giant hand and pushed forward by a sudden fierce current. The blockship was alongside – the stack looming above him, rusting plates, bridge windows smashed, a ghost ship.

He leaned over the rail. This was the moment of maximum danger, the time for jagged metal or protruding girders to open them up like a sardine can.

There was a grating on the starboard side, the cliff seemed very close, too close, and then, as they swung to port in the current, the blockship seemed to drift away into the night, was suddenly abeam.

Gericke said hoarsely, 'We're into clear water. Heavy seas. Wind force six by my estimation. Full ahead, diesels too, if you please.'

The scene in the control room was incredible. Dietz burst into tears and Friemel, in an excess of emotion, grabbed Heini Roth and hugged him.

'Remarkable,' the admiral said. 'There I was, lying in my coffin ready to go. Now I've just been told it was all a mistake.'

On the bridge, Gericke hung on tight as U-235 rode into the full force of the wind, sweeping in from the Channel. It was very dark now, with no landmarks to guide him as one great wave after another slapped over him. Only the roaring of the sea was in his ears. Better to get out of it now. 'All right, Karl,' he said. 'Bring her up and let me get dry, then we'll submerge till we're in mid-channel.'

And suddenly the roaring was louder and it was no longer the sea. He became conscious of an enormous white bow wave to starboard. There was a tremendous crash, the tearing of metal as a dark, greyhound shape ploughed right across the U-boat's forecastle and plunged on into the night.

The U-boat rolled, the conning-tower swung to port and Gericke was tossed over the side.

'My night,' he thought, for some inane reason clutching at his cap. 'Wasn't that what I said?' and then he hit the water and the first wave rolled over him.

VIII

The dim shape Gericke had glimpsed momentarily as it ploughed across the U-boat's forecastle was a Vosper MTB of the Royal Navy's Fifteenth Flotilla, racing home from patrol at thirty-five knots on receipt of the news from Falmouth over the radio.

Now she drifted helplessly, making water, all engines stopped. On the bridge, her commander, an RNVR lieutenant named Drummond, was taking the damage report from the boat's chief petty officer.

'How long have we got, chief?'

'In this sea, an hour at the most, sir. If they want to save her they'd better get a tug out here fast.'

'You're certain it was a submarine?'

'Definite, sir. Leading Seaman Cooper saw it, too.' He hesitated. 'But whether one of ours or theirs, I couldn't be sure.'

'My God,' Drummond said softly.

There was an excited cry aft of the bridge. 'Someone in the water, sir, off the port rail.'

'Searchlight,' Drummond said. 'Quickly now!'

The beam sliced across the broken water and picked out Gericke in his yellow lifejacket, his cap pulled down over his ears. He waved as he was swept in under the rail.

'Quickly!' Drummond called. 'He must be frozen half to death in there.'

Bell, the petty officer, ran down from the bridge to supervise. There was a flurry of activity at the rail and Gericke was hauled aboard. Drummond leaned over the bridge rail, watching anxiously, training the searchlight on them and then Bell looked up.

'Good God, sir, we've got ourselves a Jerry.'

IX

In London, it was raining hard and fog crouched at the ends of the streets. Janet Munro's trenchcoat was soaked through, as was the scarf bound around her hair.

They had walked for several miles in the pouring rain – Birdcage Walk, the Palace, St James's Park and Downing Street, although Jago hadn't been able to see very much. Not that he cared.

'Sure you haven't had enough?' he asked as they moved down towards Westminster Bridge.

'Not yet. I promised you something special, remember?'

'Did you?' Jago looked puzzled.

They came to the bridge and she turned on to the Embankment. 'Well, this is it,' she said. 'The most romantic place in town. Every American in London should walk along the Embankment at least once, preferably after midnight.'

'It's almost that now,' Jago said.

'Good, we'll have another cigarette and wait for the witching hour.'

They leaned on the parapet and listened to the lapping of the water. 'Have you enjoyed it, your guided tour?' she asked.

'Oh yes, ma'am, you could say that,' Jago told her. 'I was a stranger in your city, but not any more.'

'I like that,' she said. 'You're a poet, too.'

'Not me,' Jago said. 'Thank the Gershwins.' He leaned over the parapet beside her. 'You really like this old town, don't you?'

'We have a special relationship. I've seen her through good times and bad, often burning like hell, and we're still here, both of us.'

'But you don't like people much?'

Her chin tilted. He could sense anger in her, barely contained. 'Should I, darling? I wish you could give me a good reason.'

'What is it, doctor? Don't you think you're up to snuff? Do you have to let too many people die?'

'Damn you to hell, Jago.' Her hand went up as if she would strike him. Big Ben chimed the first stroke of midnight.

Jago put up his arms defensively. 'The witching hour – remember. And this is the Embankment, the most romantic place in London.'

She reached out to touch his face. 'Tell me, Jago, did they cut you up badly back there? Did they take a few years off your life?'

'Too many,' he said.

The last stroke of midnight boomed out. The rain increased into a drenching downpour and she seemed to be standing very close. Tentatively he put his hands on her shoulders. She ran a hand up behind his head and kissed him passionately on the mouth.

'Take me home, Jago,' she whispered.

— 6 —

> Barquentine *Deutschland*, 18 September 1944. Lat. 43°.4N., long. 20°.55W. Last night in the middle watch, fore upper topsail split during a bad blow. Weather continues to deteriorate. Full gale in the morning watch with big sea running.

IN SPITE OF the fact that it was only two bells of the afternoon watch, it was so dark in the saloon that Sister Angela had to light the lamp. She sat at the table which, like the chairs, was bolted to the floor. Her bible was open in front of her. Lotte sat opposite, busy with needle and thread as she mended a denim shirt.

Outside, the wind howled and the *Deutschland* rolled heavily to port taking her own time to come back again, an event which would once have caused them both considerable alarm, but not now. Water trickled down the companionway steps and slopped across the floor. It was cold and damp – everything was damp – even the blanket which she had draped around her shoulders.

Lotte, concentrating on her task in the poor light, smiled briefly, as if at some private thought. Sister Angela had seen that smile often of late; knew only too well what it meant. It was as if the girl was slipping away from her; from everything that had once seemed so important – and for what?

She was aware of anger rising inside as old wounds opened, but she resolutely held it in check. It was an unworthy emotion and solved nothing.

She said to Lotte, 'That shirt – isn't it Herr Richter's?'

Lotte looked up. 'Why, yes, sister.'

Before the conversation could be taken any further, there was a clatter on the companionway and the bosun appeared, a billycan in one hand. His head was bare, the blond hair and beard beaded with rain, and his yellow oilskin ran with water.

He smiled as he placed the can on the table. 'Hot tea, ladies. All the galley can manage at the moment.'

'Is it bad up there, Herr Richter?' Sister Angela asked.

'Just another Atlantic gale, sister,' he replied. 'Nothing special to an old hand like you.'

She smiled in spite of herself, for it was hard not to.

Lotte said, 'Your shirt, Herr Richter, will be ready for you this evening.'

'You'll spoil me, fräulein.' The *Deutschland* lurched so that he had to brace himself against the table. 'I'd better get back up there. That wasn't too good.'

He mounted the companionway and Lotte paused in her sewing. 'He never stops. One would think at times that he was the only man in the crew.'

'The finest sailor, certainly,' Sister Angela said. She paused, then carried on, 'A fine young man altogether. Has he told you much about himself?' Lotte glanced up, her face colouring.

'I only ask because Sister Käthe mentioned that she had noticed you and Herr Richter enjoying a lengthy conversation on deck yesterday evening.'

Before the girl could reply, the ship staggered under another mighty blow, swinging off course. There was a cry of alarm on deck, the doors at the head of the companionway burst open and water cascaded in.

II

Berger had the wheel with two seamen to help him as the *Deutschland* ploughed on through a wilderness of white foam. In spite of their combined efforts, the ship was swinging a couple of points on each side of her course.

Sturm and Leading Seaman Knorr were attempting to reef the fore staysail and were having a hard time of it, for the sea constantly poured over the weather bulwark, covering the hatches, swirling waist-deep, so that again and yet again, they had to stop work and simply hang on to prevent themselves from being swept away.

Richter emerged from the companionway, closed the doors behind him and turned to move towards the quarterdeck ladder. An enormous wave raced in astern, towering into the rain as if intent on engulfing them. He cried a warning to Berger, pointing, but the wave broke full upon the poop, knocking the captain's two companions from their feet.

Richter grabbed for the weather-jigger rigging and held on. Water boiled around him as the wave passed, taking all before it, so that for a moment he believed she must certainly founder under all that weight.

Slowly, the *Deutschland* started to rise and, as the water receded, he saw that there was now only Sturm up there in the weather rigging by the fore staysail.

Knorr floundered in the lee scuppers, trying to get to his feet. Richter started towards him as the *Deutschland* continued to climb and then another great sea rolled in and knocked him off his feet again. He grabbed for the edge of the main-hatch cover and held on tight, but the same sea lifted Knorr over the rail. As Richter struggled to his feet, he caught a single flash of yellow out there that was quickly gone.

Sturm started to work his way along the deck using the weather lines. Berger and his two companions were winning in their battle to control the wheel. Richter saw that the doors at the head of the companionway swung open. He stepped inside, closed them behind him and went down.

There was a foot of water in the saloon and the other nuns had emerged from their cabins in some alarm to join Sister Angela and Lotte.

'It's all right, ladies,' Richter assured them. 'Everything is under control, but I would suggest you return to your cabins and strap yourselves into those bunks until the gale blows itself out.'

There was a certain hesitation, but Sister Angela said briskly, 'Herr Richter is right. We must all do as he says at once.'

The other nuns retreated to their cabins, ankle-deep in water, skirts raised but Lotte stayed, reaching up to touch the smear of blood on Richter's right cheek.

'You are hurt, Herr Richter.'

'Nothing,' he said. 'A scratch only. Please do as I say.' He turned to Sister Angela. 'We lost a man overboard just now. Knorr. You can tell the others in your own good time. I didn't want to alarm them unnecessarily.'

She crossed herself. 'Was there nothing to be done?'

'In these seas? He was swallowed whole.'

The ship staggered again and he turned, swearing, brushed past Lotte, and went up the companionway fast. She reached out as if she would hold him back.

'Helmut,' she whispered.

She stood there, her skirts dragging in the water that slopped around her feet, something close to despair on her face. 'He'll kill himself, I know it'!

Sister Angela said gently, 'You like him, don't you? Like him a great deal, I mean?'

'Yes, sister,' Lotte replied in a low voice.

Sister Angela sat down at the table, her hands gripping the edge of the table. 'My child, you must remember that we are members of an order whose vows urge us to love all our fellow creatures equally. The danger for us in any kind of personal relationship is that it detracts from what one is able to give to others. Our vow is to be servant to humanity, Lotte.'

'I have taken no such vow, sister.'

Sister Angela braced herself against the table as the floor tilted again. She was slightly breathless now and not from any physical exertion.

'Do you know what you are saying?'

'Yes,' Lotte replied, a new firmness in her voice. 'That I am no longer certain of my vocation.'

Sister Angela reached out, grasping the girl's hand tightly. 'Think well, Lotte,' she said urgently. 'To give up God's love for . . .'

'. . . a man?' Lotte asked. 'Is it not possible then to have both?'

Sister Angela tried to stay calm and yet that ancient bitterness floated up again like bile. 'Things are not always what they seem. Human beings are frail. Once, when I was even younger than you, I loved a man, gave him my heart and, God help me, gave him my body also – and in return . . .' She choked on the words. 'And in return . . .'

Lotte said gently, 'And because one man acted so, all men are tainted? Is this what you would have me believe, sister?'

'No,' Sister Angela whispered. 'Of course not.' She squeezed Lotte's hand. 'We've talked enough for the moment. Go and lie down as Herr Richter ordered. He knows what is best for us.'

Lotte hesitated, but did as she was told. The door to her cabin clicked shut behind her. Sister Angela sat there at the table, her eyes vacant, staring into space.

'Why, Karl?' she whispered. 'Why?'

And then, as hot tears stung her eyes, the iron discipline of the years came to her aid as always. She took a deep breath to steady herself, folded her hands and started to pray for the repose of Leading Seaman Peter Knorr's soul; for all sinners everywhere whose actions only cut them off from the infinite blessing of God's love.

III

Towards evening the gale abated but it was still blowing very hard and high above the deck Helmut Richter, Sturm and Leading Seaman Kluth, balanced on the yardarm, struggled to refit the freshly-mended fore upper topsail. The rain, sweeping in from the south-east, was like bullets and bitterly cold as they punched the wet canvas, cursing as blood spurted from torn fingers.

Berger stood gazing up at the men aloft, Otto Prager at his side in black oilskin and sou'wester.

'It frightens me just to watch,' the consul said. 'I'd never get used to it, not if we sailed round the world and took a year over it.'

'It certainly separates the men from the boys,' Berger told him, as Sturm and the others started to come down.

The young lieutenant mounted to the quarterdeck. 'All square up there now, captain.' His face was pale and drawn, the memory of Knorr still with him.

Berger said, 'Don't blame yourself, boy. There was nothing to be done.'

'I almost had him,' Sturm said. 'Then he slipped from my grasp.'

Berger put a hand on his shoulder. 'Get yourself some coffee.'

Sturm went down the ladder. Berger looked over the rail and saw Richter staunching blood with a handkerchief. 'Bad?' he called.

'Finger-end, that's all.'

'See Sister Angela. She'll fix you up.'

When the bosun went down the companionway, the saloon was deserted except for Lotte who sat at the table, a book open before her. She glanced up at the sound of his foot on the stair and smiled.

'Herr Richter.'

'Fräulein.' For some reason lately he found it impossible to call her sister. 'You should be in your bunk.'

She reached for his damaged hand and started to unwrap the handkerchief. 'What have you done?'

'It's nothing,' he said. 'A split finger, that's all. Punching canvas. It happens all the time.'

The end of the middle finger was open to the bone. 'You must let me do something.'

'I'll see to it.' Sister Angela spoke from behind. 'Please return to your devotions and the task I set you. In your cabin,' she added.

Lotte coloured, picked up her book and went out quickly. It was very quiet in the saloon, the voice of the wind outside subdued, far away. Richter and Sister Angela confronted each other.

'I'll get my medical case.'

He sat at the table and lit a cigarette. 'You don't mind?' he asked when she turned.

'Your smoking? Oh no, Herr Richter. My father used to say that a man should have some vices. Of the right kind, that is.'

'A short leash, you mean?'

'Do I?' She examined the finger. 'This will need two stitches. You'd better look the other way.'

He drew on his cigarette, watching the door to Lotte's cabin, grunting a little as the needle entered his flesh.

'Where are you from, Herr Richter?'

'Vienna.'

She was surprised. 'A Viennese sailor? I didn't know there were such things. What did you do, run away to sea?'

'Strangely enough, that's exactly what I did,' Richter told her. 'My father, if you are interested, was a surgeon, and had a similar career mapped out for me.'

'And you had other ideas. Are you married?'

'No,' he said evenly.

The needle was inserted again. 'You should be. It's good for the soul, Herr Richter. There, I've finished.'

'How strange,' he said. 'I'd always understood it was good for the flesh.'

She kept her temper and contented herself with saying calmly, 'Leave her alone. She has better things to do with her life.'

'Why? Because that was the way it worked out for you?'

She stood abruptly, picked up the medical case and went

into her cabin. Richter sat there for a moment longer. As he got up, Lotte's door clicked open. 'Are you all right now, Herr Richter?' she whispered.

'Fine,' he said. 'In fact, I've never felt better, fräulein.'

She smiled again and withdrew. Richter went up the companionway steps two at a time.

IV

For Paul Gericke things progressed with extraordinary rapidity. A preliminary interrogation at Falmouth during which his own clothes had been dried, then returned to him. He had then been moved by road to Portsmouth, where he had found himself in the hands of Naval Intelligence.

They had treated him with respect. He was, after all, something of a catch for them – the most important U-boat commander to be captured since Kretschmer.

For five straight hours they had interrogated him in shifts but with a total lack of success. Gericke had resolutely stuck to the personal information required under the Geneva Convention, and nothing more.

Just after noon he was informed that he was to be moved to London. He was transferred in a naval police van, handcuffed and escorted by a petty officer, two ratings and a sub-lieutenant, all armed.

And so it was that at four-thirty in the afternoon he was in the London District PoW Cage, a requisitioned house in Kensington Palace Gardens. This time, the treatment wasn't so good, particularly from the chief petty officer who took charge of him on arrival, a massively-built man of forty-six named Carver, with the broken nose of a boxer.

'If I had my way, son,' he informed Gericke, 'there's nothing I'd fancy more than getting you inside a ring for six straight rounds and I'd make sure you'd last right up to the final bell.'

'Oh, I don't know, chief,' Gericke told him calmly. 'I should have thought you would have been at your best up a dark alley with a bottle in your hand.'

For a moment he thought Carver was going to strike him, but there were two ratings present in reception. The chief petty officer, shaking with rage, contented himself with stripping Gericke of his decorations.

The room to which he was finally taken was pleasant enough. More like a study than an office, books lining the wall, a fire in the grate and, although the tall window was heavily barred, there was a view of the garden outside. He was placed in a chair on one side of a wide desk, still handcuffed, and waited impassively for whatever was to come, an armed rating on either side of him.

After a while, the door opened. The man who walked round to the other side of the desk was a full captain in the Royal Navy. He had a DSO and ribbons for the First War – Gericke took that in automatically, along with the iron-grey hair and pale, ascetic face. He had a bad limp and leaned heavily on an ebony walking stick.

He placed a couple of manilla folders on the desk and said rather formally, 'Commander Gericke – my name is Vaughan.'

'I wish I could say I was happy to meet you.'

Vaughan nodded to one of the ratings. 'You can take the handcuffs off now, then wait outside.'

He waited for them to comply with his order and only sat down as the door clicked shut behind them. Gericke eased his cramped wrists. 'Thank you. They were beginning to be rather uncomfortable.'

'Cigarette?' Vaughan pushed a box across the table. 'Your English is really quite excellent, but then you did live over here for a couple of years, didn't you?' He opened one of the folders and put on a pair of half-moon reading glasses. '1926–28. Hull. You went to grammar school there.'

'You seem to know.'

'Yes, I do, commander,' Vaughan told him, in the same calm, neutral voice. 'Everything about you. An excellent record by the way. I congratulate you.'

Gericke restrained an impulse to laugh. 'Of course.'

'Not only the Knight's Cross, but the Oak Leaves to go with it. A rare distinction.'

'It *was*.'

'Why do you say that?'

Gericke opened his leather jerkin to indicate the tunic underneath, bare of decorations. 'The spoils of war.'

For the first time, Vaughan showed emotion. A tiny muscle twitched in his right cheek. 'Your decorations were taken from you?'

'Yes.'

'In this establishment? You will be good enough to tell me when and by whom.'

'The chief petty officer in charge of reception,' Gericke said, and added maliciously, 'I had assumed it to be the normal run of things.'

'Not while I am in charge here, I can assure you, commander.' Vaughan's face was white, pinched around the mouth as he picked up the telephone on the desk. 'Send Chief Petty Officer Carver up to twenty-two at once.'

He got his feet and stumped across to the window, leaning on his cane. There was a knock at the door a moment later and Carver entered.

'You wanted me, sir?'

Vaughan spoke without turning round. 'Carver, I understand you have in your possession certain decorations belonging to this officer.'

'Sir?' Carver started to bluster.

Vaughan swung round to face him. 'Damn your eyes, man, get them out on the table. Now!'

Carver hurriedly produced Gericke's Knight's Cross, Iron Cross First Class and wound badge and laid them on the desk. 'Is that the lot?' Vaughan asked Gericke.

Gericke nodded.

Vaughan said to Carver harshly. 'I'll deal with you later. Get out.'

As the door closed behind Carver, Gericke picked up the medals and put them in his pocket.

Vaughan sat down, took a cigarette from the box on the desk and examined the file again. 'As I was saying, quite a record. Let's see now. You joined the Tenth Flotilla at Brest after your return from the Far East, didn't you?'

'I've told you who I am, that's all that's required of me. I'm sorry, Captain Vaughan, I have nothing else to say.'

'All right,' Vaughan said. 'You compel me to become unpleasant. You really leave me no other choice.'

'Bring on the rubber hoses by all means. But it won't change anything.'

Vaughan was annoyed. 'We're not the Gestapo. We don't operate that way.'

'Then I shall be even more fascinated to hear your proposal,' Gericke assured him.

Vaughan opened the second folder. 'On 5 April 1942 you sank, in American waters near Rhode Island, an oil tanker named the *San Cristobal*.'

'Perfectly correct.'

'You are aware, of course, that this ship was a Spanish vessel registered in Bilbao and that to torpedo and sink her was contrary to the articles of war?'

'You don't say.'

'But I do and what is more to the point, our American friends intend to make you answer for it. As a courtesy, American Naval Intelligence was informed of your capture this morning. Within two hours they'd made a formal application to take you into custody. From what I hear, they intend to ship you to the States to stand trial.'

Gericke laughed. 'What nonsense! The *San Cristobal* was under charter to carry oil for the American War Department.'

'There's no mention of that fact here.'

'Strange – the rest of your information seems to have been so uniformly accurate.'

Vaughan shrugged. 'The Americans have asked for you, Gericke, that is fact, and the consequences if they do try you for this business could be most unpleasant.'

'But you could save me from all that?'

'If you were willing to co-operate.'

Gericke sighed. 'Sorry, but you really are wasting your time.'

Vaughan nodded calmly, put the manilla folder under his arm, got up and limped out without another word.

Left alone, Gericke, on impulse, pinned the Iron Cross and wound badge to his tunic and hung the Knight's Cross around his neck. Then he stood at the window and looked out through the bars. The garden was enclosed by a high wall and was badly overgrown. Rain drifted down through the branches of a large beech tree into a wilderness of rhododendrons. It was a melancholy sight.

The door opened behind him and Carver entered, followed by a rating carrying a covered tray. 'Put it down there, lad,' Carver ordered and added to Gericke. 'Something to eat, commander?'

The rating withdrew and Gericke walked to the desk. Carver leaned across and grabbed him by the front of the tunic. The eyes were cold.

'I'm going to have you, you German bastard, you see if I don't,' he whispered. He shoved Gericke back into Vaughan's chair and hurriedly left the room.

V

Just after seven on the same evening Janet Munro and Harry Jago arrived by taxi at the house in Kensington Palace Gardens. They went up the steps to the front door, which was guarded by two sentries, and into the entrance hall, where an Army Intelligence Corps sergeant sat at a trestle table.

Jago produced his pass. 'Lieutenant Jago. I'm supposed to report to a Captain Vaughan.'

'Oh yes, sir, he's expecting you. I'll get someone to take you up.'

The sergeant pressed a buzzer and Jago said, 'Okay if the lady waits for me here?'

'I don't see why not, sir.'

Jago turned to Janet, 'Sorry about this. Why the hell I'm supposed to report to a Royal Naval captain in the first place, God only knows. Let's hope it doesn't take long and we can get straight to the theatre.'

She patted his cheek. 'How could this mighty war machine of ours roll on without you?'

Before Jago could think of a suitable reply, a young ATS corporal appeared to escort him to Vaughan. Janet sat on a chair by the window, crossing one leg over the other in a manner which filled the intelligence sergeant at his desk with admiration.

'Not too bad today then, miss,' he ventured. 'Three in Hackney, two down Poplar way and one in Golders Green.'

'And that's good?' she said.

The flying bombs, the V1 variety, had been bad enough, the grating roar of their engines growing steadily louder as they approached, but at least you knew they were coming. With the V2 rockets, on the other hand, there was no warning: a supersonic bang, the roar of an explosion and total devastation.

A door on the far side to the hall opened and Gericke came through, flanked by two armed ratings. His hands were handcuffed in front of him, but he made a striking figure in the white naval cap with the Iron Cross on his tunic, the Knight's Cross around his neck.

He didn't appear to notice Janet, his head half-turned, laughing at something one of the guards had said, and they went up the stairs and disappeared from view.

The desk sergeant said, 'Jerry prisoner, miss. Naval officer. We get a lot of them through here.'

'Oh, I see.'

She stood up, crossed the hall and stood in the porch at the top of the steps. There was a staccato roaring high above in the darkness and she glanced up to see a V1 passing across the night sky, a short jet of flame sprouting from its tail.

'I wonder where that bastard will come down,' the sentry said beside her.

Death and destruction. She'd just seen one of the men responsible. *The enemy*. It was the closest she'd been to a German since before the war. For a moment, she saw Gericke again, laughing as he went up the stairs between the guards, and was conscious of a kind of anger.

Jago emerged behind her and took her arm. 'Okay, let's get out of here.'

They went down the steps and turned along the pavement. 'And what was all that about?'

'Well, I don't see why I shouldn't tell you. The British picked up a German U-boat commander last night, one of the really top boys. A guy named Paul Gericke. They've had him in here for interrogation. It seems they're giving him to us. He's being sent up to Glasgow on the night express tomorrow evening. He'll be handed over to our people and shipped out on a convoy leaving for the States three or four days from now.'

'And where do you come into it?'

'Well, he'll have a British escort, but some bright boy at Naval Headquarters remembered I was travelling on that train and decided it would be a good idea if I kept an eye out for our interests.'

'Did you meet him?'

'Just now.'

'Was he medium height – pale face, dark eyes, Iron Cross on his tunic?'

'That's our boy.'

'He was laughing as he went up the stairs,' she said. At that moment they were passing behind a row of half-demolished houses. 'He was laughing. He and his kind caused all this.'

'They tell me Berlin doesn't look too hot these days.'

She slipped an arm through his. 'You're too good to live, Harry Jago. By the way, I didn't get a chance to tell you, but Colonel Brisingham turned up at the hospital this afternoon with my travel warrant for tomorrow night's train.'

Jago was over the moon with delight. 'That means we can be together all the way to Mallaig.'

'I'm not so sure,' she said. 'Actually they've provided me with a sleeping compartment. A single berth all to myself.'

'They've what?' Jago said in astonishment. 'Have you any idea what it takes to get one of those things these days?'

'Yes,' she said. 'Eisenhower.'

Jago laughed. The rain increased and they ran across to the corner of the main road and she sheltered under a tree while he tried to whistle up a cab.

And as she waited, for some reason she kept seeing Gericke's face, laughing as he went upstairs.

VI

The clock in the charthouse chimed seven bells of the first watch. Seated at his desk in the cabin, a cigar between his teeth, Erich Berger paused to listen and then returned to his journal, the scratching of his pen sounding unnaturally loud in the silence.

> . . . the loneliest sound in the world, a ship's bell at sea by night, or is it that it simply accentuates for me the loneliness of command? I think to be a ship's master no simple task, especially in the conditions under which I find myself at the moment . . .

There was a knock on the door and Sturm entered in a flurry of rain. He wore black oilskins and sou'wester and water glistened on him in the light of the oil lamp.

'Well, Herr Sturm?' Berger said.

Sturm saluted. 'I've just made the rounds, sir. Everything nice and tight. Kluth and Weber have the wheel at present. Heading north-west by west at ten knots by estimation.'

'Full sail?'

'Every stitch she can carry.'

'And what about the weather?'

'Wind Force 5 with heavy rain, but it's surprisingly warm.'

'Excellent,' Berger went to the cupboard and found the rum bottle and two glasses. 'How long were you operating the radio for yesterday?'

Sturm accepted the glass gratefully. 'An hour and a half exactly.'

'What about the batteries?'

'Not too good, sir, but then they never were. It's not much of a set. The best Herr Prager could manage at short notice, I know. Still . . .' He hesitated. 'Do you want me to stop listening in, sir?'

'No, I don't think so. Those British and American weather reports are too useful, and the war news. But it's when we're close to home and wanting to transmit that we're going to need the power. I want to be sure we have enough in reserve.'

'Shall I leave it for tonight?'

'Half an hour,' Berger said. 'When you go off watch. I think that should suffice.'

'Very well, sir.' Sturm drained the last of his rum with reluctance. 'If you'll excuse me, I'd better get back on the quarterdeck.'

He turned and put his hand to the door – and from somewhere outside came the agonized cry of a woman.

VII

It was hot below and very close. To Lotte, this voyage seemed interminable. From nowhere to nowhere. There was a gentle and continuous snoring from beneath her. Sister Angela had moved Sister Else into the cabin without any explanation.

Lotte lay on the top bunk, the roof no more than two feet above her face, hot and uncomfortable in spite of the fact that she was wearing only a linen nightdress. She was thinking of Helmut Richter, concentrating with an intensity that was almost frightening, trying to conjure him up from the darkness – the slow smile, the wild blond hair and beard.

Lotte was a quiet, self-contained girl. Most of her life had been totally enclosed – first by the demands of a rigidly orthodox Catholic family, and then by the self-discipline of nursing training. And afterwards, the Order of the Sisters of Mercy. Nothing more demanding than God.

She had learned to live within herself. But Richter – Richter was something different – a totally new experience. When she thought of him, she smiled spontaneously.

Her body was damp with sweat. It was impossible for her to stay in that cabin another minute. She needed air – clean salt air. She dropped to the floor softly, reached for her cloak and slipped outside.

Lightning flickered on the far horizon, moving nearer. There was an eerie phosphorescence to everything, so that the ship was a place of darkness and light, warm rain drifting across the deck in a silvery haze.

Kluth leaned on the wheel, his foot against the binnacle, thoroughly enjoying himself as the *Deutschland* stormed on through the night, every sail full. Weber leaned on the rail beside him, smoking a pipe. Neither saw Lotte emerge from the companionway.

But Herbert Walz, making himself coffee in the galley, saw her. The girl kept to the shadows by the port rail and paused at the mizzen shrouds, head lifted to feel the rain.

She moved away from the rail and as she passed the galley entrance, Walz reached out and caught her round the waist.

Lotte was not certain what was happening. From surprise

as much as fear she cried out – a sharp cry of terror that sounded clearly above the wind and rain.

VIII

Helmut Richter, asleep in one of the hammocks which had been rigged in the fo'c'sle to take care of the extra crew, was awake in an instant, was up the ladder and out on deck before even Berger and Sturm had emerged from the captain's cabin.

Lotte staggered across the deck, losing her balance as the ship heeled and falling at Richter's feet. As he picked her up, the cloak fell back from her shoulders.

Sister Angela emerged from the companionway. 'Lotte!' she called.

Richter put the girl to one side and took a pace forward to stand waiting as Walz came hesitantly from the galley.

'Walz!' Richter said softly.

He stood there, bare feet apart, dressed only in seaman's denims. Lightning flickered overhead as the storm moved in. St Elmo's Fire flared at each masthead, so that the entire ship seemed to glow as it plunged forward.

'Richter!' Berger cried.

The bosun ignored him and moved forward. Walz, terrified, sprang into the ratlines and started to climb the foremast. Richter went after him picking his way with care as if he had all the time in the world.

Walz moved with remarkable speed. When he reached the lower topsail yard, he paused to look down, then drew the knife at his belt and slashed at the ratlines. Lotte cried out. There was a sudden groan from the assembled crew, followed by total silence as they held their breath.

The ratlines parted and Richter reached for the downhaul nearest to hand, swinging from it to a shroud line with the skill of a trapeze artist.

He hung there for a moment before starting upwards again. Walz, holding on to the yard, waited for him, reaching down to slash at the bosun's hand with the knife. Richter twisted out of the way, but Walz kicked him in the side of the face.

Richter slipped several feet down the line, then came to a

halt spinning round. Lotte stared up, her knuckles tight against her teeth. Sturm took a step forward.

Berger grabbed his arm. 'Leave it!' he said in a low voice.

'In God's name, Captain Berger,' Sister Angela said. 'Do something.'

'What would you suggest, sister?' Berger asked, without taking his gaze away from the scene above for a moment.

It was an extraordinary sight, with sheet lightning exploding from one horizon to the other, the strange ball of light of the St Elmo's Fire pulsating at each masthead, the eerie phosphorescence of the electrical discharge flowing along every rope and stay, picking Richter and Walz out of the darkness with total clarity.

With an incredible effort, the bosun went up the line hand over hand, grabbed for the lower topsail yard and a moment later was secure in the foot-ropes.

Walz backed away and started upwards again, climbing towards the upper topsail yard. Each flash of lightning had a dazzling white intensity to it that seemed to imprint the scene on the brain for those on deck, but in between was a brief interval of total darkness so that they might have been looking through the eyeholes of an old-fashioned moving picture machine, the action moving jerkily forward, scene by scene.

As Walz reached the yard, the bosun swung to one side on a lift, pulled himself up to a position on the extreme end of the yardarm and began inching along the foot-ropes. Walz backed away, out towards the other end of the yardarm.

Richter was very close now. He hung there no more than three feet away from Walz who struck out blindly. The point of the knife caught the bosun's right cheek. He came foward implacably and Walz gave a cry of despair.

He grabbed for the main upper topsail brace and slashed at it in a frenzy with the knife. The line parted and the yardarm, freed from restraint, swung viciously from one side to the other, the sail flapping as air spilled from it.

Richter should have been hurled into space, but managed to scramble to the temporary safety of the lower topgallant yard.

Walz swung crazily backwards and forwards. A particularly

wild roll of the *Deutschland* sent him half over the yard and he only managed to save himself by hooking an arm in the footrope.

Richter worked his way across the back of the lower topgallant from one lift to another. He paused, suspended in space, watching carefully, judging his moment, as Walz, on the end of the yardarm, swung far out over the sea.

The ship heeled, Walz swung in very fast, hanging on with one arm, striking with the knife. Richter, a rope in each hand, gave him both feet in the face. Walz cried out and went back over the yard into space.

He hit the water some distance from the starboard rail. His arm swung up in mute appeal, but in spite of the wildly flailing sail, the *Deutschland* was still making ten knots, and he receded, became one with the night, taken by the sea.

'We're heaving to, Herr Sturm. Douse jibs, if you please. Clew up forecourse, topsails and t'gallants, then get to work and repair that damage. I want to be under way again in an hour,' Berger ordered.

'Is that all you have to say?' Sister Angela's voice was low, intense. 'A man is dead.'

'It shall be so noted in the log,' Berger said impassively.

Richter dropped to the deck and Lotte ran forward, arms outstretched. When she was a yard or two away from him she swayed, half-fainting. Richter caught her quickly. He stood there for a moment looking down at her, blood oozing from his slashed cheek, then went towards the companionway.

The other nuns gathered together at the bottom, got out of the way quickly. Sister Käthe said, 'Is she all right, Herr Richter?'

Richter didn't reply. He walked across the saloon to Lotte's cabin, went in and laid her on the lower bunk. He reached for a blanket to cover her and the girl's eyes fluttered.

For a second only she stared blankly into space, then recognized him. 'Herr Richter?'

'It's all right,' Richter said.

He made a movement as if to turn away and there was instant panic. 'Don't leave me.'

He took her hand and crouched beside the bunk stroking

her forehead as one might gentle a child. 'Never,' he said softly. 'Never again. Sleep now.'

She closed her eyes, the face growing calm. After a while, the breathing became slow and regular, the hand slackened in his.

He got to his feet and turned to find the nuns peering in at the doorway, a uniform look of astonishment on their faces in the dim light. Sister Angela stood at the foot of the bed, pale and composed, hands folded. He waited for her comment, drained of emotion, quite indifferent and as always, she surprised him.

'And now, I think you'd better come with me, Herr Richter,' she said calmly. 'From the looks of things, I'd say you need another stitch or two.'

IX

In the grey light of dawn far to the north-east, U-235 surfaced at the rendezvous buoy a mile off Bergen. She presented an extraordinary sight, for in place of her prow there was only a jagged stump of twisted, rusting metal. In mid-Channel it had been discovered that eight metres of the forecastle was bent to one side. Friemel had managed to detach the damaged portion by alternating as rapidly as possible between full speed ahead and full speed back.

But the rest of the trip had been an unqualified nightmare. He had not closed his eyes in thirty-six hours and when he followed Engel up the ladder to the bridge, it was very slowly indeed.

An escort of two armed trawlers raced out to meet them, signal lamps flashing. Engel examined them through his binoculars, then turned. His face was grey, the eyes dark, no life there at all. The bandage round his forehead didn't help the general appearance.

'We made it, Herr Admiral?'

'So it would appear.'

A seaman came up the ladder behind them quickly and passed a flimsy across. 'Signal, sir.'

He offered it to Friemel, who shook his head. 'You read,' he said to Engel.

'Well done, Otto. Dönitz, Commander-in-Chief of the Kreigsmarine and BdU,' Engel said in a low voice. 'That's all it says, sir.'

'Well done.' Friemel laughed harshly. 'Well done indeed.'

There was a further flurry of activity as the minesweepers circled to take up position, men cheering from the rails as U-235 ploughed forward slowly.

From somewhere below there was a cry, a muffled cheer, feet scrambling on the iron ladder and Heini Roth erupted on to the bridge, another flimsy in his hand. His face was white with excitement. 'What is it, for God's sake?' Friemel said.

'Further signal from BdU, Herr Admiral. It simply says: Information from Abwehr that Gericke arrived London Cage on the nineteenth.'

He turned, leaned heavily on the rail, totally overcome, Friemel took a crumpled cigarette pack from his breast pocket. There was one left which he carefully inserted into his holder. Heini gave him a light, hand shaking.

Friemel inhaled deeply, then sighed. 'The last of those lousy French weeds and yet I don't think a cigarette ever tasted better in my life.'

— 7 —

Barquentine *Deutschland*, 20 September 1944. Lat. 46°.55N., long. 17°.58W. Another bad night. Wind Force 7. Rain and heavy seas. At four bells of the morning watch outer jib parted at the clew and jib boom ripped away when a huge sea came up to windward. Leading Seamen Kluth and Schmidt who had jumped to the mizzen pipe-rail were hurled into the lee scuppers. I expected to see them swept away, but by some miracle, they survived, Schmidt sustaining a fracture of the left forearm. As it was imperative to go about with such a sea running, I decided to wear ship to give Herr Sturm a chance to repair damage. At two bells of the forenoon watch, Bosun Richter reported eighteen inches of water in the bilges. I immediately ordered him to call the starboard watch from below and to commence pumping. It was two bells of the first dog watch before Herr Sturm was able to report all damage secure. Bosun Richter's watch having pumped her dry again and the storm having abated a little, I was able to bring her round and resume our original course, having lost some forty miles as we drifted to leeward. I estimate we are now some seven hundred miles due west of the Bay of Biscay.

IT WAS CONSIDERED useful propaganda to let the public see German prisoners of war being led through Euston station. Sub-Lieutenant Fisher was in charge of the escort which consisted of Carver and two leading seamen, Wright and Hardisty. They all wore gaiters and webbing belts carrying Webley .38 revolvers like any normal shore patrol, but they took Gericke through the crowd as unobtrusively as possible, just another naval prisoner, a blue raincoat draped over his shoulders.

Fisher identified himself to the guard, who led them into a luggage van. The rear section was walled off by a metal grille behind which lay a jumble of red GPO bags.

The guard produced a key. 'He can go in there if you like.'

'Fine,' Fisher said. 'Can I keep the key?'

'Don't see why not,' the guard said. 'I've got a spare. I don't suppose you're likely to steal the mail.'

He went out. Fisher unlocked the iron gate and Carver nodded to Gericke, scrupulously polite, 'If you don't mind, sir.'

Gericke moved inside, the sub-lieutenant locked the gate and handed the key to Carver. 'Right, chief. You look after things here while I see if I can find Lieutenant Jago.'

'You take your time, sir. We'll be fine in here,' Carver told him. 'A damn sight better off than they are further up the train.'

Fisher went out and Carver passed a pound note across to Leading Seaman Hardisty. 'You and your mate cut along to the station buffet and grab what you can in the way of sandwiches and fags.'

'But we've brought a load of stuff with us from the canteen, chief,' Hardisty told him.

'I know, son, I know,' Carver said. 'Which is fine, till we roll into Leeds or somewhere like it at two in the bloody morning and find the cupboard's bare. Now do as I say.'

Gericke leaned against the metal grille and examined a notice on the wall. It said:

If an air raid occurs while you are on the train:

1 Do not attempt to leave unless required by the guard to do so. You are safer where you are.
2 Pull the blinds down, both by day and night, as a protection against flying glass.
3 If room is available lie down on the floor.

Carver said, 'Thanks to you buggers, that little lot's there.'

'Tell me something, chief petty officer,' Gericke asked. 'How long have you been in the service?'

'Thirty years. I joined up in 1914 when I was sixteen.'

'Ah, a regular,' Gericke nodded. 'You surprise me. War, after all, is the name of the game for the professional. Yet you seem to object to the fact that there's one on. Perhaps the only reason you stayed on after the first lot was to wear a pretty uniform and have a girl in every port.'

Carver was furiously angry. 'You wait, you bastard.'

They heard Fisher's voice approaching. The sub-lieutenant entered followed by Captain Vaughan and Harry Jago to find Carver passing a cigarette through the mesh to Gericke.

'Care for a smoke, commander?' he was asking with perfect civility.

'That's very kind of you, chief.' Gericke accepted the cigarette and a light.

Vaughan said, 'A little primitive, but it could be worse. Any complaints, commander?'

Gericke raised his handcuffed wrists. 'Could I possibly have these removed? After all, I *am* caged in.'

'Sorry.' Vaughan shook his head. 'But if it makes you feel any better, we had an intelligence report in from our Norwegian friends in Bergen a couple of hours ago. It seems U-

235 under the command of Konteradmiral Otto Friemel arrived safely, minus seven or eight metres of her bows.'

For a moment, Gericke couldn't take it in, but in any case, there was no time to say anything for outside the guard's whistle blew, there was the sound of running feet.

Vaughan said stiffly in that careful, precise voice, 'Well, commander, I can only wish you a safe voyage, in spite of the exigencies of the North Atlantic.'

Gericke smiled. 'Ironic to find myself in the periscope sights of an old comrade.'

Vaughan saluted, beckoned to Fisher and limped out on the platform. Jago said to Gericke, 'I'll look in from time to time. It can take twelve hours or more to make Glasgow.'

'I'm in no particular hurry.'

Jago went out and Carver moved across to the grille. 'And neither am I, son,' he said softly. 'But just for starters, let's have those medals back.'

II

On Fhada, rain blew in across the harbour and drummed against the windows of the old cottage. Reeve was seated at his desk, his diary open before him. His daily entry was an old habit, engaged in from his earliest days at sea. Not so much a record of events as an attempt to formulate his thoughts. He put a match to his pipe, picked up his pen and started to write.

> . . . this life of mine, if life I can call it, has become a strange affair, a kind of metamorphosis in which everything has changed. Oliver Wendell Holmes once said that it was required of a man that he should share the action and passion of his times at peril of being judged not to have lived, and for most of my life I have followed his precept with uncommon faithfulness. But now, I find myself caught in a web of days, time passing in a kind of slow motion and to what purpose? What end?

He put down his pen and stirred the wolfhound, sprawled on the rug before the hearth, with his foot. 'Out of the way, you red devil.'

Rory moved reluctantly and Reeve added a few turves to the peat fire, then glanced at his watch. 'Almost time, Rory. Shall we see if they've anything for us today, eh? Maybe someone out there will actually remember that we still exist.'

The radio was on a table by the window. He sat down, adjusted the headphones and started to transmit. 'This is Sugar One on Fhada calling Mallaig. Are you receiving me?'

Rory crouched beside him and Reeve fondled the dog's ears and tried again. There was an almost instantaneous response. 'Hello, Sugar One, this is Mallaig receiving you loud and clear. Stand by, please. I have a message for you.'

Reeve was aware of a sudden excitement.

'Admiral Reeve? Murray here, sir.'

'What can I do for you?' Reeve demanded.

'Had a signal from London for you, sir. Just to let you know that your niece is on her way to stay with you for a few days.'

Reeve said automatically, 'That's wonderful. When does she arrive?'

'Sometime tomorrow. I can't be more exact than that, I'm afraid. You know what the trains are like these days. What about transport to Fhada, sir? I don't think I'll have anything official available.'

'That's all right,' Reeve said. 'I'll see to that end of things.' He braced himself. 'Anything else for me, Murray?'

'I'm afraid not, sir,' Murray said, and added, 'I'm sorry, admiral.'

'Don't be,' Reeve said bitterly. 'I don't think anyone else is, so why should you be different? Over and out.'

He switched off the set and sat staring into space, one hand idly playing with Rory's ears. It would be nice to see Janet again, to hear her news, but it wasn't enough. Not nearly enough.

The dog whined as his hand gripped too tightly and he stood up quickly. 'Sorry, boy. I'm not at my best today. Let's get a little fresh air.'

He took down his reefer from behind the door and went out, Rory at his heels. The wind was in the wrong direction to use a sail so he hand-pumped his way on one of the trolleys for the entire length of the line to South Inlet. When he went down to the lifeboat station the rear door of the boathouse was open. Murdoch was sitting on an old chair, sheltered from the rain, mending a net across his knee.

He looked up, the weatherbeaten face showing no emotion, his hands still working. 'A good day or a bad day is it, Carey Reeve?'

'Since when have I had a choice?'

'Like that, is it? Would you care for a dram?'

'Maybe later. My niece is arriving at Mallaig tomorrow on the London train.'

'That will be nice for you.' Murdoch spread his net. 'Young Lachlan MacBrayne is coming home on leave off that same train. His mother told me yesterday.'

'A paratrooper, isn't he?'

'That is so. If you've no objection I've promised to run across in your *Katrina* and pick him up. You would like me to bring your niece back also?'

'That would be fine,' Reeve said.

III

On the train, Gericke sprawled back on the mail sacks, eyes closed apparently asleep. Carver and the two leading seamen were playing cards. Fisher was reading a book.

There was a knock on the door and when Fisher unlocked it, Harry Jago stepped in. 'Everything okay?'

'I think so,' Fisher said. They walked across to the wire mesh screen. 'He's been asleep for the past hour.'

'Fine. If you've got time I'd like you to come up to the sleeping car and meet Dr Munro. There's a bottle of Scotch in my bag we could do a little damage to.'

'Sounds good to me,' Fisher said as they went out.

Carver lit a cigarette and scratched himself. 'They've got it made, these bloody Yanks.'

'How's that, chief?' Hardisty asked.

'This Dr Munro. A nice bit of skirt, I can tell you, going all the way to Mallaig. Her uncle's an American admiral living on some island in the Outer Hebrides. She's got a private berth up there in the sleeping car. Jago's shacked up with her.' He threw in his cards. 'Another lousy bloody hand.

Deal 'em again, Wright, only make sure you give me some good ones this time.'

He got up and stared through the mesh at Gericke. 'You awake, commander?'

Gericke made no sign, breathing softly, eyes closed and Hardisty said, 'Leave him, chief, for Christ's sake. He isn't going anywhere.'

Carver turned away reluctantly, sat down and picked up his cards. Behind him, Gericke's eyes opened for a brief moment.

IV

It was raining in Trondheim, heavy, drenching rain as Horst Necker went up the steps of the main entrance to the Operations building with Rudi Hubner. They were still in flying gear, having just returned from an eight-hour operational flight that had taken them far out into the Barents Sea and back again.

Necker was tired and bad tempered. 'They'll have to do something about that port engine. It sounds more like a bloody tractor every time we go out.'

'I know, Herr Hauptmann,' Rudi said soothingly. 'I spoke to Vogel myself. He said he was waiting for our next standdown.'

'Christ Almighty, we could be dead by then.'

He pushed open the door of the intelligence room, expecting to find Altrogge, the intelligence officer, and pulled up short, for Colonel Maier, the Gruppenkommandeur, was sitting on the edge of the desk, smoking a cigarette and leafing through some papers.

He glanced up. 'You don't look too pleased with life, Horst. Did you have trouble?'

'You could say that.' Necker dropped his parachute on a convenient chair and accepted a cigarette. 'Eight hours of nothing but bloody sea and a port engine with asthma. Otherwise the flight was sheer delight.'

Maier grinned. 'Never mind. I've brought your two-day stand-down forward. That should please you.'

'Why should it?' Necker demanded sourly. 'You'll have a damn good reason, I'm sure.'

'A change of routine. Our masters would like you to concentrate on the West Coast of Scotland and the Hebrides again for the next couple of weeks.' He smiled. 'You wanted action, Horst. You've got it. Two new Spitfire squadrons moved up to the east coast this week. That should make it interesting for you.'

'Thanks very much,' Necker said suddenly feeling surprisingly cheerful considering the circumstances. 'What's it all about?'

'Convoys from Canada have been using the northern run lately according to Intelligence. Coming up a lot closer to Iceland. From now on your patrol must take you much further out into the Atlantic. At least five hundred miles west of the Outer Hebrides.'

'We won't be able to stay there long.'

Maier pulled a chart across the desk and nodded. 'We'll give you improved drop tanks. That should add another five hundred miles. And there's a modification to your GMI system that should make it possible for you to cross Scotland without dropping below thirty-five thousand. They claim forty, but I wouldn't count on it. In any case, it should keep you out of the way of those Spitfires.'

The GMI system employed nitrous oxide which was injected into the superchargers where, during high altitude flights, it supplied additional oxygen for combustion, increasing the engine power by twenty per cent.

Necker examined the chart and nodded. 'That's a long way to go.'

Maier smiled and slapped him on the arm. 'It will seem shorter when you've had a couple of days' rest.'

V

The wind dropped considerably towards evening and the *Deutschland*, under full sail, moved on into the gathering darkness, pushed by a light breeze from the south-west.

Richter had the first watch, alone on the quarterdeck except for a petty officer torpedo mechanic named Endrass who was at the wheel. The bosun stood at the rail smoking one of his cigarillos, enjoying the night, the horned moon, the stars scattered to the far horizon, their glow diffused by a damp clinging sea mist.

At nine o'clock he went forrard to speak with the lookout in the bows. On his way back, he paused by the mizzen shrouds on the port side to check a lashing which had worked loose on the mainsail boom. There was a movement behind him and Lotte stepped out of the shadows between the lifeboats.

'Helmut!'

Her hands reached out through the darkness, her face a pale blur. Richter took them instinctively. 'Lotte – what are you doing here?'

'I've been watching you for the past half-hour, pacing from one side to the other of that wretched quarterdeck. I was beginning to think you were never coming down.'

'You must return below,' he said. 'At once.'

'Why?'

'Because Sister Angela is concerned for your welfare, I've given my word to the captain that I'll stay away from you for the rest of the voyage.'

'And you?' she said. 'Are you concerned for my welfare?'

'God help me.' He tried to release his hands 'Let be, Lotte. I've given my word – don't you see?'

'I understand only one thing,' she said. 'That all my life I have been afraid. But when I am with you . . .' Her hand tightened on his. 'Is that what love is always like, Helmut? Have you known love like this before?'

His arms went round her as his last defences crumbled. 'No, never like this, Lotte.'

She tilted her chin to peer up at him. 'As a novice, I can leave the order at will and with a minimum of fuss when we reach Kiel. And then . . .'

He kissed her gently. 'What happens in Kiel is one thing. As for now, there can be no more such meetings.'

'How much longer?' she asked.

'Two weeks if we're lucky, though we'll need to make better time than this.'

'Shall I whistle up a wind for us?' she demanded. 'A real wind?'

'No need.' He looked up at the night sky. 'I think this is only a temporary lull. Storm before morning.'

There was a slight movement behind. They turned quickly and found Sister Angela standing by the mainmast.

'Herr Richter – Lotte,' she said calmly. 'A fine night.'

It was Lotte who spoke first, reacting instinctively in Richter's defence. 'This was my fault, sister, believe me. None of Herr Richter's doing.'

'I'm well aware of that, child. I've been here for the past five minutes. But now, I really do think you should go below.'

Lotte hesitated, then started towards the companionway reluctantly. When she was half-way there, Sister Angela added, 'I'm sure Herr Richter will be happy to talk to you again tomorrow, if his duties permit.'

The girl caught her breath, paused, then turned and fled down the companionway.

Richter said. 'Do I understand from this, sister, that I actually have your permission to . . .'

'. . . pay your addresses, Herr Richter?' She smiled faintly. 'How old that makes me feel. So old.'

She turned from him and walked to Berger's door. Richter watched helplessly as she knocked and entered.

Berger was at his desk, writing. Otto Prager lay on the bunk reading a book. The consul sat up, swinging his legs to the floor and Berger laid down his pen.

'Sister?' he said politely.

Prager stood up. 'You would like me to leave, perhaps?'

He took a step towards the door, but she shook her head. 'A moment of your time only, captain. In the matter of Herr Richter and Lotte.'

'Well?' Berger asked bleakly, ready for trouble.

'I would be obliged if you would release him from his promise not to speak to her again until we reach Kiel.'

'A rather surprising change of attitude on your part, wouldn't you say?'

'A new viewpoint, perhaps. All I have ever wanted was what was right for Lotte. Her decision as to her future when we reach Kiel must be made of her own free choice with no voice to aid her but God's, I see that now. In the meantime, it would seem pointless to keep her and Herr Richter apart artificially. As I have discovered for myself, he seems a singularly honourable young man.'

Berger couldn't think of a thing to say. She gave him a moment, then added, 'And now, if you gentlemen will excuse me. I'm really very tired.'

The door closed behind her. The consul turned, total astonishment on his face. Berger, without a word, opened the cupboard and took out the rum bottle and two glasses.

VI

It was very dark as the train ploughed on into the night, rain lashing against the windows. When Harry Jago knocked on the door of the sleeping compartment and went in, Janet was in the single bunk, a blanket pulled up to her chin.

'I'm freezing.'

'Well, I could suggest a remedy for that condition,' he told her cheerfully.

'Not tonight, darling. I've had it. I could sleep for a week. You'll have to make do with the floor and a blanket.'

He shrugged his shoulders. 'Okay,' he said. 'There are guys sleeping in the luggage racks back there.' He took off his shoes, wrapped himself in one of the blankets, lay on the floor, head pillowed on a canvas holdall and was almost instantly asleep.

VII

They reached Glasgow at six-thirty on a grey, sullen morning. Janet had slept badly and awakened to find that Jago had gone. It took her a moment or so to pull herself together – to realize that they were standing still.

As she threw the blanket aside and sat up, there was a tap at the door and he looked in. 'Alive and well,' he commented. 'That's nice.'

He passed a Thermos. 'Coffee. We're in Glasgow, by the way, They seem to be disconnecting about half the coaches.'

'Then what happens?'

'We pull out in about ten minutes. Bridge of Orchy, Rannoch, Fort William and Mallaig. Another five hours if all goes well. I'm just saying goodbye to Fisher and our mutual friend, Gericke. I'll be straight back and we can have breakfast. It's all arranged.'

He went out before she could reply. For a moment only, she sat there, then got up, raised the blind and pushed down the window. The platform was almost deserted. Jago was hurrying along to a small group consisting of Lieutenant Fisher and the escort, Gericke standing in the centre, the blue raincoat over his shoulders again.

As she watched, Fisher and Jago moved to one side. She caught a brief glimpse of Gericke's sardonic face and then Carver turned him round and gave him a push. They went through the door of the station waiting-room leaving Fisher and Jago talking on the platform. Quite suddenly, Janet had had enough. She pushed up the window and pulled down the blind. When she turned back to the bunk, she was trembling.

'I'm tired,' she said softly. 'Too little sleep for too damned long. That's what it is.' And she got back into the bunk and pulled the blankets up.

'I was expecting your people to meet us,' Fisher said. 'I wonder what's keeping them?'

'God knows.' Jago looked at his watch. 'Say, I'd better get back on board. This thing pulls out again at any moment.'

'I can't hand him over quickly enough, believe me,' Fisher said. 'There's something about him. The way he looks at you.'

'I know exactly what you mean.' Jago shook hands. 'A good trip back, anyway.'

He got into the train and Fisher turned and walked towards the waiting-room where a coal fire burned in a small grate. Hardisty and Wright warmed themselves in front of it, smoking cigarettes.

'Where's the prisoner?' Fisher demanded.

'He wanted to go to the lavatory, sir.' Hardisty nodded towards a green door with the sign *Gentlemen* painted on it. 'The chief said he'd see to it.'

Fisher turned and at that moment the door opened violently and Carver staggered through, half-doubled over. He seemed to find difficulty in speaking, his mouth opening and closing as he gasped for air.

Fisher grabbed him by the lapel. 'What is it, man?' he demanded.

'He – he's got away, sir,' Carver groaned, clutching at his groin. 'The bastard's got away.'

VIII

Gericke had asked to go to the lavatory for the most genuine of reasons. The idea of escape at this stage hardly seemed to be on the cards, especially when one considered those damned handcuffs. What had happened had been a spur of the moment decision, the briefest of opportunities instantly seized.

'I'll see to this, lads,' Carver pushed him towards the door and kicked it open. 'You two have a quick smoke while the going's good.'

Inside, there was a row of stalls, a urinal, a broken wash-basin, the rain drifting in through the open window above the basin. It was the sight of that window that stirred Gericke.

The chief petty officer leaned against the door. 'All right, get on with it.'

Gericke moved towards one of the stalls, turned and held out his handcuffed wrists. 'A little awkward with these things.'

'Oh, a sit-down job, is it?' Carver laughed, eager to extract every last ounce of humiliation from the situation. 'I think we might stretch a point there, commander.' He produced the key and unlocked one handcuff. 'There, that will do you. And you'll have to leave the door open, of course. I'm sure you won't mind me watching, in the circumstances.'

'Thank you, chief,' Gericke said calmly, and lifted his right knee into Carver's crutch.

— 8 —

Barquentine *Deutschland*, 21 September 1944. Lat. 49°.52N., long. 14°.59W. Wind Force 5–6. Intermittent squalls. Heavy rain. It is now necessary to pump four hours out of each twenty-four, which seems to suffice and thanks to the size of the crew is less of a burden that it otherwise would have been. Our position now approximately two hundred and twenty miles south-west of Ireland.

FISHER MOVED out of the parcels' office with Carver hobbling at his heels, and paused outside the waiting-room. 'God damn you, Carver, I'll have you for this.'

Hardisty and Wright came round the corner on the run. 'He hasn't gone through the barrier, that's definite, sir.' Hardisty said. 'Two redcaps on duty there. They're putting the word out now.'

'Go through that damned luggage-room again,' Fisher ordered. 'He's got to be here somewhere. Nowhere he could go, not in the time.'

The two leading seamen went off. Carver said bitterly. 'When I get my hands on that German bastard I'll . . .'

'Oh, shut up, for God's sake and let me think,' Fisher said.

There was the shrill blast of a whistle, the guard's flag fluttered. A sudden hiss of steam and the train started to ease forward. One or two sailors leaned out of carriage windows to see what the fuss was about, but most of the passengers on board were still hardly stirring.

'I mean, where in the hell could he have gone?' Fisher demanded and then, as realization dawned, he almost choked. 'The train, chief!' he shouted. 'He must have got back on the train. It's the only possible explanation.'

It was already moving fast, but there was still time and he jumped for the open door of the guard's van as it passed, turning to pull Carver up behind him. Hardisty and Wright, running along the platform to join them, were too late.

'Here, what's going on?' the guard demanded.

Fisher ignored him, drew his revolver and turner to Carver. 'All right, chief, let's rout him out,' he said.

II

Janet Munro's travel voucher being marked top priority, the sleeping car steward served her first that morning, a good English breakfast of bacon, scrambled egg, marmalade and toast and tea.

Jago could hardly believe his eyes. 'Did I say there was a war on?'

'Not for people with my influence, darling.'

'I certainly joined the right ship this time.'

He sat down on the other side of the small table which the steward had pulled up from under the window. Janet poured the tea.

'You know, I've actually managed to acquire a taste for this stuff,' Jago said.

There was a knock at the door. Janet, who was nearest, reached to open it, Fisher moved in, revolver in his right hand, Carver behind him.

'What in the hell is going on?' Jago demanded.

'He gave Carver the slip back there in the station, sir,' Fisher told him. 'Asked to go to the lavatory . . .'

'Save it for your court martial, lieutenant,' Jago said brutally. 'Just tell me one thing.' He turned to Carver. 'Did you unlock his handcuffs?'

Carver licked his lips nervously. 'Just one, sir. I mean, he wanted . . .'

'I can't believe it,' Jago exploded. 'One chance – any chance – that's all a guy like that needs.' He turned away, white with anger. 'So, he's on the train, is that what you're saying?'

'I think so, sir.' Fisher hesitated and then added awkwardly, 'I mean, there wasn't anywhere else for him to go. There wasn't time.'

'You *think* so?' Jago said. 'All right then, lieutenant, where is he? German Korvettenkapitäns must be kind of thin on the ground, wouldn't you say, especially on the West Highland Line?'

Fisher glanced nervously at Carver, then back at the American. 'I – I just don't know, sir. We started with the guard's van and worked our way forward.'

'And there was no sign of him. Well, that figures. He'd hardly advertise. Is he armed?'

Carver hesitated, debating whether to lie or not, but one look from Jago was enough. 'I'm afraid so, sir. I was carrying a spare, sir. A Mauser. Just in case.'

'In case of what?' Jago demanded and then waved a hand. 'Don't bother, chief, we've got more important things to consider.' He opened his holdall and took out a service issue Colt automatic and slipped it into one pocket. 'Put those pistols away for the moment. No need to set the entire train on its ear. If he is on board, which I doubt, any confusion can only assist him.'

Fisher, delighted to hand over the reins, said eagerly, 'What are we going to do, sir?'

'Carver stays up here at one end, you and I go back to the guard's van and work our way forward. Every compartment, every lavatory. We'll find him – if he's here at all. In my personal opinion, he's on a street car right now, heading for Glasgow docks and a Portuguese or Spanish boat if he can find one.'

'In German uniform?' Janet said. 'He wouldn't last five minutes.'

'Last year a London journalist walked down Oxford Street to Piccadilly dressed as an SS colonel,' Jago said grimly. 'And no one took any kind of notice. There are so many uniforms around these days people are punch drunk.' He nodded to Fisher and Carver who moved outside. 'You stay close to home. I'll be back soon.'

III

It was a good hour later and the train was approaching the northern end of Loch Lomond when they reappeared, Fisher paler than ever, a picture of total dejection. Carver lurked in the corridor outside.

'No Gericke?' Janet said.

'What do you think?'

The guard, an old man long past his prime who had only stayed on because of the war, appeared behind Carver. 'Any luck, sir?'

Jago shook his head. 'Wherever he is, it isn't on board this train. We've checked every inch.'

The guard said, 'Not quite, sir. They coupled a flat-top on at Glasgow behind my van with three jeeps on it for delivery to the Royal Navy at Mallaig. Mind you, there's no way he could have got out there as far as I can see.'

'Is that so?' Jago said and he reached up and pulled the communication cord.

IV

Gericke had enjoyed a surprisingly comfortable trip in the back of one of the jeeps on the flat-top. He was out of the rain and the views were spectacular – just the kind of country he liked.

He had no set plan, allowing things to happen as the cards fell. The opportunity to put Carver down had been too good to miss – the decision to get back on the train so obvious that he hadn't really thought about it. He'd simply jumped for cover, head down.

And one thing was in his favour. The fact that, in regard to uniform, most naval officers looked the same the world over. All he had to do was remove the swastika and eagle from the Kriegsmarine badge on his uniform cap: and he was doing just that, the handcuffs swinging from his left wrist, when the train started to grind to a halt with such violence that he was thrown from the seat.

The game was up, so much seemed obvious, for the train was passing through a long narrow cut with sides that were almost perpendicular. Yet Gericke was reluctant to throw in the towel. He had nothing to lose. While the train was still sliding to a halt, he moved along the flat-top to the rusting iron ladder at the rear of the guard's van.

There was a catwalk on the roof and he ran along it,

jumping to the first coach, almost losing his balance as it swayed violently from side to side. He made it to the next roof and threw himself flat on his face as the train came to a halt.

There was silence, only the heavy rain, the hiss of steam and then windows going down, doors opening – excited voices. Someone was running along the side of the track. He heard Fisher say, 'Nowhere for him to go this time.'

'Exactly.' Jago called, 'So play it cool. No need for gunplay. Much better to get him back in one piece.'

They moved on. Gericke, daring all, went over the edge and slipped down the ladder to the bridge between the coaches. He opened the door before him and moved inside.

The corridor was lined with people, mostly sailors on their way to the naval depot at Mallaig, leaning out of the windows, looking back along the track. There was a great deal of speculation going on as to what it was all about. Gericke moved along the corridor, thrusting his left hand and the dangling handcuffs into his pocket.

No one took the slightest notice of him until he reached the end and then a young sailor, moving back from a window, pushed into him. He turned, took in the raincoat and uniform cap and said quickly, 'Sorry, sir.'

'That's all right.'

'What's going on back there, sir?'

'God knows,' Gericke said. 'I saw a couple of officers with guns in their hands. Maybe some prisoner or other has given them the slip.' He stood at a window for a while, just one of the crowd watching, and saw Jago and the others climb back on board. The guard's whistle sounded, there was a hiss of steam, the wheels spun and the train moved forward again.

People started to go back into their compartments and he carried on. He crossed to the sleeping car and immediately found himself in a calmer, more ordered world. The corridor was deserted and as he started along it, a door at the far end opened and the steward came out of his tiny kitchen.

He paused, 'Can I help you, sir?'

Gericke, improvising fast, remembered the conversation he had overheard earlier about Jago and the girl he was sharing a sleeping compartment with. What was her name again? Dr Munro; an American admiral's niece. It had a certain black humour to it.

'I'm Lieutenant van Lott, Royal Netherlands Navy,' he said smoothly. 'I was looking for Dr Munro.'

'Compartment fourteen. This way, sir.'

He turned, moved a little way along the corridor and knocked at a door. Gericke followed.

The door opened and Janet peered out. 'Gentleman here was looking for you, doctor. Lieutenant van Lott of the Dutch Navy.'

Janet looked Gericke over calmly. 'Thank you,' she said and added to Gericke, 'Won't you come in?'

The steward departed and Gericke moved past her into the compartment. When he turned, she was standing against the door, arms folded, watching him gravely. 'You don't look too good to me, lieutenant. What's the trouble?'

'I'm not sure. I wasn't feeling marvellous in Glasgow. Nearly got off the train there, but it's essential I get to Mallaig today. Someone told me there was a doctor on the train so I asked the steward.'

'You'd better sit down.'

He perched on the edge of the bunk. She put a hand on his forehead. 'You could be running a fever.'

'You think so?'

'But definitely.'

She was close enough for him to smell her perfume, she sat down beside him and took his pulse, crossing one knee over the other.

'You've got excellent legs, doctor.'

'It's been said before,' she said calmly and stood up. 'A large Scotch, I think, is my prescription for you.'

'You think so?'

'I'd say you're going to need it.'

She found the bottle in Jago's holdall, took a glass from the small washbasin in the corner and poured him a large one.

'Good health,' Gericke said.

'Prosit,' she replied and smiled. 'How stupid of me. That's German, isn't it?'

Gericke sighed and took the whisky down in a single swallow, 'That was really most kind of you,' he said and reached out and shot the bolt on the door.

V

Jago made his way along the swaying train, Fisher and Carver behind him. 'But what in the hell am I going to do, sir?' Fisher asked plaintively.

'Run for the hills. Blow your brains out. Why ask me?' Jago demanded. 'It's your problem, Fisher. I wasn't even there. I was back on the train.'

He had no intention of being dragged down by this young fool's incompetence. As he opened the door and entered the sleeping car, the steward was just emerging from the end compartment with a tray.

'We'll have some tea or coffee,' Jago told him, 'Anything you can rustle up.'

'In Dr Munro's compartment?' The steward hesitated. 'Actually she has someone with her at the moment, sir. A Lieutenant van Lott. Dutch naval officer.'

Jago looked at him. 'A small guy with a pale face?' he asked carefully. 'White cap, navy blue raincoat?'

'That's right, sir. I'm short of coffee, but I think I can manage tea for you gentlemen. I'll see to it directly.'

He moved along to his kitchen. Jago took the Colt automatic from his pocket and turned to Fisher. 'Well?' he said.

'I can't believe it.' Fisher looked stunned. 'It doesn't make sense.'

'Just give me a minute, sir,' Carver said eagerly, 'and I'll have the sod out of there.'

'Like hell you will. We've got Dr Munro to consider, so we play this very carefully indeed till we know what's going on. Understand?'

He moved quietly along the corridor to Janet's compartment. He tried the door handle gently without success, took a deep breath and knocked. 'Janet, you in there?' His voice was muffled.

She took a step towards the door but Gericke pulled her back, the handcuffs dangling from his wrist, plain to see now. 'I don't think so. Not at the moment.'

Jago rapped on the door again, a little more insistently. 'Heh, come on, Janet. Open up.'

Gericke sat on the edge of the bed. 'How did you know?'

'When I first saw you at the London Cage there was an eagle and swastika above the badge of that rather sweet, white cap you're wearing.'

He smiled good-humouredly. 'How could I have missed you?'

'One of your bad days, I expect. Charm, like most things, has its limitations. Now would you mind very much if we bring this little farce to an end?'

She put a hand to the bolt and Gericke produced the Mauser from his pocket and cocked it. 'I don't suppose you'd like to take my pulse again?'

'Not today, I'm fully booked.'

'Ah well, I shall always have the memory.' He clicked his heels, gave a little bow and handed the Mauser across butt first. 'Isn't that how Conrad Veidt does it in all those Hollywood movies?'

She stopped smiling. 'You fool,' she whispered. 'And in the end, where has it got you?'

He shrugged. 'The rules of the game, doctor. You have to keep moving.'

She pushed back the bolt, opened the door and stood to one side. Jago and the others crowded in, Carver grabbing Gericke roughly and turning him round, jerking his arms behind his back.

'You all right?' Jago demanded.

She handed him the Mauser. 'He behaved like a perfect gentleman.'

'I'm sorry about that,' Gericke said cheerfully over his shoulder.

She laughed harshly. 'Get him out of here, for God's sake.'

Carver shoved Gericke, whose wrists were by now handcuffed behind him, into the corridor, Jago handed him the Mauser. 'Try not to lose it again. Or him.'

'I won't, sir. You can count on that,' Carver said grimly and he put a knee behind Gericke and sent him staggering.

VI

The train stood in Fort William for twenty minutes while Fisher used the phone in the stationmaster's office. Finally he came out, climbed into the guard's van and knocked on the door of the luggage compartment. As Carver opened it, the train started to move again.

'What's the form, sir?'

'We're taking him on to Mallaig. Back to Glasgow on the afternoon train. How is he?'

'Trussed up like a Christmas turkey.'

Fisher walked over to the cage and looked inside. Gericke sprawled across the mailbags, wrists handcuffed behind him, ankles tied together with twine. The lieutenant sat down, suddenly very tired indeed, and lit a cigarette. Thank God the nightmare was over at last. No court martial, no enquiry. Well, an enquiry perhaps, but then he might not come too badly out of that. After all, it had been Carver's fault in the first place, the whole wretched affair.

VII

On the *Deutschland*, there were rumblings of discontent amounting amost to mutiny when Richter descended to the forecastle for his midday meal.

'Something's crawled in there and died if you ask me,' he heard Leading Seaman Roth observe.

The watch below were grouped around the narrow central table on which stood the cause of their dissension – two large pans which has just been brought down from the galley. The smell, when someone raised a lid, was really quite special, Richter had to admit that. Enough to take the edge off the strongest appetite.

'What's all this?' he demanded, pushing his way through.

'The food again,' Endrass told him. 'Not fit for pigs. Weber's gone too far this time.'

'He's no cook,' Richter admitted, peering into one of the pans with distaste.

'Which Walz was, whatever else he might have been.'

There was an uncomfortable silence for it was an undeniable fact of life that the cook's death had left a gap which had proved almost impossible to fill. Richter, by implication, did bear a certain responsibility for the present situation.

Riedel said, 'I served my time in sail, Herr Richter, you

know that. I was with the old Kommodore Johnsen out of Hamburg in the last grain race just before the war. One hundred and seven days, Australia to Queenstown. I know my rights and according to regulations, each man is entitled to one and quarter pounds of salt beef and three quarters of a pound of pork per day.' He dipped the ladle into the pan. 'And what do we get? A mouthful each if we're lucky.'

'Supplies are running low,' Richter said. 'That pork is half-rotten when it comes out of the barrel. You can't blame Weber for that.'

'Which is still no excuse to serve what little there is like something off the pavement,' Endrass said. 'I think we should see the captain.'

'All right.' Richter nodded. 'You and Riedel here, and you'd better bring one of those pans so he can see what we're talking about.'

Not that there was any need, for when the bosun knocked at Berger's door and entered, he found the captain and Prager seated opposite each other, plates of stew before them.

'What's this?' Berger demanded.

'Deputation from the crew, Captain. Petty Officer Endrass and Leading Seaman Riedel ask leave to speak for the men.'

Berger looked at Endrass coldly. 'Well?'

'The food, Herr Kapitän,' Endrass said. 'It's getting so the men can't stomach it any more and the stink . . .'

He lifted the lid of the pan which Riedel was holding. Berger grimaced at the first whiff. 'You've made your point. Get it out of here.' Riedel retreated. 'All right, so it's not too good, but we're all in the same boat.' He indicated his own plate and said to Richter, 'Who's in the galley now? Weber, isn't it?'

'That's right, sir, and he had to be pressed into service. Nobody wanted the job so the men drew lots.'

Berger nodded. 'I don't really see that there's anything much I can do about this. It's an old problem on sailing ships, as you know. Once the food starts going off, especially the meat, it needs an experienced cook to handle it and that's something we just don't have. I'm sure Weber is doing his best.'

'I beg leave to doubt that.' Sister Angela stood in the

doorway, a pan in one hand, the other nuns behind her. She lifted the lid, 'What would you say this is exactly?' she asked Berger.

He eyed the greasy scum on the surface with distaste. 'Pea soup, I think, sister.'

'So dirty that it's almost black,' she said. 'A rare phenomenon which is explained by the simple fact that the cook has omitted to wash the peas.'

'All right.' Berger held up a hand. 'No need to go on. So what do you want me to do about it?'

She handed the pan to Sister Käthe. 'We could start with an inspection of the galley. With your permission, of course.'

Berger, for once allowing himself to go with the tide, reached for his cap. 'For you, sister, anything. If you'd follow me, please?'

So it was that the unfortunate Weber, sitting disconsolate in the tiny galley surrounded by greasy pans and dirty plates, observed through the open doorway, a sizeable group bearing down on him headed by the captain.

He got to his feet, wiping his hands hastily on his soiled apron and Berger said, 'Outside, Weber. On the double.'

Weber did as he was told. Sister Angela paused in the doorway. She surveyed the scene inside, briefly leaning down to sniff at the rotting pork in its barrel, then turned.

'Take off your apron,' she said to Weber.

He glanced nervously at Berger, then did as he was told. She took it from him, holding it at arm's length for a moment, then tossed it over the side.

'I suggest you return this man to his normal duties. This is obviously not the place for him.'

'And the cooking?' Berger asked.

'There, you will have to show a little faith, captain. But first, I want every inch of this disgusting hovel scrubbed clean.' She turned to the nuns. 'Every pan sparkling. Then and only then will we be in a position to do something about the food. You agree, captain?'

'We are, as you so frequently remind me, in the good Lord's hands,' Berger told her.

But later, towards evening, when he went up on the quarterdeck with Prager, the aroma which drifted up from the galley on the damp air was so appetizing that for the first time in days, he felt genuine hunger.

'What's that?' he demanded of Richter who had the watch.

'I think it's what's called the woman's touch, Herr Kapitän.'

'And thank God for it,' Prager added piously.

VIII

Janet stood at the window of her sleeping compartment, looking out morosely, but even the spectacular beauties of Ben Nevis didn't improve the way she felt. She sat down at the table and picked up a book.

An hour passed, an hour and a half, and Jago continued to sleep as they moved on, passing through some of the most spectacular mountain scenery in Scotland. Glenfinnan, Lochailort and then the sea and the Sound of Arisaig, shrouded in mist and rain.

She had long since discarded the book. She sat smoking a cigarette, watching raindrops roll down the window, thinking of Gericke, mainly because the thought of him simply wouldn't go away. And that would never do. She picked up the book again and forced herself to read.

IX

Lying face-down on the mailbags Gericke couldn't see Carver, but he was conscious of his approach. The chief petty officer squatted beside him, a knife in his hand and jerked Gericke's head round.

'Very foolish,' Gericke said. 'You'd never be able to explain it away.'

Carver took the Knight's Cross from his pocket. 'Did you do something special for this one then? Big hero, is that it?' The anger welled up in him like hot lava. He sliced through the cords that bound Gericke's ankles and grabbed his arm. 'Come on – on your feet.'

Gericke stood there swaying, almost crying out with pain as blood moved in his cramped legs. Carver pushed him out through the gate, then tripped him so that he fell to his knees, head resting on the floor. Carver booted him in the ribs.

'You feel better now, sir?'

Gericke pushed himself up on his knees. 'Was this how you won those fights of yours, chief? Using men with their hands tied behind their backs as punchbags?'

Carver produced the keys to the handcuffs and swung him round. 'I'll show you if I can use myself or not.'

Gericke, his wrists free, shrugged off his raincoat, a smile on his face. Carver rushed in and swung a wild punch which the German side-stepped with ease, dropping into a fighting crouch, his right arm extended in front of him, fist clenched, his left guarding the body. And there was something terribly professional-looking about the way he moved.

The chief stamped in again, swinging a punch which Gericke once more evaded with ease, this time pivoting and delivering a left to Carver's kidneys. Carver cried out in agony and turned to face him.

'Yes, I'm afraid I haven't been really honest with you, chief,' Gericke said, sinking another left under Carver's ribs followed by a right which landed high on the cheek, splitting flesh. 'As a young man, I served my apprenticeship in a clipper ship on the nitrate run to Chile. A hard school. Plenty of discipline enforced by belaying pin, knuckle-duster and boot. I grew up fast.'

He seemed to be moving in a kind of slow motion, one punch after another finding its target and Carver's blows repeatedly landed on thin air.

The chief petty officer was in a bad way, face covered in blood, unable to speak, gasping for breath as the German drove him back across the van relentlessly.

'My friend, you are a disgrace to the uniform you wear and the country which nurtured you. Someone should have cut you down to size long ago,' Gericke said, striking Carver three terrible blows on the face that sent him back against the wall of the cage.

He slid to the floor, head lolling to one side. Gericke stood there looking down at him, then dropped to one knee and went through his pockets, retrieving his decorations.

He found the Mauser which he slipped into his own pocket, picked up his cap and put on the raincoat. He pulled back the sliding door and rain flooded in.

Janet, standing at an open window in the corridor of the sleeping car, caught a brief glimpse of him landing in heather and rolling over and over down the slope. And then there was only the mist and the rain.

— 9 —

> Barquentine *Deutschland*, 22 September 1944. Lat. 50°.59N., 15°.35W. At six bells of the midwatch, the iron collar of the mainsail boom fractured. In the ensuing tangle, the mainsail itself was split from top to bottom and we had to heave to for repairs, drifting under sea anchor until Herr Sturm reported all clear and ready to proceed at noon. The weather deteriorated into heavy rain and mist soon after. Wind NW 5–6.

THE *MARY MASTERS*, a nine-thousand-ton Liberty ship out of Halifax, Nova Scotia, with a cargo of pig iron destined for the steelworks of South Wales, had just gone through a very bad twenty-four hours. Most of the crew, including the captain, were snatching a couple of hours' sleep below.

Visiblity was poor owing to driving rain and mist and the third officer, alone on the bridge, was tired. When he raised his binoculars for perhaps the twentieth time in half an hour and the *Deutschland* sprang into view, he received a considerable shock.

He went to the voice pipe to call up the captain. 'Braithwaite, sir. Sorry to bother you, but I've sighted a sailing ship.'

'What did you say?'

'A sailing ship, sir. A quarter of a mile away on the port quarter.'

'I'll be right up.'

Braithwaite turned to examine the *Deutschland* again and a few moments later, Captain Henderson hurried on to the bridge. He was a small, white-haired man who should have retired in 1940 and had stayed on for the duration.

He reached for the binoculars and focused them. 'You old beauty,' he said softly. 'Alter course, Mr Braithwaite. I think we'll take a closer look.'

II

There were no more than half-a-dozen men visible on the decks of the *Deutschland* as Berger and Sturm stood together on the poop, watching the other vessel move in towards them.

Sturm lowered his glasses. 'A *Tommi*, Herr Kapitän. The *Mary Masters*, registered Liverpool.'

Richter came up the ladder holding the signalling lamp. 'What happens now, sir?'

'That's a merchant ship out there, not the Royal Navy.' Berger glanced up at the Swedish ensign. 'We're still the *Gudrid Andersen* until someone proves different.'

A signalling pennant was hoisted on the *Mary Masters* and Sturm examined it quickly through his glasses. 'May I be of assistance?'

Berger frowned, one hand gripping the rail. She was very near, moving on a course that would take her astern, close enough for him to see the men on the bridge clearly.

'I think we'll try a real bluff this time. You speak the best English, Herr Sturm, so you take the signalling lamp. Get ready to transmit on my orders. Plain language, if you please.'

'Aye, aye, sir.'

Sturm made a preliminary signal. There was a pause and then an answering flash.

'Here we go then,' Berger said softly. '*Gudrid Andersen* twenty-eight days out of Belém for Gothenburg. Thank you for your offer, but in no need of assistance.'

The lamp flashed in reply from the bridge of the *Mary Masters*, even closer now. Sturm waited until it had finished, then translated.

'Out of Halifax, Nova Scotia, for Swansea. Compelled to drop out of convoy yesterday owing to temporary engine fault.' The lamp flashed again. 'Do you wish me to report your position?'

'Accept his offer. After all, we don't really have a choice. You agree, Helmut?'

Richter nodded, his face grim. 'I'm afraid not, Herr Kapitän.'

'With luck, it will take them a couple of days, perhaps three, to discover that the real *Gudrid Andersen* is still in Gothenburg harbour and we'll change course as soon as they're over the horizon.'

The signal lamp clattered in Sturm's hands, the *Mary Masters* acknowledged. Most of her crew seemed to be lining the port rail, waving, calling cheerfully through the rain.

'Ask him if they are still winning the war,' Sturm turned, mouth open in astonishment. 'Get on with it, man!' Berger told him impatiently.

The reply was noticeably brief. 'Definitely. That's all he says, sir.'

'Somehow I thought they might be,' Berger said. 'Thank you and goodbye, Herr Sturm.'

The lamp clattered for the last time and as the *Mary Masters* passed astern, they heard three long blasts on her steam whistle.

'Herr Richter, return the salute.'

The bosun hurried down the ladder and ran along the deck to dip the ensign. The hooter sounded again, a lonely echo drifting across the water.

'Right, Herr Sturm, let's get to hell out of here,' Berger said.

On the bridge of the *Mary Masters*, Henderson watched the *Deutschland* slip away and she was already partly obscured by rain and mist when he lowered his binoculars.

'Everything I ever learned at sea, everything worth knowing, I learned by the age of eighteen on an old hooker just like her.'

'Is that so, sir?' Braithwaite said.

The old captain nodded. 'Watch her go, mister. Drink your fill. I don't think you'll get a second chance – not in your lifetime.'

III

There was mist on the hills, but in Mallaig it was relatively clear. Janet waited in the outer office of the naval commander's headquarters, staring out across the harbour. It was busier than when she was here before, fishing boats, several naval patrol craft, a submarine even, and a lighter unloading at the pier.

Her eyes were gritty from lack of sleep and she was impatient to be on her way. She had answered their questions, made an official statement and signed it, and still there were delays.

A young Wren was typing at a desk in the corner, but in spite of that the murmur of voices was clearly audible from the inner office. She turned from the window as the door opened. Fisher hurried out, his face flushed, and brushed past her without a word.

Jago appeared with Captain Murray, the base commander, a pleasant, grey-haired man of fifty or so. He smiled. 'Sorry about the delay, Miss Munro, but we're all through now.'

'I can go?'

'I don't see why not. You've told us all you know. As regards your passage to Fhada, Murdoch Macleod hasn't arrived yet. The arrangement was that he would report here when he did. If I were you, I'd book in at the hotel for the moment. I've told them to expect you.'

'And Gericke? What about him?'

Murray smiled. 'My dear Miss Munro, I'm filled with admiration for the gentleman.'

She was suddenly angry again. 'Good God, he *is* on the other side! Or had you forgotten that?'

'Not at all, I assure you. Professional regard for a superb seaman, that's all. However . . .' Here he turned to a one-inch ordnance survey map of the Western Highlands which was pinned to the wall. 'If he came straight over the mountain from where he left the train he would find his way blocked by Loch Morar. If he cut down on the coast road, it would only bring him to Mallaig – and he won't come here.'

'So where will he go?'

'Not very far, I'm afraid, because there isn't anywhere for

him to go. One road and the railway line coming in, as you can see. Only a question of time. He won't stay up on those hills for long, not in this weather.'

Jago picked up her bag. 'I'll walk you to the hotel.'

Murray shook hands. 'I'll send word the moment Murdoch arrives. Have a nice trip.' And he turned and went back into his office.

They walked back towards the station, heads down against the rain. Janet said, 'What about Lieutenant Fisher?'

'They'll probably post him to Cape Wrath.'

'And Carver?'

'Patching him up now at the base hospital. That must have been something to see. I mean, Gericke really sorted him out. He's finished, of course. I'm not saying he'll end up in the brig, but he'll lose all rank.'

As they came abreast of the station, a voice called, 'Dr Munro?'

A young paratrooper in red beret and camouflage jump jacket hurried across the road.

'Why, Lachlan,' Janet said. 'Were you on the train?' She turned to Jago. 'This is Lachlan MacBrayne, Harry. He's from Fhada, too.'

'Is that so?' Jago held out his hand.

Lachlan was eighteen and his untidy red hair, freckles and snub nose made him look even younger. 'Fourteen days' leave. I've just finished jump training. Murdoch is supposed to pick me up but when I checked down at the harbour he hadn't arrived.'

'He's taking me, too,' she said. 'I'm going to wait at the hotel. They'll send word when he arrives. Why not join us?'

He glanced at Jago awkwardly. 'Would it be all right, do you think?'

'Sure it would,' Jago said. 'You get your gear and follow us on.'

The boy ran back across the road.

Janet and Jago paused outside the hotel as the rain increased in a sudden rush and Janet looked up to the peaks on the other side of Loch Morar, shrouded in mist.

'I shouldn't think it would be too comfortable up there on a day like this,' Jago said.

'An understatement.'

They went up the steps into the hotel.

IV

Gericke was slightly north-west of Sitheon Mor. His intended destination was Mallaig. There was nowhere else to go; he remembered enough of the charts for the west coast of Scotland to realize that. All he had to do was keep going, straight over the top and down to Loch Morar, impossible to miss even in the worst of weather, then along the shore to the coast road. That he could last longer than a day seemed highly improbable, but at least there were boats at Mallaig. Some kind of a chance, however remote. And it was good to be free. Anything was worth that.

After jumping from the train, he had started up the hillside, coming across a mountain stream after ten minutes or so. He followed its course, moving fast with mist pressing in on either hand that gave him a safe, enclosed feeling, somehow remote from the world outside. There were birch trees at first which grew sparser as he climbed higher, working his way through bracken that in places was waist-high.

Occasionally, grouse or plover lifted out of the heather, disturbed by his passing. He kept on the move, stopping after an hour to catch his breath, sheltering under an overhang from the rain. Not that it mattered by now, for his raincoat was soaked through.

He set off again, climbing strongly. Three miles to the loch, perhaps four, and the mountains to pass over, but he was conscious of no feeling of fatigue, the first elation of freedom still carrying him on.

Half an hour later the burn petered out in a small loch and he moved on to the flank of South Morar, climbing across a boulder-strewn hillside. The mist totally enveloped him and he was by now soaked to the skin, for the first time aware of the cold.

He climbed on doggedly and two hours after leaving the train, scrambled over the edge of a great up-tilted slab of granite and found himself on a plateau. There was a special kind of cold here, a wind on his face that told him he was on top. Then a sudden current of air snatched away the grey curtain.

The view was incredible. Loch Morar below him, Mallaig on the far point four or five miles beyond and, out to sea, the islands crouching in the rain, Eigg, Rhum and Skye across the Sound of Sleat. There was a cairn of stones ten or fifteen yards away, a track snaking down towards the loch. The curtain of mist dropped back into place but he had seen enough. With renewed energy, he started down the mountainside.

V

The *Deutschland* was making good time, plunging into the waves, carrying every stitch of canvas she possessed. From the quarterdeck, Berger addressed the crew and passengers.

'The final run,' he said. 'Our meeting with the *Mary Masters* was unfortunate but we've had a lot of luck on our side. I altered course as soon as I could, just in case anyone should come looking but I don't think it likely. However, one thing is essential. Now, more than ever, we must watch those lights at night. There have been occasions when carelessness in this regard has been much in evidence.'

There was a moment of silence, every face turned up to him, expecting more and there was so little to give. He clutched the rail tightly and tried to put confidence into his voice. 'Look, it's going to be all right. Another seven or eight days, that's all and those of you with families to think of will be greeting them again, I promise you. We've come too far to fail now.' He nodded to Sturm. 'Dismiss the crew, please, Herr Sturm.'

There was a general movement as the starboard watch returned to their duties and the others went below. Berger checked the course, then descended the ladder and went into his cabin. He was pouring himself a glass of rum when there was a knock on the door and Prager entered.

'Join me?' Berger held up his glass.

'No, thanks,' Prager said, 'but I'll have one of your cheroots if you have any left.'

'Help yourself.'

Berger sat down at his desk and pulled a chart of the

Western Approaches forward. Prager said, 'You sounded good out there, Erich.'

'Did I?' Berger said wearily. 'That's something anyway.'

'Where are we? Is it permitted to ask?'

'Here,' Berger tapped on the chart with his forefinger. 'Now all we have to do is work our way up west of Ireland, the Outer Hebrides, Shetland, across to Norway. We should be safe enough then. Follow the coastline down through the Kattegat and Kiel.'

'It seemed like a dream when we started,' Prager said. 'An impossible dream.'

'Yes, it did, didn't it?'

And something touched him, a wave of greyness running through his entire body, like a cold wind brushing the face on deck at night, first warning of a storm to come.

VI

In the galley, Sister Angela and Lotte, sleeves rolled up to the elbows worked together preparing the evening meal. The door was pushed open and Richter entcred, an enamel washbasin in his hands.

He dropped it on the table. 'Salt beef. The last of the crop and it doesn't smell too good.'

Sister Angela prodded it with a knife.

'Half of it rotten, the rest teeming with life.'

'Not to worry, sister. I'm surc you'll manage to do something with it.'

He exchanged glances with Lotte, who smiled as she kneaded dough, flour to her elbows. She wasn't wearing her coif and the slender neck and cropped hair made her look strangely defenceless. Richter would have liked nothing better than an opportunity to take her in his arms.

He pulled himself together hurriedly. 'Anything else I can do?'

'Yes,' Sister Angela told him. 'There are still a few potatoes left. You can peel them. Outside.'

He took the bowl she indicated, went out and squatted by the port rail. He took out his gutting knife, sprang the blade and started on the potatoes. They were mainly rotten, sprouting roots, but he did the best he could, whistling between his teeth as he worked.

After a while, Lotte appeared, a bucket of garbage in one hand. He got up quickly, took the bucket from her and emptied it over the side. When he returned it, their hands touched briefly and she smiled. As a token, he had given her his signet ring. Impossible to wear it, of course, and for the moment she kept it hidden in her bunk under a corner of the mattress.

'It will be all right, Helmut?' she said. 'We will get through?'

'Of course we will. Why do you ask?'

'Captain Berger. It was something in his voice. Something I can't explain.'

'Nonsense, he's tired, that's all. We all are. It's been a hell of a trip.' He reached up and held her hand. 'You've nothing to worry about.'

She smiled. 'And when we get to Kiel?'

'You'll never be alone again, I promise you. From now on nothing parts us. Not ever. I swear it.'

She smiled warmly. 'Then that's all that matters,' she said and returned to the galley.

VII

Janet peered out across the harbour from the bridge of the *Dead End.* 'I always forget when I'm away just how much it rains up here.'

'Five days out of seven,' Jago said.

Jansen entered, a cup of coffee in each hand. 'Just had our orders, sir. Stornoway, by dawn's early light.'

Noting Janet's expression, Jago explained. 'He always speaks that way. In quotation.'

'A well-known disease,' Jansen told her. 'It's called education.'

A sea-going launch rounded the pier and moved into harbour. Janet leaned forward. 'I believe that's the *Katrina* now. Yes, I'm sure of it.'

Jansen said, 'I'll go and tell him you're here.'

He went out. She turned to Jago. 'Well, Harry – the end of something.'

'Or the beginning.'

'That's what I like about you, darling. The last of the great romantics and that's a quality hard to come by these days.'

VIII

There was a surprising amount of light on the pier in spite of the blackout. A crane was working, powered by a diesel engine that thumped hollowly through the night as a party of sailors unloaded oil drums from a lighter into two large trucks.

At least it gave Gericke, standing in the shadows, a view of the general state of things. There was an old gunboat which looked pre-war, with a couple of ratings on the deck. Americans, to judge from their headgear.

Beyond the gunboat was a coaster, a single stacker of eight or nine hundred tons and then a gaggle of fishing boats. And perhaps twenty yards further on as the light faded, the dim shape of a sea-going launch.

He glanced at his watch. It was just coming up to nine. Those sailors couldn't work all night, at least he hoped not, for to attempt to reach that boat as conditions were presently on the pier, was obviously impossible.

He needed somewhere to lie up for three or four hours, preferably with a roof over his head for the rain showed no sign of abating. There were half a dozen naval trucks parked at one side in a rather confined space, crammed together nose to tail.

He made a cautious reconnaissance, but there seemed to be no guard, probably because they were empty. He climbed over the tailgate of one, made himself as comfortable as possible on the floor and waited.

IX

Janet and Harry Jago were sitting in a corner of the bar of the Station Hotel when Murdoch came in. He wore seaboots and his reefer coat, a yellow oilskin over one arm, a splendidly archaic figure that made heads turn as he moved past.

'Can I get you a Scotch, Mr Macleod?' Jago asked, standing up.

'Murdoch, lad, Murdoch to my friends,' the old man said. 'And yes, a wee dram would go down just fine, you being the one with the influence to get it.'

Jago moved over to the bar and Murdoch took out his pipe. 'Do you mind, girl?'

'Not at all,' she said. 'Now tell me about the island. How's my uncle?'

Murdoch filled the pipe methodically from his oilskin pouch. Instead of answering her question, he said, 'Where would young Lachlan be?'

'In my room. I thought the bed might as well get some use and he looked as if he needed the sleep.'

Jago returned with Murdoch's Scotch. The old man raised the glass and examined the contents in the light with a connoisseur's appreciation. 'How in the devil do you manage it, lieutenant?'

'Oh, I let them have a couple of bottles now and then so they always keep one under the bar for me.'

'How is Uncle Carey? You still haven't told me?' Janet demanded.

He said carefully, 'Have they work for him yet? Have you news?'

'Yes, I think you could say that.'

He nodded. 'His only problem.'

'Mind you, it's not what he's hoping for. No more boarding parties, sword in hand, if you know what I mean.'

'I was afraid of that.' Murdoch sighed. 'He has – how can I explain it to you – a hunger for action. It is, I think, meat and drink to him. A great pity he cannot bide still for a while and a good woman to hold his hand.'

'Jean?'

'That is the impression I get.'

'And the best thing for him.' Janet was pleased. 'I'll have to see what I can do.'

'Look to your own affairs, girl,' he told her gently. 'Some things grow better on their own.'

Jago was vastly amused to see her slapped down. She kicked him under the table. 'When do you plan to leave?'

'Oh, about two o'clock in the morning if that will suit. The tide will be flowing well by then. I'll leave you now, if you don't mind. I'm promised to supper with my sister.' He produced an old tin watch from some inner pocket and consulted it gravely. 'I should have been there ten minutes ago. She'll have the skin off me. Terrible sharp since her husband died last year.'

'Is it far?' Jago stood up. 'I could get the jeep.'

'The top end of the main street. A step only. I'll see you here at one-thirty.'

He moved away through the crowded bar and Jago sat down. 'There goes one hell of an old man. Pity you had to be so open-handed with young Lachlan. There's a perfectly good bed going to waste up there.'

'Good deeds is my second name.'

He leaned across, offering her a cigarette. 'As it happens, being a young man of some resource, I have a special arrangement with the landlord.'

'Somehow I thought you might.'

'You know how it is. Home is the sailor and all that. Somewhere to lay his weary head. There *is* only one difficulty. It's a single bed.

'And two into one won't go?'

'I was always lousy at mathematics.'

'Me too.'

They got up and moved out of the bar into the hall. Rain rattled against the door in a sudden flurry of wind and she paused, one hand on the bannister. 'A hell of a night to be out.'

'Not fit for man, beast or an old stray tomcat,' he told her cheerfully. 'As my old grannie used to say.'

'I was thinking of Gericke,' she said and started upstairs.

X

Gericke actually dropped off to sleep, waking in something of a panic to find that a good two hours had passed. Not that it mattered for it was one o'clock before the sailors on the pier finished unloading. The lights were extinguished, the trucks driven away.

It was very quiet now. A dog barked hollowly somewhere in the distance. He waited for another quarter of an hour just to make sure that no one was coming back, then moved out from the shelter of the trucks and went cautiously down to the pier.

He kept to the shadows, pausing to remove his seaboots and stuffing his white cap inside his raincoat. There was a murmur of voices as the two men on watch in the gunboat chatted, the glow of a cigarette inside the wheelhouse. He moved on, soundlessly in stockinged feet, past the coaster and the fishing boats.

The launch was tied up at the bottom of a flight of stone steps. He stepped over the rail, put his seaboots down gently and descended the companionway, the Mauser in one hand.

There was a decently-sized saloon, a cabin aft with two bunks, both unoccupied, and a small toilet. The galley was forrard. Nothing could have been more satisfactory. He found a towel, dried his feet, then went back up the companionway and pulled on his seaboots.

Next, he made a cautious exploration of the wheelhouse. This was no fisherman's boat, so much was certain. A rich man's craft. Penta petrol engine, twin screws, a depth sounder, automatic steering. Such boats commonly had a range of seven or eight hundred miles, perhaps more. It all depended on what was in the tanks.

He found the correct dial which seemed to indicate that they were full or nearly so. What he needed now was an oar so that he might sweep her out of harbour before switching on the engine. He moved out on deck cautiously and pulled back into the wheel-house at the sound of voices, footsteps approaching along the pier.

He stayed in the shadows, waiting for them to stop, perhaps at one of the fishing boats, already aware with a strange kind of fatalism, that they would keep right on coming.

Someone laughed clear on the damp air, harsh, distinctive and familiar. Gericke smiled increduously as Janet Munro said, 'Don't you ever take anything seriously, Harry?'

'Not if I can help it,' Jago told her. 'You know, I've had a great idea, Murdoch. Why don't you choose the deepest spot you can find between here and Fhada and put her over the side with about eighty pounds of old chain round her ankles? I'd say the world would be a whole lot more comfortable for all of us.

'Bastard,' she replied.

'Mind your manners, girl,' Murdoch said in reproof. 'For if you do not act in a more seemly fashion, I might take the lieutenant, here, up on his suggestion.'

Gericke, smiling again, was already out of sight and halfway down the companionway.

— 10 —

Barquentine *Deutschland*, 23 September 1944. Lat.53°.59N., long. 16°.39W. Wind NW 6–7. Rain and intermittent squalls. During the mid watch, Herr Sturm requested permission to shorten sail as we were taking so much water inboard that life was becoming very uncomfortable for the passengers. I refused his request, anxious to make as much time as possible now.

JAGO SWITCHED on the light in the saloon. The blackout curtains were neatly drawn and he turned as Janet followed him down. 'That is nice. Where do you want these, by the way?'

'The aft cabin,' she said.

He kicked open the door and dropped the suitcases and medical bag on one of the bunks. As he went back into the saloon, Lachlan came down the companionway, his rifle slung over one shoulder, a kitbag under his arm.

The boy made a face. 'So help me, doctor, but I feel sick already.'

He dropped his kitbag on the floor and Janet took the rifle from him and pushed it out of sight under one of the divan seats. 'I hate those things. Never mind, Lachlan, I've got some pills in my bag. I'll give you a couple and you can get your head down and sleep all the way across.'

The boy went into the galley and she turned to Jago. 'He's always been like that, ever since he was a kid. Believe it or not, but his father was captain of a local fishing boat out of Fhada.'

'Was?'

'Apparently he was killed in action recently serving as a petty officer under Murdoch's son.'

'I know,' Jago said. 'About what happened, I mean. Not about Lachlan's father, though. They were torpedoed in the North Sea. I had the unpleasant task of bringing the good news. As I told you before, I'm just a bloody postman.'

She was suddenly angry, irritated at the recurrence of the same old theme. 'For God's sake, grow up, Harry. Stop feeling sorry for yourself.' She grabbed hold of his sweater. 'You try turning up at Fhada in that mood and I'll throw you straight back into the sea.'

'Yes, ma'am.'

He tried to kiss her, but she slipped from his arms and made for the companionway. 'I want to get out of here.'

They found Murdoch in the wheelhouse with Jansen. 'I've been trying to suggest to Mr Macleod,' the chief petty officer said, 'that maybe it would be a good idea to wait for a little more light.'

'And what was his reaction?'

'As I have been sailing these waters man and boy for at least seventy years now, I told him to mind his own business and go to hell,' Murdoch said. 'A terrible sentiment for a man of my persuasion, but there it is.'

'Admirably put,' Jago observed.

Murdoch took out his pipe. 'A couple of plates of good Scots porridge in you and you'll be ready for that dawn start to Stornoway.'

'Porridge?' Jansen said. 'A grain which in England is given to the horses, but in Scotland supports the people. It was Dr Samuel Johnson who said that first, by the way. Not me. As a matter of interest, he actually travelled in these parts.'

'Lieutenant Jago,' Murdoch said grimly, 'will you get him off now or do I pitch him headfirst over the side?'

'No offence, sir.' Jansen backed out hurriedly and stepped over the rail.

'I'm sorry,' Jago said. 'He isn't really responsible. Something they gave him when he was very young.'

'On your way, Harry.' Janet gave him a push.

Jago joined Jansen at the bottom of the steps and they cast off the lines. Janet hauled them in, then stood watching them, hands on hips. Jago blew her a kiss. She waved and went into the wheelhouse.

She stood at Murdoch's elbow peering out into the darkness. 'What's the forecast?'

'Three to four winds with rain squalls. A light fog generally in the Sea of the Hebrides just before dawn.'

'How disappointing.'

'Oh, so it's excitement you're seeking? You must wait a day or two.'

'Why do you say that?'

'Heavy weather coming.'

'Something really bad, you mean?' Janet frowned, for she knew that it was not uncommon for Fhada to be cut off from the mainland for weeks at a time. But that was usually in the winter. 'How do you know?'

'It is to be found in the wind's breath, the touch of the rain. The smell of things.' He smiled. 'Or in the sum total of a lifetime at sea, perhaps.'

She stuffed her arm through his. 'I know – you're just an old highland mystic. Can I take the wheel?'

'Later. Go you and see to the boy. You know how this trip distresses him.'

She left him and went downstairs. Lachlan was seated at the table and already looked ghastly. She went into the aft cabin, opened it and found the pills she'd promised.

'Take these with a glass of water, then get on one of the bunks. I'll bring you a cup of tea.'

She went out to the galley. Lachlan stood there by the bunk for a moment then, stomach heaving, reached for the handle of the toilet door. When he pushed it open, Gericke was sitting there, the Mauser in his right hand.

II

Janet leaned against the bulkhead in the galley and smoked a cigarette, arms folded as she waited for the kettle to boil. She was aware of the creak as the door swung open, turned casually and saw Lachlan standing there, hands clasped behind his neck.

Gericke peered over the boy's shoulder, smiling. 'Ah, there you are, doctor.'

Her heart pounded and so great was the shock that she had difficulty in speaking at all.

'You,' she whispered.

'I'm afraid so.' He stepped back, motioning with the Mauser. 'Now you will please be so good as to come out here and tie this young gentleman's hands behind him.'

He threw her a coil of thin rope which he had found behind the cabin door. Janet folded her arms quite deliberately and it landed at her feet.

'You won't shoot me. You couldn't on the train – you won't now.'

He smiled calmly. 'You're quite right. But the boy here – now he is something different. A paratrooper as well, so it may be argued that I am helping the war effort. The left kneecap first, I think.'

She picked up the coil of rope hurriedly. Lachlan looked sicker than ever. 'Sorry, doctor, but he was in the lavatory when I opened the door, sitting there bold as brass. Would he be the U-boat captain they were on about in Mallaig?'

'At your service,' Gericke said. 'Now lie down like a good boy and all will be well.'

Lachlan lay on one of the divans and Janet lashed his wrists, Gericke observing her closely.

'Satisfied?' she demanded.

'Not bad. Now the ankles.'

She did as she was told and when she was finished he said, 'And now we will go to see your friend upstairs, Mr Murdoch Macleod. Have I got the name right?'

She had recovered enough from her initial astonishment to be able to assess the situation more coolly and became aware, with a kind of clinical detachment, that she was not afraid of

Gericke in the slightest. Which was interesting. On the other hand he was very obviously a man who would kill, if he had to, without a second's hesitation.

He smiled at her. 'Of what are you thinking?'

The feeling of intimacy was really quite disturbing, but she forced herself to stay calm. 'Murdoch's an old man. One of the finest men I know. I don't want him hurt.'

It was delivered almost as a command. Gericke inclined his head. 'Very well, doctor, let's see if we can deal with this man in a civilized manner, then.'

She led the way up the companionway and opened the wheelhouse door. Murdoch stood there, his head disembodied in the light of the binnacle.

Gericke leaned in the doorway and thumbed the hammer on the Mauser very deliberately. 'You will please do exactly as you are told, Mr Macleod.'

Murdoch looked him over calmly. 'And who might you be, laddie?'

'He's Gericke, the U-boat commander who escaped from the train,' Janet informed him.

'I see,' Murdoch said. 'It's the boat you're after, is that it? And where exactly do you intend to take her?'

'Norway, by way of the Orkneys.'

'A possibility. But only just. You'd need to know what you were doing. A lot different from those sardine cans you're used to.'

'I have a master's certificate in sail,' Gericke told him. 'Is that good enough?'

Murdoch nodded gravely. 'Like that gun of yours – difficult to argue with. And what about us?'

'I'll drop you off on the way. Somewhere nice and remote on the coast of one of the larger islands. Lewis, perhaps. And now, as I am perfectly capable of reading a chart, you will oblige me by putting her on automatic pilot and coming below.'

'You feel you are familiar enough with these waters?'

'I do.'

'Then who am I to argue?'

He locked the automatic steering device in position and moved out, Janet leading the way. They descended to the saloon where he lay on the opposite divan from Lachlan and allowed her to lash his wrists and feet.

When she was finished, she said, 'Now it's my turn I suppose.'

'Good heavens no. I shouldn't dream of such a thing,' Gericke said. 'You, my dear doctor, are far too useful. First, you will make a flask of hot tea and some sandwiches, then we will continue in the wheelhouse.'

'Continue what?' she demanded suspiciously.

'Why, where we left off in the train if you like.' He smiled. 'The galley, by the way, is right behind you.

III

It was very peaceful in the wheelhouse. Janet swung from side to side in the chart-table chair and watched Gericke at the wheel.

'You like that, don't you?' she said.

'A deck under the feet, a wheel kicking in the hands?' He smiled. 'The finest feeling in the world. Well, almost.'

'Aren't you ever serious?'

'Not possible. I realized rather early in life what a bloody unpleasant business it all was. No man of intelligence could possibly take it seriously. We had a hard time when I was a boy, you see. My father was killed on the Western Front.'

'Was he a soldier?'

'No, a fighter pilot. One of the first. He lasted three years. A long time, but not long enough.'

'And your mother?'

'Died in the influenza epidemic of 1918. I went to live with her brother, my uncle Lothar in Hamburg. Poor as a church mouse, but one of the kindest men I've ever known. He was a teacher of mathematics. Had a house at Blankanese on the Elbe from which you could see every ship that entered or left Hamburg. I used to sit in my room at night for hours with the window open, watching the lights on cargo boats slipping out to sea. Going somewhere romantic – always that. And I wanted to sail with them.'

'The beginning of a love affair?'

He carried on, 'And if it was too foggy to see them there

were always the foghorns growling out there somewhere at the edge of things.'

He took one of her cigarettes from the packet on the chart table. Janet said, 'When I was a girl I used to spend summers at my uncle's place on Cape Cod. Lots of fog there. Sometimes at night you could hear the fishing boats calling to each other far out to sea.'

Gericke nodded. 'A lonely sound for a lonely place.'

She swung round on the swivel seat to face him. 'You know it?'

'I sank eleven ships off that coast between mid-March and late April of '42.' There was a slight ironic smile on his mouth. 'The Happy Time all over again. For five consecutive minutes the thought actually crossed my mind that we might win the war.'

'American ships?'

'All except one. A Spanish tanker which got in the way of the action, so to speak.'

'I see,' she said. 'So even a neutral wasn't safe from your attentions?'

He smiled sardonically. 'Sea Wolves. Isn't that what they call us?'

'And you're proud of that?' She reached for the Thermos, mainly to give her hands something to do and poured tea into the plastic cup. 'Now let me tell you something. Lieutenant Jago let me read the report on you back there on the train.'

'Strictly against regulations that, I should imagine.'

'That Spanish boat was an oil tanker, the *San Cristobal* out of Bilbao. There was a big fuss in the newspapers at the time because she was a neutral, then it turned out that she'd been chartered by the American War Department. You knew that when you sank her.'

'Naturally.' He peered down at the compass and altered course a point to starboard.

'Then why try to make me think something different?'

He smiled good-humouredly. 'But I thought that was what you wanted to believe. The brutal Hun about his evil work. Machine-gunning the lifeboats, after making sure there weren't any women available amongst the survivors, of course.'

'Damn you, Gericke!'

'Taken care of long since.'

She lit another cigarette and sat leaning her elbows on the chart table, frowning and staring into the dark glass. 'You love ships, yet you destroy them.'

'I'm perverse by nature. You should try me sometime.'

'No thanks – and still not good enough.'

'What would you prefer – some neat psychological explanation on the lines that each man kills the thing he loves? Come now, doctor. Even the great Freud once said that sometimes a cigar is only a cigar.'

'They certainly didn't teach us *that* in medical school.'

'Just put it down to the bloody war, then.'

There was a savage tone in his voice that had not been present before. For a moment she stood on the edge of something, peered into a dark and private place and drew back.

He checked the course again and stared grimly in the dark, his face set, that slight, perpetual smile missing for the first time.

'Your English,' she said lamely, 'is really very good.'

'We lived in Hull for a while. That's a port on the east coast of England.'

'I know.'

'My uncle taught English there for two years.' He smiled. 'People tell me I have a Yorkshire accent. When we returned home, I tried a year at university. Philosophy and mathematics because Uncle Lothar wanted it. It didn't work out so he allowed me to enrol in the school for naval petty officers at Finkenwärder in Hamburg. After that I went to sea as an apprentice on a square-rigger.'

'A hard school.'

'As friend Carver discovered earlier today. I sailed in clippers for a while. The Chilean nitrate trade, grain from Australia by way of the Horn. Then I served as third officer on a cargo boat to complete my navigational training. I was all of twenty-two when I took my master's tickets in both sail and steam.'

'And then?'

'Nobody wanted me. I tramped the streets of Hamburg. Visited every ship owner there was, but nothing doing. Times were hard, the Depression was at its height. We all used to meet at a bar in the Davidstrasse called the Star of David. The man who ran it had served as a bosun under sail and gave credit. I finally shipped as first mate on a clipper doing the big circle. Chile, the States, then across to Australia and home again. When I got back, everything was changed.'

'What was that?'

'It was 1933 and the Kriegsmarine was offering equivalent rank to officers of the merchant service. I couldn't get to Stralsund fast enough to sign on.'

'To learn how to sink ships?'

'It's a living.'

There was silence between them for a while. The wind had shifted and the sea was rising, the *Katrina* rocking in the turbulence. Janet said carefully, 'And women? A family? No mention of them. Haven't they ever had a place in your scheme of things?'

'Not really. Women, yes, in the most basic way. But shore leave, as I have always found, seldom lasts long enough for more permanent arrangements to grow.'

'Strictly ships that pass in the night?'

'An apt analogy.' He shrugged. 'And then the important things in life have one hell of a way of happening at exactly the wrong time. At least as regards being able to do anything about it. Don't you find that?'

He turned to face her. She was aware of a cold excitement, a need to breathe deeply – then a sudden violent squall struck *Katrina,* swinging the boat to port. Janet fell from her seat.

Gericke wrestled with the wheel and brought her head round. 'Are you all right?'

She scrambled to her feet, white and shaken. 'Yes, but I'd better get below and check on the others.' She hesitated, peering out into the dark. 'You think it will get worse?'

'I should imagine so. I'll put on the automatic steering device and come down myself.'

'Is it safe to have only that thing in control in this kind of weather?'

'A whole lot safer than allowing you to go below on your own.'

She slipped through the door and was gone. He cursed,

locking the steering and went after her, already too late, for when he entered the saloon, she had Lachlan's Lee-Enfield in her hands. She thumbed off the safety-catch, worked the bolt, ramming a cartridge into the breech, and backed off.

'Loaded, I presume?' he enquired.

'You can take my word for it,' Lachlan said, struggling to sit up.

Gericke produced his Mauser and cocked it. 'Stalemate, I think.'

'Don't make me shoot you, darling,' she said harshly. 'I will if I have to and I could hardly miss at this range.'

There was determination on her face, but a kind of panic also, as if she knew that, whatever happened, he would not pull the trigger. Suddenly, there was a desperate appeal in her eyes.

Gericke smiled very gently and placed the Mauser on the table. 'Ah well,' he said. 'It was fun while it lasted,' and he clasped both hands behind his neck.

IV

Richter, flat on his face because of the confined space, was examining the bilges with the aid of a storm lantern. The pumps had been working constantly for two hours but it was still a foot deep in there. Every so often, as the *Deutschland* plunged over a particularly large wave, filthy, rancid water washed over his head.

He finished his inspection and came up through the hatch in the aft hold, passing his lantern to Sturm. 'God, but you stink,' the young lieutenant observed.

'I know,' Richter said in disgust. 'It's like crawling along a very old sewer down there.'

'How does it look?'

'It could be worse.'

'Good.' Sturm was relieved. 'Better let the old man know straight away.'

When they went out on deck there was a terrific beam sea running and Berger, in oilskin coat and sou'wester leaned on the quarterdeck rail.

'Just in time, Herr Sturm,' he called. 'Clew up the topsails and fore lower t'gallant and make them fast, quick as you like.'

'Aye, aye, sir.'

'And get the foresail off her.'

Berger went down to his cabin and the crew tumbled into action as Sturm relayed the orders, Richter springing into the ratlines and leading the way aloft, no place for the faint-hearted in such weather. But on deck, conditions were just as hazardous. The men at the clew lines were up to their necks in water, hanging on for dear life every time another sea washed over them.

Richter, on his way down to the deck again, saw Lotte emerge from the galley. She carried a bucket in each hand and was wearing an old oilskin coat and sou'wester. At the same moment, he noticed a huge sea coming aboard.

He cried a warning, jumped for the nearest line and slid down to the deck very fast. There was a tremendous crash as the sea poured aft. Richter caught a brief glimpse of Lotte washing along with it, dropped into the welter of foam and went after her.

The *Deutschland* pointed into the slate grey sky, riding high over the next wave. Richter hauled the girl to her feet and discovered that she was still clutching the two buckets, both quite empty now. And she was laughing.

'Little fool,' he cried. 'How often do I have to tell you?'

'I don't think I'll every be dry again,' she answered.

He put a hand under her elbow and helped her along the deck to the galley. When he opened the door, there was a couple of feet of water inside, pots and pans swilling around, Sister Angela on her hands and knees.

From the look on her face, that inexhaustible patience had finally run out. Richter retreated, leaving Lotte to handle the situation.

V

Berger towelled his head dry, then sat down at his desk, selected a cheroot and lit it. The last box and only a dozen left. He inhaled the fragrance of Brazil with conscious pleasure, reached for his pen and started the daily entry in his private journal.

> . . . we are, by my estimation, perhaps a hundred miles due west of Galway Bay in Ireland and make excellent time, mainly because I have maintained a policy of carrying as much canvas as possible in rough weather. An unfortunate consequence of this is the fact that we take water inboard in large quantities and this makes things difficult for both crew and passengers. The fanlight has smashed again, water cascaded into the saloon without pause, making life wet and uncomfortable for the nuns who pray constantly during such weather, although whether their plea is for the Good Lord to take them up to heaven or save them for it, I have never been able to determine . . .

There was a knock at the door and Richter entered. Berger put down his pen. 'How was it down there, Helmut?'

'Smelly, but sound, Herr Kapitän. We worked the pumps for two hours before I went in and there was still twelve inches, but when you consider this weather and how much water we've been shipping that seems to me not too bad.'

'Good,' Berger said. 'Very good. I've a feeling we may hit rough weather all the way now and it's a comfort to know things are still no worse than they were below the waterline.'

He reached for his pen and had already started to write in his journal again as Richter went out.

VI

It was just after eight-thirty as the *Katrina* moved in towards Fhada. Gericke, seated in the swivel chair at the chart table, hands tied behind his back, looked out with interest at the grey-green hump crouching there in the rain, cliffs splashed with lime, seabirds wheeling in great clouds, cormorants, razorbills, gulls of every description.

'So this is Fhada?'

Murdoch, at the wheel, nodded. 'They say the name is derived from an old Gaelic word *Fuideidh* meaning an island that lies apart from other islands.'

'Interesting.' Gericke filled his lungs. 'I like islands. They have a special quality. In April 1941, I did a patrol in the Aegean and came down with some kind of fever. I convalesced on the island of Corfu. A marvellous place. It was April. The most beautiful wild flowers I've ever seen in my life and the butterflies . . .'

'Whatever else it is, Fhada isn't like that, darling.' Janet came in through the door carrying a mug of tea. 'I thought you might like to have yours below,' she said to Murdoch. 'Put her on automatic pilot and I'll keep my eye on things while I feed the pride of the Kriegsmarine.'

Murdoch hesitated, then locked the steering device in position. 'Ten minutes, that's all you get,' he said and went out.

'It would seem he assumed you wanted to be alone with me,' Gericke observed. 'How romantic.'

'Nothing could be further from the truth,' she said. 'I just wanted him to sit down for ten minutes and have a hot drink. He's an old man, or hadn't you noticed?'

'The doctor in you coming out. Does this happen often?'

'Not on Fhada, believe me. They're a healthy lot here.'

She unlocked the automatic pilot and took the wheel herself.

'You love the place, I think,' he said.

'It has a strange attraction for me. It's as if the outside world has ceased to exist, which it very frequently does. On Fhada, they boast winds four to seven for two-thirds of the time as early as April. From September on, anything goes. They tell a story of a constable sent from the mainland to escort a local man to serve a six weeks' sentence at Stirling prison.'

'What happened?'

'The weather was so bad that by the time it was fit for the boat to leave, the sentence was finished.'

'So – I may be in for a long stay?'

'They also boast the worst hazard to shipping on the entire west coast. The Washington Reef. That's why they stationed the first lifeboat here back in 1882. Murdoch's the present coxswain.'

'Isn't he a little old for such work?'

'He handed over to his son in '38. Came back into harness when Donald was called up by the Navy. Uncle Carey says he's a genius. One of the greatest coxswains in the history of the Lifeboat Institution.'

'I see. And how do people live here?'

'A little crofting. Sheep. A few cattle. Fishing. The population's very small now. A place of women, children and old men. All the others are away, mostly serving in merchant ships.'

As they drew nearer to the island they met the only four fishing boats still working from Fhada moving out to sea.

Janet waved. Gericke said, 'Old men.'

'And boys,' she said. 'All that will be left soon if this damned war lasts much longer.'

They moved into harbour and Gericke noticed a small dark man with a black eye patch in old seaboots and reefer coat standing at the edge of the upper jetty.

Janet placed her hands lightly on his shoulders. 'And that,' she said, 'believe it or not, is my uncle, Rear Admiral Carey Reeve, United States Navy, not quite retired.'

— 11 —

> Barquentine *Deutschland,* 23 September 1944. Further entry. Sister Angela and Herr Prager visited me formally to raise the question of low morale amongst the crew and passengers because of the lack of hot food and drink owing to the impossibility of keeping a fire going in the galley under the present weather conditions. Sister Angela made the point, which I had to accept, that my own cabin was the driest in the ship owing to its position and prevailed upon me to allow her to use it for cooking purposes with the aid of a portable oil stove. A run of two hundred and twenty-five miles this day.

IT WAS VERY quiet in the small study where Gericke sat, hands still tied behind his back. Murdoch leaned in the window seat, filling his pipe.

'This house,' Gericke said. 'Quite impressive. Who does it belong to?'

'Mrs Sinclair. She owns the island. What we call the laird in these parts. Also bailie – that's magistrate. And coroner and harbourmaster.'

'A remarkable woman.'

'You'll see soon enough. She is responsible for you in a sense. The only law we have here. Her husband was in the same trade as yourself. He went down with the *Prince of Wales* in the Pacific. That would be in 1941.'

'I see,' Gericke said. 'I shouldn't imagine I'll be too popular in that quarter.'

'We are not savages, commander. Put that from your head. During the past fortnight we have buried eight of your comrades, washed up from a U-boat that was sunk in this area on the ninth of the month. I took the services myself and almost every soul on this island attended.'

There was a moment's silence. Gericke, for once at something of a loss, said, 'I thank you. On their behalf, I thank you, sir.'

The door opened and Reeve came in. He was still wearing his reefer coat and there was rain on his face. 'I've been in touch with Captain Murray at Mallaig. He insists that in no circumstances should any attempt be made to take you back to the mainland in anything other than an official vessel. Lieutenant Jago is apparently en route for Stornoway now. He'll receive instructions by radio to call in here for you, sometime tomorrow.'

'Another day's grace before the door closes finally.'

Reeve said, 'And now Mrs Sinclair would like to see you.'

He nodded to Murdoch who moved out and Gericke followed, the admiral bringing up the rear. They went along a corridor, passed through a large stone-flagged hall and paused at a green baize door. Reeve opened it and motioned Gericke through.

It was a pleasant room, two of the walls lined with books from floor to ceiling, french windows giving a view of the garden outside. Janet and Jean stood in front of the log fire.

They turned at once. Gericke came to a halt and inclined his head formally. 'Ladies.'

'Korvettenkapitän Paul Gericke,' Reeve said. 'Mrs Sinclair.'

A handsome woman, she was wearing a Shetland sweater, brogues and a kilt, which he presumed to be in her clan's tartan, and her hair was tied back with a blue velvet bow.

She looked him over calmly and her voice was formal. 'I don't know if Admiral Reeve has explained, commander, but I am bailie here and responsible for you at law.'

'That has been made clear to me.'

'There is no policeman stationed on the island, but the police station is still here from the old days and I do have to make use of its cells on occasion.'

'I understand.'

'You will be locked up there until Lieutenant Jago arrives to take you into custody tomorrow. And you will be guarded, naturally.'

There was really nothing to say. Janet had moved to the window and was looking outside. Reeve touched Gericke's arm. 'Let's go. Murdoch and I will take you down.'

Gericke hesitated, glancing towards Janet. She did not turn round. He inclined his head again, turned without saying anything and went out followed by Reeve and Murdoch.

The door closed. 'Damn you, Paul Gericke,' Janet whispered, still staring out into the rain. 'I wish I'd never set eyes on you.'

II

The three men went down the cobbled main street, Gericke in the centre. The heavy rain kept most people indoors, but here and there a woman stood on a step watching curiously and two small boys trailed behind until Murdoch chased them away.

The old police station was at the bottom of the street and faced out over the harbour, solidly built of granite like every other dwelling in Mary's Town, with only the bars at the windows to distinguish it.

Reeve tried to open the oaken door that was bound with iron, but it refused to budge. Murdoch hammered with the toe of his boot. 'Lachlan, are you asleep in there?'

There was the sound of heavy bolts being withdrawn and

Lachlan MacBrayne peered out. He wasn't wearing his jump jacket, but was otherwise in uniform, the battledress blouse open at the neck.

'Time to lock up when we've got him inside,' Murdoch said.

There was an old desk in one corner, a chair and not much else, and a peat fire smouldered in a tiny grate.

Lachlan picked up his rifle, slung it from his shoulder, then took a large bunch of keys down from a nail on the wall. 'Will we be putting him straight in, admiral?'

'The sooner the better,' Reeve said.

They went down a flight of steps to a narrow corridor. There were three cells on either side, each closed by a gate of iron bars. Reeve untied Gericke's wrists and pushed him inside. There was an iron bed, three or four army blankets and a bucket. Lachlan closed the gate and locked it.

'That's it then.' Reeve slipped a packet of cigarettes, a box of matches and a newspaper through the bars. 'Something to read. Three days old, but you'll see you're still losing the war.'

Murdoch took a small bottle from his pocket. 'It will be cold in there after a while I'm thinking.'

'A surfeit of riches indeed.' Gericke clicked his heels. 'Gentlemen – my thanks.'

Reeve smiled in spite of himself and they went back to the office and left Gericke alone. He crossed to the barred window, peered out across the harbour, then sat on the edge of the bed, unscrewed the neck of the bottle Murdoch had given him and sampled the contents. It burned all the way down, exploding in the pit of his stomach.

He gasped for breath. 'God Almighty!' he said and stiffened as he heard steps in the corridor.

Lachlan was on the other side of the gate, the rifle still hanging from his left shoulder. He unslung it awkwardly and stood staring at Gericke, gripping the rifle light in his two hands. Gericke got up slowly, muscles tightening. As casually as possible, he took out the cigarettes Reeve had given him and put one in his mouth.

'Do you smoke?' He moved to the bars, holding out the packet.

The boy shook his head and when he spoke his voice was

hoarse. 'You had a round up the spout of that Mauser. I unloaded it myself. I saw it.'

'That's right.'

'You could have shot her. Why didn't you?'

'Could I?' Gericke said gently. 'You think that?'

The boy sighed, relaxing suddenly and rested the butt of the rifle on the floor. 'No, I don't suppose you could.' He moved away, then paused. 'I'll be making a cup of tea in a little while. Do you want one?'

'I don't think I'd like anything better.'

Lachlan said very slowly, 'I thought I could shoot you. I had it all worked out, because of my father, but when it came to it, I couldn't do it.'

'I know,' Gericke said.

The footsteps died away along the corridor. He sat down on the edge of the bed again very carefully and when he struck a match to light his cigarette, his hand was shaking.

III

The *Dead End* was five miles south-west of Idriggil Point on the Isle of Skye and making heavy weather of it. Petersen had the helm and Jago sat at the chart table checking their course. When the door swung open behind him he turned, expecting coffee and found instead Jansen, a signal flimsy in one hand and a peculiar glint in his eye.

'I think the lieutenant might find this one particularly interesting.'

'A signal?' Jago said. 'From Mallaig. Christ, we only left the damned place an hour ago. Read it to me.'

'As the lieutenant pleases.' Jansen was enjoying himself. 'Korvettenkapitän Gericke apprehended as stowaway on *Katrina*. Now on Fhada. Request you call there on your way back from Stornoway tomorrow and take into custody.'

Jago looked at him incredulously, then snatched the flimsy and read it for himself. 'It's not possible.'

'I'm afraid it has to be, sir. The good word came direct from Captain Murray himself.'

'All right – if you can find a brief moment in that crowded schedule of yours, signal Mallaig message received and understood. Will leave Stornoway at dawn tomorrow, weather permitting, and should arrive Fhada around noon. Now kindly get to hell out of here.'

Jansen withdrew, grinning hugely, and Jago picked up a pencil from the chart table and snapped it between his fingers.

IV

Janet put another log on the fire, pushing it into place with a long brass poker, then sat back and waited. Her uncle stood at the window reading the letter she had brought him.

'He says here that he's spoken to you personally.'

'That's right,' she said. 'In the back of his staff car at Guy's.' There was no immediate response and she was seized with a sudden impatience. 'He's offered you a job, Uncle Carey. The supreme commander himself. A chance to get back in the thick of things. Isn't that what you wanted?'

'Deputy Director, Supply and Personnel Co-ordination,' he said bitterly, and crumpled the letter in his hand.

'For God's sake, what do you want – blood?'

The door opened and Jean came in with tea things on a silver tray. 'Family argument?' she asked cheerfully. 'Or can anyone join in?'

'Show her,' Janet ordered. 'Go on – show her. She's as much right to know as anyone.'

Jean put the tray down on a small brass table by the fire. She crossed to Reeve, prised the letter from his grasp, smoothed it out and read it.

'But that's wonderful, Carey.' She kissed him on the cheek. 'I'm so pleased for you.'

'Good God, woman, you're as bad as she is. A desk job, don't you understand? A glorified clerk, signing papers all day.'

Jean pulled him towards the fire and Janet shook her head. 'You and Harry Jago. You just can't wait to get back into the glorious fight. Death before dishonour.'

Jean said, 'You two should be celebrating, not fighting. I've got a marvellous dinner laid on for tonight. Game pie, jugged hare and there are still four bottles of that special champagne Colin laid down in the cellar.'

'I'm sorry, Jean,' Janet told her, 'and thank you. That sounds wonderful. I'd love to come.'

Reeve stood in front of the fire, filling his pipe. 'You know Gericke interests me. It's not often one gets a chance to meet a legend face-to-face.'

'Is he really that special?' Jean asked.

'In naval circles certainly. Probably the most successful submarine commander on either side in the war. That information's not exactly on release for public consumption, mind you. But he's a remarkable man, no doubt about it.'

'Whose side are you on, for God's sake?' Janet demanded.

'Oh, don't misunderstand me. Respect of one professional for another, that's all. Mind you that attack on Falmouth was quite something. I'd love to know just how he pulled it off.'

'Then ask him to dinner, why don't you? Make up the four – isn't that the civilized thing to do? You can talk war to your heart's content.'

The sarcasm was heavy in her voice together with a certain anger.

Reeve frowned, a slight fixed smile on his mouth. 'That's not a bad idea.'

'You've got to be joking.'

'But why not?' He turned to Jean. 'Would you mind?'

She hesitated. 'I'm not sure, Carey. If you'd asked me that yesterday I'd have thought you were mad, but now . . .' She frowned. 'The enemy – everything I should hate – and yet I liked him. He's a human being.'

'Does he come or doesn't he?' Reeve demanded impatiently. 'Your decision. You are the civil power here, after all.'

'Are you suggesting he gives his parole for the evening?'

'Nothing so old-fashioned. Young Lachlan in attendance with that rifle of his, of course.'

'Why?' Janet asked. 'Why are you doing this?'

'Why not? At least I'll hear how the war's going at first hand for a change.' There was a glint in his eye, a hint of that wild and unpredictable Carey Reeve she knew and mistrusted. 'And anyway – I would have thought it might make for a rather entertaining evening.'

V

Gericke, lying on the bed, was surprised to hear that distinctive laugh from the office. He got to his feet as her step sounded in the corridor.

She stood on the other side of the gate. 'I've seen them do this scene so often in the movies that I have the dialogue off by heart. Are they treating you all right?'

'No complaints. To what do I owe the pleasure of this visit?'

'An invitation to dinner from Jean Sinclair.'

Lachlan appeared behind her looking slightly bewildered.

'A joke perhaps?' Gericke suggested.

'Half-seven for eight. As you don't have a black tie, uniform will do. Lachlan will bring you up to the house – and please don't try to do anything silly like starting to run in the wrong direction. He'll shoot you if he has to.'

He bowed slightly. 'How could I refuse such a charming invitation.'

'I know,' she said. 'The honour of the Kriegsmarine is at stake.'

She walked away briskly and the boy stared at Gericke, mouth open. Gericke smiled. 'Don't fight it, Lachlan, just go with the tide like me.'

He lay down on the bed and pillowed his head on his hands.

VI

Berger's cabin was a scene of confusion. The oil stove stood on the cabinet in a corner and his desk had been cleared to take a selection of pans. Sisters Käthe, Else and Brigitte were serving food to some of the crew and not without considerable difficulty. Outside, the wind howled in full gale and the floor tilted beneath their feet as the *Deutschland* rolled through heavy seas.

The captain stood in a corner out of the way, a glass of rum in one hand, the bottle in the other. He was just in from the quarterdeck, chilled to the bone, his oilskin streaming.

Sister Käthe looked across at him. 'Something to eat, Herr Kapitän?'

Berger shook his head. 'No time, sister. I've things to do. Any problems?.

'The men come in when they can. Three or four at a time. At least we're managing to keep a stove going in here.'

'Meaning hot food?' Berger said. 'All the difference in weather like this. I'm very grateful to you ladies. We all are, believe me.' He drained his glass. 'I'd better get back to it.'

He opened the door and went out, struggling to close it again in the high wind. The *Deutschland* fought her way through heavy seas under full sail, water pouring over the bulwarks as she rolled. There were two men on the wheel and her hatches were buried under a maelstrom which on occasions was waist-deep as he made his way to the companionway. He entered with a flood of water, got the doors closed again and went down.

Water, a foot deep, swirled about the floor of the saloon. The fanlight had been boarded over and two storm lanterns swung from hooks in the ceiling.

Four of the crew waited their turn for attention at Sister Angela's afternoon clinic. A young electrician's mate named Sporer lay on the table, his left sleeve rolled up exposing a ring of very bad sea boils on his wrist.

Sister Angela stood on one side of him, the hem of her skirt tucked into her belt. Lotte faced her holding a tray containing instruments and a small basin. Richter stood at the head of the table.

'What's all this?' Berger demanded.

'The infection is now so bad that his arm is almost paralysed.' Sister Angela reached for a scalpel. 'Hang on, Karl, like a brave boy. I'll be as quick as I can.'

Sporer, only eighteen, was frightened to death, his face damp with sweat. She nodded to Richter who placed his hands on the boy's shoulders. The *Deutschland* staggered in a sudden squall, a minor wave flowing from one side of the cabin to the other.

One of the crew lost his balance and ended on his hands and knees in the water, but Sister Angela, bracing herself against the table, leaned down and went to work.

The scalpel lanced into the boils one after another, there was an immediate stench of corruption as pus spurted. The boy cried out, bucking, in spite of Richter's weight on him – and then he fainted.

She worked on at an incredible speed, no need to be gentle now, Lotte handing her one instrument after another without a word. As she started to bandage the suppurating sores, Berger said, 'Are many of the crew suffering with those things now?'

'About half,' she said.

Berger turned and found Richter watching him. 'A long voyage, Herr Kapitän.'

Berger nodded wearily. 'So it would appear.'

VII

It was just before seven-thirty and dusk when Gericke and Lachlan turned in through the wide gate of Fhada House and moved along the gravel drive. They went up the steps and the German tugged at the chain of the old-fashioned bell-pull.

Steps approached and the door was opened by a pleasant-looking woman of sixty or so, grey hair pinned back in a bun. She was wearing a black bombazine dress and a starched white apron.

She smiled, showing no surprise at all. 'Won't you come in, sir?'

'Thank you.' Gericke stepped into the hall, Lachlan behind, the Lee-Enfield ready in both hands.

'Let me take your coat, sir.' She vanished into a small cloakroom and was back in a moment. 'The others are in the drawing room. If you'll come this way.' She paused, a hand on the door. 'Who is it again, sir?'

Gericke, convinced more than ever that he was engaged in some privileged nightmare, said, 'Korvettenkapitän Paul Gericke. I'm expected,' he added gravely.

'Oh yes, sir.' She opened the door and led the way in. 'Korvettenkapitän Gericke, madam.'

'Thank you, Mary.'

Jean Sinclair, Reeve and Janet were by the fire drinking sherry, Rory sprawled across the carpet. She held out her hand. 'I'm so glad you could come, commander.' She turned to Reeve, 'Do get Commander Gericke a drink, Carey.'

Lachlan took up a position beside the door. She said, 'Good evening, Lachlan. How is your mother?'

'She is well, Mrs Sinclair.'

'You will tell her I was asking after her.'

Gericke found himself a moment later in front of the fire, slightly bewildered, a glass of excellent sherry in one hand, a cigarette in the other.

'I hope they've made you as comfortable as possible down there,' Jean said.

But it was a remark not to be taken seriously for there was a glint in her eye, laughter hardly contained.

'I should describe the facilities at your police station as adequate rather than comfortable,' he replied smoothly.

Reeve burst out laughing. 'I like that.' He took Gericke by the arm. 'Let's leave these two to cackle on and come over here and tell me about Falmouth.'

He and Gericke moved over to the window and stood heads together. Jean said, 'He's a handsome man, isn't he?'

'Which one?' Janet said.

The older woman smiled. 'Point taken, but you know what I mean.'

Janet nodded. 'He's like no other man I've ever known. There is a quality to him I can't define. I've always been too busy for men, Jean. For any deep relationships, I mean. Medical school, then the war. Work and sleep mostly, with the occasional affair when I felt the need.'

'And Gericke?'

'I'm just a little bit afraid of him.'

'I know what you mean.'

'It's there in the eyes mostly,' Janet said.

'Or not there, haven't you noticed that? Nothing shows for he gives nothing away. He seems a man remote from life, that constant wry smile of his a sign perhaps that he thinks it all a rather black little joke. A brilliant officer, a seaman of genius; his record, those decorations prove that. And like all such men, totally unpredictable. No rule that was ever made was made for him.'

A gong sounded outside and Mary appeared in the doorway. 'Dinner is served, madam.'

Jean stood up. 'Shall we go in, gentlemen?'

She moved out with Reeve. Janet and Gericke following, Lachlan bringing up the rear.

VIII

The meal, served in a dining-room of baronial proportions, was everything Jean had promised. There was a minstrels' gallery at one end, the most enormous fireplace Gericke had ever seen, three great logs burning brightly on the open hearth. Above it hung two tattered battle flags.

There were mounted animal heads on the stone walls. Everything from leopard to Thompson's Gazelle, taking in most things in between. A magnificent suit of medieval armour, halberds, targes, and crossed claymores, muskets of every description.

'Extraordinary,' he said. 'You have a very remarkable place here, Mrs Sinclair.'

'We know,' Janet said. 'Stage six at MGM. All we need is Errol Flynn in a kilt, swinging down from that gallery, claymore in hand.'

Jean Sinclair laughed. 'Actually she's not too far from the truth, commander. This place is really the most awful fraud. Victorian Gothic. An ancestor of mine, one Fergus Sinclair, was responsible.'

'The trophies, are they from his time also?' Gericke asked.

'No, those were my grandfather's. Hunted all over the world. He was one of those men who would rather shoot anything than nothing. He used to insist on taking me deer-stalking in season when I was quite young. Something of an experience.'

'I just bet it was,' Janet commented.

'Oh yes, I learned many things. That you must never hurry. That you must never stalk and stay downwind, even at a thousand yards and always to shoot low if the target is downhill.'

'Interesting,' Gericke said. 'I must remember.'

'To weave from side-to-side when making a run for it?' Reeve said.

He was already opening a third botte of champagne, fumbling with the cork, supporting his bad arm on the edge of the table. There was a touch of aggression in his voice that had not been there earlier. Janet stopped smiling.

Jean went round the table and reached for the bottle. 'Let me, Carey. They can be difficult, those corks.'

'I can manage.' He tried to jerk the bottle away from her, one-handed, lost his grip and it smashed on the floor. 'Would you look at that,' he said bitterly.

'It's all right, Carey.' She picked up a napkin and wiped down his uniform where it had been splashed.

'That was a good year,' Reeve said slowly. He passed a hand over his eyes for a moment, then turned to Janet and Gericke. 'I must apologize. I haven't been quite myself lately.'

Jean patted him on the shoulder. 'Coffee in the drawing-room, I think.'

She nodded to Janet who glanced at Gericke, then pushed back her chair. They returned to the drawing-room and Lachlan followed without a word.

'He's not well?' Gericke asked.

She took a cigarette from a box and he gave her a light. 'You noticed his arm, and there's the eye. He got that little lot on D-Day going into action when he shouldn't. The story of his life. He's been trying to get back into the fight ever since.'

'I know the type well. His last words in this life will probably be: Follow me, men.'

She shook her head. 'The only job he's been offered, and that took all the influence in the world, is behind a desk. That's what I've come up to see him about.'

'And he didn't like it?'

'He has nothing,' she said. 'In *his* eyes, he has nothing.'

'A beautiful woman is nothing?'

'To some men,'

'But not all, I think.'

She put a hand to her throat, at a loss for words then turned quickly, sat down at the grand piano and lifted the lid.

'But then, how seriously can one take that kind of thing? The war can do strange things to people, make them act in a way they otherwise would not.'

'Or with complete honesty for once. A Bechstein, I see? Only the best. I didn't know you could play.'

'One of the more useful by-products of an expensive education, but if it's Beethoven you're after, I'm afraid I'm not your man.'

She started to play 'A Nightingale Sang in Berkeley Square' and Gericke leaned on the piano, watching her. 'You're good.'

The wolfhound came over from his place in front of the fire and flopped down beside her. 'I'm afraid so. Isn't it a bore? Even Rory agrees.'

He burst out laughing and Reeve and Jean Sinclair came in. The admiral looked considerably more cheerful and crossed to the piano. 'That really takes me back. What about "Moonlight in Vermont"?'

She moved smoothly into the new melody and Reeve went and sat by the fire with Jean, who was pouring coffee. They had their heads together and were talking softly.

'Doesn't that make you feel the world's a better place?' Janet asked.

'Envious,' Gericke whispered. 'It makes me feel envious.'

She started to play 'Lilli Marlene'. 'Is that any better?'

'Not really. Reminds me too much of the way the war is going, the British having taken that over too. Do you know "A Foggy Day in London Town"? It was extremely popular with the Luftwaffe for a while.'

She hesitated, remembering that night on the Embankment with Harry Jago. 'No, I'm afraid I never did get round to that one.'

Reeve had taken Jean Sinclair's hand. They were totally engrossed in each other. Janet closed the lid and stood up. 'I think I'd like a little air. Could I have my wrap, please?'

It was hanging over the back of a chair. Gericke got it at once and draped it around her shoulders. 'We're going on the terrace for a while to look at the evening,' she called and smiled up at Gericke. 'An old Scottish custom. Coming, Lachlan?'

Reeve glanced across. 'Oh, sure – fine.' He turned back to Jean and took her other hand.

'You see?' Gericke said. 'How a good woman can work wonders?'

'In this case, a miracle,' Janet said. 'Believe me.'

She opened the french window and moved out on the terrace. The sky was very dark, streaked with orange flame on the horizon so that to the north, the islands stood up starkly and the sea was perfectly calm.

They stood on the edge of the terrace, shoulders touching, and Lachlan paused beside the french windows. 'It's as if everything is waiting for something,' she said.

Gericke nodded. 'Once in the West Indies we surfaced off Martinique at night to charge the batteries. It was just like this. Incredibly quiet.'

'That's what I like about it here,' she said. 'The stillness. At least in the brief interludes when the wind isn't blowing.'

'The following day it blew the worst hurricane they'd known in those islands in living memory. We had to go down and stay down. Nature took care of the convoy we were after. Eleven ships out of twenty-six were sunk.'

'Did you claim a medal for that, too?'

'Now why didn't I think of that?' he said lightly.

In the pale evening light her face was barely visible. 'I'm sorry.'

Reeve appeared behind Lachlan. 'Hey, you two, the coffee's getting cold.'

'We're coming,' Janet replied.

Her wrap slipped from her shoulders, falling to the ground. Gericke picked it up and handed it to her. The last flicker of orange on the horizon seemed to flare suddenly – was extinguished as total darkness fell.

IX

At Trondheim, Necker walked across to the Operations building. He was in a thoroughly bad temper. His eyes were sore as if from lack of sleep, though he'd been sitting around for three days now with absolutely nothing to do.

When he went into the intelligence room Colonel Maier was sitting behind Altrogge's desk. The major leaned over beside him and they were examining a chart of the Western Approaches together.

Maier glanced up. 'There you are, Horst. A little action for you at last.'

'It would be nice to think so,' Necker said with a certain amount of sarcasm in his voice, 'but as the Herr Oberst is well aware, I've been called out on three separate occasions during the past thirty-six hours, only to have the operation cancelled at the last moment.'

'Not this time,' Maier said. 'It's too important. To put it briefly, you take off at 0200. Your flight plan will take you over Scotland, then south of the Outer Hebrides and west of Ireland to this map reference.' He indicated the spot with a pencil. 'According to the Abwehr, there should be a large convoy homeward bound from Halifax, Nova Scotia, in that area about now. It's essential they have the information regarding its position in Kiel before noon tomorrow.'

'Or we'll lose the war, I suppose.'

'Very funny,' Maier said coldly and got to his feet. 'You're a good pilot, Horst, but there are times when you behave with the intelligence of a fourteen-year-old. One of these days, you will make that kind of remark just once too often.'

'I'm sorry, Herr Oberst.'

'No, you're not.' Maier smiled and clapped him on the shoulder. 'Altrogge will fill you in on the wearisome details and I'll expect a personal report the moment you get back.'

He went out and Necker examined the chart. 'I'd say it's a nine-hundred-mile flight to that map reference.'

'And nine hundred back, which leaves you with six to play with when you get there. Say two hours' flying time in the target area, just to give a margin for error.'

'I don't make them,' Necker said. 'That's why I'm still here. What about those Spitfire squadrons?'

'Up here near Inverness, but they'll give you no trouble if you stay at thirty-five to thirty-eight thousand, which you can do in comfort with the improvements we've been installing. The outward journey will be in darkness anyway. A milk run.'

'If you say so,' Necker said acidly and sat down. 'All right, let's get into it in detail.'

X

Reeve opened the police station door and he and Gericke walked in, followed by Lachlan. The boy got his keys and led the way down the steps to the passageway. Gericke moved into his cell and Lachlan double-locked it.

'Herr Konteradmiral,' Gericke saluted. 'My thanks for your part in a delightful evening.'

Reeve hesitated. For a moment it seemed that he might speak. Instead, he returned the salute punctiliously and moved away along the passageway to the office, Lachlan following.

The door closed. Gericke stood there for a moment, listening, hands on the bars, then moved to the window. The stonework of the sill was cracked, the cement where the bars fitted into it, old and crumbling. He lifted his mattress, removed one of the coil springs from the iron bed and went to work on that cement with the hooked end.

There were steps in the corridor. He sat down quickly and Lachlan appeared on the other side of the gate, rifle over his shoulder, a sleeping-bag under one arm.

'What's all this?' Gericke demanded.

The boy placed a Thermos flask on the floor, unrolled the sleeping-bag, stepped into it and zipped it up around his body. Then he sat down, back against the opposite wall, rifle across his knees.

'Just keeping an eye out for you, commander. Admiral Reeve thought you might sleep better knowing I was close by.'

Gericke smiled. 'You know something, Lachlan? I think he may very well have a point there.'

He lay down on the bed, pulled the blankets up to his chin and was asleep almost instantly.

— 12 —

> Barquentine *Deutschland*, 24 September 1944. Lat. 56°N., long. 9°.51W. One hundred and ten miles south-west of the Outer Hebrides. Starts calm and strangely still as I cannot remember it in these waters within my experience. Just after midnight a ship crossed our bow for we heard her engines and saw a light plainly, presumably carelessness on the part of her crew. In the mid watch it began to rain again and the wind freshened considerably. At four bells in the morning watch, it being Sunday, Sister Angela held her usual early morning service on deck in spite of the inclement weather.

THE *DEUTSCHLAND*, with every stitch of canvas set, was making twelve knots. The sea was beginning to lift into white caps under a sky of uniform slate grey.

Rain was driving in from the south-west, yet Sister Angela stood at the rail in front of him and addressed the other nuns on the deck below with the dozen or so crew members who had felt religious enough to turn out.

Although a few of the men were Roman Catholic, the rest, when they were anything at all, were Lutherans and she had opted for a service of such a nature that it would offend no one.

She was just coming to the end of general confession, her voice clear on the damp air.

> . . . and grant, O most merciful Father, for His sake, that we may here after live a godly, righteous, and sober life, to the glory of thy holy name.

There was a moment of silence as she prayed, eyes closed, hands clasped. She crossed herself and said, 'We will now sing a hymn, specially for those at sea and well known to you all. "Eternal Father strong to save, whose arm doth bind the restless wave".'

Lotte and the other nuns took up the words bravely and Richter, standing behind her, joined in, taking the other crew members along with him in a ragged chorus. Sister Angela turned once to glance at Berger and Sturm and the captain found himself joining in helplessly.

'Oh hear us when we cry to Thee for those in peril on the sea.'

And then, as the chorus started to peter out, there was a roaring in the heavens and Berger swung round in alarm to see a black plane coming in over the sea from the south-east at no more than a hundred and fifty feet.

'God in heaven, this is it! At last this is it!' he thought and in the same moment grabbed Sister Angela and pulled her down. There was total confusion on the deck below as the crew scattered and Sister Käthe screamed piercingly.

Sturm, crouching on one knee beside Berger cried excitedly, 'Herr Kapitän – look! It's one of ours!'

Berger caught a glimpse of the Junkers as it passed over, saw the crosses on the wings clearly, the swastika tailplane, and then it banked to port and started to climb.

On the deck below men were running to the rail, two or three actually climbing the rigging, everyone cheering, and Richter and Lotte stood together, the bosun's arm around the girl's waist as they stared up into the sky.

'Now what, Herr Kapitän?' Sturm demanded.

Berger, recovering his scattered wits, got to his feet. He leaned over the rail and bawled, 'Richter, run that Swedish flag down. You'll find a Kriegsmarine ensign in the main locker in my cabin.' He turned to Sturm. 'Get on the radio, quick. Let's see if we can make contact.'

II

'Swedish?' Necker demanded. 'Are you certain?'

'Definitely, Herr Hauptmann,' Rudi assured him. 'I saw the flag plainly.'

Kranz, the rear gunner, cut in on them. 'I can confirm that, Herr Hauptmann.'

'A sailing ship,' Necker said. 'If I hadn't seen it for myself I'd never have believed it. Let's take another look.'

He throttled right back, making his pass at no more than a hundred feet this time, aware himself as they approached, that the Swedish flag was fluttering down.

'What on earth are they striking their colours for, Herr Hauptmann?' Rudi Hubner asked in bewilderment.

'Search me,' Necker said and then grunted in astonishment as another flag was run up.

As they flashed past, the flag stretched in the wind and Kranz called excitedly, 'A Kriegsmarine ensign, Herr Hauptmann! I swear it!'

'Don't worry,' Necker called. 'I saw it too. But it doesn't make any sense. I'm going round again.'

Schmidt, the wireless operator, touched his shoulder. 'I'm getting something now, Herr Hauptmann. It must be them. I'll switch over.'

A moment later, to his total astonishment, and with a clarity only to be expected at such short range, he heard Johann Sturm's voice clearly in his headphones saying, 'This is the *Deutschland* calling Big Black Eagle. Are you receiving me?'

'Big Black Eagle?' Schmidt said in bewilderment. 'What's he talking about?'

'He doesn't want to identify us, you fool, in case anyone else is picking the message up,' Necker said. 'Here, let me speak to him.'

III

Jean Sinclair was having a last cup of tea before leaving for church when Reeve and Janet arrived.

'This is a pleasant surprise,' she said. 'I don't usually have much success when I try to persuade him to turn out on a Sunday morning.'

'Business, I'm afraid,' Janet said. 'But I persuaded him to put his uniform on anyway, so grab him if you can.'

Jean looked puzzled. Reeve said, 'I've had word from Mallaig that Lieutenant Jago's got engine trouble. His deadline for fixing it is the middle of the afternoon, otherwise they'll send someone else to pick up Gericke. Whoever it is, they obviously can't make it before late evening. Possibly even tomorrow morning.'

'I see.' She glanced at her watch. 'The service, I might remind you, starts in fifteen minutes and unless you want one of Murdoch's public rebukes as we creep in at the back of the congregation, we'd better hurry.'

'All right,' he said heavily. 'I'll come, only I'll have to catch you up. I want a word with Mary about butter and eggs. I'm fresh out.'

The door closed behind him and Jean turned to Janet. 'What about you?'

'I don't think so – not this morning.'

'What are you going to do?'

'I'll think of something.'

Jean smiled. 'I'm sure you will.'

IV

Gericke had breakfasted well on porridge and fried bacon and tomatoes supplied, surprisingly enough, by Lachlan's mother. After she had gone, Lachlan resumed his place against the wall.

Gericke said, 'Sleep, Lachlan. When do you expect to get some sleep?'

'Och, I need terrible little of that. An awful problem I was to my mother as a wee boy.' Lachlan glanced at his watch. 'No sweat, commander. Murdoch takes over from me at eleven o'clock after morning service.'

'Ah yes,' Gericke said. 'He is some kind of pastor is he not?'

'That's right – and coxswain of the *Morag Sinclair*.'

'The *Morag Sinclair*?'

'The great love of Murdoch's life. She's a forty-one foot Watson-type motor lifeboat. The station's at South Inlet at the other end of the island and Murdoch lives there.'

Gericke said, 'I don't understand. Why not here?'

'Because in really rough weather the sea builds up so bad across the harbour bar it's impossible to get out. Much easier from South Inlet.'

'And this is always so?'

'No – once or twice a year it's impossible to launch from the inlet.'

'And what happens then if there is a call?'

'There's another lifeboat stationed at Barra.'

'And you, Lachlan, were you a member of the lifeboat crew before joining the army?'

'Not with my belly,' Lachlan said. 'But my father was'.

He stopped smiling and Gericke, at a loss for words, stood there gripping the bars. The outer door banged and Janet called, 'Anyone home?'

She was wearing a sheepskin coat, tweed skirt, knee-length boots and Tam o' Shanter. 'Has he been behaving himself, Lachlan?'

'No choice,' Gericke said. 'Young Lochinvar having sat against the wall looking in on me all night with that rifle across his knees.'

She passed a packet of cigarettes and a couple of magazines between the bars. 'To help you pass the time.'

'Not long now,' he said. 'Lieutenant Jago will be here at noon to take me away. Is it not so?'

'Engine trouble at Stornoway. Tonight at the earliest – maybe even tomorrow.'

He stood there looking at her through the bars as if waiting for something. Suddenly, she felt awkward, half-angry with herself for being there at all.

'I'll have to go now. I've got things to do.'

'My thanks,' Gericke said gravely and held up the magazines. 'For these – amongst other things.'

She turned and walked out quickly.

V

In the intelligence room at Trondheim, Necker paced up and down moodily, smoking a cigarette. He still wore flying clothes, his face streaked with dirt and sweat, the marks of his goggles plain.

Altrogge, at his desk, glanced up from the report he was writing. 'That won't help, Horst. Why don't you sit down. Have some coffee.'

He reached for the pot on the tray at his right hand and

Necker shook his head. 'No, thanks.' And then he exploded. 'Why all the delay? I mean, what in the hell goes on?'

'The Gruppenkommandeur is handling it personally, you know that, but with a thing like this, there are bound to be delays in channel. You'll have to be patient.' He leaned back and added carefully, 'I suspect, my friend, that you may also have to prepare yourself for a rather large rocket.'

Necker stopped his pacing. 'What are you talking about?'

'You didn't do as you were told, Horst. You didn't follow orders.'

Necker gaped at him in astonishment. 'Didn't follow orders? For God's sake, Hans, what did you expect me to do?'

The door opened and Maier entered. He carried several signal flimsies and his face was grave. 'I've been on to the Kriegsmarine in Kiel and the news has gone right up to Dönitz himself. I've had a signal acknowledging and thanking us for the information.'

'Is that all?'

'No, they also sent another signal expressing their extreme displeasure at the lack of information concerning the whereabouts of the Halifax convoy.'

'Never mind that,' Necker said. 'What about the *Deutschland?*'

Maier sat on the edge of the desk and selected a cigarette carefully. 'They know all about her from intelligence sources in the Argentine. Left Brazil some weeks ago with a crew of assorted Kriegsmarine types under a Fregattenkapitän Berger. They also have some civilian passengers on board – nuns, I believe.'

'How fantastic,' Necker said. 'To sail a thing like that from one end of the Atlantic to the other right under the noses of the British and American navies. It'll set the country on fire.'

'No it won't, my friend, for the good and sufficient reason that the news will not be released. For such an intelligent man, Horst, you can on occasion be exasperatingly stupid. You kept your radio contact with *Deutschland* to a minimum, didn't you? Improvised a crude code, for example. Why did you do that?'

'In case anyone picked up the transmission and was able to get a fix.'

'Exactly. The British Navy, Horst, can have had no more than a passing interest in the activities of a broken-down old sailing ship attempting to reach Kiel from Brazil, mainly because no one would have given a snap of the finger for her chances of getting even half-way.'

'So?'

'But now the situation changes. Our friends on the other side of the North Sea are as alive to the value of propaganda of the right sort as we are. Let them even suspect that the *Deutschland* is in that area and so close to home and they'll do anything, deploy every ship they have in those waters, to stop her getting through.'

There was silence for a moment and it was Altrogge who said, with considerable sympathy in his voice, 'So you see, Horst, no one must know. Any public announcement at this stage would be fatal.'

Necker nodded slowly, suddenly very tired, and slumped into a chair. 'The *Deutschland*, Horst, must be left to her own devices,' Maier said. 'You understand this? We can pray for her, but no more than that.'

'Yes, Herr Oberst.'

'And you were wrong, Horst. You had no right to break off from your search pattern. You could have stayed in the area another hour and a half at least. You may very well have sighted the Halifax convoy.'

Necker nodded wearily and Maier put a hand on his shoulder. 'We all make mistakes, but of this kind you are permitted only one. You understand?'

'Yes, Herr Oberst.'

'Good, now go and get something to eat, then sleep, Horst. Lots of sleep. Sometime during the next twenty-four hours you'll be going out again.'

Necker stood up. 'The same area?'

'The same.' Maier nodded. 'But the Halifax convoy this time, Horst.'

Necker went out slowly, boots drubbing. The door swung behind him. There was silence for a moment, then Maier sighed heavily. 'A funny thing, Hans,' he said to Altrogge. 'And I'll always deny having said it, of course.'

'What's that, Herr Oberst?'

'Oh, just that in his place, I've a nasty suspicion I'd have done exactly what he did.'

VI

In Stornoway, the mist had been swept away by the rising wind and rain drove in from the sea as Jago went down the ladder from the bridge and moved aft. He dropped to one knee by the open hatch and peered into the cramped engine-room.

'How's it going in there?'

Jansen squatted beside Astor and Chaney. 'Another hour, sir.'

'And are you certain it will work?'

It was Astor who looked up, slightly aggrieved. 'Me and Chaney and that limey warrant officer up at the RAF workshop, we made the new parts ourselves. Solid brass. She'll be as good as new, lieutenant.'

Jansen came up the ladder. 'He's right, sir, they've done an excellent job.'

'Good,' Jago said, hauling himself up on the bridge. 'Signal Mallaig we expect to be able to leave in one hour.' He glanced at his watch. 'Which means we'll only have overstepped Murray's deadline by ten or fifteen minutes. I'll confirm actual departure, naturally.'

He pushed open the door, went in and sat at the chart table. Jansen hesitated and said, 'The glass has fallen quite substantially within the last hour, Lieutenant.'

'So?'

'And the general forecast, not to put too fine a point on it, sir, stinks.'

Jago laughed. 'Aren't you the guy who once crossed the Atlantic single-handed?'

'The sea, lieutenant, has fulfilled a need in me for most of my life,' Jansen said gravely. 'We enjoy a very special relationship. She has shaken me up a time or two, but I have always come back for more. A game we play.'

Jago felt unaccountably chilled. 'What in the hell are you talking about?'

'God knows.' Jansen seemed embarrassed. 'Perhaps I'm

getting old.' He peered out through the doorway. 'These islands are different from anything I've ever known. The sea's different.'

'Oh, I get it,' Jago said mockingly. 'You mean it's been waiting for you up here all your life?'

'Or I've been waiting for it,' Jansen said. 'Which is something else again. Anyway, I'd better get that signal off, sir.'

He went out. Rain dashed against the bridge windows and outside the wind moaned through the steel rigging. Jago, still caught by what Jansen had said, sat there, head slightly turned as if listening to something.

There was a weather report on the desk and he picked it up. Sea areas Rockall, Bailey, Malin, the Hebrides; the picture was uniformly black. A deep depression moving in fast from the Atlantic. Heavy rain, winds four or five increasing to full gale by evening.

He crumbled the flimsy and tossed it into a corner. 'Ah well,' he said softly. 'I guess it just isn't my day.'

VII

On the *Deutschland*, Berger sat at the charts in his cabin, plotting the course for the next few days. He was aware of the pump clanking monotonously outside, the rising wind. Otto Prager lay on the bunk reading a book. He sat up and removed his spectacles.

'That damn thing seems to be going on for ever.'

'You think so?'

There was a knock at the door and Sturm entered, 'You wanted me, Herr Kapitän?'

'How goes it?'

'Two hours yesterday – two and a half today.'

'And still not dry?'

'Almost.' Sturm hesitated. 'We ship water constantly, captain, which doesn't help. It seems to me, sir, that if we took in sail . . .'

'Not a stitch, Herr Sturm.' Berger slammed a hand on the table. 'Not one rag do you touch without my permission. You understand?'

'As you say, sir.'

'Now return to your duties and send Richter in here.'

Sturm withdrew and Prager got up and crossed to the desk. 'He's changed, that boy. A month ago he would have jumped to attention and clicked his heels if you'd spoken to him like that, but now . . .'

'. . . he's a man,' Berger cut in. 'He has the *Deutschland* to thank for that. Nothing will ever be the same again.'

'He's right then?'

'Only in part. That we are shipping a great deal of water is true, which doesn't help an already indifferent situation below the waterline. That the main reason for this is my insistence on hanging out all my canvas in rough weather is also true. But bad weather is the best friend we have, for it makes us difficult to find. We can use it, Otto, to make time, which at this stage in the game is what we need to do at all costs.' He smoothed the chart with both hands. 'I mustn't fail. Not now. Not having come so far.'

Prager put a hand on his shoulder. 'We owe you a great deal, Erich. All of us.'

There was a knock at the door and Richter came in. He wore an oilskin jacket and his hands were covered in Stockholm tar. 'Herr Kapitän?'

'Ah, Richter. You've been aloft, I see.'

The bosun glanced at his hands. 'A block came loose on the top foremast.'

'Have you attended to the saloon skylight?'

'We've boarded it up permanently, Herr Kapitän. Dark for the ladies down there now, but better than water flooding through at all hours.'

'Good,' Berger said. 'Now, I'd like your opinion on our general situation.'

Richter appeared to hesitate. 'You are the master, sir, not I.'

'I know, man,' Berger said impatiently. 'But except for myself, you've had more time at sea under sail than anyone else. You, at least, know what I'm talking about.'

Richter shrugged. 'As the Herr Kapitän pleases.'

Berger half-turned the western-approaches chart and tapped it with his fingers. 'Most blockade runners in the past have attempted the Denmark Strait between Greenland and Iceland, then across to Norway. You agree?'

'One doesn't exactly expect to find traffic up there, Herr Kapitän.'

'But not for us, eh? Why?'

'A possibility of spare ice floating around in the Greenland section and we'd have to spend too much time north of the Arctic Circle.'

'I agree. And once past the Hebrides, where should our present route take us? The Orkneys passage?'

'No, sir,' Richter said. 'In my opinion we'd do better to make our turn somewhere north of the Shetlands, then cut straight across for Bergen.'

'Good, Helmut. Very good. It's nice to have one's judgement confirmed.' Berger rolled up the chart. 'There is just one other thing. Herr Sturm thinks we're carrying too much canvas. Do you agree with him?'

'Not if the Herr Kapitän wishes to make time,' Richter said. 'However, I would point out that the glass is falling. In my opinion, we're in for a bad night.'

Berger, who had started to smile, frowned in irritation. 'All right, I wasn't born yesterday. You think I don't know the glass is falling?'

The bosun went out. Berger unrolled the chart and looked down at it, scowling.

VIII

Gericke moved his bed towards the gate to avoid the rain which was driving in through the broken window every so often when the wind gusted. When he had things arranged to his satisfaction, he went back and peered through the bars.

It was just after seven, night falling fast and as wild a scene as he had ever seen, ragged waves stretching to the horizon, driving rain, sky of lead verging to black, yet here and there slashed with orange and gold.

Suddenly, far out to sea beyond the end of the pier, he saw the *Dead End* rise high over a wave, then plunge down again, her prow biting deep.

There was a step in the passageway and he turned to see

Janet on the other side. She wore a sou'wester and an oilskin coat that glistened with rain and she carried a covered basket. She dropped to one knee and pushed the basket through the small flap at the bottom of the gate.

'That should keep you going. What the Scots call a good ham tea.'

Gericke picked the basket up and put it on his bunk. 'Your friend, Lieutenant Jago. He's making his run into harbour now and from the looks of that sea, I'd say he must be damn glad to get in.'

'Harry?' she said, her face lighting up. 'Here?'

She turned and ran out and Gericke reached for a cigarette as Lachlan came along from the office, a mug of tea in his hand which he passed through.

'Have you a match, Lachlan?'

'I have, commander,' Lachlan gave him a box between the bars. 'You can keep them.'

Gericke lit his cigarette and moved to the window. The gunboat was bouncing against the pier now, her crew hanging on to her lines.

He saw Jago come out on the bridge, then Janet, her yellow oilskin clear against the evening light, running along the pier. Jago waved, came down the ladder and stepped over the rail. A moment later she was in his arms.

'So that's the way of it,' Gericke whispered. And as the wind gusted, driving rain in through the bars, he turned away.

IX

At Fhada House the wind howled down the chimney, sending the logs roaring. Jago reached out his hands to the blaze. 'That's marvellous, Mrs Sinclair. I was beginning to think I'd never get warm again. One hell of a trip.'

'Another coffee?'

'No, thanks. I've really done very well.'

He glanced across at Janet who played the piano softly. Jean said, 'I'm sorry the admiral couldn't come.'

'Well, as he said, he prefers to stick close to the radio on a night like this.'

'I know,' she said. 'There could be a call for the lifeboat.

I wish they'd get that submarine cable connected. It makes things very difficult for everyone. Carey, you know, is our only link with civilization.'

The clock chimed eleven and Jago smiled. 'I really think I should be getting back now. Early start in the morning.' He turned. 'I'm ready when you are, Janet.'

'I'm staying the night, darling,' Janet said, still continuing to play.

'Oh, I see. Well, I'd better get going then.'

She showed no inclination to move. Jean Sinclair took him out into the hall. As she helped him into his reefer, she said, 'You did say an early start in the morning, didn't you, lieutenant?'

'That's right, ma'am.'

She shook her head. 'I don't think so. Not tomorrow, probably not for two or three days now.' She smiled. 'I know what I'm talking about. When the wind starts blowing over Fhada like this, anything can happen.'

Jago grinned, suddenly much more cheerful. 'Can you positively guarantee that?'

'I think so."

As she opened the door, struggling to hold it still against the wind, he kissed her on the right cheek. 'Anyone ever tell you you're an angel?' he said and plunged out into the gale.

When Jean returned to the drawing-room, Janet was standing by the fire pulling on her sheepskin. 'Has he gone?'

'Obviously.'

'Good.' Janet moved past her into the hall and Jean followed. 'What are you playing at?'

'To be perfectly honest, I don't know,' Janet said and added, 'I've just had a great idea. To hell with men.'

'It's a thought.' Jean opened the door. 'I'd sleep on it if I were you.'

'Exactly,' Janet said and she moved out into the driving rain.

X

'Personally I think the search for the Halifax convoy to be a waste of time,' Hans Altrogge said. 'But they still insist you have a look.'

It was just before midnight and the intelligence room was a place of shadows. Necker leaned over the chart and nodded. 'I agree. A waste of fuel, the whole exercise.'

'Not entirely, Horst.' Altrogge opened a briefing file. 'There's something building up out there in the Atlantic, something pretty unusual according to our weather station at Kap Bismarck in Greenland.'

'How unusual?'

'Deep depression coming in very fast and exceptionally severe storms forecast. Nothing to worry you, of course, not at thirty-five thousand.'

'And what if I have to go down?'

'We must hope you won't have to. One thing is certain, the trip should be worthwhile for the weather statistics you can bring back, if nothing else.' 'All right,' Necker said. 'When do we leave?'

'0500,' Altrogge glanced at his watch. 'Time to get some sleep in. You could manage three or four hours.'

'I'll think about it,' Necker said and went out.

— 13 —

> Barquentine *Deutschland,* 25 September 1944. Lat. 56°.20N., long. 9°.39W. A bad night. Winds Force 6–8 increasing. Heavy rain and a pounding sea. At two bells in the midwatch I gave orders to furl the fore upper topgallant and fore upper topsail. This was accomplished with considerable difficulty. Richter, Winzer and Kluth have the wheel at this moment which I snatch to enter the log. The barometer continues to fall. I greatly fear things will get worse before they get better.

ON FHADA it was Reeve who first became aware, for certain, that something completely out of the ordinary in the way of weather was building up. High winds always had made him nervous and restless. Unable to sleep, he got out of bed around 2 a.m., made a pot of coffee and sat at the radio for a while to see what he could pick up.

The air seemed alive with voices, crackling through the static. Some were faint and far away, others close at hand, but all had one thing in common: fear. Those who could were already running for shelter.

At one point a Royal Naval supply ship, south of Iceland, came in urgently to report a wind speed of seventy-five knots increasing, with heavy seas and rain. She was trying to make Reykjavik.

It was almost three o'clock when he tuned in to the first really vital transmission from RAF Coastal Command at Stornoway.

> Suspect polar air depression imminent in sea areas Malin and Hebrides. Be prepared for winds of hurricane force within the next few hours. Expected direction north-east.

Reeve sat thinking about it for a moment, then padded into the kitchen, closing the door quietly behind him. He had often joked that the telephone in the wall was so old that Alexander Graham Bell himself must have installed it, but just now it was a lifeline. He turned the handle vigorously for some considerable time, knowing there would be no one on duty at the post office on the quay. It would be necessary to raise Mrs MacBrayne from her bed.

There was no response at first. He tried again and as he did so, the kitchen door opened and Janet entered, her dressing-gown over her shoulders. 'What's going on?'

He waved her to silence as Mrs MacBrayne's sleepy voice said, 'Hello?'

'Katrina? Reeve here. Can you put me through to Murdoch at South Landing. Sorry to bother you, but it's urgent.'

She was instantly alert. 'Is the boat called out, admiral?'

'Not yet, but it could be before too long, the way things are building up.'

'Hold on now. I'll put you through directly.'

He turned to Janet. 'Put the kettle on, sweetheart, we'll have some coffee. We could be in for a long night.'

She was still slightly bemused, but went obediently to the stove, opened it and fed wood into the still glowing ashes.

Reeve waited impatiently. After a while, Katrina MacBrayne came back on. 'I can't get through, admiral.'

'You mean there's no reply?'

'Och, no. The line's dead. Down in this wind, I'm thinking. Is there anything I can do?'

'No, I'll see to it. But I think the crew should be alerted.'

'But there is no crew, admiral. The fishing boats were working the grounds South Uist way this afternoon. They'll run for shelter to Lochboisdale to wait for it to blow over. If they call the boat out tonight, there'll be no one fit to handle her except old men and boys.'

'Right, Katrina,' Reeve said briskly. 'Leave it to me. I'll be in touch.'

He replaced the receiver and turned to Janet. 'I've got a job for you.' He took her by the hand, led her into the living-room and sat her down at the radio. He adjusted the dial quickly and locked it in. 'That's the band that most of the local stuff comes through on. You can get dressed if you want, make your coffee, only keep listening. Any messages for me or for Fhada direct, write them down.'

'But what about you?' she demanded. 'Where are you going?' 'To see Murdoch,' he said simply, went into his bedroom and started to dress quickly.

II

Reeve carried a storm lantern, but it only seemed to accentuate the darkness. Rain fell relentlessly and the wind gusted with such force that it was out of the question to raise the sail on the trolley.

He pumped his way across the spine of the island one-handed, rain cascading from his oilskins. The wind snatched away the storm lantern when he was half way there and he completed the journey in darkness.

He negotiated the track down to the lifeboat station with the aid of the electric torch he'd slipped into his pocket in case of emergencies before leaving. He could hear Rory barking and then the cottage door was opened, light flooding out, and Murdoch appeared. The wolfhound bounded through the rain to greet Reeve. His hand fastened in its ruff and they went down to the cottage together.

Murdoch drew him inside. 'A bad night to be out, admiral.'

'Worse at sea.' Reeve took off his sou'wester and oilskin and crouched at the fire. 'I've been trying to get you on the telephone. The line must be down.'

'Is the boat called out then?'

'No. Not that you could do much if it was. You haven't got a crew, Murdoch. The fishing boats didn't get back in this evening.'

'I wouldn't say that,' Murdoch told him calmly. 'There is Hamish Macdonald, Francis Patterson, James and Dougal Sinclair.'

Reeve stared at him. 'Hamish Macdonald is seventy if he's a day. The Sinclair brothers must be the oldest twins in the business. I don't know about Patterson . . .'

'We were born in the same year, admiral.'

'Come off it, Murdoch,' Reeve said angrily. 'There's a

world of difference between you and those old guys and you know it.'

'The *Morag* is a fine boat. If she capsizes, she rights herself again. Even if her engine compartments flood, her engines will still keep turning. You know the *Morag*, admiral. It is not like the old days when young muscle was needed for the oars. Hamish and the others have fished these waters all their lives. They know their business. It is enough.'

'Well, I hope to God they don't have to be put to the test.'

Murdoch produced a bottle from a cupboard by the fire and found a couple of glasses. 'Here, now, this will put marrow in your bones again.'

Reeve gulped, tears springing to his eyes as the *Uisgebeatha* exploded in the pit of his stomach. 'Damn you, Murdoch, that not only hits the spot—it takes it right out. Anyway, you need eight to man the boat so you're still three short. What would you do about that?'

'There is always Lachlan.'

'Who spews his guts at the first ripple on the water. You must be joking.' A sudden gust of wind slammed solidly against the roof of the house and the building shook. He shivered. 'I don't like the sound of that. I caught a storm warning from Coastal Command on the radio before leaving. Winds of hurricane force within the next few hours from the south-west.'

Murdoch frowned. 'Let us hope they are wrong. If that is the way of it, it's the devil's own job we'd have in launching.'

'You think so?'

'I know it, admiral.'

Reeve reached for his oilskin. 'I'd better be getting back. At first light we'll see if we can find where your line's down.'

'And if I'm needed before then?' Murdoch took his own yellow oilskin down from behind the door. 'Better I come with you now and see what is happening out there in the wide world.'

III

It was a quarter to five when they reached Reeve's cottage and when they went into the living-room, Jean was sitting with Janet at the radio.

'Hello, Carey,' she said. 'I couldn't sleep in this wind so I thought I'd come along and see how you were making out. I'll get some tea.'

She went into the kitchen. Janet said, 'Things have been warming up. The Stornoway boat was called out an hour ago to assist a fleet tanker in difficulties off Cape Wrath. Barra, twenty minutes later.'

'Where to?'

'Somewhere up in the North Minch.'

'Our turn soon, I'm thinking,' Murdoch said as Jean returned with cups of tea on a tray. 'No, not now, Mrs Sinclair. I have one or two people to see. I'll be back later.'

He went out and Janet said, 'Where's he off to?'

'Oh, rousting out Hamish Macdonald, the Sinclair twins and a few other members of the pensioners' club, just in case they're needed,' Reeve told her.

'You must be joking. They're old men.'

'You try telling Murdoch that.' There were various other notes on the table and he picked one up. 'What's this, another weather report?'

'That's right. From the Meteorological Office.'

It was substantially the same as before. Sea areas Hebrides, Bailey, Malin, an intense depression giving rise to hurricane force winds with heavy rain and sleet.

A moment later, a voice crackled over the radio, 'Mallaig calling Sugar One on Fhada. Mallaig calling Sugar One on Fhada.'

The reception was poor, crackling with static, other voices crowding in. Reeve took the mike. 'Reeve here. Receiving you strength five, Mallaig.'

'I have Captain Murray for you, admiral.'

There was only the static for a moment and then Murray's voice broke in. 'Hullo, sir, how are things with you?'

'Terrible. What about your side of the pond?'

'Total chaos. Two lighters sunk right here in the damned

harbour and a nine-hundred-ton coaster loaded with fuel drums broken loose from her moorings. We've been trying to contact Jago during the past hour; routine check on all naval vessels. No success, I'm afraid. Any suggestions?'

'Last I saw of him he was safely tied up at the pier. I'll take a look and call back.'

'Be obliged if you would, admiral. By the way, you're in for at least another really bad day. We've reports of winds gusting up to a hundred knots. The weather boys tell me we can expect an almost vertical fall in barometric pressure.'

'For those few kind words, I thank you,' Reeve told him. 'Over and out.'

IV

It was bitterly cold in the cell. Gericke had slept little during the night and at five-thirty, he got up and went to the window, pulling a blanket around his shoulders.

It was still dark outside, but occasionally the horizon exploded with electricity, giving a split-second instant picture of the scene in the harbour. There were several small boats adrift down there as far as he could see, two of them upturned.

The noise of the wind was higher now, a grating moan that was a constant irritation. He looked out again and in another flash of sheet lightning saw a figure in an oilskin, lantern in hand, ploughing along the pier towards the gunboat. There was a step in the passageway and Lachlan peered through the bars, an oil lamp in one hand.

'You must be cold in there, commander.'

'Yes, I think you could say that.'

'I've a good fire up there in the office. If you'd give me your hand on it, I'd let you sit by it for a while.' The boy grinned. 'Not that there's anywhere for you to go—not in this lot.'

'Why, thank you, Lachlan,' Gericke said without hesitation. 'My hand and my word. You are very kind.'

The boy unlocked the gate and Gericke followed him up to the office. The peat fire glowed white-hot in the draught. Lachlan handed him a mug of tea as a great gust of wind struck the roof, loosening tiles.

'God help me, but it frightens me, that wind, commander.

Frightens me to death. The same since I was a wee boy. Isn't that a terrible thing to have to confess?'

'That one is afraid?' Gericke smiled and offered him a cigarette. 'Have one of these, Lachlan, and join the club.'

V

Mary's Town had never been a good anchorage and, though sheltered from the wind when it was from the south-west, a considerable sea was apt to build up inside the harbour.

The *Dead End* had had a bad night. Twice she had dragged her lines, on the first occasion being hurled back against the pier by a severe gust with considerable force, and she was under regular attack from loose boats in the harbour.

Jago and his crew had been at action stations for much of the night, engaged in a constant battle to save the old gunboat from dashing her brains out against the pier. By five thirty, he was exhausted.

He was aware of the storm lantern on the pier, but didn't realize it was Reeve coming aboard until the admiral mounted the ladder to the bridge.

'How goes it?'

'We're hanging on, sir, that's about all. I think I'd rather be taking my chances in the open.'

'Don't kid yourself. You think this is bad? Wait till it gets worse. Murray's been in touch. He can't raise you.'

'I know, our radio's taken a pounding. I'll be surprised if they can ever put it together again.'

'Okay, I'll notify Murray you're still in one piece. If you can spare an hour when it gets lighter, come on up to my cottage. I've an idea I might need you.'

'Will do, sir.'

Reeve judged his moment to step over the rail and hurried back along the pier.

VI

Berger kicked open the door of his cabin and lurched inside followed by a tremendous gust of wind and rain. The oil lamp above his desk was swinging in its gimbals, light and dark chasing each other back and forth in the corners.

Otto Prager, who had been lying on the bunk, sat up in alarm. 'What is it, Erich?'

Berger was soaked to the skin in spite of his oilskins. His face was wild. 'I lost another man.'

He leaned heavily on the desk for a moment, then made his way round to the other side with all the care of a drunken man as the floor heaved. He sagged into his chair.

'I'm sorry,' Prager said.

'Aren't we all?'

Berger opened the top drawer, took out the ship's log and picked up his pen.

> . . . Five bells in the morning watch and conditions as bad as I have ever known. We have reduced sail to main lower topsail and storm staysail with great difficulty. Conditions aloft were atrocious. At four bells two enormous waves swept down upon the ship. She rose the first, but while in the trough on the other side, the second wave struck, reaching half-way up the foremast. There were eight men in the rigging at that time by my orders, amongst them Leading Electrician's Mate Hans Bergman who was swept away.

'So far,' Berger said bitterly. 'Poor lad. All this bloody way—and for what?'

'You need sleep, Erich.'

'You're right,' Berger said. 'Wake me in half an hour.'

He laid his head on his hands and closed his eyes. Prager sat watching him, the light from the wildly swinging oil lamp flickering backwards and forwards across the room and outside the thousand several voices of the wind seemed to rise to a crescendo.

'It's the sea, Otto,' Berger said softly without opening his eyes, 'I think maybe it's decided to come for us.'

VII

In the saloon, the nuns grouped around the table, heads bowed, hands clasped. Water dripped in through the skylight, but the boards, for the present, seemed to be holding. And here, as in the rest of the ship, there was not a dry inch to be found, water pouring down the companionway, swilling in and out of the cabins.

Sister Angela prayed aloud in a firm, steady voice: 'Thou, O Lord, that stillest the raging of the sea, hear, hear us and save us, that we perish not . . .'

The doors at the top of the companionway opened and Richter clattered down the steps, carrying a large billy-can which he set on the table. His cap was soaked, his tangled beard and oilskin streaming with water. He stood there waiting, chest heaving. Sister Angela faltered, then continued her prayer to the end and crossed herself.

'Captain's compliments, sister. Hot coffee. Just made on the oilstove in his cabin.'

'My thanks to Captain Berger. How are things?'

'Bad,' Richter said. 'We lost another man. Young Bergman. Swept from the rigging.'

'We will pray for him.'

'Yes, you might well do that, sister.'

He turned and went back up the companionway. 'Let us pray, Sisters, for the soul of Hans Bergman, that he may find peace.'

But Lotte, at the other end of the table, turned suddenly, mounted the companionway before a word could be said and went out on deck.

It was a sight to take her breath away. Although it was well past dawn there was no day: the sky was black, mountainous swirling clouds touched with violet and red as if somewhere beyond in the gloom great fires burned. Lightning flickered constantly and the wind howled like a mad dog, slashing at her face.

Everyone on deck had his hands full and no one noticed her. Sturm had the wheel, with Winzer and Kluth, and four men manned the pump, each one tethered to the mainmast by a line.

The sea swept in over the ship in a solid mass, taking all before it. Lotte hung on to the ladder. The *Deutschland* seemed to lie right over, then righted herself.

Without their lifelines the men on the pump would have

been washed away. They floundered on the deck like stranded fish and Richter, who had jumped into the ratlines, dropped down to go to their aid.

There was a sudden violent report, almost like an explosion, high above. He looked up. The lifts had parted on the fore topgallant. As he watched, the yard swung violently and the sail broke free.

It fluttered wildly in the gale, the entire mast vibrating. Richter knew that it could only be a question of time before it snapped the fore topmast itself like a rotten stick. He ran to the gale, snatched one of the fire-axes from its mounting, and sprang into the ratlines.

He paused to jam the axe into his belt, turned and saw Berger on the quarterdeck waving wildly. Impossible to hear what he was calling, but it was plain enough from his gestures that he wanted Richter down out of there.

But if that sail was left and brought the mast down . . . Richter kept on climbing, gritting his teeth. His oilskin was worse than useless, more a hindrance than a help for it offered little protection against such heavy and continuous rain. The rigging was swollen, every rope stiff, and each time he raised an arm to pull himself up, a cold stream of water slopped in between clothes and skin. The wind was pulling and tearing at his clothes like a living thing.

He paused on the foretop for a moment to catch his breath. The sea boiled white foam as far as the eye could see, rain and hail driving in, lightning glimmered balefully in the blackness of the sky.

He paused beneath the sail. It thundered free with a terrible roar. Facing death now, judging his moment, he moved close to the mast, got inside the flailing sail, hung on tight with one hand and swung the fire-axe, attacking the ring that held the yard to the mast.

The sail enveloped him, almost tearing him away. Then the line from one corner tightened, pulling it straight for a moment. He glanced down and found Berger standing on the foretop just below him, hanging on to the line.

He nodded, Richter swung the axe again, aware of the entire topmast vibrating. Once, twice, the axe cut clean through metal, the yard swung, the line parted. Berger released the line – only just in time, as the yard, the lower topgallant sail still fluttering wildly from it, whirled away on the wind.

Berger clapped Richter on the shoulder. Slowly, painfully, they descended, taking their time. Richter dropped to the deck and, as he moved forward, saw Lotte by the quarterdeck ladder. She was gazing at him, a kind of awe on her face. As if by instinct, he held out his arms and she ran into their shelter.

VIII

Jago and his men moved the gunboat into the inner harbour at first light where the groundswell was less of a problem. As soon as the *Dead End* was secure he left Jansen in charge and went up to the cottage. Jean Sinclair let him in the front door and when he went into the living-room, Reeve and Murdoch were at the radio.

'How goes it?'

'Terrible,' the admiral said. 'A bloody shambles.'

In Mallaig, another coaster had been driven ashore and two more lighters sunk. Three trawlers had foundered off Stornoway so quickly that nothing could be done, overwhelmed in that terrible sea. South of Iceland, the Royal Canadian Navy corvette *Macmichael* had disappeared, never to be seen again, along with the eighty-five officers and men who comprised her crew. And the Halifax convoy, striking for the North Channel into the Irish Sea, was hopelessly scattered.

But still, there had not been a specific call for the Fhada lifeboat. Murdoch sat patiently smoking his pipe, listening to the jumbled messages over the radio. Jago went into the kitchen where he found Janet with Jean making sandwiches.

'Hey,' he said. 'You're a woman after all.'

'Watch it, darling.' She pointed the knife under his chin.

He helped himself to tea. 'I see the boat hasn't been called out.'

'It will be. That's what Murdoch's waiting for. The crew are all ready down at the lifeboat station.' She shook her head. 'Honest to God, Harry, you've never seen anything like it. There isn't one of them who isn't a grandfather. It's pathetic.'

'Pathetic? A bunch of guys are willing to put themselves

on the line in the worst sea I've ever seen in my life and that's all you can find to say?'

'They wouldn't last five minutes out there. What would be the point?'

He went back into the living-room and took a chair next to Reeve. It was just after seven-thirty. At ten to eight there was another weather forecast from Stornoway.

US Destroyer Carbisdale a hundred-ten miles north-west of Butt of Lewis reports winds of hurricane force, gusting to one-hundred-twenty knots.

'A hundred and twenty,' Jago said in awe.

'A bad blow indeed,' Murdoch said gravely. 'As bad as I have known.'

Janet brought in tea and sandwiches on a tray, put them down and went back to Jean in the kitchen without a word. Jago helped himself to a sandwich and leaned forward to pat Rory on the head. The clock on the mantelpiece struck eight times.

As the last stroke died away, a voice sounded over the radio in broken English. 'Three-masted barquentine *Deutschland* adrift and helpless. I estimate my present position some twenty miles south-west of Fhada in Outer Hebrides. For God's sake help us. I have women on board.'

The message faded, drowned in a sea of static. Reeve turned to stare at Jago. 'Did he say *Deutschland*?'

'That's what it sounded like to me, admiral.'

'A three-masted barquentine,' Murdoch said. 'I did not think I would live to see the day.' Janet and Jean had come from the kitchen and stood listening. Reeve said, 'It just can't be, for Christ's sake.'

Berger's voice swelled through the static. 'This is barquentine *Deutschland* in urgent need of assistance, twenty miles south-west of Fhada. I have women on board.'

'There he is again, admiral,' Jago said. 'That guy *has* to be for real.'

Reeve reached for the microphone, and then, as Berger started to repeat his message again, another voice broke in on channel. '*Deutschland*, hier ist Grosser Schwarzer Adler.'

What followed was wholly in German. Reeve sat back helplessly. 'What in the hell goes on here? One minute we have some guy screaming for assistance—the next, a lot of Kraut I don't understand a word of.'

There was a moment's silence before Janet said carefully, 'Gericke would, Uncle Carey.'

IX

On the *Deutschland* things had gone from bad to worse. By seven-fifteen it became obvious that she could no longer support the main lower topsail and Berger gave Sturm the necessary orders.

To clew up that sail proved to be incredibly difficult. Although the men had to work at no great height above the deck, they still had the appalling wind to contend with. Every rope was foul, swollen to twice its normal size, the blocks jammed at a touch, and all the time the wind tore at them, keen as a surgeon's lancet, splitting flesh with its driven spray.

Finally it was done and the men descended wearily to the deck. The wind now dominated everything, striking thc ship one blow after another as it gusted. Ragged clouds passed by overhead, seeming low enough to touch the mastheads, sheet lightning flickered and the rain fell relentlessly.

Another four men worked frantically at the pump. Berger, as he watched them at the quarterdeck rail, felt strangely impotent. Such puny insignificance in the midst of all this vastness. What could it hope to achieve?

He turned to check on Sturm and the two men who had the wheel with him, and his mouth opened in a soundless cry as a tremendous following sea rolled in across the stern.

The *Deutschland* shuddered, Berger found himself on his back, clutching at the rail for life itself, as hundreds of tons of water swept on towards the prow. There was no sign of Winzer or Kluth, but Sturm was still there hanging on to the wheel.

Berger staggered aross the quarterdeck to join him. The *Deutschland* put her lee rail under the water. They fought like demons. Berger cursing in a frenzy, and slowly, so slowly, she started to answer the helm. But the blow had been mortal. The mizzen topmast and much of the rigging had gone. The life-boats had been swept away. The galley shack had totally disappeared.

Richter came up the ladder. Berger shouted in his ear, 'Two more men on this wheel, Richter, then a damage report, quick as you can.'

The bosun disappeared. A few moments later Holzer and Endrass came up to take over the wheel. 'You're in charge here, Herr Sturm. I'll see what the situation is below.'

As Berger reached his cabin door, Richter came up the companionway. 'Are the sisters safe?'

Richter nodded. 'Shaken up and badly scared. But we've other problems now, Herr Kapitän. Twenty inches of water in the bilges and rising.'

Berger turned to look at the *Deutschland*. Rigging lines danced on the wind, the fore lower topsail had torn free and half of it still fluttered from the yardarm like a ragged grey flag. Here and there planking protruded from the deck and the pipe rails were smashed. The entire ship shuddered as she wearily climbed another great wave and a squall hit her.

Richter knew what he was thinking; could smell defeat. 'It's no good, is it, Helmut?' the captain said. 'We're finished.'

'I'm afraid so, Herr Kapitän.'

Berger nodded. 'Take over from Herr Sturm and tell him to bring the radio to my cabin right away.'

X

Necker had left Trondheim at five and the flight over Scotland at thirty-five thousand feet, far above the weather, had been completely without incident. He had arrived in the target area, however, to find a very different situation.

Clouds boiled below him, dark and menacing, tinged with orange and fire, twisting and curling like black smoke. Schmidt said, 'They're having a hell of a time down there today. My English is only fair, but I know SOS when I hear it. I'll cut you in, sir.'

There was another message coming through now. Sea areas Malin and Hebrides. Wind gusting to one-hundred-thirty. Barometer reading nine-seven-o and still falling.

It was Schmidt who said, 'I know one thing, Herr Hauptmann. The Halifax convoy won't be a convoy any longer. She'll have been smashed to pieces.'

But Necker, gazing down into that black smoke below, was thinking of the *Deutschland.* He said to Rudi, 'You've got the position where we saw the *Deutschland* yesterday. Average let's say ten knots on a north-east by north course. See what your dead reckoning can do with that for her present whereabouts.'

'But Herr Hauptmann,' Rudi protested. 'Our orders . . .'

Necker said coldly, 'Do as you're told, and shut up.'

It only took the boy a couple of minutes to produce the desired information and he passed it across. Necker altered course immediately, switching on his intercom at the same time.

'Listen to me, you lot. They told us this was the finest all-weather plane in the world. Claimed it would even operate under hurricane conditions. Let's see if they're right. I'm going down into that shit to find out what's happening to the *Deutschland.* My decision.'

He pushed the column forward, taking the Junkers into a shallow dive, and started to descend. Within a few minutes they were enveloped in cloud and heavy rain, lightning flickering at the wing tips.

They continued to descend at speed, buffeted from side to side in the heavy wind. Necker had to hang on to the column with all his strength. At one point, they slewed to port, the wind striking a series of blows on the fuselage that stripped pieces from the wings, but he regained control and maintained his dive.

They were at ten thousand still descending, still enveloped in dark, swirling clouds. Rudi had unclipped his oxygen mask and stared out through the windscreen, his face very white.

And it was all a waste of time, Necker told himself. In such weather it was highly unlikely that the *Deutschland* would have been able to maintain her original course, and her speed, after all, was only an estimation.

At three thousand, the Junkers burst out of the clouds into a great bowl of luminous light and torrential rain, a sea of foam stretching to the horizon. And there she was – quite incredibly, about half a mile away to the south-west.

'Rudi,' Necker said, 'I owe you a bottle of champagne,' and he banked steeply to port.

Rudi had the binoculars out. 'She looks in bad shape, Herr Hauptmann.'

Schmidt broke in, 'Something's wrong, sir. They're transmitting a distress call. In English. Berger is asking for help.'

'Hook me in,' said Necker grimly. 'And I'll talk to him myself.'

— 14 —

> Barquentine *Deutschland,* 25 September 1944. Winds of hurricane strength and the *Deutschland,* being in my opinion in imminent danger of foundering, I started to transmit distress calls at the end of the morning watch. Our signal, I fear, is very weak owing to the effect of salt water on the batteries. However, shortly afterwards our friend from the Luftwaffe reappeared. To our mutual astonishment, a third party joined in from the neighbouring island of Fhada.

'*DEUTSCHLAND* CALLING. Are you still with us, Necker? We lost you in low cloud.'

'I still have you in sight,' Necker replied. 'Don't worry. I'll stay close.'

The exchange crackled through static, remote and somehow far away. Gericke, at the radio, said slowly, '*Deutschland*?'

'Well, speak to him,' Reeve said. 'Find out what's going on.'

'Very well.' Gericke reached for the microphone and started to transmit in German. '*Deutschland*, this is Fhada calling. Come in, please.'

There was silence and then Berger's voice crackled faintly. 'Necker, who was that, for God's sake?'

'I don't know.'

'*Deutschland*. Fhada calling. Will you please come in with fullest details on your present position. We may be able to assist.'

There was a further silence and then Necker's voice: '. . . haven't any idea . . . suggest you answer . . . see what happens.'

Once more there was silence, other fainter messages crowding in as if from far away. Jago said, 'What's going on out there, commander?'

'We're only picking up one side of the conversation now. Necker, whoever he is. As for the *Deutschland*, she's either foundered or lost radio contact.'

'There's only one sure way to find out,' Reeve said. 'Speak to Necker this time.'

'All right.' Gericke tried again. 'Fhada calling Necker. Come in, please. Fhada calling Necker. Come in, please. I cannot raise the *Deutschland*. Urgent I speak with you.'

Only the silence. Jean Sinclair said softly. 'He doesn't trust you, commander.'

Gericke tried again. 'Necker, this is Korvettenkapitän Paul Gericke of the Kriegsmarine calling from Fhada. I beg you to reply to me.'

There was more static, then Necker's voice strongly. 'Paul Gericke – the U-boat ace?'

'That's right.'

'But how can this be?'

'I am a prisoner of war. Those in charge here have asked me to monitor your calls because they cannot understand German. Who are you?'

'Hauptmann Horst Necker serving with KG 40 out of Trondheim. Shipping and weather reconnaissance. I'm circling the *Deutschland* at the moment in a JU 88.'

'I can't get any kind of reply from them.' Gericke said. 'What's wrong?'

'Their signal has weakened. Sea water in the batteries.'

'Can you still monitor them?'

'Yes, if I stay close.'

The admiral said impatiently, 'Come on, Gericke, what's going on out there?'

Gericke told him. Reeve turned to Murdoch. 'Think you can reach them?'

'We can try,' Murdoch said. 'It would help if that aircraft stayed overhead to give us a mark. Visibility at sea level will be very bad.'

'That's asking one hell of a lot,' Jago said. 'Of Necker, I mean. Can you imagine what it's like trying to keep that plane in the air in this weather?'

Gericke reached for the microphone again. 'Gericke calling Necker. We have a lifeboat here ready to leave at once. It would greatly assist if you could stay in the area as marker.'

Necker replied: 'In the worst conditions I've ever known. But she's handling all right so far. We'll do what we can. Present position is as follows.' He gave the essential facts slowly and clearly. 'How long before this lifeboat reaches us?'

Gericke passed the details to Murdoch. The old man nodded. 'About an hour. I'm leaving now.'

'I'm coming with you.' Reeve reached for his oilskin. But Murdoch shook his head. 'You are welcome to watch, admiral – nothing more. I have my crew.'

'Now look here,' Reeve started to say hotly.

'I am coxswain of the Fhada lifeboat, Carey Reeve,' the old man said. 'Life or death this day, by my decision only. You can see us off with pleasure, but no more.'

Reeve turned to Gericke. 'Stay on that radio. I'll be back as soon as I've seen the boat launched.'

'Very well,' Gericke said.

Murdoch plunged out into the gale with Reeve and Jago at his heels.

II

High up on the spine of the island the wind was ferocious, a living thing that seemed to be doing its utmost to force the trolley back. It took the combined efforts of Murdoch and Jago pumping together to make any kind of progress.

When they came to end of the track above the lifeboat station, the sea was enough to take the breath away. A ragged broken carpet of white water, one enormous wave after another flowing in a kind of slow motion. Now and then in the trough, the jagged black teeth of the reef gaped beyond the mouth of the inlet.

'Think you can make it?' Reeve bawled into Murdoch's ear.

'Perhaps,' the old man replied.

There were people clustered around the lifeboat house. Mainly women and a few children. As the three men hurried down the track there was the sound of running behind and Lachlan overtook them.

'I came as soon as I heard,' he said, slightly breathless. 'And half Mary's Town behind me. Will you be needing me, Murdoch?'

'There are six of us, Lachlan. We can manage fine.'

Murdoch moved on through the small crowd and entered the boathouse. His crew already waited in the boat wearing yellow oilskins and lifejackets.

The doors at the end of the slipway were open. He pulled on an oilskin and moved a yard or two down the slope from where he could see into the mouth of the inlet. He looked up at his crew.

'There is a chance it can be done. One in ten only, but worth a try. There is a ship out there in a bad way and women on board. And if we don't go now, we don't go at all, not the way the sea builds up out here. If any one of you thinks better of it, speak up and get out of the boat.'

This last remark was delivered in the same calm, matter-of-fact tone as the rest. White-bearded Francis Patterson replied with a touch of impatience, 'Can we be off now, Murdoch, or are we going to hang about and jaw all day?'

'So be it,' Murdoch said and went up the ladder.

The women in the small crowd moved down to the Strand, talking anxiously amongst themselves in low voices.

The *Morag Sinclair* emerged from the mouth of the boat-house a moment later, sliding down the slipway at considerable speed, and entered the water, her prow biting deep, spray fanning high into the air.

She moved on through the heavy swell, lifting as a great wave smashed in through the narrow mouth of the inlet. For a moment, the reef gaped again through broken water. There was silence from the crowd, only the wind howling.

'It's no good,' Reeve said. 'They'll never make it. It's madness. Those waves must be thirty feet high. If they hit at the wrong moment, they'll be chewed to pieces out there.'

But the *Morag* kept going, out through the entrance in a burst of speed. 'He's trying to catch the next big swell for clearance over the reef,' Jago cried.

Perhaps it might have worked, Murdoch's one chance in ten. But at that moment, the wind gusted with such violence that a woman screamed somewhere in the crowd. The *Morag Sinclair* staggered, then veered sharply to port and seemed to poise high on the swell above the black rocks suddenly revealed.

'She's going to strike!' Reeve cried.

An enormous wave bored in, rising thirty or forty feet into the mouth of the inlet, carrying the lifeboat broadside on, helpless before it. She struck close inshore, water boiling over her in fury, washing two of the crew straight over the side.

Harry Jago was running now, down into the surf, reaching out for a yellow oilskin. He was aware of Francis Patterson's face surfacing beside him, eyes closed, teeth-bared.

And then there were others beside him, waist-deep in the freezing water. Admiral Reeve, with his one good arm, floundering, the black patch lifting to reveal the ugly puckered scar, the eyeless socket. Jago turned the yellow oilskin over to find James Sinclair and heaved him backwards through the surf to where willing hands stretched out to help.

The next few minutes were a total confusion of shouts and screams, the *Morag Sinclair* grinding in through the surf on each succeeding wave. A line was thrown, another, and people running from the boathouse brought more.

Jago found himself heaving, bending his back in the surf, Lachlan and Reeve beside him. Once, falling flat on his face, he took a moment to collect himself and was astonished to see a dozen women on the next rope, skirts swirling up about their hips.

The wind blew sand straight into his face. He closed his eyes and kept on hauling, the rope burning his shoulder. Then he was on his hands and knees. This time, when he opened his eyes painfully and looked about him, everyone seemed to be roughly in the same position. And the *Morag Sinclair*, tilted to one side, was safe on the beach.

Jago and Reeve got to their feet and went forward. Murdoch appeared at the rail above them. His face was very pale and twisted with pain.

'Are you all right?' Reeve called.

'I took a knock when we broached. It's nothing.'

Jago circled the boat. 'Only superficial damage and the screws are intact.'

'That's something,' Reeve said. 'At least there's been no loss of life. A miracle.'

Murdoch hooked a ladder over and came down it awkwardly as the crowd surged forward. His left arm swung loosely at his side in a way which Jago thought was distinctly unhealthy.

The old man swayed and Jago tried to steady him. 'Are you all right?'

Murdoch pushed him away. 'Never mind me.' He turned to Reeve. 'There is a boat out there helpless, and women on board, and nothing to be done about it.'

Jago heard someone say, 'There's always the *Dead End*.' Only afterwards did he realize it was he himself who had spoken.

III

Jago sat at the chart table, Jansen at his side and the crew crowded in around the door. 'That's it,' he said. 'Now you know the score. It's going to be rough out there. Volunteers only this trip. Any man who wants to can collect his duffel and step over that rail to the pier and I won't think any the worse of him. Not to put too fine a point on it, I'd say that should particularly commend itself to those of you who are married.'

It was Petersen who spoke for all of them. 'We've been together a long time, lieutenant. We've been in the water together more than once and this is the first time I ever heard you talk crap. Begging your pardon, sir.'

'I think what he's trying to ask in his own delectable way, lieutenant, is when do we leave?' Jansen said.

Jago glanced at his watch. 'The admiral's due at any

moment with the *Deutschland*'s present position. I'd say we'll be moving out of here within the next ten to fifteen minutes.' He looked up. 'So what are you all hanging about for?'

IV

Janet left Murdoch lying on the bed, closed the door softly and went into the living-room. Gericke was at the radio, Reeve and Jean beside him.

The admiral turned. 'How is he?'

'The arm's broken. I've put it in a splint for the time being and given him a pain-killing injection. He should sleep for a while. How are things going?'

'Not so good. We've not been able to raise Necker again. Probably an electrical storm.'

Gericke was still trying in the background, speaking urgently into the mike in German. 'Come in, Necker. Come in, please.'

Necker's voice sounded faint, but clear enough for them all to sense the urgency. 'Necker here, Gericke. I've been calling for the past half-hour. What's happening?'

'We've not been connecting, that's all.' Gericke told him. 'Too much disturbance. There's been a delay. The lifeboat couldn't get away, but there's a gunboat leaving now from Mary's Town. Please confirm present position.' Necker did so and Gericke went on, 'What about the *Deutschland*? Are you still in touch?'

'Only with difficulty. The signal is very weak. Another hour to wait, then?'

'I'm afraid so.'

Gericke had written the details of the *Deutschland*'s position on a scrap of paper which he pushed across at Reeve. The admiral slipped it into his pocket. 'I'll get this down to Jago.'

As he turned to the door, Jean caught his sleeve, 'Carey, you wouldn't do anything silly, like try to go along for the ride, would you?'

'At my age?' He grinned and kissed her lightly. 'Sweetheart. You've got to be joking.'

He went out quickly. Jean turned, her face troubled. 'He's going to go, Janet. I know it.'

Janet said bitterly, 'What did you expect?'

She went into the kitchen and slammed the door. Gericke reached for Jean's hand and held it tight for a moment. Necker's voice cut in on them.

'Have they left yet?'

'On their way.'

'I have a problem. An hour and fifteen minutes, then we must head for home. A question of fuel.'

'I understand,' Gericke said. 'You must leave when you think fit. Your decision.'

He switched off and turned to Jean with a smile. 'And now, if you dare venture in there, I think we could all do with one of your nice hot cups of tea.'

V

The *Dead End* was ready and waiting, her engines turning, when Reeve went on to the bridge, Jago was bending over the chart and the admiral passed Gericke's message across.

Jago quickly worked out the target position and nodded. 'That's it, sir. We can get moving now.'

'I'd like to come with you.'

Petersen, at the wheel, glanced sideways, Jansen looked stolidly ahead. Jago said, 'Well, now, admiral, I'm not so sure that's a good idea.'

'I could order you to take me.'

'And I could point out, with the utmost respect, that as commander of this old bucket, I'm the only one whose words count round here.'

Reeve came right down. 'All right, lieutenant, I'm asking not ordering. I'll even say please if that helps.'

'My command, sir. You understand that?'

'Perfectly.'

Jago nodded and turned to Jansen. 'Okay, chief, let's move it.'

VI

Necker's voice exploded from the radio, full of excitement. 'Come in, Gericke! Come in!'

'Receiving you loud and clear,' Gericke replied. 'What is it?'

'I can see it. I can see the gunboat, half a mile to starboard, in heavy seas, but making progress.'

'He can see the *Dead End*,' Gericke said.

'My God,' Janet breathed and her hand fastened tightly on his shoulder.

'I'll stay on the air,' Gericke said. 'Please keep close contact from now on.'

The bedroom door clicked open and Murdoch appeared, his left arm in a sling. His face was drawn and full of pain, a slightly dazed expression in the eyes. 'What is it?' he demanded.

Janet went to his side and drew him towards a chair. 'You shouldn't be up. You should have stayed in bed.'

The old man sat down heavily and it was to Gericke he spoke now. 'What is happening, commander?'

'Lieutenant Jago has gone out there in the gunboat.'

'And the admiral?'

'We think he has gone with them.'

'They should have taken me. I know how this game is played. They do not.' There was only resignation in Murdoch's voice now. 'God help all of them.'

VII

The *Deutschland* wallowed in gigantic seas, plunging drunkenly down the slope of each successive wave, climbing with extreme difficulty to the crest of the next. There was two or three feet of water in the saloon and it was rising. The nuns, in Prager's charge, were secure for the moment in Berger's cabin.

On the quarterdeck, Richter and two of the men had the wheel. Berger stood at the rail, hanging on tightly as one sea after another washed in. Below, four of the crew, tethered to the mainmast, pumped frantically, a losing battle.

He looked up to the Junkers, circling overhead, his brain numbed by the incessant cold, faintly surprised to find that she was still there. Sturm stumbled out of the cabin below and hauled himself up the ladder.

The wind tore away his voice even when he put his mouth close to Berger's ear. The captain shook his head. Sturm grabbed his arm and pointed to starboard. As Berger turned, the *Dead End* came over the crest of a wave two hundred yards away, poised dramatically, then plunged down out of sight.

VIII

Every window on the bridge of the gunboat was smashed, the door ripped from its hinges and Petersen and Chaney struggled to hold the wheel between them. Reeve had jammed himself into a corner and Jago and Jansen crouched at the chart table, observing the *Deutschland*.

Jago had long since passed the point of feeling the intense cold, indeed of feeling anything. His body had ceased to exist, only the brain turned still, sharp and keen. The trip had been a nightmare. He knew that to have got this far was some kind of miracle. But that didn't matter. They were here.

'Now what?' Jansen cried into his ear.

The *Deutschland* leaned over, her lee rail under water, then swung to port again.

'I don't know,' Jago said. 'Perhaps if we go in there under the lee. If they're quick.'

This was unknown territory, a situation so extreme that it was not covered by any manual of seamanship. He was hesitating. And that was fatal. Two men at the quarterdeck rail were waving frantically. One of them, he presumed, was Berger, beckoning him to come in.

Reeve broke the spell, crying hoarsely, 'Let's go, for God's sake! Let's go!'

Jago turned to Petersen. 'Okay, straight in to her lee rail. This is crunch time.'

He went out on the bridge, followed by Reeve. Jansen went down to the deck, calling the other five crew members to him and they moved to the rail to get ready.

The *Dead End* went in fast and Chaney turned the wheel frantically at the last moment as a wave caught them. Her prow smashed into the barquentine's rail. As the wave receded, the *Deutschland* rolled to port and the *Dead End* dropped sickeningly fifteen feet below her. In the same moment a great sea rolled in across the *Deutschland*'s port rail, rising forty feet up her masts, sweeping everything before it.

Jago, on his knees in a world of green water, hanging on to the rail, felt the gunboat sag beneath him. Another wave washed in as he grabbed for Reeve, throwing both of them bodily forward. When it receded, he found himself face-down beside the admiral on the deck of the *Deutschland*.

Berger reached them a moment before the next wave struck and hauled Jago to his feet. The lieutenant grabbed at the mainmast ratlines to steady himself, turned and saw, to his horror, the *Dead End* in the process of going down close to the rail, the *Deutschland*'s mizzen mast, torn from its mountings by the first enormous sea, lying across her in a tangle of wreckage.

The surviving members of his crew were already on the move, jumping for their lives to the deck of the *Deutschland*. Petersen, blood on his face, but not Chaney. Crawford, Lloyd – but no sign of Jansen.

Another wave swept in and Jago held tight, aware that the *Deutschland* was foundering beneath his feet, already up to his waist in water, as the combined weight of the mizzen mast and the gunboat pulled her over.

Richter came down the quarterdeck ladder, an axe in one hand, and started to attack the tangled web of lines that still held them tied to the mast. In a daze Jago turned to watch him. And then Reeve was tugging at his arm and pointing.

Jansen was out there, head and shoulders above the tangle where the mast had struck. He was bareheaded, one arm free. Jago stumbled towards Richter and pulled him away.

The German had him by the oilskin with one hand holding him off and Reeve was screaming into his ear. 'It's got to be done, Jago. Otherwise we all go.'

Jago turned to look out at Jansen as if in a dream, could have sworn he smiled and then quite distinctly heard the chief call, 'Get it done, lieutenant.'

Suddenly, unable to breathe, he tore the axe from Richter's grasp. 'Damn you,' he cried. 'Damn you all to hell!'

There were tears in his eyes. The axe rose, descended, cutting deep, rose again and again in a frenzy.

The *Deutschland* lifted as the mast tore away from the gunboat and Jago was hurled on his back. He got to his feet in time to see the mast and what was left of the *Dead End* drifting rapidly away. He caught a final glimpse of Jansen, his arm moving in slow motion, as if in a kind of benediction. Then another wave rolled in and there was nothing.

Jago hurled the axe into the sea, turned and stumbled away.

IX

At almost the same moment Necker's voice sounded on the radio again. 'She's foundering. The gunboat has foundered.'

Gericke turned and said gravely, 'I'm afraid the *Dead End* has gone down.'

Jean Sinclair slumped into a chair, stunned. Janet said frantically, 'It can't be.'

'Come in, Necker. Come in. Please confirm your last message.'

There was silence, the crackle of static. Janet said in a dull voice, 'All gone. All of them. Uncle Carey, Harry . . .'

Necker's voice cut in on her. 'Have been in communication with the *Deutschland.* The gunboat foundered under her lee rail when the mizzen mast fell on her. There were six survivors from her crew, all of whom are now safe on board *Deutschland.*'

'Six survivors,' Gericke translated rapidly.

Jean grabbed his arm. 'Who? I must know who?'

'Admiral Reeve, Lieutenant Jago and four others,' Necker continued.

Gericke turned to Jean. 'He's safe, Mrs Sinclair, for the moment at any rate, on board the *Deutschland.*' He glanced at Janet. 'And so is your lieutenant.'

Necker's voice broke in again. 'What happens now? What shall I say to the *Deutschland*?'

Gericke sat there for a long moment. Then he told him.

When he had finished, Necker said, 'Are you sure? You will see to it personally?'

'My word on it.'

'I'll tell them what you say. The trouble is, I'm already ten minutes past the critical point as regards my fuel for the return trip.'

'There is nothing more you can do here, my friend. Speak to the *Deutschland* and go home.'

There was a brief pause. Janet said, 'What's going on? What have you been saying?'

Gericke motioned her to silence. Necker's voice sounded again. 'I've spoken to Berger. Told him what you intend.'

'Has he told the admiral?'

'Yes, he's sent a rather peculiar message for you.'

'What is it?'

'He says isn't it about time you realized you'd lost the war. Does that make any sense?'

'Of a sort. And now, my friend, you must be leaving.'

Necker said, 'Goodbye, sir. It's been an honour to know you.'

'And you, Herr Hauptmann.'

And then there was only that damned static again. Gericke switched off the set and reached for a cigarette. 'So,' he said.

'What's going on?' Janet began, but Murdoch waved her down.

'Be still, girl.' He leaned close to Gericke. 'Well, commander?'

'Necker's had to leave. He's already dangerously short of fuel, but before he went, I asked him to send a last message to the *Deutschland*.'

'And what would that be?'

'I told them to hang on because we'd be coming for them in the lifeboat.'

'But that's impossible,' Jean said. 'She's on the beach at South Inlet.'

'And even if we could launch her again,' Murdoch said, 'she will never make it over that reef and out to sea, not as the wind is. I told you that.'

'I'm not suggesting that you launch her from South Inlet, but from here in the harbour.'

Murdoch shook his head. 'Madness. It can't be done and if it could – if you dragged that boat from one end of the island to the other, who could take her out there?' He looked down at his broken arm. 'One hand is not enough – not in weather like this.'

'I told them I would come myself,' Gericke said simply. 'I told them exactly what I intended.' He turned to the two women. 'The admiral knows and so does Jago. They must also know that it is their only chance of life now.'

The door burst open and Lachlan ran in to collapse against the table, chest heaving as if he had run for some considerable distance.

'What is it, lad?' Murdoch demanded sternly. 'Pull yourself together now.'

'I've been up on Feith na Falla,' Lachlan said, struggling for breath. 'Along with half the town. The *Deutschland* has just come into view.'

X

As Janet and Gericke went over the crest and stood on top of the hill the wind almost knocked them back again. She held on to his arm tightly and Murdoch and Lachlan, Jean Sinclair between, followed after them.

There were dozens of women there many of them wearing the oilskins of absent husbands, most with shawls bound tightly around their heads against the wind.

The sea raged in fury, a boiling cauldron. Visibility, because of blown spindrift and sleet, was poor and yet they were able to see her a couple of miles out, lifting on the crest of a wave, two masts only now and the rag of a staysail still intact.

Murdoch raised his binoculars. 'Aye, she is in a bad way sure enough,' he said and then swung the binoculars slightly to the north-west.'

Lachlan said, 'She is going straight on to the Washington.'

'I fear so.'

Someone in the crowd cried out and then another voice was raised – another. Women were moving forward, arms outstretched – calling out, as if by the simple power of their voices, they could haul her back. Prevent what was happening.

Gericke said nothing, but simply reached for Murdoch's binoculars and focused them on that place where the sea boiled in fury, spray lifting a hundred feet into the air over jagged rocks. The *Deutschland* was no more than three hundred yards away from the reef, drifting in fast to a rising chorus from the women on the hill.

'She'll strike,' Murdoch said, taking back the binoculars. 'Can't avoid it now.'

He stood there, legs apart, watching intently through the binoculars and when he finally turned, his face was surprisingly calm. 'The old Washington will hold her tight for a while. Time enough if we move fast.' He waved his arm at the crowd. 'Follow me – all of you!'

He went straight down the hill. Gericke and Janet, Jean Sinclair and Lachlan followed. As the word spread, others went after them until, in a few moments, the top of the hill was deserted.

The track emerged at the side of the church. When they reached that point, the old man went through the lych-gate hurried up the path and entered the porch. A moment later, the bell started to toll.

XI

Horst Necker burst out of cloud at eight thousand feet over the Moray Firth, in serious trouble and still descending. Things hadn't been right since leaving the *Deutschland*, but it was only within the past five minutes that the source of the trouble had become apparent – a fracture in one of the fuel pipes connecting the GMI system.

'I'll have to go down to floor level,' he said over the intercom. 'No choice. Anyone who wants to pray, start now.'

There was a chance that in this weather the *Tommis* would be too preoccupied to bother about one stray intruder on their radar screen. In fact, although Necker wasn't aware of it, Spitfires had already scrambled at Huntly airfield near Inverness and were seeking him out.

'I have a Kurier! I have a Kurier!' Kranz, the rear gunner's voice sounded in his ears.

Necker went into a corkscrew instantly, the reflex of several years of combat flying coming to his aid. He was aware of the chatter of the machine-guns, glanced up to see a Spitfire zoom overhead and turn away to port, and then the entire aircraft seemed to stagger. Miraculously he was still in control.

'Everyone still in one piece?' he said over the intercom.

There was no reply. Rudi, blood on his face where a splinter had sliced his cheek, scrambled to the rear. Necker kept on going down, jinking from side to side, aware of the shock waves as cannon shell punched holes in the fuselage.

Rudi got back into his seat. 'Kranz is dead. Schmidt is unconscious. Some sort of head wound. I've put a field dressing on him.'

'Good boy. Now hang on while I show these bastards how to fly.'

He took the Junkers right down to sea level – a hazardous undertaking; with forty foot swells, it was possible to find on occasion that the seas ahead were above the plane.

And the Spitfires didn't like it, although two of them still hung on grimly for a while, even at that suicidal level.

Once, Necker looked down and observed strange waterspouts all around and wondered for a moment what they were – until the Junkers shuddered again under the impact of cannon shell.

Twenty minutes at three hundred miles an hour. Not so good with that fractured pipe. The engines would be overheating, but not long now, unless he had hopelessly miscalculated.

The aircraft staggered under a well-aimed burst of machine-gun fire. The windscreen shattered, Necker felt as if he had been kicked in the left shoulder, turned and found the port engine smoking. He feathered it at once and switched to the extinguishers. The Junkers slowed, the needle falling right down to one hundred and fifty.

He hung on grimly, still no more than fifty feet above the sea. Rudi plucked at his arm excitedly. 'They've gone, Herr Hauptmann. Cleared off. I don't understand.'

'That's what I was hoping for. We're just over a hundred miles from the coast. That's usually the limit of their radius on a sea chase.'

Rudi was staring at the blood on his glove and touched Necker's arm again gingerly. 'You're wounded.'

'So I believe,' Necker said. 'You know at flying school,

they told us it was impossible to keep one of these birds in the air on one engine. Let's see if we can prove them wrong.'

'What shall I do, Herr Hauptmann?'

'Take off your belt, fasten it round the left rudder pedal.'

Rudi did as he was told and with his help, it was now possible to hold the crippled Junkers on course again.

'Pull tight, Rudi, all the way home.' Necker grinned, beginning to feel the pain in his shoulder now and not caring. 'See how simple it is when you know how? Stick with me and you'll live forever.'

XII

When Murdoch mounted into the pulpit at St Mungo's there were something like seventy people in the congregation, mainly women, a handful of old men and children. It was strangely silent, the wind muted by the thickness of massive stone walls.

He stood for a moment, head bowed in prayer, then looked up. 'There is a boat out there on the Washington. You all know this. And the *Morag Sinclair* is beached at South Inlet. The only question is what can be done?' No one said a word. 'Commander Gericke has a solution. That we haul the *Morag* from South Inlet to Mary's Town and launch her in the harbour.'

There was a gasp from the congregation. Someone said clearly, 'Impossible.'

'Not so,' Murdoch said. 'Such a thing has been done before. In Northumbria, early in the war, at Newbiggin. Should we be capable of less? Or must those poor souls on the Washington perish?'

Katrina MacBrayne answered him in a clear savage voice. 'Bloody Germans all. Why should we lift a finger?'

'I could say that Admiral Reeve is out there, too, and five survivors from that Yankee gunboat. I could say that there are women out there, for there are. But what would be the point? I am not here to argue. I am here to tell you. Is this all your God means? Is this what our worship together has meant? You have lost a husband to the war, Katrina MacBrayne. I have given a son – a week back some of you women wept at the graveside of German boys laid to rest in our own churchyard. Pain is the same both sides. Everyone loses. But what does that prove? That there is no God in this life? No, by heaven, for he gives us choice in our actions. We choose the way, not he.'

The silence was intense; total. 'People die out there if we do nothing and who they are doesn't matter. You see the state I'm in. Not fit to handle a wheel. But when the *Morag* leaves harbour, Commander Gericke stands in my place and I, by God, will be at his right hand.' He slammed his fist down hard on the lectern. 'There has been enough of talking. I am going to South Inlet to get that boat. Those who will can follow. As for the rest – to hell with you.'

He came down out of the pulpit and marched up the aisle like a strong wind.

— 15 —

> Barquentine *Deutschland*, 25 September 1944. At four bells in the forenoon watch in winds of hurricane strength we struck on the Washington Reef three miles north-west of Fhada in the Outer Hebrides. We are in the hands of the Almighty now and although help is promised, I fear there is little hope for us.

THE *DEUTSCHLAND* lay hard on the reef, her back broken, the fore topmast swinging down in a tangle of rigging, the sea breaking over her, one wave after another. Her stern jutted high into the air. Those who had been able to make their way aft in time, clustered on the quarterdeck. There were still several men forrard, some tied to the mainmast, others high in the rigging.

Berger, Reeve and Jago huddled together at the quarterdeck

rail. Sturm hauled himself up the ladder and crouched beside them and spoke to Berger, shouting to make himself heard.

Berger's English, though far from perfect, was good enough to get by. He turned to Reeve, his mouth close to the admiral's ear. 'The women seem safe enough for the moment, in my cabin. Sturm says the bulkhead's breached but it's mainly holding together.'

'Not for long,' Reeve said as the *Deutschland* lifted, then crunched down on to the reef again.

'Gericke will come. He said he would.'

For a moment Reeve saw again the *Morag Sinclair* on the beach at South Inlet and wanted to tell the German the truth. But what would be the point? At least the end, when it came, would be quick.

Berger leaned over the rail, in spite of the breaking waves and tried to count the men in the rigging and on the deck by the mainmast. 'Not good. It looks like we lost five when we struck.'

The telegraphist was forty feet up in the ratlines where he had climbed to avoid the worst of the waves. Jago saw him plainly. The man waved and actually managed a smile. A mountain of water curled in. When it subsided, he was gone.

'We've got to get those men out of there,' Jago shouted.

Reeve plucked at his sleeve. 'Don't be crazy. You won't last two minutes on that open deck.'

Jago shook him off, crawled to the quarterdeck ladder and descended cautiously. He hung on at the bottom as another wave washed in, holding his breath, refusing to let go. As it subsided, Richter dropped down beside him.

He carried a coil of rope over one shoulder and tied one end quickly about Jago's waist, then looped the rest around the ladder. Jago started forward and Richter paid the rope out gradually.

Jago struggled desperately alone in a world of cold green water. He lost his footing at one point, fetching up in the scuppers, but braced himself hard against the rope, and carried on, sometimes on hands and knees, until he was almost within touching distance of Petersen, tethered to the mainmast. Another wave bounced Petersen towards him on the end of his line and Jago grabbed him by the leg, then the belt, hauling himself over Petersen's prostrate body until he reached the mainmast and was able to stand.

He unfastened the rope from around his waist and tied it to the mast, then waved to Richter. The German lashed the other end securely to the ladder so that there was now a lifeline stretching to the mast three feet above deck level.

Jago gestured to the men in the rigging and they started to descend. Petersen and the others, who had been tethered to the mast, had already untied themselves and were making their way across one by one, the rest followed. Jago waited until last, made a final check to make absolutely certain the deck and rigging were clear and went after them.

II

In Berger's cabin, Prager and the nuns were still reasonably protected from the full fury of the storm, in spite of breaches in the bulkhead. Prager crouched against the bunk, the rum bottle in both hands. He had almost emptied it, had ceased to feel the cold.

'Not long now, Gertrude,' he whispered. 'Not long.'

Sister Angela prayed aloud at one end of the desk, hands clasped. 'Save, Lord, or else we perish. The living, the living shall praise thee. O send thy word of command to rebuke the raging winds and the roaring sea; that we, being delivered from this distress, may live to serve thee, and to glorify thy name all the days of our life.'

The door opened and Richter entered, slamming it behind him. He looked around the cabin, frowning. Sister Angela said, 'Herr Richter?'

'Where's Lotte?'

She was very cold and when she unclasped her hands, she found, to her surprise, that they were shaking. 'Lotte?' She looked around, a dazed expression on her face. 'Has anyone seen Lotte?'

Sister Brigitte was sobbing. No one seemed to have anything to say. Richter crossed to Prager and hauled him to his feet. 'You were supposed to bring them up from the saloon just before we struck. Didn't Lotte come with you?'

'Definitely,' Prager said. 'I was right behind her.'

Sister Käthe said, 'She went back.'

Richter started violently. 'That's not possible.'

'I heard her say she'd forgotten something.' Sister Käthe said vacantly. 'Then she went out.'

Richter wrenched open the door and plunged outside. He started down the companionway, but the deck and entire superstructure was buckled and twisted, the way into the saloon blocked by a tangle of wreckage.

'Lotte?' he cried. 'Lotte?' But there was no reply.

It was Jago who saw him first, crossing the deck below, using the lifeline they had rigged. He tugged at Berger's sleeve. 'What's he up to?'

'God knows,' Berger replied.

As they watched, Richter took out his gutting knife, sprung the blade, slashed at the ropes securing the cargo hatch, surprisingly still intact, and disappeared into the forrard hold.

III

The *Morag Sinclair* was almost at the top of the track leading up from the lifeboat station. She sat on a trolley with enormous broad iron wheels, not used since the time of the pulling lifeboat, when muscle and oars provided the power. Gericke had thought it impossible to lift her into position. But the solution was simple. They had pushed her out into the surf, as in the old days, floated her on to the trolley and hauled them in together.

Now, close to the crest of the hill, the lines were hauled by eleven farmhorses, forty-one women, eighteen children and eleven men.

Gericke and Lachlan moved behind, blocking the wheels every few yards with baulks of timber. Sleet mingled with the rain, cutting cruelly into the flesh.

Someone in a long oilskin coat fell down a yard or two ahead of Janet. She left her place on the line and ran to help, discovering, to her horror, that it was a frail, white-haired women of seventy at least. There was blood on her hands. She looked down at it, a dazed expression on her face, then raised her long skirt and tore strips from her petticoat.

She started to wind them around her hands and Janet tried to pull her over to the side of the track. 'You must sit down.'

The old woman pushed her away. 'Leave me be, girl.' She staggered up the track and resumed her place.

'Oh God, this is madness,' Janet said to herself.

Murdoch was beside her, pulling her to her feet. 'Are you all right, girl?'

'Yes – yes, I'm fine.'

'Then why have you left your place?'

He glared at her like some Old Testament prophet about to invoke the wrath of God and smite the wrongdoer. She turned from his anger and, slipping and stumbling, ran forward along the column to resume her place beside Jean.

Time was meaningless now, a long agony as she strained, and voices swelled around her, women urging each other on, reaching beyond the agony to another place. Then, quite suddenly and to a ragged cheer, they went over the crest and started to move faster, following the path beside the railway track.

IV

There was five to ten feet of water in the forrard hold; depending on where he stood, for it was inclined sharply to starboard. The storm lantern hung from a hook in the bulkhead, its light playing across the dark water, which erupted suddenly as Richter surfaced.

But there was no route through there. The communicating hatchway was hopelessly jammed. And even if it hadn't been, it was debatable whether he would be able to hold his breath for long enough to get through all that wreckage under water.

So there was only one way, it seemed. He rapped at the bulkhead with his knuckles. Still reasonably sound. It would take time. But then he didn't really have anywhere else to go. He picked up the two-handed fire-axe he'd brought down with him and swung it over his head.

V

The *Morag Sinclair* was half-way along the track beside the railway line, high up on the spine of the island, progress slowing a little as they moved, totally exposed, into the full fury of the wind.

The scene behind was like a battlefield, people huddled beside the track at intervals where they had dropped, totally exhausted. It was a nightmare that couldn't be allowed to continue, Janet knew that, and yet still she bowed her back beside Jean, the rope biting cruelly into her shoulder and her hands dripping blood.

When she looked out over the sea, it seemed more troubled than ever, a vast wash of foam, a sky of writhing black smoke that boiled down as if it would envelop the earth.

Ahead of her, old Dougal Sinclair stumbled out of the line, crossed the railway track and fell down in the heather. Janet relinquished her grip and went after him wearily. He looked very peaceful lying there on his back, the blue eyes staring up into the dark sky. It was a moment or two before she realized how fixed that stare was and quickly unbuttoned his oilskin and jacket, reaching inside to feel for his heart.

Gericke dropped to one knee beside her. 'What is it?' he demanded. 'Are you all right?'

'He's dead,' she said bitterly. 'Are you satisfied now?'

VI

Reeve crouched against the quarterdeck rail of the *Deutschland*, his pocket telescope raised, and looked towards Fhada. 'No good,' he cried to Jago. 'They can probably see us from up there on Feith na Falla, but I can't even see the island.'

'They're not coming, admiral. Nobody's coming. We've had it.'

At least in the Solomons it had been warm. He closed his eyes and a wave washed in, lifting the *Deutschland* bodily and crashing her down again.

'Christ Jesus, but I thought we were going straight over the edge of the reef that time,' Reeve said.

Berger shouted in his ear. 'She's breaking up now. Next

time that happens, or the time after, she comes apart at the seams.'

Reeve's face was bleached from the constant salt water, wrinkled like a fish's belly, and he looked a hundred years old. Jago leaned close. 'You wanted action, admiral. You got it in spades. What a way to go.'

VII

Richter had just smashed his way through from the forrard hold when the *Deutschland* lifted and started to roll. Oh God, he thought, this is it.

She settled on the rocks again, with a nasty grating sound as more planks tore loose. He waited for the swirling water to subside. Strangely enough he wasn't afraid, consumed totally by a passionate need to know what had happened to Lotte.

He squeezed past the mainmast mounting and the pump, found a nail on which to hang the storm lantern and started to attack the bulkhead which would give him access to the aft hold.

VIII

The *Morag Sinclair* was beginning to move fast now as the track sloped down to cross the railway line above Mary's Town, and suddenly the situation was totally changed. The forty or so people who were left on the lines, their roles reversed, were hanging on grimly to stop the boat running away from them on its trolley.

Murdoch hurried alongside, shouting instructions to Gericke and Lachlan as they attempted to slow her by blocking the wheels with the same baulks of timber they had used at South Inlet.

The *Morag* was really moving – rocking alarmingly on her trolley, swinging from side to side, leaving a trail of smashed windows as she coasted down the High Street. She emerged on to the front by the pier at some considerable speed, Gericke and Lachlan running alongside, frantically jamming the wheels with their timber pieces and slowly and very, very gradually, she started to slide to a halt.

There was the silence of total exhaustion. Murdoch heaved himself up the ladder and over the side and nodded to Gericke. 'You, too, commander.'

Gericke followed him, aware with something of a surprise, that his arms were having difficulty in holding the weight of his body.

Murdoch looked out over the crowd. 'What is wrong with you, then? She's only fifteen tons. One more heave now.'

No one made a sound and then, somehow, women who had collapsed were on their feet again, reaching wearily for their lines. They dragged the lifeboat forward to the top of the stone slipway at the head of the pier and ran her down into the harbour.

Watching her there, grinding against the pier, Janet couldn't quite take it all in. She was aware of Jean crying helplessly beside her, tears pouring down her cheeks, heard Gericke say, 'Get those petrol drums along here quickly now,' for they had emptied the tanks at South Inlet to lighten her.

Murdoch, in the aft cockpit, was calling up to the pier. 'Lachlan, are you there, boy? No time for your sick belly now. I need you – and you, Hamish, and Francis Patterson. Are you still game?'

They went forward, those old men, even James Sinclair, whose brother lay dead back beside the track. Janet turned, started to run back up the High Street, finding a new strength in her purpose, never stopping until she reached the cottage. She went inside, snatched her medical bag and ran back down the hill to the harbour.

She pushed her way on to the pier through the crowd and saw them on deck below, fastening their lifejackets, each man in yellow oilskins, even Gericke. She went down the stone steps to the lower landing and scrambled over the rail.

Murdoch turned to confront her. 'And what is this, girl?'

'There are six of you, Murdoch. Five and a half if you consider that arm of yours. You should crew eight.'

Gericke got between them, his hands on her shoulders. 'This is no job for a woman, Janet. You must see that.'

'Who got your bloody boat here for you?' She held up her

medical bag. 'I'm not here as a woman. I'm here as a doctor. And you might be damned glad to have me along before this is through.'

Gericke opened his mouth to reply, but Murdoch pulled him out of the way. 'No time to argue. You go to hell your own way, girl. Get down in the cockpit.' He gave her a push. 'You'll find an oilskin and lifejacket. Put them on and stay out of the way.'

Gericke's face was pale. He hesitated, then moved to the wheel. A second later, Lachlan, who was acting as bowman, had cast off and they were moving away from the pier out into the harbour.

IX

At the quarterdeck rail, Jago, Reeve and Berger still huddled together. The *Deutschland* had eased herself over a little further to starboard and seemed to lift now with each wave.

It was Reeve who, turning to look in the direction of Fhada for the hundredth time, caught the first glimpse of the *Morag Sinclair* a mile to starboard.

'She's coming!' he cried, tugging frantically at Jago's arm. 'I see her.'

Jago pulled himself to his feet, holding on to the rail and peered into the rain through swollen eyelids. 'No,' he said hoarsely. 'You're imagining things.'

But Reeve cried out again excitedly, clutching at Berger. This time the lifeboat was plain and a sudden cheering broke out amongst the men assembled on the quarterdeck.

Berger waved Sturm across. 'Go down to my cabin and bring up the sisters.'

Sturm crawled away wearily. At that moment another wave thundered against the *Deutschland* sliding her bodily across the reef. Part of the prow broke off and the storm staysail, intact all this time, fluttered away like a great bird.

'They'd better hurry,' Jago said. 'From the feel of that last one, I'd say we don't have too much time.'

X

Richter had hacked his way through three bulkheads and

scrambled into the aft hold as the men on deck started to cheer. He hesitated, put down the axe, turned and crawled back through the hole he had just made. He clung on to the base of the mainmast as the ship moved again on the reef, but emerged from the forrard hatch a few moments later in time to catch a glimpse of the *Morag Sinclair* on the crest of a wave some distance away.

How much time did he have? Impossible to know. He dropped down into the hold, forced his way back through the water, negotiating the holes he had made in the bulkheads, until he stood again in the aft hold.

At some time in the *Deutschland*'s earlier history, the hold had been halved to make room for the additional cabin accommodation. The intervening bulkhead having been added at a later date, it had nothing like the strength of construction of the ones he had already negotiated. He picked up his axe, waded towards it and started to attack it furiously.

XI

The *Morag Sinclair* took water constantly, green sheets passing over her from stem to stern, exploding into the aft cockpit with stunning force. Janet was terrified. The waves seemed so enormous that each time they attempted to scale one, the task seemed an impossibility, the *Morag* climbing in slow motion. When she swooped down the other side into the trough, it was as if she never intended to come up again.

But Gericke seemed unperturbed as he wrestled with the wheel, Murdoch at his shoulder.

Lifeboatmen, as a rule, don't wear lifelines, believing them to be too constricting in an emergency. So it was that at one moment, as Lachlan turned from beside her, reaching up to the rail and slipped, a sea washed in, taking him out with it over the starboard rail. Janet screamed and as Gericke glanced over his shoulder in alarm, the starboard rail dipped under and the boy miraculously floated inboard.

Murdoch reached down and shook him like a rat. 'Lifeline!' he shouted. 'Get a lifeline on!' He turned to Hamish MacDonald. 'Lifelines for everyone. My orders – like it or not.' He crouched down over Janet. 'You too, girl.'

She reached for the line that was passed to her and had barely hooked herself on when disaster struck. The *Morag* hovered on the crest of a mountainous wave, broached as she went down. At the same moment, the wind gusted in fury, striking her starboard bow. She capsized.

To Janet, the world was stinking green water, washing over, filling heart and mind and brain, kicking and struggling in a desperate desire to live. The *Morag* was partially under, still pushing forward, screws turning.

Slowly, she righted herself. Janet was aware of Gericke clinging to the wheel with one hand, reaching out to her with the other, Murdoch pulling himself up beside them. Lachlan was safe, Hamish MacDonald, Sinclair. But Francis Patterson had gone.

From then on, so vicious was the weather, so impenetrable the curtain of rain and sleet and flying spindrift that they caught no further sight of the wreck until they lurched over the top of an enormous wave and saw her a hundred and fifty yards away, the survivors clustered on the quarterdeck, waving.

'Now what?' Gericke demanded.

'Take your time, boy,' Murdoch said. 'And let me work this out.'

XII

Richter broke through the final bulkhead. He crawled into the saloon. It was dark in there, only the gurgle of the water, the howling of the gale outside. As with the rest of the ship, it was steeply inclined, the starboard cabins under water.

'Lotte?' he called.

There was no reply. Could be none. He had been a fool to think otherwise. He floundered through the water, crawled up the slope to where the door of her cabin swung crazily, braced himself in the entrance and raised the lamp.

She lay trapped across the bunk, a tangle of wreckage across her stomach and legs. Her face was very pale, her eyes closed, but now she opened them slowly.

'Helmut,' she whispered. 'I knew you would come.'

'What happened? Why did you come back?'

'Your ring, Helmut. I'd hidden it here under the mattress in the corner of my bunk. I forgot it when we were ordered on deck. Wasn't that silly of me?'

He was already heaving on the beam, straining with all his strength, but it refused to budge. 'How strange,' she said. 'I've been so cold for days, so very cold, yet now, I can't feel a thing.'

The *Deutschland* shook herself and started to move as if ready now to ease off the reef. He wrenched frantically at the beam again, then said, 'I must get help, Lotte. I'll be back in a little while. I'll have to take the lantern, but don't be afraid.'

'You won't leave me?'

'Never again. Remember my promise?'

He left her there and ploughed back through the water, working his way from hold to hold. The *Deutschland* was in constant motion, nosing forward, slithering further over the edge of the Washington, her prow dipping.

Richter hauled himself up the ladder in time to see the *Morag* moving in. The nuns were already making their way across from the shelter of Berger's cabin, the men on the quarterdeck crowding down the ladder.

There were cries of fear and one of the women screamed high and shrill as the *Deutschland* moved again with a terrible rending and tearing sound.

Richter had to hang on tight to the ladder for a moment. He dropped down, waist-deep in water, waded towards the hole in the bulkhead and climbed through. The *Deutschland* was in constant motion now, water swirling all around him, but when he reached the saloon, there was that strange eerie quiet. And she was still there waiting for him when he went into the cabin. He hung up the lantern and sat down beside her.

'You came back.'

'Of course.'

'What's happening, Helmut?'

'They're coming for us, Lotte. They finally got here.' He took her hand and held it tightly.

XIII

To Murdoch, debating on the best way to go in, that sudden tremble as the *Deutschland* slid towards the edge was enough.

'She's going, lad, she's going!' He slapped Gericke on the shoulder. 'Give her everything you've got, full power and straight in over the rail. Two minutes is all we get.'

Gericke boosted power, the *Morag* surged forward, catching even those on the quarterdeck by surprise, slicing in across the rail until her bows rested on the deck.

There was no need to say a word for already the nuns were scurrying from Berger's cabin, shepherded by Sturm, and Prager and Reeve, Jago and the rest of them, were getting off the quarterdeck fast.

The *Deutschland* shook herself again and men cried out in fear, Sister Käthe screaming, falling across the rail. Janet reached over, dragged her bodily, pushed her down into the cockpit and the cabin.

'She'll take us with her, boy!' Murdoch shouted. 'Reverse those engines. Get ready!' He waved his arm and called furiously, 'Come on, damn you! She's going!'

There was a final mad scramble, men vaulting over the rails in panic, Berger last of all, the ship's log and his personal journal in an oilskin wrapper under his arm. Gericke reversed the engines full power as the *Deutschland* sagged again, and the *Morag* shot away.

Sister Angela crouched in a corner of the small cabin. She tried to get up, peering at the faces crowded around her. 'Lotte?' she said. 'Where's Lotte?'

There was no reply – could be none. She turned, grabbed Janet's arm fiercely and said in English. 'Lotte isn't here – neither is Herr Richter. They must still be on board.'

Janet scrambled out of the cabin into the cockpit. Jago was there, Reeve above him crouched beside Gericke and Murdoch. She shook Jago's arm. 'There's still someone on board.'

He seemed to find difficulty in speaking. 'Not possible.'

She reached up and pulled at Gericke's oilskin. 'Paul – there's still someone on board.'

He glanced down at her, startled. In the same moment, the *Deutschland* started to slide off the reef.

XIV

Berger, at the starboard rail, had tears in his eyes. As water boiled around her, his hand went up in a brief salute. For a moment, the main topmast was visible, then that too dropped beneath the surface and there was nothing – only the sea's leavings. A few planks, a tangle of rope, a barrel spinning.

Gericke, his face grave, turned the wheel, taking the *Morag* away from the Washington, round in a great curve, ready to start the slow and painful fight back through those mountainous seas to Fhada.

— 16 —

Barquentine *Deutschland*, 25 September 1944. At three bells of the afternoon watch with the *Deutschland* sinking beneath us, the sixteen survivors of her original complement were snatched from the Washington Reef by the lifeboat *Morag Sinclair*, Coxswain Murdoch Macleod and Korvettenkapitän Paul Gericke of the Kriegsmarine combining in a remarkable feat of seamanship. Afterwards they conveyed us to the neighbouring island of Fhada through heavy and mountainous seas. I was distressed to learn that in one way or another seven people gave their lives to save ours. Words, for the first time, fail me. So ends this log. Erich Berger, Master

REEVE POURED himself a large Scotch and drank it slowly. He was tired right through, more conscious of his age than he had ever been. The wind hammered against the roof of the cottage, and he winced.

'No more, please,' he whispered. 'Enough is enough.'

He hobbled painfully across to his desk. What he needed

now was sleep, but first there was work to be done. He reached for his pen and opened his journal. There was a knock at the door and Harry Jago entered, struggling to close it again against the wind. His face was swollen, the flesh split in a dozen places. Like Reeve, he seemed to find difficulty in walking.

'You don't look too good, Harry.' The admiral pushed the bottle of Scotch across the desk, 'Help yourself.'

Jago went into the kitchen and came back with a glass. When he spoke, it was very slowly. 'I feel like a dead man walking.'

'I know what you mean. How's Janet?'

'Indestructible. It's like a field hospital at Fhada House, and she hasn't stopped since we got in.'

'She's had plenty of practice. It's been a long war,' the admiral said. 'Still foul out there?'

'Nothing like as bad. Winds seven to eight, I'd say, and falling a little. She'll have blown herself out by morning.'

He emptied his glass and Reeve filled it again. 'I've been in touch with Murray on the radio. Chaotic over there apparently, but he's going to send a boat in the morning. Says he'll try and make it himself.'

'What about the survivors? What will happen to them?'

'I don't know. Internment for the nuns, prison camp for Berger and his men.' There was a long pause and Jago stared down into his glass.

'You don't like that, do you?'

'It just doesn't have any meaning for me any more. Not any of it.'

'I know how you feel. All that bloody way and they nearly made it.'

The Scotch by now was dulling the pain. 'And Gericke?' Jago asked.

'What about him? There's still a war on, Harry.'

'I know,' Jago said. 'There always is some place. Does he go back in his cell?'

'That isn't my decision. Jean's the civil power here, you know that.'

Jago emptied his glass at a swallow. 'Well, I think I'll get back up to the house and see how my boys are doing.'

'Then bed, Harry. Go to bed.' Reeve managed a smile. 'That's an order.'

'Admiral.' Jago drew himself up and managed a salute.

He had almost reached the door, had his hand out, when Reeve said softly, 'Harry?'

Jago turned. 'Yes, sir.'

'All of a sudden I feel old, Harry. Too damned old. I just wanted to tell somebody that.'

II

There was still quite a swell in the harbour as Gericke went along the pier, head down against the rain. The *Morag Sinclair* danced at her moorings, a brave sight in her blue and white paint. Only a closer inspection revealed the ferocious battering she had taken from the sea.

He stood there, hands thrust deep into the pockets of the reefer someone had given him, and suddenly he heard himself hailed. He turned and saw Murdoch on the lower landing further along the pier, standing beside the *Katrina.*

As Gericke went down the stone steps, Lachlan came out of the wheelhouse. There was an oil drum on deck and he levered it over on to the landing with an ease which indicated that it was empty.

'What's this?' Gericke asked.

'Lachlan and I have been filling the *Katrina*'s tanks,' the old man said. 'That she may be ready for sea if wanted.'

The boy nodded to Gericke. 'Commander.'

'I didn't have a chance to tell you before, but you were fine out there, Lachlan.' Gericke held out his hand. 'I was proud to know you.'

Lachlan flushed crimson, stared at the hand for a moment, grabbed it briefly, then turned and hurried away.

'There is good stuff there, I am thinking,' Murdoch said. 'Too good to be off to bloody war again in a few days.' He started to fill his pipe, awkwardly because of his broken arm. 'Have you spoken with Janet since returning?'

'She's had her hands more than full.'

'Things must have eased considerably for her by now.' The

old man turned and looked out to sea through the driving rain. 'Still rough, but not too rough.'

'I suppose not.'

Murdoch nodded. 'Go see her now, boy.'

'Yes, I believe I will.'

He started to walk away and Murdoch called, 'Commander.'

'Yes?'

'Good luck to you.'

For a long, long moment they looked at each other, then Gericke turned and hurried away along the pier.

III

As he went into the kitchen of Fhada House, Jean Sinclair turned from the stove with a bowl of hot water. 'Hello,' she said. 'Are you looking for Janet?'

'Yes. Is she available?'

'Pretty busy last time I saw her. She has one of the sailors from the *Deutschland* on the table in the dining-room. A broken arm.'

'And the rest?'

'Mostly sleeping now. I think every bed in the house must be in use.' She held up the bowl. 'Sorry, I'll have to move on. Janet's waiting for this.'

He opened the door. 'And Captain Berger. Where is he?'

'First bedroom on the right, top of the stairs.'

She went away quickly and Gericke climbed the stairs. He paused at the door she had indicated, knocked and entered. Johann Sturm and Leading Seaman Petersen lay on top of the bed, side by side, sleeping heavily. Berger was seated in a chair at a small table by the window, his head resting on his arms.

The log of the *Deutschland* was open before him. Gericke stood at his shoulder for a moment and read its last entry, then turned and tiptoed out.

As the door clicked behind him, Berger stirred and looked up, peering around the room through swollen eyelids. 'Who's there?' he called hoarsely.

But there was no one. No one at all. His head sank down on his arms. He slept again.

IV

Reeve was writing in his journal with care and considerable precision, mainly because he was more than a little drunk, when the door opened violently and Janet came in, Jago at her heels.

'Is Paul here?'

He laid down his pen and regarded her with drunken gravity. 'Ah, Gericke, you mean. I didn't realize you two were on first-name terms.'

He was mocking her and she flared angrily. 'Has he been here?'

'Half an hour ago. Maybe a little longer. As a matter of fact we had a drink together, then he asked if he could leave something for you.'

'What?' she demanded.

'He said it was a private matter. I think you'll find it in the bedroom, whatever it is.'

She went out quickly into the hall and opened her bedroom door. The Knight's Cross with Oak Leaves for a second award lay, neatly arranged, on her pillow. She stared down at it, stupefied for a moment, then picked it up and ran back into the living room.

'Uncle Carey!' She held it out to him, her voice breaking.

Reeve nodded. 'Now I understand. On his way out he said, tell her she's earned it.'

There was a knock at the door and Murdoch moved in. 'Ah, there you are, admiral.'

'And what can I do for you?'

'A matter of official business only. The *Katrina* appears to be missing from her moorings.'

'Is that a fact!' Reeve said. 'It's a damned good thing I'm insured.'

Janet ran out of the door. Jago turned to Reeve, leaning on the desk. 'Are you going to notify Mallaig? They'll get to him soon enough up there in the Minch.'

'Very unfortunate, Harry, but the radio appears to have

packed in since I last talked to Murray. Valve gone, I think, and I don't have any spares. Just have to wait till they get here tomorrow. Nothing else to be done.'

Jago took a long, long breath, then turned and went out. Murdoch said gravely, 'Is that good Scotch you have there in that bottle, Carey Reeve?'

'And another in the cupboard when we've finished that. I've been holding out on you.'

'Later, then, I will come back if I may. But now, I must see to my people.'

He walked out. Reeve poured himself another whisky and resumed his writing.

> ... and so I see, when all is said and done, that this has been an old story. Murdoch, Harry Jago and Gericke – men against the sea, who have won this time. But in the end, what is the nature of their achievement ...?

God, but he was tired – more tired than he had ever been. The wind rattled the window as if trying to get in, but it could not touch him now. He pillowed his head on one arm for a moment and was instantly asleep, the pen still firm in his good hand and resting on that final entry.

WRATH OF THE LION

— 1 —

THE GRATICULES misted over, momentarily obscured by a curtain of green water, but as the tip of the periscope broke through to the surface the small untidy freighter jumped into focus with astonishing clarity. Lieutenant Fenelon gripped the handles of the eyepiece and his breath escaped in a long sigh.

Beside him Jacaud said, 'The *Kontoro?*'

Fenelon nodded. 'Not more than five hundred yards away.'

Jacaud dropped his cigarette and ground it into the deck with his heel. 'Let me see.'

Fenelon stood back, conscious of the hollowness at the base of his stomach. He was twenty-six years of age and had never seen action, never known what war was like except through the eyes of other men. But this – this was a new sensation. He felt strangely dizzy and passed a hand across his eyes as he waited.

Jacaud grunted and turned. He was a big, dangerous-looking man badly in need of a shave, a jagged scar bisecting his right cheek.

'Nice of them to be on time.'

Fenelon took another look. The *Kontoro* moved slowly to the right across the little black lines etched on the glass of the periscope and his throat went dry. He was already beginning to taste a little of that special excitement that takes possession of the hunter when his quarry is in plain sight.

'One torpedo,' he said softly. 'That's all it would take.'

Jacaud was watching him, a strange, sardonic smile on his face. 'What would be the point? No one would ever know.'

'I suppose not.' Fenelon called the control room from his voice-pipe. 'Steer one-oh-five and prepare to surface.'

He whipped the periscope down, the hiss it made as it slid into its well mingling with the clamour of the alarm klaxon. As he turned, brushing sweat from his eyes, Jacaud took a Lüger from his pocket. He removed the clip, checked it with the rapidity of the expert and slammed it back into the butt with a click that somehow carried with it a harsh finality.

He lit another cigarette. When he looked up he was no longer smiling.

II

In the wheelhouse of the *Kontoro* Janvier, the first officer, yawned as he bent over the chart. He made a quick calculation and threw down his pencil. By dead reckoning they were forty miles west of Ushant and the weather forecast wasn't good. Winds of gale force reported imminent in sea areas Rockall, Shannon, Sole and Finisterre.

For the moment there was only an unnatural calm, the sea lifting in a great oily swell. Janvier was tired, his eyes gritty from lack of sleep. A native of Provence, he had never managed to get used to the cold of these northern seas and he shivered with distaste as he gazed out into the grey dawn.

Behind him the door to the companionway clicked open and the steward entered holding a steaming cup of coffee in each hand. He gave one to Janvier and the other to the helmsman, taking his place at the wheel for a few moments while the man drank.

Janvier opened the door and walked out on to the bridge. He stood at the rail drinking his coffee and breathing deeply of the cold morning air, feeling considerably more cheerful. Once across Biscay there was the long run south to look forward to – Madeira, then the Cape and sun all the way. He finished his coffee, emptied the dregs over the side and started to turn.

A hundred yards to starboard there was a sudden surge in the oily water. It boiled in a white froth and a submarine broke through to the surface, strange and alien like some primeval creature in the dawn of time.

Janvier stood at the rail, trapped by surprise. As he watched, the conning-tower hatch opened and a young officer in peaked cap appeared, followed by a sailor who immediately hoisted a small ensign. A sudden gust of wind lifted it stiffly, the red, white and blue of the tricolour standing out vividly against the grey clouds.

The steward emerged from the wheelhouse and stood at the rail. 'What do you make of her, sir?'

Janvier shrugged. 'God knows. Better get the captain.'

A third sailor appeared in the conning-tower, a signal-lamp in his hands. The submarine moved in closer, narrowing the gap, and the lamp started to wink rapidly.

A reserve naval officer, Janvier had no difficulty in reading the signal for himself. When he had deciphered it he stood at the rail frowning for a moment, then went into the wheelhouse and unhooked the signal-lamp.

As he moved back to the rail, the light flickered again from the conning-tower, repeating her request. As Janvier replied with the 'Message received' signal, the captain came up the ladder from the well-deck, the quartermaster close behind.

Henri Duclos was nearly fifty, and after thirty years at sea, five of them as a corvette captain with the Free French Navy, he found it difficult to be surprised by anything.

'What's all this?' he demanded.

'They've made the same signal twice,' Janvier told him. ' "Heave to. I wish to come aboard." '

'What have you replied?'

'Message received.'

Duclos went into the wheelhouse and came back with a pair of binoculars. He examined the submarine for a moment and grunted. 'She's French all right. I can see the uniforms. Small for a sub, though.' He handed the binoculars to the quartermaster. 'What do you make of her?'

The old man took his time and then nodded. '*L'Alouette*. I saw her in Oran last year when the fleet was exercising. An ex-U-boat. Experimental job the Germans were working on at the end of the war. One of those the navy took over.'

'So now we know who she is,' Duclos said. 'The point is, what in the hell does she want with us?' He turned to Janvier. 'Ask her to be more explicit.'

There was a pause while the lamps flickered again, and Janvier turned blankly. 'She says: "Imperative I board you. Matter of national importance. Please observe radio silence." '

The lamp on the conning-tower of the submarine was still. 'What shall I reply, sir?' Janvier said.

Duclos raised the binoculars to his eyes for a moment then

took them down. 'What can you reply? If it's important enough for them to send a blasted sub after us, then it's important. Signal: "Come aboard." ' He grimaced at the quartermaster. 'I was looking forward to all that sun. My rheumatism's been killing me lately. Let's hope we don't have to go into Brest.'

The quartermaster shrugged. 'Stranger things are happening in the Republic these days.'

'Which republic?' Duclos demanded sardonically. 'Stand to all hands and get a ladder over the side.'

The quartermaster moved away and Janvier lowered the lamp. 'They thank us for our co-operation.'

'Do they, now?' Duclos observed. 'Let's hope they aren't wasting our time. Stop all engines.'

Janvier moved into the wheelhouse and Duclos took out his pipe and filled it from a worn leather pouch, watching the submarine as he did so. The forward hatch was opened and a large yellow dinghy hauled out and inflated. As the freighter started to slow, the two vessels drifted together until finally the gap had narrowed to no more than twenty or thirty yards.

The submarine commander climbed down the ladder from the conning-tower and paused at the bottom, watching the half-dozen sailors working on the dinghy. He was slim and rather boyish in his reefer jacket and rubber boots, and the peaked cap was tilted rakishly to one side. He glanced up at Duclos, smiled and waved, then walked along the hull and stepped down into the dinghy.

He was followed by half a dozen sailors, most of whom carried sub-machine-guns slung across their backs. Four of them paddled the boat across the narrow strip of water towards the ladder that had been dropped over the side of the *Kontoro*. Two sailors, still standing by the forward hatch of the submarine, carefully paid out a connecting line.

'Carrying a lot of hardware, aren't they?' Janvier said.

Duclos nodded. 'I don't like the look of this at all. It could be messy enough to rub off on all of us. Perhaps they're after someone in the crew. An OAS man trying to get out of the country or something like that.'

The sailors came over the side quickly. Three of them unslung their sub-machine-guns and stayed in the well-deck and the young officer mounted the ladder to the upper deck, briskly followed by the other three.

He held out his hand and smiled. 'Captain Duclos? My name is Fenelon. Sorry about all this, but I'm only obeying orders, you understand.'

The man who came up the ladder next had a scarred and brutal face and cropped hair. Like Fenelon, he wore a naval reefer jacket and rubber boots, but no cap. He leaned casually against the rail and lit a cigarette. The other two sailors spaced themselves behind Fenelon, machine-guns ready.

Duclos began to feel distinctly uneasy. 'Look, what's going on? What's this all about?'

'All in good time,' Fenelon said. 'You complied with my request to maintain radio silence?'

'Of course.'

'Good.' Fenelon turned and nodded briefly to one of the sailors, who crossed the deck to the wireless room which stood at the rear of the wheelhouse, opened the door and went inside.

A cry of alarm was followed by a burst of fire. A moment later the radio operator staggered through the door, blood on his face. He dropped to his knees and Janvier moved quickly to pick him up.

'The radio,' the man moaned. 'He put a burst through it.'

There was a sudden, ugly murmur from the crew in the well-deck that was answered by a volley of firing, bullets hissing through the steel rigging lines. Duclos glanced over the rail and saw that a heavy machine-gun had been mounted on a swivel on the rim of the sub's conning-tower. Even allowing for the difference in height between the two vessels, it was still capable of reducing most of the deck area of the *Kontoro* to a bloody shambles.

He turned slowly, his face pale. 'Who are you?'

Fenelon smiled. 'Exactly what we seem, captain. The commanding officer and crew of the submarine *L'Alouette*. Under special orders, but serving France, I assure you.'

'What do you want?' Duclos said.

'One of your passengers, Pierre Bouvier. I understand he is travelling with you as far as Madeira?'

Duclos's rage, hardly contained, flooded out in a roar of

anger. 'By God, I'll see you in hell first! I'm still captain of this ship.'

Still leaning comfortably against the rail, Jacaud pulled the Lüger from his pocket and shot him neatly through the left leg. Duclos screamed as the heavy slug splintered his knee-cap and rolled over on the deck, face twisted in agony.

'To encourage the rest of you,' Jacaud said calmly. 'Now get Bouvier up here.'

As Janvier turned, a quiet voice said: 'No need, monsieur. He is here.'

The man who stepped out of the saloon companionway was well past middle age. Tall and thin with stooping shoulders, he had the angular bony face of the ascetic and thinning grey hair. He wore a raincoat over pyjamas and a small, grey-haired woman clutched his arm fearfully. Behind them, two other passengers, clothes hastily pulled on, hesitated in the doorway.

'You are Pierre Bouvier?' Fenelon demanded.

'That is correct.'

Jacaud nodded to one of the sailors. 'Bring him over here.'

The woman's voice lifted at once, but Bouvier quietened her and allowed himself to be led forward. The sailor placed him with his back to the rail and went and stood beside Jacaud. 'What do you want with me?' Bouvier said.

'A month ago at Fort-Neuf you were public prosecutor at a trial,' Fenelon said. 'A trial at which six good friends of ours received the death sentence.'

'So, the OAS is in this?' Bouvier shrugged. 'I did my duty as I saw it. No man can do more.'

'You will, I am sure, allow us the same privilege, monsieur.' Fenelon produced a document from his pocket, unfolded it and read rapidly. ' "Pierre Bouvier, I must inform you that you have been tried in your absence and found guilty of the crime of treason against the Republic by a military tribunal of the Council of National Resistance." '

He paused and Bouvier cut in gently, 'And the sentence of the court is death?'

'Naturally,' Fenelon said. 'Have you anything to say?'

Bouvier shrugged and an expression of contempt crossed

his face. 'Say? Say what? There is no charge to answer. I know it and you know it. Frenchmen everywhere will—'

Jacaud plucked the sub-machine-gun from the hands of the sailor standing next to him, aimed quickly and fired a long burst that drove Bouvier back against the rail. He spun round, the material of his raincoat bursting into flame as bullets hammered across his back, and fell to the deck.

His wife cried his name once, took a single step forward and fainted, one of the passengers catching her as she fell backwards.

From the well-deck there was a strange, muted sigh from the crew and then there was only silence. Jacaud tossed the machine-gun to the sailor he had taken it from and went down the ladder without a backward glance. Fenelon looked as if he might be sick at any moment. He nodded to his men and hurriedly followed the big man, missing a step half-way down and almost falling to the deck.

They went over the side one by one and from the conning tower of the submarine the heavy machine-gun covered them menacingly. When they were all in the dinghy the sailors standing by the forward hatch hauled on the line quickly.

They left the dinghy to drift and everyone scrambled down through the hatch except Fenelon, who walked along the hull and climbed the ladder to the conning-tower. He stood looking up at the freighter for a moment as the two vessels drifted apart, and on the *Kontoro* there was a strange, uncanny silence.

The two sailors dismounted the machine-gun and disappeared. Fenelon remained only a moment or two longer before following. The conning-tower hatch clanged shut, the sound echoing flatly across the water.

On the *Kontoro* it was as if a spell had been broken and everyone surged forward to the rail. Janvier had never felt quite so helpless in his life before and for some unaccountable reason was strangely close to tears.

In the distance the wind was already beginning to lift the waves into whitecaps and he remembered the gale warning. *L'Alouette* sank beneath the waves like a grey ghost, the tricolour waved bravely, then that too disappeared and there was only the sea.

2

A THIN SEA FOG rolled in from Southampton Water as the taxi turned the corner and pulled in to the kerb. Anne Grant peered out through the window at the dim bulk of the building rearing into the night.

The original structure had been Georgian, so much was obvious, but the years had left their mark. A line of uneven steps lifted to the door, the paint cracked and peeling in the diffused yellow light of a street-lamp. Above it a small glass sign said 'Regent Hotel'.

She tapped on the partition and the driver opened it. 'Are you sure this is the place?'

'Regent Hotel, Farthing Lane. That's what you said and that's where I've brought you,' the man replied. 'It's only a doss-house, lady. The sort of place sailors come to for a kip on their first night ashore. What did you expect – the Ritz?'

She opened the door and got out, hesitating for a moment as she gazed up at the damp, crumbling façade of the hotel. Except for the lapping of water against the wharf pilings on the other side of the street, it was completely quiet. When a café door was opened somewhere in the middle distance the music and laughter might have been coming from another planet. She gave the driver ten shillings, told him to wait and went up the steps.

The corridor was dimly lit, a flight of stairs rising into the shadows at the far end. She wrinkled her nose in distaste at the stale smell compounded of cooking odours and urine, and moved forward.

There was a door to the left, the legend 'Bar' etched in acid on its frosted-glass panel. When she opened it she found herself in a long, narrow room, the far end shrouded in darkness. An old marble-topped bar fronted one wall, a cracked mirror behind it, and a man leaned beside the beer pumps reading a newspaper.

In one corner a drunk sprawled across a table face-down, his breath whistling uneasily through the stillness. Two men sat beside a small coal fire talking softly as they played cards. They turned to look at her and she closed the door and walked past them.

The barman was old and balding, with the sagging, disillusioned face of a man who had got past being surprised at anything. He folded his paper neatly and pushed it under the bar.

'What can I do for you?'

'I'm looking for a Mr van Sondergard,' she said. 'I understand he's staying here.'

Beyond the barman the two men by the fire were watching her in the mirror. One of them was small and squat with an untidy black beard. His companion was at least six feet tall with a hard, raw-boned face and hands that never stopped moving, shuffling the cards ceaselessly. He grinned and she returned his gaze calmly for a moment and looked away.

'Sondergard?' the barman said.

'She'll be meaning the Norwegian,' the tall man said in a soft Irish voice.

'Oh, that fella?' The barman nodded. 'Left yesterday.'

He ran a cloth over the surface of the bar and Anne Grant said blankly: 'But that isn't possible. I only hired him last week through the seamen's pool. I've a new motor-cruiser waiting at Lulworth now. He's supposed to run her over to the Channel Islands tomorrow.'

'You'll have a job catching him,' the Irishman cut in. 'He shipped out as quartermaster on the *Ben Alpin* this morning. Suez and all point east.' He got to his feet and crossed the room slowly. 'Anything I can do?'

Before she could reply a voice cut in harshly: 'How about some service this end for a change?'

She turned in surprise, realizing for the first time that a man stood in the shadows at the far end of the bar. The collar of his reefer jacket was turned up and a peaked cap shaded a face that was strangely white, the eyes like dark holes.

The barman moved towards him and the Irishman leaned against the bar and grinned at Anne. 'How about a drink?'

She shook her head gently, turned and walked to the door. She went out into the corridor and paused at the top of the steps. The taxi had gone and the fog was much thicker now, rolling in across the harbour, swirling round the street-lamps like some living thing.

She went down the steps and started along the pavement. When she reached the first lamp she paused and looked back. The Irishman and his friend were standing in the doorway. As she turned to move on, they came down the steps and moved after her.

II

Neil Mallory lit another cigarette, raised his whisky up to the light, then set it down. 'This glass is dirty.'

The barman walked forward, a truculent frown on his face. 'And what do you expect me to do about it?'

'Get me another one,' Mallory said calmly.

It was some indefinable quality in the voice, a look in the dark eyes, that made the barman swallow his angry retort and force a smile. He filled a fresh glass and pushed it across. 'We aim to please.'

'That's what I thought,' Mallory said his eyes following the Irishman and his friend as they went through the door after the woman. He took the whisky down in one easy swallow and went after them.

He stood at the top of the steps listening, but the fog smothered everything, even sound. A ship moved across the water, its fog-horn muted, alien and strange, touching something deep inside him. He shivered involuntarily. It was at that moment that Anne Grant cried out.

He went down the steps and stood listening, head slightly forward. The cry sounded again from the left, curiously flat and muffled by the fog, and he started to run.

He turned the corner on to a wharf at the far end of the street, running silently on rubber-soled feet, and took them by surprise. The two men were holding the struggling woman on the ground in the yellow light of a street-lamp.

As the Irishman turned in alarm, Mallory lifted a foot into his face. The man staggered back with a cry, rolled over the edge of the wharf and fell ten feet into the soft sludge of the mudbank.

The bearded man pulled a knife from his pocket and Mallory backed away. The man grinned and rushed him. As the knife came up Mallory grabbed for the wrist, twisting the arm up and out to one side, taut as a steel bar. The man screamed like a woman and dropped the knife. Mallory struck him a savage blow across the side of the neck with his forearm and he crumpled to the ground.

Anne Grant leaned against the wall, her face pale in the sickly yellow light, blood streaking one cheek from a deep scratch. She laughed shakily and brushed a tendril of dark hair from her forehead.

'You don't do things by halves, do you?'

'What's the point?' he said.

Her jersey suit was soiled and bedraggled, the blouse ripped to the waist. When she moved forward she limped heavily on her right foot. She stopped to pick up her handbag and the bearded man groaned and rolled on his back.

She looked down at him for a moment, then turned to Mallory. 'Are you going to call the police?'

'Do you want me to?'

'Not particularly.' She started to shake slightly. 'Suddenly it seems colder.'

He slipped off his reefer jacket and hung it around her shoulders. 'What you need is a drink. We'll go back to the hotel. You can use my room while I get you a taxi.'

She nodded down at the bearded man. 'Will he be all right?'

'His kind always are.'

He took her arm. They walked to the corner and turned into the street. It started to rain, a thin drizzle that beaded the iron railings like silver. There was a dull, aching pain in her ankle and the old houses floated in the fog, unreal and insubstantial, part of the dark dream from which she had yet to awaken, and the pavement seemed to move beneath her feet.

His arm was instantly around her, strong and reassuring,

and she turned and smiled into the strange, pale face, the dark eyes. 'I'll be all right. A little dizzy, that's all.'

The hotel sign swam out of the fog to meet them and they went through the entrance and mounted the rickety stairs. His room was at the end of the corridor and he opened the door, switched on the light and motioned her inside.

'Make yourself at home. I'll be back in a couple of minutes.'

The room had that strange, rather dead, atmosphere typical of cheap hotels the world over. There was a strip of worn carpet on the floor, an iron bed, a cheap wardrobe and locker. The one touch of luxury was the wash-basin in the corner by the window and she hobbled across to it.

Surprisingly, there was plenty of hot water and she washed her face and hands, then examined herself in the mirror that was screwed to the wall above the basin. The scratch on her cheek was only superficial, but her suit was ruined. Otherwise she seemed to have sustained no real damage. She was sitting on the edge of the bed examining her ankle when he returned.

He placed a half-bottle of brandy and two glasses on top of the bedside locker and dropped to one knee beside her. 'Any damage?'

She shook her head. 'A nasty graze, that's all.'

He pulled a battered fibre suitcase from under the bed and took out a heavy fisherman's sweater which he dropped into her lap. 'You'd better put that on. You're wet through.'

When she had pulled it over her head and rolled up the long sleeves, he rested her right foot on his knee and bandaged the damaged ankle expertly with a folded handkerchief. She watched quietly.

He was of medium height, with broad shoulders, and wore the sort of clothes common to sailors. A cheap blue flannel shirt and heavy working trousers in some dark material, held up by a broad leather belt with a brass buckle. But this was no ordinary man. He had a strange, hard, enigmatic face, the face of a man few would care to trifle with. The skin was clear and bloodless; black, crisp hair in a point to the forehead. The eyes were the strangest feature, so dark that all light died in them.

On the wharf he had been terrible in his anger, competent and deadly, and when he looked up suddenly his dark eyes stared through her like glass. For the first time that night genuine fear moved inside her and then his whole face creased into a smile of quite devastating charm, so great, that he seemed to undergo a complete personality change.

'You look about ten years old in that sweater.'

She smiled warmly and held out her hand. 'My name is Anne Grant and I'm very grateful to you.'

'Mallory,' he said. 'Neil Mallory.'

He touched her hand briefly, opened the brandy, poured a generous measure into one of the glasses and passed it to her. 'I got the barman to phone for a taxi. It might be some time before it gets here.'

'I'd like to know why the driver who brought me didn't wait,' she said. 'I asked him to.'

'They're not too keen on hanging around the dock area at night. It's a rough place and taxi-drivers are obvious targets.' He grinned. 'That goes double for good-looking young women, by the way.'

She smiled ruefully. 'Don't rub it in. I'd no idea what I was letting myself in for, but I was getting desperate. I'd been waiting in Lulworth for someone for most of the day. When it became obvious that he wasn't going to show up I decided to come looking for him.'

'Van Sondergard?' Mallory said. 'I heard you ask the barman about him.'

'Did you know him?'

'He had a room along the corridor from here. I had a drink with him once when he came in the bar. Nothing more than that. Where did you meet him?'

'I didn't,' she said. 'The whole thing was arranged through the seamen's pool. I told them I need someone to take a motor-cruiser across to the Channel Islands for me and captain her for a month or so until my sister-in-law and I were capable of looking after her ourselves. I also told them we'd prefer someone who'd done a little skin-diving. They put me in touch with Sondergard.' She sighed. 'He seemed rather keen on the idea. I'd love to know what changed his mind.'

'It was very simple really. He was sitting in the bar half drunk, feeling rather sorry for himself, when one of his old captains walked in, due out on the morning tide for Suez and short of a quartermaster. Three drinks was all it took for Sondergard to pack his duffel and go off with him. Sailors have a habit of doing things like that.'

He swallowed his brandy, took out an old leather cigarette case and offered her one. 'Are you a sailor, Mr Mallory?' she asked as he struck a match and held it forward in cupped hands.

He shrugged. 'Amongst other things. Why?'

'I wasn't sure. If I'd been asked I'd have said you were a soldier.'

'What makes you say that?'

'I think you could say I know the breed. My father was one and so was my husband. He was killed in Korea.'

There didn't seem anything to say and Mallory lit a cigarette and walked to the window. He peered outside, then turned.

'The motor-cruiser you mentioned, what kind is it?'

'A thirty-footer by Akerboon. Twin screw, steel hull.'

'Only the best?' He looked suitably impressed. 'How's she powered?'

'Penta petrol engine. She'll do about twenty-two knots at full stretch.'

'Depth-sounder, automatic steering, every latest refinement?' He grinned. 'I'd say she must have cost you all of seven thousand pounds.'

'Not me,' she said. 'My father-in-law. All I did was obey orders. He told me exactly what he wanted.'

'Sounds like a man who's used to getting his own way.'

She smiled. 'A habit he finds hard to break. He's a major-general.'

'Grant?' Mallory frowned. 'Are you talking about Iron Grant? The Western Desert man?'

She nodded. 'That's right. He's been living in the Channel Islands since he left the army. I keep house for him.'

'What does the old boy do with himself these days?'

'He's almost blind now,' she said, 'but he's still amazingly active and he's made quite a reputation for himself as a war historian. He uses a tape-recorder and his daughter Fiona and I type up his notes for him.'

'You said you wanted Sondergard to have had some experience as a skin-diver? Why was that?'

'It wasn't essential, but he could have been useful. In the fifteenth century a small fishing village and fortress on Île de Roc were inundated. The ruins are now about eight fathoms down a few hundred yards off-shore. We're making a survey. Fiona and I have been doing most of the diving so far.'

'Sounds interesting,' he said. 'You shouldn't find any difficulty in getting another man from the pool to take on a job like that.'

As he looked out of the window and down into the yellow fog she said quietly, 'I was wondering whether you might be interested?'

He turned slowly, a slight frown on his face. 'You don't know anything about me.'

'What is there to know? You told me yourself you were a sailor.'

'From necessity,' he said. 'Not choice.'

'You couldn't handle *Foxhunter*, you mean?'

'Is that her name? Oh, yes, I've handled boats like that before. I've even done a little skin-diving.'

'Eighty pounds a month and all found,' she said. 'Does that tempt you?'

He grinned reluctantly. 'It does indeed, Mrs Grant.'

She held out her hand in a strangely boyish gesture. 'I'm glad.'

He held it for a moment, looking into her eyes gravely. Her smile faded, and again she was conscious of that vague irrational fear. Something must have shown on her face. Mallory's hand tightened on hers and he smiled gently. In that single moment her fear disappeared and an inexplicable tenderness flooded through her. A horn sounded outside in the street and he helped her to her feet.

'Time to go. Where are you staying?'

'An hotel in the town centre.'

'You should cause quite a sensation going through the foyer,' he told her as he took her arm and helped her across to the door.

The fog was clearing a little as he handed her into the taxi. She wound down the window and leaned out to him. 'I've several things to attend to tomorrow, so I can't get down to Lulworth again until the evening. I'll see you down there.'

He nodded. 'You could do with a morning in bed.'

She smiled wanly in the pale light, but before she could reply the taxi moved away. Mallory stood looking into the fog, listening to the sound of the engine die into the distance, then turned and went up the steps.

When he entered the bar the barman was still reading his newspaper. 'Where are they?' Mallory asked.

The man lifted the flap and jerked his thumb at the rear door. 'In there.'

When Mallory opened the door he found the Irishman sitting at a wooden table beside a coal fire, a basin of hot water in front of him. His clothes were plastered with mud and he was wiping blood from a gash that ran from his ear to the point of his chin. The man with the black beard lay on an old horse-hair sofa, clutching his right arm and moaning softly.

The Irishman lurched to his feet, his eyes wild. 'You bastard. What were you trying to do, kill us?'

'I told you to frighten the girl a little, that's all, but you tried to be clever. Anything you got, you asked for.' Mallory took several banknotes from his wallet and tossed them on the table. 'That should settle the account.'

'Ten quid?' the Irishman cried. 'Ten lousy quid! What about Freddy? You've broken his arm.'

'No skin off my nose,' Mallory said calmly. 'Tell him to try the Health Service.'

He walked out and the Irishman slumped into his chair again, head swimming. The barman came in and stood looking at him. 'How do you feel?'

'Bloody awful. Who is that bastard?'

'Mallory?' The barman shrugged. 'I know one thing. He's the coldest fish I've ever met and I've known a few.' He looked down at the bearded man and shook his head. 'Freddy doesn't look too good. Maybe I should phone for an ambulance?'

'You can do what the hell you like,' the Irishman said violently.

The barman moved to the door, shaking his head. 'You know what they say. When you sup with the Devil you need a long spoon. I reckon you and Freddy got a little too close.'

He sighed heavily and disappeared into the bar.

— 3 —

THE ROOM WAS half in shadow, the only light the shaded lamp on the desk. The man who sat sideways in the swivel chair, gazing out through the broad window at the glittering lights of London, was small, the parchment face strangely ageless. It was the face of an extraordinary human being, a man who had known pain and who had succeeded in moving beyond it.

The green intercom on his desk buzzed once and he swung round in the chair and flicked a switch. 'Yes?'

'Mr Ashford is here, Sir Charles.'

'Send him in.'

The door opened soundlessly and Ashford advanced across the thick carpet, a tall, greying man in his forties with the worried face of the professional civil servant who had spent too much of his life close to the seats of power.

He sat down in the chair opposite, opened his briefcase and produced a file which he placed carefully on the desk. Sir Charles pushed a silver cigarette box across to him.

'What's the verdict?'

'Oh, the PM agrees with you entirely. The whole thing must be investigated. But we don't want the newspapers getting on to it. You'll have to be damn careful.'

'We usually are,' Sir Charles said frostily.

'There's just one thing the PM isn't too happy about.' Ashford opened the file on the desk. 'This fellow Mallory. Is he really the best man for the job?'

'More than that,' Sir Charles said. 'He's the best man I've got and he's worked with the Deuxième Bureau before with some success. In fact, they've asked for him twice. His mother was French, of course. They like that.'

'It's this shocking affair in Perak in 1954 that the PM isn't happy about. Dammit all, the man was lucky to escape prison.'

Sir Charles pulled the file across the desk and turned it round. 'This is the record of a quite exceptional officer.' He put on a pair of rimless spectacles and started to read aloud, selecting items at random. ' "Special Air Service during the war . . . dropped into France three times . . . betrayed to the Gestapo . . . survived six months at Sachsenhausen . . . paratroop captain in Palestine . . . major in Korea . . . two years in a Chinese prison camp in Manchuria . . . released 1953 . . . posted to Malaya, January 1954, on special service." ' He closed the file and looked up. 'A lieutenant-colonel at thirty. Probably the youngest in the army at that time.'

'And kicked out at thirty-one,' Ashford countered.

Sir Charles shrugged. 'He was told to clear the last Communist guerrilla out of Perak and he did it. A little ruthlessly perhaps, but he did it. His superiors then heaved a sigh of relief and threw him to the wolves.'

'And you were waiting to catch him, I suppose?'

Sir Charles shook his head. 'I let him drift for a year. Bombay, Alexandria, Algiers. I knew where he was. When I was satisfied that the iron was finally in his soul I pulled him in. He's worked for me ever since.'

Ashford sighed and got to his feet. 'Have it your own way, but if anything goes wrong . . .'

Sir Charles smiled softly. 'I know, I end up like Neil Mallory. Out on my ear.'

Ashford flushed, turned and crossed the room quickly. The door closed behind him and Sir Charles sat there thinking about it all. After a while he flicked a switch on the intercom. 'Send in Mallory.'

He lit a cigarette and stood by the window, gazing out over the city, still the greatest in the world, whatever anyone tried to say. When he opened the window he could smell the river and the sound from a ship's hooter drifted faintly on the quiet air as it moved down from the Pool.

He was tired and there was a slight ache somewhere behind his right eye. Something he should really see his doctor about. On the other hand, perhaps it was better not to know? He wondered whether Mallory would survive long enough ever to take his place behind the desk in this quiet room. It would have been a comforting thought, but he knew it was rather unlikely.

The door clicked open behind him and closed again. When he turned Mallory was standing beside the desk. An easy-fitting suit of dark worsted outlined his broad shoulders and in the diffused white light his aquiline face gave an impression of strength and breeding, not out of place anywhere.

Sir Charles moved back to his chair and sat down. 'How are you, Neil?'

'Pretty fit, sir. I've just had six weeks on the island.'

'I know. How's your shoulder?'

'No more trouble. They've done a good job.'

Sir Charles nodded. 'You'll have to be a little more careful next time, won't you?' He opened a file, took out a typewritten document and pushed it across. 'Have a look at that.'

He occupied himself with some other papers and Mallory skimmed through the three closely typed sheets of foolscap. When he had finished he handed them back, face expressionless.

'Where's the *Kontoro* now?'

'The destroyer which found her took her straight into Brest. For the time being the French are holding the lid down tight. Complete security and so on. They can't keep it quiet for more than three or four days. These things always leak out sooner or later.'

'What are they trying to do about it?'

'The usual round-up of anyone who's even remotely suspected of being connected with the OAS or CNR. On top of that, the Deuxième Bureau and the Brigade Criminelle, backed by every available military security agent, have been given one order: Find that Submarine.'

'I shouldn't have thought that would be too difficult.'

'I'm not so sure,' Sir Charles said. 'For one thing this is no ordinary submarine. She's quite small. A thing the Germans were working on at the end of the war.'

'What's her radius?'

'Not much over a thousand.'

'Which means she could be based in Spain or even Portugal?'

'The French are working along those lines right now, but they've got to be careful. On top of that, they're combing the entire Biscay coast, every creek, every island.' He sighed heavily. 'I've a horrible feeling that they're completely wasting their time.'

'I wondered when you were coming to that,' Mallory said.

Sir Charles grinned impishly like a schoolboy, opened a drawer and took out a map which he unfolded across the desk. It was a large-scale Admiralty chart of the Channel Islands and the Golfe de St Malo.

'Ever hear of Philippe de Beaumont?'

'The paratroop colonel? The one who helped bring de Gaulle back to power?'

'That's right. He was one of the leaders of the military coup of May 1958 and a member of the original Committee of Public Safety. Philippe, Comte de Beaumont. Last survivor of one of the greatest of the French military families.'

'And he's living in the Channel Islands?'

'He was the great advocate of a French Algeria. When de Gaulle came down on the side of independence he resigned his commission and left France.' Sir Charles drew a circle on the chart about thirty miles south-west of Guernsey. 'There's an island called Île de Roc owned by old Hamish Grant.'

'You mean Iron Grant, the Western Desert general?'

'That's right. Been living there for five years with his daughter Fiona, writing up the war. His daughter-in-law Mrs Anne Grant seems to run things. Her husband was killed in Korea. About a mile west of Île de Roc there's a smaller island called St Pierre.'

'And de Beaumont's living there?'

'He bought it from Grant two years ago. There's a sort of castle up on top of the rock, one of those mock-Gothic jobs some crank built during the nineteenth century.'

'And you think he's up to no good?'

'Let's put it this way. The French have checked on him for two years now and can't find even the hint of a connection with either the OAS or CNR, although he's known to be sympathetic to their aims. Frankly, even their Foreign Office think he's simply a *grand seigneur* who won't come home because he's annoyed with the general.'

'And you don't agree?'

'I might have done until yesterday evening.'

'What happened to change your mind?'

'I've had a man keeping an eye on de Beaumont for a year now, just as a precaution. There's a small hotel on Île de Roc. He was working there as barman. He went missing Tuesday. Yesterday evening he drifted in on the evening tide. The police went over from Guernsey and picked up the body. Needless to say there isn't even a hint of foul play.'

'You think he may have seen something?' Sir Charles shrugged. 'I don't see why not. *L'Alouette* left Brest on a routine training patrol two days ago. She could have called at St Pierre and our man could have seen her. It's pretty obvious that he came across something, and the Deuxième agree with me. They're sending a man across to work with you on this thing.'

'I wondered when we were coming to that,' Mallory said.

Sir Charles pushed a file across. 'Raoul Guyon, aged twenty-nine. He was a captain in a colonial parachute regiment. Went straight to Indo-China from St Cyr in 1952.'

Mallory looked down at the photograph. It showed a young man, slim-hipped and wiry, the sleeves of his camouflaged jacket rolled up to expose sunburnt arms. The calm, sun-blackened face, dark eyes, were shaded by a peaked cap that somehow gave him a strangely sinister, forbidding appearance.

'Why did he leave the army?'

'God knows,' Sir Charles said. 'I should imagine six years in Algeria was enough for any man. He asked to be placed on unpaid leave and Legrande of the Deuxième offered him a job.'

'When do I meet him?'

'You don't, for the moment. Apparently, he's quite a talented painter. He's using that as a cover. Should book in at the hotel on Île de Roc sometime tomorrow.'

'What about me?'

'A little more complicated, I'm afraid. If de Beaumont *is* up to no good, then he'll be expecting company. We need to make your background convincing enough to fool him for at least a day or two, and I might as well tell you now that's all the time we can allow.'

'What do I do?' Mallory asked.

Sir Charles opened another file and passed a photo across. The girl who stared out at Mallory was somewhere in her twenties, dark hair close-cropped like a young boy's, almond-shaped eyes slanting across high cheekbones. She was not beautiful in any conventional sense and yet in a crowd she would have stood out.

'Anne Grant?' he said instinctively.

Sir Charles nodded. 'She came over this morning to finalize the purchase of a thirty-foot motor-cruiser called *Foxhunter*. It's moored at Lulworth now. Apparently, she hired a seaman through the pool to skipper the thing for a couple of months till she and her sister-in-law get used to it for themselves. A big boat for a couple of girls.'

Mallory nodded. 'I ran one in and out of Tangiers for a while back in '59. Remember?'

'Think you could handle one again?'

Mallory grinned. 'I don't see why not.'

Sir Charles nodded in satisfaction. 'First you'll have to get rid of this seaman. After that all you have to do is make sure you get his job.'

'That shouldn't prove too difficult.' Mallory hesitated and went on: 'Couldn't we work something out with General Grant? Let him know what we're after? He'd be certain to co-operate.'

Sir Charles shook his head. 'Before you knew where you were he'd be running the whole damned show. In any case, I'm never happy about bringing amateurs into these things if it can be avoided. They give the game away too easily. Use him by all means, but only in an extreme situation where there's no other way.' He got to his feet abruptly. 'I want results on this one, Neil, and I want them fast. Cut any corners you have to. I'll back you all the way.'

One corner of Mallory's mouth twitched ironically. 'I seem to remember someone saying that to me once before.'

Sir Charles's face was grave and dispassionate, the eyes calm, and Mallory knew beyond a shadow of a doubt that if necessary the old man would not have the slightest compunction in throwing him to the wolves.

'I'm sorry, Neil,' he said.

'At least I know where I stand with you.' Mallory shrugged. 'That's something.'

Sir Charles took an old gold watch from his pocket and checked it quickly. 'You'll have to get moving. I've arranged for you to be fully briefed by G3 at eight o'clock. They'll give you everything. Money, seaman's papers and a special transmitter. Report your arrival. After that, radio silence till you have some news. I've arranged for three MTBs to proceed to Jersey, ostensibly for shallow-water exercises. The moment we get anything positive from you they'll move in so fast de Beaumont won't know what's hit him.'

Mallory walked to the door. As he opened it, the old man said: 'Good luck, Neil. With the right kind this could turn out to be a pretty straightforward one.'

'Aren't they all?' Mallory said dryly, and the door closed gently behind him.

— 4 —

PROFESSOR YOSHIYAMA was little more than five feet in height and wore a judo jacket and trousers many times washed, a black belt around his waist. The face was the man's most outstanding feature, the skin the colour of parchment and almost transparent. There was nothing weak there. Only strength and intelligence and a kind of gentleness. It could have been that of a saint or scholar. It was, in fact, the face of a great master who had practised his art for more than fifty years.

His voice was dry and rather pedantic, the vowels clipped slightly, but the dozen men sitting cross-legged on the floor were giving him all their attention. High in the balcony of the gymnasium, Mallory leaned on the rail and watched.

'The literal meaning of the two Japanese characters which make up the word karate is empty hands,' Yoshiyama said. 'This refers to the fact that karate developed as a system of self-defence relying solely on unarmed techniques. The system was first developed centuries ago on the island of Okinawa during a time when the inhabitants were forbidden to carry arms on pain of death.'

There was a strangely old-fashioned flavour to everything he said, as if he were repeating a lesson painfully learned. He turned to a large wall chart which carried an outline of a human figure with all vital points, and their respective striking areas, clearly marked.

'The system consists of techniques of blocking or deflecting an attack and of counter-attacking by punching, striking or kicking.' He turned, his face bland, expressionless. 'But there is more to karate than well-practised tricks and physical force.' He tapped his head. 'There is also the mental application. You will be taught how to focus all your strength and energy on a single target at any given time. Let me show you what I mean.'

He nodded briefly and his two assistants picked up three lengths of planking. They were perhaps two feet long, each plank an inch thick. The two men took up their positions in front of Yoshiyama, holding the three planks between them and slightly above waist-level. In a single incredibly fluid motion the old man's left foot stamped forward and his right fist moved up from the waist, knuckles extended. There was a report like a gunshot and the planks split from end to end.

A quick murmur rose from the class and Yoshiyama turned, quite unperturbed. 'It is also possible to snap a brick in half with the edge of the hand.' He permitted himself one brief smile. 'But this requires practice. Major Adams, please,'

A small, wiry, middle-aged man with greying hair and a black patch over his right eye stood up at the back of the class and came forward. Like Yoshiyama, he wore a black belt, but where his left arm should have been a metal limb dangled.

'You will observe that Major Adams is rather a small man,' Yoshiyama said. 'He is also no longer in the prime of life. If we add to this the fact that he has only one arm one would not in normal circumstances give him much hope of surviving any kind of physical assault. As it happens, however, his circumstances are far from normal.'

He nodded to one of his assistants and moved out of the way. The assistant, a young, powerfully-built Japanese, ran to the far side of the gymnasium. He selected a knife from a table which contained an assortment of weapons, turned and ran forward, a blood-curdling cry surging from his throat.

He swerved to one side, came to a dead stop, then moved in quickly, the knife slashing at the major's face. Adams moved with incredible speed, warding off the attacking arm with an extended knife-hand block. At the same moment he fell diagonally forward to one side and delivered a roundhouse kick to the groin. In what was virtually the same motion he kicked at his opponent's knee-joint with the same foot. The Japanese somersaulted, ended flat on his back, and the foot thudded across his windpipe.

For a moment they lay there and then both men scrambled to their fect grinning widely. 'In other circumstances, and had the blows been delivered with full force, my assistant would now be dead.' Yoshiyama said simply.

Adams picked up a towel, started to wipe sweat from his face and caught sight of Mallory in the gallery. He nodded briefly, said something to Yoshiyama and moved across to the door. Mallory met him in the corridor outside.

'What are you trying to do, go out in a blaze of glory?'

Adams grinned. 'Every so often I get so sick of the sight of that damned desk that I could blow my top. Yoshiyama provides a most efficient safety-valve.' He ran a hand over his right hip and winced slightly. 'That last fall hurt like hell. I must be getting old.'

As they mounted the stairs at the end of the corridor, Mallory thought about Adams. One of the best agents the department had ever had; all the guts in the world and a mind like a steel trap until the night he'd got too close for someone's comfort and they'd tied a Mills bomb to the handle of his hotel bedroom in Cairo.

And now he was a desk man, running G3, the intelligence

section that was the pulse-beat of the whole organization. Some people would have said he was lucky, but not Adams.

He opened a door and walked through a small, neat office. A middle-aged, desiccated-looking spinster with neat grey hair and rimless spectacles sat behind the typewriter. She glanced up, an expression of disapproval on her face, and Adams grinned.

'Don't say it, Milly. Just tell them I'm ready.'

He led the way into his own office. Like Sir Charles's, it commanded a fine view of the river, the desk standing by the window. He opened a cupboard, took out a heavy bathrobe and pulled it on.

'Sorry about the delay. I thought Sir Charles would keep you for an hour at least.'

'More like fifteen minutes,' Mallory said. 'He always goes straight to the heart of things with the sticky ones.'

'I wouldn't call it that,' Adams said. 'Interesting more than anything else. Whole thing could be just a storm in a teacup. Let's go into the projection room.'

He opened the far door and they descended a few steps into a small hall. There were several rows of comfortable seats and a large screen. The place was quite deserted. They sat down and Mallory offered Adams a cigarette.

'Any gaps in this one?'

Adams exhaled with a sigh of pleasure and shook his head. 'I don't think so. Nothing important, anyway. Has the old man told you much?'

'He's outlined the job, told me who the principals are. No more than that.'

'Let's get started, then.' Adams turned and glanced up at the projection box where a dim light showed. 'Ready when you are.'

A section of film started to run a few moments later. It showed a submarine entering port slowly, her crew lining the deck.

'To start with, that's what all the fuss is about,' Adams said. '*L'Alouette*. Taken at Oran a couple of years ago.'

'She looks rather small. There can't be more than a dozen men on deck.'

'Originally a German U-boat. Type XXIII. Just over a

hundred feet long. Does about twelve kilometres submerged. Crew of sixteen.'

'What about armament?'

'Two 21″ torpedoes in the bow and she doesn't carry spares.'

'Doesn't leave much room for mistakes.'

Adams nodded. 'They never really amounted to anything. This one was built at Deutsches Werft in 1945 and sunk with all hands in the Baltic. She was raised in '46, refitted and handed over to the French.'

The film ended and a slide appeared. It showed a young French naval officer, eyes serious beneath the uniform cap, the rather boyish face schooled to gravity.

'Henri Fenelon, full lieutenant. He's her commander. Age twenty-six, unmarried. Born in Nantes. Father still lives there. Runs a small wine-exporting business.'

Mallory studied the face for a moment or two. 'Looks weak to me. Ever been in action?'

Adams shook his head. 'Why do you ask?'

Mallory shrugged. 'He looks as if he could crack easily. What's his political background?'

'That's the surprising thing. We can't find any evidence of an OAS connection at all.'

'Probably did it for adventure,' Mallory said. 'He only needed half a dozen men in the crew to agree with him. They could have coerced the rest.'

'Sounds feasible,' Adams said. 'Let's move on.'

Various slides followed. There was an Admiralty chart of Île de Roc, with the harbour, the hotel and General Grant's house all clearly marked. St Pierre was little more than a rock lifting a hundred or so feet out of the sea and crowned by the Victorian Gothic castle.

Mallory shook his head. 'God knows how they ever managed to build the damned thing out there.'

'1861,' Adams said. 'A self-made industrialist called Bryant. Bit of a megalomaniac. Saw himself as king of the castle and so on. Cost him better than a hundred thousand to build the place and that was real money in those days.'

'I can't see a jetty. Is it on the other side?'

'There's a cave at the base of the cliffs. If you look carefully you can see the entrance. The jetty's inside.'

The castle faded and another picture took its place. It was that of a distinguished-looking man with silvering hair, eyes calm in a sensitive, aquiline face.

'De Beaumont?' Mallory said.

Adams nodded. 'Philippe, Comte de Beaumont. One of the oldest of the great French families. He's even a rather distant blood relation of you-know-who, which makes the whole thing even more complicated.'

'I know quite a lot about his military history,' Mallory said. 'After all, he's something of a hero to paratroopers the world over. He came over here during the war and joined de Gaulle, didn't he?'

'That's right. Received just about every decoration possible. Afterwards he went to Indo-China as a colonel of colonial paratroops. The Viets picked him up at the surrender of Dien-Bien-Phu in 1954. After his release he returned to France and was posted to Algeria. He was always at loggerheads with the top brass. Once had an argument with the old man himself at an official reception over what constitutes war in the modern sense.'

'That should have been enough to get him put out to grass on its own.'

Adams shrugged. 'They needed him, I suppose. After all, he *was* the most outstanding paratroop colonel in Algeria at that time. Handled all the dirtier jobs the top brass didn't want to soil its fingers with.'

'So he helped bring de Gaulle back to power?'

'That's right. A prime mover in the Algérie Française movement. The general, of course, kicked him right in the teeth by granting independence to Algeria after all.'

'And de Beaumont cleared out?'

'After Challe's rather abortive little coup last year. Whether or not he was actually mixed up in that little lot we can't be certain. The point is that he left France and bought this place on St Pierre from Hamish Grant. Caused quite a stir in the French papers at the time.'

'And he's kept his nose clean since then?'

'As a whistle.' Adams grinned. 'Even the French can't turn anything up on him. He runs a boat, by the way. Forty-foot twin-screw motor-yacht named *Fleur de Lys*. The very latest thing for deep-sea cruising with depth-sounder, automatic pilot and 100 h.p. DAF diesels. A bit of a recluse, but he's been seen in St Helier occasionally. What do you think?'

'I'd say he has the kind of inbred arrogance that can only come from a thousand years of always being right, or at least thinking you were,' Mallory said. 'Men like him can never sit still. They usually have to be plotting at one thing or another. Comes from that natural assumption that anything conflicting with their own views must be wrong.'

'Interesting,' Adams said. 'He has more the look of a seventeenth-century puritan to me. One of the thin-lipped intolerant variety. A damned good colonel in the New Model Army.'

'Jesus and no quarter?' Mallory shook his head. 'He's no bigot. Simply a rather arrogant aristocrat with a limited field of vision and an absolute conviction of the rightness of his own actions. When he decides on a plan of attack he follows it through to the bitter end. That's what made him such an outstanding officer. For men like him the rot sets in only if they step outside themselves and see just how much the whole damned thing is costing.'

'An interesting analysis, considering you've only seen his photo.'

'I know about him as a soldier,' Mallory said. 'At Dien-Bien-Phu they offered to fly him out. He was too valuable to lose. He refused. In his last message he said they'd been wrong from headquarters staff down to himself. That the whole Dien-Bien-Phu strategy had been a terrible mistake. He said that if his men had to stay and pay the price the least he could do was stay and pay it with them.'

'Which probably accounted for his popularity with the troops,' Adams said.

'Men like him are never loved by anyone,' Mallory said. 'Even themselves.'

De Beaumont's picture was replaced by another. The face which stared down at them was strong and brutal, the eyes cold, hair close-cropped.

'Paul Jacaud,' Adams said. 'Aged forty. Parents unknown. He was raised by the madame of a waterfront brothel in Marseilles. Three years in the Resistance, joined the paratroops after the war. He was sergeant-major in de Beaumont's regiment. Medaille Militaire plus a courtmartial for murder that failed for lack of evidence.'

'And still with his old boss?'

'That's right. You can make what you like out of that. Let's have a look at the angels now.'

A picture of Hamish Grant flashed on the screen, a famous one taken in the Ardennes in the winter of '44. Montgomery stood beside him, grinning as they examined a map. He was every inch Iron Grant, great shoulders bulging under a sheepskin coat.

'Quite a man,' Mallory said.

'And he hasn't changed much. Of course, his sight isn't too good, but he's still going strong. Written a couple of pretty good campaign histories of the last war.'

'What about the family?'

'He's a widower. Son was killed in Korea. At the moment his household consists of his daughter Fiona, daughter-in-law Anne and an ex-Gurkha *naik* called Jagbir who was with him during the war. This is the daughter.'

Fiona Grant had long blonde hair and a heart-shaped face that was utterly appealing. 'Rather a handful, that one,' Adams said. 'She was raised in the south of France, which didn't help. They tried Roedean, but that was a complete fiasco. She was finally settled in a Paris finishing school, which apparently suited her. She's at home at the moment.'

'I like her,' Mallory said. 'She's got a good mouth.'

'Then see what you think of this one. Anne Grant, the old man's daughter-in-law.'

It was the same photograph that Sir Charles had shown him and Mallory stared up at it, his throat for some unaccountable reason going dry. It was as if they had met before and yet he knew that to be impossible. The almond-shaped eyes seemed to come to life, holding his gaze, and he shook his head slightly.

'She's over here now to finalize the purchase of a new boat.'

'Sir Charles told me that much. What about this man Sondergard she's hired through the pool?'

'We'll ship him out somewhere. There's no difficulty there.

I've already got a little scheme in mind to bring you and Anne Grant together.'

They next saw the picture of a Frenchwoman called Juliette Vincente who was working at the hotel on Île de Roc. Nothing was known against her and she seemed quite harmless, as did Owen Morgan, her employer. When the Welshman's face faded away, Mallory straightened in his seat, thinking they had finished. To his surprise another face appeared.

He turned to Adams in surprise. 'But this is Raoul Guyon, the man I'm going to work with. I've already seen his picture. What's the idea?'

Adams shrugged. 'I'm not sure, but I'm not really happy about the way the French are handling this business. I've got a hunch that old spider Legrande and the Deuxième aren't telling us all they could. In the circumstances it might prove useful to know everything there is to know about Raoul Guyon. He's rather unusual.'

Mallory looked again at the photo Sir Charles had shown him. The slim, wiry figure in the camouflage uniform, the sun-blackened face, the calm, expressionless eyes.

'Tell me about him.'

'Raoul Guyon, aged twenty-nine. Went straight to Indo-China from St Cyr in 1952. He's the only known survivor of his particular cadet class for that year, which is enough to set any man apart for a start.'

'He wasn't at Dien-Bien-Phu?'

Adams shook his head. 'No, but he was at plenty of other hot spots. He was up to his ears in it in Algeria. There was some talk of a girl. Moorish, I think. She was murdered by the FLN and it had a big effect on him. He was badly wounded a day or two later.'

There followed a picture of Guyon half-raised on a stretcher, his chest heavily bandaged, blood soaking through. The face was sunken, beyond pain, the eyes stared into an abyss of loneliness.

'There's a lad who's been through the fire,' Mallory said.

'And then some. Commander of the Legion of Honour, Croix de la Valeur Militaire and half a dozen mentions in despatches. On top of that, he paints like an angel.'

'A man to be reckoned with.'

'And don't you forget it.'

For the next twenty minutes they continued to sit there, discussing questions of time and place, some important technical data and various other items, all of which were relevant to the success of the operation. When they finally returned to the office Adams sat behind his desk and nodded at a large and well-filled in-tray.

'Look at that,' he said with an expression of disgust. 'God in heaven, but I'd trade places with you, Neil.'

Mallory grinned. 'I wonder? Is there anything else?'

Adams shook his head. 'Call in at the technical branch. They've got a rather neat line in transmitters for you. They'll give you a call-sign, suitable code and so on. Come back in half an hour. I'll have some identity papers and things ready plus a rough outline of my little scheme to bring you and Mrs Grant together.'

'Now *that* I look forward to,' Mallory said.

And the strange thing was that he really did. As he went along the corridor and descended the stairs to the technical branch the memory of her haunted him. Those strange eyes searching, looking for something.

He sighed heavily. Taking it all in all, it looked as if this whole affair could become really complicated.

— 5 —

'*FOXHUNTER!* Ahoy! Ahoy! *Foxhunter!*'

The boat lay at anchor fifty yards out from the beach, her cream and yellow hull a vivid splash of colour against the white cliffs of the cove. A small wind moved in from the sea, lifting the water across the shingle, and darkness was falling fast.

Anne Grant shivered slightly as a light drizzle drifted across her face. She was tired and hungry and her ankle had started to ache again. She opened her mouth to hail the boat a second time and Neil Mallory appeared on deck. He dropped over the stern into the dinghy and rowed towards her.

He was wearing knee-length rubber boots and when the prow of the fibre-glass dinghy ground on the wet shingle he stepped into the shallows and swung it round so that the stern was beached.

He held out his hand for the girl's suitcase and smiled. 'How do you feel?'

'All the better for being here,' she said. 'It's been a long day. I had a lot of running around to do.'

She was wearing a tweed suit with a narrow skirt and a sheepskin coat. He helped her into the stern seat, pushed off and rowed for the boat.

Anne took in the flared, raking bow and long, sloping deckhouse of *Foxhunter* with a conscious pleasure. As she breathed deeply of the good sea air she smiled at Mallory.

'What do you think of her?'

'*Foxhunter?*' He nodded. 'She's a thoroughbred all right, but that's still an awful lot of boat for two women to handle as a regular thing. How old is your sister-in-law?'

'Fiona is eighteen, whatever that proves. I think you underrate us.'

'What about the engines?' he said. 'They'll need looking after.'

'We've no worries there. Owen Morgan, who runs the hotel on the island, is a retired ship's engineer. He'll give us any help we need and there's always Jagbir.'

'Who's he?' Mallory said quickly, remembering that he wasn't supposed to know.

'The general's orderly. He was a *naik* in a Gurkha regiment. They've been together since the early days of the war. He hasn't had what you would call a formal education, but he's still the best cook I've ever come across, and he has an astonishing aptitude for anything mechanical.'

'Sounds like a good man to have around the house,' Mallory said.

They bumped against the side of *Foxhunter* and he handed her up the short ladder and followed with her suitcase. 'What time would you like to leave?'

She took the case from him. 'As soon as you like. Have you eaten?'

'Not since noon.'

'I'll change and make some supper. We can leave afterwards.'

When she had gone Mallory pulled the dinghy round to the stern and hoisted it over the rail. By now darkness was falling fast and he turned on the red and green navigation lights and went below.

He found her working at the stove in the galley, wearing old denims and a polo-necked sweater that somehow made her look more feminine than ever. She looked over her shoulder and smiled.

'Bacon and eggs all right?'

'Suits me,' he said.

When it was ready they sat opposite each other at the saloon table and ate in companionable silence. As she poured coffee a sudden flurry of rain drummed against the roof.

She looked up at him, eyebrows raised. 'That doesn't sound too good. What's the forecast?'

'Three-to-four wind, rain squalls. Nothing to get worked up about. Are you worried?'

'Not in the slightest.' She smiled slightly. 'I always like to know what I'm getting into, that's all.'

'Don't we all, Mrs Grant?' He got to his feet. 'I think we ought to get started.'

When he went on deck the wind had increased, scattering the drizzle in silver cobwebs through the navigation lights. He went into the wheelhouse, pulled on his reefer jacket and spent a couple of minutes looking at the chart.

The door swung open, a flurry of wind lifting the chart like a sail, and Anne Grant appeared at his elbow. She was wearing her sheepskin coat and a scarf was tied around her head, peasant-fashion.

'All set?' he said.

She nodded, her eyes gleaming with excitement in the light from the chart table. He pressed the starter. The engines coughed once asthmatically, then roared into life. He took *Foxhunter* round in a long, sweeping curve and out through the entrance of the cove into the Channel.

The masthead light swung rhythmically from side to side as the swell started to roll beneath them and spray hit the window. A couple of points to starboard the red and green navigation lights of a steamer were clearly visible a mile out to sea. Mallory reduced speed to ten knots and they ploughed forward into the darkness, the sound of the engines a muted throbbing on the night air.

He grinned at her. 'Nothing much wrong there. With any kind of luck we should have a clear run.'

'When do you want me to take over?'

He shrugged. 'No rush. Get some sleep. I'll call you when I feel tired.'

The door banged behind her and a small trapped wind whistled round the wheelhouse and died in a corner. He pulled the hinged seat down from the wall, lit a cigarette and settled back comfortably, watching the foam curl along the prow.

This was the sort of thing he looked forward to on a voyage. To be alone with the sea and the night. The world outside retreated steadily as *Foxhunter* moved into the darkness and he started to work his way methodically through his briefing from beginning to end, considering each point carefully before moving on to another.

It was in recalling that de Beaumont had been in Indo-China that he remembered that Raoul Guyon had been there also. Mallory frowned and lit another cigarette. There might be a connection, although Adams hadn't said anything about such a possibility. On the other hand, Guyon hadn't been a Viet prisoner, which made a difference. One hell of a difference.

He checked the course, altering it a point to starboard, and settled back again in the seat, turning the collar of his reefer jacket up around his face. Gradually his mind wandered away on old forgotten paths and he thought of people he had known, incidents which had happened, good and bad, with a sort of measured sadness. His life seemed to be like a dark sea rolling towards the edge of the world, hurrying him to nowhere.

He checked his watch, and found, with a sense of surprise, that it was after midnight. The door opened softly, coinciding with a spatter of rain on the window, and Anne Grant came in carrying a tray.

'You promised to call me,' she said reproachfully. 'I couldn't believe my eyes when I wakened and saw the time. You've been up here a good four hours.'

'I feel fine,' he said. 'Could go on all night.'

She placed the tray on the chart table and filled two mugs from a covered pot. 'I've made tea. You didn't seem to care for the coffee at supper.'

'Is there anything you don't notice?' he demanded.

She handed him a mug and smiled in the dim light. 'The soldier's drink.'

'What are you after?' he said. 'The gory details?'

She pulled down the other seat and handed him a sandwich. 'Only what you want to tell me.'

He considered the point and knew that, as always, a partial truth was better than a direct lie. 'I was kicked out in 1954.'

'Go on,' she said.

'My pay didn't stretch far enough.' He shrugged. 'You know how it is. I was in charge of a messing account and borrowed some cash to tide me over. Unfortunately the auditors arrived early that month. They usually do in cases like mine.'

'I don't believe you,' she said deliberately.

'Suit yourself.' He got to his feet and stretched. 'She's on automatic pilot, so you'll be all right for a while. I'll be up at quarter to four to change course.'

She sat there looking at him without speaking, her eyes very large in the half-light, and he turned, opened the door and left her there.

He went down to the cabin and flopped on his bunk, staring up at the bulkhead through the darkness. There had been women before, there always were, but only to satisfy a need, never to get close to. That had been the way for a long time and he had been content. Now this strange, quiet girl with her cropped hair had come into his life and quietly refused to be pushed aside. His last conscious thought was of her face glowing in the darkness, and she was smiling at him.

II

He was not aware of having slept, only of being awake and looking at his watch and realizing with a sense of shock that it was half-three. He pulled on his jacket and went on deck.

There was quite a sea running and cold rain stung his face as he walked along the heaving deck and opened the glass-panelled door of the wheelhouse. Anne Grant was standing at the wheel, her face disembodied in the compass light.

'How are things going?' he asked.

'I'm enjoying myself. There's been a sea running for about half an hour now.'

He glanced out of the window. 'Likely to get worse before it gets better. I'll take over.'

She made way for him, her soft body pressing against his as they squeezed past each other. 'I don't think I could sleep now even if I wanted to.'

He grinned. 'Make some more tea, then, and come back. Things might get interesting.'

He increased speed a little, racing the heavy weather that threatened from the east, and after a while she returned with the tea. The wheel kicked like a living thing in his hands and he strained his eyes into the grey waste of the morning.

The sea grew rougher, waves rocking *Foxhunter* from side to side, and again Mallory increased speed until the prow seemed to lift clean out of the water each time a wave rolled beneath them.

Half an hour later they raised Alderney and he became aware of that great tidal surge that drives in through the Channel Islands, raising the level of the water in the Golfe de St Malo by as much as thirty feet.

He altered course for Guernsey and asked Anne to get the forecast on the radio in the saloon. She took her time over it and when she came back she carried more tea and sandwiches on a tray.

'It's pretty hopeful,' she said. 'Wind moderating, rain squalls dying away.'

'Anything else?'

'Some fog patches in the islands, but nothing to worry about.'

Gradually the wind died, the sea calmed and they ran into a clear September morning with a slight mist rising from the water. Mallory opened a window and inhaled the freshness. When he turned she was smiling at him.

'You can handle a boat, Mr Mallory. I'll say that for you.'

'Don't forget to mention the fact in my reference.'

She smiled, picked up the tray and went out again. He leaned over the chart and checked the course. *Foxhunter* rounded Les Hanois lighthouse on the western tip of Guernsey an hour and a half later and seagulls and cormorants cried harshly in the sky, sweeping in across the deck from the great cliffs.

Already visibility was becoming worse, fog drifting in patches across the open sea as Guernsey dropped behind the horizon. He set the automatic pilot, leaned over the chart and Anne Grant came in.

'How are we doing?'

'With any kind of luck we should reach Île de Roc in an hour to an hour and a half. Depends on the fog. If we run into any really bad patches things could get tricky.'

'There's a large-scale Admiralty chart of the island and its approaches in the top drawer,' she said. 'I bought it specially.'

He took it out and they leaned over it together. Île de Roc was perhaps two miles long and three across, the only anchorage a bay at the southern end. The entire area was encircled by a network of sunken reefs with only two deep-water channels giving anything like a safe passage through.

'I'll take her if you like,' Anne said. 'I know these waters like the back of my hand and you need to.'

'The damned place looks like a death-trap.' Mallory shook his head. 'I wouldn't like to be drifting in on those shores on a dirty night.'

'A lot of good ships have done just that. You see St Pierre a mile to the north? In the old days whenever a gale was blowing in from the Atlantic ships were often swept between the two islands to founder on the reef which links them. At low tide the water-level drops as much as thirty feet and you can see some of those old wrecks.'

'Dangerous waters to go swimming in.'

She nodded. 'Especially at the wrong time. As a matter of

fact, the barman from Owen Morgan's hotel was drowned only the other day. His body drifted in the evening before I left.'

'Not so good.' Mallory moved on quickly. 'I see there's a castle marked on St Pierre.'

'A Gothic mausoleum. It's out on a twenty-year lease to a French count, Philippe de Beaumont.'

'The place is going to be busier than I thought.'

She shook her head. 'We don't see much of him. He stays pretty close to home and we don't get many visitors on the island. The hotel only has six bedrooms. They're booked right through the summer, of course, but Owen usually ends the season at the beginning of September. He likes to enjoy the last of the good weather himself.'

'He won't need much staff, then?'

'Only during the season and then he uses Guernsey girls. He's had a French cook living in full-time for nearly a year now. She should have left at the end of the season, but stayed on.'

'Sounds a rather obvious set-up.'

She shrugged. 'It's their own affair and she's a nice girl. I hope he marries her.'

The fog lifted a little and on either hand the sea broke in a white foam over great reefs. Mallory smiled grimly. 'I think this is where you start doing your stuff.'

She took over the wheel and altered course half a point. A moment later, through a sudden break in the fog, the towering cliffs of the island loomed into view and then the grey curtain dropped into place again.

Mallory reduced speed and Anne Grant took the cruiser forward into the fog. She seemed completely unperturbed and he shrugged fatalistically, pulled down the other seat and took out a cigarette.

At that moment the whole boat rocked violently and Mallory and the girl were thrown across to the other side of the wheelhouse. *Foxhunter* yawed alarmingly and Mallory shoved the girl away and scrambled across to the spinning wheel.

As he pulled the boat back on course, Anne Grant moved beside him and they peered out into the fog. Perhaps a hundred feet to starboard he caught a glimpse of something solid moving through the water and a sizable wave rolled back to rock *Foxhunter* again.

'And what in the hell was that?' he said.

'Probably a basking shark. They're common enough in these waters, but it must have been a big one to leave a wake like that.'

Mallory stared out into the fog, a frown on his face, remembering the force of that wave. Could a shark, however big it was, have set up such a disturbance? He was still thinking about it when they emerged from the last patch of fog and Île de Roc reared out of the sea a quarter of a mile away.

To the west was St Pierre, much smaller, a little blurred because visibility at that distance still wasn't good. Between the two islands the sea frothed and roared over the great underwater bridge.

'We're in the clear now,' Anne Grant said, and he gave *Foxhunter* everything she had as they roared through the water towards the great round cove which opened to meet them.

The water was a deep translucent blue, reminding him strangely of the Mediterranean. A stone jetty jutted fifty feet out from the shore and above it was the hotel, a two-storeyed, white-painted building sheltering in a hollow from the winter gales.

A fifteen-foot launch was moored on the far side of the cove. A young, dark-haired man in sun-glasses was sitting in the stern looking over the side. As he turned towards them a swimmer surfaced and Mallory caught a flash of blonde hair.

When they were a hundred feet from the jetty he cut the engines and *Foxhunter* settled back into the water, drifting in on her own momentum. Anne Grant was already getting the fenders over the side and Mallory ran out to help her. The moment they touched he jumped for the jetty with a line and ran it twice around an iron bollard. *Foxhunter* jerked once, bumped against the jetty and was still.

As he moved to fasten the other line, an engine roared into life, the sound echoing harshly from the cliffs, and the launch came towards the jetty. The swimmer was aleady almost there. Anne Grant moved to the port rail and Mallory joined her.

'Fiona,' she said simply.

As the girl arrived Mallory leaned down and hauled her up and over the rail. She crouched on deck for a moment, laughing and shaking herself like a young puppy.

'But it's marvellous, Anne. Simply marvellous.'

She didn't even look eighteen, long blonde hair trailing damply to her shoulders. She wore a pair of bathing pants and the upper half of a rubber diving suit in bright yellow that fitted her slim figure like a second skin.

She examined Mallory with interest and her eyes widened in approval. 'And where did you find *him?*'

Anne laughed and kissed her affectionately. 'Now, don't start, Fiona. This is Neil Mallory. He's going to run the boat for us for a month or two till we get the hang of things.'

Fiona Grant pushed a tendril of wet hair out of her eyes and held out her hand. 'I don't know about Anne, but speaking for myself I'll try not to learn too fast.'

The launch was no more than twenty or thirty feet away now and its occupant cut the engine and it drifted in towards *Foxhunter*.

'Who's this, for goodness' sake?' Anne demanded.

Fiona slipped a wet arm in hers. 'A simply marvellous man, Anne. He's French. Staying here for a week or two to paint and do a little skin-diving.'

'But I thought Owen closed the hotel last week?'

'He did, but luckily I was on the jetty when he came in. I persuaded Owen to change his mind.'

The launch bumped against the side and Mallory caught the thrown line. As he looped it round the rail, the Frenchman vaulted on to the deck. He wore a slim-fitting jersey that left his sunburnt arms bare, and the dark glasses gave him the same slightly sinister and anonymous look the peaked military cap had done in the photo in his file.

Fiona took his arm and turned to face them. 'Anne, I'd like you to met Raoul Guyon,' she said.

— 6 —

THE ANCIENT, grey-stone house was firmly rooted into a hollow in the hill, great beech trees flanking it on either side. At some time a large glass conservatory had been added, running along the whole length of the building, and a series of shallow steps dropped down to a stone terrace.

From the terrace the cliffs fell a good two hundred feet into a small funnel-shaped inlet that would have made a wonderfully sheltered mooring had it not been for the jagged line of rocks stretching across the entrance.

Anne Grant leaned on the wall, a cool drink in her hand, and looked out to sea. It had turned into a beautiful day, surprisingly warm for September, with a scattering of white clouds trailing to the horizon. She felt completely relaxed and at peace, happy to be home again. A foot crunched on gravel. When she turned, her father-in-law stood at the top of the steps.

Major-General Hamish Grant, DSO, MC and bar, had been well named Iron Grant. Six feet four inches in height, with a great breadth of shoulder, his hair was a snow-white mane swept back behind his ears. He wore an old pair of khaki service trousers and a corduroy jacket.

He probed at the top step with his walking stick. 'You there, Anne?'

'Here I am, Hamish.'

She went up the steps and took his arm and his great, craggy face broke into a warm smile. 'Fiona seemed tremendously excited about the new boat, but she was hardly in the house for a moment before she was changed and off out again.'

In a corner of the terrace stood a table containing a tray of drinks and shaded by a large striped umbrella. She led him across and he eased his great bulk into a wicker chair.

'She's gone down to the hotel to meet Raoul Guyon, this

young French painter who's staying there. She promised to show him some of the island before lunch.'

'What about this fellow Mallory?'

'He should be here at any moment. I asked him to pick up the diving equipment. There was no real hurry, but I thought you might like to meet him.'

'I certainly would, if only to thank him for the way he handled this Southampton affair.' He frowned. 'Mallory. Neil Mallory. There's something familiar about that name. Irish, of course.'

'He certainly doesn't have an accent.'

'And you say he was cashiered for cooking the mess books? That certainly doesn't fit in with the sort of man who'd take on a couple of thugs in a back alley.'

'That's what I thought. He's a strange man, Hamish. At times there's something almost frightening about him. He's so curiously remote and detached from things. I think you'll like him.'

'I'd love to know why they slung him out,' the general said. 'Mind you, the War Office, God bless 'em, do some pretty daft things these days.'

'I'd rather you didn't raise the subject,' she said. 'Promise?'

He frowned for a moment and then shrugged. 'I don't see why not. After all, a man's past is his own affair. Can he sail the boat, that's the main thing?'

She nodded. 'Perfectly.'

'Then what have we got to grumble about?' He squeezed her hand. 'Get me a brandy and soda like a good girl and tell me some more about *Foxhunter*.'

She didn't get the chance. As she was pouring his drink, Jagbir appeared at the top of the steps, Mallory a yard or two behind him.

The Gurkha was short and squat, no more than five feet tall, and wore a neat, sand-coloured linen jacket. He had the ageless, yellow-brown face of the Asiatic and limped heavily on his left foot, relic of a bad wound received at Cassino.

He spoke good English with the easy familiarity of the old servant. 'Mr Mallory's here, general.'

The general sipped a little of his brandy and put the glass down again. 'What's on the stove?'

'Curried chicken. When would you like to have it?'

'Any time you like. Serve it out here.'

Mallory stood at the top of the steps waiting, cap in hand, and Anne smiled up at him. 'Would you care to have lunch with us, Mr Mallory?'

He shook his head. 'It's good of you to offer, but I've already arranged to eat at the hotel.'

She dismissed Jagbir with a quick nod, trying to hide her disappointment, and Mallory came down the steps.

'This is Mr Mallory, general,' she said formally.

Hamish Grant turned towards Mallory, his head slightly to one side. 'Come a bit closer, man. I don't see very well.'

Mallory moved to the table and looked down into the cloudy, opalescent eyes. The general reached out and touched him gently on the chest. 'My daughter-in-law tells me you're a good sailor.'

'I hope so,' Mallory said.

'What was your last ship?'

'An oil-tanker. S.S. *Pilar*. Tampico to Southampton.'

The general turned to Anne. 'Did you check his papers?' She shook her head and he looked up at Mallory again. 'Let's see them.'

Mallory took a wallet from his hip pocket, extracted a folded document and union card and tossed them on the table.

'See when he was last paid off and check the union card. There should be a photo.'

She checked the documents quickly and nodded. 'Paid off S.S. *Pilar*, Southampton, 1 September.' She smiled as she handed them back. 'It isn't a very good photo.'

Mallory didn't reply and the general continued: 'The terms Mrs Grant agreed with you, you're quite satisfied with them?'

'Perfectly.'

'There'll be a bonus of one hundred pounds for you on top. Some token of my gratitude for the way you handled this Southampton business.'

'That won't be necessary, sir,' Mallory said coolly.

Blood surged into the general's face in an instant. 'By God, sir, if I say it is necessary it *is* necessary. You'll take orders like everyone else.

Mallory adjusted his cap and turned to Anne. 'You mentioned some diving equipment you wanted me to take down to the boat?'

She took a hurried glance at the general's purple face and said quickly: 'You'll find a station wagon in the courtyard at the rear. Jagbir's already loaded it. I'll be down later this afternoon.'

'I'll expect you.' Mallory turned to the general. 'Anything else, sir?'

'No, damn your eyes!' the general exploded.

A smile tugged at the corner of Mallory's mouth. His hand started upwards in an instinctive salute. He caught himself just in time, glanced once at Anne, turned, and ran lightly up the steps.

The general started to laugh. 'Pour me another brandy.'

Anne uncorked the bottle and reached for his glass. 'Am I right in assuming all that was quite deliberate?'

'Of course,' Hamish Grant said, 'and I'll add to your mystery, my dear. There goes a man who once was used to command, and high command at that. I didn't spend forty years in the army for nothing.'

II

High on the cliffs on the western side of the island Raoul Guyon and Fiona Grant topped a steep hill and paused. Before them the island seemed to tumble over the cliffs and the great jagged spine which joined them to St Pierre was visible under the water.

'There,' she said, making a sweeping gesture with one hand. 'Did I lie to you?'

'You were right,' he said. 'Absolutely magnificent.'

'I'll expect to see you up here with your easel first thing in the morning.'

You'll be disappointed. I always work from preliminary sketches, never from life.'

She had moved a few feet away, stooping to pick up a flower, and now she turned quickly. 'Fraud.'

He took a small sketch-pad and pencil from the pocket of his corduroy jacket and dropped to the ground. 'Stay where you are, but look out to sea.'

She obeyed him at once. 'All right, but this had better be good.'

'Don't chatter,' he said. 'It distracts me.'

The sun glinted on her straw-coloured hair and her image blurred so that in that one brief moment of time she might have been a painting by Renoir. She looked incredibly young and innocent and yet the wind from the sea moulded the thin cotton dress to her firm young figure with a disturbing sensuousness.

Guyon grunted and pocketed his pencil. 'All right.'

She dropped beside him and snatched the pad from his hand. In the same moment her smile died and colour stained her cheeks. Inescapably caught in a few brief strokes of the pencil for all eternity, she stood gazing out to sea, and by some strange genius all that was good in her, all the innocence and longing of youth, was there also.

She looked up at him in wonderment. 'It's beautiful.'

'But you are,' he said calmly. 'Has no one ever told you this before?'

'I learned rather early in life that it's dangerous to let them.' She smiled ruefully. 'Until my mother died four years ago we lived in a villa near St Tropez. You know it?'

'Extremely well.'

'In St Tropez, in season, anything female is in demand and fourteen-year-old girls seem to have a strong appeal for some men.'

'So I've heard,' he said gravely.

'Yes, life had its difficulties, but then the general bought this little island and I went to school for a couple of years. I didn't like that at all.'

'What did you do, run away?'

She pushed her long hair back from her face and laughed. 'Persuaded the general to send me to a finishing school in Paris. Now *that* was really something.' Guyon grinned and lit a cigarette. 'Tell me, why do you always call him general?'

She shrugged. 'Everyone does – except for Anne, of course. She's special. When she married my brother Angus she was only my age. He was killed in Korea.'

She paused, a few wild flowers held to her face as she stared pensively into the past, and Guyon lay back, gazing up at the sky, sadness sweeping through him as he remembered another time, another girl.

Algiers, 1958. After five months chasing *fellaghas* in the cork forests of the Grande Kabylie he had found himself in that city of fear, leading his men through the narrow streets of the Kasbah and Bab el Qued, locked in the life-or-death struggle that was the Battle of Algiers.

And then Nerida had come into his life, a young Moorish girl fleeing from a mob after a bomb outrage on the Boulevard du Telemly. He closed his eyes and saw again her dark hair tumbling across a pillow, moonlight streaming through a latticed window. The long nights when they had tried to forget tomorrow.

But the morning had come, the cold grey morning when she had been found on the beach, stripped and defiled, head shaven, body mutilated. The proper ending for a woman who had betrayed her people for a *Frangaoui*. The sniper's bullet of the following day which had sent him back to France on a stretcher had almost carried a welcome oblivion.

Nerida. The scent of her was strong in his nostrils and he reached out and pulled her down, crushing his lips against hers. Her body was soft and yielding and when she swung on to her back her mouth answered sweet as honey. He opened his eyes and Fiona Grant smiled lazily up at him.

'Now what brought that on?'

He leaned on one elbow for a moment and rubbed a hand across his eyes. 'Put it down to the sea air. I'm sorry.'

'I'm not.'

'Then you should be.' He pulled her to her feet. 'Didn't you tell me you were expected for lunch?'

She held on to his hand. 'Come back with me. I'd like you to meet the general.'

'Some other time. I've arranged to eat at the hotel.'

She turned from him like a hurt child. He restrained a strong impulse to take her in his arms, reminded himself strongly that he had work to do – important work – and walked away. When he reached the top of the rise he hesitated and turned reluctantly.

She was standing where he had left her, head drooping, something touchingly despondent about her. The strong sunlight, streaming through the thin cotton of her dress, outlined her firm young thighs perfectly.

'Damn her!' he said softly to himself. 'She might as well have nothing on.'

He sighed heavily and went back down the slope.

III

Mallory lay on his bunk in *Foxhunter* watching the blue smoke from his cigarette twist and swirl in the current from the air-conditioner. He'd had an excellent meal at the hotel in company with Owen Morgan, but there had been no sign of the Frenchman.

His mind went back again to his meeting with Hamish Grant at the house on the cliffs. There had been method behind the old man's bullying, of that he was certain. He had been a soldier himself for too long to subscribe to the opinion that all generals were rather stupid, dull-witted blimps who spent their time either needlessly sending men to their deaths or over-indulging at the table.

Behind the worn, leather-coloured face, the half-blind eyes, was a will of iron and a first-rate brain. Iron Grant, who had force-marched his division through the hell that was the Qattara Depression rather than surrender to Rommel, who had led the way down the ramp of the first landing craft to hit Sword Beach on D-day, was an adversary to be reckoned with by any standards.

And then there was his daughter-in-law. Mallory closed his eyes, trying to picture her face. There was a calmness about her, a sureness that he found disturbing. Even on the wharf at Southampton she had not seemed afraid. It was as if life had done its worst, could do no more. As if nothing could ever really hurt her again. It came to him quite suddenly that she must have loved her husband very much and he was aware of a vague, irrational jealousy.

He heard no sound and yet it was as if a wind had passed over his face and every muscle came alive and singing, ready for instant action. The lower step of the companionway creaked and he reached for the butt of the revolver under his pillow.

'No need, my friend,' Raoul Guyon said quietly.

As Mallory opened his eyes, the young Frenchman dropped on to the opposite bunk and produced a packet of cigarettes.

'We missed you at lunch,' Mallory said. 'What happened?'

Guyon shrugged. 'Something came up. You know how it is?'

'I certainly do. There's grass on your jacket.'

'A fine day for lying on one's back and contemplating heaven,' Guyon said brazenly.

'Not when there's a job to be done.' Mallory opened a cupboard under the bunk, took out a bottle of whisky and two glasses and set them on the table. 'Business and pleasure don't mix.

'On occasion, I'm happy to say that they do. Am I not supposed to be a fun-loving young artist on vacation?' Guyon poured himself a generous measure of whisky and raised his glass. '*Santé*.'

Slim-hipped, lean and sinewy, Raoul Guyon possessed that strange quality to be found in the airborne troops of every country, a kind of arrogant self-sufficiency bred of the hazards of the calling. While unaware of this in himself, he recognized it at once in the Englishman, but there was more than that. Much more. Mallory was the same strange mixture of soldier and monk, of man-of-action and mystic, that he had seen in the great paratroop colonels in Algiers. Men like Philippe de Beaumont. Strange, wild, half-mad fanatics, marred by their experiences in the Viet prison camps, for the time controlling the destiny of a great nation.

But Mallory also had passed through the fire of a Communist prison camp and, like Philippe de Beaumont, he had tried to put into practice those lessons hard learned from his Chinese taskmasters and with the same disastrous result.

Mallory lit a cigarette and leaned back against the bulkhead. 'How good is your skin-diving?'

Guyon shrugged. 'I know what I'm doing. A little out of practice, that's all.'

'Anne Grant wants me to take her out over the reef this afternoon. She's brought a couple of aquamobiles back from the mainland. Wants to try them out. I thought if you asked Fiona nicely you might get yourself invited.'

'As a matter of fact, I already have. All part of my business-cum-pleasure activities.'

'You don't waste much time.' Mallory grinned. 'We'll see how things look. We can make a full-scale reconnaissance later tonight.'

'You really think there may be something in this business?'

Mallory shrugged. 'I wouldn't like to say. As I was bringing the boat in this morning something damned big passed us underwater. Anne Grant said it was a shark. Apparently they're pretty common round here.'

'Do you think it's worth reporting?'

Mallory shook his head. 'My boss is interested in facts, not possibilities. I've signalled my arrival and nothing more.' He opened the cupboard again, took out what was apparently a small transistor radio and held it up. 'Amazing what they can do with electronics these days. There are three motor torpedo boats based on St Helier now, supposed to be on shallow-water exercises. If I give them the word they'll be in here like a shot.'

'What's the signal?'

'Their codeword is Leviathan. When we need them we simply signal Code Four. That's all that's needed.'

Mallory put the set in a drawer in the table and Guyon helped himself to more whisky. 'I was in touch with my own people before I left Guernsey this morning. They've drawn a complete blank where *L'Alouette* is concerned. It's creating something of a situation.'

'What in the hell are the OAS trying to prove?' Mallory said. 'This sort of thing isn't going to get them anywhere in the long run.'

'Desperate men seek desperate remedies. Eight times since 1960 either the OAS or the CNR have conspired to kill de Gaulle. They came closest last month when they ambushed his car on the way to Villacoublay Airport. They picked the leader of that little affair up only last week.'

'So this latest business is to prove to people they're still a force to be reckoned with?'

'More than that. That they have a long arm which can reach out to punish those who oppose them. This isn't the first member of the judiciary to be assassinated. At this rate there will soon be no one willing to be connected with the trials of OAS members, especially when to take part carries an automatic death sentence.'

'What about Bouvier?'

'He was public prosecutor at a military tribunal which only last month tried six members of the OAS. Two were sentenced to death. His execution was stage-managed to have the maximum dramatic effect and the government can't hope to keep it secret beyond the end of the week.'

'Which doesn't give us long to handle things here.' Mallory frowned. 'Have you ever met de Beaumont personally?'

'Only as one of the crowd. He was a member of the original Committee of Public Safety which brought de Gaulle back to power. When it became obvious that the general wouldn't play along with his dream of an integrated Algeria he fell to plotting, or so we think.'

'Was anything ever proved against him?'

Guyon shook his head. 'It was thought that he was the power behind the scenes in General Challe's abortive coup in 1961, but there was no evidence. Before any could be collected he asked to be placed on unpaid leave and left France. He's cxtremely wealthy, by the way. One of his uncles married into industry after the first war.'

'What does Legrande think about him?'

Guyon laughed. 'Legrande has little respect for the aristocracy. He would see the guillotine set up in the old situation and smile at the prospect. He has no proof that de Beaumont is directly connected with the OAS, but he is unhappy about him. He would be quite content to see him dead. He has a naturally tidy mind.'

'And what's your own opinion?'

'Of de Beaumont?' Guyon hesitated. 'He's a dangerous man and no fool. For a year he was in charge of all military intelligence in Algeria, but he was always at loggerheads with the brass-hats. He saw war as the Communists see war – as something to be won – and he believed that the end justified the means. Something the *boi-dois* had beaten into him in the Viet camps.' Guyon half smiled. 'This much at least I would expect you to have in common with him. Legrande told me that you, too, were behind the Communist wire for a time.'

'You make him sound interesting,' Mallory said. 'I'd like to meet him. I've a feeling that would tell me all I need to know.'

'Very possibly.' Guyon emptied his glass. 'Is there anything else you wish me to do?'

'This Frenchwoman who's living at the hotel with Morgan, Juliette Vincente? In my briefing they said she was harmless. What do you think?'

'Our preliminary report certainly didn't indicate anything unusual. Her mother and father have a small farm in Normandy. One brother, killed doing his military service in Algeria in 1958. She worked at an hotel in St Malo for six months before coming here.'

Mallory nodded. 'Sounds all right, but run the usual check on your room, just to make sure it hasn't been searched.'

Guyon put on his sun-glasses and got to his feet. 'I'll get changed. See you in about half an hour and we'll have a look at that reef.' He paused in the doorway and stretched. 'It really is a beautiful day. I'm quite looking forward to it.'

After he had gone Mallory sat on the edge of the bunk going over things in his mind, trying to work out what might happen, but he knew that he was wasting his time.

If there was one lesson he had learned above all others it was that in this game nothing was certain. Chance ruled every move. He opened one of the lockers, took out the diving gear and started to check it.

— 7 —

MALLORY vaulted over the rail into the translucent blue water, paused for a moment to adjust the flow of air from his aqualung and swam down in a long sweeping curve that brought him under the hull of *Foxhunter* to where Fiona Grant swayed beside the anchor chain like some exotic flower in her yellow diving suit. A moment later her sister-in-law appeared beside them in a cloud of silver bubbles.

Fiona jack-knifed at once and followed the anchor chain down into the blue mist, her long hair streaming out behind, and Mallory and Anne went after her.

They were perhaps a hundred yards out from the shore on the southern side of the island and the water was saturated with sunlight, so that even when they reached bottom at forty feet visibility was good.

The sea-bed was covered by a great spreading forest of seaweed six or seven feet deep which moved rhythmically with every ebb and flow of current, changing colour like some living thing. Fiona swam into it, fish scattering to avoid her. Mallory paused, hovering over the undulating mass, and Anne tapped him on the shoulder and moved away.

They plunged over a great black spine of rock and a wall complete with arched Norman window loomed out of the shadows a few feet to the right. Anne swam effortlessly through it and Mallory followed.

It was obvious that only the strong tidal currents on this side of the island had prevented the building from being completely silted over centuries before. It had no roof and the walls had crumbled until they stood no higher than four feet above the sand. Beyond, the sea-bed sloped gently into another forest of seaweed, broken walls and jumbled blocks of worked masonry strewn on every side.

Fiona Grant appeared from the gloom and swam towards them. She poised a couple of feet away, put a hand into the nylon bag which was looped to her left wrist and produced a piece of red pottery which she waved triumphantly. Anne raised her thumb and they all turned, swam back across the rocks and struck upwards to *Foxhunter*'s curved hull.

They surfaced by the small ladder suspended over the side, and Anne went up first. Mallory followed her, pulled off his mask and turned to give Fiona a hand. She squatted on the deck, taking the pieces of pottery from her bag one by one and laying them out carefully.

Raoul Guyon had set up an easel next to the wheelhouse and was sketching Hamish Grant, who sat in the bows. The

Frenchman put down his pencil and moved across to join them.

The general turned his head sharply. 'What's going on?'

'Fiona's found some pottery,' Anne said.

Guyon turned to Mallory, a strange, alien-looking figure in his webbed feet and black rubber suit. 'What's it like down there?'

'Interesting,' Mallory said. 'You should try it.'

'Perhaps later. I'd like to get my sketches of the general finished and the light is just right.'

Fiona unstrapped her aqualung, squatted down on the deck again and started to sort through the pieces of pottery, completely absorbed by her task.

Anne turned to Mallory. 'That's the last we'll see of her today.'

'Do you want to go down again?'

She shook her head. 'I'd like to try out the aquamobiles. You take one and I'll have the other. We'll go round the point to the St Pierre reef. I'll show you the middle passage and there's at least one interesting wreck.'

Guyon helped Mallory bring the two aquamobiles up from the saloon. They were bullet-shaped underwater scooters driven by battery-operated propellers, designed to operate at depths of up to a hundred and fifty feet. They carried their own spotlights for use when visibility was bad.

Anne and Mallory went over the side and Guyon passed down the heavy scooters. Anne moved away at once and Mallory went after her.

The sea was calm, the sun bright on the face of the water, but as they approached the great finger of rock jutting out into the sea at the western end of the island Mallory became aware of cross-currents tugging at his body. Anne raised an arm in a quick signal and disappeared.

The sensation of speed underwater was extraordinary. To Mallory it seemed as if he were hurtling through space as he chased the yellow-clad figure in front of him and yet his effective speed was not much more than three knots.

The red nose of the scooter whipped through the blue-green water, pulling him across a jumbled mass of black rocks. For a moment currents seemed to pull his body in several directions at once and then he was round the point and into calmer water.

They surfaced by a weed-covered shoulder of rock and Anne sat on its slope half out of the water and pulled up her mask. On either side, and stretching across to St Pierre, was white water, surf breaking everywhere over the jagged rocks which made up the central reef mass.

'At low tide most of the reef is twenty feet above water,' she said. 'Stretching all the way to St Pierre like a giant's causeway.'

'Could it be crossed on foot?'

She looked dubious. 'I wouldn't like to try. It's only clear for an hour. Something to do with another flood which moves in this way from the Atlantic.'

A mile away the great, jagged rock of St Pierre lifted out of the sea. The castle was perched on the ultimate edge of the cliffs, its strange, pointed Gothic towers in sharp relief against the blue sky. The sea creamed over rocks two hundred feet below.

'What do you think of it?' she said.

'It must have cost a fortune to build even on the golden tide of Victorian prosperity.' He shaded his eyes and frowned. 'I can't see a jetty.'

'It's under the island. If you look carefully beyond the last line of rocks you'll see the entrance in the cliffs. At high water there's only a ten- or twelve-foot clearance.'

'Is the water very deep in there?' he said casually.

She nodded. 'Even at low water there's a good ten fathoms. There's a fault in the sea-bed which splits the reef along the centre. It runs right under St Pierre.'

'Would that be your famous middle passage?'

'That's right, and it's well worth seeing.'

She clamped her rubber mouthpiece between her teeth, pulled down the mask and eased herself back under the water. Visibility was still good and Mallory could see the great boulders of the reef four or five fathoms beneath, and then quite suddenly Anne tilted her scooter over a shelf of granite and went down into space.

They moved through a misty tunnel of rock, sunlight slanting through fissures and cracks in the roof in wavering bands of light. In places the passage was reminiscent of a cathedral nave, the rock arched up on either side to support the roof, and then the dimness brightened and they moved into a section which was open to the sea.

Anne was twenty or thirty feet in front and she paused, waiting for him. When he approached she jack-knifed. Mallory went after her, the scarlet nose of his scooter cleaving the water, fish crowding to either side. At ten fathoms he moved into a mysterious green dusk with visibility considerably reduced.

Beneath him she had paused, hovering over a ledge. When he joined her he saw, to his astonishment, a three-ton Bedford truck wedged on its side in a large fissure. The canvas tilt had long since disappeared, but when he moved in close he saw painted on the side the white star which all Allied vehicles had carried on D-Day and after.

They moved away again and a moment later the outline of a ship's stern loomed out of the gloom. Every rail, every line, was festooned with strange submarine growths and he followed the curving side to where a ragged torpedo hole gaped darkly at him. Beneath, tilted into a crevasse, was a Churchill tank, beyond it the shapes of trucks, a solitary field-gun's barrel slanting towards the surface.

Mallory followed Anne across the deck to the wheelhouse. The open door swung gently in the current, the deck around it smashed and broken as if by some internal explosion. The wheel was still intact and also the compass in its mounting, encrusted with scales. When Mallory moved inside he had a strange sensation that someone should be there, that something was missing. A bad end for a good ship, he thought, and moved out again. She tapped him on the shoulder, and together they rose towards the luminosity that was the surface.

They hauled themselves on to the flat top of a large rock, dry in the sun, and Anne pulled up her mask and breathed deeply several times.

'What's the story?' Mallory said.

She shrugged. 'One of the D-Day armada that never made it. She was torpedoed near Guernsey. When her engines stopped the tide carried her straight in across the reef. Apparently, the crew got away earlier in the life-boats.'

'Where did you get the story?'

'From Owen Morgan. There are plenty of wrecks in these waters and Owen knows them all – and their histories. Something of a hobby with him.'

'Interesting,' Mallory said. 'I'd like to take another look. Feel up to it?'

'I don't think so. I'll wait for you here. Don't stay too long. When the tide starts turning there's quite an under-current through the passage.'

He was aware of it almost at once, like an invisible hand pushing him to one side as he went down over the edge of the reef. The pressure of the water clawed at his mask as the scooter pulled him down and he swerved as a steel mast pierced the gloom.

He hovered over the tilting deck, considering his next move. The sight of the black, gaping entrance to a companionway decided him. He moved inside, switching on the light mounted on top of the scooter.

He moved along the angled corridor and opened the first door he came to. It fell inwards slowly, the room beyond it dark, and he was aware of a strange, irrational fear. He pushed forward boldly, and the light, spreading through the water, showed him a table bolted to the floor, a bunk against one wall and bottles and assorted debris floating against the ceiling.

He swam out and moved further along the corridor to where it disintegrated into a twisted mass of metal, electric wires draped from the roof and, most poignant sight of all, the broken remnants of a human skeleton crushed beneath a girder.

He moved back along the corridor quickly and, the moment he emerged from the companionway, struck up towards the reef. At twenty feet he paused to decompress for several minutes, aware of the current tugging at his body. He surfaced a few yards from the rock and found Anne Grant waist-deep on the edge of the reef, adjusting her equipment.

'We'll have to get moving,' she shouted, as he approached and pushed up his mask. 'It must be later than I thought. I can feel the tide moving already.'

'Is that bad?' he said.

She nodded. 'Even the aquamobiles aren't going to do us much good with a five-knot current flowing the other way.'

She moved off at once and he went after her. Behind them the entire length of the reef was surging into breakers and he could feel the relentless pressure of the current. He started to flutter-kick with all his strength, and gradually the point grew nearer. Anne turned, gave him a quick wave and they went down.

He could see the weeds on the sea-bed beneath him leaning over on one side, pointing back towards the reef, and the pressure was now a solid wall that he was trying to break through. He kicked again, was dimly aware of the black rocks passing beneath him and then they were round into calm water and his aquamobile seemed to leap forward with a surge of power.

He surfaced and saw Anne at once, over the right and some distance in front of him. He raised a hand, urging her on, and followed. When he rounded the final point of rock she was perhaps fifty yards in front of him and moving strongly towards *Foxhunter*.

A speedboat was moored beside the ladder, the sunlight gleaming on its scarlet trim, and someone sat in a canvas chair next to General Grant, a tall, distinguished-looking man in dark glasses and linen jacket who stood up and moved to the rail, shading his eyes as Anne approached.

She reached the ladder and he moved to give her a hand. When she climbed up on deck Mallory was still twenty or thirty yards away and he reduced speed.

As he came in under the counter of the speedboat the man who was sitting at the wheel turned to look down at him. He was a large, dangerous-looking individual with a hard face, a jagged scar bisecting the right cheek. Mallory recognized him at once from the photograph he had been shown at his briefing.

He pushed up his mask. 'Hello there.'

Jacaud looked down at him calmly, nodded, then turned away. Mallory pulled himself to the bottom of the ladder where Raoul Guyon was already waiting, a hand outstretched for the aquamobiles.

Mallory went over the rail, squatted on deck and took off

his aqualung. Anne Grant was standing a yard or two away, an attractive figure in her yellow diving suit as she talked to the man in the linen jacket.

There was little doubt who he was. The handsome, aristocratic face, the easy poise, spoke of a man who was supremely aware of the fact that God had created the de Beaumonts first.

'Such a nice surprise,' she was saying.

'Pure luck that I passed, I assure you. I was trying out my new speedboat.' De Beaumont raised her hand to his mouth. 'My dear Anne, you grow more delightful each time I see you.'

She coloured charmingly and the general cut in: 'And now that we've got you you won't get away so easily. You must come to dinner tonight. It's been far too long.'

'Please do,' Anne said.

He shrugged, still holding her hand. 'How can I refuse?'

Raoul Guyon was standing with Fiona beside the deck-house and Anne turned towards him. 'Have you met Monsieur Guyon?'

'I have indeed,' de Beaumont said. 'I've been looking at these delightful sketches he's done of the general. If he can spare the time perhaps you could persuade him to come across to St Pierre one day and sketch me?'

'A pleasure,' Guyon said.

Anne turned towards Mallory. 'And this is Mr Neil Mallory. He's running the boat for us for a month or two till Fiona and I get used to things.'

De Beaumont stood for a moment, looking towards Mallory, and then he slowly removed his sun-glasses. His eyes were a strange, metallic blue and very cold, no warmth in them at all, and yet something moved there, something that instantly put Mallory on the alert.

'Mr Mallory.' De Beaumont held out his hand.

Mallory took it and the grip tightened. The Frenchman looked into his eyes for a long moment, then turned back to Anne.

'And now I must go. At what time this evening?'

'Seven,' she said. 'We'll look forward to seeing you.'

He went down the ladder into the speedboat and nodded

to Jacaud. The engine roared into life and the boat turned away in a surge of power.

De Beaumont raised his hand in farewell, took a gold cigarette case from an inner pocket, selected a cigarette and lit it.

'Shall I tell Marcel to be ready to run you across tonight?' Jacaud said.

De Beaumont nodded. 'And Pierre, but I shall also require you, Jacaud.'

'Something interesting?'

'I have just seen a ghost,' de Beaumont said calmly. 'A ghost from the past, and ghosts are always interesting.'

He settled back in the seat and Jacaud spun the wheel in his hands and took the speedboat round the point, his face quite expressionless.

II

Mallory stood at the wheel of *Foxhunter* thinking about de Beaumont. There had been something there, of that he was sure, but what could it possibly be? They had certainly never met.

The door clicked open behind him and Raoul Guyon came in and leaned against the chart table, lighting a cigarette.

'What did you think of him?'

Mallory shrugged. 'Very charming, very elegant. Seems soft until you look in his eyes. Are you dining with them tonight?'

Guyon shook his head. 'I've been invited for drinks afterwards. What was it like on the reef? Anything interesting?'

Mallory told him everything that had happened. When he had finished Guyon nodded. 'From the sound of it, this cavern under the island would seem like an adequate hiding place for *L'Alouette*.'

'That's what we'll have to find out.'

'And how do we do that?'

'We'll use the aquamobiles. Try the middle passage approach I told you about.'

'Straight into the cavern. Do you think they'll let us?'

'That's what we'll have to find out. We'll go in some time

tonight. The forecast's good and there's a moon. If the weather holds it shouldn't be too difficult. We'll go round the point in the dinghy. That should give us a good start.'

Guyon sighed. 'Legrande told me this one would be interesting. Little did he know. I'll see you later.'

The door closed behind him and Mallory increased speed. The strange thing was that as *Foxhunter* ran back towards the jetty he wasn't thinking of the danger that lay ahead, of the long swim through the dark night. He was thinking of two metallic blue eyes and wondering what it was that he had seen in them.

— 8 —

THROUGH the french windows the lawn shimmered palely and the great beeches were silhouetted against the evening sky. Beyond was the timelss sad sough of the sea.

Inside, the room was warm and comfortable, the light softly diffused and a log hissed and spluttered on the hearthstone. There was a grand piano in one corner, two old comfortable couches drawn to the fire and a print or two on the walls.

It was a room that was lived in, a quiet, comfortable place, and the five people gathered loosely about the fire talked quietly to each other, Fiona Grant's occasional laugh breaking to the surface like a bubble of air in a quiet pool.

De Beaumont and his host wore dinner jackets and the Frenchman looked elegant, completely at his ease as he talked to Anne Grant and the general.

Fiona was wearing a simple green dress in some heavy silk material and sat on the arm of an old tapestry chair. Guyon stood beside her smoking a cigarette, one hand on the high mantelpiece. He was not in evening dress, but a well-cut suit of dark blue fitted his wiry figure to perfection, giving him a touch of distinction.

He leaned close to Fiona, muttered something in her ear, and she chuckled and stood up. 'Raoul and I are going for a little walk. Anyone feel like joining us?'

'And what would you do if we said yes?' her father demanded.

'Brain you!' She kissed him affectionately and moved to the door. 'I'll get a coat, Raoul. It could turn chilly.'

Raoul smiled at de Beaumont. 'Will I see you again before you leave, colonel?'

De Beaumont shook his head. 'Unlikely, I'm afraid. I keep early hours these days. Strict instructions from my doctor.'

Guyon held out his hand. 'For the present, then.'

'And don't forget about that portrait,' de Beaumont reminded him. 'I meant what I said.'

The young Frenchman nodded to the others and walked across to the door quickly as Fiona called from the hall.

'Seems a nice enough young chap,' the general observed.

'Fiona obviously thinks so,' Anne said. 'And he's certainly talented. He was in the army in Algeria for several years before he took up painting.'

'He's remarkably talented,' de Beaumont said. 'He'll make a name for himself with little difficulty.'

The general turned his head as Jagbir came in and handed round drinks from a tray. 'Any sign of Mr Mallory yet?'

'No, general.'

The general opened a silver box at his elbow and took out a long black cheroot. 'I wonder what's happened to him?'

'Probably something to do with the boat,' Anne said. 'And he is walking, remember.'

De Beaumont fitted a cigarette into a silver holder and said carefully, 'Have you known him long?'

Hamish Grant shook his head. 'Anne picked him up in Southampton. As a matter of fact, he got her out of a rather nasty scrape.'

'And this is the basis upon which you hired him?'

'His papers were all in order. He'd only just signed off a tanker from Tampico a day or so before. Why do you ask?'

De Beaumont stood up, paced restlessly across to the french windows and turned. 'This is really most difficult for me. I don't want you to think that I am interfering, yet on the other hand I feel that I should speak.'

'You know something about him?' the general said. 'Something to his discredit?'

De Beaumont came back to his chair and sat down. 'You're aware, of course, that during the latter part of my army career I was commanding officer of a parachute regiment in Algeria. During the first few months of 1959 I was seconded to the general staff in Algiers and placed in charge of military security.'

'How does this concern Mallory?'

'We kept a special file on people who were thought to be working for the FLN or the various other nationalist organizations. Neil Mallory was in that file. He was captain of a sea-going motor-yacht berthed in Tangiers. He was a smuggler, engaged in the extremely profitable business of running contraband tobacco into Spain and Italy. He was also thought to be running guns for the FLN.'

Hamish Grant emptied his glass, placed it carefully down on the table at his elbow and shrugged. 'In other words he was a tough, rather unscrupulous young man who'd make a pound wherever there was one to be made. You've told me nothing I hadn't already worked out for myself.' He pushed his glass across to Anne. 'Pour me another, my dear.'

'It was the years before Tangiers I found most interesting when I read this file,' de Beaumont said. 'That's why I recalled him so easily. Remember a book you loaned me about a year ago? A War Office manual entitled *A New Concept of Revolutionary Warfare*? You told me it had been written by a brilliant young officer in 1953 during the months following his release from a Chinese prison camp in Korea. I believe it caused quite a stir at the time.'

The general stiffened, one hand tightening on the handle of his walking stick. 'God in heaven,' he said, 'Mallory! Lieutenant-Colonel Neil Mallory.'

'What was it they called him after that unpleasantness in Malaya?' de Beaumont said gently. 'The Butcher of Perak?'

The glass into which Anne Grant was at the moment pouring whisky splintered sharply against the floor. She stood gazing fixedly at de Beaumont, a puzzled expression on her face, then crossed quickly to her father-in-law.

'What does he mean?'

Hamish Grant patted her hand. 'You're sure it's the same man?'

De Beaumont shrugged. 'The circumstances can hardly be coincidental. Admittedly, until today I had only seen his photograph, but it's a distinctive face. Not the sort one forgets easily.'

'But what is it, Hamish?' Anne demanded.

De Beaumont was clearly embarrassed. 'Perhaps it would be better if I went. Forgive me for having cast a shadow on what otherwise has been a truly delightful evening, but as a friend I felt that I had no choice but to tell you what I knew of this man.'

'You were quite right.' Hamish Grant got to his feet. 'I'm very grateful to you. We'll see you again soon, I hope?'

'But of course.'

The general sat down again and de Beaumont and Anne moved into the hall. 'I'll get Jagbir to run you down to the jetty in the station wagon,' she said.

De Beaumont shook his head. 'No need. A fine evening. The walk will do me good.'

When he raised her hand to his lips it was limp and unresponsive. He picked up his coat, opened the door and smiled. 'Good night, Anne.'

'Good night, Colonel de Beaumont,' she said formally, and the door closed.

He stood on the top step, a slight smile on his face. She was annoyed because he had brought to light something discreditable in Mallory's past and that annoyance could only be the automatic reaction of a woman already deeply involved, which was interesting.

He moved down the steps towards the main gate and Jacaud stepped out of the bushes. 'What happened?'

De Beaumont shrugged. 'Patience, my dear Jacaud. I have set things in motion. Now we must await developments.'

A foot crunched on gravel and Jacaud pulled him quickly into the shadows. A moment later Mallory walked by and went towards the house.

'What do we do now?' Jacaud whispered. 'Return to St Pierre?'

De Beaumont shook his head. 'The night is young and interesting things have yet to happen. I think we will go down to the hotel and sample some of our good friend Owen's contraband brandy. We can await developments there.'

He chuckled gently and led the way out through the gates to the narrow dirt road, white in the gloaming.

II

'Who was he, Hamish?' Anne said calmly. 'I want to know.'

'Neil Mallory?' Hamish shrugged. 'An outstanding paratroop officer. First-rate war record, decorated several times. Afterwards, Palestine, Malaya, a different kind of war. He went to Korea in '51, was wounded and captured somewhere on the Imjin. Prisoner for two years.'

'And then what?'

'From what one can make out he was the sort of man people were rather afraid of, especially his superiors. A little like Lawrence or Orde Wingate, God rest his soul. The sort of desperate eccentric who doesn't really fit in where peacetime soldiering's concerned.'

'De Beaumont said he was a colonel? He must have been very young.'

'Probably the youngest in the army at the time. He wrote this book *A New Concept of Revolutionary Warfare* for the War Office in 1953. It aroused a lot of talk at the time. Most people seemed to think he'd turned Communist. Kept quoting from Mao Tse-tung's book on guerrilla warfare as if the damned thing were a bible.'

'What happened?'

'He'd been promoted lieutenant-colonel after the Korean business. They had to find him something to do so they sent him to Malaya. Things weren't too good at that time. In some areas the Communist guerrillas virtually controlled everything. They gave Mallory command of some local troops. It wasn't really a regiment. Not much more than a hundred men. Recruiting was bad at the time. Little stocky Malayan peasants straight out of the rice fields. I know the type.'

'Did they make good soldiers?'

'In three months they were probably the most formidable jungle troops in Malaya. Within six they'd proved themselves so efficient in the field they'd earned a nick-name: 'Mallory's Tigers'."

'What happened in Perak?'

'The climax of the drama, or the tragedy, if you like, because that's what it was. At that time Perak was rotten with Communist guerrillas, especially on the border with Thailand. The powers-that-be told Mallory to go in and clean them out once and for all.'

'And did he?'

'I think you could say that, but when he'd finished he'd earned himself a new name.'

'The Butcher of Perak?'

'That's right. A man who'd ordered the shooting of many prisoners, who had interrogated and tortured captives in custody. A man who was proved to have acted with a single-minded and quite cold-blooded ferocity.'

'And he was cashiered?'

The general shook his head. 'I should imagine that would have involved others. No, they simply retired him. Gave the usual sort of story to the newspapers. Took the line that he'd never really recovered from his experiences in Chinese hands and so on. Nobody could argue with that and the whole thing simply faded away.'

She sat staring into the fire for several moments, then shook her head. 'The man you describe must have been a monster, and Neil Mallory isn't that, I'm sure.'

He stretched out a hand and covered hers. 'You're attracted to him, aren't you?' She made no reply and he sighed. 'God knows it was bound to happen. A long time since Angus went, Anne. A long, long time.'

The door opened and Jagbir appeared, Mallory at his shoulder. 'Mr Mallory is here, general.'

Hamish Grant straightened in his chair, shoulders squared, and said calmly, 'Show Colonel Mallory in, Jagbir.'

Mallory paused just inside the room, his face very white in the soft light, the strange dark eyes showing nothing. 'Who told you?'

'De Beaumont,' the general said. 'When he was head of French Military Intelligence in Algiers in '59 they had a general file on people like you. I understand you were running guns out of Tangiers to the FLN. Is that correct?'

For the moment Mallory was aware only of a feeling of profound relief. That de Beaumont should recognize him from the North African days was unfortunate, but at least the front he had used in Tangiers had obviously been accepted and that was the main thing.

'Does it matter?' he said. 'My past, I mean?'

'Good heavens, man, I'm not interested in what you got up to in Tangiers. It's what happened in Perak that I want to know about.'

'And suppose I say that's none of your damned business?'

The old man stayed surprisingly calm, but Anne moved forward and touched Mallory on the sleeve. 'Please, Neil, I must know.'

Her eyes seemed very large as she gazed up at him, and he turned abruptly, crossed to the french window and went down the steps of the terrace outside.

He stood at the wall above the inlet in the desolate light of gloaming, and, below, the lights of a ship out to sea seemed very far away.

He was tired, drained of all emotion, aware out of some strange inner knowledge that whatever a man did came to nothing in the final analysis.

A step sounded on gravel behind him. When he turned, Hamish Grant and his daughter-in-law were standing at the bottom of the steps. They moved to the table, the old man lowered himself into one of the chairs and Anne Grant approached Mallory.

For a long time she stood peering up at him, her face in shadow, and then she swayed forward, burying her face against his chest, and his arms went round her instinctively.

The old man was silhouetted sharply against the pale night sky and the sea, hands crossed on top of his stick, rooted into the ground like some ancient statue.

'Right, Colonel Mallory,' he said in a voice that would brook no denial, 'I'm ready when you are.'

— 9 —

LIEUTENANT GREGSON paced nervously up and down, smoking a cigarette, trying to look as unconcerned as the half-dozen Malay soldiers who squatted in the long grass talking quietly. At the edge of the clearing the body of a man was suspended by his ankles above the smouldering embers of a fire, the flesh peeling from his skull.

The smell was nauseating, so bad that Gregson could almost taste it. He shuddered visibly and wondered what was keeping the colonel. He was only twenty-two, slim with good shoulders but the face beneath the red beret was fine-drawn, the eyes set too deeply in their sockets.

He heard the sound of the Land-Rover coming along the track and snapped his fingers quickly. There was no need. The soldiers had risen as one man with the easy, relaxed discipline of veterans and stood waiting. A moment later Sergeant Tewak pushed his way into the clearing, followed by the colonel.

Mallory wore a paratrooper's beret and a camouflaged uniform open at the neck, no badges of rank in evidence. He stood staring at the body, dark eyes brooding in that strange white face, and restlessly tapped a bamboo swagger stick against his right knee.

When he spoke his voice was calm. 'When did you find him?'

'About an hour ago. I thought you might want to see him exactly as they left him.'

Mallory nodded. 'Leave Sergeant Tewak in charge here. He can bring the body into Maluban in your Land-Rover. You can come back with me.'

He turned abruptly into the jungle and Gregson gave the necessary orders to Tewak and followed. When he reached the Land-Rover Mallory was already sitting behind the wheel and Gregson climbed into the passenger seat.

The colonel drove away rapidly and Gregson lit a cigarette and said carefully, 'I hope you're not blaming yourself in any way, sir?'

Mallory shook his head. 'He was a good soldier, he knew the risks he was taking. If they'd accepted him we'd have learned a hell of a lot. Probably enough to have put them out of business in the whole of Perak. But they didn't.'

Remembering the pathetic, tortured body, the stench of burning flesh, Gregson shuddered. 'They didn't give him much of a chance, did they, sir?'

'They seldom do,' Mallory observed dryly. 'There are one or two chairborne flunkeys in Singapore who could have learned something this afternoon. Unfortunately they never seem to come this far in.' He took a cigarette from his breast pocket, one hand on the wheel, and lit it. 'There was a signal from HQ while you were away. They're sending me a plane Friday. There's to be an enquiry.'

Gregson turned quickly. 'The Kelantang affair?'

Mallory nodded. 'Apparently the papers got hold of it back home.' He slowed to negotiate a steep hill. 'I don't think I'll be coming back.'

'But that's ridiculous,' Gregson said angrily. 'There isn't a guerrilla left in Kelantang. The Tigers have had more success in six months than any other unit since the emergency began.'

'They don't like my methods,' Mallory said. 'It's as simple as that.'

'Neither did I, at first, but I know now that it's the only way. If you don't fight fire with fire you might as well pack up and go home.'

'And they won't let us do either.' Mallory said. 'Britain never likes to let go of anything. That's my Irish father speaking and he had the best of reasons for knowing.'

The Land-Rover went over a small rise as it emerged from the jungle, and beneath them, beside the river, was Maluban. There were perhaps forty or fifty thatched houses on stilts, the saw-mill and rubber warehouse on the far side of the jetty.

It was very still, the jungle brooding in that quiet period

before night fell, and as Mallory took the Land-Rover down into the village a whistle sounded shrilly and the workers started to emerge from the mill.

He braked to a halt outside his command post, a weathered, clapboard bungalow raised on concrete stilts, saluted the sentry and ran up the steps briskly. Inside, a corporal sat at a radio transmitter in one corner. He started to rise and Mallory pushed him down.

'Anything?' he asked in Malayan.

'Not since you left, sir.'

Mallory moved to the large map of the area which was pinned to one wall. He ran a finger along the course of the river. 'Jack must be about there now. A good forty miles.'

Gregson nodded and indicated a small village to the south-west. 'Harry should be at Trebu by nightfall. Between them they'll have swept most of the western side of the river.'

'Without turning up a damned thing. What's our effective strength here at the moment?'

'Including Sergeant Tewak and the six men bringing in the body, a dozen. Eight men in the sick-bay and all genuine.'

'You don't need to tell me.' Mallory picked up his swagger stick. 'Mr Li's giving a dinner party tonight. I'll probably be there till midnight. Call me if anything turns up.'

'Something special?'

Mallory nodded. 'He's got a journalist staying with him for a few days. A woman called Mary Hume.'

'Isn't she the one who used to be an MP?'

'That's right. One of these professional liberals who spend their time visiting the trouble spots and kicking the poor old army up the backside in print.'

'Never mind,' Gregson said. 'Old Li's food is always interesting.'

'Some consolation.' Mallory moved to the door, turned and, for almost the first time since Gregson had known him, smiled. 'Friday – that's just three days. Not much time to clean up Perak, eh?'

When he had gone Gregson went back to the map. There was a hell of a lot of country and he knew in his bones that the patrols they had out along the river were wasting their time. There were perhaps sixty Chinese guerrillas in Perak, certainly no more. And yet they were enough to terrorize an entire state, to fill the people themselves with such fear that all hopes of co-operation were impossible.

And on Friday the colonel was to fly to Kuala Lumpur to face an enquiry that could well lead to his court martial and disgrace. Gregson cursed softly. If only Mallory could have flown out with the news that he and his Tigers had done it again. Had destroyed the last effective guerrilla band in the north. That would have given them something to think about at HQ.

He went into the bedroom at the rear, poured himself a drink and stood on the verandah looking across the small strip of rough grass that was the garden. A loose board creaked and he turned and saw Suwon, Mr Li's secretary, coming up the steps.

She was perhaps twenty and her skin had that creamy look peculiar to Eurasian women, her lips an extra fullness that gave her a faintly sensual air. Her scarlet dress was of heavy red silk, slashed on either side above the knee, and moulded her ripe figure.

He grinned crookedly and raised his glass. 'Surprise, surprise. I thought you'd be at the party.'

'I will be later,' she said. 'But I wanted to see you.'

'Now that's most flattering.'

He moved close and she held a hand against his chest. 'Please, Jack, this is serious. The wife of Sabal, the ferryman, has just been to see me. She's scared out of her wits.'

'What's the trouble?'

'They've been hiding a wounded terrorist at their house for three days now, under the usual threats. He was shot in that patrol clash on the other side of the river last week. His friends took him to Sabal's house because of its isolation. You know where it is?'

Gregson's stomach was hollow with excitement and when he put down his glass his hand was shaking. 'About half a mile upriver. So they've decided to hand him over?'

She shrugged. 'If the man doesn't have medical treatment soon he'll die. Sabal is a Buddhist. He couldn't let that happen.'

'You've told no one else?'

She shook her head. 'I've no desire to become a target. You know how easily these things leak out. That's why I came the back way.'

He buckled on his belt and revolver. 'No one will know who tipped me off, I promise you that.'

'It's Sabal and his family I'm really worried about.'

'No need to be. I'll only take a couple of men with me. Make it look like a routine call.' He kissed her lightly on the mouth. 'You'd better get going. They'll be looking for you at dinner. And not a word about this to anyone. I'd like to surprise the colonel.'

He went out through the other room and she heard his voice raised as he called to the duty corporal. A few moments later the Land-Rover drove away. She stood there, a shadow slanting across her eyes like a mask. It was as if she were waiting for something. Only when the sound of the engine had finally died into the distance did she turn and walk away.

II

A moth fluttered despairingly beside the oil lamp and shrivelled in the heat. What was left of it fluttered to the table. Mr Li brushed it away and reached for the decanter. It was obvious that he had European blood in him. His eyes lifted slightly at the corners, but they were shrewd and kindly, the lips beneath the straight nose well formed and full of humour.

'More brandy, Mrs Hume?'

She was in her early forties, her greying hair cut short in the current fashion, still attractive in her simple print dress, a kashmir shawl around her shoulders against the cool of the evening.

She pushed her glass across and Mr Li continued, 'You have no idea of the pleasure it gives me to entertain a British Member of Parliament in my own home.'

'I'm afraid you're a little out of date, Mr Li,' she answered lightly as Suwon came in with the coffee. 'I'm no longer interested in politics. Simply a working journalist on an assignment.'

'To discover for yourself the state of things in the border country?' Mr Li smiled. 'How fortunate that Colonel Mallory agreed to accept my hospitality during his stay. I am sure there can be no greater authority on the troubled times through which we are passing.'

'I've already seen something of Colonel Mallory's methods,' Mary Hume said coldly, and turned to Mallory, who sat at one end of the long table in a beautifully tailored drill uniform, the medal ribbons and SAS wings above his left pocket a splash of colour in the lamplight. 'I drove through a village called Pedak about ten miles south of here on the way in. Every house burned to the ground on your orders. Women and children homeless and the rains due.'

Suwon leaned over Mallory's shoulder to pour coffee into his cup and he was aware of her fragrance. 'One of my patrols was ambushed in Pedak two days ago. Four men killed and two wounded. The villagers could have warned them. They didn't.'

'Because they were afraid,' she said angrily. 'Surely that's obvious. The Communist guerrillas must have forced them to keep silent with threats.'

'Quite right,' Mallory replied calmly. 'That's why I burned their houses. Next time they'll think twice.'

'But you're giving them an impossible choice,' she said. 'To betray their own countrymen.'

'Something people like you never seem to get straight. The men who were ambushed and killed, my soldiers, were Malays. The guerrillas who killed them are Chinese.'

'Not all of them.'

'Some are Malayan Chinese, I wouldn't argue on that point, but the majority are Chinese Communists, trained and armed by the Army of the People's Republic and infiltrated into Malaya from Thailand.'

'What Colonel Mallory says is quite true, Mrs Hume,' Mr Li put in. 'These terrorists are bad people. They have made things very difficult for us in this area.'

'For business, you mean,' she said acidly.

'But of course.' Mr Li was not at all put out. 'Many of the great rubber estates have virtually gone out of business and things will soon be as bad in the timber trade. At the mill my workers are already on half-time. These are the people who really suffer, you know. Two weeks ago the Catholic mission at Kota Banu was attacked. The priest-in-charge was away at the time, but two nuns and thirteen young girls were killed.'

'You're wasting your time, Li,' Mallory said. 'That isn't the sort of story Mrs Hume wants to hear. That rag of hers usually prints items like that in the bottom left-hand corner of page seven.'

He picked up his brandy and walked out on the open verandah, aware of Li's voice raised in apology behind him. In the gathering darkness beyond the river the jungle started to come alive, tree-frogs setting the air vibrating, while howler monkeys challenged each other, swinging through the trees, and through it all the steady, pulsating beat of the crickets.

At his shoulder Mary Hume said in a dry, matter-of-fact voice: 'They're saying in Singapore that you executed your prisoners during the Kelantang operation. Is it true?'

'I was hard on the heels of another gang. I needed every man I had.' Mallory shrugged. 'Prisoners would have delayed me.'

'And now there's to be an enquiry. They'll kick you out, you know.'

He shrugged. 'Isn't that what you want?'

She frowned. 'You don't like me, do you, Colonel Mallory?'

'Not particularly.'

'May I ask why? I'm only doing my job.'

'As I remember, that was the excuse you offered in Korea when you and one or two choice specimens like you accepted an invitation from the Chinese to see what things were really like over on that side.'

'I see now,' she said, and her voice died away in a long sigh.

'You wrote some excellent articles on how good the prison camps were,' Mallory said. 'How well we were all treated. I read them after I was released. Of course, they never showed you over my camp, Mrs Hume, which is hardly surprising. Around about the time you were starting your conducted tour I was doing six months in a rather small bamboo cage. As a matter of fact, about twenty of us were. A salutary experience, particularly as winter was just beginning.'

'I reported the facts as I saw them,' she said calmly.

'People like you always do.' He swallowed about half of his

brandy and went on: 'One thing really does interest me. Why has it always got to be your own country? Why is it never the other side? I mean, what exactly *is* eating away at your guts?'

She was obviously only controlling her anger by a supreme effort of will, and when she replied her voice vibrated slightly. 'Where a moral principle is involved I refuse to be hampered by a spurious nationalism.'

'Is that a fact?' Mallory said. 'Well, I've got news for you, Mrs Hume. I'd rather have that lot out there in the jungle than you and your kind any day. At least they fight for what they believe in. I can respect them for that.'

'Even when they butcher nuns and young girls?' she taunted.

'We managed things like that on a much more impressive scale during the war. After all, for a purist like yourself there can't be much difference between the terrorist's grenade and the bombs released at the touch of a button from forty thousand feet.' She was suddenly very still and he said softly: 'But then I was forgetting. Wasn't your husband a bomber pilot during the war? I'm sure his opinion would be most interesting.'

'My husband is dead, Colonel Mallory. He was killed in the war.'

'I know, Mrs Hume,' Mallory said softly.

She turned abruptly and went back inside and Mallory took out a cigarette, striking a match against the verandah rail.

There was a rustle in the bushes below and Sergeant Tewak said quietly: 'Colonel, there is bad news at the command post. It would be well for you to come.'

Mallory glanced over his shoulder quickly. Mr Li and Mary Hume sat at the table, talking earnestly, heads together, and Suwon busied herself preparing drinks at the sideboard. He vaulted over the rail and followed Tewak through the bushes.

The little Malay hurried along without speaking, leading the way out through the rear gate and down the hill to the village. The streets were quiet, but outside the command post Mallory found what seemed to be the whole detachment standing in twos and threes, each man armed and in marching order.

As Tewak led the way round to the store hut at the side of the bungalow Mallory was aware of the emptiness that snatched at the pit of his stomach. The Malay opened the door, switched on the light and led the way in.

The body was covered by a groundsheet and lay on a trestle table in the centre of the room. Mallory knew it was Gregson at once because of the American paratrooper's boots which he had bought at a second-hand shop in Singapore three months previously. Tewak pulled back the groundsheet and waited, his face like stone.

The teeth were clenched, lips drawn back in the death-agony. His hands had been tied behind him, the eyes gouged out, quite obviously while he was still alive. The rest of him was like a piece of raw meat.

Mallory took a deep breath and turned away. 'When did it happen?'

'About half an hour ago. He was tipped off that a wounded terrorist was hiding at the house of Sabal the ferryman. I arrived back about an hour after he'd left. He only took two men. When he didn't return I thought I'd better investigate.'

'Are they all dead?'

'Also Sabal and his wife and their four children.'

Mallory nodded slowly, a slight frown on his face. He looked down at the body on the table, once more covered with the groundsheet.

'Go to Mr Li's bungalow. There's an Englishwoman there, a Mrs Hume. Tell her I want to see her. If she refuses to come, use force.'

The door closed softly and Mallory took out a cigarette and lit it, thinking about Gregson, about the senseless, needless cruelty of his going. It had been intended as a threat, so much was obvious, and had been directed at him personally. Whoever controlled the sixty or so terrorists in Perak had simply used Gregson as a calling card.

A few minutes later the door opened and Mary Hume was pushed inside. Behind her Mallory was conscious of Li's troubled face in the doorway.

She was trembling with anger, her face very white as she moved forward. Mallory cut in quickly before she could speak.

'So sorry to trouble you, Mrs Hume, but one of my young officers was very anxious to meet you.'

As the frown deepened across her forehead, he pulled the

groundsheet away quickly. She stood staring at the table, an expression of wonderment frozen into place, and then her head started to move from side to side, the lips trembling. Mr Li took her gently in his arms and held her close.

'This was not a good thing to do, colonel.'

'You go to hell,' Mallory said, 'and you can take her with you,' and he turned and covered Gregson carefully.

In the distance thunder rumbled and then lightning flared. In the split second of its illumination Mallory saw each item of furniture in his bedroom clearly. He tossed his swagger stick and beret on the bed and opened the shutters. As he stepped on to the verandah the rain came with a sudden, great rush, filling the air with its voice.

He breathed deeply, taking the air into his lungs, and a quiet voice said, 'The night air is not good when the rains start, colonel.'

Suwon stood a few feet away by the rail and as lightning flared again her face seemed to jump out of the darkness, the embroidered dragon on the scarlet dress coming alive like some strange night creature.

'I was hoping you'd come,' he said.

She moved very close until their bodies touched and her scent was warm in his nostrils, the sharply pointed breasts hard against him. She placed one hand behind his neck, her mouth slack with desire, and he said softly, 'Why did you tell Gregson that a wounded terrorist was hiding out at Sabal's house?'

As his hands slid round to the small of her back her body tensed, taut as a bow-string. She gave a terrified gasp, turned and stumbled down the steps to the lawn. As she started across, lightning exploded again and in that brief moment of illumination Sergeant Tewak and half a dozen men moved forward in a semicircle. As Tewak reached her the sky seemed to split wide open with a crash of thunder that made the earth tremble, drowning her cry of terror as she was turned roughly and pushed towards the steps.

In his room Mallory lit the lamp, pulled out a chair and sat down. Suwon's dress was saturated, clinging to her like a second skin, and her face was very white as Tewak brought her forward.

'Earlier this evening you visited the command post by way of the garden. You told Lieutenant Gregson there was a wounded terrorist at Sabal's house.' She started to shake her head weakly in denial and Mallory went on: 'Don't waste time in stupid lies. The duty corporal overheard the entire conversation.'

Tears started to roll down her face and he said: 'Gregson is dead, but I don't blame you for that. Only the person who gave you your orders. Who was it? You needn't be afraid. I'll see you're protected.'

She shook her head desperately and tried to pull free from Tewak's iron grip. She was wasting her time. The Malay raised his eyebrows. Mallory nodded and Tewak smashed his clenched fist into her mouth, sending her staggering across the room on to the bed.

When Mallory pulled her forward her lips were crushed and bleeding and a couple of teeth were missing.

'Two weeks ago your friends burned down a Catholic mission and butchered thirteen little girls,' he said calmly. 'Last July they derailed a train and killed or injured nearly a hundred peasants. As far as I'm concerned you're expendable. Now either you tell me what I want to know or I'll let Tewak really go to work on you, and one thing I can promise – you'll never want to look in a mirror again.'

Tewak started to take off his belt and she shook her head weakly, the breath bubbling out through her broken mouth.

'Mr Li,' she moaned. 'It was Mr Li.'

III

Li examined himself in the bathroom mirror, a pair of tweezers in one hand. Very carefully he plucked a couple of gold hairs from his upper lip, then opened a large, gold-capped bottle of perfumed astringent and poured some into his palms. He carefully massaged his face, wincing slightly at the stinging coldness, turned and moved into his bedroom.

Mallory was standing by the open window that led to the verandah. He wore his red beret and the swagger stick in his right hand beat restlessly against his thigh. It was the eyes which told Li his fate, those strange, unfathomable eyes like holes in the white face, staring through and beyond him.

There was nothing to say, nothing at all. He stood there, a slight, careful smile on his face, hands thrust into the pockets of his silk dressing-gown, and Mallory made a slight gesture with his hand that brought Tewak and his men into the room.

Mr Li moved to a small coffee table, selected a cigarette from a jade box and lit it. 'Who told you?'

Mallory shook his head. 'Suwon was a mistake. Girls like her value their looks too much. They haven't got anything else to trade with.'

The bookcase against the far wall came down with a splintering crash and three of the soldiers rammed the butt ends of their rifles against the wooden panelling. A moment later a large segment fell out, revealing a cupboard, perhaps three feet square, containing a wireless transmitter and several files.

Mallory examined the find, nodded and turned quickly. 'So far, so good. Now let's get down to business. According to our intelligence reports you have between sixty and seventy guerrillas operating in Perak. I'd like to know where they are.'

'You're wasting your time, my dear Mallory,' Li said. 'And that's something you can't really spare, isn't it? When is it they're coming for you – Friday? Thirty-six hours, that's all.'

He started to laugh and Tewak raised a hand. Mallory shook his head. 'No sense in wasting time on the preliminaries. Bring him into the living-room, there's a fire there.'

Li was aware of a coldness clutching at his inside. The stories he had heard about this man Mallory, of his Tigers and the way they operated. No one really believed it because the English didn't fight in that way. Didn't use such methods, which was their greatest weakness. Brainwashing and psychological pressures he had been prepared for, but this . . .

They hustled him into the other room and across to the wide stone fireplace in which he had ordered the servants to light a log fire against the dampness of the rains. Mallory nodded and Li's dressing-gown and pyjama jacket were ripped away, baring him to the waist. His hands were jerked roughly behind his back and lashed with a length of rope.

There was a disturbance outside the door and Mallory

heard Mary Hume's voice raised shrilly. He crossed the room and moved past his men into the corridor. The dark circles under her eyes accentuated the paleness of her face and she had obviously been crying.

'What's going on in there?' she said. 'I demand to know.'

'I'm questioning Mr Li,' Mallory told her. 'We've just discovered that he's not quite what he seems to be.'

'I don't believe you,' she said.

'Well, that's just too bad. At a later date I'll be happy to show you the transmitting set he had hidden in his room, but right now I'm busy.' He turned to the corporal on his left. 'Escort Mrs Hume to her room and see that she doesn't leave it.'

He went back into the living-room, slamming the door on her sudden, indignant outburst, and crossed to the fire. He sat down in the chair opposite Li, took out a cigarette and lit it.

'Have you ever been tortured?' Li made no reply and Mallory continued: 'In 1943 I was working under cover in France. I was only twenty. The Gestapo got hold of me. The first two days I didn't do too bad, but by the end of the week I was telling them everything they wanted to know. Of course, by that time London had changed everything round, so it didn't really matter.'

'How very interesting,' Li said.

'I thought you might say that.' Mallory picked up a poker and inserted it into the fire. 'I'm afraid I can't wait for a week, you understand that, but I don't think I'll have to. I've had the extra advantage of two years in a Communist prison camp. They taught me a lot, those friends of yours.'

Li gazed at the poker in fascinated horror and his throat went dry. He moistened his lips and croaked: 'You wouldn't dare. The marks would be on my body for all to see. Mrs Hume would be a witness to all that had taken place.'

'They told me to clean out Perak,' Mallory said, 'and I've only got till Friday morning to do it. That means cutting a few corners. You understand, I'm sure.'

He took the poker from the fire. It was white hot and he turned and said gently, 'Tell me where your men are, that's all I want to know.'

'You're wasting your time,' Li said. 'You might as well shoot me and get it over with.'

'I don't think so.' Mallory considered him carefully and shook his head. 'I'd say you might last two hours, but I doubt it.'

IV

It was perhaps three hours later when Li regained consciousness on his bed in the cool darkness of his room. His hands had been roughly bandaged and pain coursed through his entire body, sending his senses reeling.

And he had talked. That was the shameful thing. He had poured out everything to the terrible Englishman with the white face and the dark eyes that pierced straight through to the soul.

He pushed himself upright and slowly hobbled across the floor, grinding his teeth together to keep from crying out. He paused at the window and peered outside. The verandah was deserted. There was no one in sight. He pushed the window open and crossed to the steps. He stood there for a moment, inhaling the freshness of the rain, a faint excitement stirring inside him, driving the pain from his mind. He would win. He would beat Mallory in the end and that was the important thing.

He stumbled down the steps and started across the lawn. He was perhaps half-way across when he heard the click of a bolt as a weapon was cocked. He turned, mouth opening to cry out, conscious that even now Mallory had won.

The line of fire erupting from the bushes spun him around twice and drove him down against the earth. For a moment only there was the scent of wet grass in his nostrils, then nothing.

In his office at the command post Mallory heard the rattle of the sub-machine-gun clearly. He paused for a moment, head raised, then returned to the map in front of him. A few minutes later the door opened and Tewak entered, shaking rain from his groundsheet.

Mallory sat back. 'What happened?'

'The sentry got him as he was crossing the garden. Mrs

Hume's outside. Apparently she ran out of the house when she heard the shooting. She saw his condition.'

'Bring her in,' Mallory said.

She was wearing an old Burberry that was far too big for her, the shoulders soaked by the rain. Tewak led her forward and she slumped into a chair and sat looking at Mallory, her face old and careworn.

'I saw Mr Li,' she said dully. 'I saw what you'd done to him.'

'Mr Li was directly responsible for the murder by torture of Lieutenant Gregson and his men,' Mallory said. 'He was responsible for the deaths of thirteen schoolgirls two weeks ago and very many more innocent people during the past two years.'

'You tortured him,' she said. 'Tortured him in cold blood, then shot him down.'

'If he'd gone to Singapore he'd have been tried and very probably sentenced to ten years at the most as a political offender,' Mallory said. 'His friends would have got him out before then, believe me.'

'You fool,' she whispered. 'You've lost everything. Everything. Don't you see that?'

Mallory leaned forward. 'There are sixty-three Communist guerrillas in Perak, Mrs Hume. That's something I got out of Li. About thirty of them are camped at this moment on an abandoned rubber estate near Trebu. I've got a large patrol in that area now. They'll be in position to attack at 2 a.m. The rest are going to pass downriver hidden in two fishing boats within the next hour. Apparently, they'd intended to destroy the railway bridge at Pegu at dawn. I'm afraid they'll be disappointed.'

She frowned slightly, as if finding difficulty in taking in what he had said. 'But you've only got a handful of men. You can't possibly hope to defeat such a large group.'

'Solicitude for my welfare at this stage, Mrs Hume? You're slipping.' He got to his feet and buckled on his revolver. 'Don't worry, we have our ways.' He crossed to the door, opened it and turned. 'Stay here, and this time I mean it.'

Mary Hume opened her mouth to protest, but no sound came, and suddenly she was afraid. Afraid of this terrible young man. There was nothing she could do, nothing to prevent the tragedy that was taking place. Out of some strange, inner knowledge she knew that Neil Mallory, in the process of destroying the evil that he hated, was also destroying himself. The most surprising thing of all was that she cared.

V

Mallory moved across to the jetty and paused beside the two men who squatted behind the heavy machine-gun. Another was positioned on top of a small hill fifty yards away and between them they covered the river with an arc of fire.

At the end of the jetty Tewak waited with the rest of the men. Two of them crouched behind the narrow wall, the heavy tanks of their flame-throwers bulging obscenely.

The rain rushed into the river with a heavy, sibilant whispering, and Mallory was aware of a strange, aching sadness. It was as if he had done all this before in another time, another place. As if life were a circle turning endlessly. Everything that had happened during the previous few hours lacked definition, like a dream only half remembered.

And then Tewak grunted. There was the slapping of water against a keel, a sensation of an even darker mass moving through the darkness, and Mallory tapped Tewak lightly on the shoulder.

The little sergeant picked up a portable spot and switched it on. The white beam lanced through the night, picking out two large fishing boats as they slipped downstream, side by side, sails furled, a man in each stern working a sweep.

There was a cry of alarm and the first boat half lifted out of the water as it collided with the ferry hawser which Tewak and his men had suspended across the river an hour earlier.

The boat spun round, crashing into its fellow, and there was another cry, followed by a burst of small-arms fire directed towards the jetty.

Mallory called out and the men with the flame-throwers stood up. Liquid fire arched through the night, splashing across the two boats. Immediately their super-structure and sails started to burn and men poured on to their decks from below.

The two heavy machine-guns opened up, raking the decks, chopping down the guerrillas as soon as they appeared. Tewak dropped the spot, picked up his sub-machine-gun and joined in with the rest of the men.

It was over within a few minutes. A handful jumped from the blazing inferno and struck out desperately for safety, but the flame-throwers searched them out, the fire licking hungrily across the surface of the water, catching them one by one.

By this time the river and the village were brilliantly illuminated and Mallory stood there watching, taking no part in what was happening. He glanced at his watch. It was just after 2 a.m. and he wondered how Harrison was getting on.

He turned and found Mary Hume standing a few yards away. When he walked towards her he saw that she was crying.

'You butcher,' she said. 'You butcher. I'll see you hang for this night's work.'

'I'm sure you will, Mrs Hume,' he said calmly and went past her along the jetty.

Twenty-four hours left now till that plane arrived, that was all, but it was enough. If he moved fast along the river bank to meet up with Harrison and his men coming south they'd be certain to sweep up any survivors of the clash at the rubber estate. Another twenty-four hours and after that . . .

As he went up the bank towards the command post the first fishing boat sank beneath the surface with a hiss of steam.

— 10 —

A MATCH flared outlining Hamish Grant's craggy features as he lit a cheroot. 'And the enquiry?'

It was quite dark now and, below, waves creamed over the rocks in the entrance of the tiny inlet. It was a warm, soft night, stars strung away to the horizon, and when a cloud moved from the face of the moon the terrace was bathed in a hard, white light.

Mallory turned from looking out to sea and shrugged. 'A foregone conclusion. They used terms like: "Previous gallant service." Hinted that I hadn't really recovered from the ordeal of two years in a Chinese prison camp.'

'And spared you the ultimate disgrace.'

'They didn't actually cashier me, if that's what you mean. You could say I was eased into retirement as quietly as possible. For the good of the service, of course.'

'Naturally,' the old man said. 'A bad business. That sort of thing rubs off on everyone concerned.'

'What I did to Li he would have done to me,' Mallory said. 'The purpose of terrorism is to terrorize. Lenin said that. It's on page one of every Communist handbook on revolutionary warfare. You can only fight that kind of fire with fire. Otherwise you might as well lie down and let the waves wash over you. That's what I brought out of that Chinese prison camp, general.'

'An interesting point of view.'

'The only one in the circumstances. I did what had to be done. When I'd finished there was no more terror by night in Perak. No more Kota Banus. No more butchering of little girls. God knows, that should count for something.'

There was silence. In the moonlight Anne Grant's face seemed very pale, the eyes dark and secret, telling him nothing. When a cloud crossed the moon she became a motionless silhouette, her face turned towards him, but still she didn't speak.

Mallory sighed and tossed his cigarette over the wall in a glowing curve. 'In the circumstances, perhaps you'll excuse me, general? This has turned out to be one of those evenings when I could do with a drink.'

He turned and went up the steps, the sound of his going fading quickly into the darkness. After a while Hamish Grant said quietly: 'It's not often one meets a man like that. Someone who's willing to carry the guilt for the rest of us. It takes a rather special brand of courage.'

She turned towards him, her face a pale blur, and then, as if coming to a decision, stood up. 'Do you mind?'

He reached for her hand and held it tightly. 'Leave me the car, will you? I might join you later.'

II

'And that was that,' Mallory told himself. 'That was very much that.' No question of what she had thought of him. Her silence, that stillness, had been answer enough. And the strange thing was that it mattered, that for the first time in years the protective shell he had grown had cracked and now he was defenceless.

His chin was on his breast, hands in pockets, as he turned on to the springy turf beside the road, white in the moonlight that ran down to the harbour.

A small wind seemed to crawl across his face and he drew in his breath sharply. He heard no sound and yet he knew that she walked beside him. He spoke calmly, but with a faint Irish intonation, inherited from his father, always apparent in moments of great stress.

'And what would you be wanting, Anne Grant?'

'A drink, Neil Mallory,' she said, matching his mood, 'and perhaps another. Would that be asking too much?'

He paused and turned to face her, hands still thrust into his pockets. In the moonlight she looked very beautiful, more beautiful than he had ever thought a woman could be, and there were tears in her eyes. He slipped an arm about her shoulders and together they went down the hill towards the lights of the hotel.

III

In the long grass on the hill above the cliffs Raoul Guyon lay on his back and stared into an infinity of stars, his hands clasped behind his head. Beside him Fiona Grant sat cross-legged, combing her hair.

She turned and smiled, her face clear in the moonlight. 'Well, are you going to make an honest woman of me?"

'As always, you have a gift for the difficult question,' he said.

'A plain yes or no would do. I'm reasonably civilized.'

'A word no woman is entitled to use,' he said solemnly, and lit a cigarette. 'Life is seldom as simple as yes or no, Fiona.'

'I don't agree,' she said. 'It's people who make it complicated. My father likes you, if that's got anything to do with it, and I can't see what they'd have to complain about at your end. After all, I could pass for French.'

'I'm quite sure my mother would adore you. On the other hand, we Bretons are very old-fashioned in certain matters. She would never allow me to marry a girl who couldn't bring a sizable dowry with her.'

'Would eleven thousand pounds do?' Fiona said. 'My favourite uncle died last March.'

'I'm sure *maman* would be most impressed,' Guyon told her.

She squirmed against him, laying her head on his chest. 'In any case, why should we worry about money? I know most artists have to struggle, but how many of them paint like you?'

'A good point.'

And she was right. Already he had sold many paintings, working between assignments on the family farm near Loudeac that his mother still managed so competently. Mornings on the banks of the Oust with leaves drifting from the beech trees into the river and the smell of wet earth. Country that he had grown up in and loved. He was aware, with a strange wonderment, that he wanted to take this girl there, to see again with her the old grey farmhouse rooted into its hollow amongst the trees, walk with her over the familiar country that he loved so much.

'Of course, there could always be someone else,' she said.

Her voice was light and yet there was a poignancy there. It was as if she was aware of how near to hurt she might be, and he pulled her close instinctively.

'There was a girl once, Fiona, in Algiers a long time ago. She gave me peace when I needed it more than anything else on earth. She paid for that gift with her life. A high price. I've been trying to escape from her ever since.'

There was a short silence, and then she said gently: 'Have you ever considered that it might be Algeria that you're running from? That somehow this girl has come to symbolize everything that ever happened there?'

In that single instant he knew that what she had said was true. That by some strange perception she had struck right to the very heart of things.

'I know I'm young, Raoul,' she continued, 'and on the whole I've only seen the lighter side, but I know this: the war in Algeria wasn't the first to send men home with blood on their hands and it won't be the last. But that's life. There wouldn't be any sweet without sour. People get by.'

'At a guess I'd say you must be about a thousand years old.'

He kissed her passionately and she linked her arms behind his neck and pressed her body against him. After a while she rolled away and lay on her back, breathless, eyes sparkling.

'And now do you think I might get to see that farm in Brittany?'

He pulled her to her feet and held her at arm's length. 'Did I ever have a choice?'

She reached up to kiss him and then turned and ran away down the hill. Guyon gave her a start of perhaps twenty yards and then went after her, laughter bubbling up spontaneously inside him for the first time in years.

IV

The bar at the hotel was a long, pleasant room with white-washed walls, its windows facing out to sea. Two large oil lamps were suspended from one of the oak beams that supported the low roof.

Jacaud and two other men sat at a table in a corner and played cards. Owen Morgan leaned on the bar beside them, watching the play, a small, greying man with hot Welsh eyes and a face hardened by a lifetime of the sea.

Beside an open window Mallory and Anne faced each other across a small table, smoking cigarettes. Far out to sea the lights of a ship moved slowly across the horizon like something from another world and Anne sighed.

'A big one. I wonder where she's going?'

'Tangiers, the Azores. Take your choice.'

'An invitation?'

'Of the most improper kind,' he said, and smiled.

'You should do that more often,' she said. 'It suits you.'

Before he could reply a shadow fell across the table. Juliette Vincente was standing there, a half-bottle of champagne and two glasses on her tray. She was perhaps thirty-five, a plain, rather simple-looking woman in a blue woollen dress, thickening slightly at the waist, but her skin was fresh and clean, the cheeks touched with crimson.

'From Monsieur le Comte, madame,' she said simply, and placed the bottle and glasses on the table.

At the far end of the bar two or three broad steps lifted to another room where de Beaumont sat beside a pleasant fire. Anne nodded and he raised his glass.

'Small return for a delightful meal.'

'Shall I ask him over?' Mallory said.

She shook her head. 'Not unless you want to.'

A moment or two later the station wagon braked to a halt outside and Raoul Guyon and Fiona got out, turning to help the general. The old man led the way up the steps confidently and entered the bar.

'Over here, Hamish!' Anne called, and he turned and came towards them.

Mallory got to his feet and brought a chair forward and Fiona slipped into the window-seat beside Anne. Guyon picked up the bottle and nodded approvingly.

'Heidsieck 1952. How typical for the English to reserve the best for themselves. I must really do something to upset the balance.'

He moved across to the bar and Hamish Grant produced a brown leather cheroot case and proffered it to Mallory. 'Try one of these. Filthy things, but nothing quite like 'em. Picked up the habit in India.'

Mallory took one and offered the old man a light as Guyon returned. 'Our good friend Owen is raiding his cellar. He can't guarantee that everything will have necessarily come in through the proper channels, but no matter. He tells me that the revenue man only comes once a year and always warns him in advance.'

'Understandable,' the general said. 'They were in the navy together.'

Owen Morgan appeared a few moments later and came across with a wide grin. 'No need for ice,' he said to Guyon as he offered a bottle for inspection. 'It's cold enough where that's been.'

'Excellent,' Guyon said. 'I'll open it while you fetch some glasses.'

His gaiety was quite infectious and within a few moments he had them all laughing with a description of an outrageous and quite untruthful incident from his past. The conversation which followed moved along spontaneously.

Once or twice Mallory noticed the three men in the corner looking towards them, obviously irritated after some particularly loud burst of laughter from Fiona or Guyon. One of them hammered on the table and called loudly to Owen Morgan for more cognac.

Mallory leaned across to Anne. 'The one on the left with the haircut. He was at the wheel of de Beaumont's boat this afternoon. Who is he?'

'They called him Jacaud,' she said. 'That's all I can tell you. He seems to go everywhere with de Beaumont. I think the others are afraid of him.'

'Hardly surprising,' Guyon put in. 'There's about fifteen stone of bone and muscle there, mostly muscle from the look of him.'

Jacaud got to his feet, crossed the bar and mounted the steps to the other room. He leaned on de Beaumont's table and they held a short conversation. Mallory watched them over the rim of his glass. Once, de Beaumont turned and looked towards them. He gazed coolly at Mallory for a moment, then turned back to Jacaud.

The big Frenchman rejoined his friends and Owen Morgan turned on the radio, the sound of music filling the room. Guyon pulled Fiona to her feet and grinned.

'Come on, let's liven the place up a little.'

They made an attractive couple as they circled the room. The beautiful young girl on the threshold of womanhood, and Guyon, his lean, sun-tanned face animated and full of life.

Anne Grant watched them wistfully and coloured when she saw that Mallory was looking at her. 'Fiona always makes me feel old,' she said.

'But not too old.' Mallory turned to the general. 'You'll excuse us, sir?'

The general touched the champagne bottle lightly and raised his glass. 'Enjoy yourselves while you can. I'll make do with this.'

They moved into the centre of the floor. She slipped one arm about his neck and danced with her head on his shoulder, her body pressed so closely against him that he could feel the line from breast to thigh.

For a moment he forgot about everything except the fact that he was dancing with a warm, exciting girl whose perfume filled his nostrils and caused a pleasant ache of longing in the pit of his stomach.

It had been a long time since he had slept with a woman but that wasn't the whole explanation. That Anne Grant attracted him was undeniable, but there was something more there, something deeper that for the moment was beyond his comprehension.

The music stopped, a pause between records, and they went back to their table. The others followed a few moments later, and as Fiona seated herself there was a burst of loud laughter from Jacaud and his two friends in the corner, followed by a remark in French, coarse, to the point and quite unprintable.

Guyon swung round, his face hardening. The three men returned his gaze boldly. He took one quick step towards them and Mallory caught him by the sleeve and pulled him down into his chair.

'Let it go.'

Guyon was shaking with suppressed anger. 'You heard what he said?'

Fiona leaned forward and put a hand on his arm. 'Don't let it upset you, Raoul. They've had a little too much to drink, that's all.'

A shadow fell across the table and Mallory looked up into the face of the man he had heard Owen Morgan refer to as Marcel a little earlier. He was of medium height and wore denim pants and a blue seaman's jersey. He was very drunk and clutched at the edge of the table to steady himself.

'I think you'd be better off sitting down,' Mallory told him in French.

Marcel ignored him, leaned across the table, knocking over a glass, and grabbed Anne by one arm. 'You dance with me now?' he mouthed in broken English.

Mallory grabbed for the man's right arm just above the elbow, his thumb hooking in the pressure point. As Marcel swung round, mouth opening in a cry of agony, Guyon kicked him under the right knee-cap. Marcel staggered backwards, lost his balance and sprawled across the other table. Jacaud pushed him to one side, got to his feet and moved forward.

He stood there, swaying slightly as if drunk, and yet the slate-grey eyes were as cold as ice, eternally watchful.

'Two to one, messieurs,' he said in excellent English. 'You made the odds.'

Owen Morgan came round the bar on the run, face very white, eyes blazing. The big Frenchman sent him staggering backwards with a single, contemptuous shove of his hand and laughed harshly.

'He asked for it, Jacaud,' de Beaumont called sharply. 'Let it end there.'

Jacaud ignored him and de Beaumont made no move to come down into the bar, gave no indication of being able or willing to control the situation. He stayed by the fire, a watchful expression on his face.

In that moment Mallory realized that the whole thing had been arranged. That for some reason of his own de Beaumont had deliberately engineered the situation.

Guyon started to rise and Mallory pulled him down again. 'My affair.'

Jacaud stood there swaying a little, still keeping up the pretence of being drunk, his great hands hooked slightly, every muscle tensed and ready. He lurched forward and stood over them.

'Of course, my friend might be willing to settle for a drink.' He nodded at the table. 'A bottle of champagne would do.'

'Anything to oblige,' Mallory said calmly.

He reached for the bottle and, as he turned, reversed his grip and smashed it across the side of the Frenchman's skull. As Anne cried out, Jacaud staggered and fell to one knee. Mallory picked up a chair, moved in fast and smashed it down across the great shoulders. Jacaud grunted, started to heel over and Mallory smashed the broken chair down again and again until it splintered. He tossed it to one side and waited.

Slowly, painfully, Jacaud reached for the edge of the bar and pulled himself up. He hung there for a moment, then turned to Mallory, wiping blood from his face casually.

And then, incredibly, he charged, head down like a wounded bull, the great hands reaching out to destroy. Mallory judged his moment exactly, swerved to one side, allowing the Frenchman to plunge past, and slashed him across the kidneys with a karate blow delivered with the edge of his hand.

Jacaud screamed and fell to the floor. For a little while he stayed there on his hands and knees, and when he got to his feet he was slobbering like an animal. He lurched forward and Mallory kicked his feet from under him. Jacaud crashed to the floor, rolled over and lay still.

In the silence which followed, de Beaumont came down the steps slowly. He dropped to one knee beside Jacaud, examined him and looked up. 'You are a hard man, Colonel Mallory.'

'When I have to be,' Mallory said. 'You could have done something to stop this. Why didn't you?'

He turned without waiting for a reply and went back to the table. 'I think that might do for one night. Shall we go?'

Hamish Grant's face was pale, the nostrils flaring slightly as he got to his feet. 'You know, I really think it's about time I bought you a drink, Neil. I've got some rather special whiskey back at the house. So Irish that you can taste the peat. I'd like to have your opinion on it.'

Anne's face was very white and she was trembling. Mallory squeezed her hand reassuringly and they all walked towards the door. De Beaumont moved to block the way.

'One moment, general. Perhaps I might be allowed to tender my apologies for this distressing affair. At the best of times Jacaud has a short temper. When he's been drinking . . .'

'No need for that, de Beaumont,' Hamish Grant said coldly. 'I think the matter has been handled quite adequately.'

De Beaumont stood there, his smile frozen into place, and then he turned away sharply and they moved outside.

Fiona got behind the wheel, Guyon beside her, and the general and Anne climbed into the back. Mallory slammed the door and leaned in at the open window.

'If you don't mind, general, I'd like to take you up on that drink another time. I've had enough excitement for one night.'

As Anne's head turned sharply towards him he turned quickly, giving them no time to argue, and went down the slope towards the jetty. A few moments later the engine coughed into life behind him and the station wagon moved away.

He turned right at the jetty, following a steeply shelving path which brought him down to a strip of sand, white in the moonlight, waves curling in across the shingle with a gentle sucking sound.

He sat on a boulder and lit a cigarette with fingers that trembled slightly. He inhaled deeply, drawing the smoke into his lungs and released it with a long sigh.

Behind him Anne Grant said, 'You don't do things by halves, do you?'

'What's the point?' he said simply.

'We seem to have held this conversation before.'

When she whispered his name they came together naturally and easily. Her hands pulled his head down as her mouth sought his and her sweetness drove every other thought from his mind. He picked her up in his arms and laid her down gently in the soft sand.

— 11 —

THE WIND WAS freshening, lifting the waves into white-caps, and as the dinghy rounded the point water slopped over the gunwale. Guyon carefully eased his weight into the centre and started to bale. He wore a heavy sweater and reefer jacket against the cold. A pair of night-glasses hung around his neck and one of the aquamobiles lay in the prow behind him.

Mallory sat in the stern wearing a black rubber diving suit, the heavy aqualung already strapped into place on his back.

As a cross-current started to turn the dinghy in towards the cliffs he opened the throttle on the outboard motor to compensate and glanced at the luminous dial of his watch.

It was 11:45 and there was very little cloud, the sky brilliant with stars, and the moonlight danced across the waves, leaving a trail of silver behind it. The dinghy lifted high on a large swell and swung in towards the great finger of rock which marked the western tip of the island. Mallory opened the throttle again. For a moment the dinghy seemed to stand still and then it forged ahead.

They rounded the point, fighting the cross-currents, Guyon cursing steadily as water slopped over the sides, and then they were sweeping into calmer water. Beyond, St Pierre and the Gothic towers of the castle were dark against the sky.

Mallory throttled down again and the dinghy coasted on, the sound of her motor a murmur on the wind. The great reef running between the two islands was deceptively innocent in the moonlight. Waves rolling in from the sea splashed lazily across the rocks, now and then a curtain of white spray lifting into the night like silver lace.

He took the dinghy into the calm waters of the middle passage until they reached the first point where the roof closed in and water boiled across great jagged black teeth. He cut the motor and the dinghy slowed and ground gently against a sloping, weed-covered shoulder of rock. Guyon hooked the painter into a crevasse and looked towards St Pierre through the night-glasses.

'About a quarter of a mile. A long swim.'

'Not with the aquamobile,' Mallory said.

Guyon got it over the side, the dinghy heeling dangerously. 'Rather you than me. The water's like ice. How long will you be?'

Mallory shrugged. 'No more than half an hour. I've no intention of hanging around at the other end.'

He fitted the rubber mouthpiece between his teeth and adjusted his air supply, touched the knife briefly at his belt and clambered awkwardly over the side on to the reef. He waded into the water, swam to the other side of the dinghy and reached for the aquamobile. Guyon smiled once and Mallory nodded and sank beneath the surface.

Moonlight filtered down through the water, probing into the depths. When he passed beneath the surface of the reef and came into the middle passage he entered a darker, more sinister world.

He switched on the powerful light and its beam pierced through the darkness in front of him, splaying against the rocks that arched above his head.

He tilted the nose of the aquamobile and went down gently, levelling out at twenty feet. Although his top speed was no more than three knots, he seemed to rush at a terrifying speed into the wall of grey mist that was the edge of his visibility. The great, arched nave of the reef stretched into infinity before him, the water breaking against his mask.

And then he was through and moving into a strange, unreal landscape of jumbled rocks and pale forests of seaweed waving languidly in the diffused moonlight. He surfaced and looked up at the cliffs of St Pierre, the pointed towers of the castle dark against the sky.

The moonlight splashed across the face of the cliffs, picking out the dark mouth of the cave. It was now high water and there was no more than a ten- or twelve-foot clearance. Mallory turned the nose of the aquamobile down and levelled out at forty feet. He switched off the spot and moved into a grey phosphorescent mist.

The great fault in the sea-bed dropped beneath him. At least ten fathoms, Anne had said, slicing into the heart of the island. The mist seemed to swing to one side like a curtain, revealing the entrance of the cave, a good sixty feet across as it widened on its way down.

He drifted in, grey-green walls moving past on either side. The water lightened, the grey merging into aquamarine as artificial light seeped down from the surface. He moved in close to the wall and went forward cautiously.

He stopped abruptly, switching off the aquamobile. From this point on the rough wall of the cave merged into the jetty, great square blocks of masonry like the foundations of some ancient fort descending into the depths. He started up cautiously and immediately the grey-black underbelly of the submarine appeared from the mist.

He had found what he was looking for and to stay any

longer was to invite trouble. He turned and flutter-kicked towards the entrance. The light dimmed and he was aware of the current tugging at him.

He swam out into that strange, grey, phosphorescent world and paused to switch on the aquamobile. In that same moment it was torn from his grasp with a metallic clang and a shock-wave, spreading through the water, burst around him.

He turned and saw the frogman suspended in the water about twenty feet away, a weird sea-creature, full of menace, the moonlight glinting on his visor as he reloaded his speargun.

Mallory drove forward, pulling the heavy knife from its sheath. When he was perhaps ten feet away the gun exploded again in a shower of silver bubbles. He swung desperately to one side. The spear hurtled past and he moved in fast, his knife cleaving through rubber and flesh.

The man's body bucked agonizingly, blood rising in a dark cloud as Mallory pulled out the knife and snatched at the air-pipe. As it came free in his hand, air burst out at pressure, bubbles swirling past him on the way to the surface.

He could see the man's face quite clearly now, eyes bulging, teeth clamped together in agony. Quite suddenly he went over backwards in a graceful curve, like a leaf spiralling earthwards in autumn, the weight of his aqualung taking him down.

Mallory struck up towards the surface, chasing his aquamobile, which was rising slowly. He grabbed the handles and switched on, already aware of further shock-waves rippling through the water, bouncing from his body.

The aquamobile surged forward, helped by the turning tide. The sea-bed started to shelve again, and, below, he was aware of the pale forest of seaweed, the ribbons of black rock that were the beginnings of the reef.

Once again he was aware of a shock-wave curling around his body and he glanced to his right. Perhaps fifty yards away and coming up fast through moon-drenched water was a large underwater scooter, at least twice as long as his aquamobile, a frogman trailing behind.

Mallory kicked desperately, urging the aquamobile forward. And then the rocks swarmed up out of the gloom on either side and he rushed into the darkness of the middle passage. He switched on his spot, planing down to avoid the overhanging roof. He was aware of a muffled throbbing in his ear, and glanced back. A wide band of diffused light spreading through the mist told him that his pursuer wasn't far behind.

He passed through a section where moonlight streamed in through cracks and fissures in the roof and knew that he was about half-way along the passage, somewhere above the wreck of the freighter. As he came into the clear section he plunged down and at ten fathoms a tapering steel mast loomed out of the gloom. Mallory held on with one hand and waited.

The darkness moved in on him with terrible, suffocating pressure and the mast seemed to move a little as if the old freighter had rolled. He remembered the dark companionway, dead men's bones crushed under a steel girder, and shivered, suddenly aware of the cold.

He could sense the turbulence in the water, waves rippling down. When he looked up there was the weird, incandescent glow of the spot-lamp on the other scooter as it passed overhead. He waited for a moment or two, then went up slowly.

At twenty feet he levelled out, switched on the motor, but not the spot, and went after the other scooter. Only in patches was visibility really bad and at this depth the moonlight streamed in through fissures in the rock like regularly spaced lamps along a dark road.

When he emerged at last from the great central nave into clear water he switched off the aquamobile and surfaced.

Raoul Guyon sat in the stern of the dinghy. A yard or two away the frogman stood waist-deep in water on the shelving reef beside his scooter, a loaded spear-gun in his hands. It was almost as if they were holding a conversation.

Mallory released his grip on the aquamobile, went under the surface and swam forward. He erupted in a surge of power, slid his right arm about the man's neck and fell backwards, towing him into deep water, tearing the air-hose from his mouth.

They sank down through the clear water, the spear-gun spiralling off to one side. Mallory wrenched again with his free hand, pulling away the mask, and the man's face turned up, contorted with fear.

Mallory hung on, even when a clutching hand reached

backwards, wrenching away his own air-hose. He compressed his lips and tightened his grip. Blood began to seep from the man's nostrils in two clouds and a moment later he swung loosely against Mallory's arm. Mallory unlocked his fingers and the body bounced away, spun round twice and started to sink.

There was a roaring in his ears and his temples pounded. He kicked for the surface and bumped against the side of the dinghy, gasping and choking for breath. Guyon reached over and grasped his outstretched hand and Mallory stumbled up the sloping shelf of rock and crouched on his hands and knees, chest heaving.

Guyon jumped knee-deep into the water beside him and helped him up, pulling away the mask, his face strained and anxious in the moonlight. When he spoke his voice sounded faint and far away and Mallory shook his head several times.

The roaring subsided abruptly and he gasped: 'No time for questions. I ran into a little trouble. We'd better get moving.'

'You found *L'Alouette*?'

'She's there, all right. Moored to the jetty under the island just like we thought. Room for a couple more from the look of the place.'

He unbuckled the heavy aqualung, swung it into the prow and clambered aboard the dinghy. As he started the outboard motor Guyon unhooked the painter and followed him. A second later and the dinghy was moving back towards Île de Roc, following the twisting channel between the great rocks which already reared up on either side as the tide turned.

'What happens now?' Guyon said.

'We call up Leviathan the moment we get back. Those motor torpedo boats from St Helier will be here before you know it.'

The dinghy rocked in the turbulence as it swept on a fast current between high black walls and turned towards the point. Behind them a full-throated roar shattered the night and Guyon raised the night-glasses and looked back. When he took them down his face looked very white in the moonlight.

'It's that damned speedboat of de Beaumont's. Coming up fast on this side of the reef. Must be doing all of fifteen knots.'

Mallory glanced back, catching a brief glimpse of the thin

pencil of light that was the speedboat's spot, and opened the throttle of the dinghy's outboard motor. The strong current was running against them now as they tried to breast the point, and the light craft was twisted round, a wave splashing across her prow.

'Throw the aqualung overboard,' Mallory shouted.

Guyon scrambled to his knees, reached for the straps, heaved and slid the aqualung over. There was an immediate difference, the prow riding over the next wave, and they turned the point and moved into what should have been calmer water.

The turning tide at this point clashed headlong with the usual strong coastal current, and all around them great patches of white water joined with others, sending irregular waves cascading against the cliffs, the undertow sucking them out again.

The dinghy wallowed in the trough between two great swells, her speed cut in half, and, behind, the roar of the speedboat drew inexorably nearer.

'We'll never make it to the harbour,' Guyon called. 'A couple more minutes and they'll see us.'

A great heaving swell was building up to starboard. As it swept in, lifting the dinghy high into the air, Mallory caught a glimpse of Hamish Grant's house tucked into a fold at the top of the cliffs, a light shining in one of the ground-floor rooms. He swung the tiller over and the current drove the dinghy in towards the cliffs at tremendous speed.

The gap in the inlet had been at least twenty yards across, but the real problem was that line of jagged rocks blocking the entrance as surely as if it had been a steel portcullis. The one slim hope was that the waves, sweeping in, would raise the water-level and carry them over.

He shouted to Guyon: 'This is going to be rough. Hang on and get ready to swim.'

The Frenchman looked back once, his lips moving in reply, but the roaring of the sea drowned his words. Mallory held on to the tiller with both hands. Strange, swirling currents twisted them round and the dinghy was carried helplessly in.

The opening of the cove appeared suddenly in the face of the cliff, water boiling through in a great surge. At one side white spray foamed high in the air, while, all around, dirty cream patches formed as rocks showed through.

The dinghy slewed broadside into the entrance, lifted high and smashed down upon a great green slab of rock. The tiller was wrenched from Mallory's hand and the outboard motor was torn away with a section of the stern.

The dinghy slithered forward across the reef and ground to a halt, a jagged edge of rock smashing through the hull. Guyon went head first over the prow with a cry and Mallory went after him.

The Frenchman tried to stand and Mallory plunged through the boiling surf, hands outstretched to meet him. For a moment they clung together and then another wave, cascading in across the reef, bowled them over.

Guyon went under, and Mallory, striking after him, found himself in deep water. He grabbed the Frenchman by the collar of his jacket and struck out, the current pushing them forward. His feet touched sand and he stood up, pulling Guyon after him. Water boiled waist-high again, tugging at their limbs. As it receded they lurched forward, feet slipping in the shingle, and staggered up the narrow strip of beach at the base of the cliffs.

II

Someone was playing the piano, an old, pre-war Cole Porter number with something of the night in it, something of warmth and love and hope that seemed to belong to another age than this.

Crouching in the bushes below the terrace Mallory was caught for a brief moment, unable to go forward or back. Guyon groaned beside him, coughing up water; Mallory pulled him to his feet and they staggered up the steps.

The french window was ajar, one end of a red velvet curtain billowing out as a gust of wind lifted it. He took a deep breath and opened it wide.

The fire burned brightly on the stone hearth and Hamish Grant's hair gleamed like silver in the lamplight as he leaned in his wing-backed chair, smoking a cheroot. Anne sat opposite, staring into the fire while Fiona played the piano.

It was Fiona who saw them first. She gave a sudden gasp, her hands striking a false chord, and jumped to her feet. Anne stood up slowly and Hamish Grant turned his head and looked directly at the window.

'Sorry about this,' Mallory said as he moved forward, one arm still around Guyon's shoulders.

Guyon retched suddenly and started to cough again. Mallory helped him to a chair by the fire and the Frenchman fell into it with a groan.

Anne stayed surprisingly calm. 'Brandy, Fiona,' she said. 'Quickly. Two glasses.'

Mallory moved forward, water streaming from his rubber suit, and streched out his hands to the fire, shivering involuntarily as the warmth enveloped him. Hamish Grant reached out to the dark figure, dimly seen, and touched the wet rubber suit.

'A strange time to go swimming.'

'In the circumstances we didn't have much choice.' Mallory turned to Anne, who gazed up at him searchingly. 'You're on the phone here, aren't you?'

She nodded. 'Linked to Guernsey by cable, but it hasn't been working since yesterday's storm. That often happens. There's the radio telephone on *Foxhunter*, of course. Is it important?'

'You could say that.' Mallory turned to Guyon, who was gulping the brandy Fiona had passed to him. 'I'll have to get down to the harbour straight away. I can use the transmitter.'

'We'll both go,' Guyon said. 'There could be trouble waiting down there.'

'Any chance of an explanation?' Hamish Grant enquired mildly.

Mallory took the glass of brandy Fiona offered, swallowed half of it down and coughed as the fiery liquor caught at the back of his throat. 'I'd say you were entitled to one in the circumstances. I was sent here by British Intelligence and Captain Guyon by the same branch on the other side of the Channel. We were asked to do a quick check on de Beaumont.'

'I see,' Hamish Grant said. 'I take it he's up to no good?'

'Very much so. His present activities are a direct threat to the interests of his own government and the fact that he's seen fit to operate from British territory presents a serious complication. On top of that, we don't like what he's doing anyway.'

Hamish Grant smiled faintly. 'How strange. Two great nations side by side through the centuries. We have our quarrels, but somehow they're always in the family. The moment the chips are down we move in to help each other so fast it's almost frightening.'

'Can I ask what happened to van Sondergard?' Anne asked.

'I paid him double what you would have done and shipped him out.'

'And the incident on the wharf? That was arranged, too?'

He nodded. 'It got a little out of hand. That's why I had to get so rough. I'm sorry.'

'I'm not,' she said simply.

He reached out and touched her face and something glowed deep in her eyes. Her hand went up, holding his against her cheek, and she turned her head, touching her lips to his cold palm. For a brief moment it was as if they were alone. As if the others had ceased to exist. It was Hamish Grant who broke the spell.

'I should imagine dry clothes should be the first step and you'll need the car.'

'I'll get it out of the garage,' Fiona said quickly.

She was standing at the side of Guyon's chair. She smiled down at him, then went out through the french windows. Guyon got to his feet and he and Mallory followed Anne out of the room, leaving a trail of sea-water across the carpet.

She found dry socks, some old service slacks and a couple of heavy sweaters from Hamish Grant's wardrobe and left the two men in his room to change. When they went downstairs ten minutes later Jagbir was pouring coffee into cups arranged on a table beside the fire. Hamish Grant still sat in his chair, but there was no sign of the girls.

The little Gurkha offered them coffee, no visible excitement on his face, and the old man said: 'There was a mention of possible trouble when you go down to the harbour. The violent sort, I presume. Are you armed?'

Guyon answered: 'I had a revolver in the pocket of my reefer coat. I lost it coming through the surf.'

'You'll find another in the top right-hand drawer of the desk behind you,' the old man said. 'Half a box of cartridges somewhere at the back. There should be a Lüger there as well, but that's already loaded.'

Guyon opened the drawer and came back, the revolver in one hand, the Lüger in the other. 'You can have the Lüger,' the old man went on. 'I'll keep the Webley myself, if you don't mind.'

Guyon slipped the Lüger into his pocket and started to load the Webley. Anne and Fiona came in. They were both wearing heavy sheepskin coats and Anne was binding a scarf about her head, peasant-fashion.

She smiled at Mallory. 'Ready when you are.'

He shook his head gently. 'Not on your life. You stay right here.'

A slight crease appeared between her eyes and Fiona started to protest. Hamish Grant cut in sharply, 'They'll have enough to worry about without you two.'

Fiona turned to Anne, but her sister-in-law sighed and shook her head. 'He's right, Fiona. We'd only be in the way.' She smiled up at Mallory. 'So we sit and wait? How long for?'

'With any luck the whole thing should be wrapped up into a neat parcel by breakfast. And, I warn you, I'll have an appetite.'

'I'll hold you to that.'

He touched her hand briefly and led the way out into the hall. The shooting brake was parked at the bottom of the steps, its engine ticking over, and he climbed behind the wheel and waited for Guyon. The young Frenchman was standing at the top of the steps with Fiona, Anne in the doorway behind them. The young girl reached up, kissed him and hurried inside. He came down the steps and got into the passenger seat, his face grim.

Mallory drove away quickly, turning out through the gates along the white road and down the hill towards the harbour. The hotel was in darkness and the cove was exactly as they had left it, *Foxhunter* moored to one side of the jetty, Guyon's hired launch on the other.

Mallory braked to a halt at the end of the jetty, switched

off the engine and got out. Moonlight silvered the water and the night sky was like a warm dark velvet cushion scattered with diamonds.

'So far, so good,' he said to Guyon, and led the way along the jetty.

He jumped to *Foxhunter*'s deck and went into the wheelhouse. He switched on the light and cursed softly. The radio telephone had been wrenched from its fastening on the far wall and lay in the corner, smashed beyond repair, a fire-axe beside it.

'They beat us to it after all.'

He pushed past Guyon, hurried down the companionway and through the saloon to the aft cabin. He dropped to one knee, opened the locker beneath his bunk and rummaged inside.

'Is this what you are looking for, Colonel Mallory?' Raoul Guyon said softly.

Mallory got to his feet and turned. Guyon stood on the other side of the table, a drawer open, holding the small electronic transmitter that was Mallory's only link with the department.

'Good man,' Mallory said, and took a step forward.

Guyon dropped the set to the floor and ground his heel into it twice, at the same time taking the Lüger from his coat pocket.

Mallory stood staring at him, a slight frown on his face, and a voice said: 'Excellent, Captain Guyon. I was really beginning to despair of you.'

As Mallory turned, de Beaumont stepped out of the shadows of the dark galley, Jacaud at his side, a sub-machine-gun in his hands.

— 12 —

THEY WERE CLOSE to the island now and Marcel cut the engine to half-speed and took *Foxhunter* in slowly towards the dark arch. The speedboat bobbed behind them on a long towline and as Mallory looked out to sea a shadow moved in from the horizon, blanketing the stars.

Guyon stood by the rail a few feet away talking to de Beaumont in a low voice and Jacaud leaned against the wheelhouse, the sub-machine-gun in his hands. One of his eyes was half closed, the right side of his face swollen and disfigured by a huge purple bruise, and his eyes stared at Mallory unwinkingly.

They moved into the dark entrance and Mallory shivered, chilled by the damp air, and then they were through. From end to end the cave was about a hundred yards long and perhaps fifty feet across. Beneath the surface, as he had discovered earlier, it was even wider.

The long stone jetty was brightly illuminated by two arc-lamps and they coasted in to tie up behind a magnificent forty-foot, steel-hulled motor-yacht, the name *Fleur de Lys* painted across her counter.

The submarine was moored on the far side, squat and black in the water, and looked even smaller than Mallory had imagined. A dozen or so men in the uniform of the French Navy worked busily, loading stores on board under the supervision of a slim, rather boyish-looking lieutenant in peaked cap and reefer jacket. As they went up the short ladder to the jetty, he came forward, saluting de Beaumont casually.

'How are things going, Fenelon?' de Beaumont asked. 'Any snags?'

Fenelone shook his head. 'We'll be ready on schedule.'

'Good, I'll give you a final briefing at 9 a.m.' Fenelon went back to his men and de Beaumont turned to Mallory. 'Magnificent, isn't she? And just the thing for our purposes. Small, compact – only needs a crew of sixteen. You're familiar with the type?'

'Only on paper.'

'This one has quite a history. Built at Deutsches Werft in 1945 and sunk with all hands within a month of commissioning. After she was raised she was transferred to the French.'

'And now she's yours,' Mallory said. 'A chequered career.'

A body was against the far wall, covered by a tarpaulin, webbed feet turned to one side, blood streaking the pool of sea-water in which it lay.

'We couldn't find the other one. The current must have taken him under the reef.' De Beaumont shook his head. 'A nasty way to die.'

The words seemed to carry an implicit threat, but Mallory refused to be drawn, and de Beaumont smiled faintly and led the way across to where a flight of stone steps lifted a hundred feet into the gloom, curving round one wall of the cave. They mounted the steps and emerged on to a stone landing, and de Beaumont led the way to the far end of a passage, passing several doors. One or two stood open to show narrow service bunks and grey blankets neatly folded. From a side entrance there came the smell of cooking.

He opened another door and they entered a large hall, great curved beams of oak arching into the gloom. There was a wide marble staircase and, above it, a gallery. At one side logs blazed in an immense medieval fireplace.

'Quite a sight, isn't it? The money these Victorian industrialists must have had to throw around, and every stone brought in by boat.'

His tone was casual, mannered. He might have been a rather complacent host showing a friend over his new place. They went up the great staircase and moved along the gallery to the far end. De Beaumont opened a door to disclose a narrow spiral staircase. At intervals there were slotted windows and Mallory could see far out to sea as they mounted higher and higher.

They reached a stone landing and paused outside a door. De Beaumont went in, leaving it ajar. The room contained a great deal of radio equipment and an operator sat before a transmitting set, headphones clamped to his ears. He stood up when de Beaumont appeared. There was a murmur of conversation and then the colonel came back outside.

He continued up the spiral staircase, Mallory, Guyon and Marcel following behind, Jacaud bringing up the rear. At last they emerged on a small landing and de Beaumont opened his final door.

The room was circular in shape and quite large. It was comfortably furnished, Persian carpets covering the floor, logs burning brightly in the wide fireplace. The walls were lined with books except for a section perhaps twenty feet long covered by a velvet curtain. De Beaumont pulled it to one side, revealing a curved glass window.

'One of my little improvements. On a clear day you can see France.' He indicated a chair by the fire. 'If you please.'

Mallory sat in the chair and Jacaud moved to stand behind him, the sub-machine-gun held ready. Marcel stood by the window, a revolver in his right hand held against his thigh. Guyon remained by the door and Mallory looked across at him. Guyon returned his gaze calmly, giving nothing away, and Mallory turned to de Beaumont, who was now sitting in the opposite chair.

'I will not insult your intelligence by fencing with you, Colonel Mallory,' he said. 'For some time I was a prisoner of the Viets in Indo-China. There is little they failed to teach me at first hand about the extraction of information from the unco-operative. Jacaud was senior warrant officer of my regiment. He shared my experiences. I need hardly add that he would welcome an opportunity to experiment.'

'No need to go on,' Mallory said. 'I get the point.'

'Excellent,' de Beaumont said. 'We can get down to business. As you may now have deduced for yourself, Captain Guyon is something of a double agent. When the Deuxième offered him employment they were not aware that he was already a loyal member of the OAS. A most convenient arrangement. He confirms the fact that the Bureau had no real grounds for suspecting *L'Alouette* to be in hiding here. That his assignment to Île de Roc to work with you was at the request of British Intelligence. I'd like to know why.'

'We had a man here watching you,' Mallory said. 'Just routine, because of who you are and what you are. He drifted in on the tide the other evening. Accidental drowning was the coroner's verdict.'

'He had a habit of taking long walks on the cliffs after dark with a pair of night-glasses,' de Beaumont said. 'Rather dangerous. Someone should have warned him.'

'You made a mistake there,' Mallory said. 'To my chief it meant only one thing. Our man had seen something important. With the French combing every creek and inlet on their side of the Channel it gave him a rather nasty feeling to think that she might be sitting it out in the Channel Islands.'

'A pity,' de Beaumont said. 'Now I must move out rather sooner than I had intended. On the other hand, neither my immediate nor long-term plans will be affected in the slightest.' He stood up and smiled politely. 'In happier circumstances I should have enjoyed talking to you. We must have a great deal in common. I'm sure you'll understand that my time is limited.'

'Naturally,' Mallory said ironically and got to his feet.

He had often wondered about this moment, how it would come and when. The strange thing was that he was not afraid. More curious than anything else. Jacaud moved restlessly behind him and Marcel came away from the wall, the gun still held against his leg.

De Beaumont took a revolver from his pocket, crossed to Guyon and handed it to him. 'Will you do the honours, captain? A soldier's end, I think.'

Guyon's hand tightened on the butt of the revolver and he looked across at Mallory, his face very white. Quite suddenly he grabbed de Beaumont by the front of his coat, pulling him forward, and rammed the barrel of the revolver against his throat.

There was a moment of stillness and then de Beaumont laughed gently. 'You know, our friends in Paris have been worried about you for some time now, Guyon. I can understand why. You're slipping. I should have thought an officer of your experience would have been able to tell the difference in weight between a revolver loaded with blanks and one loaded with live ammunition.'

He reached up and took the revolver from Guyon's hand and Guyon looked across at Mallory and smiled wryly. 'Sometimes we can be too clever, my friend.'

'Nice to have you back,' Mallory said.

De Beaumont opened the door and nodded to Marcel. 'Take him below and watch him carefully. I'll send Colonel Mallory down later.'

He closed the door behind them, turned to Mallory and smiled. 'And now that we all know exactly where we are we can perhaps relax for half an hour.' He took a bottle and two glasses from a cupboard in the corner and returned to his chair. 'This is really quite an excellent cognac. I think you'll enjoy it.'

Mallory sat in the opposite chair, aware of Jacaud at his back, and waited for what was to come. He accepted a glass of cognac, drank a little and leaned back. 'I can't understand what you hope to gain from all this. Murder and assassination will only lose you what little support you command.'

'A matter of opinion,' de Beaumont said. 'The only politics which seem to matter in this modern world are the politics of violence. Palestine, Cyprus and Algeria were all examples of victory achieved by a deliberate and carefully planned use of violence and assassination. We can do the same.'

'The circumstances are completely different. In the cases you've quoted, nationalistic elements were opposed to a colonial power. In your own, Frenchmen are murdering Frenchmen.'

'They are not worthy of the name, the swine we have dealt with so far. Loud-mouths, professional liberals and scheming politicians who feathered their own nests while I and men like me rotted in the Viet prison camps.' De Beaumont laughed bitterly. 'I remember our homecoming only too well. Booed all the way into Marseilles by Communist dock workers.'

'Ancient history,' Mallory said. 'Nobody wants to know. In any case, unless they'd been through the same experience themselves they wouldn't know what you're talking about.'

'But you have,' de Beaumont said. 'Deep inside, I think you know what I mean. You learned a hard lesson from the Chinese. You put it down in cold print in that book of yours. What happened when you put it into practice?'

He stared into the fire, a frown on his face. 'It was going to be different in Algeria, we were certain of that. We fought the *fells* in the *jebel* of the Atlas Mountains, in the heat of the Sahara, in the alleys of Algiers, and we were beating them. In the end we had them by the throat.'

He turned to Mallory. 'I was in the army plot of the 13 May 1958. They gave us no choice. They would have arrested my friends and me, tried us on trumped-up atrocity charges, designed to please the loud-mouths and fellow-travellers back home in Paris. We put de Gaulle in power because we believed in the ideal of a French Algeria, a greater France.'

'And once he was in control he did exactly the opposite to what you had intended,' Mallory said. 'One of the great ironies of post-war history.'

De Beaumont swallowed some more cognac and continued. 'Even more ironic that I, Phillipe de Beaumont, descendant of one of the greatest of French military families, should have helped place in power the man who has destroyed the greatness of his country.'

'That remains to be seen,' Mallory said. 'I'd say that Charles de Gaulle was moved by one thing only – deep patriotism. Whatever he's done he's done because he thought it best for France.'

De Beaumont shrugged. 'So we disagree? It's of little moment. After his visit to St Malo on the 3rd of next month he will no longer present a problem.'

'I don't know what you have in mind, but I wouldn't count on anything. How many times have your people failed now? Eight, isn't it?'

'I flatter myself that my own organization has been rather more successful. These affairs need the trained mind, Mallory. Everything I handle is a military operation. *L'Alouette* affair, I have handled personally from the beginning. My colleagues in Paris know nothing about it. I work strictly on my own and use them as an information service only.'

Mallory shook his head. 'You can't last much longer. You're working on too big a scale. Already *L'Alouette*'s becoming more of a liability than anything else.'

'You couldn't be more wrong.' De Beaumont got to his feet, took a couple of charts from the cupboard beside his chair and crossed to a small table. 'Come over here. You'll find this interesting.'

They were Admiralty charts of the area between Guernsey and the French coast and he joined them together quickly. 'Here is Île de Roc and St Pierre, thirty miles south-west of Guernsey. The nearest French soil is Pointe du Château, only twenty miles away. You know the area?'

Mallory shook his head. 'The closest I've been is Brest.'

'A dangerous coast of small islands and reefs, lonely and wild. You will notice Île de Monte only a quarter of a mile off the coast, the Gironde Marshes opposite. There is a small cottage on an island perhaps half a mile into the marsh on the main creek. Eight miles from a road and very lonely. Not even a telephone. There are only two people in residence at the moment.'

'And you want them?'

'Only the man. Henri Granville.'

Mallory straightened, a frown on his face. 'You mean Granville the judge, the Procureur-Général who retired last month?'

'I congratulate you on your intimate knowledge of French affairs. He arrived there with his wife yesterday. They are quite alone. Of course, no one is supposed to know. He's fond of solitude – solitude and birds. Unfortunately for him, a contact of mine in Paris got news of his movements last night and let me know at once. I'm sending Jacaud across in *L'Alouette* later today. His execution should cause quite a stir.'

'You're crazy,' Mallory said. 'He must be eighty if he's a day. On top of that, he's one of the best-loved men in France. God in heaven, everybody loves Granville! Politics doesn't enter into it.'

'On three occasions now he has presided at tribunals which have condemned old comrades of mine to death,' de Beaumont said. 'Now he must pay the consequences. By striking at Granville we prove once and for all that we are a force to be reckoned with. That no man, however powerful, no matter what his public standing, is safe from our vengeance.'

'Henri Granville never condemned anyone in his life without good reason. Harm him in any way and you'll bring the mountain in on you.' Mallory shook his head. 'You'll never get away with it.'

De Beaumont smiled faintly, crossed to the fire and poured more cognac into his glass. 'You think not?' He swallowed a little of the cognac and sighed. 'I will postpone your execution till this evening. By that time Jacaud will have returned. It will give me some satisfaction in sending you to your death with the knowledge that Henri Granville has preceded you.'

'Which remains to be seen,' Mallory said.

De Beaumont turned and indicated a tattered battle standard hanging above the fireplace. 'An ancestor of mine carried that himself at Waterloo when his standard-bearer was shot. It was with me at Dien-Bien-Phu. I managed to hang on to it during all those bitter months of captivity. You will notice it bears the motto of the de Beaumonts.'

' "Who dares, wins",' Mallory said.

'I would remember that if I were you.'

'Something you seem to have forgotten,' Mallory said. 'When that ancestor of yours picked up that standard at Waterloo he didn't carry it forward on his own. There was a regiment of guards backing him up all the way and I seem to remember that at Dien-Bien-Phu you commanded a regiment of colonial paratroops. But, then, that's France I'm speaking about. The real France. Something you wouldn't know anything about.'

For a moment something glowed in de Beaumont's eyes, but he pushed back his anger and forced a smile. 'Take him below, Jacaud. He and Guyon can spend their last hours together trying to solve an impossible problem. The thought will amuse me.'

Jacaud gave Mallory a push towards the door. As he opened it, de Beaumont said calmly: 'And, Jacaud, when I next see Colonel Mallory I expect him to be in his present condition. You understand?'

Jacaud turned sharply, a growl rising in his throat. For a moment he seemed about to defy de Beaumont and then he turned suddenly and pushed Mallory forward.

They went down the spiral staircase, Mallory leading, all the time aware of the machine-gun at his back. The gallery was in half-darkness, the fire a heap of glowing ashes, as they crossed the hall and went through the door which led to the living-quarters and the cave.

At the end of a long whitewashed corridor they found Marcel sitting on a chair outside a door, reading a newspaper, the revolver stuck in his belt.

He looked up at Jacaud, eyes raised enquiringly. 'When?'

'This evening when I get back from the mainland.' Jacaud turned to Mallory and patted the sub-machine-gun. A red glow seemed to light up behind the cold eyes. 'Personally, Colonel Mallory.'

Mallory moved into the cell. As the door clanged behind him, Guyon swung his legs to the floor and sat looking at him.

He grinned suddenly. 'You wouldn't by any chance have such a thing as a cigarette on you, would you?'

— 13 —

'I HAD LOST all belief or interest in right or wrong. In the end you believe only in your friends, the comrade who had his throat cut the previous night. That was what six years in Algeria had done for me.'

Raoul Guyon stood by the small barred window gazing into the night. When he turned he looked tired.

'And this is why you joined the OAS?' Mallory said.

Guyon shook his head. 'I was in Algiers in 1958. So much blood that I was sickened by it. There was a young Moorish girl. For a little while we tried to shelter from the storm together. They found her on the beach one morning, stripped, mutilated. I had to identify the body. The following day I was badly wounded and sent back to France to convalesce. When I returned my comrades seemed to have the only solution. To bring back de Gaulle.'

'You took part in the original plot?'

Guyon shrugged. 'I was on the fringe. Just one more junior officer. But to me de Gaulle stood for order out of chaos. Afterwards most of us were posted to other units. I spent five months on patrol with the Camel Corps in the Hoggar.'

'And did you find what you were looking for?'

'Almost,' Guyon said. 'There was a day of heat and thirst when I almost had it, when the rocks shimmered and the mountains danced in a blue haze and I was a part of it. Almost, but not quite.'

'What happened after that?'

'I was posted back to Algeria to one of the worst districts. A place of barbed wire and fear, where violence erupted like a disease and life was no longer even an act of faith. I was wounded again last year just before General Challe's abortive coup. Not seriously, but enough to give me a legitimate excuse to put in a request to be placed on unpaid leave. The night before I left, Legrande visited me in my hotel room. Offered me work with the Deuxième Bureau.'

'And you accepted?'

'In a strange way it offered me some sort of escape. Later, in Paris, I was approached by OAS agents. As an ex-paratroop officer and supporter of the original coup which had placed de Gaulle in power, I must have seemed an obvious choice.'

'And you informed Legrande?'

'As soon as I could get in touch with him. That was the funny thing. I didn't even have to make a choice. It was almost as if it had been made for me. He told me to accept the offer. From his point of view an agent with contacts in that direction would obviously be valuable.'

'And yet we were informed that the Deuxième had no real suspicions about de Beaumont. Surely you must have had some sort of a lead on him through your Paris connections with the other side?'

'Not really. I was only on the edge of their organization. De Beaumont's name was mentioned as one sympathetic to their aims. On the other hand, his political opinions are well known in France. There was certainly never any hint that he might be an active worker.'

'And all this time you were completely accepted?'

'I certainly thought so. As a new recruit to the Deuxième,

it was obvious that my sources would be limited, but I passed on selected information on Legrande's orders. I certainly never managed to get close to any of the really big men, but I was working towards it. On two occasions he even allowed me to warn some of the lesser fry when their arrest was imminent.'

'What about *L'Alouette?*'

'That was the thing which puzzled us from the beginning. The complete absence of information as to her whereabouts, even in OAS circles. Because of that Legrande told me to inform my Paris contacts that I had been assigned to the Channel Islands merely to run a routine check on de Beaumont, just to make sure that he was behaving himself. Legrande felt that at least it would prove once and for all whether a definite link existed.'

'Something he didn't see fit to inform us at our end.'

'I'm sorry about that, but Legrande never lives in the present – only the future. He envisaged a possible situation in which my other activities could prove useful. Under the circumstances it seemed wiser to present myself as Raoul Guyon, an accredited agent of the Bureau and nothing more.'

'I see the old fox is still a believer in playing his cards as they fall,' Mallory said. 'It shows in his poker game.'

'A remark strangely similar to one he made about you just before I left.'

Mallory grinned. 'One thing at least has come out of all this. De Beaumont definitely does have a link with the OAS in Paris because he was warned that you were coming. The one thing I don't understand is why he didn't think it strange that you hadn't told them about *L'Alouette* affair.'

'The first thing he asked me coming across on the boat. A difficult question to answer.'

'And how did you?'

'Told him the Bureau believed the whole business to be the work of an independent group. That this was confirmed for me personally by the obvious ignorance of the affair in OAS circles. That as an ex-paratroop officer who had taken part in the coup of June '58, only to be betrayed by de Gaulle, I would much prefer to work with him.'

'And he accepted that?'

'He seemed to at the time.'

'It all sounds pretty shaky to me.'

'It obviously did to de Beaumont.' Guyon grinned wryly. 'On the other hand, I didn't have time to think up anything better and I did make my own move against you just before they did, remember?'

'That was quick thinking.'

The young Frenchman shrugged. 'When I saw what they had done to the radio telephone it seemed logical to assume they were still on board, that we were under observation. It seemed wise to establish my credentials while I still could and I remembered seeing you put the transmitter in the table drawer earlier in the afternoon.'

'And you'd never met him previously?'

Guyon shook his head. 'As I told you before, only as one of a crowd. Naturally, I knew a great deal about him. He was one of the really great paratroop officers, you know.'

'I've been going over everything he said to me upstairs,' Mallory said. 'None of it really makes sense. In the end he must lose. The murder of a fine old man like Henri Granville on its own will be sufficient to lose him, and those who think like him, a great deal of sympathy, and yet he goes on. I wonder why?'

'He was always a strange, ascetic man. A cross between religious fanatic and soldier. The surrender at Dien-Bien-Phu, the humiliation of the Viet camps and our subsequent withdrawal from Indo-China were a source of lasting shame to him. Like many of his kind, he swore it would never happen again.'

'And in spite of everything he could do it did.'

Guyon nodded. 'De Beaumont is the last of one of our most noble families, his only heir a brother who is a professor of political history at the Sorbonne. A man with pronounced left-wing sympathies. One of his ancestors was one of the few nobles to give wholehearted support to the revolution in 1789, another was a general under Napoleon. For one hundred and fifty years the de Beaumonts have been one of the greatest of French families.'

'Something of a national calamity if he had to be arrested.'

'Exactly. The government was more than happy when he

chose to reside in the Channel Islands. At the time it seemed to dispose of him as an immediate problem.'

'Which he has now become,' Mallory said, 'and in more ways than one.'

'You are thinking of his threat to dispose of de Gaulle during his visit to St Malo next month?' Guyon shook his head, lay on the other bed, pillowing his head on his hands. 'I'm not too worried about that. They won't get de Gaulle. He's indestructible, that one. Like one of those rocks out there on the reef after a storm. A little more weathered, but still standing.'

'Which leaves us with the Granville affair,' Mallory said. 'And the hell of it is there doesn't seem to be a damned thing we can do about it.'

He lit a cigarette and lay on his back, gazing at the ceiling, going over the events of the previous couple of hours in his mind. After a while he said softly: 'The first rule in this game is that the job must come before everything else. Most men I've worked with, in your position, would have played along with de Beaumont, would even have executed me if necessary.'

'Perhaps I saw the situation differently,' Guyon said.

'You moved so fast you didn't even notice the difference in weight the blanks made. Why?'

'Something I've been asking myself on and off for the past hour or more. It's not easy to explain. Let's just say that suddenly people have become important to me again and leave it at that.'

He turned his face to the wall and Mallory lay there, smoking his cigarette, thinking how strange it was that a young man, all feeling burned out of him by the flames of two savage wars, should be brought back to life by that oldest and most elemental of human emotions – love.

II

He was cold and stiff and his limbs ached. He pulled the blanket over his legs and checked his watch. It was almost 5 a.m. and he lay in the darkness listening to the rain and the wind. After a while he drifted into sleep again.

He became aware that someone was prodding him and

opened his eyes. Raoul Guyon squatted beside him. Grey light seeped into the room through the barred window and Mallory swung his legs to the floor.

'Still raining?'

Guyon nodded. 'Hasn't let up all night. It's almost eight.'

Mallory walked to the door and peered through the iron grille into the corridor outside. A young sailor sat in a chair reading a book, a heavy service revolver in the holster at his waist.

Mallory crossed to the window. The casement opened easily enough, but the bars set in the ledge on either side were strong and firm. He looked into the grey morning, out along the reef to Île de Roc. Rain slanted down and visibility was poor, a cold mist drifting close to the surface of the water.

'I wonder what they're doing over there?' Guyon said at his shoulder.

'They must have realized by now that something's gone wrong.' Mallory shrugged. 'If they've any sense at all they'll have brought in Owen Morgan and gone to Guernsey for help in your launch.'

'Surely de Beaumont will have considered that possibility?'

'He probably has. That's what's worrying me.'

There was a rattle of bolts and the door opened. As they both turned, Marcel entered and stood to one side, a revolver in his right hand. The young sailor followed, carrying a tray which he placed on the bed. They withdrew without saying a word, bolting the door again.

The food was simple, bread and cheese and hot coffee, and Mallory suddenly realized how hungry he was. They sat on either side of the tray to eat and finished off by sharing his last cigarette.

Afterwards he lay on the bed waiting for something to happen, while Guyon paced restlessly up and down the cell, the rain hammering against the window. It was almost ten o'clock when the door opened again and de Beaumont entered, Marcel at his back.

He seemed in a good humour and smiled cheerfully. 'Good morning, gentlemen. I trust you spent a good night? Your quarters are adequate?'

'I've seen worse,' Mallory admitted.

'Anything I can get you?'

'The condemned man's last wish?' Mallory shrugged. 'We could do with some cigarettes. That's about all'.

Marcel took a packet of Gauloises from his pocket and threw them on the bed. 'Anything else?' de Beaumont said politely.

Mallory put a cigarette in his mouth and tossed the packet to Guyon. 'I don't think so.'

'Then you will excuse me? You'll be interested to know that Jacaud and his men left for Pointe du Château fifteen minutes ago as scheduled. Under the circumstances I think it's time I paid a visit to our friends on Île de Roc.'

'I wouldn't count on anyone being there to meet you.'

'Oh, they'll be there, all right. I can assure you of that.'

De Beaumont smiled faintly as if enjoying some private joke, nodded to Marcel and passed outside. The door closed and the bolts were rammed home with a harsh finality. Guyon turned with a gesture of despair and Mallory motioned him to silence. When he went to the door the young sailor was back on his chair reading a magazine.

Mallory crossed to the window and looked outside. A minute or two later he heard the sound of an engine and *Foxhunter* came into view, running alongside the reef towards Île de Roc.

'There he goes.'

Guyon moved to the window, peered out, and frowned. 'But why has he taken *Foxhunter?*'

'Easier to handle than *Fleur de Lys* on the short run and there's too much sea for the speedboat.'

Guyon, thinking of Fiona, dropped his cigarette and stamped on it viciously. 'I didn't like his last remark. He sounded far too sure of himself. As if he knew for certain that the general and the girls would still be on the island.'

'I imagine he does,' Mallory said. 'It's been a long night. He could have been up to anything, but that isn't important at the moment. He probably only intends to bring them back here for safe custody until he's ready to move out.'

'You may be right.'

'It's Henri Granville I'm thinking about, sitting in the middle of the Gironde Marshes not knowing that sometime after noon there'll be a knock at the door. I can see the smile on Jacaud's face now.'

'And nothing we can do about it.'

'Plenty, if we could get out of here. There's always the radio room in the tower, or the *Fleur de Lys* would be a better bet. A boat of that size is bound to have a radio telephone.'

Guyon shook his head. 'Those marshes are one of the most isolated places on the entire coast. Even if we managed to contact my people in Paris it would still be too late for Henri Granville. They'd never reach him in time.'

'But we could,' Mallory said. '*L'Alouette* will have to make the entire run submerged. That will take her a good three hours.'

'It's almost an hour since she left,' Guyon pointed out.

'*Fleur de Lys* has twice the speed. We could still beat Jacaud to the punch.'

'Only if we get out of here within the next half-hour,' Guyon said. 'And I stopped believing in miracles a long time ago.'

'We don't need a miracle. Just a little luck,' Mallory pulled him down on the bed. 'Now listen carefully.'

III

It was cold in the passage and the young sailor shivered and got to his feet. He stamped vigorously to restore his circulation and walked a few paces away from the chair. He was bored. He was also a little afraid. In the beginning the whole affair had seemed like a great adventure, a crusade. Now he was not so sure. He turned to move back to his chair and a muffled cry sounded from inside the cell.

He stood there, a puzzled frown on his face. There was another cry, followed by the crash of a bed going over. He arrived at the grille in time to see Guyon drive his fist into Mallory's face, knocking him against the wall.

'You got me into this, you bastard!' the young Frenchman cried. 'I'll kill you! I'll kill you!'

He flung himself forward and Mallory ducked under another blow, moved in close and tripped him. A moment later and he was kneeling on Guyon's chest, hands twisted into his collar as he throttled him expertly.

The young sailor gave a cry of alarm. He pulled back the

bolts and moved into the cell, revolver ready in his right hand. He reached for Mallory's collar and to his amazement Guyon erupted from the floor, grabbed his wrist savagely and twisted the revolver from his grasp. The sailor's mouth opened in a cry of alarm that was cut short as Mallory's fist moved in a short arc against the side of the jaw.

Mallory picked up the revolver, nodded to Guyon and they went outside quickly. All was quiet. Guyon bolted the door and they hurried along the passage.

A strange quiet reigned until they reached the main corridor when they heard voices in the distance and the clatter of pans from the kitchen. They passed along to the far end and Mallory opened the door cautiously and stepped on to the landing at the top of the steps which led down to the cave.

The jetty was deserted and *Fleur de Lys* and the speed-boat were the only craft moored to the wall. They went down the stone steps quickly, paused for a moment at the bottom, then hurried across to *Fleur de Lys*.

When they went into the wheelhouse they saw at once that the radio telephone had been removed from its housing on the wall. Mallory grinned tightly. 'He's a cautious bastard, I'll say that for him.'

'Only to be expected.' Guyon shrugged. 'A good soldier tries to forsee every eventuality.' He looked around and shook his head. 'This looks one hell of a size for two of us.'

'We'll manage,' Mallory said. 'We'll have to. There's plenty of fuel in the tank, which is the main thing. Go get those lines off the jetty and we'll move out.'

Guyon went forward quickly and untied the first line. As he started aft there was a harsh cry. When he glanced up he saw a sailor standing on the landing at the top of the steps. He ran along the deck and cast off the other line. The sailor drew a revolver and fired two wild shots as he came down the steps.

He was too late. The engines were already roaring into life and Mallory took *Fleur de Lys* out through the entrance. Spray splashed against the window, waves breaking over the deck as he turned through the lee-side of the reef and set course for Pointe du Château.

— 14 —

HAMISH GRANT opened the door and stood listening to the sound of quiet breathing. Fiona was stretched on the sofa and Anne slept in the wing-backed chair, a rug over her legs.

As he started to close the door she opened her eyes and said softly, 'What time is it?'

'Just after eight. Jagbir's made some fresh tea.'

She got to her feet, draped the rug over Fiona and followed him out. 'Any sign of them?'

The old man shook his head. 'Not yet.'

The kitchen looked out over the courtyard, a large and pleasant room, beams supporting a low ceiling. Jagbir was frying eggs at the stove. When he saw Anne he poured a cup of tea and gave it to her and she stood in front of the fire, drinking it slowly.

Beyond, through the wide window, clouds hung threateningly over the fields, rain dripped from the gutters and brown leaves crawled across the cobbles. She went to the window and gazed out into the rain, thinking of Mallory.

Hamish Grant moved beside her and squeezed her hand. 'He did say it would take till breakfast-time. I shouldn't worry too much if I were you.'

'I'm not,' she said. 'One thing I *am* sure of is his ability to look after himself, but I'd have thought we'd have heard from them by now.'

'We very probably will before much longer.'

She finished her tea and moved to the door. 'I think I'll run down to the harbour and see what's happening.'

'I'll send Jagbir with you.'

She shook her head. 'Let him get on with breakfast. I shan't be long. No need to wake Fiona till I get back. She could do with the sleep.'

She went along the hall, pulled on her sheepskin coat and let herself out of the front door. Rain fell steadily and she fastened a scarf about her hair as she went down the drive and turned through the gates.

Visibility was poor, a grey, clinging mist drifting in patches across the water, and the central hill of the island looked very green against the leaden sky. She hurried along the road and paused on the brow of the hill to look down into the harbour. Only one boat was moored there, Raoul Guyon's launch, and the shooting brake was parked at the end of the jetty.

She went down the hill quickly, taking a short cut across the wet grass. The shooting brake was beaded with moisture, the engine cold. She stood there for a moment, a frown on her face, then walked along the jetty and stepped on to the deck of Guyon's launch. She went into the small saloon, stood looking about her for a moment, then turned to go.

She paused, wrinkling her nose, aware of the heavy, acrid taint of oil on the fresh morning air. It seeped into a pool from under the door of the engine compartment. She opened it and looked into a twisted mass of smashed pipes and broken valves.

She crouched on one knee, gazing at the engine, her mind frozen. As she started to rise, steps boomed hollowly on the wooden planking of the jetty and Owen Morgan called, 'Hello below!'

Anne went up the companionway and came out on deck as he stepped down from the jetty. He wore an old blue pilot coat and rubber boots. Rain frosted his grey hair. He started to grin, but his smile faded at the sight of her troubled face.

'What's wrong?'

'Take a look at the engine.'

He went down the companionway quickly. When he reappeared his face was grave. 'Why would anyone want to do a thing like that?'

'To make sure we couldn't get off the island,' she said.

He frowned quickly. 'Look, how about letting me in on all this? Where's *Foxhunter?* I heard her go out early this morning.'

'That must have been Colonel Mallory and Monsieur Guyon,' she said. 'They should have been back by now. I'm very much afraid something may have happened to them.'

'Are they in some kind of trouble?'

'They could be, but there isn't time to explain now, Owen. We must get to Guernsey as soon as possible. What about your launch?'

'I hauled her up the slipway and into the boathouse ready for winter only two days ago,' he said. 'No trouble to bring her down again if it's all that urgent. I can have her ready for sea in half an hour.'

'Do that,' Anne said. 'I'll go back to the house for the others. I'll explain things more fully when I get back.'

She hurried along the jetty, climbed behind the wheel and switched on the engine. It required a lot of choke before it would turn over and Owen was already half-way up the slope towards the boathouse at the side of the hotel when she finally moved away.

The Welshman's skin crawled with excitement. Whatever was wrong, it was certainly serious. So much had been evident from Anne Grant's manner and actions, and to a man whose entire life had been a series of adventures the prospect of action carried all the kick of a good stiff drink. When he was only a few yards away from the boathouse he remembered that the heavy door was padlocked. He turned and moved up the slope quickly to the side door of the hotel.

When he went into the kitchen Juliette was standing at the sink washing the breakfast dishes. 'Where's the key to the boathouse?' he demanded.

She turned, her eyebrows arching in surprise. 'On the nail behind the door where it always is. What's wrong?'

'I've got to get the boat out,' he said. 'The Grants want me to run them over to Guernsey. Can't explain why. I don't even know myself. But it must be something serious.'

He took down the key and went out again. After he had gone Juliette Vincente stood at the sink, gazing blankly at the door. After a moment she dried her hands carefully, hung up the towel and went up the back stairs to her bedroom.

II

Owen Morgan opened the heavy doors of the boathouse and moved inside. The launch was seated firmly into a deep concrete slot, a steel cable coiled around a winch at her stern, holding her in place.

He jumped down on to the deck, pulled off the top of the engine housing and paused suddenly, his throat going dry. The engine was in exactly the same state as the one in Guyon's boat. Delicate pipes and valves smashed beyond repair, a heavy hammer from his own tool-kit lying in the ruins.

As he got to his feet there was the scrape of a shoe on stone behind him. He turned and looked up at Juliette. She wore his old corduroy jacket against the cold, her hands thrust deep into the pockets.

'What's wrong, Own?' she asked.

And then in one single, inexplicable flash of intuition he knew that she was responsible and his eyes widened. 'Why, Juliette?' he said. 'Why did you do it?'

'My brother was killed in Algeria, Owen.' Her voice was flat, lifeless. 'He died for France. They repaid him by giving what he'd died for away. I couldn't stand by and allow that to happen.'

Anger flared inside him like flames through dry leaves. 'What sort of bloody nonsense are you telling me, girl? What about my boat?'

He started to clamber up beside her and she backed away, taking a revolver from her pocket. He stood facing her, very still, the skin on his face so white that it was almost transparent, a bewildered expression on his face.

'It's me, Juliette. Owen.' He took a step forward.

'Move past me very slowly, Owen,' she said. 'Your hands behind your back. Don't make me kill you.'

He stood poised, feet apart, and wild laughter erupted from his mouth. 'Kill me, girl? You?'

In a moment he drove forward, one hand reaching for the gun, the other grabbing for her coat. In that same instant something seemed to move in her eyes and he knew with the most appalling certainty that he had made the last mistake of his life.

The sound of the shot re-echoed deafeningly between the walls of the boathouse and the force of the bullet, smashing through his body, sent him staggering backwards. He swayed on the edge of the ramp, hands clutching at his stomach, the blood erupted from his mouth in a bright stream and he fell back on the deck.

Juliette Vincente moved to the edge of the ramp and looked down at him. He lay very still, his dark eyes fixed on a point a million miles beyond her. She put the revolver back into her pocket, went outside and started to close the heavy doors. When she turned, *Foxhunter* was just coming round the point into the harbour.

III

In the kitchen Hamish Grant sat at one end of the table, the remains of his breakfast before him, and listened gravely to what Anne had to tell him.

When she had finished he shook his head briefly. 'No use trying to pretend things look good. They don't. But one thing *is* certain. There isn't much we can do on our own.'

'Then Guernsey is our only hope?'

He nodded and got to his feet. 'I think it would be better if we all went. It never pays to take chances and things could get rather unhealthy.'

Fiona came in from the hall carrying his old British warm. 'You'll need this on, Father. It's rather cold.'

It was the first time she had called him anything but general since she was quite small, and his heart went out to her. He reached for her face, dimly seen, and patted her cheek.

'Not to worry, Fiona. We'll get things sorted out.'

She held his hand tightly for a moment, then turned and led the way into the hall. Anne was already sitting behind the wheel of the brake, the engine ticking over. The general and Jagbir got into the rear, Fiona in the front, and Anne drove away quickly.

IV

It was still raining heavily and she turned on the wipers, leaning forward, watching for pot-holes in the dirt road. As the brake climbed to the crest of the hill she changed to a lower gear, ready for the descent to the harbour. They went over the top of the rise, Fiona gave a cry of alarm and Anne braked quickly.

De Beaumont, Marcel and three sailors stood in the road, looking out towards the sea. About a quarter of a mile offshore, and running strongly south-west towards the French coast, was *Fleur de Lys*. Marcel had one arm outstretched as he pointed. He turned to speak to de Beaumont and saw the shooting brake.

As they fanned across the road, Anne slammed her foot hard against the accelerator in a reflex action that took the old brake forward in a surge of power. She saw the mouths open in alarm, voiceless above the roaring of the engine, and then they were scattering to either side. The brake shot through and bounced down on the road, swerving on the bend at the bottom, cutting across the grass towards the jetty.

She braked hard and the vehicle slewed in a long, breath-taking skid that for one awful moment seemed to be taking them over the edge to the beach and the rocks below. They came to a stop, the front bumper lodged against a boulder, and she opened the door and got out.

There was no sign of Owen Morgan or his launch and when she looked up at the boathouse the great doors were still closed. She turned and found the general scrambling out at the rear, helped by Jagbir. As the little Gurkha straightened, his coat fell open to show the ivory-and-silver hilt of his *kukri*, the curved blade in its leather sheath thrust into his waistband.

As Fiona came round from the other side there was a faint cry up on the hill. Anne looked up and saw de Beaumont and his men running towards them. One of them paused, raised his rifle and fired a warning shot that whined across the jetty into the water.

Hamish Grant turned quickly. 'What about, Owen?'

'No sign of him or the launch,' Anne said. 'But *Foxhunter*'s moored at the end of the jetty.'

Any brief hope that they might be able to take over the launch before de Beaumont and his men arrived disappeared as a sailor came out of the wheelhouse, looked towards them, then hurried back inside.

'We'd better get up to the hotel,' Anne said.

They started up the hill, Fiona leading the way, Hamish Grant using his walking stick to help him. There was another cry from de Beaumont and the sailor who had been guarding *Foxhunter* rushed out on deck with a rifle and loosed off a quick shot which splintered the woodwork of one of the boathouse doors.

Anne could taste blood in her mouth and there was a pain in her chest. She took Hamish Grant's hand and scrambled on, her feet slipping on the wet turf, and then they were on to the terrace and moving into the porch.

Fiona flung open the door and led the way inside. The bar was quite empty, a small fire burning in the grate. The stillness was so complete that Anne could hear her heart pounding.

Hamish Grant leaned against a table, struggling for breath, and she called out: 'Owen, Owen Morgan! Where are you?'

There was no footfall and yet a quiet voice said with startling suddenness from behind her, 'He isn't here.'

Anne turned quickly and looked into the calm face of Juliette Vincente. 'For God's sake, Juliette. Where is he? What's going on?'

'I think that perhaps you have come to the wrong place, madame.' Juliette's hand came out of her pocket, holding the pistol. 'And now we will all wait quietly for the Comte de Beaumont.'

In the same moment Jagbir drove forward, the terrible Gurkha battle-cry bursting from his throat. His hand swung from under his coat, the razor-sharp blade of the *kukri* hissing softly through space.

Juliette Vincente pulled the trigger twice, bullets smashing into the little Gurkha's body, and then he was on top of her. As she fired again at close quarters the heavy blade swung down, half severing her neck. They fell together, Jagbir on top, the *kukri* as firmly clenched in his right hand in death as it had been in life.

As Fiona screamed, the door swung open. Hamish Grant turned, pulling the Webley from his pocket, thrusting it towards the dark formless shadow against the light that was de Beaumont.

Behind him the window shattered and the barrel of a rifle was rammed painfully into his back. 'If the general is wise he will drop it,' Marcel said.

Hamish Grant stood there, trapped in the moment of decision, and already it was too late. De Beaumont moved forward and pulled the Webley gently from his grasp.

'And now, old friend, perhaps you will be sensible?'

— 15 —

FLEUR DE LYS rolled her slim length into the wind, plunging over a wave as water broke across her prow. In the wheelhouse Mallory leaned over the chart table. Behind him the wheel clicked to one side eerily to compensate as the vessel veered to starboard, the automatic pilot in control.

The Admiralty charts he had found in the flat drawers underneath the table were very comprehensive. The one which covered the Pointe du Château coastline and the Gironde Marshes told him everything he needed to know.

The door of the saloon companionway swung open and Guyon appeared. He wore a yellow oilskin jacket and carried a large mug of coffee in each hand.

'How are we doing?'

Mallory checked his watch. 'Almost noon. Not long now. We're doing about fifteen knots.'

'I heard the weather forecast on the radio in the galley just before I came up,' Guyon said. 'It wasn't good. Winds increasing and fog indicated in the coastal area.'

'We're running into it already.'

Mallory drank some of his coffee and Guyon peered through the window. In the distance the fog waited like a damp shroud and heavy grey skies dropped towards the sea. Already the waves were lifting into whitecaps in the north-west.

'How far would you say we're behind *L'Alouette* now?' Guyon said.

Mallory shrugged. 'Submerged, she only has half our speed. Allowing for the start she had, it's going to run things a little close.'

He leaned over the chart again. 'She'll have to surface inshore of Île de Yeu before moving into the main creek flowing out of the marshes.'

'What depth is it there?'

Mallory traced its course with a pencil. 'Four or five fathoms. Strong tidal currents constantly changing. Not to be relied on, I know what *that* means. One day there's a sandbank. The next, six fathoms of clear water. These tidal marshes are all the same.'

'But we could get in with *Fleur de Lys?*'

'I think so. Probably not as far as the central island where the cottage is. It's marked on the chart. Half a mile in.'

Guyon straightened and the inimitable wry grin twisted his mouth. 'Things might get interesting, eh?'

'I think you could say that.'

Gradually the mist enfolded them until they were running through a strange, enclosed world and Mallory took over the wheel and reduced speed to ten knots. About thirty minutes later they emerged into a patch of clear water and saw the coastline of Pointe du Château no more than half a mile to port.

As they approached, a string of rocks and small islands lifted out of the sea, running parallel to the coast, trailing away towards the great hog-back of the Île de Yeu, looming out of the mist in the distance.

Mallory called to Guyon to take over the wheel and went back to the chart. When he straightened, his eyes glittered strangely.

'I think we can save a little time here, but it means taking a chance. *L'Alouette* will have to use the inshore passage. She has no other choice. This side of Île de Yeu, there's another passage marked between the island and the reef. Three fathoms.'

'We might take the bottom out of her,' Guyon said.

Mallory shrugged. 'It's de Beaumont's boat, not mine.'

Guyon grinned tightly. 'Then I suggest you take the wheel.'

Mallory changed course a point and the young Frenchman went down the saloon companionway. When he returned he carried two lifejackets.

'When I was a child a gypsy woman told my mother I must always beware of water. Superstitious nonsense, of course, but unfortunately my Breton blood says otherwise. I'd hate to prove her right at this stage.'

Mallory changed to the automatic pilot, slipped his arms through the straps of the lifejacket and took over the wheel again. They were running parallel with the islands now and *Fleur de Lys* rocked in the turbulence, waves slapping solidly against her hull.

Rain hammered against the window, cascading in a sheet which blurred the outlines of all solid objects, adding a strangely dreamlike quality to the whole scene. Île de Yeu was very close and he could see white water boiling in a frenzy across the jagged spine of the reef.

He swung the wheel hard to port. *Fleur de Lys* shuddered protestingly, a wave slammed against her hull and the deck tilted. Guyon was thrown across the wheelhouse and Mallory fell to one knee. The wheel started to spin but already his hands were back in position. As he brought her head round she lurched forward towards the narrow band of clear water between the reef and the island.

He gave her everything the engines had to offer and the boat responded magnificently. The passage rushed towards them at a seemingly impossible speed and then they were into it, water crashing across great rocks on either side, white, curling fingers reaching out to enfold them.

All around, boulders were appearing and disappearing, waves foaming over them and Raoul Guyon hung on to the chart table, his face white.

Strange, swirling currents snatched at the rudder and for one agonizing moment *Fleur de Lys* slewed to port. Mallory heaved on the wheel. There was a slight, audible shudder that ran through the entire craft as she slid across a sandbank, and then they were into clear water.

Fog rolled from the land in patches and they could smell the foetid odour of the marshes that was carried towards them on the offshore breeze. Mallory reduced speed and they moved in, the engine rumbling protestingly on a low note.

The marshes drifted out of the fog, dark and sinister, waiting to receive them, and overhead a long wavering skein of geese passed like wind-blown spirits of the dead. Long, narrow sandbanks lifted out of the water and, landward, miles of rough grass marsh, a maze of creeks, waterlogged mud and wavering barriers of reeds.

They turned the end of a long sandbar and the mouth of the creek opened before them. Guyon leaned forward with a cry of alarm. Squatting just inside the entrance like some land-blown whale was *L'Alouette*, her grey-black plates shining with moisture. Fenelon stood in the conning tower with Jacaud and below three sailors were fitting an outboard motor to the stern of a large rubber dinghy.

Mallory took *Fleur de Lys* forward in a surge of power, her bow wave cascading across the hull of the submarine, knocking one of the sailors into the water. There was a startled cry and as they passed there was no more than ten feet between them. Mallory was aware of the shocked dismay on Fenelon's face, of Jacaud frowning in disbelief, and then they were through and safe in the fog.

He reduced speed to five knots and opened the window. Fog was sucked in, sharp and cold, the taste of it bitter as death. He strained his eyes into the gloom, watching the reeds drift by. A few minutes later they slid gently to a halt with a slight jar.

Mallory quickly reversed the engines. For a moment nothing seemed to be happening and then quite suddenly *Fleur de Lys* slid backwards.

'That settles that,' he said. 'We obviously aren't going to get any further.'

He cut the engines, went out on deck and climbed on top of the wheelhouse. The reeds were very thick at this point, but to the left there was a small lagoon, circular in shape and perhaps a hundred feet in diameter.

He pointed to it as Guyon scrambled up beside him. 'Our one chance.'

He jumped to the deck, went into the wheelhouse and started the engines. as they rumbled into life he spun the wheel and crashed the boat into the reeds as she gathered speed.

For a moment they seemed an impenetrable barrier and then they slowly parted and *Fleur de Lys* passed through into the lagoon. Mallory cut the engines and she moved slowly to the far end and came to a halt, her prow grounding gently against a sandbank.

'No time to waste,' he said. 'One of us stays with the boat. The other goes for Granville and his wife.'

'That had better be me,' Guyon said. 'We have mutual acquaintances. I think he would trust me.'

Mallory pulled the chart forward. 'You'll do better by going on foot and swimming the intervening channels.' He opened a drawer and produced a pocket compass.

'Keep due west and you can't miss the central island. About a quarter of a mile away.'

'Getting Granville back here might be difficult,' Guyon said. 'He's an old man.'

'But used to these marshes. That's why he comes here, remember. You'll have to make out the best way you can.' Mallory produced the revolver he had taken from the young sailor at the castle and held it out. 'Not much, but better than nothing.'

Guyon pushed it into the pocket of his oilskin jacket and went out on deck quickly. He jumped from the prow to the sandbank and plunged into the reeds.

Mallory lit a cigarette and stood on deck in the quiet rain. Perhaps five minutes later he heard the sound of an outboard motor passing along the main channel. It moved into the distance, muffled by the fog, and then there was only silence.

II

As Guyon went through the reeds a curlew whistled hauntingly somewhere to the left and wildfowl called as they lifted from the water, disturbed by his passing. He came out on higher ground, checked the compass and ran forward, alone in a land of shining mudflats, lonely creeks and everywhere the reeds.

He came to the end of solid ground and waded across a narrow creek, his feet sinking into soft mud. He could taste the salt on his lips and it stung his eyes painfully, but he kept on moving, pushing through the reeds into the grey shroud.

Gradually the ground became firmer again until he was able to run across sand and coarse marsh-grass. A few moments later he stood on the banks of a shallow lake and the house loomed out of the fog on its island fifty yards away.

The evil, scum-covered waters reached out to meet him as he moved forward, and he took out the revolver and held it above his head. It was not likely that the water would affect it, but there was no point in taking chances.

It was surprisingly easy going, the mud giving way to hard sand, and he was soon moving up on to dry land again. As he ran towards the single-storeyed house a narrow wooden jetty loomed out of the fog and he paused abruptly. No boat was moored there, not even a marsh punt. He stood there, a frown on his face, considering the fact, then turned and went towards the house.

He could smell woodsmoke and saw it lifting in a blue tracer from the rough stone chimney. He went up rickety wooden steps to the porch, opened the door and went in.

The room was furnished simply but comfortably, loose rugs scattered across the polished wooden floor. There were several bookcases, all filled, a sofa and two easy chairs in front of the fireplace.

Logs smouldered fitfully on the stone hearth, heavily banked with ashes that they might not burn too quickly. They told Guyon all he needed to know. Henri Granville and his wife were not there. But, then, they should have always counted on that as a possibility.

Ornithology was the old man's great hobby. He had even written a book on the subject. It was quite obvious that at this moment he and his wife were sitting in their boat somewhere among the reeds which covered so many square miles of the marshes, probably even in some bird-hide since dawn taking photos.

He moved outside and went down to the jetty. Faintly, throught the mist, came the sound of an outboard motor. Jacaud and his men. For them the solution would be obvious. They would simply wait for Granville to put in an appearance. No need even to go looking for him.

There was only one answer to the problem and Guyon waded into the lake and pushed towards the other side. He moved up on to high ground and ran along the shore towards the sound of the motor.

III

In spite of the clammy cold of the marshes sweat trickled from Fenelon's armpits. Ever since that first moment of shock when *Fleur de Lys* had passed them in the mouth of the estuary he had felt sick and frightened. And then de Beaumont's message over the radio, the mind numbing as the operator decoded it.

The message was quite plain. In the circumstances they were to return at once. But that hadn't been good enough for Jacaud. He had insisted on going on into the marsh and Fenelon had wilted under his cold fury.

The reeds lifted like pale ghosts on either hand, the only sound the steady rattle of the outboard motor. He sat in the stern at the tiller, two sailors in the centre with rifles. Jacaud sat on the edge of the rounded prow, his sub-machine-gun slung around his neck as he gazed into the fog like some great bird of prey.

He turned, his granite, brutal face running with moisture. 'We must be almost there. Cut the motor. We'll start paddling.'

'You're wasting your time, Jacaud,' Guyon called gaily. 'I beat you to it. By now Henri Granville and his wife are well on their way out of here.'

As the dinghy drifted forward, a sandbank reached out from the reeds like a pointing finger. Guyon stood on a small hillock at the far end. His hand swung up and he fired twice. One of the sailors groaned and went over the side, still clutching his rifle.

Jacaud slipped the sub-machine-gun over his head. It came

up in a long, stuttering burst of fire, slicing through the reeds. He was too late. Guyon had disappeared like a ghost into the fog. He laughed mockingly somewhere near at hand and then there was silence.

The remaining sailor leaned over the side to pull in his comrade. Jacaud turned and struck up his arm. 'Leave him. We haven't time.'

The sailor recoiled from the killing fury, the devil's face that confronted him. The curious thing was that when Jacaud spoke his voice was quite calm.

'Back to *L'Alouette* and give that motor everything it's got. Mallory's got to return to Île de Roc. He's no choice. His girl-friend's still there. If we're lucky we can catch them on their way out to sea.'

IV

To Mallory the rattle of gunfire in the distance was like a physical blow and he walked the deck in impotent fury, hoping desperately that whatever had gone wrong Guyon had been able to handle it. Perhaps ten minutes later he heard the sound of the outboard motor returning along the creek. He stood very still, one foot on the rail, listening as it passed downstream.

He clambered on top of the wheelhouse and looked towards the west, straining into the fog. It was a good fifteen minutes before he heard the sound of brent geese calling bitterly as they lifted from the reeds. As the beating of their wings subsided, he was aware of movement towards the left.

He took a chance, cupped his hands and called: 'Raoul! Over here!'

A couple of minutes later Guyon emerged from the fog and stumbled across the sandbank. Mallory ran to the prow and hauled him on board. Guyon was soaked to the skin and bitterly cold, his face pale and drawn.

'Have they passed yet?'

Mallory nodded. 'What happened?'

Guyon explained briefly, shivering repeatedly as the wind cut through his damp clothes. 'What do we do now?'

'Get to hell out of here and fast,' Mallory said. 'Unless I'm very much mistaken Jacaud will wait for us at the estuary. If we can get down there fast enough we might stand a chance of getting out to sea before they're ready.'

'And back to Île de Roc?'

'That's the general idea. You'd better go below. Find yourself some dry clothes and a drink. I'll get things moving up here.'

He went into the wheelhouse and started the engines. When he put them into reverse *Fleur de Lys* parted easily from the soft mud and he swung the wheel hard over, bringing her prow round until she pointed towards the wall of reeds that barred them from the creek.

He took her forward with a burst of speed, repeating his earlier manoeuvre. Once again it proved successful. The reeds parted protestingly and the boat burst into the creek. He turned the wheel to starboard and she swung round, grazing the mud of the opposite bank.

He took her downstream slowly, the engines a murmur in the rain. Guyon came up from the saloon wearing khaki slacks, rubber boots and a heavy white sweater with a turtle collar. In one hand he carried a bottle of brandy, in the other a tin mug.

'How do you feel?' Mallory said.

Guyon grinned and held up the brandy. 'How would you expect? It's Courvoisier. Like some?'

'I certainly would.'

Mallory took the brandy down in two quick gulps. As a warm glow started to seep through his entire body he took out the packet of Gauloises that Marcel had given them and threw them to Guyon.

'Better have one while the going's good. Things might get pretty warm within the next ten minutes.'

He took one himself and opened the window of the wheelhouse. Rain kicked into his face and there was a slight wind blowing in from the sea across the marshes, lifting the fog into weird shapes.

Visibility was down to thirty or forty yards, but the reeds were beginning to drop back and the channel widened perceptibly. The water lifted in long swelling ripples and waves kicked against the bottom of the boat. They were almost there now and as a curving sandbank appeared a few yards to port he cut the engines and the current carried them in. There was a slight shudder and they stopped.

'What's the idea?' Guyon asked.

'I'd like to know what the opposition are up to. You stay here. I shan't be long.'

Mallory jumped to the sandbank, landing knee-deep in water, waded out and followed its length into the fog until he could no longer see *Fleur de Lys*. A few minutes later he stood at the end, water splashing in across the sand, and looked out towards Île de Yeu. There was no sign of *L'Alouette* and he turned and ran back the way he had come splashing through the shallows as the tide began to lift over the sandbank.

Fleur de Lys was already swinging out into the deepening channel and he took Guyon's proffered hand and scrambled over the rail.

'Not a sign of them. As far as I'm concerned I'm going to give her everything she's got and head out to sea. They'll have to come up with something pretty good to stop us.'

He went into the wheelhouse, started the engines and reversed into the channel. Visibility was becoming rather better as the fog lifted and *Fleur de Lys* roared down the centre of the channel, her bow wave surging across the water on either side.

The mouth of the estuary appeared, clear and open to the sea, and Mallory swung the wheel to port to negotiate the great sandbank fifty yards beyond the entrance. As they turned the point, the current pushing against them, they found *L'Alouette* waiting.

Jacaud was in the conning tower, a heavy machine-gun mounted on a swivel pin. The moment they came into view he started to fire. Bullets swept across the deck and Mallory ducked as glass shattered in the wheelhouse.

Guyon crouched in the doorway, resting the revolver across one raised arm, trying for a steady shot, but it was impossible. As bullets hammered into their hull, Mallory spun the wheel and the young Frenchman lost his balance.

It was the fog which saved them, a long, solid bank rolling in across the reef before the wind, and it swallowed them in an instant. Guyon picked himself up and stood listening to the impotent chatter of the machine-gun as Jacaud continued to fire. After a while there was silence.

He turned to face Mallory, his breath easing out in a long sigh. 'I'd say that called for another drink.'

As they emerged from the fog-bank, Mallory took them out to sea, giving the engines full power. He turned with a grin. 'Nothing wrong there, thank God.'

Guyon went into the saloon and returned with the Courvoisier. 'He's made one hell of a mess down there. Holes all over the place. I don't think de Beaumont will be pleased.'

Mallory swallowed some of his brandy and lit a cigarette. 'We'll find out about that soon enough.'

Guyon went into the saloon and Mallory inhaled deeply on his cigarette with a conscious pleasure. Everything was going to be all right, he was certain of that. Sometimes one got these feelings. The wind had freshened even more and spray spattered against the shattered windows of the wheelhouse. He pulled down the helmsman's seat and sat.

Some time later Guyon came in with sandwiches and hot coffee and Mallory switched to the automatic pilot. 'Want me to take over?' Guyon asked.

Mallory shook his head. 'In these conditions it should only take us two hours at the most to get there.'

V

It was perhaps half an hour later that he became aware that they were slowing perceptibly. His attempts to adjust the controls met with no success and he switched to automatic pilot and went below.

Guyon was lying on one of the saloon divans, his head on his hands, eyes closed. As Mallory entered, he opened them and sat up.

'What's wrong?'

'God knows,' Mallory said, 'but we're losing speed badly and she isn't answering to the wheel like she should.'

The *Fleur de Lys* heeled to starboard and there was a great rushing of water beneath their feet. He dropped to one knee, pulled back the carpet and peered inside. When he looked up his face was grave.

'There must be two dozen bullet holes along the waterline. We're leaking like a sieve. No wonder the damned thing's slowed down.'

They went on deck quickly and into the wheelhouse. The electric pump was housed in a cupboard in one corner and the condition of the doors, splintered by bullets, told him what he would find.

He surveyed the smashed and twisted metal briefly, then turned, his face grim. 'You'll find a hand-pump aft of the main engine housing. Do the best you can with that. Stick it as long as you can and I'll spell you.'

'I see,' Raoul Guyon said. 'Things look bad, eh?'

'Only if *L'Alouette* catches us in this condition,' Mallory said grimly.

Guyon moved out along the deck without a word and a moment later Mallory became aware of the harsh, rhythmic clangour of the hand-pump. He looked out of the window at the brownish-white stream of water gushing across the deck, took over the wheel and waited for *Fleur de Lys* to lighten.

— 16 —

WHEN FENELON first caught sight of *Fleur de Lys* his mind froze, refusing to accept for the moment what he knew to be an impossibility. The graticules misted over, temporarily obscured by a wave, and he raised the periscope a little more.

Fleur de Lys jumped into view, her familiar lines quite unmistakable. He said quickly to the rating at his side: 'Fetch Monsieur Jacaud here. Tell him to hurry.'

Jacaud arrived a few moments later. 'What's going on?'

'Take a look.'

The big man gripped the handles of the periscope tightly

and lowered his head. When he turned to look at Fenelon a muscle twitched in his right cheek.

'I wonder what went wrong?'

Fenelon shrugged. 'Perhaps you damaged her engines with the machine-gun, or even holed her. Does it matter? Shall I surface? We should be able to board her with very little trouble.'

Jacaud shook his head and something glowed in the cold eyes. 'I've got a better idea. Remember the *Kontoro*? You said that one torpedo was all it would take. Let's see what you can do.'

Fenelon felt the blood surge to his temples and his heart pounded wildly. 'My God, it's perfect! They won't even know what hit them.'

'I don't mind that,' Jacaud said, 'as long as there's nothing left afterwards.'

L'Alouette carried two 21″ torpedoes, both mounted in the bow. Fenelon took a deep breath, pulled himself together and started to issue firm, crisp orders.

'Enemy's bearing, one-two-five. Course, one-three-one. Speed, six knots. Range, one thousand five hundred.'

These facts, fed into a complicated electrical device, provided the angle of deflection, enabling the torpedoes to be aimed the right distance ahead of the target so that both should arrive in the same place at the same time.

A moment later the petty officer called, 'Deflection, one-three degrees right, sir.'

Fenelon raised the periscope handles, his face pressed to the rubber eyepiece. 'Stand by both tubes.'

'Both tubes ready, sir.'

Fenelon could feel the sweat trickling down his face and his heart seemed to leap inside him. So often he had heard of this moment, had it described to him by men who knew. But for him this was the first.

'Stand by to fire.'

Fleur de Lys seemed to leap into focus, every line of her clear and clean. His hands tightened on the handles. 'Fire one.'

The submarine lurched as the missile shot away and the hydrophone operator reported, 'Torpedo running.'

'Fire two.'

Again the submarine shuddered.

'Torpedo running.'

Fenelon turned to Jacaud. 'Care to watch?'

The big man pushed him roughly to one side and bent to the handles.

II

On board *Fleur de Lys*, Guyon still sweated at the pump and the boat ran on, the automatic pilot in control while Mallory stood on top of the wheelhouse and swept the sea with a pair of glasses.

That *L'Alouette* would catch up with them now was certain. They were making no more than six knots and barely holding back the water. Submerged, the submarine had three or four knots on them. They were well out of the main shipping lane, he knew that. Their only hope was the chance of an odd fishing boat putting in an appearance, hardly likely considering the weather.

He swung the glasses again in a wide arc and stiffened as something lifted out of the water to starboard. It was a periscope, the tell-tale bow wave giving it away, and then he saw the great, surging streak of foam boiling under the surface of the water as it ran towards them.

'Torpedo!' he cried, and jumped to the deck, losing his balance and rolling over. He picked himself up, scrambled into the wheelhouse and grabbed for the wheel. He spun it round desperately, and slowly she started to turn. Guyon appeared beside him, adding his weight, shoving the wheel over, and then a great swell, rolling in from the west, gave them the final push.

Mallory left Guyon at the wheel and rushed to the rail. He was just in time to see the wash of the torpedo passing to starboard. A few seconds later it was followed by the second.

III

In the submarine Jacaud gave a growl of rage, turned and

grabbed Fenelon by the jacket. 'You missed, damn you! You missed!'

'But that's impossible.'

Fenelon bent to the periscope and Jacaud pulled him away. 'From now on I'm giving the orders. Take her in close and surface. I'm going to finish Mr Bloody Mallory off personally.'

IV

On the *Fleur de Lys* Mallory was back at the wheel and Guyon worked the pump furiously. But it was no good. The boat rolled heavily, waves breaking across her prow, the weight of the water inside holding her down.

L'Alouette had fired both her tubes and no additional torpedoes were carried by Type XXIII submarines, Mallory knew that. He looked out of the window, watching the fog roll in again in patches. There was no other vessel in sight, and his heart sank. In the circumstances Jacaud's next move seemed obvious.

Somehow there was still a shock of surprise as the sea boiled in a great cauldron no more than fifty yards away and *L'Alouette* broke through to the surface. Even as the water still spilled from her plates Jacaud appeared in the conning-tower. A rating came up beside him and they started to mount the heavy machine-gun on its firing-pin.

Guyon stood in the doorway, the revolver ready in his right hand. 'Now what?'

'I think that's obvious,' Mallory said flatly. 'If I'm going to go I'm taking him with me. It's been nice knowing you.

'And you, *mon colonel*.' Raoul Guyon drew himself together as if on parade. 'An honour, sir.'

He moved along the deck to the prow and Mallory swung the wheel and brought *Fleur de Lys* into the wind. A moment later and she was bearing down on *L'Alouette*.

Jacaud started to fire, bullets hammering into the prow, and Malory braced himself, hands firm on the wheel. Guyon lay flat on the deck, one arm around a stanchion, waiting for the moment of impact. There were two rounds left in the revolver and he was praying that at the last he might have the chance of putting them both into Jacaud.

In the conning-tower of *L'Alouette* Jacaud still fired the machine-gun, raising it slightly, aiming for Mallory in the wheelhouse. Fenelon appeared beside him, his face white and terrified, mouth open in a soundless scream.

Mallory was aware of all these things, of the bullets hammering into the wheelhouse as he ducked out of sight and then *Fleur de Lys* was lifted high on a swell. She seemed to poise there for a moment, then slid down the other side into *L'Alouette*, her prow grinding against the side of the conning-tower where it joined the hull.

There was a terrible crash, a groan of tortured metal as the bow crunched into the plates, cutting through the ballast tanks, crushing the pressure hull. *L'Alouette* heeled, the conning-tower leaning over, spilling the machine-gun into the water, and Jacaud and Fenelon hung on desperately.

Guyon was on his feet, leaning over the rail. As he took aim and fired *Fleur de Lys* lurched to one side and he went head first into the sea.

Fleur de Lys kept on moving, her steel hull sliding over the submarine, pushing it down into the water. Suddenly she was across, her prow plunging into a wave. Mallory got to his feet, grabbed the wheel and struggled to bring her round.

Incredibly, she anwered, and lifted sluggishly over the swell, her engines still beating. He turned and looked out through the shattered windows at the submarine.

She had righted herself now, but the sea was breaking over her hull in sinister fashion. The forward hatch opened and several sailors emerged. Jacaud came down the outside ladder to join them.

They were pointing at something in the sea and Mallory saw Raoul Guyon, a swell lifting him up and carrying him in towards the submarine. As he was washed across the grey hull they pounced on him.

There was nothing Mallory could do and he kept on going, passing into the fog. When he glanced back five minutes later *L'Alouette* was lost to view.

Gradually the engines lost power and progress became slower. The fog was very patchy, blown by a strengthening wind, and in the distance he could see Île de Roc low on the horizon. The engines stopped altogether, five minutes later, with a hiss of steam.

He went down into the flooded saloon, found the bottle of Courvoisier and went back on deck. The fog had cleared even more now, but the wind was cold and the waves were lifting again.

He unshipped the dinghy and waited until the green waters started to slop across the deck, then he slid it over the stern and climbed in. He rowed away, paused and watched *Fleur de Lys* slide under the surface.

The water boiled for a little while, then calmed into a great white patch of froth, a coil of rope, a box and one or two loose spars floating in the centre. It was always a saddening sight, the loss of a good ship. He inflated his lifejacket, raised the bottle of Courvoisier to his lips and started to row.

V

L'Alouette drifted low in the water, her powerful diesels still working, pushing her towards the island. Progress was agonizingly slow and in the conning-tower Jacaud waited, a cigarette in his mouth, watching the island grow nearer in the gathering dusk.

Below, things were bad and getting worse every minute. The crew worked knee-deep in water and it took the petty officer all his time to keep them under control.

Fenelon lay on the bunk in his tiny cabin, lips moving soundlessly as he stared up at the bulkhead. He shivered as if he had the ague and when someone attempted to speak to him he gazed at the man with vacant eyes.

Guyon lay huddled in a corner of the conning-tower bridge, blood oozing from a nasty gash in his forehead, knocked insensible by Jacaud the moment they had hauled him from the sea.

Jacaud stirred him with his boot, wondering exactly how he was going to kill him. It would have been easy to leave him in the sea or even to put a bullet through his head the moment they hauled him aboard, but that would have been too simple. Guyon deserved something special. He was a traitor and had been all along the line.

The throb of the diesels faltered and stopped and in the silence which followed there was a startled cry from inside the submarine. The forward hatch opened and the crew poured out. They brought with them several inflatable dinghies, including the one with the outboard motor which Jacaud had used in the marshes.

Jacaud picked Guyon up, slung him over one shoulder with easy strength and went down the ladder. He walked along the hull and paused a couple of yards away from the frightened sailors. They were no more than a quarter of a mile from the great reef which linked Île de Roc and St Pierre, the tide carrying them in. Jacaud did not intend to wait and see what happened to *L'Alouette* when she was pounded across those terrible rocks.

He nodded to the petty officer. 'I'm taking the one with the outboard motor. You're coming with me.'

There was a chorus of startled cries from the men and one of them rushed forward. 'Why you? Why not us?'

Jacaud took a Lüger from his pocket and shot the man twice in the chest, the bullets knocking him into the water. There was a sudden silence and they all crowded back.

A few moments later the largest dinghy was moving away, the petty officer in the stern operating the outboard motor. Jacaud sat in the prow facing him and Guyon sprawled in the bottom.

The power of the current was already swinging the doomed submarine in towards the reef and there was a confused shouting on deck. One by one, the men crowded into the remaining dinghies and the current immediately swept them away.

VI

Below in *L'Alouette* Fenelon lay in his cabin, forgotten by everyone. It was only when the water reached his bunk that he came to his senses. He sat up, stared down at it for a moment, then suddenly seemed to come to life.

He moved outside and started forward. At that moment the lights went out. He screamed as darkness enfolded him and started to feel his way along desperately.

As he reached the control room, light streaming in through the open conning-tower, water started to cascade down the ladder and the whole world seemed to turn upside down.

He was aware of the crash, the rending of the metal plates and then a green cascade mercifully engulfed him. The sea swung *L'Alouette* in across the reef. For a brief moment she poised on the edge, then plunged down into the darkness of the middle passage.

— 17 —

THE OARS dipped and rose and Mallory pulled with all his strength, but his arms were tired and already there was a blister in one palm from a splinter in the rough handles.

It was more than an hour since *Fleur de Lys* had gone down and he had rowed steadily for most of that time, making little progress. The fog still hung low over the water in long, wraithlike patches. On one occasion he seemed to hear a faint cry. When he looked back there was a brief flash of yellow on top of a wave as one of the submarine's rubber dinghies was swept out to sea.

After a while he stopped and rested on the oars. Île de Roc was still half a mile away and it was quite obvious that the run of the tide was sweeping him on a parallel course with the island that would eventually take him out to sea.

Even if he fetched up in the steamer lane that ran up-Channel from Ushant it would be dark in another hour. He was under no illusions about his ability to survive a night in the Channel in such a frail craft.

There were two good doubles left in the bottle of Courvoisier. He took them down slowly and tossed the empty bottle into the sea. As a thin rain drifted down on the wind he reached for the oars and started to row again.

The freshening wind dispelled the last traces of fog and an ugly chop formed on the water. He pulled steadily, staring into the gathering twilight, his mind a blank, everything he had of brain and muscle concentrated on his impossible task.

When he paused twenty minutes later and looked over his shoulder he saw to his astonishment that he was now quite close to the island. There was a slapping sound against the keel of the dinghy and it swung round, swirling past a long finger of rock, moving in fast, caught by some inshore current.

He bent to the oars with renewed vigour, forgetting the pain in his right hand, the blood that dripped steadily down. The current helped, carrying him closer inshore every minute. The waves were higher now as they pounded in over the rocks and water started to slop across the dinghy's stern.

He heaved on the oars, trying to keep her head round, but it was too much for him. He let them go, knelt in the bottom and waited, holding on with both hands.

The cliffs were very close now, the surf white as it crashed in across the narrow beach, breaking over ledges of rock. Behind Mallory a great, heaving swell rolled in, gathering momentum, sweeping him in before it. A sudden rending crash jarred his spine. Water foamed around, spray lifting high into the air. The dinghy ground forward across jagged rocks, her boards splintering, and came to a halt, the prow wedged into a crevasse.

Mallory hung on, and as the sea receded with a great sucking noise he scrambled out of the dinghy and stumbled across the final line of rocks. A moment later he was safe on the strip of beach at the base of the cliffs.

II

He sat down, holding his head in his hands, and the world spun away. The taste of the sea was in his throat and he retched, bringing up a quantity of salt-water.

After a while he got to his feet and turned to examine the cliffs behind. They were no more than seventy or eighty feet high and sloped gently backwards, cracked and fissured by great gullies.

It was an easy enough climb and he scrambled over the edge a few minutes later and turned to look out to sea. The fog had disappeared completely now, but darkness was falling fast and the moon was already rising above the horizon.

He hurried through the wet grass, following the slope in a gentle curve that brought him over the edge of the hill ten minutes later on the far side of the harbour from the Grants' house.

The cove looked strangely deserted, no smoke rising from the chimney of the hotel. He was aware of Guyon's launch, of the shooting brake tilted against a rock, the long skid-marks trailing back up the grassy slope to the road. He went down the slope on the run.

He walked round to the front of the hotel, calling loudly without receiving any reply. When he opened the door and stepped into the bar he was already prepared for something out of the ordinary, some evidence of a struggle at least.

Jagbir and Juliette Vincente still crouched together by the bar, a pool of dried blood spreading into the rush matting.

It was very quiet, too quiet, and for a moment Mallory seemed to hear the sea roaring in his ears and there was an element of unreality to it all. It was as if none of this were really happening, and he turned and stumbled outside.

He wasted five minutes in going down to the jetty in the forlorn hope that Guyon's launch might be seaworthy. It was almost completely dark when he breasted the hill and trotted towards the Grants' house.

He went in through the kitchen and quiet enveloped him, that strange, secret stillness a house wraps about itself when no one is there, and an overwhelming loneliness surged through him.

He spoke aloud, his voice hoarse and broken: 'Anne?'

But only the house listened to him and the quiet ones. He stumbled into the sitting-room, opened the cabinet and poured himself a brandy. He stood there, sipping it quietly remembering her here by the fireside in the soft lamplight a thousand years ago.

The darkness seemed to move in on him with a strange

whispering, and he closed his eyes tightly, fighting the panic, the despair which rose inside him. The moment passed. He put down the glass and went out through the french windows.

The moon was clear and very bright, stars strung away to the horizon. When he topped the hill on the western side of the island St Pierre and the castle were etched out of black cardboard, breathtakingly beautiful like something from a child's fairy-tale.

Beneath him the tide was already on the turn, white water breaking across the great reef, rocks thrusting their heads into the moonlight. Minute by minute the water would continue to drop until for one brief hour a jagged causeway linked the two islands. One hour only and then the tide would come roaring in. But there was no point in thinking about that. Such had been his haste since landing from the dinghy that he had not even had time to rid himself of his lifejacket. He touched it mechanically, moved along the cliffs till he came to a sloping ravine that slanted to the beach below, and started down.

III

Marcel unbolted the heavy door and de Beaumont moved inside. There was no window, but the room was brightly illuminated by a naked bulb which hung from the centre of the low ceiling. Guyon and Hamish Grant sat on a couple of old packing cases, talking in low tones.

They came to their feet, the old man leaning on his walking stick. Guyon was very pale, dark circles under his eyes, and the gash on his forehead was red and angry.

'It seems I must congratulate you, Captain Guyon,' de Beaumont said calmly.

Guyon shook his head. 'No need. You were doomed from the beginning. A pity you didn't realize that a few lives ago.'

'I wouldn't be too sure. The game isn't over yet.'

'It will be the moment Colonel Mallory makes land.'

'And what if he doesn't? From what I hear, *Fleur de Lys* was in a sinking condition when last seen.'

'You're forgetting Granville and his wife. They must have contacted the authorities now. The sands are running out, de

Beaumont. You were wrong from the start, always have been. We don't need you and your bully-boys to tell us how to govern France.'

Marcel took a step forward and de Beaumont pushed him back. 'Let him go on.'

'A country's greatness lies in the hearts of her people, not in the size of her possessions, and France is people. In one way or another, blood and suffering is all they've been given since 1939 and they've had enough. But not you, Colonel. You couldn't stop if you wanted to.'

'Anything I have done I have done to the greater glory of France,' de Beaumont said.

'Or the greater glory of Philippe de Beaumont? Which is it? Can you tell the difference? Have you ever been able to?'

De Beaumont's face seemed to sag, and for the first time since Guyon had known him he looked like an old man. He turned and walked out. Marcel hesitated and then followed him. The door closed and the bolts rasped into place.

'Quite a speech,' Hamish Grant said out of the long silence which followed.

'Accomplishing precisely nothing,' Guyon said wearily, and sat down, his head in his hands.

'Worth hearing, though.' The old man patted him gently on the shoulder, resumed his seat and they waited.

IV

De Beaumont stood in front of the great glass window of the tower room and looked out over the sea. Far, far to the west the rim of the ocean was tipped with orange fire. Île de Roc dark against the sky.

The beauty of it was too much for a man and he opened the casement and inhaled the good salt air and out beyond the island the lights of a ship seemed very far away.

Life was a series of beginnings and endings, that much at least he had learned. He remembered Dien-Bien-Phu, standing on the edge of a foxhole in the rain as the tricolour was hauled down and little yellow peasants from the rice fields had swarmed over the broken ground to take him and what was left of his men.

And then Algeria. Years of bloodshed. Of death in the streets and death in the hills. He had believed implicitly that the end justified the means, but what if that end was never realized? What if one were left only with the blood on the hands? Blood which had been shed to no purpose, which could never be washed off.

He felt curiously sad and drained of all emotion. A small wind moaned around the tower and then there was only the silence. In that single moment the heart turned to ashes inside him. Looking out over the moonlit sea he knew with a bitter certainty that he had been wrong. That in the final analysis all that he had done came to nothing. That everything Raoul Guyon had said was true.

He walked to the fireplace and looked up at the old battle standard for a long moment. He nodded, as if coming to some secret, hidden decision.

He picked up the telephone and pressed an extension button. When the receiver was lifted at the other end he said briefly, 'Send up Jacaud.'

He replaced the phone, moved across to a narrow door, opened it and stepped into the small turret bedroom. Anne Grant sat in a chair by the window. Fiona lay on the bed.

They got to their feet and faced him. He bowed courteously and stood to one side. 'If you would be so kind.'

They hesitated perceptibly, then brushed past him. He closed the door, moved to the fire and turned.

'What have you done with my father?' Fiona demanded.

'There is no need to alarm yourself. He will come to no harm. I give you my word.'

'And Raoul Guyon?'

De Beaumont smiled faintly. 'A great deal has taken place of which you are not aware. Captain Guyon is at this moment with General Grant. Except for a nasty cut on the head he seemed in fair condition when I saw him an hour ago.'

'You haven't mentioned Colonel Mallory,' Anne said carefully.

De Beaumont shrugged. 'All I can say with truth, my dear, is that at this precise moment I haven't the slightest idea where he is.'

There was a knock at the door, it opened and Jacaud

entered. He came forward and waited, the cold eyes in the brutal, animal face giving nothing away.

'Have *Foxhunter* refuelled and made ready for sea,' de Beaumont said.

'I've already seen to it. Are we leaving?'

'I should imagine it would be the sensible thing to do. Even if Mallory hasn't managed a landfall yet Granville must certainly be in touch with the French authorities by now. Admittedly they will then have to contact British Intelligence, but I shouldn't imagine it will be long before we're faced with some sort of official delegation.'

'Where are we going – Portugal?'

'Perhaps you, but not me, Jacaud.' Philippe de Beaumont extracted a cigarette from his case and fitted it carefully into his holder. 'We leave in half an hour for Jersey. When you have landed me in St Helier you are a free man. You and the others may go where you please.'

Jacaud's eyes narrowed. 'Jersey? Why would you want to go there?'

'Because they possess a more than adequate airport, my dear Jacaud, and an early-morning flight to Paris. I intend to be on it.'

'You must be mad. You couldn't walk ten yards along the Champs Élysées without somebody recognizing you.'

'No need,' de Beaumont said calmly. 'You see, I intend to place myself in the hands of the authorities.'

For once Jacaud's iron composure was shattered. 'Give yourself up? You'd face certain execution.'

'That would be for the court to decide.' De Beaumont shook his head. 'I've been wrong, Jacaud. We all have. I thought I wanted what was best for France. I see now that what I really wanted was what was best for me. Further bloodshed and violence would accomplish nothing. The events of the past few days have taught me that.'

'And what about the women and the old man? What do we do with them?'

'We can release them before we leave. They'll be picked up before long.'

'And Guyon?'

'Him we will also leave.'

Rage erupted from Jacaud's mouth in a growl of anger. 'I'll see that one on his back if it's the last thing I do on top of earth. God in heaven, I could have left him to drown.'

'Sergeant-Major Jacaud!' De Beaumont's voice was like cold steel. 'I have given you certain orders. You will see that they are carried out. Understand?'

For a dangerous moment the fire glimmered in Jacaud's eyes, and then, quite suddenly, he subsided. 'I beg the colonel's pardon.'

'Accepted. Release Captain Guyon and General Grant and bring them up here. We leave in half an hour.'

Jacaud opened the door and went out. De Beaumont sighed, and said almost to himself: 'Twenty-three years of blood and war. Too much for any man.'

It was Anne who answered him, her face very pale. 'Before God, Colonel de Beaumont, I pity you.'

He took her hand and kissed it gently, then crossed to the door to the turret room and opened it. 'Perhaps you would wait in here?'

They walked past him. He closed the door and went to the fireplace. He looked up at the standard for a long moment, then sat down at his writing desk and picked up a pen.

V

Marcel sat at the table in his tiny room, a bottle of cognac in front of him. He was reading an old magazine, turning the pages slowly, his mind elsewhere. They should have been out of this place the moment Jacaud had returned with the news of the loss of *L'Alouette*, so much was obvious. He wondered what de Beaumont had wanted, and raised his glass to his lips. Behind him the door crashed open and Jacaud entered.

His face was white, the skin drawn tightly over the prominent cheekbones, and there was a strange, smoky look in his eyes that made Marcel's flesh crawl.

'What is it? What happened up there?'

Jacaud grabbed the glass, filled it with cognac and swallowed it down. 'He wants us to take him to Jersey. From there he intends to fly to Paris to hand himself over to the authorities.'

'He must be mad,' Marcel's face turned a sickly yellow colour. 'Are you going to let him?'

'Am I hell. If they get him they get all of us. It would only be a matter of time.'

'What about the prisoners?'

'He's going to release them.'

Marcel jumped up in alarm. 'We've got to get out of here. This whole thing's going sour.'

'We're getting out of here all right, but on our own,' Jacaud said. 'Just you and me. Everyone else can go to the devil. But first I've got to settle with de Beaumont. He knows too much for his own good.'

'And Guyon?'

'I'll have to forgo that pleasure. You take care of him and the old man. I'll see you on the jetty in fifteen minutes.'

He went out and Marcel raised the bottle of cognac to his lips, swallowed deeply and tossed it into a corner.

VI

It was quiet in the corridor and he moved quickly along to the end and paused outside a stout wooden door. He took a revolver from his pocket and checked it quickly. There were four rounds in the cylinder and he unbolted the door, kicked it open and moved inside.

Raoul Guyon and General Grant rose to meet him. Marcel closed the door behind him and moved forward.

'You first, captain,' he said, and his hand swung up.

Guyon flung himself to one side and the bullet chipped stone from the wall. In the same moment Hamish Grant slashed at the light with his walking stick, plunging the room into darkness.

Marcel cried out sharply and fired twice. He was aware of a shadow moving over towards the right in the split-second flash and fired twice again. The second time the hammer clicked on an empty chamber. He flung the useless weapon into the darkness with a sob and reached for the door.

There was the scrape of a foot behind him and a great arm slid around his neck. He was aware of the pain, of the relentless brute strength, and struggled wildly. Hamish Grant increased the pressure, his fingers locked together like steel bands, and the Frenchman went limp.

The old man dropped him to the floor and said hoarsely, 'Raoul, where are you?'

There was a movement in the darkness beside him. 'Here, general.'

Hamish Grant put out a hand and touched him on the shoulder. 'Are you hit?'

'Not a chance,' Guyon said. 'But let's get out of here. We must find the girls.'

The old man opened the door cautiously and walked into the passage. Something moved, a dark shadow against the light. He reached out, a snarl rising in his throat, and his wrists were gripped tightly.

A tired, familiar voice said: 'All right, general. It's me.'

— 18 —

MALLORY struggled across a great slippery mass of rounded stones and paused on top of a natural escarpment. He had never felt greater loneliness in his entire life. On each side stretched the sea, and before him, clear in the moonlight, the sinister, twisted maze of jagged rocks and great boulders that made up the reef.

At high water the escarpment upon which he was now standing would be a good five fathoms deep, and he moved on, slipping and stumbling across a morass of slimy seaweed, sinking up to his knees in places.

It had taken him three-quarters of an hour to get half-way along the reef. With each passing moment it became more and more apparent that unless he could increase his rate of progress the tide would sweep back in to pound him across these cruel rocks.

He came out on to a strip of wet sand shining in the moonlight, and started to run. For perhaps a hundred yards the sand held true and then petered out into gravel and broken stone.

He entered a forest of dark pointing fingers which lifted into the moonlight like some strange prehistoric monument and wasted ten minutes finding his way through. As he struggled out along a shelving bank of seaweed he paused and looked down at moonlight shining on the waters of the middle passage.

It stretched before him, a dark tunnel with at least twenty feet of headroom at low water. The wind blowing in from the sea, scattering spray in his face, decided him. At his present rate of progress he was certain to be caught. There was only one remaining chance of beating the tide and he slid over the edge.

Strangely enough, when he entered the water he wasn't aware of the cold and his lifejacket worked perfectly. He turned on to his back and started to swim, using both arms in a powerful back stroke.

The passage was shadowy in the moonlight and very still and the sound of the sea outside seemed to come from another place. He remembered what lay beneath him, fathoms deep in the darkness, and pushed the thought away, concentrating all his strength on the task in hand.

It was perhaps fifteen minutes later that he became aware of a different note outside and spray foamed through the crannies above his head, slashing across his face. The water-level started to rise at once and with every passing minute the roof came nearer.

He turned on his face and swam forward, thrashing wildly with his feet. A few moments later he came out into a jagged basin. As a swell lifted him up he grabbed for a ledge and hauled himself out of the water.

The tide was already moving in, licking hungrily at the rocks, and far out to sea a flash of sheet lightning illuminated the sky. He came to the end of the main body of the reef and before him a long, thin spine of rock and gravel stretched three hundred yards to St Pierre.

He started to run, aware of the roaring of the sea, hungry for him as she swept in to drown the land, erupting with phosphorescence, blue-green lights dancing on the water, dissolving as rapidly as they appeared.

To the right, lightning flared again and a dark band of shadow moved across the sky, snuffing out the stars. He came to a long strip of shingle and started to run.

Half-way across, the sea splashed in knee-deep. He struggled forward, aware of its strength as it tugged at him. It was already at his waist when he reached the sprawling mass of boulders heaped at the base of the island. As his feet missed bottom, he thrashed forward, grabbed for a ledge and hauled himself out.

Still the sea rose, and he moved on, aware only of the menace behind. He skirted the base of the cliffs and finally reached a point of jagged rock no more than twenty feet from the entrance to the cave.

He jumped into the water and started to swim desperately, but there was no need. The tide swept him into the entrance on the crest of a great swell. A moment later he bumped against the wall of the jetty at *Foxhunter*'s stern. He swam round to a flight of stone steps and climbed out of the water.

He was tired, more tired than he had ever been in his life, and the roaring of the sea seemed to have got inside his head. He pulled off his lifejacket, padded across the jetty and went up the steps, keeping to the wall. When he reached the landing all was quiet. He opened the door cautiously and moved forward.

There were three doors on this section of the corridor, all leading to rooms used as quarters by *L'Alouette*'s crew. He searched them quickly, hoping for a weapon, but found nothing.

As he emerged from the last he heard the muffled reports of several gunshots fired close at hand. He stood listening intently. Another shot sounded. He went along the passage, every sense alert, and paused at the end.

Behind him a door opened. He whirled round, hands coming up, and Hamish Grant stepped into the light.

II

The great hall was a place of shadows. No fire burned in the hearth and a single light at the far end gave the only illumination. Mallory moved out of the doorway and stood listening, but there was no sound, and he moved forward followed by Guyon and Hamish Grant.

There was a small lamp bracketed to the wall of the gallery and for some reason it seemed to grow dimmer as he went upstairs. He paused, swaying a little, and Guyon's anxious voice seemed to come from a great distance.

'Are you all right?'

Mallory opened his eyes, nodded and moved on, putting one foot in front of the other mechanically. It was only when they reached the door to the tower and he pushed it open that he realized how exhausted he was. There was no strength left in him at all.

Guyon and the old man crowded into the narrow hall and Mallory bolted the door. 'Whatever happens now, no one else gets in,' he said, and the words seemed to be spoken by someone else.

He took a deep breath, summoning together every final resource of body and mind, and led the way up the stairs. The walls spiralled round, the night sky gleaming through the slotted windows, and somewhere thunder rumbled menacingly.

When they emerged on the first landing the door to the radio room stood open and there was no one there. Mallory moved across to the set and switched it on. There was a faint crackling of static. He picked up the microphone and high in the tower three shots were fired in rapid succession. A moment later Fiona Grant screamed.

III

Jacaud paused on the landing, took the Lüger from the pocket of his reefer coat and removed the clip. It was by no means full, he could tell that by the weight, but there was no time to reload. He slammed it back into the butt, replaced the Lüger in his pocket and opened the door.

De Beaumont was sitting at his desk writing, his hair silver in the soft light. He blotted the sheet of paper carefully, put down his pen and looked up.

A frown appeared on his face. 'What's happened, Jacaud? Where are General Grant and Guyon?'

'Marcel is taking care of them now,' Jacaud said calmly.

'Taking care of them? I don't understand.'

'Don't you, my brave colonel?' Jacaud laughed harshly. 'Did you really think I'd stand to one side and allow you to fly off to Paris to play *le grand seigneur*, a de Beaumont to the end?'

'How dare you!' de Beaumont said hoarsely.

'For you it's always been a game,' Jacaud said. 'A great and wonderful game with bugles blowing and standards flying in the breeze like some medieval set-piece. That's the way you've lived and that's the way you want to die, but not this time, colonel. They'll squeeze you so hard you'll tell them everything that's ever happened to you since you were three years old. Unfortunately for you, that includes me.'

De Beaumont grabbed a glass paperweight, hurled it with all his force and reached for the handle of the drawer containing his revolver. Jacaud jumped to one side, the paperweight smashing against the wall, and fired.

The bullet caught de Beaumont in the left shoulder, spinning him round, and Jacaud fired again twice, the impact driving de Beaumont forward. He clutched at the mantelpiece, the linen material of his jacket bursting into flames, and reached up towards the old battle standard. He started to fall, his fingers catching at the fringe, and it fluttered down to cover him like a scarlet shroud.

The door of the turret room opened and Anne and Fiona Grant appeared. The young girl screamed once, her hands going up to her face. Jacaud ignored them. He walked slowly across the room and stood looking down at de Beaumont, a dazed expression in his eyes.

Behind him the door swung open with a crash. As he turned, Raoul Guyon hurled himself forward. Jacaud's first bullet chipped the wall beside the door, his second caught Guyon just above the left breast, stopping him in his tracks.

Guyon groaned and fell to one knee. Jacaud raised the Lüger, took careful aim and fired again.

As the hammer fell on an empty chamber, Anne Grant flung herself forward, grabbing at his arm. He hit her back-handed, slamming her against the wall, and reached into his pocket for some spare rounds.

IV

Mallory seemed to fill the doorway, the eyes dark shadows in a face that was lined with fatigue. He started forward, swaying slightly from side to side, eyes never leaving Jacaud, no expression on his face, a dead man walking.

Jacaud dropped the Lüger, seized the heavy brass poker from the fireplace and weighed it in his hand, a savage smile on his face.

'Come on!' he said. 'Come on, you bastard!'

Mallory stood there, hands hanging loosely at his sides, fatigue washing over his face, and Jacaud sprang forward, the brass poker swinging down, gleaming in the lamplight.

To Mallory that blow was like a branch swaying in the wind. As the poker came down he grabbed for the wrist, twisting the arm up and out to one side, taut as a steel bar, using the same terrible grip he had used on the jetty at Southampton so long ago.

Jacaud screamed, dropping the poker, and the muscles of his shoulder started to tear. Mallory reached for the wrist with his other hand and twisted it round and up.

Again there was a tearing sound as muscle gave and Jacaud screamed again. Still keeping that terrible hold in position, Mallory ran him head first across the room towards the great window. It dissolved in a snowstorm of flying glass and Jacaud dived into darkness, his last cry swept away on the wind like some departing spirit.

Raoul Guyon was propped against Fiona's knee, his face hollow with pain, and Hamish Grant stood in the doorway. When Mallory turned, blood on his face from the flying glass, they were all looking towards him strangely.

He started to fall and strong arms caught him, easing him

down to the floor, and he looked up at Anne Grant, that dark, dear face so full of love for him.

'Raoul?' he said. 'How's Raoul? Is it serious?'

'He's going to be fine.'

There was something else, something important. He frowned desperately and then remembered. 'The radio room – downstairs. We must call Jersey. There are three motor torpedo boats just waiting for the right signal.'

'It's all right,' she said. 'Everything's all right. We'll take care of it.'

She pillowed his head against her breast, her arms about him. He turned into their softness, the sound of the sea in his ears, and slept.